Detective Gryce, N.Y.P.D.
Volume: 3

Detective Gryce, N.Y.P.D. Volume: 3

The Circular Study

Hand and Ring

The Doctor, His Wife, and the Clock

Anna Katherine Green

LEONAUR

Detective Gryce, N.Y.P.D.
Volume: 3
The Circular Study
Hand and Ring
and
The Doctor, His Wife, and the Clock
by Anna Katherine Green

First published under the titles
The Circular Study
Hand and Ring
and
The Doctor, His Wife, and the Clock

Leonaur is an imprint of Oakpast Ltd

Copyright in this form © 2011 Oakpast Ltd

ISBN: 978-0-85706-771-5 (hardcover)
ISBN: 978-0-85706-772-2 (softcover)

http://www.leonaur.com

Publisher's Notes

The views expressed in this book are not necessarily
those of the publisher.

Contents

The Circular Study   7

Hand and Ring   153

The Doctor, His Wife, and the Clock   535

The Circular Study

Contents

BOOK 1. A STRANGE CRIME

Red Light   11

Mysteries   15

The Mute Servitor   21

A New Experience For Mr. Gryce   25

Five Small Spangles   31

Suggestions From an Old Friend   41

Amos's Son   52

In The Round of the Staircase   60

High and Low   68

Bride Roses   72

Misery   83

Thomas Explains   90

Despair   93

Memoranda   98

BOOK 2. REMEMBER EVELYN

The Secret of the Cadwaladers   101

The Oath   113

Eva   118

Felix   133

Why the Iron Slide Remained Stationary   136

Answered   146

Last Words   150

BOOK 1: A STRANGE CRIME

1

Red Light

Mr. Gryce was melancholy. He had attained that period in life when the spirits flag and enthusiasm needs a constant spur, and of late there had been a lack of special excitement, and he felt dull and superannuated. He was even contemplating resigning his position on the force and retiring to the little farm he had bought for himself in Westchester; and this in itself did not tend to cheerfulness, for he was one to whom action was a necessity and the exercise of his mental faculties more inspiring than any possible advantage which might accrue to him from their use.

But he was not destined to carry out this impulse yet. For just at the height of his secret dissatisfaction there came a telephone message to headquarters which roused the old man to something like his former vigour and gave to the close of this gray fall day an interest he had not expected to feel again in this or any other kind of day. It was sent from Carter's well-known drug store, and was to the effect that a lady had just sent a boy in from the street to say that a strange crime had been committed in ——'s mansion round the corner. The boy did not know the lady, and was shy about showing the money she had given him, but that he had money was very evident, also, that he was frightened enough for his story to be true. If the police wished to communicate with him, he could be found at Carter's, where he would be detained till an order for his release should be received.

A *strange* crime! That word "strange" struck Mr. Gryce, and made him forget his years in wondering what it meant. Meanwhile the men about him exchanged remarks upon the house brought thus unexpectedly to their notice. As it was one of the few remaining landmarks of the preceding century, and had been made conspicuous moreover by the shops, club-houses, and restaurants pressing against it on either side, it had been a marked spot for years even to those who knew nothing of its history or traditions.

And now a crime had taken place in it! Mr. Gryce, in whose ears that word "strange" rang with quiet insistence, had but to catch the eye of the inspector in charge to receive an order to investigate the affair. He started at once, and proceeded first to the drug store. There he found the boy, whom he took along with him to the house indicated in the message. On the way he made him talk, but there was nothing the poor waif could add to the story already sent over the telephone. He persisted in saying that a lady (he did not say woman) had come up to him while he was looking at some toys in a window, and, giving him a piece of money, had drawn him along the street as far as the drug store. Here she showed him another coin, promising to add it to the one he had already pocketed if he would run in to the telephone clerk with a message for the police. He wanted the money, and when he grabbed at it she said that all he had to do was to tell the clerk that a strange crime had been committed in the old house on —— Street. This scared him, and he was sliding off, when she caught him again and shook him until his wits came back, after which he ran into the store and delivered the message.

There was candour in the boy's tone, and Mr. Gryce was disposed to believe him; but when he was asked to describe the lady, he showed that his powers of observation were no better than those of most of his class. All he could say was that she was a stunner, and wore shiny clothes and jewels, and Mr. Gryce, recognizing the lad's limitations at the very moment he found himself in view of the house he was making for, ceased to question him, and directed all his attention to the building he was approaching.

Nothing in the exterior bespoke crime or even disturbance. A shut door, a clean stoop, heavily curtained windows (some of which were further shielded by closely drawn shades) were eloquent of inner quiet and domestic respectability, while its calm front of brick, with brownstone trimmings, offered a pleasing contrast to the adjoining buildings jutting out on either side, alive with signs and humming with business.

"Some mistake," muttered Gryce to himself, as the perfect calm reigning over the whole establishment struck him anew. But before he had decided that he had been made the victim of a hoax, a movement took place in the area under the stoop, and an officer stepped out, with a countenance expressive of sufficient perplexity for Mr. Gryce to motion him back with the hurried inquiry: "Anything wrong? Any blood shed? All seems quiet here."

The officer, recognizing the old detective, touched his hat. "Can't get in," said he. "Have rung all the bells. Would think the house empty if I had not seen something like a stir in one of the windows overhead. Shall I try to make my way into the rear yard through one of the lower windows of Knapp & Co.'s store, next door?"

"Yes, and take this boy with you. Lock him up in some one of their offices, and then break your way into this house by some means. It ought to be easy enough from the back yard."

The officer nodded, took the boy by the arm, and in a trice had disappeared with him into the adjoining store. Mr. Gryce remained in the area, where he was presently besieged by a crowd of passers-by, eager to add their curiosity to the trouble they had so quickly scented. The opening of the door from the inside speedily put an end to importunities for which he had as yet no reply, and he was enabled to slip within, where he found himself in a place of almost absolute quiet. Before him lay a basement hall leading to a kitchen, which, even at that moment, he noticed to be in trimmer condition than is usual where much housework is done, but he saw nothing that bespoke tragedy, or even a break in the ordinary routine of life as observed in houses of like size and pretension.

Satisfied that what he sought was not to be found here, he followed the officer upstairs. As they emerged upon the parlour floor, the latter dropped the following information:

"Mr. Raffner of the firm next door says that the man who lives here is an odd sort of person whom nobody knows; a bookworm, I think they call him. He has occupied the house six months, yet they have never seen anyone about the premise but himself and a strange old servant as peculiar and uncommunicative as his master."

"I know," muttered Mr. Gryce. He did know, everybody knew, that this house, once the seat of one of New York's most aristocratic families, was inhabited at present by a Mr. Adams, noted alike for his more than common personal attractions, his wealth, and the uncongenial nature of his temperament, which precluded all association with his kind. It was this knowledge which had given zest to this investigation. To enter the house of such a man was an event in itself: to enter it on an errand of life and death—Well, it is under the inspiration of such opportunities that life is reawakened in old veins, especially when those veins connect the heart and brain of a sagacious, if octogenarian, detective.

The hall in which they now found themselves was wide, old-fashioned, and sparsely furnished in the ancient manner to be observed in such time-honoured structures. Two doors led into this hall, both of which now stood open. Taking advantage of this fact, they entered the nearest, which was nearly opposite the top of the staircase they had just ascended, and found themselves in a room barren as a doctor's outer office. There was nothing here worth their attention, and they would have left the place as unceremoniously as they had entered it if they had not caught glimpses of richness which promised an interior of uncommon elegance, behind the half-drawn folds of a *portière* at the further end of the room.

Advancing through the doorway thus indicated, they took one look about them and stood appalled. Nothing in their experience (and they had both experienced much) had prepared them for the thrilling, the solemn nature of what they were here called upon to contemplate.

Shall I attempt its description?

A room small and of circular shape, hung with strange tapestries relieved here and there by priceless curios, and lit, although it was still daylight, by a jet of rose-coloured light concentrated, not on the rows and rows of books around the lower portion of the room, or on the one great picture which at another time might have drawn the eye and held the attention, but on the upturned face of a man lying on a bearskin rug with a dagger in his heart and on his breast a cross whose golden lines, sharply outlined against his long, dark, swathing garment, gave him the appearance of a saint prepared in some holy place for burial, save that the dagger spoke of violent death, and his face of an anguish for which Mr. Gryce, notwithstanding his lifelong experience, found no name, so little did it answer to a sensation of fear, pain, or surprise, or any of the emotions usually visible on the countenances of such as have fallen under the unexpected stroke of an assassin.

2

Mysteries

A moment of indecision, of awe even, elapsed before Mr. Gryce recovered himself. The dim light, the awesome silence, the unexpected surroundings recalling a romantic age, the motionless figure of him who so lately had been the master of the house, lying outstretched as for the tomb, with the sacred symbol on his breast offering such violent contradiction to the earthly passion which had driven the dagger home, were enough to move even the tried spirit of this old officer of the law and confuse a mind which, in the years of his long connection with the force, had had many serious problems to work upon, but never one just like this.

It was only for a moment, though. Before the man behind him had given utterance to his own bewilderment and surprise, Mr. Gryce had passed in and taken his stand by the prostrate figure.

That it was that of a man who had long since ceased to breathe he could not for a moment doubt; yet his first act was to make sure of the fact by laying his hand on the pulse and examining the eyes, whose expression of reproach was such that he had to call up all his professional sangfroid to meet them.

He found the body still warm, but dead beyond all question, and, once convinced of this, he forbore to draw the dagger from the wound, though he did not fail to give it the most careful attention before turning his eyes elsewhere. It was no ordinary weapon. It was a curio from some oriental shop. This in itself seemed to point to suicide, but the direction in which the blade had entered the body and the position of the wound were not such as would be looked for in a case of self-murder.

The other clews were few. Though the scene had been one of bloodshed and death, the undoubted result of a sudden and fierce attack, there were no signs of struggle to be found in the well-ordered apartment. Beyond a few rose leaves scattered on the floor, the room was a scene of peace and quiet luxury. Even the large table which occupied the centre of the room and near which the master of the house had been standing when struck gave no token of the tragedy which had been enacted at its side. That is, not at first glance; for though its large top was covered with articles of use and ornament, they all stood undisturbed and presumably in place, as if the shock which had laid their owner low had failed to be communicated to his belongings.

The contents of the table were various. Only a man of complex tastes and attainments could have collected and arranged in one small compass pipes, pens, portraits, weights, measures, Roman lamps, Venetian glass, rare porcelains, medals, rough metal work, manuscript, a scroll of music, a pot of growing flowers, and—and—(this seemed oddest of all) a row of electric buttons, which Mr. Gryce no sooner touched than the light which had been burning redly in the cage of fretted ironwork overhead changed in a twinkling to a greenish glare, filling the room with such ghastly tints that Mr. Gryce sought in haste another button, and, pressing it, was glad to see a mild white radiance take the place of the sickly hue which had added its own horror to the already solemn terrors of the spot.

"Childish tricks for a man of his age and position," ruminated Mr. Gryce; but after catching another glimpse of the face lying upturned at his feet he was conscious of a doubt as to whether the owner of that countenance could have possessed an instinct which was in any wise childish, so strong and purposeful were his sharply cut features. Indeed, the face was one to make an impression under any circumstances. In the present instance, and with such an expression stamped upon it, it exerted a fascination which disturbed the current of the detective's thoughts whenever by any chance he allowed it to get between him and his duty. To attribute folly to a man with such a mouth and such a chin was to own one's self a poor judge of human nature. Therefore, the lamp overhead, with its electric connection and changing slides, had a meaning which at present could be sought for only in the evidences of scientific research observable in the books and apparatus everywhere surrounding him.

Letting the white light burn on, Mr. Gryce, by a characteristic effort, shifted his attention to the walls, covered, as I have said, with tapestries and curios. There was nothing on them calculated to aid him in his research into the secret of this crime, unless—yes, there

16

was something, a bent-down nail, wrenched from its place, the nail on which the cross had hung which now lay upon the dead man's heart. The cord by which it had been suspended still clung to the cross and mingled its red threads with that other scarlet thread which had gone to meet it from the victim's wounded breast. Who had torn down that cross? Not the victim himself. With such a wound, any such movement would have been impossible. Besides, the nail and the empty place on the wall were as far removed from where he lay as was possible in the somewhat circumscribed area of this circular apartment. Another's hand, then, had pulled down this symbol of peace and pardon, and placed it where the dying man's fleeting breath would play across it, a peculiar exhibition of religious hope or mad remorse, to the significance of which Mr. Gryce could not devote more than a passing thought, so golden were the moments in which he found himself alone upon this scene of crime.

Behind the table and half-way up the wall was a picture, the only large picture in the room. It was the portrait of a young girl of an extremely interesting and pathetic beauty. From her garb and the arrangement of her hair, it had evidently been painted about the end of our civil war. In it was to be observed the same haunting quality of intellectual charm visible in the man lying prone upon the floor, and though she was fair and he dark, there was sufficient likeness between the two to argue some sort of relationship between them. Below this picture were fastened a sword, a pair of epaulettes, and a medal such as was awarded for valor in the civil war.

"Mementoes which may help us in our task," mused the detective.

Passing on, he came unexpectedly upon a narrow curtain, so dark of hue and so akin in pattern to the draperies on the adjoining walls that it had up to this time escaped his attention. It was not that of a window, for such windows as were to be seen in this unique apartment were high upon the wall, indeed, almost under the ceiling. It must, therefore, drape the opening into still another communicating room. And such he found to be the case. Pushing this curtain aside, he entered a narrow closet containing a bed, a dresser, and a small table. The bed was the narrow cot of a bachelor, and the dresser that of a man of luxurious tastes and the utmost nicety of habit. Both the bed and dresser were in perfect order, save for a silver-backed comb, which had been taken from the latter, and which he presently found lying on the floor at the other end of the room.

This and the presence of a pearl-handled parasol on a small stand near the door proclaimed that a woman had been there within a short space of time. The identity of this woman was soon established in his eyes by a small but unmistakable token connecting her with the one who had been the means of sending in the alarm to the police. The token of which I speak was a little black spangle, called by milliners and mantua-makers a sequin, which lay on the threshold separating this room from the study; and as Mr. Gryce, attracted by its sparkle, stooped to examine it, his eye caught sight of a similar one on the floor beyond, and of still another a few steps farther on. The last one lay close to the large centre-table before which he had just been standing.

The dainty trail formed by these bright sparkling drops seemed to affect him oddly. He knew, minute observer that he was, that in the manufacture of this garniture the spangles are strung on a thread which, if once broken, allows them to drop away one by one, till you can almost follow a woman so arrayed by the sequins that fall from her. Perhaps it was the delicate nature of the clew thus offered that pleased him, perhaps it was a recognition of the irony of fate in thus making a trap for unwary mortals out of their vanities. Whatever it was, the smile with which he turned his eye upon the table toward which he had thus been led was very eloquent.

But before examining this article of furniture more closely, he attempted to find out where the thread had become loosened which had let the spangles fall. Had it caught on any projection in doorway or furniture? He saw none. All the chairs were cushioned and—But wait! there was the cross! That had a fretwork of gold at its base. Might not this *filigree* have caught in her dress as she was tearing down the cross from the wall and so have started the thread which had given him this exquisite clew?

Hastening to the spot where the cross had hung, he searched the floor at his feet, but found nothing to confirm his conjecture until he had reached the rug on which the prostrate man lay. There, amid the long hairs of the bearskin, he came upon one other spangle, and knew that the woman in the shiny clothes had stooped there before him.

Satisfied on this point, he returned to the table, and this time subjected it to a thorough and minute examination. That the result was not entirely unsatisfactory was evident from the smile with which he eyed his finger after having drawn it across a certain spot near the inkstand, and also from the care with which he lifted that inkstand and

18

replaced it in precisely the same spot from which he had taken it up. Had he expected to find something concealed under it? Who can tell? A detective's face seldom yields up its secrets.

He was musing quite intently before this table when a quick step behind him made him turn. Styles, the officer, having now been over the house, had returned, and was standing before him in the attitude of one who has something to say.

"What is it?" asked Mr. Gryce, with a quick movement in his direction.

For answer the officer pointed to the staircase visible through the antechamber door.

"Go up!" was indicated by his gesture.

Mr. Gryce demurred, casting a glance around the room, which at that moment interested him so deeply. At this the man showed some excitement, and, breaking silence, said:

"Come! I have lighted on the guilty party. He is in a room upstairs."

"He?" Mr. Gryce was evidently surprised at the pronoun.

"Yes; there can be no doubt about it. When you see him—but what is that? Is he coming down? I'm sure there's nobody else in the house. Don't you hear footsteps, sir?"

Mr. Gryce nodded. Someone was certainly descending the stairs.

"Let us retreat," suggested Styles. "Not because the man is dangerous, but because it is very necessary you should see him before he sees you. He's a very strange-acting man, sir; and if he comes in here, will be sure to do something to incriminate himself. Where can we hide?"

Mr. Gryce remembered the little room he had just left, and drew the officer toward it. Once installed inside, he let the curtain drop till only a small loophole remained. The steps, which had been gradually growing louder, kept advancing; and presently they could hear the intruder's breathing, which was both quick and laboured.

"Does he know that any one has entered the house? Did he see you when you came upon him upstairs?" whispered Mr. Gryce into the ear of the man beside him.

Styles shook his head, and pointed eagerly toward the opposite door. The man for whose appearance they waited had just lifted the *portière* and in another moment stood in full view just inside the threshold.

Mr. Gryce and his attendant colleague both stared. Was this the murderer? This pale, lean servitor, with a tray in his hand on which rested a single glass of water?

Mr. Gryce was so astonished that he looked at Styles for explanation. But that officer, hiding his own surprise, for he had not expected this peaceful figure, urged him in a whisper to have patience, and both, turning toward the man again, beheld him advance, stop, cast one look at the figure lying on the floor and then let slip the glass with a low cry that at once changed to something like a howl.

"Look at him! Look at him!" urged Styles, in a hurried whisper. "Watch what he will do now. You will see a murderer at work."

And sure enough, in another instant this strange being, losing all semblance to his former self, entered upon a series of pantomimic actions which to the two men who watched him seemed both to explain and illustrate the crime which had just been enacted there.

With every appearance of passion, he stood contemplating the empty air before him, and then, with one hand held stretched out behind him in a peculiarly cramped position, he plunged with the other toward a table from which he made a feint of snatching something which he no sooner closed his hand upon than he gave a quick side-thrust, still at the empty air, which seemed to quiver in return, so vigorous was his action and so evident his intent.

The reaction following this thrust; the slow unclosing of his hand from an imaginary dagger; the tottering of his body backward; then the moment when with wide open eyes he seemed to contemplate in horror the result of his own deed;—these needed no explanation beyond what was given by his writhing features and trembling body. Gradually succumbing to the remorse or terror of his own crime, he sank lower and lower, until, though with that one arm still stretched out, he lay in an inert heap on the floor.

"It is what I saw him do upstairs," murmured Styles into the ear of the amazed detective. "He has evidently been driven insane by his own act."

Mr. Gryce made no answer. Here was a problem for the solution of which he found no precedent in all his past experience.

3

The Mute Servitor

Meanwhile the man who, to all appearance, had just re-enacted before them the tragedy which had so lately taken place in this room, rose to his feet, and, with a dazed air as unlike his former violent expression as possible, stooped for the glass he had let fall, and was carrying it out when Mr. Gryce called to him:

"Wait, man! You needn't take that glass away. We first want to hear how your master comes to be lying here dead."

It was a demand calculated to startle any man. But this one showed himself totally unmoved by it, and was passing on when Styles laid a detaining hand on his shoulder.

"Stop!" said he. "What do you mean by sliding off like this? Don't you hear the gentleman speaking to you?"

This time the appeal told. The glass fell again from the man's hand, mingling its clink (for it struck the floor this time and broke) with the cry he gave—which was not exactly a cry either, but an odd sound between a moan and a shriek. He had caught sight of the men who were seeking to detain him, and his haggard look and cringing form showed that he realized at last the terrors of his position. Next minute he sought to escape, but Styles, gripping him more firmly, dragged him back to where Mr. Gryce stood beside the bearskin rug on which lay the form of his dead master.

Instantly, at the sight of this recumbent figure, another change took place in the entrapped butler. Joy—that most hellish of passions in the presence of violence and death—illumined his wandering eye and distorted his mouth; and, seeking no disguise for the satisfaction he felt, he uttered a low but thrilling laugh, which rang in unholy echo through the room.

Mr. Gryce, moved in spite of himself by an abhorrence which the irresponsible condition of this man seemed only to emphasize, waited till the last faint sounds of this diabolical mirth had died away in the high recesses of the space above. Then, fixing the glittering eye of this strange creature with his own, which, as we know, so seldom dwelt upon that of his fellow-beings, he sternly said:

"There now! Speak! Who killed this man? You were in the house with him, and should know."

The butler's lips opened and a string of strange gutturals poured forth, while with his one disengaged hand (for the other was held to his side by Styles) he touched his ears and his lips, and violently shook his head.

There was but one interpretation to be given to this. The man was deaf and dumb.

The shock of this discovery was too much for Styles. His hand fell from the other's arms, and the man, finding himself free, withdrew to his former place in the room, where he proceeded to enact again and with increased vivacity first the killing of and then the mourning for his master, which but a few moments before had made so suggestive an impression upon them. This done, he stood waiting, but this time with that gleam of infernal joy in the depths of his quick, restless eyes which made his very presence in this room of death seem a sacrilege and horror.

Styles could not stand it. "Can't you speak?" he shouted. "Can't you hear?"

The man only smiled, an evil and gloating smile, which Mr. Gryce thought it his duty to cut short.

"Take him away!" he cried. "Examine him carefully for blood marks. I am going up to the room where you saw him first. He is too nearly linked to this crime not to carry some trace of it away with him."

But for once even this time-tried detective found himself at fault. No marks were found on the old servant, nor could they discover in the rooms above any signs by which this one remaining occupant of the house could be directly associated with the crime which had taken place within it. Thereupon Mr. Gryce grew very thoughtful and entered upon another examination of the two rooms which to his mind held all the clews that would ever be given to this strange crime.

The result was meagre, and he was just losing himself again in contemplation of the upturned face, whose fixed mouth and haunting expression told such a story of suffering and determination, when

22

there came from the dim recesses above his head a cry, which, forming itself into two words, rang down with startling clearness in this most unexpected of appeals:

"Remember Evelyn!"

Remember Evelyn! Who was Evelyn? And to whom did this voice belong, in a house which had already been ransacked in vain for other occupants? It seemed to come from the roof, and, sure enough, when Mr. Gryce looked up he saw, swinging in a cage strung up nearly to the top of one of the windows I have mentioned, an English starling, which, in seeming recognition of the attention it had drawn upon itself, craned its neck as Mr. Gryce looked up, and shrieked again, with fiercer insistence than before:

"Remember Evelyn!"

It was the last uncanny touch in a series of uncanny experiences. With an odd sense of nightmare upon him, Mr. Gryce leaned forward on the study table in his effort to obtain a better view of this bird, when, without warning, the white light, which since his last contact with the electrical apparatus had spread itself through the room, changed again to green, and he realized that he had unintentionally pressed a button and thus brought into action another slide in the curious lamp over his head.

Annoyed, for these changing hues offered a problem he was as yet too absorbed in other matters to make any attempt to solve, he left the vicinity of the table, and was about to leave the room when he heard Styles's voice rise from the adjoining antechamber, where Styles was keeping guard over the old butler:

"Shall I let him go, Mr. Gryce? He seems very uneasy; not dangerous, you know, but anxious; as if he had forgotten something or recalled some unfulfilled duty."

"Yes, let him go," was the detective's quick reply. "Only watch and follow him. Every movement he makes is of interest. Unconsciously he may be giving us invaluable clews." And he approached the door to note for himself what the man might do.

"Remember Evelyn!" rang out the startling cry from above, as the detective passed between the curtains. Irresistibly he looked back and up. To whom was this appeal from a bird's throat so imperatively addressed? To him or to the man on the floor beneath, whose ears were forever closed? It might be a matter of little consequence, and it might be one involving the very secret of this tragedy. But whether important or not, he could pay no heed to it at this juncture, for the old butler, coming from the front hall whither he had hurried on being released by Styles, was at that moment approaching him, carrying in one hand his master's hat and in the other his master's umbrella.

Not knowing what this new movement might mean, Mr. Gryce paused where he was and waited for the man to advance. Seeing this, the mute, to whose face and bearing had returned the respectful immobility of the trained servant, handed over the articles he had brought, and then noiselessly, and with the air of one who had performed an expected service, retreated to his old place in the antechamber, where he sat down again and fell almost immediately into his former dazed condition.

"Humph! mind quite lost, memory uncertain, testimony valueless," were the dissatisfied reflections of the disappointed detective as he replaced Mr. Adams's hat and umbrella on the hall rack. "Has he been brought to this state by the tragedy which has just taken place here, or is his present insane condition its precursor and cause?" Mr. Gryce might have found some answer to this question in his own mind if, at that moment, the fitful clanging of the front door bell, which had hitherto testified to the impatience of the curious crowd outside, had not been broken into by an authoritative knock which at once put an end to all self-communing.

The coroner, or some equally important person, was at hand, and the detective's golden hour was over.

4

A New Experience For Mr. Gryce

Mr. Gryce felt himself at a greater disadvantage in his attempt to solve the mystery of this affair than in any other which he had entered upon in years. First, the victim had been a solitary man, with no household save his man-of-all-work, the mute. Secondly, he had lived in a portion of the city where no neighbours were possible; and he had even lacked, as it now seemed, any very active friends. Though some hours had elapsed since his death had been noised abroad, no one had appeared at the door with inquiries or information. This seemed odd, considering that he had been for some months a marked figure in this quarter of the town. But, then, everything about this man was odd, nor would it have been in keeping with his surroundings and peculiar manner of living for him to have had the ordinary associations of men of his class.

This absence of the usual means of eliciting knowledge from the surrounding people, added to, rather than detracted from, the interest which Mr. Gryce was bound to feel in the case, and it was with a feeling of relief that a little before midnight he saw the army of reporters, medical men, officials, and such others as had followed in the coroner's wake, file out of the front door and leave him again, for a few hours at least, master of the situation.

For there were yet two points which he desired to settle before he took his own much-needed rest. The first occupied his immediate attention. Passing before a chair in the hall on which a small boy sat dozing, he roused him with the remark:

"Come, Jake, it's time to look lively. I want you to go with me to the exact place where that lady ran across you today."

The boy, half dead with sleep, looked around him for his hat.

"I'd like to see my mother first," he pleaded. "She must be done up about me. I never stayed away so long before."

"Your mother knows where you are. I sent a message to her hours ago. She gave a very good report of you, Jake; says you're an obedient lad and that you never have told her a falsehood."

"She's a good mother," the boy warmly declared. "I'd be as bad—as bad as my father was, if I did not treat her well." Here his hand fell on his cap, which he put on his head.

"I'm ready," said he.

Mr. Gryce at once led the way into the street.

The hour was late, and only certain portions of the city showed any real activity. Into one of these thoroughfares they presently came, and before the darkened window of one of the lesser shops paused, while Jake pointed out the two stuffed frogs engaged with miniature swords in mortal combat at which he had been looking when the lady came up and spoke to him.

Mr. Gryce eyed the boy rather than the frogs, though probably the former would have sworn that his attention had never left that miniature conflict.

"Was she a pretty lady?" he asked.

The boy scratched his head in some perplexity.

"She made me a good deal afraid of her," he said. "She had very splendid clothes; oh, gorgeous!" he cried, as if on this question there could be no doubt.

"And she was young, and carried a bunch of flowers, and seemed troubled? What! not young, and carried no flowers—and wasn't even anxious and trembling?"

The boy, who had been shaking his head, looked nonplussed.

"I think as she was what you might call troubled. But she wasn't crying, and when she spoke to me, she put more feeling into her grip than into her voice. She just dragged me to the drug-store, sir. If she hadn't given me money first, I should have wriggled away in spite of her. But I likes money, sir; I don't get too much of it."

Mr. Gryce by this time was moving on. "Not young," he repeated to himself. "Some old flame, then, of Mr. Adams; they're apt to be dangerous, very dangerous, more dangerous than the young ones."

In front of the drug-store he paused. "Show me where she stood while you went in."

The boy pointed out the identical spot. He seemed as eager as the detective.

"And was she standing there when you came out?"

"Oh, no, sir; she went away while I was inside."

"Did you see her go? Can you tell me whether she went up street or down?"

"I had one eye on her, sir; I was afraid she was coming into the shop after me, and my arm was too sore for me to want her to clinch hold on it again. So when she started to go, I took a step nearer, and saw her move toward the kerbstone and hold up her hand. But it wasn't a car she was after, for none came by for several minutes."

The fold between Mr. Gryce's eyes perceptibly smoothed out.

"Then it was some cabman or hack-driver she hailed. Were there any empty coaches about that you saw?"

The boy had not noticed. He had reached the limit of his observations, and no amount of further questioning could elicit anything more from him. This Mr. Gryce soon saw, and giving him into the charge of one of his assistants who was on duty at this place, he proceeded back to the ill-omened house where the tragedy itself had occurred.

"Any one waiting for me?" he inquired of Styles, who came to the door.

"Yes, sir; a young man; name, Hines. Says he's an electrician."

"That's the man I want. Where is he?"

"In the parlour, sir."

"Good! I'll see him. But don't let anyone else in. Anybody upstairs?"

"No, sir, all gone. Shall I go up or stay here?"

"You'd better go up. I'll look after the door."

Styles nodded, and went toward the stairs, up which he presently disappeared. Mr. Gryce proceeded to the parlour.

A dapper young man with an intelligent eye rose to meet him. "You sent for me," said he.

The detective nodded, asked a few questions, and seeming satisfied with the replies he received, led the way into Mr. Adams's study, from which the body had been removed to an upper room. As they entered, a mild light greeted them from a candle which, by Mr. Gryce's orders, had been placed on a small side table near the door. But once in, Mr. Gryce approached the larger table in the centre of the room, and placing his hand on one of the buttons before him, asked his companion to be kind enough to blow out the candle. This he did, leaving the room for a moment in total darkness. Then with a sudden burst of illumination, a marvellous glow of a deep violet colour shot over the whole room, and the two men turned and faced each other both with inquiry in their looks, so unexpected was this theatrical effect to the one, and so inexplicable its cause and purpose to the other.

"That is but one slide," remarked Mr. Gryce. "Now I will press another button, and the colour changes to—pink, as you see. This one produces green, this one white, and this a bilious yellow, which is not becoming to either of us, I am sure. Now will you examine the connection, and see if there is anything peculiar about it?"

Mr. Hines at once set to work. But beyond the fact that the whole contrivance was the work of an amateur hand, he found nothing strange about it, except the fact that it worked so well.

Mr. Gryce showed disappointment.

"He made it, then, himself?" he asked.

"Undoubtedly, or someone else equally unacquainted with the latest method of wiring."

"Will you look at these books over here and see if sufficient knowledge can be got from them to enable an amateur to rig up such an arrangement as this?"

Mr. Hines glanced at the shelf which Mr. Gryce had pointed out, and without taking out the books, answered briefly:

"A man with a deft hand and a scientific turn of mind might, by the aid of these, do all you see here and more. The aptitude is all."

"Then I'm afraid Mr. Adams had the aptitude," was the dry response. There was disappointment in the tone. Why, his next words served to show. "A man with a turn for mechanical contrivances often wastes much time and money on useless toys only fit for children to play with. Look at that bird cage now. Perched at a height totally beyond the reach of any one without a ladder, it must owe its very evident usefulness (for you see it holds a rather lively occupant) to some contrivance by which it can be raised and lowered at will. Where is that contrivance? Can you find it?"

The expert thought he could. And, sure enough, after some ineffectual searching, he came upon another button well hid amid the tapestry on the wall, which, when pressed, caused something to be disengaged which gradually lowered the cage within reach of Mr. Gryce's hand.

"We will not send this poor bird aloft again," said he, detaching the cage and holding it for a moment in his hand. "An English starling is none too common in this country. Hark! he is going to speak."

But the sharp-eyed bird, warned perhaps by the emphatic gesture of the detective that silence would be more in order at this moment

28

than his usual appeal to "remember Evelyn," whisked about in his cage for an instant, and then subsided into a doze, which may have been real, and may have been assumed under the fascinating eye of the old gentleman who held him. Mr. Gryce placed the cage on the floor, and idly, or because the play pleased him, old and staid as he was, pressed another button on the table—a button he had hitherto neglected touching—and glanced around to see what colour the light would now assume.

But the yellow glare remained. The investigation which the apparatus had gone through had probably disarranged the wires. With a shrug he was moving off, when he suddenly made a hurried gesture, directing the attention of the expert to a fact for which neither of them was prepared. The opening which led into the antechamber, and which was the sole means of communication with the rest of the house, was slowly closing. From a yard's breadth it became a foot; from a foot it became an inch; from an inch——

"Well, that is certainly the contrivance of a lazy man," laughed the expert. "Seated in his chair here, he can close his door at will. No shouting after a deaf servant, no awkward stumbling over rugs to shut it himself. I don't know but I approve of this contrivance, only——" here he caught a rather serious expression on Mr. Gryce's face—"the slide seems to be of a somewhat curious construction. It is not made of wood, as any sensible door ought to be, but of——"

"Steel," finished Mr. Gryce in an odd tone. "This is the strangest thing yet. It begins to look as if Mr. Adams was daft on electrical contrivances."

"And as if we were prisoners here," supplemented the other. "I do not see any means for drawing this slide back."

"Oh, there's another button for that, of course," Mr. Gryce carelessly remarked.

But they failed to find one.

"If you don't object," observed Mr. Gryce, after five minutes of useless search, "I will turn a more cheerful light upon the scene. Yellow does not seem to fit the occasion."

"Give us rose, for unless you have someone on the other side of this steel plate, we seem likely to remain here till morning."

"There is a man upstairs whom we may perhaps make hear, but what does this contrivance portend? It has a serious look to me, when you consider that every window in these two rooms has been built up almost under the roof."

"Yes; a very strange look. But before engaging in its consideration I should like a breath of fresh air. I cannot do anything while in confinement. My brain won't work."

Meanwhile Mr. Gryce was engaged in examining the huge plate of steel which served as a barrier to their egress. He found that it had been made—certainly at great expense—to fit the curve of the walls through which it passed. This was a discovery of some consequence, causing Mr. Gryce to grow still more thoughtful and to eye the smooth steel plate under his hand with an air of marked distrust.

"Mr. Adams carried his taste for the mechanical to great extremes," he remarked to the slightly uneasy man beside him. "This slide is very carefully fitted, and, if I am not mistaken, it will stand some battering before we are released."

"I wish that his interest in electricity had led him to attach such a simple thing as a bell."

"True, we have come across no bell."

"It would have smacked too much of the ordinary to please him."

"Besides, his only servant was deaf."

"Try the effect of a blow, a quick blow with this silver-mounted alpenstock. Someone should hear and come to our assistance."

"I will try my whistle first; it will be better understood."

But though Mr. Gryce both whistled and struck many a resounding knock upon the barrier before them, it was an hour before he could draw the attention of Styles, and five hours before an opening could be effected in the wall large enough to admit of their escape, so firmly was this barrier of steel fixed across the sole outlet from this remarkable room.

5

Five Small Spangles

Such an experience could not fail to emphasize Mr. Gryce's interest in the case and heighten the determination he had formed to probe its secrets and explain all its extraordinary features. Arrived at headquarters, where his presence was doubtless awaited with some anxiety by those who knew nothing of the cause of his long detention, his first act was to inquire if Bartow, the butler, had come to his senses during the night.

The answer was disappointing. Not only was there no change in his condition, but the expert in lunacy who had been called in to pass upon his case had expressed an opinion unfavourable to his immediate recovery.

Mr. Gryce looked sober, and, summoning the officer who had managed Bartow's arrest, he asked how the mute had acted when he found himself detained.

The answer was curt, but very much to the point.

"Surprised, sir. Shook his head and made some queer gestures, then went through his pantomime. It's quite a spectacle, sir. Poor fool, he keeps holding his hand back, so."

Mr. Gryce noted the gesture; it was the same which Bartow had made when he first realized that he had spectators. Its meaning was not wholly apparent. He had made it with his right hand (there was no evidence that the mute was left-handed), and he continued to make it as if with this movement he expected to call attention to some fact that would relieve him from custody.

"Does he mope? Is his expression one of fear or anger?"

"It varies, sir. One minute he looks like a man on the point of falling asleep; the next he starts up in fury, shaking his head and pounding the walls. It's not a comfortable sight, sir. He will have to be watched night and day."

"Let him be, and note every change in him. His testimony may not be valid, but there is suggestion in every movement he makes. Tomorrow I will visit him myself."

The officer went out, and Mr. Gryce sat for a few moments communing with himself, during which he took out a little package from his pocket, and emptying out on his desk the five little spangles it contained, regarded them intently. He had always been fond of looking at some small and seemingly insignificant object while thinking. It served to concentrate his thoughts, no doubt. At all events, some such result appeared to follow the contemplation of these five sequins, for after shaking his head doubtfully over them for a time, he made a sudden move, and sweeping them into the envelope from which he had taken them, he gave a glance at his watch and passed quickly into the outer office, where he paused before a line of waiting men. Beckoning to one who had followed his movements with an interest which had not escaped the eye of this old reader of human nature, he led the way back to his own room.

"You want a hand in this matter?" he said interrogatively, as the door closed behind them and they found themselves alone.

"Oh, sir—" began the young man in a glow which made his more than plain features interesting to contemplate, "I do not presume——"

"Enough!" interposed the other. "You have been here now for six months, and have had no opportunity as yet for showing any special adaptability. Now I propose to test your powers with something really difficult. Are you up to it, Sweetwater? Do you know the city well enough to attempt to find a needle in this very big haystack?"

"I should at least like to try," was the eager response. "If I succeed it will be a bigger feather in my cap than if I had always lived in New York. I have been spoiling for some such opportunity. See if I don't make the effort judiciously, if only out of gratitude."

"Well, we shall see," remarked the old detective. "If it's difficulty you long to encounter, you will be likely to have all you want of it. Indeed, it is the impossible I ask. A woman is to be found of whom we know nothing save that she wore when last seen a dress heavily be-spangled with black, and that she carried in her visit to Mr. Adams, at the time of or before the murder, a parasol, of which I can procure you a glimpse before you start out. She came from, I don't know where, and she went—but that is what you are to find out. You are not the only man who is to be put on the job, which, as you see, is next door to a hopeless one, unless the woman comes forward and proclaims herself. Indeed, I should despair utterly of your success if it were not for one small fact which I will now proceed to give you as my special and confidential agent in this matter.

"When this woman was about to disappear from the one eye that was watching her, she approached the kerbstone in front of Hudson's fruit store on 14th Street and lifted up her right hand, so. It is not much of a clew, but it is all I have at my disposal, except these five spangles dropped from her dress, and my conviction that she is not to be found among the questionable women of the town, but among those who seldom or never come under the eye of the police. Yet don't let this conviction hamper you. Convictions as a rule are bad things, and act as a hindrance rather than an inspiration."

Sweetwater, to whom the song of the sirens would have sounded less sweet, listened with delight and responded with a frank smile and a gay:

"I'll do my best, sir, but don't show me the parasol, only describe it. I wouldn't like the fellows to chaff me if I fail; I'd rather go quietly to work and raise no foolish expectations."

"Well, then, it is one of those dainty, nonsensical things made of gray chiffon, with pearl handle and bows of pink ribbon. I don't believe it was ever used before, and from the value women usually place on such fol-de-rols, could only have been left behind under the stress of extraordinary emotion or fear. The name of the owner was not on it."

"Nor that of the maker?"

Mr. Gryce had expected this question, and was glad not to be disappointed.

"No, that would have helped us too much."

"And the hour at which this lady was seen on the kerbstone at Hudson's?"

"Half-past four; the moment at which the telephone message arrived."

"Very good, sir. It is the hardest task I have ever undertaken, but that's not against it. When shall I see you again?"

"When you have something to impart. Ah, wait a minute. I have my suspicion that this woman's first name is Evelyn. But, mind, it is only a suspicion."

"All right, sir," and with an air of some confidence, the young man disappeared.

Mr. Gryce did not look as if he shared young Sweetwater's cheerfulness. The mist surrounding this affair was as yet impenetrable to him. But then he was not twenty-three, with only triumphant memories behind him.

His next hope lay in the information likely to accrue from the published accounts of this crime, now spread broadcast over the country. A man of Mr. Adams's wealth and culture must necessarily have possessed many acquaintances, whom the surprising news of his sudden death would naturally bring to light, especially as no secret was made of his means and many valuable effects. But as if this affair, destined to be one of the last to engage the powers of this sagacious old man, refused on this very account to yield any immediate results to his investigation, the whole day passed by without the appearance of any claimant for Mr. Adams's fortune or the arrival on the scene of any friend capable of lifting the veil which shrouded the life of this strange being. To be sure, his banker and his lawyer came forward during the day, but they had little to reveal beyond the fact that his pecuniary affairs were in good shape and that, so far as they knew, he was without family or kin.

Even his landlord could add little to the general knowledge. He had first heard of Mr. Adams through a Philadelphia lawyer, since dead, who had assured him of his client's respectability and undoubted ability to pay his rent. When they came together and Mr. Adams was introduced to him, he had been struck, first, by the ascetic appearance of his prospective tenant, and, secondly, by his reserved manners and quiet intelligence. But admirable as he had found him, he had never succeeded in making his acquaintance. The rent had been uniformly paid with great exactitude on the very day it was due, but his own visits had never been encouraged or his advances met by anything but the cold politeness of a polished and totally indifferent man. Indeed, he had always looked upon his tenant as a bookworm, absorbed in study and such scientific experiments as could be carried on with no other assistance than that of his deaf and dumb servant.

Asked if he knew anything about this servant, he answered that his acquaintance with him was limited to the two occasions on which he had been ushered by him into his master's presence; that he knew nothing of his character and general disposition, and could not say whether his attitude toward his master had been one of allegiance or antagonism.

And so the way was blocked in this direction.

Taken into the room where Mr. Adams had died, he surveyed in amazement the huge steel plate which still blocked the doorway, and the high windows through which only a few straggling sunbeams could find their way.

Pointing to the windows, he remarked:

"These were filled in at Mr. Adams's request. Originally they extended down to the wainscoting."

He was shown where lath and plaster had been introduced and also how the plate had been prepared and arranged as a barrier. But he could give no explanation of it or divine the purpose for which it had been placed there at so great an expense.

The lamp was another curiosity, and its varying lights the cause of increased astonishment. Indeed he had known nothing of these arrangements, having been received in the parlour when he visited the house, where there was nothing to attract his attention or emphasize the well-known oddities of his tenant.

He was not shown the starling. That loquacious bird had been removed to police headquarters for the special delectation of Mr. Gryce.

Other inquiries failed also. No clew to the owner of the insignia found on the wall could be gained at the pension office or at any of the G. A. R. posts inside the city. Nor was the name of the artist who had painted the portrait which adorned so large a portion of the wall a recognized one in New York City. Otherwise a clew might have been obtained through him to Mr. Adams's antecedents. All the drawers and receptacles in Mr. Adams's study had been searched, but no will had been found nor any business documents. It was as if this strange man had sought to suppress his identity, or, rather, as if he had outgrown all interest in his kind or in anything beyond the walls within which he had immured himself.

Late in the afternoon reports began to come in from the various tradesmen with whom Mr. Adams had done business. They all had something to say as to the peculiarity of his habits and the freaks of his mute servant. They were both described as hermits, differing from the rest of their kind only in that they denied themselves no reasonable luxury and seemed to have adopted a shut-in life from a pure love of seclusion. The master was never seen at the stores. It was the servant who made the purchases, and this by means of gestures which were often strangely significant. Indeed, he seemed to have great power of expressing himself by looks and actions, and rarely caused a mistake or made one. He would not endure cheating, and always bought the best.

Of his sanity up to the day of his master's death there was no question; but more than one man with whom he had had dealings was ready to testify that there had been a change in his manner for the past few weeks—a sort of subdued excitement, quite unlike his former methodical bearing. He had shown an inclination to testiness, and was less easily pleased than formerly. To one clerk he had shown a nasty spirit under very slight provocation, and was only endured in the store on account of his master, who was too good a customer for them to offend. Mr. Kelly, a grocer, went so far as to say he acted like a man with a grievance who burned to vent his spite on some one, but held himself in forcible restraint.

Perhaps if no tragedy had taken place in the house on —— Street these various persons would not have been so ready to interpret thus unfavourably a nervousness excusable enough in one so cut off from all communication with his kind. But with the violent end of his master in view, and his own unexplained connection with it, who could help recalling that his glance had frequently shown malevolence?

But this was not evidence of the decided character required by the law, and Mr. Gryce was about to regard the day as a lost one, when Sweetwater made his reappearance at headquarters. The expression of his face put new life into Mr. Gryce.

"What!" he cried, "you have not found her?"

Sweetwater smiled. "Don't ask me, sir, not yet. I've come to see if there's any reason why I should not be given the loan of that parasol for about an hour. I'll bring it back. I only want to make a certain test with it."

"What test, my boy? May I ask, what test?"

"Please to excuse me, sir; I have only a short time in which to act before respectable business houses shut up for the night, and the test I speak of has to be made in a respectable house."

"Then you shall not be hindered. Wait here, and I will bring you the parasol. There! bring it back soon, my boy. I have not the patience I used to have."

"An hour, sir; give me an hour, and then——"

The shutting of the door behind his flying figure cut short his sentence.

That was a long hour to Mr. Gryce, or would have been if it had not mercifully been cut short by the return of Sweetwater in an even more excited state of mind than he had been before. He held the parasol in his hand.

"My test failed," said he, "but the parasol has brought me luck, notwithstanding. I have found the lady, sir, and——"

He had to draw a long breath before proceeding.

"And she is what I said," began the detective; "a respectable person in a respectable house."

"Yes, sir; very respectable, more respectable than I expected to see. Quite a lady, sir. Not young, but——"

"Her name, boy. Is it—Evelyn?"

Sweetwater shook his head with a look as naive in its way as the old detective's question.

"I cannot say, sir. Indeed, I had not the courage to ask. She is here——"

"Here!" Mr. Gryce took one hurried step toward the door, then came gravely back. "I can restrain myself," he said. "If she is here, she will not go till I have seen her. Are you sure you have made no mistake; that she is the woman we are after; the woman who was in Mr. Adams's house and sent us the warning?"

"Will you hear my story, sir? It will take only a moment. Then you can judge for yourself."

"Your story? It must be a pretty one. How came you to light on this woman so soon? By using the clew I gave you?"

Again Sweetwater's expression took on a touch of *naïveté*.

"I'm sorry, sir; but I was egotistical enough to follow my own idea. It would have taken too much time to hunt up all the drivers of hacks in the city, and I could not even be sure she had made use of a public conveyance. No, sir; I bethought me of another way by which I might reach this woman. You had shown me those spangles. They were portions of a very rich trimming; a trimming which has only lately come into vogue, and which is so expensive that it is worn chiefly by women of means, and sold only in shops where elaborate garnitures are to be found. I have seen and noticed dresses thus trimmed, in certain windows and on certain ladies; and before you showed me the spangles you picked up in Mr. Adams's study could have told you just how I had seen them arranged. They are sewed on black net, in figures, sir; in scrolls or wreaths or whatever you choose to call them; and so conspicuous are these wreaths or figures, owing to the brilliance of the spangles composing them, that any break in their continuity is plainly apparent, especially if the net be worn over a colour, as is frequently the case.

"Remembering this, and recalling the fact that these spangles doubtless fell from one of the front breadths, where their loss would attract not only the attention of others, but that of the wearer, I said to myself, 'What will she be likely to do when she finds her dress thus disfigured?' And the answer at once came: 'If she is the lady Mr. Gryce considers her, she will seek to restore these missing spangles, especially if they were lost on a scene of crime. But where can she get them to sew on? From an extra piece of net of the same style. But she will not be apt to have an extra piece of net. She will, therefore, find herself obliged to buy it, and since only a few spangles are lacking, she will buy the veriest strip.' Here, then, was my clew, or at least my ground for action. Going the rounds of the few leading stores on Broadway, 23d Street, and Sixth Avenue, I succeeded in getting certain clerks interested in my efforts, so that I speedily became assured that if a lady came into these stores for a very small portion of this bespangled net, they would note her person and, if possible, procure some clew to her address.

"Then I took up my stand at Arnold's emporium. Why Arnold's? I do not know. Perhaps my good genius meant me to be successful in this quest; but whether through luck or what not, I was successful, for before the afternoon was half over, I encountered a meaning glance from one of the men behind the counter, and advancing toward him, saw him rolling a small package which he handed over to a very pretty and rosy young girl, who at once walked away with it. 'For one of our leading customers,' he whispered, as I drew nearer. 'I don't think she is the person you want.' But I would take no chances. I followed the young girl who had carried away the parcel, and by this means came to a fine brownstone front in one of our most retired and aristocratic quarters.

"When I had seen her go in at the basement door, I rang the bell above, and then—well, I just bit my lips to keep down my growing excitement. For such an effort as this might well end in disappointment, and I knew if I were disappointed now—But no such trial awaited me. The maid who came to the door proved to be the same merry-eyed lass I had seen leave the store. Indeed, she had the identical parcel in her hand which was the connecting link between the imposing house at whose door I stood and the strange murder in ——Street. But I did not allow my interest in this parcel to become apparent, and by the time I addressed her I had so mastered myself as to arouse no suspicion of the importance of my errand. You, of course, foresee the question I put to the young girl. 'Has your mistress lost a parasol? One has been found—' I did not finish the sentence, for I perceived by her look that her mistress had met with such a loss, and as this was all I wanted to know just then, I cried out, 'I will bring it. If it is hers, all right,' and bounded down the steps.

"My intention was to inform you of what I had done and ask your advice. But my egotism got the better of me. I felt that I ought to make sure that I was not the victim of a coincidence. Such a respectable house! Such a respectable maidservant! Should she recognize the parasol as belonging to her mistress, then, indeed, I might boast of my success. So praying you for a loan of this article, I went back and rang the bell again. The same girl came to the door. I think fortune favoured me today. 'Here is the parasol,' said I, but before the words were out of my mouth I saw that the girl had taken the alarm or that some grievous mistake had been made. 'That is not the one my mistress lost,' said she. 'She never carries anything but black.' And the door was about to close between us when I heard a voice from within call out peremptorily: 'Let me see that parasol. Hold it up, young man. There! at the foot of the stairs. Ah!'

"If ever an exclamation was eloquent that simple 'ah!' was. I could not see the speaker, but I knew she was leaning over the banisters from the landing above. I listened to hear her glide away. But she did not move. She was evidently collecting herself for the emergency of the moment. Presently she spoke again, and I was astonished at her tone: 'You have come from Police Headquarters,' was the remark with which she hailed me.

"I lowered the parasol. I did not think it necessary to say yes.

"'From a man there, called Gryce,' she went on, still in that strange tone I can hardly describe, sir.

"'Since you ask me,' I now replied, 'I acknowledge that it is through his instructions I am here. He was anxious to restore to you your lost property. Is not this parasol yours? Shall I not leave it with this young girl?'

"The answer was dry, almost rasping: 'Mr. Gryce has made a mistake. The parasol is not mine; yet he certainly deserves credit for the use he has made of it, in this search. I should like to tell him so. Is he at his office, and do you think I would be received?'

"'He would be delighted,' I returned, not imagining she was in earnest. But she was, sir. In less time than you would believe, I perceived a very stately, almost severe, lady descend the stairs. She was dressed for the street, and spoke to me with quite an air of command. 'Have you a cab?' she asked.

"'No,' said I.

"'Then get one.'

"Here was a dilemma. Should I leave her and thus give her an opportunity to escape, or should I trust to her integrity and the honesty of her look, which was no common one, sir, and obey her as every one about her was evidently accustomed to do?

"I concluded to trust to her integrity, and went for the cab. But it was a risk, sir, which I promise not to repeat in the future. She was awaiting me on the stoop when I got back, and at once entered the hack with a command to drive immediately to Police Headquarters. I saw her as I came in just now sitting in the outer office, waiting for you. Are you ready to say I have done well?"

Mr. Gryce, with an indescribable look of mingled envy and indulgence, pressed the hand held out to him, and passed out. His curiosity could be restrained no longer, and he went at once to where this mysterious woman was awaiting him. Did he think it odd that she knew him, that she sought him? If so, he did not betray this in his manner, which was one of great respect. But that manner suddenly changed as he came face to face with the lady in question. Not that it lost its respect, but that it betrayed an astonishment of a more pronounced character than was usually indulged in by this experienced detective. The lady before him was one well known to him; in fact, almost an associate of his in certain bygone matters; in other words, none other than that most reputable of ladies, Miss Amelia Butterworth of Gramercy Park.

6

Suggestions From an Old Friend

The look with which this amiable spinster met his eye was one which a stranger would have found it hard to understand. He found it hard to understand himself, perhaps because he had never before seen this lady when she was labouring under an opinion of herself that was not one of perfect complacency.

"Miss Butterworth! What does this mean? Have you——"

"There!" The word came with some sharpness. "You have detected me at my old tricks, and I am correspondingly ashamed, and you triumphant. The gray parasol you have been good enough to send to my house is not mine, but I was in the room where you picked it up, as you have so cleverly concluded, and as it is useless for me to evade your perspicacity, I have come here to confess."

"Ah!" The detective was profoundly interested at once. He drew a chair up to Miss Butterworth's side and sat down. "You were there!" he repeated; "and when? I do not presume to ask for what purpose."

"But I shall have to explain my purpose not to find myself at too great a disadvantage," she replied with grim decision. "Not that I like to display my own weakness, but that I recognize the exigencies of the occasion, and fully appreciate your surprise at finding that I, a stranger to Mr. Adams, and without the excuse which led to my former interference in police matters, should have so far forgotten myself as to be in my present position before you. This was no affair of my immediate neighbour, nor did it seek me. I sought it, sir, and in this way. I wish I had gone to Jericho first; it might have meant longer travel and much more expense; but it would have involved me in less humiliation and possible publicity.

"Mr. Gryce, I never meant to be mixed up with another murder case. I have shown my aptitude for detective work and received, ere now, certain marks of your approval; but my head was not turned by them—at least I thought not—and I was tolerably sincere in my determination to keep to my own *metier* in future and not suffer myself to be allured by any inducements you might offer into the exercise of gifts which may have brought me praise in the past, but certainly have not brought me happiness. But the temptation came, not through you, or I might have resisted it, but through a combination of circumstances which found me weak, and, in a measure, unprepared. In other words, I was surprised into taking an interest in this affair. Oh, I am ashamed of it, so ashamed that I have made the greatest endeavour to hide my participation in the matter, and thinking I had succeeded in doing so, was congratulating myself upon my precautions, when I found that parasol thrust in my face and realized that you, if no one else, knew that Amelia Butterworth had been in Mr. Adams's room of death prior to yourself. Yet I thought I had left no traces behind me. Could you have seen——"

"Miss Butterworth, you dropped five small spangles from your robe. You wore a dress spangled with black sequins, did you not? Besides, you moved the inkstand, and—Well, I will never put faith in circumstantial evidence again. I saw these tokens of a woman's presence, heard what the boy had to say of the well-dressed lady who had sent him into the drug-store with a message to the police, and drew the conclusion—I may admit it to you—that it was this woman who had wielded the assassin's dagger, and not the deaf-and-dumb butler, who, until now, has borne the blame of it. Therefore I was anxious to find her, little realizing what would be the result of my efforts, or that I should have to proffer her my most humble apologies."

"Do not apologize to me. I had no business to be there, or, at least, to leave the five spangles you speak of, behind me on Mr. Adams's miserable floor. I was simply passing by the house; and had I been the woman I once was, that is, a woman who had never dipped into a mystery, I should have continued on my way, instead of turning aside. Sir, it's a curious sensation to find yourself, however innocent, regarded by a whole city full of people as the cause or motive of a terrible murder, especially when you have spent some time, as I have, in the study of crime and the pursuit of criminals. I own I don't enjoy the experience. But I have brought it on myself. If I had not been so curious—But it was not curiosity I felt. I will never own that I am subject to mere curiosity; it was the look on the young man's face. But I forget myself. I am rambling in all directions when I ought to be telling a consecutive tale. Not my usual habit, sir; this you know; but I am not quite myself at this moment. I declare I am more upset by this discovery of my indiscretion than I was by Mr. Trohm's declaration of affection in Lost Man's Lane! Give me time, Mr. Gryce; in a few minutes I will be more coherent."

"I am giving you time," he returned with one of his lowest bows. "The half-dozen questions I long to ask have not yet left my lips, and I sit here, as you must yourself acknowledge, a monument of patience."

"So you thought this deed perpetrated by an outsider," she suddenly broke in. "Most of the journals—I read them very carefully this morning—ascribed the crime to the man you have mentioned. And there seems to be good reason for doing so. The case is not a simple one, Mr. Gryce; it has complications—I recognized that at once, and that is why—but I won't waste another moment in apologies. You have a right to any little fact I may have picked up in my unfortunate visit, and there is one which I failed to find included in any account of the murder. Mr. Adams had other visitors besides myself in those few fatal minutes preceding his death. A young man and woman were with him. I saw them come out of the house. It was at the moment I was passing——"

"Tell your story more simply, Miss Butterworth. What first drew your attention to the house?"

"There! That is the second time you have had to remind me to be more direct. You will not have to do so again, Mr. Gryce. To begin, then, I noticed the house, because I always notice it. I never pass it without giving a thought to its ancient history and indulging in more or less speculation as to its present inmates. When, therefore, I found myself in front of it yesterday afternoon on my way to the art exhibition, I naturally looked up, and—whether by an act of providence or not, I cannot say—it was precisely at that instant the inner door of the vestibule burst open, and a young man appeared in the hall, carrying a young woman in his arms. He seemed to be in a state of intense excitement, and she in a dead faint; but before they had attracted the attention of the crowd, he had placed her on her feet, and, taking her on his arm, dragged her down the stoop and into the crowd of passers-by, among whom they presently disappeared.

"I, as you may believe, stood rooted to the ground in my astonishment, and not only endeavoured to see in what direction they went, but lingered long enough to take a peep into the time-honoured interior of this old house, which had been left open to view by the young man's forgetting to close the front door behind him. As I did so, I heard a cry from within. It was muffled and remote, but unmistakably one of terror and anguish: and, led by an impulse I may live to regret, as it seems likely to plunge me into much unpleasantness, I rushed up the stoop and went in, shutting the door behind me, lest others should be induced to follow.

"So far, I had acted solely from instinct; but once in that semi-dark hall, I paused and asked what business I had there, and what excuse I should give for my intrusion if I encountered one or more of the occupants of the house. But a repetition of the cry, coming as I am ready to swear from the farthest room on the parlour floor, together with a sharp remembrance of the wandering eye and drawn countenance of the young man whom I had seen stagger hence a moment before, with an almost fainting woman in his arms, drew me on in spite of my feminine instincts; and before I knew it, I was in the circular study and before the prostrate form of a seemingly dying man. He was lying as you probably found him a little later, with the cross on his breast and a dagger in his heart; but his right hand was trembling, and when I stooped to lift his head, he gave a shudder and then settled into eternal stillness. I, a stranger from the street, had witnessed his last breath while the young man who had gone out——"

"Can you describe him? Did you encounter him close enough for recognition?"

"Yes, I think I would know him again. I can at least describe his appearance. He wore a checked suit, very natty, and was more than usually tall and fine-looking. But his chief peculiarity lay in his expression. I never saw on any face, no, not on the stage, at the climax of the most heart-rending tragedy, a greater accumulation of mortal passion struggling with the imperative necessity for restraint. The young girl whose blond head lay on his shoulder looked like a saint in the clutch of a demon.

She had seen death, but he—But I prefer not to be the interpreter of that expressive countenance. It was lost to my view almost immediately, and probably calmed itself in the face of the throng he entered, or we would be hearing about him today. The girl seemed to be devoid of almost all feeling. I should not remember her."

"And was that all? Did you just look at that recumbent man and vanish? Didn't you encounter the butler? Haven't you some definite knowledge to impart in his regard which will settle his innocence or fix his guilt?"

"I know no more about him than you do, sir, except that he was not in the room by the time I reached it, and did not come into it during my presence there. Yet it was his cry that led me to the spot; or do you think it was that of the bird I afterward heard shouting and screaming in the cage over the dead man's head?"

"It might have been the bird," admitted Mr. Gryce. "Its call is very clear, and it seems strangely intelligent. What was it saying while you stood there?"

"Something about Eva. 'Lovely Eva, maddening Eva! I love Eva! Eva! Eva!'"

"Eva? Wasn't it 'Evelyn? Poor Evelyn?'"

"No, it was Eva. I thought he might mean the girl I had just seen carried out. It was an unpleasant experience, hearing this bird shriek out these cries in the face of the man lying dead at my feet."

"Miss Butterworth, you didn't simply stand over that man. You knelt down and looked in his face."

"I acknowledge it, and caught my dress in the *filigree* of the cross. Naturally I would not stand stock still with a man drawing his last breath under my eye."

"And what else did you do? You went to the table——"

"Yes, I went to the table."

"And moved the inkstand?"

"Yes, I moved the inkstand, but very carefully, sir, very carefully."

"Not so carefully but that I could see where it had been sitting before you took it up: the square made by its base in the dust of the table did not coincide with the place afterwards occupied by it."

"Ah, that comes from your having on your glasses and I not. I endeavoured to set it down in the precise place from which I lifted it."

"Why did you take it up at all? What were you looking for?"

"For clews, Mr. Gryce. You must forgive me, but I was seeking for clews. I moved several things. I was hunting for the line of writing which ought to explain this murder."

"The line of writing?"

"Yes. I have not told you what the young girl said as she slipped with her companion into the crowd."

"No; you have spoken of no words. Have you any such clew as that? Miss Butterworth, you are fortunate, very fortunate."

Mr. Gryce's look and gesture were eloquent, but Miss Butterworth, with an access of dignity, quietly remarked:

"I was not to blame for being in the way when they passed, nor could I help hearing what she said."

"And what was it, madam? Did she mention a paper?"

"Yes, she cried in what I now remember to have been a tone of affright: 'You have left that line of writing behind!' I did not attach much importance to these words then, but when I came upon the dying man, so evidently the victim of murder, I recalled what his late visitor had said and looked about for this piece of writing."

"And did you find it, Miss Butterworth? I am ready, as you see, for any revelation you may now make."

"For one which would reflect dishonour on me? If I had found any paper explaining this tragedy, I should have felt bound to have called the attention of the police to it. I did notify them of the crime itself."

"Yes, madam; and we are obliged to you; but how about your silence in regard to the fact of two persons having left that house immediately upon, or just preceding, the death of its master?"

"I reserved that bit of information. I waited to see if the police would not get wind of these people without my help. I sincerely wished to keep my name out of this inquiry. Yet I feel a decided relief now that I have made my confession. I never could have rested properly after seeing so much, and——"

"Well?"

"Thinking my own thoughts in regard to what I saw, if I had found myself compelled to bridle my tongue while false scents were being followed and delicate clews overlooked or discarded without proper attention. I regard this murder as offering the most difficult problem that has ever come in my way, and, therefore——"

"Yes, madam."

"I cannot but wonder if an opportunity has been afforded me for retrieving myself in your eyes. I do not care for the opinion of any one else as to my ability or discretion; but I should like to make you forget my last despicable failure in Lost Man's Lane. It is a sore remembrance to me, Mr. Gryce, which nothing but a fresh success can make me forget."

"Madam, I understand you. You have formulated some theory. You consider the young man with the tell-tale face guilty of Mr. Adams's death. Well, it is very possible. I never thought the butler was rehearsing a crime he had himself committed."

"Do you know who the young man is I saw leaving that house so hurriedly?"

"Not the least in the world. You are the first to bring him to my attention."

"And the young girl with the blonde hair?"

"It is the first I have heard of her, too."

"I did not scatter the rose leaves that were found on that floor."

"No, it was she. She probably wore a bouquet in her belt."

"Nor was that frippery parasol mine, though I did lose a good, stout, serviceable one somewhere that day."

"It was hers; I have no doubt of it."

"Left by her in the little room where she was whiling away the time during which the gentlemen conversed together, possibly about that bit of writing she afterward alluded to."

"Certainly."

"Her mind was not expectant of evil, for she was smoothing her hair when the shock came——"

"Yes, madam, I follow you."

"And had to be carried out of the place after——"

"What?"

"She had placed that cross on Mr. Adams's breast. That was a woman's act, Mr. Gryce."

"I am glad to hear you say so. The placing of that cross on a layman's breast was a mystery to me, and is still, I must own. Great remorse or great fright only can account for it."

"You will find many mysteries in this case, Mr. Gryce."

"As great a number as I ever encountered."

"I have to add one."

"Another?"

"It concerns the old butler."

"I thought you did not see him."

"I did not see him in the room where Mr. Adams lay."

"Ah! Where, then?"

"Upstairs. My interest was not confined to the scene of the murder. Wishing to spread the alarm, and not being able to rouse any one below, I crept upstairs, and so came upon this poor wretch going through the significant pantomime that has been so vividly described in the papers."

"Ah! Unpleasant for you, very. I imagine you did not stop to talk to him."

"No, I fled. I was extremely shaken up by this time and knew only one thing to do, and that was to escape. But I carried one as yet unsolved enigma with me. How came I to hear this man's cries in Mr.

Adams's study, and yet find him on the second floor when I came to search the house? He had not time to mount the stairs while I was passing down the hall."

"It is a case of mistaken impression. Your ears played you false. The cries came from above, not from Mr. Adams's study."

"My ears are not accustomed to play me tricks. You must seek another explanation."

"I have ransacked the house; there are no back stairs."

"If there were, the study does not communicate with them."

"And you heard his voice in the study?"

"Plainly."

"Well, you have given me a poser, madam."

"And I will give you another. If he was the perpetrator of this crime, how comes it that he was not detected and denounced by the young people I saw going out? If, on the contrary, he was simply the witness of another man's blow—a blow which horrified him so much that it unseated his reason—how comes it that he was able to slide away from the door where he must have stood without attracting the attention and bringing down upon himself the vengeance of the guilty murderer?"

"He may be one of the noiseless kind, or, rather, may have been such before this shock unsettled his mind."

"True, but he would have been seen. Recall the position of the doorway. If Mr. Adams fell where he was struck, the assailant must have had that door directly before him. He could not have helped seeing any one standing in it."

"That is true; your observations are quite correct. But those young people were in a disordered state of mind. The condition in which they issued from the house proves this. They probably did not trouble themselves about this man. Escape was all they sought. And, you see, they did escape."

"But you will find them. A man who can locate a woman in this great city of ours with no other clew than five spangles, dropped from her gown, will certainly make this parasol tell the name of its owner."

"Ah, madam, the credit of this feat is not due to me. It was the initial stroke of a young man I propose to adopt into my home and heart; the same who brought you here tonight. Not much to look at, madam, but promising, very promising. But I doubt if even he can discover the young lady you mean, with no other aid than is given by this parasol. New York is a big place, ma'am, a big place. Do you know how Sweetwater came to find you? Through your virtues, ma'am; through your neat and methodical habits. Had you been of a careless turn of mind and not given to mending your dresses when you tore them, he might have worn his heart out in a vain search for the lady who had dropped the five spangles in Mr. Adams's study. Now luck, or, rather, your own commendable habit, was in his favour this time; but in the prospective search you mentioned, he will probably have no such assistance."

"Nor will he need it. I have unbounded faith in your genius, which, after all, is back of the skilfulness of this new pupil of yours. You will discover by some means the lady with the dove-coloured plumes, and through her the young gentleman who accompanied her."

"We shall at least put our energies to work in that direction. Sweet-water may have an idea——"

"And I may have one."

"You?"

"Yes; I indulged in but little sleep last night. That dreadful room with its unsolved mystery was ever before me. Thoughts would come; possibilities would suggest themselves. I imagined myself probing its secrets to the bottom and——"

"Wait, madam; how many of its so-called secrets do you know? You said nothing about the lantern."

"It was burning with a red light when I entered."

"You did not touch the buttons arranged along the table top?"

"No; if there is one thing I do not touch, it is anything which suggests an electrical contrivance. I am intensely feminine, sir, in all my instincts, and mechanisms of any kind alarm me. To all such things I give a wide berth. I have not even a telephone in my house. Some allowance must be made for the natural timidity of woman."

Mr. Gryce suppressed a smile. "It is a pity," he remarked. "Had you brought another light upon the scene, you might have been blessed with an idea on a subject that is as puzzling as any connected with the whole affair."

"You have not heard what I have to say on a still more important matter," said she. "When we have exhausted the one topic, we may both feel like turning on the fresh lights you speak of. Mr. Gryce, on what does this mystery hinge? On the bit of writing which these young people were so alarmed at having left behind them."

"Ah! It is from that you would work! Well, it is a good point to

49

start from. But we have found no such bit of writing."

"Have you searched for it? You did not know till now that any importance might be attached to a morsel of paper with some half-dozen words written on it."

"True, but a detective searches just the same. We ransacked that room as few rooms have been ransacked in years. Not for a known clew, but for an unknown one. It seemed necessary in the first place to learn who this man was. His papers were consequently examined. But they told nothing. If there had been a scrap of writing within view or in his desk——"

"It was not on his person? You had his pockets searched, his clothes——"

"A man who has died from violence is always searched, madam. I leave no stone unturned in a mysterious case like this."

Miss Butterworth's face assumed an indefinable expression of satisfaction, which did not escape Mr. Gryce's eye, though that member was fixed, according to his old habit, on the miniature of her father which she wore, in defiance of fashion, at her throat.

"I wonder," said she, in a musing tone, "if I imagined or really saw on Mr. Adams's face a most extraordinary expression; something more than the surprise or anguish following a mortal blow? A look of determination, arguing some superhuman resolve taken at the moment of death, or—can you read that face for me? Or did you fail to perceive aught of what I say? It would really be an aid to me at this moment to know."

"I noted that look. It was not a common one. But I cannot read it for you——"

"I wonder if the young man you call Sweetwater can. I certainly think it has a decided bearing on this mystery; such a fold to the lips, such a look of mingled grief and—what was that you said? Sweetwater has not been admitted to the room of death? Well, well, I shall have to make my own suggestion, then. I shall have to part with an idea that may be totally valueless, but which has impressed me so that it must out, if I am to have any peace tonight. Mr. Gryce, allow me to whisper in your ear. Some things lose force when spoken aloud."

And leaning forward, she breathed a short sentence into his ear which made him start and regard her with an amazement which rapidly grew into admiration.

"Madam!" he cried, rising up that he might the better honour her with one of his low bows, "your idea, whether valueless or not, is one which is worthy of the acute lady who proffers it. We will act on it, ma'am, act at once. Wait till I have given my orders. I will not keep you long."

And with another bow, he left the room.

7

Amos's Son

Miss Butterworth had been brought up in a strict school of manners. When she sat, she sat still; when she moved, she moved quickly, firmly, but with no unnecessary disturbance. Fidgets were unknown to her. Yet when she found herself alone after this interview, it was with difficulty she could restrain herself from indulging in some of those outward manifestations of uneasiness which she had all her life reprobated in the more nervous members of her own sex. She was anxious, and she showed it, like the sensible woman she was, and was glad enough when Mr. Gryce finally returned and, accosting her with a smile, said almost gayly:

"Well, that is seen to! And all we have to do now is to await the result. Madam, have you any further ideas? If so, I should be glad to have the benefit of them."

Her self-possession was at once restored.

"You would?" she repeated, eying him somewhat doubtfully. "I should like to be assured of the value of the one I have already advanced, before I venture upon another. Let us enter into a conference instead; compare notes; tell, for instance, why neither of us look on Bartow as the guilty man."

"I thought we had exhausted that topic. Your suspicions were aroused by the young couple you saw leaving the house, while mine—well, madam, to you, at least, I may admit that there is something in the mute's gestures and general manner which conveys to my mind the impression that he is engaged in rehearsing something he has seen, rather than something he has done; and as yet I have seen no reason for doubting the truth of this impression."

"I was affected in the same way, and would have been, even if I had not already had my suspicions turned in another direction. Besides, it is more natural for a man to be driven insane by another's act than by his own."

"Yes, if he loved the victim."

"And did not Bartow?"

"He does not mourn Mr. Adams."

"But he is no longer master of his emotions."

"Very true; but if we take any of his actions as a clew to the situation, we must take all. We believe from his gestures that he is giving us a literal copy of acts he has seen performed. Then, why pass over the gleam of infernal joy that lights his face after the whole is over? It is as if he rejoiced over the deed, or at least found immeasurable satisfaction in it."

"Perhaps it is still a copy of what he saw; the murderer may have rejoiced. But no, there was no joy in the face of the young man I saw rushing away from this scene of violence. Quite the contrary. Mr. Gryce, we are in deep waters. I feel myself well-nigh submerged by them."

"Hold up your head, madam. Every flood has its ebb. If you allow yourself to go under, what will become of me?"

"You are disposed to humour, Mr. Gryce. It is a good sign. You are never humourous when perplexed. Somewhere you must see daylight."

"Let us proceed with our argument. Illumination frequently comes from the most unexpected quarter."

"Very well, then, let us put the old man's joy down as one of the mysteries to be explained later. Have you thought of him as a possible accomplice?"

"Certainly; but this supposition is open to the same objection as that which made him the motive power in this murder. One is not driven insane by an expected horror. It takes shock to unsettle the brain. He was not looking for the death of his master."

"True. We may consider that matter as settled. Bartow was an innocent witness of this crime, and, having nothing to fear, may be trusted to reproduce in his pantomimic action its exact features."

"Very good. Continue, madam. Nothing but profit is likely to follow an argument presented by Miss Butterworth."

The old detective's tone was serious, his manner perfect; but Miss Butterworth, ever on the look-out for sarcasm from his lips, bridled a little, though in no other way did she show her displeasure.

"Let us, then, recall his precise gestures, remembering that he must have surprised the assailant from the study doorway, and so have seen the assault from over his master's shoulder."

"In other words, directly in front of him. Now what was his first move?"

"His first move, as now seen, is to raise his right arm and stretch it behind him, while he leans forward for the imaginary dagger. What does that mean?"

"I should find it hard to say. But I did not see him do that. When I came upon him, he was thrusting with his left hand across his own body—a vicious thrust and with his left hand. That is a point, Mr. Gryce."

"Yes, especially as the doctors agree that Mr. Adams was killed by a left-handed blow."

"You don't say! Don't you see the difficulty, then?"

"The difficulty, madam?"

"Bartow was standing face to face with the assailant. In imitating him, especially in his unreasoning state of mind, he would lift the arm opposite to the one whose action he mimics, which, in this case, would be the assailant's right. Try, for the moment, to mimic my actions. See! I lift this hand, and instinctively (nay, I detected the movement, sir, quickly as you remembered yourself), you raise the one directly opposite to it. It is like seeing yourself in a mirror. You turn your head to the right, but your image turns to the left."

Mr. Gryce's laugh rang out in spite of himself. He was not often caught napping, but this woman exercised a species of fascination upon him at times, and it rather amused than offended him, when he was obliged to acknowledge himself defeated.

"Very good! You have proved your point quite satisfactorily; but what conclusions are to be drawn from it? That the man was not left-handed, or that he was not standing in the place you have assigned to him?"

"Shall we go against the doctors? They say that the blow was a left-handed one. Mr. Gryce, I would give anything for an hour spent with you in Mr. Adams's study, with Bartow free to move about at his will. I think we would learn more by watching him for a short space of time than in talking as we are doing for an hour."

It was said tentatively, almost timidly. Miss Butterworth had some sense of the temerity involved in this suggestion even if, according to her own declaration, she had no curiosity. "I don't want to be disagreeable," she smiled.

She was so far from being so that Mr. Gryce was taken unawares, and for once in his life became impulsive.

"I think it can be managed, madam; that is, after the funeral. There are too many officials now in the house, and——"

"Of course, of course," she acceded. "I should not think of obtruding myself at present. But the case is so interesting, and my connection with it so peculiar, that I sometimes forget myself. Do you think"—here she became quite nervous for one of her marked self-control—"that I have laid myself open to a summons from the coroner?"

Mr. Gryce grew thoughtful, eyed the good lady, or rather her folded hands, with an air of some compassion, and finally replied:

"The facts regarding this affair come in so slowly that I doubt if the inquest is held for several days. Meanwhile we may light on those two young people ourselves. If so, the coroner may *overlook* your share in bringing them to our notice."

There was a sly emphasis on the word, and a subtle humour in his look that showed the old detective at his worst. But Miss Butterworth did not resent it; she was too full of a fresh confession she had to make.

"Ah," said she, "if they had been the only persons I encountered there. But they were not. Another person entered the house before I left it, and I may be obliged to speak of him."

"Of him? Really, madam, you are a mine of intelligence."

"Yes, sir," was the meek reply; meek, when you consider from whose lips it came. "I ought to have spoken of him before, but I never like to mix matters, and this old gentleman——"

"Old gentleman!"

"Yes, sir, very old and very much of a gentleman, did not appear to have any connection with the crime beyond knowing the murdered man."

"Ah, but that's a big connection, ma'am. To find some one who knew Mr. Adams—really, madam, patience has its limits, and I must press you to speak."

"Oh, I will speak! The time has come for it. Besides, I'm quite ready to discuss this new theme; it is very interesting."

"Suppose we begin, then, by a detailed account of your adventures in this house of death," dryly suggested the detective. "Your full adventures, madam, with nothing left out."

"I appreciate the sarcasm, but nothing has been left out except what I am about to relate to you. It happened just as I was leaving the house."

"What did? I hate to ask you to be more explicit. But, in the interests of justice——"

"You are quite right. As I was going out, then, I encountered an elderly gentleman coming in. His hand had just touched the bell handle. You will acknowledge that it was a perplexing moment for me. His face, which was well preserved for his years, wore an air of expectation that was almost gay. He glanced in astonishment at mine, which, whatever its usual serenity, certainly must have borne marks of deep emotion. Neither of us spoke. At last he inquired politely if he might enter, and said something about having an appointment with someone in the study. At which I stepped briskly enough aside, I assure you, for this might mean—What did you say? Did I close the door? I assuredly did. Was I to let the whole of—— Street into the horrors of this house at a moment when a poor old man—No, I didn't go out myself. Why should I? Was I to leave a man on the verge of eighty—excuse me, not every man of eighty is so hale and vigorous as yourself—to enter such a scene alone? Besides, I had not warned him of the condition of the only other living occupant of the house."

"Discreet, very. Quite what was to be expected of you, Miss Butterworth. More than that. You followed him, no doubt, with careful supervision, down the hall."

"Most certainly! What would you have thought of me if I had not? He was in a strange house; there was no servant to guide him, he wanted to know the way to the study, and I politely showed him there."

"Kind of you, madam,—very. It must have been an interesting moment to you."

"Very interesting! Too interesting! I own that I am not made entirely of steel, sir, and the shock he received at finding a dead man awaiting him, instead of a live one, was more or less communicated to me. Yet I stood my ground."

"Admirable! I could have done no better myself. And so this man who had an appointment with Mr. Adams was shocked, really shocked, at finding him lying there under a cross, dead?"

"Yes, there was no doubting that. Shocked, surprised, terrified, and something more. It is that something more which has proved my perplexity. I cannot make it out, not even in thinking it over. Was it the fascination which all horrible sights exert on the morbid, or was it a sudden realization of some danger he had escaped, or of some difficulty yet awaiting him? Hard to say, Mr. Gryce, hard to say; but you may take my word for it that there was more to him in this meeting than an unexpected stumbling upon a dead man where he expected to find a live one. Yet he made no sound after that first cry, and hardly any movement. He just stared at the figure on the floor; then at his face, which he seemed to devour, at first with curiosity, then with hate, then with terror, and lastly—how can I express myself?—with a sort of hellish humour that in another moment might have broken into something like a laugh, if the bird, which I had failed to observe up to this moment, had not waked in its high cage, and, thrusting its beak between the bars, shrilled out in the most alarming of tones: 'Remember Evelyn!'

"That startled the old man even more than the sight on the floor had done. He turned round, and I saw his fist rise as if against some menacing intruder, but it quickly fell again as his eyes encountered the picture which hung before him, and with a cringe painful to see in one of his years, he sidled back till he reached the doorway. Here he paused a minute to give another look at the man outstretched at his feet, and I heard him say:

"'It is Amos's son, not Amos! Is it fatality, or did he plan this meeting, thinking——'

"But here he caught sight of my figure in the antechamber beyond, and resuming in an instant his former debonair manner, he bowed very low and opened his lips as if about to ask a question. But he evidently thought better of it, for he strode by me and made his way to the front door without a word. Being an intruder myself, I did not like to stop him. But I am sorry now for the consideration I showed him; for just before he stepped out, his emotion—the special character of which, I own to you, I find impossible to understand—culminated in a burst of raucous laughter which added the final horror to this amazing adventure. Then he went out, and in the last glimpse I had of him before the door shut he wore the same look of easy self-satisfaction with which he had entered this place of death some fifteen minutes before."

"Remarkable! Some secret history there! That man must be found. He can throw light upon Mr. Adams's past. 'Amos's son,' he called him? Who is Amos? Mr. Adams's name was Felix. Felix, the son of Amos. Perhaps this connection of names may lead to something. It is not a common one, and if given to the papers, may result in our receiving a clew to a mystery which seems impenetrable. Your stay in Mr. Adams's

57

house was quite productive, ma'am. Did you prolong it after the departure of this old man?"

"No, sir, I had had my fill of the mysterious, and left immediately after him. Ashamed of the spirit of investigation which had led me to enter the house, I made a street boy the medium of my communication to the police, and would have been glad if I could have so escaped all responsibility in the matter. But the irony of fate follows me as it does others. A clew was left of my presence, which involves me in this affair, whether I will or no. Was the hand of Providence in this? Perhaps. The future will tell. And now, Mr. Gryce, since my budget is quite empty and the hour late, I will take my leave. If you hear from that bit of paper——"

"If I hear from it in the way you suggest I will let you know. It will be the least I can do for a lady who has done so much for me."

"Now you flatter me—proof positive that I have stayed a minute longer than was judicious. Good evening, Mr. Gryce. What? I have not stayed too long? You have something else to ask."

"Yes, and this time it is concerning a matter personal to yourself. May I inquire if you wore the same bonnet yesterday that you do today?"

"No, sir. I know you have a good reason for this question, and so will not express my surprise. Yesterday I was in reception costume, and my bonnet was a jet one——"

"With long strings tied under the chin?"

"No, sir, short strings; long strings are no longer the fashion."

"But you wore something which fell from your neck?"

"Yes, a boa—a feather boa. How came you to know it, sir? Did I leave my image in one of the mirrors?"

"Hardly. If so, I should not have expected it to speak. You merely wrote the fact on the study table top. Or so I have dared to think. You or the young lady—did she wear ribbons or streamers, too?"

"That I cannot say. Her face was all I saw, and the skirt of a dove-coloured silk dress."

"Then you must settle the question for me in this way. If on the tips of that boa of yours you find the faintest evidence of its having been dipped in blood, I shall know that the streaks found on the top of the table I speak of were evidences of your presence there. But if your boa is clean, or was not long enough to touch that dying man as you leaned over him, then we have proof that the young lady with the dove-coloured plumes fingered that table also, instead of falling at once into the condition in which you saw her carried out."

"I fear that it is my boa which will tell the tale: another proof of the fallibility of man, or, rather, woman. In secret search for clews I left behind me traces of my own presence. I really feel mortified, sir, and you have quite the advantage of me."

And with this show of humility, which may not have been entirely sincere, this estimable lady took her departure.

Did Mr. Gryce suffer from any qualms of conscience at having elicited so much and imparted so little? I doubt it. Mr. Gryce's conscience was quite seared in certain places.

8

In The Round of the Staircase

The next morning Mr. Gryce received a small communication from Miss Butterworth at or near the very time she received one from him. Hers ran:

You were quite correct. So far as appears, I was the only person to lean over Mr. Adams's study table after his unfortunate death. I have had to clip the ends of my boa.

His was equally laconic:

My compliments, madam! Mr. Adams's jaws have been forced apart. A small piece of paper was found clinched between his teeth. This paper has been recovered, and will be read at the inquest. Perhaps a few favoured persons may be granted the opportunity of reading it before then, notably yourself.

Of the two letters the latter naturally occasioned the greater excitement in the recipient. The complacency of Miss Butterworth was superb, and being the result of something that could not be communicated to those about her, occasioned in the household much speculation as to its cause.

At Police Headquarters more than one man was kept busy listening to the idle tales of a crowd of would-be informers. The results which had failed to follow the first day's publication of the crime came rapidly in during the second. There were innumerable persons of all ages and conditions who were ready to tell how they had seen this and that one issue from Mr. Adams's house on the afternoon of his death, but when asked to give a description of these persons, lost themselves in generalities as tedious as they were unprofitable. One garrulous old woman had observed a lady of genteel appearance open the door to an elderly gentleman in a great-coat; and a fashionably dressed young woman came in all breathless to relate how a young man with a very pale young lady on his arm ran against her as she was going by this house at the very hour Mr. Adams was said to have been murdered. She could not be sure of knowing the young man again, and could not say if the young lady was blonde or brunette, only that she was awfully pale and had a beautiful gray feather in her hat.

Others were ready with similar stories, which confirmed, without adding to, the facts already known, and night came on without much progress having been made toward the unravelling of this formidable mystery.

On the next day Mr. Adams's funeral took place. No relatives or intimate friends having come forward, his landlord attended to these rites and his banker acted the part of chief mourner. As his body was carried out of the house, a half-dozen detectives mingled with the crowd blocking the thoroughfare in front, but nothing came of their surveillance here or at the cemetery to which the remains were speedily carried. The problem which had been presented to the police had to be worked out from such material as had already come to hand; and, in forcible recognition of this fact, Mr. Gryce excused himself one evening at headquarters and proceeded quite alone and on foot to the dark and apparently closed house in which the tragedy had occurred.

He entered with a key, and once inside, proceeded to light up the whole house. This done, he took a look at the study, saw that the cross had been replaced on the wall, the bird-cage rehung on its hook under the ceiling, and everything put in its wonted order, with the exception of the broken casings, which still yawned in a state of disrepair on either side of the doorway leading into the study. The steel plate had been shoved back into the place prepared for it by Mr. Adams, but the glimpses still to be seen of its blue surface through the hole made in the wall of the antechamber formed anything but an attractive feature in the scene, and Mr. Gryce, with something of the instinct and much of the deftness of a housewife, proceeded to pull up a couple of rugs from the parlour floor and string them over these openings. Then he consulted his watch, and finding that it was within an hour of nine o'clock, took up his stand behind the curtains of the parlour window. Soon, for the person expected was as prompt as himself, he saw a carriage stop and a lady alight, and he hastened to the front door to receive her. It was Miss Butterworth.

"Madam, your punctuality is equal to my own," said he. "Have you ordered your coachman to drive away?"

"Only as far as the corner," she returned, as she followed him down the hall. "There he will await the call of your whistle."

"Nothing could be better. Are you afraid to remain for a moment alone, while I watch from the window the arrival of the other persons we expect? At present there is no one in the house but ourselves."

"If I was subject to fear in a matter of this kind, I should not be here at all. Besides, the house is very cheerfully lighted. I see you have chosen a crimson light for illuminating the study."

"Because a crimson light was burning when Mr. Adams died."

"Remember Evelyn!" called out a voice.

"Oh, you have brought back the bird!" exclaimed Miss Butterworth. "That is not the cry with which it greeted me before. It was 'Eva! Lovely Eva!' Do you suppose Eva and Evelyn are the same?"

"Madam, we have so many riddles before us that we will let this one go for the present. I expect Mr. Adams's valet here in a moment."

"Sir, you relieve me of an immense weight. I was afraid that the privilege of being present at the test you propose to make was not to be accorded me."

"Miss Butterworth, you have earned a seat at this experiment. Bartow has been given a key, and will enter as of old in entire freedom to do as he wills. We have simply to watch his movements."

"In this room, sir? I do not think I shall like that. I had rather not meet this madman face to face."

"You will not be called upon to do so. We do not wish him to be startled by encountering any watchful eye. Irresponsible as he is, he must be allowed to move about without anything to distract his attention. Nothing must stand in the way of his following those impulses which may yield us a clew to his habits and the ways of this peculiar household. I propose to place you where the chances are least in favour of your being seen by him—in this parlour, madam, which we have every reason to believe was seldom opened during Mr. Adams's lifetime."

"You must put out the gas, then, or the unaccustomed light will attract his attention."

"I will not only put out the gas, but I will draw the *portières* close, making this little hole for your eye and this one for mine. A common expedient, madam; but serviceable, madam, serviceable."

The snort which Miss Butterworth gave as she thus found herself drawn up in darkness before a curtain, in company with this plausible old man, but feebly conveyed her sensations, which were naturally complex and a little puzzling to herself. Had she been the possessor of a lively curiosity (but we know from her own lips that she was not), she might have found some enjoyment in the situation. But being where she was solely from a sense of duty, she probably blushed behind her screen at the position in which she found herself, in the cause of truth and justice; or would have done so if the opening of the front door at that moment had not told her that the critical moment had arrived and that the deaf-and-dumb valet had just been introduced into the house.

The faintest "Hush!" from Mr. Gryce warned her that her surmise was correct, and, bending her every energy to listen, she watched for the expected appearance of this man in the antechamber of Mr. Adams's former study.

He came even sooner than she was prepared to see him, and laying down his hat on a table near the doorway, advanced with a busy air toward the *portière* he had doubtless been in the habit of lifting twenty times a day. But he barely touched it this time. Something seen, or unseen, prevented him from entering. Was it the memory of what he had last beheld there? Or had he noticed the rugs hanging in an unaccustomed way on either side of the damaged casings? Neither, apparently, for he simply turned away with a meek look, wholly mechanical, and taking up his hat again, left the antechamber and proceeded softly upstairs.

"I will follow him," whispered Mr. Gryce. "Don't be afraid, ma'am. This whistle will bring a man in from the street at once."

"I am not afraid. I would be ashamed——"

But it was useless for her to finish this disclaimer. Mr. Gryce was already in the hall. He returned speedily, and saying that the experiment was likely to be a failure, as the old man had gone to his own room and was preparing himself for bed, he led the way into the study, and with purpose, or without a purpose—who knows?—idly touched a button on the table top, thus throwing a new light on the scene. It was Miss Butterworth's first experience of this change of light, and she was observing the effect made by the violet glow now thrown over the picture and the other rich articles in the room when her admiration was cut short, and Mr. Gryce's half-uttered remark also, by the faint sound of the valet's descending steps.

Indeed, they had barely time to regain their old position behind the parlour *portières* when Bartow was seen hurrying in from the hall with his former busy air, which this time remained unchecked.

Crossing to his master's study, he paused for an infinitesimal length of time on the threshold, as if conscious of something being amiss, then went into the room beyond, and, without a glance in the direction of the rug, which had been carefully relaid on the spot where his master had fallen, began to make such arrangements for the night as he was in the habit of making at this hour. He brought a bottle of wine from the cupboard and set it on the table, and then a glass, which he first wiped scrupulously clean. Then he took out his master's dressing gown and slippers, and, placing them to hand, went into the bedroom.

By this time the two watchers had crept from their concealment near enough to note what he was doing in the bedroom. He was stooping over the comb which Mr. Gryce had left lying on the floor. This small object in such a place seemed to surprise him. He took it up, shook his head, and put it back on the dresser. Then he turned down his master's bed.

"Poor fool!" murmured Miss Butterworth as she and her companion crept back to their old place behind the parlour curtains, "he has forgotten everything but his old routine duties. We shall get nothing from this man."

But she stopped suddenly; they both stopped. Bartow was in the middle of the study, with his eyes fixed on his master's empty chair in an inquiring way that spoke volumes. Then he turned, and gazed earnestly at the rug where he had last seen that master lying outstretched and breathless; and awakening to a realization of what had happened, fell into his most violent self and proceeded to go through the series of actions which they were now bound to consider a reproduction of what he had previously seen take place there. Then he went softly out, and crept away upstairs.

Mr. Gryce and Miss Butterworth stepped at once into the light, and surveyed each other with a look of marked discouragement. Then the latter, with a sudden gleam of enthusiasm, cried quickly:

"Turn on another colour, and let us see what will happen. I have an idea it will fetch the old man down again."

Mr. Gryce's brows went up.

"Do you think he can see through the floor?"

But he touched a button, and a rich blue took the place of the violet.

Nothing happened.

Miss Butterworth looked disturbed.

"I have confidence in your theories," began Mr. Gryce, "but when they imply the possibility of this man seeing through blank walls and obeying signals which can have no signification to any one on the floor above——"

"Hark!" she cried, holding up one finger with a triumphant air. The old man's steps could be heard descending.

This time he approached with considerable feebleness, passed slowly into the study, advanced to the table, and reached out his hands as if to lift something which he expected to find there. Seeing nothing, he glanced in astonishment up at the book shelves and then back to the table, shook his head, and suddenly collapsing, sank in a doze on the nearest chair.

Miss Butterworth drew a long breath, eyed Mr. Gryce with some curiosity, and then triumphantly exclaimed:

"Can you read the meaning of all that? I think I can. Don't you see that he came expecting to find a pile of books on the table which it was probably his business to restore to their shelves?"

"But how can he know what light is burning here? You can see for yourself that there is no possible communication between this room and the one in which he has always been found by any one going above."

Miss Butterworth's manner showed a hesitation that was almost naive. She smiled, and there was apology in her smile, though none in her voice, as she remarked with odd breaks:

"When I went upstairs—you know I went upstairs when I was here before—I saw a little thing—a very little thing—which you doubtless observed yourself and which may explain, though I do not know how, why Bartow can perceive these lights from the floor above."

"I shall be very glad to hear about it, madam. I thought I had thoroughly searched those rooms——"

"And the halls?"

"And the halls; and that nothing in them could have escaped my eyes. But if you have a more patient vision than myself——"

"Or make it my business to look lower——"

"How?"

"To look lower; to look on the floor, say."

"On the floor?"

"The floor sometimes reveals much: shows where a person steps the oftenest, and, therefore, where he has the most business. You must have noticed how marred the woodwork is at the edge of the carpeting on that little landing above."

"In the round of the staircase?"

"Yes."

Mr. Gryce did not think it worth his while to answer. Perhaps he had not time; for leaving the valet where he was, and Miss Butterworth where she was (only she would not be left, but followed him), he made his way upstairs, and paused at the place she had mentioned, with a curious look at the floor.

"You see, it has been much trodden here," she said; at which gentle reminder of her presence he gave a start; possibly he had not heard her behind him, and after sixty years of hard service even a detective may be excused a slight nervousness. "Now, why should it be trodden here? There is no apparent reason why any one should shuffle to and fro in this corner. The stair is wide, especially here, and there is no window——"

Mr. Gryce, whose eye had been travelling over the wall, reached over her shoulder to one of the dozen pictures hanging at intervals from the bottom to the top of the staircase, and pulling it away from the wall, on which it hung decidedly askew, revealed a round opening through which poured a ray of blue light which could only proceed from the vault of the adjoining study.

"No window," he repeated. "No, but an opening into the study wall which answers the same purpose. Miss Butterworth, your eye is to be trusted every time. I only wonder you did not pull this picture aside yourself."

"It was not hanging crooked then. Besides I was in a hurry. I had just come from my encounter with this demented man. I had noticed the marks on the landing, and the worn edges of the carpet, on my way upstairs. I was in no condition to observe them on my way down."

"I see."

Miss Butterworth ran her foot to and fro over the flooring they were examining.

"Bartow was evidently in the habit of coming here constantly," said she, "probably to learn whether his master had need of him. Ingenious in Mr. Adams to contrive signals for communication with this man! He certainly had great use for his deaf-and-dumb servant. So one mystery is solved!"

"And if I am not mistaken, we can by a glance through this loophole obtain the answer to another. You are wondering, I believe, how

Bartow, if he followed the movements of the assailant from the doorway, came to thrust with his left hand, instead of with his right. Now if he saw the tragedy from this point, he saw it over the assailant's shoulder, instead of face to face. What follows? He would imitate literally the movements of the man he saw, turn in the same direction and strike with the same hand."

"Mr. Gryce, we are beginning to untangle the threads that looked so complicated. Ah, what is that? Why, it's that bird! His cage must be very nearly under this hole."

"A little to one side, madam, but near enough to give you a start. What was it he cried then?"

"Oh, those sympathetic words about Eva! 'Poor Eva!'"

"Well, give a glance to Bartow. You can see him very well from here."

Miss Butterworth put her eye again to the opening, and gave a grunt, a very decided grunt. With her a grunt was significant of surprise.

"He is shaking his fist; he is all alive with passion. He looks as if he would like to kill the bird."

"Perhaps that is why the creature was strung up so high. You may be sure Mr. Adams had some basis for his idiosyncrasies."

"I begin to think so. I don't know that I care to go back where that man is. He has a very murderous look."

"And a very feeble arm, Miss Butterworth. You are safe under my protection. My arm is not feeble."

A-Table. B-Small Stand. C-Door to Bedroom D-Evelyn's Picture
E-Loophole on Stair Landing. F- Entrance to Study.

Since my readers may not understand how an opening above the stairway might communicate with Mr. Adams's study, I here submit a diagram of the same. The study walls were very high, forming a rounded extension at the back of the house.

9

High and Low

At the foot of the stairs, Mr. Gryce excused himself, and calling in two or three men whom he had left outside, had the valet removed before taking Miss Butterworth back into the study. When all was quiet again, and they found an opportunity to speak, Mr. Gryce remarked:

"One very important thing has been settled by the experiment we have just made. Bartow is acquitted of participation in this crime."

"Then we can give our full attention to the young people. You have heard nothing from them, I suppose?"

"No."

"Nor from the old man who laughed?"

"No."

Miss Butterworth looked disappointed.

"I thought—it seemed very probable—that the scrap of writing you found would inform you who these were. If it was important enough for the dying man to try to swallow it, it certainly should give some clew to his assailant."

"Unfortunately, it does not do so. It was a veritable scrawl, madam, running something like this: 'I return your daughter to you. She is here. Neither she nor you will ever see me again. Remember Evelyn!' And signed, 'Amos's son.'"

"Amos's son! That is Mr. Adams himself."

"So we have every reason to believe."

"Strange! Unaccountable! And the paper inscribed with these words was found clinched between his teeth! Was the handwriting recognized?"

"Yes, as his own, if we can judge from the specimens we have seen of his signature on the fly-leaves of his books."

"Well, mysteries deepen. And the retaining of this paper was so important to him that even in his death throe he thrust it in this strangest of all hiding-places, as being the only one that could be considered safe from search. And the girl! Her first words on coming to herself were: 'You have left that line of writing behind.' Mr. Gryce, those words, few and inexplicable as they are, contain the key to the whole situation. Will you repeat them again, if you please, sentence by sentence?"

"With pleasure, madam; I have said them often enough to myself. First, then: 'I return your daughter to you!'"

"So! Mr. Adams had some one's daughter in charge whom he returns. Whose daughter? Not that young man's daughter, certainly, for that would necessitate her being a small child. Besides, if these words had been meant for his assailant, why make so remarkable an effort to hide them from him?"

"Very true! I have said the same thing to myself."

"Yet, if not for him, for whom, then? For the old gentleman who came in later?"

"It is possible; since hearing of him I have allowed myself to regard this as among the possibilities, especially as the next words of this strange communication are: 'She is here.' Now the only woman who was there a few minutes previous to this old gentleman's visit was the light-haired girl whom you saw carried out."

"Very true; but why do you reason as if this paper had just been written? It might have been an old scrap, referring to past sorrows or secrets."

"These words were written that afternoon. The paper on which they were scrawled was torn from a sheet of letter paper lying on the desk, and the pen with which they were inscribed—you must have noticed where it lay, quite out of its natural place on the extreme edge of the table."

"Certainly, sir; but I had little idea of the significance we might come to attach to it. These words are connected, then, with the girl I saw. And she is not Evelyn or he would not have repeated in this note the bird's catch-word, 'Remember Evelyn!' I wonder if she is Evelyn?" proceeded Miss Butterworth, pointing to the one large picture which adorned the wall.

"We may call her so for the nonce. So melancholy a face may well suggest some painful family secret. But how explain the violent part played by the young man, who is not mentioned in these abrupt and hastily penned sentences! It is all a mystery, madam, a mystery which we are wasting time to attempt to solve."

"Yet I hate to give it up without an effort. Those words, now. There were some other words you have not repeated to me."

"They came before that injunction, 'Remember Evelyn!' They bespoke a resolve. 'Neither she nor you will ever see me again.'"

"Ah! but these few words are very significant, Mr. Gryce. Could he have dealt that blow himself? May he have been a suicide after all?"

"Madam, you have the right to inquire; but from Bartow's pantomime, you must have perceived it is not a self-inflicted blow he mimics, but a maddened thrust from an outraged hand. Let us keep to our first conclusions; only—to be fair to every possibility—the condition of Mr. Adams's affairs and the absence of all family papers and such documents as may usually be found in a wealthy man's desk prove that he had made some preparation for possible death. It may have come sooner than he expected and in another way, but it was a thought he had indulged in, and—madam, I have a confession to make also. I have not been quite fair to my most valued colleague.

"The study—that most remarkable of rooms—contains a secret which has not been imparted to you; a very peculiar one, madam, which was revealed to me in a rather startling manner. This room can be, or rather could be, cut off entirely from the rest of the house; made a death-trap of, or rather a tomb, in which this incomprehensible man may have intended to die. Look at this plate of steel. It is worked by a mechanism which forces it across this open doorway. I was behind that plate of steel the other night, and these holes had to be made to let me out."

"Ha! You detectives have your experiences! I should not have enjoyed spending that especial evening with you. But what an old-world tragedy we are unearthing here! I declare"—and the good lady actually rubbed her eyes—"I feel as if transported back to medieval days. Who says we are living in New York within sound of the cable car and the singing of the telegraph wire?"

"Some men are perfectly capable of bringing the medieval into Wall Street. I think Mr. Adams was one of those men. Romanticism tinged all his acts, even the death he died. Nor did it cease with his death. It followed him to the tomb. Witness the cross we found lying on his bosom."

"That was the act of another's hand, the result of another's superstition. That shows the presence of a priest or a woman at the moment he died."

"Yet," proceeded Mr. Gryce, with a somewhat wondering air, "he must have had a grain of hard sense in his make-up. All his contrivances worked. He was a mechanical genius, as well as a lover of mystery."

"An odd combination. Strange that we do not feel his spirit infecting the very air of this study. I could almost wish it did. We might then be led to grasp the key to this mystery."

"That," remarked Mr. Gryce, "can be done in only one way. You have already pointed it out. We must trace the young couple who were present at his death struggle. If they cannot be found the case is hopeless."

"And so," said she, "we come around to the point from which we started—proof positive that we are lost in the woods." And Miss Butterworth rose. She felt that for the time being she, at least, had come to the end of her resources.

Mr. Gryce did not seek to detain her. Indeed, he appeared to be anxious to leave the place himself. They, however, stopped long enough to cast one final look around them. As they did so Miss Butterworth's finger slowly rose.

"See!" said she, "you can hardly perceive from this side of the wall the opening made by the removal of that picture on the stair landing. Wouldn't you say that it was in the midst of those folds of dark-coloured tapestry up there?"

"Yes, I had already located that spot as the one. With the picture hung up on the other side, it would be quite invisible."

"One needs to keep one's eyes moving in a case like this. That picture must have been drawn aside several times while we were in this room. Yet we failed to notice it."

"That was from not looking high enough. High and low, Mr. Gryce! What goes on at the level of the eye is apparent to everyone."

The smile with which he acknowledged this parting shot and prepared to escort her to the door had less of irony than sadness in it. Was he beginning to realize that years tell even on the most sagacious, and that neither high places nor low would have escaped his attention a dozen years before?

10

Bride Roses

"A blonde, you say, sir?"

"Yes, Sweetwater; not of the usual type, but one of those frail, ethereal creatures whom we find it so hard to associate with crime. He, on the contrary, according to Miss Butterworth's description (and her descriptions may be relied upon), is one of those gentlemanly athletes whose towering heads and powerful figures attract universal attention. Seen together, you would be apt to know them. But what reason have we for thinking they will be found together?"

"How were they dressed?"

"Like people of fashion and respectability. He wore a brown-checked suit apparently fresh from the tailor; she, a dove-coloured dress with white trimmings. The parasol shows the colour of her hat and plumes. Both were young, and (still according to Miss Butterworth) of sensitive temperament and unused to crime; for she was in a fainting condition when carried from the house, and he, with every inducement to self-restraint, showed himself the victim of such powerful emotion that he would have been immediately surrounded and questioned if he had not set his burden down in the vestibule and at once plunged with the girl into the passing crowd. Do you think you can find them, Sweetwater?"

"Have you no clews to their identity beyond this parasol?"

"None, Sweetwater, if you except these few faded rose leaves picked up from the floor of Mr. Adams's study."

"Then you have given me a problem, Mr. Gryce," remarked the young detective dubiously, as he eyed the parasol held out to him and let the rose-leaves drop carelessly through his fingers. "Somehow I do not feel the same assurances of success that I did before. Perhaps I more fully realize the difficulties of any such quest, now that I see how much rests upon chance in these matters. If Miss Butterworth had not been a precise woman, I should have failed in my former attempt, as I am likely to fail in this one. But I will make another effort to locate the owner of this parasol, if only to learn my business by failure. And now, sir, where do you think I am going first? To a florist's, with these faded rose-leaves. Just because every other young fellow on the force would make a start from the parasol, I am going to try and effect one from these rose-leaves. I may be an egotist, but I cannot help that. I can do nothing with the parasol."

"And what do you hope to do with the rose-leaves? How can a florist help you in finding this young woman by means of them?"

"He may be able to say from what kind of a rose they fell, and once I know that, I may succeed in discovering the particular store from which the bouquet was sold to this more or less conspicuous couple."

"You may. I am not the man to throw cold water on any one's schemes. Every man has his own methods, and till they are proved valueless I say nothing."

Young Sweetwater, who was now all nerve, enthusiasm, and hope, bowed. He was satisfied to be allowed to work in his own way.

"I may be back in an hour, and you may not see me for a week," he remarked on leaving.

"Luck to your search!" was the short reply. This ended the interview. In a few minutes more Sweetwater was off.

The hour passed; he did not come back; the day, and still no Sweetwater. Another day went by, enlivened only by an interchange of notes between Mr. Gryce and Miss Butterworth. Hers was read by the old detective with a smile. Perhaps because it was so terse; perhaps because it was so characteristic.

Dear Mr. Gryce:
I do not presume to dictate or even to offer a suggestion to the New York police, but have you inquired of the postman in a certain district whether he can recall the postmark on any of the letters he delivered to Mr. Adams?
A. B.

His, on the contrary, was perused with a frown by his exacting colleague in Gramercy Park. The reason is obvious.

Dear Miss Butterworth:
Suggestions are always in order, and even dictation can be en-

dured from you. The postman delivers too many letters on that
block to concern himself with postmarks. Sorry to close another thoroughfare.

E. G.

Meanwhile, the anxiety of both was great; that of Mr. Gryce exces-
sive. He was consequently much relieved when, on the third morning,
he found Sweetwater awaiting him at the office, with a satisfied smile
lighting up his plain features. He had reserved his story for his special
patron, and as soon as they were closeted together he turned with
beaming eyes toward the old detective, crying:

"News, sir; good news! I have found them; I have found them
both, and by such a happy stroke! It was a blind trail, but when the
florist said that those petals might have fallen from a bride rose—well,
sir, I know that any woman can carry bride roses, but when I remembered that the clothes of her companion looked as though they had
just come from the tailor's, and that she wore gray and white—why, it
gave me an idea, and I began my search after this unknown pair at the
Bureau of Vital Statistics."

"Brilliant!" ejaculated the old detective. "That is, if the thing
worked."

"And it did, sir; it did. I may have been born under a lucky star,
probably was, but once started on this line of search, I went straight to
the end. Shall I tell you how? Hunting through the list of such persons
as had been married within the city limits during the last two weeks,
I came upon the name of one Eva Poindexter. Eva! that was a name
well-known in the house on —— Street. I decided to follow up this
Eva."

"A wise conclusion! And how did you set about it?"

"Why, I went directly to the clergyman who had performed the
ceremony. He was a kind and affable *dominie*, sir, and I had no trouble
in talking to him."

"And you described the bride?"

"No, I led the conversation so that he described her."

"Good; and what kind of a woman did he make her out to be?
Delicate? Pale?"

"Sir, he had not read the service for so lovely a bride in years. Very
slight, almost fragile, but beautiful, and with a delicate bloom which
showed her to be in better health than one would judge from her
dainty figure. It was a private wedding, sir, celebrated in a hotel par-

lour; but her father was with her——"

"Her father?" Mr. Gryce's theory received its first shock. Then the old man who had laughed on leaving Mr. Adams's house was not the father to whom those few lines in Mr. Adams's handwriting were addressed. Or this young woman was not the person referred to in those lines.

"Is there anything wrong about that?" inquired Sweetwater.

Mr. Gryce became impassive again.

"No; I had not expected his attendance at the wedding; that is all."

"Sorry, sir, but there is no doubt about his having been there. The bridegroom——"

"Yes, tell me about the bridegroom."

"Was the very man you described to me as leaving Mr. Adams's house with her. Tall, finely developed, with a grand air and gentlemanly manners. Even his clothes correspond with what you told me to expect: a checked suit, brown in colour, and of the latest cut. Oh, he is the man!"

Mr. Gryce, with a suddenly developed interest in the lid of his inkstand, recalled the lines which Mr. Adams had written immediately before his death, and found himself wholly at sea. How reconcile facts so diametrically opposed? What allusion could there be in these lines to the new-made bride of another man? They read, rather, as if she were his own bride, as witness:

I return your daughter to you. She is here. Neither she nor you will ever see me again. Remember Evelyn!

Amos's Son.

There must be something wrong. Sweetwater must have been led astray by a series of extraordinary coincidences. Dropping the lid of the inkstand in a way to make the young man smile, he looked up.

"I'm afraid it's been a fool chase, Sweetwater. The facts you relate in regard to this couple, the fact of their having been married at all, tally so little with what we have been led to expect from certain other evidences which have come in——"

"Pardon me, sir, but will you hear me out? At the Imperial, where they were married, I learned that the father and daughter had registered as coming from a small place in Pennsylvania; but I could learn nothing in regard to the bridegroom. He had not appeared on the scene till the time for the ceremony, and after the marriage was seen to take his bride away in one carriage while the old gentleman departed in another. The latter concerned me little; it was the young couple I had been detailed to find. Employing the usual means of search, I tracked them to the Waldorf, where I learned what makes it certain that I have been following the right couple. On the afternoon of the very day of Mr. Adams's death, this young husband and wife left the hotel on foot and did not come back. Their clothes, which had all been left behind, were taken away two days later by an elderly gentleman who said he was her father and whose appearance coincides with that of the person registering as such at the Imperial. All of which looks favourable to my theory, does it not, especially when you remember that the bridegroom's name——"

"You have not told it."

"Is Adams, Thomas Adams. Same family as the murdered man, you see. At least, he has the same name."

Mr. Gryce surveyed the young man with admiration, but was not yet disposed to yield him entire credence.

"Humph! I do not wonder you thought it worth your while to follow up the pair, if one of them is named Adams and the other Eva. But, Sweetwater, the longer you serve on the force the more you will learn that coincidences as strange and unexpected as these do occur at times, and must be taken into account in the elucidation of a difficult problem. Much as I may regret to throw cold water on your hopes, there are reasons for believing that the young man and woman whom we are seeking are not the ones you have busied yourself about for the last two days. Certain facts which have come to light would seem to show that if she had a husband at all, his name would not be Thomas Adams, but Felix, and as the facts I have to bring forward are most direct and unimpeachable, I fear you will have to start again, and on a new tack."

But Sweetwater remained unshaken, and eyed his superior with a vague smile playing about his lips.

"You have not asked me, sir, where I have spent all the time which has elapsed since I saw you last. The investigations I have mentioned did not absorb more than a day."

"Very true. Where have you been, Sweetwater?"

"To Montgomery, sir, to that small town in Pennsylvania from which Mr. Poindexter and his daughter registered."

"Ah, I see! And what did you learn there? Something directly to the point?"

"I learned this, that John Poindexter, father of Eva, had for a friend in early life one Amos Cadwalader."

"Amos!" repeated Mr. Gryce, with an odd look.

"Yes, and that this Amos had a son, Felix."

"Ah!"

"You see, sir, we must be on the right track; coincidences cannot extend through half a dozen names."

"You are right. It is I who have made a mistake in drawing my conclusions too readily. Let us hear about this Amos. You gathered something of his history, no doubt."

"All that was possible, sir. It is closely woven in with that of Poindexter, and presents one feature which may occasion you no surprise, but which, I own, came near nonplussing me. Though the father of Felix, his name was not Adams. I say was not, for he has been dead six months. It was Cadwalader. And Felix went by the name of Cadwalader, too, in the early days of which I have to tell, he and a sister whose name——"

"Well?"

"Was Evelyn."

"Sweetwater, you are an admirable fellow. So the mystery is ours."

"The history, not the mystery; that still holds. Shall I relate what I know of those two families?"

"At once: I am as anxious as if I were again twenty-three and had been in your shoes instead of my own for the last three days."

"Very well, sir. John Poindexter and Amos Cadwalader were, in their early life, bosom friends. They had come from Scotland together and settled in Montgomery in the thirties. Both married there, but John Poindexter was a prosperous man from the first, while Cadwalader had little ability to support a family, and was on the verge of bankruptcy when the war of the rebellion broke out and he enlisted as a soldier. Poindexter remained at home, caring for his own family and for the two children of Cadwalader, whom he took into his own house.

"I say his own family, but he had no family, save a wife, up to the spring of '80. Then a daughter was born to him, the Eva who has just married Thomas Adams. Cadwalader, who was fitted for army life, rose to be a captain; but he was unfortunately taken prisoner at one of the late battles and confined in Libby Prison, where he suffered the tortures of the damned till he was released, in 1865, by a forced exchange of prisoners. Broken, old, and crushed, he returned home, and no one living in the town at that time will ever forget the day he

77

alighted from the cars and took his way up the main street. For not having been fortunate enough, or unfortunate enough, perhaps, to receive any communication from home, he advanced with a cheerful haste, not knowing that his only daughter then lay dead in his friend's house, and that it was for her funeral that the people were collecting in the green square at the end of the street. He was so pale, broken, and decrepit that few knew him.

"But there was one old neighbour who recognized him and was kind enough to lead him into a quiet place, and there tell him that he had arrived just too late to see his darling daughter alive. The shock, instead of prostrating the old soldier, seemed to nerve him afresh and put new vigour into his limbs. He proceeded, almost on a run, to Poindexter's house, and arrived just as the funeral *cortège* was issuing from the door. And now happened a strange thing. The young girl had been laid on an open bier, and was being carried by six sturdy lads to her last resting place. As the father's eye fell on her young body under its black pall, a cry of mortal anguish escaped him, and he sank on his knees right in the line of the procession.

"At the same minute another cry went up, this time from behind the bier, and John Poindexter could be seen reeling at the side of Felix Cadwalader, who alone of all present (though he was the youngest and the least) seemed to retain his self-possession at this painful moment. Meanwhile the bereaved father, throwing himself at the side of the bier, began tearing away at the pall in his desire to look upon the face of her he had left in such rosy health four years before. But he was stopped, not by Poindexter, who had vanished from the scene, but by Felix, the cold, severe-looking boy who stood like a guard behind his sister. Reaching out a hand so white it was in itself a shock, he laid it in a certain prohibitory way on the pall, as if saying no. And when his father would have continued the struggle, it was Felix who controlled him and gradually drew him into the place at his own side where a minute before the imposing figure of Poindexter had stood; after which the bearers took up their burden again and moved on.

"But the dramatic scene was not over. As they neared the churchyard another procession, similar in appearance to their own, issued from an adjoining street, and Evelyn's young lover, who had died almost simultaneously with herself, was brought in and laid at her side. But not in the same grave: this was noticed by all, though most eyes and hearts were fixed upon Cadwalader, who had escaped his loathsome prison and returned to the place of his affections for *this*.

"Whether he grasped then and there the full meaning of this double burial (young Kissam had shot himself upon hearing of Evelyn's death), or whether all explanations were deferred till he and Felix walked away together from the grave, has never transpired. From that minute till they both left town on the following day, no one had any word with him, save Poindexter, whom he went once to see, and young Kissam's mother, who came once to see him. Like a phantom he had risen upon the sight of the good people of Montgomery, and like a phantom he disappeared, never to be seen by any of them again, unless, as many doubt, the story is true which was told some twenty years ago by one of the little village lads.

"He says (it was six years after the tragic scene I have just related) that one evening as he was hurrying by the churchyard, in great anxiety to reach home before it was too dark, he came upon the figure of a man standing beside a grave, with a little child in his arms. This man was tall, long-bearded, and terrifying. His attitude, as the lad describes it, was one of defiance, if not of cursing. High in his right hand he held the child, almost as if he would hurl him at the village which lies under the hill on which the churchyard is perched; and though the moment passed quickly, the boy, now a man, never has forgotten the picture thus presented or admitted that it was anything but a real one. As the description he gave of this man answered to the appearance of Amos Cadwalader, and as the shoe of a little child was found next morning on the grave of Cadwalader's daughter, Evelyn, it has been thought by many that the boy really beheld this old soldier, who for some mysterious reason had chosen nightfall for this fleeting visit to his daughter's resting-place.

"But to others it was only a freak of the lad's imagination, which had been much influenced by the reading of romances. For, as these latter reasoned, had it really been Cadwalader, why did he not show himself at John Poindexter's house—that old friend who now had a little daughter and no wife and who could have made him so comfortable? Among these was Poindexter himself, though some thought he looked oddly while making this remark, as if he spoke more from custom than from the heart. Indeed, since the unfortunate death of Evelyn in his house, he had never shown the same interest in the Cadwaladers.

"But then he was a man much occupied with great affairs, while the Cadwaladers, except for their many griefs and misfortunes, were regarded as comparatively insignificant people, unless we except Felix, who from his earliest childhood had made himself feared even by grown people, though he never showed a harsh spirit or exceeded the bounds of decorum in speech or gesture. A year ago news came to Montgomery of Amos Cadwalader's death, but no particulars concerning his family or burial place. And that is all I have been able to glean concerning the Cadwaladers."

Mr. Gryce had again become thoughtful.

"Have you any reason to believe that Evelyn's death was not a natural one?"

"No, sir. I interviewed the old mother of the young man who shot himself out of grief at Evelyn's approaching death, and if any doubt had existed concerning a matter which had driven her son to a violent end, she could not have concealed it from me. But there seemed to have been none. Evelyn Cadwalader was always of delicate health, and when a quick consumption carried her off no one marvelled. Her lover, who adored her, simply could not live without her, so he shot himself. There was no mystery about the tragic occurrence except that it seemed to sever an old friendship that once was firm as a rock. I allude to that between the Poindexters and Cadwaladers."

"Yet in this tragedy which has just occurred in —— Street we see them brought together again. Thomas Adams marries Eva Poindexter. But who is Thomas Adams? You have not mentioned him in this history."

"Not unless he was the child who was held aloft over Evelyn's grave."

"Humph! That seems rather far-fetched. What did you learn about him in Montgomery? Is he known there?"

"As well as any stranger can be who spends his time in courting a young girl. He came to Montgomery a few months ago, from some foreign city—Paris, I think—and, being gifted with every personal charm calculated to please a cultivated young woman, speedily won the affections of Eva Poindexter, and also the esteem of her father. But their favourable opinion is not shared by every one in the town. There are those who have a good deal to say about his anxious and unsettled eye."

"Naturally; he could not marry all their daughters. But this history you have given me: it is meagre, Sweetwater, and while it hints at something deeply tragic, does not supply the key we want. A girl who died some thirty years ago! A father who disappeared! A brother who, from being a Cadwalader, has become an Adams! An Eva whose name, as well as that of the long-buried Evelyn, was to be heard in constant repetition in the place where the murdered Felix lay with those inscrutable lines in his own writing, clinched between his teeth! It is a snarl, a perfect snarl, of which we have as yet failed to pull the right thread. But we'll get hold of it yet. I'm not going to be baffled in my old age by difficulties I would have laughed at a dozen years ago."

"But this right thread? How shall we know it among the fifty I see entangled in this matter?"

"First, find the whereabouts of this young couple—but didn't you tell me you had done so; that you know where they are?"

"Yes. I learned from the postmaster in Montgomery that a letter addressed to Mrs. Thomas Adams had been sent from his post-office to Belleville, Long Island."

"Ah! I know that place."

"And wishing to be assured that the letter was not a pretence, I sent a telegram to the postmaster at Belleville. Here is his answer. It is unequivocal: 'Mr. Poindexter of Montgomery, Pa. Mr. Thomas Adams and Mrs. Adams of the same place have been at the Bedell House in this place five days.'"

"Very good; then we have them! Be ready to start for Belleville by one o'clock sharp. And mind, Sweetwater, keep your wits alert and your tongue still. Remember that as yet we are feeling our way blindfold, and must continue to do so till some kind hand tears away the bandage from our eyes. Go! I have a letter to write, for which you may send in a boy at the end of five minutes."

This letter was for Miss Butterworth, and created, a half-hour later, quite a stir in the fine old mansion in Gramercy Park. It ran thus:

Have you sufficient interest in the outcome of a certain matter to take a short journey into the country? I leave town at 1p.m. for Belleville, Long Island. If you choose to do the same, you will find me at the Bedell House, in that town, early in the afternoon. If you enjoy novels, take one with you, and let me see you reading it on the hotel *piazza* at five o'clock. I may be reading too; if so, and my choice is a book, all is well, and you may devour your story in peace. But if I lay aside my book and take up a paper, devote but one eye to your story and turn the other on the people who are passing you. If after you have done so, you leave your book open, I shall understand that you fail to recognize these persons. But if you shut the volume, you may expect to see me also fold up my newspaper; for by so doing you will have signalled me that you have identified the young man and woman you saw leaving Mr. Adams's house on the fatal afternoon of your first entrance.   E. G.

11

Misery

It is to be hoped that the well-dressed lady of uncertain age who was to be seen late that afternoon in a remote corner of the hotel *piazza* at Belleville had not chosen a tale requiring great concentration of mind, for her eyes (rather fine ones in their way, showing both keenness and good nature) seemed to find more to interest them in the scene before her than in the pages she so industriously turned over.

The scene was one calculated to interest an idle mind, no doubt. First, there was the sea, a wide expanse of blue, dotted by numerous sails; then the beach, enlivened by groups of young people dressed like popinjays in every colour; then the village street, and, lastly, a lawn over which there now and then strayed young couples with tennis rackets in their hands or golf sticks under their arms. Children, too— but children did not seem to interest this amiable spinster. (There could be no doubt about her being a spinster.) She scarcely glanced at them twice, while a young married pair, or even an old gentleman, if he were only tall and imperious-looking, invariably caused her eyes to wander from her book, which, by the way, she held too near for seeing, or such might have been the criticism of a wary observer.

This criticism, if criticism it would be called, could not have been made of the spruce, but rather feeble octogenarian at the other end of the *piazza*. He was evidently absorbed in the novel he held so conspicuously open, and which, from the smiles now and then disturbing the usual placidity of his benevolent features, we can take for granted was sufficiently amusing. Yet right in the midst of it, and certainly before he had finished his chapter, he closed his book and took out a newspaper, which he opened to its full width before sitting down to peruse its columns.

At the same moment the lady at the other end of the *piazza* could be seen looking over her spectacles at two gentlemen who just at that moment issued from the great door opening between her and the elderly person just alluded to. Did she know them, or was it only her curiosity that was aroused? From the way she banged together her book and rose, it looked as if she had detected old acquaintances in the distinguished-looking pair who were now advancing slowly toward her. But if so, she could not have been overjoyed to see them, for after the first hint of their approach in her direction she turned, with an aspect of some embarrassment, and made her way out upon the lawn, where she stood with her back to these people, caressing a small dog in a way that betrayed her total lack of sympathy with these animals, which were evidently her terror when she was sufficiently herself to be swayed by her natural impulses.

The two gentlemen, on the contrary, with an air of total indifference to her proximity, continued their walk until they reached the end of the *piazza*, and then turned and proceeded mechanically to retrace their steps.

Their faces now being brought within view of the elderly person who was so absorbed in his newspaper, the latter shifted that sheet the merest trifle, possibly because the sun struck his eyes too directly, possibly because he wished to catch sight of two very remarkable men. If so, the opportunity was good, as they stopped within a few feet of his chair. One of them was elderly, as old as, if not older than, the man watching him; but he was of that famous Scotch stock whose members are tough and hale at eighty. This toughness he showed not only in his figure, which was both upright and graceful, but in the glance of his calm, cold eye, which fell upon everybody and everything unmoved, while that of his young, but equally stalwart companion seemed to shrink with the most acute sensitiveness from every person he met, save the very mild old reader of news near whom they now paused for a half-dozen words of conversation.

"I don't think it does me any good," was the young man's gloomy remark. "I am wretched when with her, and doubly wretched when I try to forget myself for a moment out of her sight. I think we had better go back. I had rather sit where she can see me than have her wonder—Oh, I will be careful; but you must remember how unnerving is the very silence I am obliged to keep about what is destroying us all. I am nearly as ill as she."

Here they drew off, and their apparently disinterested hearer turned the page of his paper. It was five minutes before they came back. This time it was the old gentleman who was speaking, and as he was more discreet than his companion or less under the influence of his feelings, his voice was lower and his words less easy to be distinguished.

"Escape? South coast—she will forget to watch you for—a clinging nature—impetuous, but foolishly affectionate—you know that— no danger—found out—time—a cheerful home—courage—happiness—all forgotten."

A gesture from the young man as he moved away showed that he did not share these hopes. Meanwhile Miss Butterworth—you surely have recognized Miss Butterworth—had her opportunities too. She was still stooping over the dog, which wriggled under her hand, yet did not offer to run away, fascinated perhaps by that hesitating touch which he may or may not have known had never inflicted itself upon a dog before. But her ears, and attention, were turned toward two girls chatting on a bench near her as freely as if they were quite alone on the lawn. They were gossiping about a fellow-inmate of the big hotel, and Miss Butterworth listened intently after hearing them mention the name Adams. These are some of the words she caught:

"But she is! I tell you she is sick enough to have a nurse and a doctor. I caught a glimpse of her as I was going by her room yesterday, and I never saw two such big eyes or such pale cheeks. Then, look at him! He must just adore her, for he won't speak to another woman, and just moves about in that small, hot room all day. I wonder if they are bride and groom? They are young enough, and if you have noticed her clothes——"

"Oh, don't talk about clothes. I saw her the first day she came, and was the victim of despair until she suddenly got sick and so couldn't wear those wonderful waists and jackets. I felt like a dowdy when I saw that pale blue——"

"Oh, well, blue becomes blondes. You would look like a fright in it. I didn't care about her clothes, but I did feel that it was all up with us if she chose to talk, or even to smile, upon the few men that are good enough to stay out a week in this place. Yet she isn't a beauty; she has not a good nose, nor a handsome eye, nor even an irreproachable complexion. It must be her mouth, which is lovely, or her walk—did you notice her walk? It was just as if she were floating; that is, before she fell down in that faint. I wonder why she fainted. Nobody was doing anything, not even her husband. But perhaps that was what troubled her. I noticed that for some cause he was looking very serious—

and when she had tried to attract his attention two or three times and failed, she just fell from her chair to the floor. That roused him. He has hardly left her since."

"I don't think they look very happy, do you, for so rich and handsome a couple?"

"Perhaps he is dissipated. I have noticed that the old gentleman never leaves them."

"Well, well, he may be dissipated; handsome men are very apt to be. But I wouldn't care if——"

Here the dog gave a yelp and bolted. Miss Butterworth had unconsciously pinched him, in her indignation, possibly, at the turn these rattle-pated young ladies' conversation was taking. This made a diversion, and the young girls moved off, leaving Miss Butterworth without occupation. But a young man who at that moment crossed her path gave her enough to think about.

"You recognize them? There is no mistake?" he whispered.

"None; the one this way is the young man I saw leave Mr. Adams's house, and the other is the old gentleman who came in afterward."

"Mr. Gryce advises you to return home. He is going to arrest the young man." And Sweetwater passed on.

Miss Butterworth strolled to a seat and sat down. She felt weak; she seemed to see that young wife, sick, overwhelmed, struggling with her great fear, sink under this crushing blow, with no woman near her capable of affording the least sympathy. The father did not impress her as being the man to hold up her fainting head or ease her bruised heart. He had an icy look under his polished exterior which repelled this keen-eyed spinster, and as she remembered the coldness of his ways, she felt herself seized by an irresistible impulse to be near this young creature when the blow fell, if only to ease the tension of her own heartstrings, which at that moment ached keenly over the part she had felt herself obliged to play in this matter.

But when she rose to look for Mr. Gryce, she found him gone; and upon searching the *piazza* for the other two gentlemen, she saw them just vanishing round the corner in the direction of a small smoking-room. As she could not follow them, she went upstairs, and, meeting a maid in the upper hall, asked for Mrs. Adams. She was told that Mrs. Adams was sick, but was shown the door of her room, which was at the end of a long hall. As all the halls terminated in a window under which a sofa was to be found, she felt that circumstances were in her favour, and took her seat upon the sofa before her in a state of great complacency. Instantly a sweet voice was heard through the open transom of the door behind which her thoughts were already concentrated.

"Where is Tom? Oh, where is Tom? Why does he leave me? I'm afraid of what he may be tempted to do or say down on those great *piazzas* alone."

"Mr. Poindexter is with him," answered a voice, measured, but kind. "Mr. Adams was getting very tired, and your father persuaded him to go down and have a smoke."

"I must get up; indeed I must get up. Oh! the camphor— the——"

There was a bustle; this poor young wife had evidently fainted again.

Miss Butterworth cast very miserable glances at the door.

Meanwhile in that small and retired smoking-room a terrible scene was in progress. The two gentlemen had lit their cigars and were sitting in certain forced attitudes that evinced their non-enjoyment of the weed each had taken out of complaisance to the other, when an old man, strangely serious, strangely at home, yet as strangely a guest of the house like themselves, came in, and shut the door behind him.

"Gentlemen," he at once announced, "I am Detective Gryce of the New York police, and I am here—but I see that one of you at least knows why I am here."

One? Both of them! This was evident in a moment. No denial, no subterfuge was possible. At the first word uttered in the strange, authoritative tone which old detectives acquire after years of such experiences, the young man sank down in sudden collapse, while his companion, without yielding so entirely to his emotions, showed that he was not insensible to the blow which, in one moment, had brought destruction to all their hopes.

When Mr. Gryce saw himself so completely understood, he no longer hesitated over his duty. Directing his full attention to Mr. Adams, he said, this time with some feeling, for the misery of this young man had impressed him:

"You are wanted in New York by Coroner D——, whose business it is to hold an inquest over the remains of Mr. Felix Adams, of whose astonishing death you are undoubtedly informed. As you and your wife were seen leaving that gentleman's house a few minutes before he expired, you are naturally regarded as valuable witnesses in determining whether his death was one of suicide or murder."

It was an accusation, or so nearly one, that Mr. Gryce was not at all surprised to behold the dark flush of shame displace the livid terror which but an instant before had made the man before him look like one of those lost spirits we sometimes imagine as flitting across the open mouth of hell. But he said nothing, seemingly had no power to do so, and his father-in-law was about to make some effort to turn aside this blow when a voice in the hall outside was heard inquiring for Mr. Adams, saying that his wife had fainted again and required his help.

The young husband started, cast a look full of despair at Mr. Poindexter, and thrusting his hand against the door as if to hold it shut, sank on his knees before Mr. Gryce, saying:

"She knows! She suspects! Her nature is so sensitive."

This he managed to utter in gasps as the detective bent compassionately over him. "Don't, don't disturb her! She is an angel, a saint from heaven. Let me bear the blame—he was my brother—let me go with you, but leave her in ignorance——"

Mr. Gryce, with a vivid sense of justice, laid his hand on the young man's arm.

"Say nothing," he enjoined. "My memory is good, and I would rather hear nothing from your lips. As for your wife, my warrant does in no way include her; and if you promise to come with me quietly, I will even let you bid her *adieu*, so that you do it in my presence."

The change which passed over the young man's face at these significant words was of a nature to surprise Mr. Gryce. Rising slowly, he took his stand by Mr. Poindexter, who, true to his inflexible nature, had scarcely moved in limb and feature since Mr. Gryce came in.

"What have you against me?" he demanded. And there was a surprising ring to his voice, as if courage had come with the necessity of the moment. "Of what am I accused? I want you to tell me. I had rather you would tell me in so many words. I cannot leave in peace until you do."

Mr. Poindexter made a movement at this, and cast a half-suspicious, half-warning glance at his son-in-law. But the young man took no notice of his interference. He kept his eye on the detective, who quietly took out his warrant.

At this instant the door shook.

"Lock it!" was the hoarse command of the accused man. "Don't let anyone pass that door, even if it is to bring the tidings of my wife's death."

Mr. Gryce reached out his hand, and turned the key in the lock. Young Adams opened the paper which he had taken from the detective's hand, and while his blood-shot eyes vainly sought to master the few lines there written, Mr. Poindexter attracted the attention of Mr. Gryce, and, fixing him with his eye, formed his lips with three soundless words:

"For murder? Him?"

The detective's bow and a very long-drawn sigh from his son-in-law answered him simultaneously. With a curious lift of his upper lip, which showed his teeth somewhat unpleasantly for a moment, he drew back a step, and sank into his previous immobility.

"I am indebted to you," declared the young man. "Now I know where I stand. I am quite ready to go with you and stand trial, if such be deemed necessary by the officials in New York. You," he cried, turning with almost an air of command to the old gentleman beside him, "will watch over Eva. Not like a father, sir, but like a mother. You will be at her side when she wakes, and, if possible, leave her only when she sleeps. Do not let her suffer—not too much. No newspapers, no gossiping women. Watch! watch! as I would watch, and when I come back—for I will come back, will I not?" he appealed to Mr. Gryce, "my prayers will bless you and——" A sob stuck in his throat, and he turned for a minute aside; then he took the detective's arm quite calmly and remarked:

"I do not want to say goodbye to my wife. I cannot bear it. I had rather go straight from here without another glance at her unconscious face. When I have told my story, for I shall tell it to the first man who asks me, I may find courage to write her. Meanwhile, get me away as quickly as you can. Time enough for the world to know my shame tomorrow."

Mr. Gryce tapped on the window overlooking the *piazza*. A young man stepped in.

"Here is a gentleman," he cried, "who finds himself forced to return in great haste to New York. See that he gets to the train in time, without fuss and without raising the least comment. I will follow with his portmanteau. Mr. Poindexter, you are now at liberty to attend your suffering daughter." And with a turn of the key, he unlocked the door, and one of the most painful scenes of his long life was over.

12

Thomas Explains

Mr. Gryce was not above employing a little *finesse*. He had expressed his intention of following Mr. Adams, and he did follow him, but so immediately that he not only took the same train, but sat in the same car. He wished to note at his leisure the bearing of this young man, who interested him in quite a different way from what he had anticipated, a way that vaguely touched his own conscience and made him feel his years as he had no right to feel them when he had just brought to an end an intricate and difficult pursuit.

Seated at a distance, he watched with increasing interest the changes which passed over his prisoner's handsome countenance. He noted the calmness which now marked the features he had so lately seen writhing in deepest agony, and wondered from what source the strength came which enabled this young man to sit so stoically under the eyes of people from whose regard, an hour before, he had shrunk with such apparent suffering. Was it that courage comes with despair? Or was he too absorbed in his own misery to note the shadow it cast about him? His brooding brow and vacant eye spoke of a mind withdrawn from present surroundings. Into what depths of remorse, who could say? Certainly not this old detective, seasoned though he was by lifelong contact with criminals, some of them of the same social standing and cultured aspect as this young man.

At the station in Brooklyn he rejoined his prisoner, who scarcely looked up as he approached. In another hour they were at Police Headquarters and the serious questioning of Mr. Adams had begun.

He did not attempt to shirk it. Indeed, he seemed anxious to talk. He had a burden on his mind, and longed to throw it off. But the burden was not of the exact nature anticipated by the police. He did not acknowledge having killed his brother, but confessed to having been the incidental cause of that brother's death. The story he told was this:

"My name is Cadwalader, not Adams. My father, a Scotchman by birth, was a naturalized citizen of Pennsylvania, having settled in a place called Montgomery when a young married man. He had two children then, one of whom died in early life; the other was my brother Felix, whose violent death under the name of Adams you have called me here to explain. I am the fruit of a later marriage, entered into by my father some years after leaving Montgomery. When I was born he was living in Harrisburg, but, as he left there shortly after I had reached my third year, I have no remembrances connected with that city. Indeed, my recollections are all of very different scenes than this country affords.

"My mother having died while I was still an infant, I was sent very early in life to the Old World, from which my father had originally come. When I returned, which was not till this very year, I found my father dying, and my brother a grown man with money—a great deal of money—which I had been led to think he was ready to share with me. But after my father was laid away, Felix" (with what effort he uttered that name!) "Felix came to New York, and I was left to wander about without settled hopes or any definite promise of means upon which to base a future or start a career. While wandering, I came upon the town where my father had lived in early youth, and, hunting up his old friends, I met in the house of one who had come over from Scotland with my father a young lady" (how his voice shook, and with what a poignant accent he uttered that beloved name) "in whom I speedily became interested to the point of wishing to marry her.

"But I had no money, no business, no home to give her, and, as I was fain to acknowledge, no prospects. Still I could not give up the hope of making her my wife. So I wrote to my brother, Felix Cadwalader, or, rather, Felix Adams, as he preferred to be called in later years for family reasons entirely disconnected with the matter of his sudden demise, and, telling him I had become interested in a young girl of good family and some wealth, asked him to settle upon me a certain sum which would enable me to marry her with some feeling of self-respect. My only answer was a repetition of the vague promise he had thrown out before. But youth is hopeful, even to daring, and I decided to make her mine without further parley, in the hope that her beauty and endearing qualities would win from him, at first view, the definite concession he had so persistently denied me.

91

"This I did, and the fault with which I have most to reproach myself is that I entered into this alliance without taking her or her father into my confidence. They thought me well off, possibly rich, and while Mr. Poindexter is a man of means, I am sure, if he had known I had nothing but the clothes I wore and the merest trifle in the way of pocket money, he would have cried halt to the marriage, for he is a very ambitious man and considers his daughter well worth a millionaire's devotion—as she is.

"Felix (you must pardon me if I show no affection for my brother—he was a very strange man) was notified of my marriage, but did not choose to witness it, neither did he choose to prohibit it; so it was conducted quietly, with strangers for witnesses, in a hotel parlour. Then, with vague hopes, as well as certain vague fears, I prepared to take my young bride into the presence of my brother, who, hardened as he was by years of bachelorhood, could not be so entirely impervious to feminine charms as not to recognize my wife as a woman deserving of every consideration.

"But I had counted without my host. When, two days after the ceremony which had made us one, I took her to the house which has since become so unhappily notorious, I found that my brother had but shown me one facet, and that the least obdurate, of his many-sided nature.

"Brilliant as steel, he was as hard, and not only professed himself unmoved by my wife's many charms, but also as totally out of sympathy with such follies as love and marriage, which were, he said, the fruit of unoccupied minds and a pastime wholly unworthy of men boasting of such talents and attainments as ourselves. Then he turned his back upon us, and I, moved by an anger little short of frenzy, began an abuse for which he was so little prepared that he crouched like a man under blows, and, losing minute by minute his self-control, finally caught up a dagger lying close at hand, and crying, 'You want my money? Well, then, take it!' stabbed himself to the heart with one desperate blow.

"I fear I shall not be believed, but that is the story of this crime, gentlemen."

13

Despair

Was it? Tragedies as unpremeditated as this had doubtless occurred, and inconsistencies in character shown themselves in similar impetuosities, from the beginning of time up till now. Yet there was not a man present, with or without the memory of Bartow's pantomime, which, as you will recall, did not tally at all with this account of Mr. Adams's violent end, who did not show in a greater or less degree his distrust and evident disbelief in this tale, poured out with such volubility before them.

The young man, gifted as he was with the keenest susceptibilities, perceived this, and his head drooped.

"I shall add nothing to and take nothing from what I have said," was his dogged remark. "Make of it what you will."

The inspector who was conducting the inquiry glanced dubiously at Mr. Gryce as these words left Thomas Adams's lips; whereupon the detective said:

"We are sorry you have taken such a resolution. There are many things yet left to be explained, Mr. Adams; for instance, why, if your brother slew himself in this unforeseen manner, you left the house so precipitately, without giving an alarm or even proclaiming your relationship to him?"

"You need not answer, you know," the inspector's voice broke in. "No man is called upon to incriminate himself in this free and independent country."

A smile, the saddest ever seen, wandered for a minute over the prisoner's pallid lips. Then he lifted his head and replied with a certain air of desperation:

"Incrimination is not what I fear now. From the way you all look at me I perceive that I am lost, for I have no means of proving my story."

This acknowledgment, which might pass for the despairing cry of an innocent man, made his interrogator stare.

"You forget," suggested that gentleman, "that you had your wife with you. She can corroborate your words, and will prove herself, no doubt, an invaluable witness in your favour."

"My wife!" he repeated, choking so that his words could be barely understood. "Must she be dragged into this—so sick, so weak a woman? It would kill her, sir. She loves me—she———"

"Was she with you in Mr. Adams's study? Did she see him lift the dagger against his own breast?"

"No." And with this denial the young man seemed to take new courage. "She had fainted several moments previously, while the altercation between my brother and myself was at its height. She did not see the final act, and—gentlemen, I might as well speak the truth (I have nothing to gain by silence), she finds it as difficult as you do to believe that Mr. Adams struck himself. I—I have tried with all my arts to impress the truth upon her, but oh, what can I hope from the world when the wife of my bosom—an angel, too, who loves me—oh, sirs, she can never be a witness for me; she is too conscientious, too true to her own convictions. I should lose—she would die———"

Mr. Gryce tried to stop him; he would not be stopped.

"Spare me, sirs! Spare my wife! Write me down guilty, anything you please, rather than force that young creature to speak———"

Here the inspector cut short these appeals which were rending every heart present. "Have you read the newspapers for the last few days?" he asked.

"I? Yes, yes, sir. How could I help it? Blood is blood; the man was my brother; I had left him dying—I was naturally anxious, naturally saw my own danger, and I read them, of course."

"Then you know he was found with a large cross on his breast, a cross which was once on the wall. How came it to be torn down? Who put it on his bosom?"

"I, sir. I am not a Catholic but Felix was, and seeing him dying without absolution, without extreme unction, I thought of the holy cross, and tore down the only one I saw, and placed it in his arms."

"A pious act. Did he recognize it?"

"I cannot say. I had my fainting wife to look after. She occupied all my thoughts."

"I see, and you carried her out and were so absorbed in caring for her you did not observe Mr. Adams's valet——"

"He's innocent, sir. Whatever people may think, he had nothing to do with this crime——"

"You did not observe him, I say, standing in the doorway and watching you?"

Now the inspector knew that Bartow had not been standing there, but at the loophole above; but the opportunity for entrapping the witness was too good to lose.

Mr. Adams was caught in the trap, or so one might judge from the beads of perspiration which at that moment showed themselves on his pale forehead. But he struggled to maintain the stand he had taken, crying hotly:

"But that man is crazy, and deaf-and-dumb besides! or so the papers give out. Surely his testimony is valueless. You would not confront me with him?"

"We confront you with no one. We only asked you a question. You did not observe the valet, then?"

"No, sir."

"Or understand the mystery of the coloured lights?"

"No, sir."

"Or of the plate of steel and the other contrivances with which your brother enlivened his solitude?"

"I do not follow you, sir." But there was a change in his tone.

"I see," said the inspector, "that the complications which have disturbed us and made necessary this long delay in the collection of testimony have not entered into the crime as described by you. Now this is possible; but there is still a circumstance requiring explanation; a little circumstance, which is, nevertheless, one of importance, since your wife mentioned it to you as soon as she became conscious. I allude to the half dozen or more words which were written by your brother immediately preceding his death. The paper on which they were written has been found, and that it was a factor in your quarrel is evident, since she regretted that it had been left behind you, and he—Do you know where we found this paper?"

The eyes which young Adams raised at this interrogatory had no intelligence in them. The sight of this morsel of paper seemed to have deprived him in an instant of all the faculties with which he had been carrying on this unequal struggle. He shook his head, tried to reach out his hand, but failed to grasp the scrap of paper which the inspector held out. Then he burst into a loud cry:

"Enough! I cannot hold out, with no other support than a wicked lie. I killed my brother for reasons good as any man ever had for killing another. But I shall not impart them. I would rather be tried for murder and hanged."

It was a complete breakdown, pitiful from its contrast with the man's herculean physique and fine, if contracted, features. If the end, it was a sad end, and Mr. Gryce, whose forehead had taken on a deep line between the eyebrows, slowly rose and took his stand by the young man, who looked ready to fall. The inspector, on the contrary, did not move. He had begun a tattoo with his fingers on the table, and seemed bound to beat it out, when another sudden cry broke from the young man's lips:

"What is that?" he demanded, with his eyes fixed on the door, and his whole frame shaking violently.

"Nothing," began the inspector, when the door suddenly opened and the figure of a woman white as a wraith and wonderful with a sort of holy passion darted from the grasp of a man who sought to detain her, and stood before them, palpitating with a protest which for a moment she seemed powerless to utter.

It was Adams's young, invalid wife, whom he had left three hours before at Belleville. She was so frail of form, so exquisite of feature, that she would have seemed some unearthly visitant but for the human anguish which pervaded her look and soon found vent in this touching cry:

"What is he saying? Oh, I know well what he is saying. He is saying that he killed his brother, that he held the dagger which rid the world of a monster of whose wickedness none knew. But you must not heed him. Indeed you must not heed him. He is innocent; I, his wife, have come twenty miles, from a bed of weakness and suffering, to tell you so. He——"

But here a hand was laid gently, but firmly on her mouth. She looked up, met her husband's eyes filled with almost frantic appeal, and giving him a look in return that sank into the heart of every man who beheld it, laid her own hand on his and drew it softly away.

"It is too late, Tom, I must speak. My father, my own weakness, or your own peremptory commands could not keep me at Belleville when I knew you had been brought here. And shall I stop now, in the presence of these men who have heard your words and may believe them? No, that would be a cowardice unworthy of our love and the true lives we hope to lead together. Sirs!" and each man there held his breath to catch the words which came in faint and fainter intonation from her lips, "I know my husband to be innocent, because the hand that held the dagger was mine. I killed Felix Cadwalader!"

★★★★★★

The horror of such a moment is never fully realized till afterward. Not a man there moved, not even her husband, yet on every cheek a slow pallor was forming, which testified to the effect of such words from lips made for smiles and showing in every curve the habit of gentle thought and the loftiest instincts. Not till someone cried out from the doorway, "Catch her! she is falling!" did any one stir or re-lease the pent-up breath which awe and astonishment had hitherto held back on every lip. Then he in whose evident despair all could read the real cause of the great dread which had drawn him into a false confession, sprang forward, and with renewed life showing itself in every feature, caught her in his arms.

As he staggered with her to a sofa and laid her softly down, he seemed another man in look and bearing; and Mr. Gryce, who had been watching the whole wonderful event with the strongest interest, understood at once the meaning of the change which had come over his prisoner at that point in his memorable arrest when he first real-ized that it was for himself they had come, and not for the really guilty person, the idolized object of his affections.

Meanwhile, he was facing them all, with one hand laid tenderly on that unconscious head.

"Do not think," he cried, "that because this young girl has steeped her hand in blood, she is a wicked woman. There is no purer heart on earth than hers, and none more worthy of the worship of a true man. See! she killed my brother, son of my father, beloved by my mother, yet I can kiss her hand, kiss her forehead, her eyes, her feet, not because I hate him, but because I worship her, the purest—the best——" He left her, and came and stood before those astonished men. "Sirs!" he cried, "I must ask you to listen to a strange, a terrible tale."

14

Memoranda

"It is like and unlike what I have just related to you," began young Adams. "In my previous confession I mixed truth and falsehood, and to explain myself fully and to help you to a right understanding of my wife's act, I shall have to start afresh and speak as if I had already told you nothing."

"Wait!" cried Mr. Gryce, in an authoritative manner. "We will listen to you presently;" and, leaning over the inspector, he whispered a few words, after which he took out a pencil and jotted down certain sentences, which he handed over to this gentleman.

As they had the appearance of a memorandum, and as the inspector glanced more than once at them while Mr. Adams (or Cadwalader, as he should now rightfully be called) was proceeding with his story, I will present them to you as written.

Points to be made clear by Mr. Adams in his account of this crime:

1. Why a woman who was calm enough to stop and arrange her hair during the beginning of an interview should be wrought up to such a pitch of frenzy and exasperation before it was over as to kill with her own hand a man against whom she had evidently no previous grudge. (Remember the comb found on the floor of Mr. Adams's bedroom.)

2. What was the meaning of the following words, written just previous to this interview by the man thus killed: "I return you your daughter. Neither you nor she shall ever see me again. Remember Evelyn!"

3. Why was the pronoun "I" used in this communication? What position did Mr. Felix Adams hold toward this young girl quali-

fying him to make use of such language after her marriage to his brother?

4. And having used it, why did he, upon being attacked by her, attempt to swallow the paper upon which he had written these words, actually dying with it clinched between his teeth?

5. If he was killed in anger and died as monsters do (her own word), why did his face show sorrow rather than hate, and a determination as far as possible removed from the rush of over-whelming emotions likely to follow the reception of a mortal blow from the hand of an unexpected antagonist?

6. Why, if he had strength to seize the above-mentioned paper and convey it to his lips, did he not use that strength in turning on a light calculated to bring him assistance, instead of leaving blazing the crimson glow which, according to the code of sig-nals as now understood by us, means: "Nothing more required just now. Keep away."

7. What was the meaning of the huge steel plate found between the casings of the doorway, and why did it remain at rest within its socket at this, the culminating moment of his life?

8. An explanation of how old Poindexter came to appear on the scene so soon after the event. His words as overheard were: "It is Amos's son, not Amos!" Did he not know whom he was to meet in this house? Was the condition of the man lying before him with a cross on his bosom and a dagger in his heart less of a surprise to him than the personality of the victim?

9. Remember the conclusions we have drawn from Bartow's pantomime. Mr. Adams was killed by a left-handed thrust. Watch for an acknowledgment that the young woman is left-handed, and do not forget that an explanation is due why for so long a time she held her other arm stretched out behind her.

10. Why did the bird whose chief cry is "Remember Evelyn!" sometimes vary it with "Poor Eva! Lovely Eva! Who would strike Eva?" The story of this tragedy, to be true, must show that Mr. Adams knew his brother's bride both long and well.

11. If Bartow is, as we think, innocent of all connection with this crime save as witness, why does he show such joy at its result? This may not reasonably be expected to fall within the scope of Thomas Adams's confession, but it should not be ig-nored by us. This deaf-and-dumb servitor was driven mad by a fact which caused him joy. Why?

12. Notice the following schedule. It has been drawn up after repeated experiments with Bartow and the various slides of the strange lamp which cause so many different lights to shine out in Mr. Adams's study:

White light—Water wanted.

Green light—Overcoat and hat to be brought.

Blue light—Put back books on shelves.

Violet light—Arrange study for the night.

Yellow light—Watch for next light.

Red light—Nothing wanted; stay away.

The last was on at the final scene. Note if this fact can be explained by Mr. Adams's account of the same.

With these points in our mind, let us peruse the history of this crime and of the remote and possibly complicated causes which led to it.

15

The Secret of the Cadwaladers

Thomas Cadwalader suggested rather than told his story. We dare not imitate him in this, nor would it be just to your interest to relate these facts with all the baldness and lack of detail imposed upon this unhappy man by the hurry and anxiety of the occasion. Remarkable tragedies have their birth in remarkable facts, and as such facts are but the outcome of human passions, we must enter into those passions if we would understand either the facts or their appalling consequences. In this case, the first link of the chain which led to Felix Adams's violent death was forged before the birth of the woman who struck him. We must begin, then, with almost forgotten days, and tell the story, as her pleader did, from the standpoint of Felix and Thomas Cadwalader.

Thomas Cadwalader—now called Adams—never knew his mother; she died in his early infancy. Nor could he be said to have known his father, having been brought up in France by an old Scotch lawyer, who, being related to his mother, sometimes spoke of her, but never of his father, till Thomas had reached his fifteenth year. Then he put certain books into his hands, with this remarkable injunction:

"Here are romances, Thomas. Read them; but remember that none of them, no matter how thrilling in matter or effect, will ever equal the story of your father's bitterly wronged and suffering life."

"My father!" he cried; "tell me about him; I have never heard."

But his guardian, satisfied with an allusion which he knew must bear fruit in the extremely susceptible nature of this isolated boy, said no more that day, and Thomas turned to the books. But nothing after that could ever take his mind away from his father. He had scarcely thought of him for years, but now that that father had been placed before him in the light of a wronged man, he found himself continually hunting back in the deepest recesses of his memory for some long-forgotten recollection of that father's features calculated to restore his image to his eyes. Sometimes he succeeded in this, or thought he did; but this image, if image it was, was so speedily lost in a sensation of something strange and awe-compelling enveloping it, that he found himself more absorbed by the intangible impressions associated with this memory than by the memory itself. What were these impressions, and in what had they originated?

In vain he tried to determine. They were as vague as they were persistent. A stretch of darkness—two bars of orange light, always shining, always the same—black lines against these bars, like the tops of distant gables—an inner thrill—a vague affright—a rush about him as of a swooping wind—all this came with his father's image, only to fade away with it, leaving him troubled, uneasy, and perplexed. Finding these impressions persistent, and receiving no explanation of them in his own mind, he finally asked his guardian what they meant.

But that guardian was as ignorant as himself on this topic; and satisfied with having roused the boy's imagination, confined himself to hints, dropped now and then with a judiciousness which proved the existence of a deliberate purpose, of some duty which awaited him on the other side of the water, a duty which would explain his long exile from his only parent and for which he must fit himself by study and the acquirement of such accomplishments as render a young man a positive power in society, whether that society be of the Old World or the New. He showed his shrewdness in thus dealing with this pliable and deeply affectionate nature. From this time forth Thomas felt himself leading a life of mystery and interest.

To feel himself appointed for a work whose unknown character only heightened its importance gave point to every effort now made by this young man, and lent to his studies that vague touch of romance which made them a delight, and him an adept in many things he might otherwise have cared little about. At eighteen he was a graduate from the Sorbonne, and a musical virtuoso as well. He could fence, ride, and carry off the prize in games requiring physical prowess as well as mental fitness. He was, in fact, a prodigy in many ways, and was so considered by his fellow-students. He, however, was not perfect; he lacked social charm, and in so far failed of being the complete gentleman. This he was made to realize in the following way:

One morning his guardian came to him with a letter from his father, in which, together with some words of commendation for his present attainments, that father expressed a certain dissatisfaction with his general manner as being too abrupt and self-satisfied with those of his own sex, and much too timid and deprecatory with those of the other. Thomas felt the criticism and recognized its justice; but how had his father, proved by his letter to be no longer a myth, become acquainted with defects which Thomas instinctively felt could never have attracted the attention of his far from polished guardian?

His questions on this point elicited a response that confounded him. He was not the only son of his father; he had a brother living, and this brother, older than himself by some twenty years or more, had just been in Paris, where, in all probability, he had met him, talked with him, and perhaps pressed his hand.

It was a discovery calculated to deepen the impression already made upon Thomas's mind. Only a purpose of the greatest importance could account for so much mystery. What could it be? What was he destined to do or say or be? He was not told, but while awaiting enlightenment he was resolved not to be a disappointment to the two anxious souls who watched his career so eagerly and exacted from him such perfection. He consequently moderated his manner, and during the following year acquired by constant association with the gilded youth about him that indescribable charm of the perfect gentleman which he was led to believe would alone meet with the approval of those he now felt bound to please. At the end of the year he found himself a finished man of the world. How truly so, he began to realize when he noted the blush with which his presence was hailed by women and the respect shown him by men of his own stamp. In the midst of the satisfaction thus experienced his guardian paid him a final visit.

"You are now ready," said he, "for your father's summons. It will come in a few weeks. Be careful, then. Form no ties you cannot readily break; for, once recalled from France, you are not likely to return here. What your father's purpose concerning you may be I do not know, but it is no ordinary one. You will have money, a well-appointed home, family affection, all that you have hitherto craved in vain, and in return you will carry solace to a heart which has awaited your healing touch for twenty years. So much I am ordered to say; the rest you will hear from your father's own lips."

Aroused, encouraged, animated by the wildest hopes, the most extravagant anticipations, Thomas awaited his father's call with feverish impatience, and when it came, hastened to respond to it by an immediate voyage to America. This was some six months previous to the tragedy in ---- Street. On his arrival at the wharf in New York he was met, not by his brother, as he had every reason to expect, but by a messenger in whose face evil tidings were apparent before he spoke. Thomas was soon made acquainted with them. His father, who he now learned was called Cadwalader (he himself had always been called Adams), was ill, possibly dying. He must therefore hasten, and, being provided with minute instructions as to his way, took the train at once for a small village in northern Pennsylvania.

All that followed was a dream to him. He was hurried through the night, with the motion of the ship still in his blood, to meet—what? He dared not think. He swam in a veritable nightmare. Then came a stop, a hurrying from the train, a halt on a platform reeking with rain (for the night was stormy), a call from someone to hurry, the sight of a panting horse steaming under a lamp whose blowing flame he often woke in after nights to see, a push from a persuasive hand, then a ride over a country road the darkness of which seemed impenetrable, and, finally, the startling vision of an open door, with a Meg Merrilies of a woman standing in it, holding a flaming candle in her hand. The candle went out while he looked at it, and left only a voice to guide him—a voice which, in tones shaken by chill or feeling, he could not tell which, cried eagerly:

"Is that you, laddie? Come awa in. Come awa in. Dinna heed the rain. The maister's been crying on you a' day. I'm glad you're no ower late."

He got down, followed the voice, and, stumbling up a step or two, entered a narrow door, which was with difficulty held open behind him, and which swung to with a loud noise the minute he crossed the threshold. This or the dreariness of the place in which he found himself disturbed him greatly. Bare floors, stained walls, meagre doorways, and a common pine staircase, lighted only by the miserable candle which the old woman had relit—were these the appointments of the palatial home he had been led to expect? These the surroundings, this the abode of him who had exacted such perfection on his part, and to satisfy whose standard he had devoted years of hourly, daily effort, in every department of art and science? A sickening revolt seized him, aggravated by the smiles of the old woman, who dipped and curtsied before him in senile delight. She may have divined his feelings, for, drawing him inside, she relieved him of his overcoat, crying all the while, with an extravagant welcome more repulsive than all the rest:

104

"O the fine laddie! Wad your puir mither could see you the noo! Bonnie and clever! No your faither's bairn ava! All mither, laddie, all mither!"

The room was no better than the hall.

"Where is my father?" he asked, authoritatively, striving to keep down his strong repugnance.

"Dinna ye hear him? He's crying on ye. Puir man, he's wearying to see ye."

Hear him? He could scarcely hear her. The driving rain, the swish of some great boughs against the house, the rattling of casements and doors, and the shrieking of wind in the chimney made all other sounds well-nigh inaudible. Yet as he listened he seemed to catch the accents of a far-off voice calling, now wistfully, now imperatively, "Thomas! Thomas!" And, thrilled with an emotion almost superstitious in its intensity, he moved hastily toward the staircase.

But the old woman was there before him. "Na! Na!" she cried. "Come in by and eat something first."

But Thomas shook his head. It seemed to him at that moment as if he never could eat or sleep again, the disillusion was so bitter, his disappointment so keen.

"You will na? Then haste ye—haste ye. But it's a peety you wadna ha'e eaten something. Ye'll need it, laddie; ye'll need it."

"Thomas! Thomas!" wailed the voice.

He tore himself away. He forced himself to go upstairs, following the cry, which at every moment grew louder. At the top he cast a final glance below. The old woman stood at the stair-foot, shading the candle from the draught with a hand that shook with something more than age. She was gazing after him in vague affright, and with the shadow of this fear darkening her weazen face, formed a picture from which he was glad to escape.

Plunging on, he found himself before a window whose small panes dripped and groaned under a rain that was fast becoming a torrent. Chilled by the sight, he turned toward the door faintly outlined beside it, and in the semi-darkness seized an old-fashioned latch rattling in the wind that permeated every passageway, and softly raised it.

Instantly the door fell back, and two eyes blazing with fever and that fire of the soul of which fever is the mere physical symbol greeted him from the midst of a huge bed drawn up against the opposite wall. Then two arms rose, and the moaning cry of "Thomas! Thomas!" changed to a shout, and he knew himself to be in the presence of his father.

Falling on his knees in speechless emotion, he grasped the wasted hands held out to him. Such a face, rugged though it was and far from fulfilling the promise held out to him in his dreams, could not but move any man. As he gazed into it and pressed the hands in which the life blood only seemed to linger for this last, this only embrace, all his filial instincts were aroused and he forgot the common surroundings, the depressing rain, his own fatigue and bitter disappointment, in his lifelong craving for love and family recognition.

But the old man on whose breast he fell showed other emotions than those by which he was himself actuated. It was not an embrace he craved, but an opportunity to satisfy an almost frenzied curiosity as to the appearance and attributes of the son who had grown to manhood under other eyes. Pushing him gently back, he bade him stand in the light of the lamp burning on a small pine table, and surveyed him, as it were, from the verge of his own fast failing life, with moans of mingled pain and weariness, amid which Thomas thought he heard the accents of a supreme satisfaction.

Meanwhile in Thomas himself, as he stood there, the sense of complete desolation filled his breast almost to bursting. To have come home for this! To find a father only to be weighed in the scales of that father's judgment! To be admired, instead of loved!

As he realized his position and listened to the shrieking of the wind and rain, he felt that the wail of the elements but echoed the cry of his own affections, thus strangled in their birth. Indeed the sensations of that moment made so deep an impression upon him that he was never afterward able to hear a furious gust of wind or rain without the picture rising up before him of this great hollow room, with the trembling figure of his father struggling in the grasp of death and holding it at bay, while he gauged with worldly wisdom the physical, mental, and moral advantages of the son so long banished and so lately restored to his arms.

A rush of impetuous words followed by the collapse of his father's form upon the pillow showed that the examination was over. Rushing forward, he grasped again that father's hands, but soon shrank back, stunned by what he heard and the prospect it opened before him. A few of his father's words will interpret the rest. They came in a flood, and among others Thomas caught these:

"The grace of God be thanked! Our efforts have not failed. Handsome, strong, noble in look and character, we could ask nothing more, hope for nothing more. My revenge will succeed! John Poindexter will find that he has a heart, and that that heart can be wrung. I do not need to live to see it. For me it exists now; it exists here!" And he struck his breast with hands that seemed to have reserved their last strength for this supreme gesture.

John Poindexter! Who was he? It was a new name to Thomas. Venturing to say so, he reeled under the look he received from his father's eyes.

"You do not know who John Poindexter is, and what he has done to me and mine? They have kept their promise well, too well, but God will accord me strength to tell you what has been left unsaid by them. He would not bring me up to this hour to let me perish before you have heard the story destined to make you the avenger of innocence upon that enemy of your race. Listen, Thomas. With the hand of death encircling my heart, I speak, and if the story find you cold—But it will not. Your name is Cadwalader, and it will not."

Constrained by passions such as he had never imagined even in dreams, Thomas fell upon his knees. He could not listen otherwise. His father, gasping for breath, fixed him with his hollow eyes, in which the last flickering flames of life flared up in fitful brightness.

"Thomas"—the pause was brief—"you are not my only child."

"I know it," fell from Thomas's white lips. "I have a brother; his name is Felix."

The father shook his head with a look suggestive of impatience.

"Not him! Not him!" he cried. "A sister! a sister, who died before you were born—beautiful, good, with a voice like an angel's and a heart—she should be standing by my side today, and she would have been if—if he—but none of that. I have no breath to waste. Facts, facts, just facts! Afterward may come emotions, hatred, denunciation, not now. This is my story, Thomas.

"John Poindexter and I were friends. From boyhood we shared each other's bed, food, and pleasures, and when he came to seek his fortune in America I accompanied him. He was an able man, but cold. I was of an affectionate nature, but without any business capacity. As proof of this, in fifteen years he was rich, esteemed, the master of a fine house, and the owner of half a dozen horses; while I was the same nobody I had been at first, or would have been had not Providence given me two beautiful children and blessed, or rather cursed, me with the friendship of this prosperous man.

"When Felix was fourteen and Evelyn three years older, their mother died. Soon after, the little money I had vanished in an unfortunate enterprise, and life began to promise ill, both for myself and for my growing children. John Poindexter, who was honest enough then, or let me hope so, and who had no children of his own, though he had been long married, offered to take one of mine to educate. But I did not consent to this till the war of the rebellion broke out; then I sent him both son and daughter, and went into the army.

"For four years I fought for the flag, suffering all that a man can suffer and live, and being at last released from Libby Prison, came home with a heart full of gratitude and with every affection keyed up by a long series of unspeakable experiences, to greet my son and clasp once more within my wasted arms the idolized form of my deeply loved daughter. What did I find? A funeral in the streets—hers—and Felix, your brother, walking like a guard between her speechless corpse and the man under whose protection I had placed her youth and innocence.

"Betrayed!" shrieked the now frenzied parent, rising on his pillow. "Her innocence! Her sweetness! And he, cold as the stone we laid upon her grave, had seen her perish with the anguish and shame of it, without a sign of grief or a word of contrition."

"O God!" burst from lips the old man was watching with frenzied cunning.

"Ay, God!" repeated the father, shaking his head as if in defiance before he fell back on his pillow. "He allowed it and I—But this does not tell the story. I must keep to facts as Felix did—Felix, who was but fifteen years old and yet found himself the only confidant and solace of this young girl betrayed by her protector. It was after her burial——"

"Cease!" cried a voice, smooth, fresh, and yet strangely commanding, from over Thomas's shoulder. "Let me tell the rest. No man can tell the rest as I can."

"Felix!" ejaculated Amos Cadwalader below his breath.

"Felix!" repeated Thomas, shaken to his very heart by this new presence. But when he sought to rise, to turn, he felt the pressure of a hand on his shoulder and heard that voice again, saying softly, but peremptorily:

"Wait! Wait till you hear what I have to say. Think not of me, think only of her. It is she you are called upon to avenge; your sister, Evelyn."

Thomas yielded to him as he had to his father. He sank down beneath that insistent hand, and his brother took up the tale.

"Evelyn had a voice like a bird. In those days before father's return, she used to fill old John Poindexter's house with melody. I, who, as a boy, was studious, rather than artistic, thought she sang too much for a girl whose father was rotting away in a Southern prison. But when about to rebuke her, I remembered Edward Kissam, and was silent. For it was his love which made her glad, and to him I wished every happiness, for he was good, and honest, and kind to me. She was eighteen then, and beautiful, or so I was bound to believe, since every man looked at her, even old John Poindexter, though he never looked at any other woman, not even his own wife.

"And she was good, too, and pure, I swear, for her blue eyes never faltered in looking into mine until one day when—my God! how well I remember it!—they not only faltered, but shrank before me in such terror, that, boy though I was, I knew that something terrible, something unprecedented had happened, and thinking my one thought, I asked if she had received bad news from father. Her answer was a horrified moan, but it might have been a shriek. 'Our father! Pray God we may never see him or hear from him again. If you love him, if you love me, pray he may die in prison rather than return here to see me as I am now.'

"I thought she had gone mad, and perhaps she had for a moment; for at my look of startled distress a change took place in her. She remembered my youth, and laughing, or trying to laugh away her frenzy, uttered some hurried words I failed to understand, and then, sinking at my knee, laid her head against my side, crying that she was not well; that she had experienced for a long time secret pains and great inward distress, and that she sometimes feared she was not going to live long, for all her songs and merry ways and seeming health and spirits.

"'Not live, Evelyn?' It was an inconceivable thought to me, a boy. I looked at her, and seeing how pale, how incomprehensibly pale she was, my heart failed me, for nothing but mortal sickness could make such a change in any one in a week, in a day. Yet how could death reach her, loved as she was by Edward, by her father, and by me. Thinking to rouse her, I spoke the former's name. But it was the last word I should have uttered. Crouching as if I had given her a blow, she put her two hands out, shrieking faintly: 'Not that! Never that! Do not speak his name. Let me never hear of him or see him again. I am dead—do you not understand me?—dead to all the world from this day—except to you!' she suddenly sobbed, 'except to you!'

"And still I did not comprehend her. But when I understood, as I soon did, that no mention was to be made of her illness; that her door was to be shut and no one allowed to enter, not even Mrs. Poindexter or her guardian—least of all, her guardian—I began to catch the first intimation of that horror which was to end my youth and fill my whole after life with but one thought—revenge. But I said nothing, only watched and waited. Seeing that she was really ill, I constituted myself her nurse, and sat by her night and day till her symptoms became so alarming that the whole household was aroused and we could no longer keep the doctor from her. Then I sat at her door, and with one ear turned to catch her lightest moan, listened for the step she most dreaded, but which, though it sometimes approached, never passed the opening of the hall leading to her chamber.

"For one whole week I sat there, watching her life go slowly out like a flame, with nothing to feed it; then as the great shadow fell, and life seemed breaking up within me, I dashed from the place, and confronting him where I found him walking, pale and disturbed, in his own hall, told him that my father was coming; that I had had a dream, and in that dream I had seen my father with his face turned toward this place. Was he prepared to meet him? Had he an answer ready when Amos Cadwalader should ask him what had become of his child?

"I had meant to shock the truth from this man, and I did so. As I mentioned my father's name, Poindexter blanched, and my fears became certainty. Dropping my youthful manner, for I was a boy no longer, I flung his crime in his face, and begged him to deny it if he could. He could not, but he did what neither he nor any other man could do in my presence now and live—he smiled. Then when he saw me crouching for a spring—for, young as I was, I knew but one impulse, and that was to fly at his throat—he put out his powerful hand, and pinning me to the ground, uttered a few short sentences in my ear.

"They were terrible ones. They made me see that nothing I might then do could obliterate the fact that she was lost if the world knew what I knew, or even so much as suspected it; that any betrayal on my part or act of contrition on his would only pile the earth on her innocent breast and sink her deeper and deeper into the grave she was then digging for herself; that all dreams were falsities; that Southern prisons seldom gave up their victims alive; and that if my father should escape the jaws of Libby and return, it was for me to be glad if he found a quiet grave instead of a dishonoured daughter. Further, that if I crossed him, who was power itself, by any boyish exhibition of hate, I would find that any odium I might invoke would fall on her and not on him, making me an abhorrence, not only to the world at large, but to the very father in whose interest I might pretend to act.

"I was young and without worldly experience. I yielded to these arguments, but I cursed him where he stood. With his hand pressing heavily upon me, I cursed him to his face; then I went back to my sister.

"Had she, by some supernatural power, listened to our talk, or had she really been visited by some dream, that she looked so changed? There was a feverish light in her eye, and something like the shadow of a smile on her lips. Mrs. Poindexter was with her; Mrs. Poindexter, whose face was a mask we never tried to penetrate. But when she had left us alone again, then Evelyn spoke, and I saw what her dream had been.

"'Felix,' she cried as I approached her trembling with my own emotions and half afraid of hers, 'there is still one hope for me. It has come to me while you have been away. Edward—he loves me—did—perhaps he would forgive. If he would take me into his protection (I see you know it all, Felix) then I might grow happy again—well—strong—good. Do you think—oh, you are a child, what do you know?—but—but before I turn my face forever to the wall try if he will see me—try, try—with your boy's wit—your clever schemes, to get him here unknown to—to—the one I fear, I hate—and then, then, if he bids me live, I will live, and if he bids me die, I will die; and all will be ended.'

"I was an ignorant boy. I knew men no more than I knew women, and yielding to her importunities, I promised to see Edward and plan for an interview without her guardian's knowledge. I was, as Evelyn had said, keen in those days and full of resources, and I easily managed it. Edward, who had watched from the garden as I had from the door, was easily persuaded to climb her lattice in search of what he had every reason to believe would be his last earthly interview with his darling. As his eager form bounded into the room I tottered forth, carrying with me a vision of her face as she rose to meet—what? I dared not think or attempt to foresee. Falling on my knees I waited the issue. Alas! It was a speedy one.

"A stifled moan from her, the sound of a hoarse farewell from him, told me that his love had failed her, and that her doom was sealed.

Creeping back to her side as quickly as my failing courage admitted, I found her face turned to the wall, from which it never again looked back; while presently, before the hour was passed, shouts ringing through the town proclaimed that young Kissam had shot himself. She heard, and died that night. In her last hour she had fancies. She thought she saw her father, and her prayers for mercy were heart-rending. Then she thought she saw him, that demon, her executioner, and cringed and moaned against the wall.

"But enough of this. Two days after, I walked between him and her silent figure outstretched for burial. I had promised that no eye but mine should look upon her, no other hand touch her, and I kept my word, even when the impossible happened and her father rose up in the street before us. Quietly, and in honour, she was carried to her grave, and then—then, in the solitude of the retreat I had found for him, I told our father all, and why I had denied him the only comfort which seemed left to him—a last look at his darling daughter's face."

16

The Oath

A sigh from the panting breast of Amos Cadwalader followed these words. Plainer than speech it told of a grief still fresh and an agony still unappeased, though thirty years had passed away since the unhappy hour of which Felix spoke.

Felix, echoing it, went quickly on:

"It was dusk when I told my story, and from dark to dawn we sat with eyes fixed on each other's face, without sleep and without rest. Then we sought John Poindexter.

"Had he shunned us we might have had mercy, but he met us openly, quietly, and with all the indifference of one who cannot measure feeling, because he is incapable of experiencing it himself. His first sentence evinced this. 'Spare yourselves, spare me all useless recriminations. The girl is dead; I cannot call her back again. Enjoy your life, your eating and your drinking, your getting and your spending; it is but for a few more years at best. Why harp on old 'griefs?' His last word was a triumph. 'When a man cares for nothing or nobody, it is useless to curse him.'

"Ah, that was it! That was the secret of his power. He cared for nothing and for no one, not even for himself. We felt the blow, and bent under it. But before leaving him and the town, we swore, your father and I, that we would yet make that cold heart feel; that some day, in some way, we would cause that impassive nature to suffer as he had made us suffer, however happy he might seem or however closely his prosperity might cling to him. That was thirty years ago, and that oath has not yet been fulfilled."

Felix paused. Thomas lifted his head, but the old man would not let him speak. "There are men who forget in a month, others who forget in a year. I have never forgotten, nor has Felix here. When you were born (I had married again, in the hope of renewed joy) I felt, I know not why, that Evelyn's avenger was come. And when, a year or so after this event, we heard that God had forgotten John Poindexter's sins, or, perhaps, remembered them, and that a child was given him also, after eighteen years of married life, I looked upon your bonny face and saw—or thought I saw—a possible means of bringing about the vengeance to which Felix and I had dedicated our lives.

"You grew; your ardent nature, generous temper, and facile mind promised an abundant manhood, and when your mother died, leaving me for a second time a widower, I no longer hesitated to devote you to the purpose for which you seemed born. Thomas, do you remember the beginning of that journey which finally led you far from me? How I bore you on my shoulder along a dusty road, till arrived within sight of his home, I raised you from among the tombs and, showing you those distant gables looming black against the twilight's gold, dedicated you to the destruction of whatever happiness might hereafter develop under his infant's smile? You do? I did not think you could forget; and now that the time has come for the promise of that hour to be fulfilled, I call on you again, Thomas. Avenge our griefs, avenge your sister. *Poindexter's girl has grown to womanhood.*"

At the suggestion conveyed in these words Thomas recoiled in horror. But the old man failed to read his emotion rightly. Clutching his arm, he proceeded passionately:

"Woo her! Win her! They do not know you. You will be Thomas Adams to them, not Thomas Cadwalader. Gather this budding flower into your bosom, and then—Oh, he must love his child! Through her we have our hand on his heart. Make her suffer—she's but a country girl, and you have lived in Paris—make her suffer, and if, in doing so, you cause him to blench, then believe I am looking upon you from the grave I go to, and be happy; for you will not have lived, nor will I have died, in vain."

He paused to catch his failing breath, but his indomitable will triumphed over death and held Thomas under a spell that confounded his instincts and made him the puppet of feelings which had accumulated their force to fill him, in one hour, with a hate which it had taken his father and brother a quarter of a century to bring to the point of active vengeance.

"I shall die; I am dying now," the old man panted on. "I shall never live to see your triumph; I shall never behold John Poindexter's eye glaze with those sufferings which rend the entrails and make a man question if there is a God in heaven. But I shall know it where I am. No mounded earth can keep my spirit down when John Poindexter feels his doom. I shall be conscious of his anguish and shall rejoice; and when in the depths of darkness to which I go he comes faltering along my way——

"Boy, boy, you have been reared for this. God made you handsome; man has made you strong; you have made yourself intelligent and accomplished. You have only to show yourself to this country girl to become the master of her will and affection, and these once yours, remember *me! Remember Evelyn!*"

Never had Thomas been witness to such passion. It swept him along in a burning stream against which he sought to contend and could not. Raising his hand in what he meant as a response to that appeal, he endeavoured to speak, but failed. His father misinterpreted his silence, and bitterly cried:

"You are dumb! You do not like the task; are virtuous, perhaps— you who have lived for years alone and unhampered in Paris. Or you have instincts of honour, habits of generosity that blind you to wrongs that for a longer space than your lifetime have cried aloud to heaven for vengeance. Thomas, Thomas, if you should fail me now——"

"He will not fail you," broke in the voice of Felix, calm, suave, and insinuating. "I have watched him; I know him; he will not fail you."

Thomas shuddered; he had forgotten Felix, but as he heard these words he could no longer delay looking at the man who had offered to stand his surety for the performance of the unholy deed his father exacted from him. Turning, he saw a man who in any place and under any roof would attract attention, awake admiration and—yes, fear. He was not a large man, not so large as himself, but the will that expressed itself in frenzy on his father's lips showed quiet and inflexible in the gray eye resting upon his own with a power he could never hope to evade. As he looked and comprehended, a steel band seemed to compress his heart; yet he was conscious at the same time that the personality before which he thus succumbed was as elegant as his own and as perfectly trained in all the ways of men and of life.

Even the air of poverty which had shocked him in his father's person and surroundings was not visible here. Felix was both well and handsomely clad, and could hold his own as the elder brother in every respect most insisted upon by the Parisian gentleman. The long and, to Thomas, mysterious curtain of dark-green serge which stretched behind him from floor to ceiling threw out his pale features with a remarkable distinctness, and for an instant Thomas wondered if it had been hung there for the purpose of producing this effect. But the demand in his brother's face drew his attention, and, bowing his head, he stammered:

"I am at your command, Felix. I am at your command, father. I cannot say more. Only remember that I never saw Evelyn, that she died before I was born, and that I——"

But here Felix's voice broke in, kind, but measured:

"Perhaps there is some obstacle we have not reckoned upon. You may already love some woman and desire to marry her. If so, it need be no impediment——"

But here Thomas's indignation found voice.

"No," said he; "I am heart-whole save for a few lingering fancies which are fast becoming vanishing dreams."

He seemed to have lived years since entering this room.

"Your heart will not be disturbed now," commented Felix. "I have seen the girl. I went there on purpose a year ago. She's as pale as a snow-drop and as listless. You will not be obliged to recall to mind the gay smiles of Parisian ladies to be proof against her charms."

Thomas shrugged his shoulders.

"She must be made to know the full intoxication of hope," Felix proceeded in his clear and cutting voice. "To realize despair she must first experience every delight that comes with satisfied love. Have you the skill as well as heart to play to the end a *rôle* which will take patience as well as dissimulation, courage as well as subtlety, and that union of will and implacability which finds its food in tears and is strengthened, rather than lessened, by the suffering of its victim?"

"I have the skill," murmured Thomas, "but——"

"You lack the incentive," finished Felix. "Well, well, we must have patience with your doubts and hesitations. Our hate has been fostered by memories of her whom, as you say, you have never seen. Look, then, Thomas. Look at your sister as she was, as she is for us. Look at her, and think of her as despoiled, killed, forgotten by Poindexter. Have you ever gazed upon a more moving countenance, or one in which beauty contends with a keener prophecy of woe?"

Not knowing what to expect, anticipating almost to be met by her shade, Thomas followed the direction of his brother's lifted hand, and beheld, where but a minute before that dismal curtain had hung, a blaze of light, in the midst of which he saw a charming, but tragic, figure, such as no gallery in all Europe had ever shown him, possibly because no other limned face or form had ever appealed to his heart. It did not seem a picture, it seemed her very self, a gentle, loving self that breathed forth all the tenderness he had vainly sought for in his living relatives; and falling at her feet, he cried out:

"Do not look at me so reproachfully, sweet Evelyn. I was born to avenge you, and I will. John Poindexter shall never go down in peace to his tomb."

A sigh of utter contentment came from the direction of the bed.

"Swear it!" cried his father, holding out his arms before him in the form of a cross.

"Yes, swear it!" repeated Felix, laying his own hand on those crossed arms.

Thomas drew near, and laid his hand beside that of Felix.

"I swear," he began, raising his voice above the tempest, which poured gust after gust against the house. "I swear to win the affections of Eva Poindexter, and then, when her heart is all mine, to cast her back in anguish and contumely on the breast of John Poindexter."

"Good!" came from what seemed to him an immeasurable distance. Then the darkness, which since the taking of this oath had settled over his senses, fell, and he sank insensible at the feet of his dying father.

★★★★★★

Amos Cadwalader died that night; but not without one awful scene more. About midnight he roused from the sleep which had followed the exciting incidents I have just related, and glancing from Thomas to Felix, sitting on either side of the bed, fixed his eyes with a strange gleam upon the door.

"Ah!" he ejaculated, "a visitor! John Poindexter! He comes to ask my forgiveness before I set out on my dismal journey."

The sarcasm of his tone, the courtesy of his manner, caused the hair to stir on the heads of his two sons. That he saw his enemy as plainly as he saw them, neither could doubt.

"Does he dread my meeting with Evelyn? Does he wish to placate me before I am joined to that pathetic shade? He shall not be disappointed. I forgive you, John Poindexter! I forgive you my daughter's shame, my blighted life. I am dying; but I leave one behind who will not forgive you. I have a son, an avenger of the dead, who yet lives to—to——"

He fell back. With these words, which seemed to seal Thomas to his task, Amos Cadwalader died.

17

Eva

Felix had not inherited his father's incapacity for making money. In the twenty years that had passed since Thomas had been abroad he had built up a fortune, which he could not induce his father to share, but which that father was perfectly willing to see devoted to their mutual revenge. There was meaning, therefore, in the injunction Felix gave his brother on his departure for Montgomery:

"I have money; spend it; spend what you will, and when your task is completed, there will still be some left for your amusement."

Thomas bowed. "The labourer is worthy of his hire," was his thought. "And you?" he asked, looking about the scanty walls, which seemed to have lost their very excuse for being now that his father had died. "Will you remain here?"

Felix's answer was abrupt, but positive. "No; I go to New York to-morrow. I have rented a house there, which you may one day wish to share. The name under which I have leased it is Adams, Felix Adams. As such you will address me. Cadwalader is a name that must not leave your lips in Montgomery, nor must you forget that my person is known there, otherwise we might not have been dependent on you for the success of our revenge." And he smiled, fully conscious of being the handsomer man of the two. "And now how about those introductions we enjoined you to bring from Paris?"

★★★★★★

The history of the next few weeks can best be understood by reading certain letters sent by Thomas to Felix, by examining a diary drawn up by the same writer for his own relief and satisfaction. The letters will be found on the left, and the diary on the right, of the double columns hereby submitted. The former are a summary of facts; the latter is a summary of feelings. Both are necessary to a right comprehension of the situation.

Dear Felix:
I am here; I have seen her. She is, as you have said, a pale blonde. Tomorrow I present my credentials to John Poindexter. From what I have already experienced I anticipate a favourable reception.
Yours aff., Thomas

FIRST ENTRY

I could not write Felix the true story of this day. Why? And why must I write it here? To turn my mind from dwelling on it? Perhaps. I do not seem to understand my own feelings, or why I begin to dread my task, while ardently pressing forward to accomplish it.

I have seen her. This much I wrote to Felix, but I did not say where our meeting took place or how. How could I? Would he understand how one of Poindexter's blood could be employed in a gracious act, or how I, filled with a purpose that has made my heart dark as hell ever since I embraced it, could find that heart swell and that purpose sink at my first glimpse of the face whose beauty I have sworn to devote to agony and tears? Surely, surely Felix would have been stronger, and yet——

I went from the cars to the cemetery. Before entering the town or seeing to my own comfort, I sought Evelyn's grave, there to renew my oath in the place where, nineteen years ago, my father held me up, a four-year-old child, in threat, toward John Poindexter's home. I had succeeded in finding the old and neglected stone which marked her resting-place, and was bending in the sunset light to examine it, when the rustle of a woman's skirts attracted my attention, and I perceived advancing toward me a young girl in a nimbus of rosy light which seemed to lift her from the ground and give to her delicate figure and strangely illumined head an ethereal aspect which her pure features and tender bearing did not belie.

In her arms she carried a huge cluster of snow-white lilies, and when I observed that her eyes were directed not on me, but on the grave beside which I stood, I moved aside into the shadow of some bushes and watched her while she strewed these flowers—emblems of innocence—over the grave I had just left.

What did it mean, and who was this young girl who honoured with such gracious memorials the grave of my long-buried sister? As she rose from her task I could no longer restrain either my emotion or the curiosity with which her act had inspired me. Advancing, I greeted her with all the respect her appearance called for, and noting that her face was even more beautiful when lifted in speech than when bent in gravity over her flowers, I asked her, in the indifferent tone of a stranger, who was buried in this spot, and why she, a mere girl, dropped flowers upon a grave the mosses of whose stone proved it to have been dug long before she was born.

Her answer caused me a shock, full as my life has lately been of startling experiences. "I strew flowers here," said she, "because the girl who lies buried under this stone had the same birthday as myself. I never saw her, it's true, but she died in my father's house when she was no older than I am today, and since I have become a woman and realize what loss there is in dying young, I have made it a custom to share with her my birthday flowers. She was a lily, they say, in appearance and character, and so I bring her lilies."

It was Eva Poindexter, the girl I—And she was strewing flowers on Evelyn's grave

LETTER 2

Dear Felix:

I have touched the hand of John Poindexter. In order to win a place in the good graces of the daughter I must please the father, or at least attract his favourable notice. I have reason to think I have done this.

Very truly, Thomas.

ENTRY 2

I no longer feel myself a true man. John Poindexter is cold in appearance, hard in manner, and inflexible in opinion, but he does not inspire the abhorrence I anticipated nor awaken in me the one thought due to the memory of my sister. Is it because he is Eva's father? Has the loveliness of the daughter cast a halo about the parent? If so, Felix has a right to execrate me and my father to——

Dear Felix:

The introductions furnished me have made me received every-where. There is considerable wealth here and many fine houses. Consequently I find myself in a congenial society, of which she is the star. Did I say that he was, as of old, the chief man of the town?

Yours truly, Thomas.

ENTRY 3

She is beautiful. She has the daintiness of the lily and the flush of the rose. But it is not her beauty that moves me; it is the strange sweetness of her nature, which, nevertheless, has no weakness in it; on the contrary, it possesses peculiar strength, which becomes instantly apparent at the call of duty. Could Felix have imagined such a Poindexter? I cannot contemplate such loveliness and associate it with the execrable sin which calls down vengeance upon this house. I cannot even dwell upon my past life. All that is dark, threatening, secret, and revengeful slips from me under her eye, and I dream of what is pure, true, satisfying, and en-nobling. And this by the influence of her smile, rather than of her words. Have I been given an angel to degrade? Or am I so blind as to behold a saint where others (Felix, let us say) would see only a pretty woman with unexpected attractions?

LETTER 4

Dear Felix:

Rides, dances, games, nonsense generally. My interest in this young girl is beginning to be publicly recognized. She alone seems ignorant of it. Sometimes I wonder if our scheme will fail through her impassibility and more than conventional in-nocence. I am sometimes afraid she will never love me. Yet I have exerted myself to please her. Indeed, I could not have exerted myself more. Today I went twenty-five miles on horse-back to procure her a trifle she fancied.

Yours aff., Thomas.

ENTRY 4

All will not go as easily as Felix imagines. Eva Poindexter may be a country girl, but she has her standards, too, and mere grace and attainment are not sufficient to win her. Have I the other qualities she demands? That remains to be seen. I have one she never dreams of. Will its shadow so overwhelm the rest that her naturally pure spirit will shrink from me just at the moment when I think her mine? I cannot tell, and the doubt creates a hell within me. Something deeper, stronger, more imperious than my revenge makes the winning of this girl's heart a necessity to me. I have forgotten my purpose in this desire. I have forgotten everything except that she is the one woman of my life, and that I can never rest till her heart is wholly mine. Good God! Have I become a slave where I hoped to be master? Have I, Thomas Cadwalader, given my soul into the keeping of this innocent girl? I do not even stop to inquire. To win her—that is all for which I now live.

LETTER 5

Dear Felix:
She may not care for me, but she is interested in no one else. Of this I am assured by John Poindexter, who seems very desirous of aiding me in my attempt to win his daughter's heart. Hard won, close bound. If she ever comes to love me it will be with the force of a very strong nature. The pale blonde has a heart. Yours aff., Thomas.

ENTRY 5

If it were passion only that I feel, I might have some hope of re-straining it. But it is something more, something deeper, something which constrains me to look with her eyes, hear with her ears, and throb with her heart. My soul, rather than my senses, is enthralled. I want to win her, not for my own satisfaction, but to make her happy. I want to prove to her that goodness exists in this world—I, who came here to corrode and destroy; I, who am still pledged to do so. Ah, Felix, Felix, you should have chosen an older man for your purpose, or remembered that he who could be influenced as I was by family affections possesses a heart too soft for such infamy

LETTER 6

Dear Felix:
Will you send me a few exquisite articles from Tiffany's? I see that her father expects me to give her presents. I think she will

accept them. If she does, we may both rest easy as to the state of her affections.

Very truly, Thomas

ENTRY 6

The name of Evelyn is never mentioned in this house. Sometimes I think that he has forgotten her, and find in this thought the one remaining spur to my revenge. Forgotten her! Strange, that his child, born long after his victim's death, should remember this poor girl, and he forget! Yet on the daughter the blow is planned to fall—if it does fall. Should I not pray that it never may? That she should loathe instead of love me? Distrust, instead of confide in my honour and affection? But who can pray against himself? Eva Poindexter must love me, even if I am driven to self-destruction by my own remorse, after she has confided her heart to my keeping.

LETTER 7

Dear Felix:

This morning I passed under the window you have described to me as Evelyn's. I did it with a purpose. I wanted to test my own emotions and to see how much feeling it would arouse in me. Enough.

Eva accepted the brooch. It was the simplest thing you sent.

Aff., Thomas.

ENTRY 7

I cannot bring myself to pass a whole day away from her side. If Felix were here and could witness my assiduity, he would commend me in his cold and inflexible heart for the singleness with which I pursue my purpose. He would say to me, in the language of one of his letters: "You are not disappointing us." Us! As if our father still hovered near, sharing our purposes and hope. Alas! if he does, he must penetrate more deeply than Felix into the heart of this matter; must see that with every day's advantage—and I now think each day brings its advantage—I shrink further and further from the end they planned for me; the end which can alone justify my advance in her affections. I am a traitor to my oath, for I now know I shall never disappoint Eva's faith in me. I could not.

Rather would I meet my father's accusing eyes on the verge of

that strange world to which he has gone, or Felix's recriminations here, or my own contempt for the weakness which has
made it possible for me to draw back from the brink of this
wicked revenge to which I have devoted myself.

LETTER 8

Dear Felix:

A picnic on the mountains. It fell to me to escort Miss Poindexter down a dangerous slope. Though no words of affection
passed between us (she is not yet ready for them), I feel that I
have made a decided advance in her good graces.
Yours, Thomas.

ENTRY 8

I hate John Poindexter, yes, I hate him, but I can never hate his
daughter. Only Felix could so confound the father with the
child as to visit his anger upon this gentle embodiment of all
that is gracious, all that is trustworthy, all that is fascinating in
woman. But am I called upon to hate her? Am I not in a way
required to love her? I will ask Felix. No, I cannot ask Felix.
He would never comprehend her charm or its influence over
me. He would have doubts and come at once to Montgomery.
Good God! Am I proving such a traitor to my own flesh and
blood that I cannot bear to think of Felix contemplating even
in secret the unsuspicious form of his enemy's daughter?

LETTER 9

Dear Felix:

I do not hear from you. Are you well, or did your journey affect
your health? I have no especial advance to report. John Poindexter seems greatly interested in my courtship. Sometimes he
gives me very good advice. How does that strike you, Felix?
Aff., Thomas.

ENTRY 9

I have touched her hand! I have felt her sweet form thrilling
against mine as we descended the mountain ledges together!
No man was near, no eye—there were moments in which
we were as much alone in the wide paradise of these wooded
slopes as if the world held no other breathing soul. Yet I no
more dared to press her hand, or pour forth the mad worship

of my heart into her innocent ears, than if the eyes of all Paris had been upon us. How I love her! How far off and faint seem the years of that dead crime my brother would invoke for the punishment of this sweet soul! Yes, and how remote that awful hour in which I knelt beneath the hand of my dying father and swore—Ah, that oath! That oath!

Letter 10

Dear Felix:
Miss Poindexter has told me unreservedly that she cares for me. Are you satisfied with me now?
In haste, Thomas.

Entry 10

The thing I dreaded, the thing I might have foreseen, has occurred. Felix has made his appearance in Montgomery. I received a communication to that effect from him today; a communication in which he commands me to meet him tonight, at Evelyn's grave, at the witching hour of twelve. I do not enjoy the summons. I have a dread of Felix, and begin to think he calculates upon stage devices to control me. But the day has passed for that. I will show him that I can be no more influenced in that place and at that hour than I could be in this hotel room, with the sight of her little glove—is there sin in such thefts?— lying on the table before us. Evelyn! She is a sacred memory. But the dead must not interfere with the living. Eva shall never be sacrificed to Evelyn's manes, not if John Poindexter lives out his life to his last hour in peace; not if Felix—well; I need to play the man; Felix is a formidable antagonist to meet, alone, in a spot of such rancorous memories, at an hour when spirits—if there be spirits—haunt the precincts of the tomb.

Letter 11

Dear Felix:
Have a fresh draft made. I need cigars, clothes, and—a wedding ring. But no, let me stop short there. We will be married without one, unless you force it upon us. Eva's colour is blue.
Very truly, Thomas.

Entry 11

I should not have known Felix had I met him in the street.

How much of a stranger he appeared, then, in the faint moon-light which poured upon that shaded spot! His very voice seemed altered, and in his manner I remarked a hesitation I had not supposed him capable of showing under any circumstances. Nor were his words such as I expected. The questions I dreaded most he did not ask. The recriminations I looked for he did not utter. He only told me coldly that my courtship must be shortened; that the end for which we were both prepared must be hastened, and gave me two weeks in which to bring matters to a climax.

Then he turned to Evelyn's grave, and bending down, tried to read her name on the mossy stone. He was so long in doing this that I leaned down beside him and laid my hand on his shoulder. He was trembling, and his body was as cold as the stone he threw himself against. Was it the memory of her whom that stone covered which had aroused this emotion? If so, it was but natural. To all appearance he has never in all his life loved any one as he did this unhappy sister; and struck with a respect for the grief which has outlived many a man's lifetime, I was shrinking back when he caught my hand, and with a convulsive strain, contrasting strongly with his tone, which was strangely measured, he cried, "Do not forget the end! Do not forget John Poindexter! his sin, his indifference to my father's grief; the accumulated sufferings of years which made Amos Cadwalader a hermit amongst men.

"I have seen the girl; she has changed—women do change at her age—and some men, I do not say you, but some men might think her beautiful. But beauty, if she has it, must not blind your eyes, which are fixed upon another goal. Overlook it; overlook her—you have done so, have you not? Pale beauties cannot move one who has sat at the feet of the most dazzling of Parisian women. Keep your eyes on John Poindexter, the debt he owes us, and the suffering we have promised him. That she is sweet, gentle, different from all we thought her, only makes the chances of reaching his heart the greater. The worthier she may be of affections not indigenous to that hard soul, the surer will be our grip upon his nature and the heavier his downfall."

The old spell was upon me. I could neither answer nor assert myself. Letting go my hand, he rose, and with his back to the village—I noticed he had not turned his face to it since coming to this spot—he said: "I shall return to New York tomorrow. In two weeks you will telegraph your readiness to take up your abode with me. I have a home that will satisfy you; and it will soon be all your own."

Here he gripped his heart; and, dark as it was, I detected a strange convulsion cross his features as he turned into the moonlight. But it was gone before we could descend.

"You may hear from me again," he remarked somewhat faintly as he grasped my hand, and turned away in his own direction. I had not spoken a word during the whole interview.

LETTER 12

Dear Felix:

Congratulations: visits from my neighbours; all the *éclat* we could wish or a true lover hate. The ring you sent fits as if made for her. I am called in all directions by a thousand duties. I am on exhibition, and every one's curiosity must be satisfied.

In haste, Thomas.

ENTRY 12

I shall never understand Felix. He has not left the town, but is staying here in hiding, watching me, no doubt, to see if the signs of weakening he doubtless suspects in me have a significance deep enough to overthrow his planned revenge. I know this, because I have seen him more than once during the last week, when he thought himself completely invisible. I have caught sight of him in Mr. Poindexter's grounds when Eva and I stood talking together in the window. I even saw him once in church, in a dark corner, to be sure, but where he could keep his eye upon us, sitting together in Mr. Poindexter's pew. He seemed to me thin that day. The suspense he is under is wearing upon him. Is it my duty to cut it short by proclaiming my infidelity to my oath and my determination to marry the girl who has made me forget it?

LETTER 13

Dear Felix:

Eva is not pleased with the arrangements which have been made for our wedding. John Poindexter likes show; she does not. Which will carry the day?

Yours aff., Thomas.

ENTRY 13

She loves me. Oh, ecstasy of life! Eva Poindexter loves me. I forced it from her lips today. With my arms around her and her head on my shoulder, I urged her to confession, and it came. Now let Felix do what he will! What is old John Poindexter to me? Her father. What are Amos Cadwalader's hatred and the mortal wrong that called so loudly for revenge? Dead issues, long buried sorrows, which God may remember, but which men are bound to forget. Life, life with her! That is the future toward which I look; that is the only vengeance I will take, the only vengeance Evelyn can demand if she is the angel we believe her. I will write to Felix tomorrow.

LETTER 14

Dear Felix:

A compromise has been effected. The wedding will be a quiet one, but not celebrated here. As you cannot wish to attend it, I will not mention the place or hour of my marriage, only say that on September 27th at 4 p. m. you may expect my wife and myself at your house.

Aff., Thomas.

ENTRY 14

I have not written Felix. I had not the courage.

ENTRY 15

I have had a dream. I thought I saw the meeting of my father with the white shade of Evelyn in the unimaginable recesses of that world to which both have gone. Strange horrors, stranger glories met as their separate paths crossed, and when the two forms had greeted and parted, a line of light followed the footsteps of the one and a trail of gloom those of the other. As their ways divided, I heard my father cry:

"There is no spot on your garments, Evelyn. Can it be that the wrongs of earth are forgotten here? That mortals remember what the angels forget, and that our revenge is late for one so blessed?"

I did not hear the answer, for I woke; but the echo of those words has rung in my ears all day. "Is our revenge late for one so blessed?"

I have summoned up courage. Felix has been here again, and the truth has at last been spoken between us. I had been pressing Eva to name our wedding day, and we were all standing— that is, John Poindexter, my dear girl, and myself—in the glare of the drawing-room lights, when I heard a groan, too faint for other ears to catch, followed by a light fall from the window overlooking the garden. It was Felix. He had been watching us, had seen my love, heard me talk of marriage, and must now be in the grounds in open frenzy, or secret satisfaction, it was hard to tell which.

Determined to know, determined to speak, I excused myself on some hurried plea, and searched the paths he knew as well as I. At last I came upon him. He was standing near an old dial, where he had more than once seen Eva and me together. He was very pale, deathly pale, it seemed to me, in the faint starlight shining upon that open place; but he greeted me as usual very quietly and with no surprise, almost, in fact, as if he knew I would recognize his presence and follow him.

"You are playing your *rôle* well," said he; "too well. What was that I heard about your marrying?"

The time had come. I was determined to meet it with a man's courage. But I found it hard. Felix is no easy man to cross, even in small things, and this thing is his life, nay, more—his past, present, and future existence.

I do not know who spoke first. There was some stammering, a few broken words; then I heard myself saying distinctly, and with a certain hard emphasis born of the restraint I put upon myself:

"I love her! I want to marry her. You must allow this. Then——"

I could not proceed. I felt the shock he had received almost as if it had been communicated to me by contact. Something that was not of the earth seemed to pass between us, and I remember raising my hand as if to shield my face. And then, whether it was the blowing aside of some branches which kept the moonlight from us, or because my eyesight was made clearer by my emotion, I caught one glimpse of his face and became conscious of a great suffering, which at first seemed the wrenching of my own heart, but in another moment impressed itself upon me as that of his, Felix's.

I stood appalled.

My weakness had uprooted the one hope of his life, or so I thought; and that he expressed this by silence made my heart yearn toward him for the first time since I recognized him as my brother. I tried to stammer some excuse. I was glad when the darkness fell again, for the sight of his bowed head and set features was insupportable to me. It seemed to make it easier for me to talk; for me to dilate upon the purity, the goodness which had robbed me of my heart in spite of myself. My heart! It seemed a strange word to pass between us two in reference to a Poindexter, but it was the only one capable of expressing the feeling I had for this young girl. At last, driven to frenzy by his continued silence, which had something strangely moving in it, I cried:

"You have never loved a woman, Felix. You do not know what the passion is when it seizes upon a man jaded with the hollow pleasures of an irresponsible life. You cannot judge; therefore you cannot excuse. You are made of iron——"

"Hush!" It was the first word he had spoken since I had opened my heart to him. "You do not know what you are saying, Thomas. Like all egotists, you think yourself alone in experience and suffering. Will you think so when I tell you that there was a time in my life when I did not sleep for weeks; when the earth, the air, yes, and the heavens were full of nothing but her name, her face, her voice? When to have held her in my arms, to have breathed into her ear one word of love, to have felt her cheek fall against mine in confidence, in passion, in hope, would have been to me the heaven which would have driven the devils from my soul forever?

"Thomas, will you believe I do not know the uttermost of all you are experiencing, when I here declare to you that there has been an hour in my life when, if I had felt she could have been brought to love me, I would have sacrificed Evelyn, my own soul, our father's hope, John Poindexter's punishment, and become the weak thing you are today, and gloried in it, I, Felix Cadwalader, the man of iron, who has never been known to falter? But, Thomas, I overcame that feeling. I crushed down that love, and I call upon you to do the same. You may marry her, but——"

What stopped him? His own heart or my own impetuosity? Both, perhaps, for at that moment I fell at his feet, and seizing his hand, kissed it as I might a woman's. He seemed to grow cold and stiff under this embrace, which showed both the delirium I was laboring under and the relief I had gotten from his words. When he withdrew his hand, I feel that my doom was about to be spoken, and I was not wrong. It came in these words:

"Thomas, I have yielded to your importunity and granted you the satisfaction which under the same circumstances I would have denied myself. But it has not made me less hard toward you; indeed, the steel with which you say my heart is bound seems tightening about it, as if the momentary weakness in which I have indulged called for revenge. Thomas, go on your way; make the girl your wife—I had rather you would, since she is—what she is—but after she has taken your name, after she believes herself secure in her honourable position and your love, then you are to remember our compact and your oath—back upon John Poindexter's care she is to be thrown, shortly, curtly, without explanation or excuse; and if it costs you your life, you are to stand firm in this attitude, using but one weapon in the struggle which may open between you and her father, and that is, your name of Cadwalader. You will not need any other. Thomas, do you swear to this? Or must I direct my own power against Eva Poindexter, and, by telling her your motive in courting her, make her hate you forever?"

"I will swear," I cried, overpowered by the alternative with which he threatened me. "Give me the bliss of calling her mine, and I will follow your wishes in all that concerns us thereafter."

"You will?" There was a sinister tone in this ejaculation that gave a shock to my momentary complacency. But we are so made that an anticipated evil affects us less than an immediate one; and remembering that weeks must yet elapse, during which he or John Poindexter or even myself might die, I said nothing, and he went icily on:

"I give you two months, alone and untrammelled. Then you are to bring your bride to my house, there to hear my final decision. There is to be no departure from this course. I shall expect you, Thomas; you and her. You can say that you are going to make her acquainted with your brother."

"I will be there," I murmured, feeling a greater oppression

than when I took the oath at my father's death-bed. "I will be there."

There was no answer. While I was repeating those four words, Felix vanished.

ENTRY 17

Today I wrote again to Felix. He is at home, must be, for I have neither seen nor felt his presence since that fateful night. What did I write? I don't remember. I seem to be living in a dream. Everything is confused about me but Eva's face, Eva's smile. They are blissfully clear. Sometimes I wish they were not. Were they confused amid these shadows, I might have stronger hope of keeping my word to Felix. Now, I shall never keep it. Eva once my wife, separation between us will become impossible. John Poindexter is ill.

ENTRY 18

The wedding is postponed. John Poindexter is very ill. Pray God, Felix hears nothing of this. He would come here; he would confront his enemy on his bed of sickness. He would denounce him, and Eva would be lost to me.

ENTRY 19

Mr. Poindexter is better, but our plans will have to be altered. We now think we will be married quietly, possibly in New York.

ENTRY 20

We have decided to be married in New York. Mr. Poindexter needs the change, and Eva and I are delighted at the prospect of a private wedding. Then we will be near Felix, but not to subject ourselves to his will. Oh, no!

ENTRY 21

Married! She is mine. And now to confront Felix with my determination to hold on to my happiness. How I love her, and how I pity him! John Poindexter's wickedness is forgotten, Evelyn but a fading memory. The whole world seems to hold but three persons—Eva, Felix, and myself. How will it end? We meet at his home tomorrow.

18

Felix

Meanwhile there was another secret struggle going on in the depth of a nature from which all sympathy was excluded both by the temperament of the person concerned and the circumstances surrounding him.

I can but hint at it. Some tragedies lie beyond the ken of man, and this one we can but gather from stray scraps of torn-up letters addressed to no one and betraying their authorship only through the writer's hand. They were found long after the mystery of Felix Cadwalader's death had been fully accounted for, tucked away under the flooring of Bartow's room. Where or how procured by him, who can tell?

★★★★★★

"Madness!

"I have seen Eva Poindexter again, and heaven and hell have contended for me ever since. Eva! Eva! the girl I thought of only as our prey. The girl I have given to my brother. She is too lovely for him: she is too lovely for any man unless it be one who has never before thrilled to any woman's voice, or seen a face that could move his passions or awaken his affection. Is it love I feel? Can I, Felix, who have had but one thought, known but one enthusiasm, retain in this breast of iron a spot however secret, however small, which any woman, least of all his daughter, could reach? Never! I am the prey of frenzy or the butt of devils. Yet only the inhabitants of a more celestial sphere brighten around me when I think of those half-raised eyes, those delicately parted lips, so devoid of guile, that innocent bearing, and the divine tenderness, mingled with strength, by which she commands admiration and awakens love. I must fly. I must never see her again. Thomas's purpose is steady. He must never see that mine rocks like an idol smitten by a thunderbolt.

"If Thomas had not been reared in Paris, he too—But I am the only weak one. Curses on my——

"Did I say I would fly? I cannot, not yet. One more glimpse of her face, if only to satisfy myself that I have reason for this madness. Perhaps I was but startled yesterday to find a celestial loveliness where I expected to encounter pallid inanity. If my emotion is due to my own weakness rather than to her superiority, I had better recognize my folly before it proves my destruction.

I will stay and——

Thomas will not, shall not——

dexter's daughter——

hate, hate for Thom——

"My self-esteem is restored. I have seen her again—him—they were together—there was true love in his eye—how could I expect him not to love her—and I was able to hide my anguish and impose his duty on him. She loves him—or he thinks so—and the work goes on. But I will not stay to watch its accomplishment. No, no.

"I told him my story tonight, under the guise of a past experience. Oh, the devils must laugh at us men! They have reason to. Sometimes I wonder if my father in the clearness of his new vision does not join them in their mirth.

"Home with my unhappy secret! Home, where nothing comes to distract me from my gnawing griefs and almost intolerable thoughts. I walk the floors. I cry aloud her name. I cry it even under the portrait of Evelyn. There are moments when I am tempted to write to Thomas—to forbid him——

"Eva! Eva! Eva! Every fibre in my miserable body utters the one word. But no man shall ever know. Thomas shall never know how the thought of her fills my days and nights, making my life a torment and the future——

"I wait for his letters (scanty they are and cold) as the doomed criminal awaits his executioner. Does she really love him? Or will that exquisite, that soulful nature call for a stronger mate, a more concentrated temperament, a—a——

"I thought I saw in one of my dark hours my father rising up from his grave to curse me. Oh! he might curse on if——

"What have I said about no man knowing? Bartow knows. In his dumbness, his deafness, he has surprised my secret, and shows that he has done so by his peering looks, his dissatisfied ways, and a jealousy

134

at which I could shout aloud in mirth, if I were not more tempted to shriek aloud in torment. A dumb serving-man, picked up I have almost forgotten where, jealous of my weakness for John Poindexter's daughter! He was never jealous of my feeling for Evelyn. Yet till the day I dared fate by seeking out and looking for the second time upon the woman whose charms I had scorned, her name often resounded through these rooms, and my eyes dwelt upon but one spot, and that was where her picture hangs in the woeful beauty which has become my reproach.

"I have had a great surprise. The starling, which has been taught to murmur Evelyn's name, today shrieked out, 'Eva! Eva!' My first impulse was to wring its neck, my next to take it from its cage and hide it in my bosom. But I did neither. I am still a man.

"Bartow will wring that bird's neck if I do not. This morning I caught him with his hand on the cage and a murderous light in his eye, which I had no difficulty in understanding. Yet he cannot hear the word the wretched starling murmurs. He only knows it is a word, a name, and he is determined to suppress it. Shall I string the cage up out of this old fellow's reach? His deafness, his inability to communicate with others, the exactness with which he obeys my commands as given him by my coloured slides, his attention to my every wish, consequent upon his almost animal love for my person, are necessary to me now, while the bird—Ah! there it goes again, 'Eva! Eva!'

"Is it hate or love I feel, abhorrence or passion? Love would seek to save, but I have no thought of saving her, since she has acknowledged her love for Thomas, and since he—Oh, it is not now for Evelyn's sake I plan revenge, but for my own! These nights and days of torture—the revelation I have had of my own nature—the consent I was forced to give to a marriage which means bliss to them and anguish beyond measure to me—all this calls for vengeance, and they will not escape, these two. I have laid my plans deep. I have provided for every contingency. It has taken time, thought, money. But the result is good. If they cross the threshold of my circular study, they must consent to my will or perish here, and I with them.

"Oh, they shall never live and be happy! Thomas need not think it. John Poindexter need not think it! I might have forgotten the oath made on my father's crossed arms, but I will never forget the immeasurable griefs of these past months or the humiliation they have brought me. My own weakness is to be avenged—my unheard-of, my intolerable weakness. Remember Evelyn? Remember Felix! Ah, again! Eva! Eva! Eva!"

19

Why the Iron Slide Remained Stationary

The rest must be told in Thomas's own words, as it forms the chief part of the confession he made before the detectives:

According to my promise, I took my young wife to Felix's house on the day and at the hour proposed. We went on foot, for it was not far from the hotel where we were then staying, and were received at the door by an old servant who I had been warned could neither speak nor hear. At sight of him and the dim, old-fashioned hall stretching out in aristocratic gloom before us, Eva turned pale and cast me an inquiring look. But I reassured her with a smile that most certainly contradicted my own secret dread of the interview before us, and taking her on my arm, followed the old man down the hall, past the open drawing-room door (where I certainly thought we should pause), into a room whose plain appearance made me frown, till Bartow, as I have since heard him called, threw aside the *portière* at one end and introduced us into my brother's study, which at that moment looked like fairyland, or would have, if Felix, who was its sole occupant, had not immediately drawn our attention to himself by the remarkable force of his personality, never so impressive as at that moment.

Eva, to whom I had said little of this brother, certainly nothing which would lead her to anticipate seeing either so handsome a man or one of such mental poise and imposing character, looked frightened and a trifle awe-struck. But she advanced quite bravely toward him, and at my introduction smiled with such an inviting grace that I secretly expected to see him more or less disarmed by it.

And perhaps he was, for his already pale features turned waxy in the yellow glare cast by the odd lantern over our heads, and the hand he had raised in mechanical greeting fell heavily, and he could barely stammer out some words of welcome. These would have seemed quite inadequate to the occasion if his eyes which were fixed on her face, had not betrayed the fact that he was not without feeling, though she little realized the nature of that feeling or how her very life (for happiness is life) was trembling in the balance under that indomitable will.

I who did know—or thought I did—cast him an imploring glance, and, saying that I had some explanations to make, asked if Mrs. Adams might not rest here while we had a few words apart.

He answered me with a strange look. Did he feel the revolt in my tone and understand then as well as afterward what the nature of my compliance had been? I shall never know. I only know that he stopped fumbling with some small object on the table before him, and, bowing with a sarcastic grace that made me for the first time in my intercourse with him feel myself his inferior, even in size, led the way to a small door I had failed to notice up to this moment.

"Your wife will find it more comfortable here," he observed, with slow pauses in his speech that showed great, but repressed, excitement. And he opened the door into what had the appearance of a small but elegant sleeping-apartment. "What we have to say cannot take long. Mrs. Adams will not find the wait tedious."

"No," she smiled, with a natural laugh, born, as I dare hope, of her perfect happiness. Yet she could not but have considered the proceeding strange, and my manner, as well as his, scarcely what might be expected from a bridegroom introducing his bride to his only relative.

"I will call you—" I began, but the vision of her dimpled face above the great cluster of roses she carried made me forget to complete my sentence, and the door closed, and I found myself face to face with Felix.

He was breathing easier, and his manner seemed more natural now that we were alone, yet he did not speak, but cast a strange, if not inquiring, glance about the room (the weirdest of apartments, as you all well know), and seeming satisfied with what he saw, why I could not tell, led the way up to the large table which from the first had appeared to exert a sort of uncanny magnetism upon him, saying:

"Come further away. I need air, breathing place in this close room, and so must you. Besides, why should she hear what we have to say? She will know the worst soon enough. She seems a gentle-hearted woman."

"An angel!" I began, but he stopped me with an imperious gesture.

"We will not discuss your wi—Mrs. Adams," he protested. "Where is John Poindexter?"

"At the hotel," I rejoined. "Or possibly he has returned home. I no longer take account of his existence. Felix, I shall never leave my wife. I had rather prove recreant to the oath I took before I realized the worth of the woman whose happiness I vowed to destroy. This is what I have come to tell you. Make it easy for me, Felix. You are a man who has loved and suffered. Let us bury the past; let us——"

Had I hoped I could move him? Perhaps some such child's notion had influenced me up to this moment. But as these words left my lips, nay, before I had stumbled through them, I perceived by the set look of his features, which were as if cast in bronze, that I might falter, but that he was firm as ever, firmer, it seemed to me, and less easy to be entreated.

Yet what of that? At the worst, what had I to fear? A struggle which might involve Eva in bitter unpleasantness and me in the loss of a fortune I had come to regard almost as my own. But these were petty considerations. Eva must know sooner or later my real name and the story of her father's guilt. Why not now? And if we must start life poor, it was yet life, while a separation from her——

Meanwhile Felix had spoken, and in language I was least prepared to hear.

"I anticipated this. From the moment you pleaded with me for the privilege of marrying her, I have looked forward to this outcome and provided against it. Weakness on the part of her bridegroom was to be expected; I have, therefore, steeled myself to meet the emergency; for your oath must be kept!"

Crushed by the tone in which these words were uttered, a tone that evinced power against which any ordinary struggle would end in failure, I cast my eyes about the room in imitation of what I had seen him do a few minutes before. There was nothing within sight calculated to awaken distrust, and yet a feeling of distrust (the first I had really felt) had come with the look he had thrown above and around the mosque-like interior of the room he called his study. Was it the calm confidence he showed, or the weirdness of finding myself amid Oriental splendours and under the influence of night effects in high day and within sound of the clanging street cars and all the accompanying bustle of every-day traffic? It is hard to say; but from this moment on I found myself affected by a vague affright, not on my own account, but on hers whose voice we could plainly hear humming a gay tune in the adjoining apartment. But I was resolved to suppress all betrayal of uneasiness. I even smiled, though I felt the eyes of Evelyn's pictured countenance upon me; Evelyn's, whose portrait I had never lost sight of from the moment of entering the room, though I had not given it a direct look and now stood with my back to it. Felix, who faced it, but who did not raise his eyes to it, waited a moment for my response, and finding that my words halted, said again:

"That oath must be kept!"

This time I found words with which to answer. "Impossible!" I burst out, flinging doubt, fear, hesitancy, everything I had hitherto trembled at to the winds. "It was in my nature to take it, worked upon as I was by family affection, the awfulness of our father's approaching death, and a thousand uncanny influences all carefully measured and prepared for this end. But it is not in my nature to keep it after four months of natural living in the companionship of a man thirty years removed from his guilt, and of his guileless and wholly innocent daughter. And you cannot drive me to it, Felix. No man can force another to abandon his own wife because of a wicked oath taken long before he knew her. If you think your money——"

"Money?" he cried, with a contempt that did justice to my disinterestedness as well as his own. "I had forgotten I had it. No, Thomas, I should never weigh money against the happiness of living with such a woman as your wife appears to be. But her life I might. Carry out your threat; forget to pay John Poindexter the debt we owe him, and the matter will assume a seriousness for which you are doubtless poorly prepared. A daughter dead in her honeymoon will be almost as great a grief to him as a dishonoured one. And either dead or dishonoured he must find her, when he comes here in search of the child he cannot long forget. Which shall it be? Speak!"

Was I dreaming? Was this Felix? Was this myself? And was it in my ears these words were poured?

With a spring I reached his side where he stood close against the table, and groaned rather than shrieked the words:

"You would not kill her! You do not meditate a crime of blood—here—on her—the innocent—the good——"

"No," he said; "it will be you who will do that. You who will not wish to see her languish—suffer—go mad—Thomas, I am not the raving being you take me for. I am merely a keeper of oaths. Nay, I am more. I have talents, skill. The house in which you find yourself is proof of this. This room—see, it has no outlet save those windows, scarcely if at all perceptible to you, above our heads, and that opening shielded now by a simple curtain, but which in an instant, without my moving from this place, I can so hermetically seal that no man, save he be armed with crowbar and pickaxe, could enter here, even if man could know of our imprisonment, in a house soon to be closed from top to bottom by my departing servant."

"May God protect us!" fell from my lips, as, stiff with horror, I let my eyes travel from his determined face, first to the windows high over my head and then to the opening of the door, which, though but a few steps from where I stood, was as far as possible from the room into which my darling had been induced to enter.

Felix, watching me, uttered his explanations as calmly as if the matter were one of every-day significance. "You are looking for the windows," he remarked. "They are behind those goblin faces you see outlined on the tapestries under the ceiling. As for the door, if you had looked to the left when you entered, you would have detected the edge of a huge steel plate hanging flush with the casing. This plate can be made to slide across that opening in an instant just by the touch of my hand on this button. This done, no power save such as I have mentioned can move it back again, not even my own. I have forces at my command for sending it forward, but none for returning it to its place. Do you doubt my mechanical skill or the perfection of the electrical apparatus I have caused to be placed here? You need not, Thomas; nor need you doubt the will that has only to exert itself for an instant to— Shall I press the button, brother?"

"No, no!" I shouted in a frenzy, caused rather by my knowledge of the nature of this man than any especial threat apparent in his voice or gesture. "Let me think; let me know more fully what your requirements are—what she must suffer if I consent—and what I."

He let his hand slip back, that smooth white hand which I had more than once surveyed in admiration. Then he smiled.

"I knew you would not be foolish," he said. "Life has its charms even for hermits like me; and for a *beau garçon* such as you are———"

"Hush!" I interposed, maddened into daring his full anger. "It is not my life I am buying, but hers, possibly yours; for it seems you have planned to perish with us. Is it not so?"

"Certainly," was his cold reply. "Am I an assassin? Would you expect me to live, knowing you to be perishing?"

I stared aghast. Such resolve, such sacrifice of self to an idea was beyond my comprehension.

"Why—what?" I stammered. "Why kill us, why kill your-self——"

The answer overwhelmed me.

"Remember Evelyn!" shrilled a voice, and I paused, struck dumb with a superstitious horror I had never believed myself capable of experiencing. For it was not Felix who spoke, neither was it any ut-terance of my own aroused conscience. Muffled, strange, and startling it came from above, from the hollow spaces of that high vault lit with the golden glow that henceforth can have but one meaning for me—death.

"What is it?" I asked. "Another of your mechanical contrivances?"

He smiled; I had rather he had frowned.

"Not exactly. A favourite bird, a starling. Alas! he but repeats what he has heard echoed through the solitude of these rooms. I thought I had smothered him up sufficiently to insure his silence during this interview. But he is a self-willed bird, and seems disposed to defy the wrappings I have bound around him; which fact warns me to be speedy and hasten our explanations. Thomas, this is what I require: John Poindexter—you do not know where he is at this hour, but I do—received a telegram but now, which, if he is a man at all, will bring him to this house in a half-hour or so from the present moment.

"It was sent in your name, and in it you informed him that matters had arisen which demanded his immediate attention; that you were on your way to your brother's (giving him this address), where, if you found entrance, you would await his presence in a room called the study; but that—and here you will see how his coming will not aid us if that steel plate is once started on its course—if the possible should occur and your brother should be absent from home, then he was to await a message from you at the *Plaza*. The appearance of the house would inform him whether he would find you and Eva within; or so I telegraphed him in your name.

"Thomas, if Bartow fulfils my instructions—and I have never know him to fail me—he will pass down these stairs and out of this house in just five minutes. As he is bound on a long-promised journey, and as he expects me to leave the house immediately after him, he has drawn every shade and fastened every lock. Consequently, on his exit, the house will become a tomb, to which, just two weeks from today, John Poindexter will be called again, and in words which will lead to a demolition which will disclose—what? Let us not forestall the future, our horrible future, by inquiring.

"But Thomas, shall Bartow go? Shall I not by signs he comprehends more readily than other men comprehend speech indicate to him on his downward passage to the street that I wish him to wait and open the door to the man whom we have promised to overwhelm in his hour of satisfaction and pride? You have only to write a line—see! I have made a copy of the words you must use, lest your self-command should be too severely taxed. These words left on this table for his inspection—for you must go and Eva remain—will tell him all he needs to know from you. The rest can come from my lips after he has read the signature, which in itself will confound him and prepare the way for what I have to add. Have you anything to say against this plan? Anything, I mean, beyond what you have hitherto urged? Anything that I will consider or which will prevent my finger from pressing the button on which it rests?"

I took up the paper. It was lying on the table, where it had evidently been inscribed simultaneously with or just before our entrance into the house, and slowly read the few lines I saw written upon it. You know them, but they will acquire a new significance from your present understanding of their purpose and intent:

I return you back your daughter. Neither she nor you will ever see me again. Remember Evelyn!

Amos's Son.

"You wish me to sign these words, to put them into my own handwriting, and so to make them mine? Mine!" I repeated.

"Yes, and to leave them here on this table for him to see when he enters. He might not believe any mere statement from me in regard to your intentions."

I was filled with horror. Love, life, human hopes, the world's friendships—all the possibilities of existence, swept in one concentrated flood of thought and feeling through my outraged consciousness, and I knew I could never put my name to such a blasphemy of all that was sacred to man's soul. Tossing the paper in his face, I cried:

"You have gone too far! Better her death, better mine, better the destruction of us all, than such dishonour to the purest thing heaven ever made. I refuse, Felix—I refuse. And may God have mercy on us all!"

The moment was ghastly. I saw his face change, his finger tremble where it hovered above the fatal button; saw—though only in imagination as yet—the steely edge of that deadly plate of steel advancing beyond the lintel, and was about to dare all in a sudden grapple with this man, when a sound from another direction caught my ear, and looking around in terror of the only intrusion we could fear, beheld Eva advancing from the room in which we had placed her.

That moment a blood-red glow took the place of the sickly yellow which had hitherto filled every recess of this weird apartment. But I scarcely noticed the change, save as it affected her pallor and gave to her cheeks the colour that was lacking in the roses at her belt.

Fearless and sweet as in the hour when she first told me that she loved me, she approached and stood before us.

"What is this?" she cried. "I have heard words that sound more like the utterances of some horrid dream than the talk of men and broth-ers. What does it mean, Thomas? What does it mean, Mr. ——"

"Cadwalader," announced Felix, dropping his eyes from her face, but changing not a whit his features or posture.

"Cadwalader?" The name was not to her what it was to her father. "Cadwalader? I have heard that name in my father's house; it was Eve-lyn's name, the Evelyn who——"

"Whom you see painted there over your head," finished Felix, "my sister, Thomas's sister—the girl whom your father—but I spare you, child though you be of a man who spared nothing. From your hus-band you may learn why a Cadwalader can never find his happiness with a Poindexter. Why thirty or more years after that young girl's death, you who were not then born are given at this hour the choice between death and dishonour. I allow you just five minutes in which to listen. After that you will let me know your joint decision. Only you must make your talk where you stand. A step taken by either of you to right or left, and Thomas knows what will follow."

Five minutes, with such a justification to make, and such a deci-sion to arrive at! I felt my head swim, my tongue refuse its office, and stood dumb and helpless before her till the sight of her dear eyes raised in speechless trust to mine flooded me with a sense of triumph amid all the ghastly terrors of the moment, and I broke out in a tumult of speech, in excuses, explanations, all that comes to one in a more than mortal crisis.

She listened, catching my meaning rather from my looks than my words. Then as the minutes fled and my brother raised a warning hand, she turned toward him, and said:

"You are in earnest? We must separate in shame or perish in this prison-house with you?"

His answer was mere repetition, mechanical, but firm:

"You have said it. You have but one minute more, madam."

She shrank, and all her powers seemed leaving her, then a reaction came, and a flaming angel stood where but a moment before the most delicate of women weakly faltered; and giving me a look to see if I had the courage or the will to lift my hand against my own flesh and blood (alas for us both! I did not understand her) caught up an old Turkish dagger lying only too ready to her hand, and plunged it with one sideways thrust into his side, crying:

"We cannot part, we cannot die, we are too young, too happy!"

It was sudden; the birth of purpose in her so unexpected and so rapid that Felix, the ready, who was prepared for all contingencies, for the least movement or suggestion of escape, faltered and pressed, not the fatal button, but his heart.

One impulsive act on the part of a woman had overthrown all the fine-spun plans of the subtlest spirit that ever attempted to work its will in the face of God and man.

But I did not think of this then; I did not even bestow a thought upon the narrowness of our escape, or the price which the darling of my heart might be called upon to pay for this supreme act of self-defence. My mind, my heart, my interest were with Felix, in whom the nearness of death had called up all that was strongest and most commanding in his strong and commanding spirit.

Though struck to the heart, he had not fallen. It was as if the will which had sustained him through thirty years of mental torture held him erect still, that he might give her, Eva, one look, the like of which I had never seen on mortal face, and which will never leave my heart or hers until we die. Then as he saw her sink shudderingly down and the delicate woman reappear in her pallid and shrunken figure, he turned his eyes on me and I saw,—good God!—a tear well up from those orbs of stone and fall slowly down his cheek, fast growing hollow under the stroke of death.

"Eva! Eva! I love Eva!" shrilled the voice which once before had startled me from the hollow vault above.

Felix heard, and a smile faint as the failing rush of blood through his veins moved his lips and brought a revelation to my soul. He, too, loved Eva!

When he saw I knew, the will which had kept him on his feet gave way, and he sank to the floor murmuring:

"Take her away! I forgive. Save! Save! She did not know I loved

144

her."

Eva, aghast, staring with set eyes at her work, had not moved from her crouching posture. But when she saw that speaking head fall back, the fine limbs settle into the repose of death, a shock went through her which I thought would never leave her reason unimpaired.

"I've killed him!" she murmured. "I've killed him!" and looking wildly about, her eyes fell on the cross that hung behind us on the wall. It seemed to remind her that Felix was a Catholic. "Bring it!" she gasped. "Let him feel it on his breast. It may bring him peace— hope."

As I rushed to do her bidding, she fell in a heap on the floor.

"Save!" came again from the lips we thought closed forever in death. And realizing at the words both her danger and the necessity of her not opening her eyes again upon this scene, I laid the cross in his arms, and catching her up from the floor, ran with her out of the house. But no sooner had I caught sight of the busy street and the stream of humanity passing before us, than I awoke to an instant recognition of our peril. Setting my wife down, I commanded life back into her limbs by the force of my own energy, and then dragging her down the steps, mingled with the crowd, encouraging her, breathing for her, living in her till I got her into a carriage and we drove away.

For the silence we have maintained from that time to this you must not blame Mrs. Adams. When she came to herself—which was not for days—she manifested the greatest desire to proclaim her act and assume its responsibility. But I would not have it. I loved her too dearly to see her name bandied about in the papers; and when her father was taken into our confidence, he was equally peremptory in enjoining silence, and shared with me the watch I now felt bound to keep over her movements.

But alas! His was the peremptoriness of pride rather than love. John Poindexter has no more heart for his daughter than he had for his wife or that long-forgotten child from whose grave this tragedy has sprung. Had Felix triumphed he would never have wrung the heart of this man. As he once said, when a man cares for nothing and nobody, not even for himself, it is useless to curse him.

As for Felix himself, judge him not, when you realize, as you now must, that his last conscious act was to reach for and put in his mouth the paper which connected Eva with his death. At the moment of death his thought was to save, not to avenge. And this after her hand had struck him.

145

20

Answered

A silence more or less surcharged with emotion followed this final appeal. Then, while the various auditors of this remarkable history whispered together and Thomas Adams turned in love and anxiety toward his wife, the inspector handed back to Mr. Gryce the memorandum he had received from him.

It presented the following appearance:

Answered
*1.*Why a woman who was calm enough to stop and arrange her hair during the beginning of an interview should be wrought up to such a pitch of frenzy and exasperation before it was over as to kill with her own hand a man she had evidently had no previous grudge against. (Remember the comb found on the floor of Mr. Adams's bedroom.)

Answered
2. What was the meaning of the following words, written just previous to this interview by the man thus killed: "I return you your daughter. Neither you nor she will ever see me again. Remember Evelyn!"

Answered
3. Why was the pronoun "I" used in this communication? What position did Mr. Felix Adams hold toward this young girl qualifying him to make use of such language after her marriage to his brother?

Answered
4. And having used it, why did he, upon being attacked by her, attempt to swallow the paper upon which he had written these words, actually dying with it clinched between his teeth?

Answered

5. If he was killed in anger and died as monsters do (her own word), why did his face show sorrow rather than hate, and a determination as far as possible removed from the rush of overwhelming emotions likely to follow the reception of a mortal blow from the hand of an unexpected antagonist?

Answered

6. Why, if he had strength to seize the above-mentioned paper and convey it to his lips, did he not use that strength in turning on a light calculated to bring him assistance, instead of leaving blazing the crimson glow which, according to the code of signals as now understood by us, means: "Nothing more required just now. Keep away?"

Answered

7. What was the meaning of the huge steel plate found between the casings of the doorway, and why did it remain at rest within its socket at this, the culminating, moment of his life?

Answered

8. An explanation of how old Poindexter came to appear on the scene so soon after the event. His words as overheard were: "It is Amos' son, not Amos!" Did he not know whom he was to meet in this house? Was the condition of the man lying before him with a cross on his bosom and a dagger in his heart less of a surprise to him than the personality of the victim?

Not Answered

9. Remember the conclusions we have drawn from Bartow's pantomime. Mr. Adams was killed by a left-handed thrust. Watch for an acknowledgment that the young woman is left-handed, and do not forget that an explanation is due why for so long a time she held her other arm stretched out behind her.

Answered

10. Why did the bird whose chief cry is "Remember Evelyn!" sometimes vary it with "Poor Eva! Lovely Eva! Who would strike Eva?" The story of this tragedy, to be true, must show that Mr. Adams knew his brother's bride both long and well.

Answered

11. If Bartow is, as we think, innocent of all connection with this crime save as witness, why does he show such joy at its result? This may not reasonably be expected to fall within the scope of Thomas Adams's confession, but it should not be ig-

nored by us. This deaf-and-dumb servitor was driven mad by the fact which caused him joy. Why?[1]

Answered

12. Notice the following schedule. It has been drawn up after repeated experiments with Bartow and the various slides of the strange lamp which cause so many different lights to shine out in Mr. Adams's study:

White light—Water wanted.

Green light—Overcoat and hat to be brought.

Blue light—Put back books on shelves.

Violet light—Arrange study for the night.

Yellow light—Watch for next light.

Red light—Nothing wanted; stay away.

The last was on at the final scene. Note if this fact can be explained by Mr. Adams's account of the same.

★★★★★★

Two paragraphs alone lacked complete explanation. The first, No. 9, was important. The description of the stroke dealt by Mr. Adams's wife did not account for this peculiar feature in Bartow's pantomime. Consulting with the inspector, Mr. Gryce finally approached Mr. Adams and inquired if he had strength to enact before them the blow as he had seen it dealt by his wife.

The startled young man looked the question he dared not ask. In common with others, he knew that Bartow had made some characteristic gestures in endeavouring to describe this crime, but he did not know what they were, as this especial bit of information had been carefully held back by the police. He, therefore, did not respond hastily to the suggestion made him, but thought intently for a moment before he thrust out his left hand and caught up some article or other from the inspector's table and made a lunge with it across his body into an imaginary victim at his right. Then he consulted the faces about him with inexpressible anxiety. He found little encouragement

---

1. It must be remembered that the scraps of writing in Felix's hand had not yet been found by the police. The allusions in them to Bartow show him to have been possessed by a jealousy which probably turned to delight when he saw his master smitten down by the object of that master's love and his own hatred. How he came to recognize in the bride of another man the owner of the name he so often saw hovering on the lips of his master, is a question to be answered by more astute students of the laws of perception than myself. Probably he spent much of his time at the loophole on the stairway, studying his master till he understood his every gesture and expression.

in their aspect.

"You would make your wife out left-handed," suggested Mr. Gryce. "Now I have been watching her ever since she came into this place, and I have seen no evidence of this."

"She is not left-handed, but she thrust with her left hand, because her right was fast held in mine. I had seized her instinctively as she bounded forward for the weapon, and the convulsive clutch of our two hands was not loosed till the horror of her act made her faint, and she fell away from me to the floor crying: 'Tear down the cross and lay it on your brother's breast. I would at least see him die the death of a Christian.'"

Mr. Gryce glanced at the inspector with an air of great relief. The mystery of the constrained attitude of the right hand which made Bartow's pantomime so remarkable was now naturally explained, and taking up the blue pencil which the inspector had laid down, he wrote, with a smile, a very decided "answered" across paragraph No. 9.

21

Last Words

A few minutes later Mr. Gryce was to be seen in the outer room, gazing curiously at the various persons there collected. He was seeking an answer to a question that was still disturbing his mind, and hoped to find it there. He was not disappointed. For in a quiet corner he encountered the amiable form of Miss Butterworth, calmly awaiting the result of an interference which she in all probability had been an active agent in bringing about.

He approached and smilingly accused her of this. But she disclaimed the fact with some heat.

"I was simply there," she explained. "When the crisis came, when this young creature learned that her husband had left suddenly for New York in the company of two men, then—why then, it became apparent to everyone that a woman should be at her side who understood her case and the extremity in which she found herself. And I was that woman."

"You are always that woman," he gallantly replied, "if by the phrase you mean being in the right place at the right time. So you are already acquainted with Mrs. Adams's story?"

"Yes; the ravings of a moment told me she was the one who had handled the dagger that slew Mr. Adams. Afterward, she was able to explain the cause of what has seemed to us such a horrible crime. When I heard her story, Mr. Gryce, I no longer hesitated either as to her duty or mine. Do you think she will be called upon to answer for this blow? Will she be tried, convicted?"

"Madam, there are not twelve men in the city so devoid of intelligence as to apply the name of crime to an act which was so evidently one of self-defence. No true bill will be found against young Mrs. Adams. Rest easy."

The look of gloom disappeared from Miss Butterworth's eyes.

"Then I may return home in peace," she cried. "It has been a desperate five hours for me, and I feel well shaken up. Will you escort me to my carriage?"

Miss Butterworth did not look shaken up. Indeed, in Mr. Gryce's judgment, she had never appeared more serene or more comfortable. But she was certainly the best judge of her own condition; and after satisfying herself that the object of her care was reviving under the solicitous ministrations of her husband, she took the arm which Mr. Gryce held out to her and proceeded to her carriage.

As he assisted her in, he asked a few questions about Mr. Poindexter.

"Why is not Mrs. Adams's father here? Did he allow his daughter to leave him on such an errand as this without offering to accompany her?"

The answer was curtness itself:

"Mr. Poindexter is a man without heart. He came with us to New York, but refused to follow us to Police Headquarters. Sir, you will find that the united passions of three burning souls, and a revenge the most deeply cherished of any I ever knew or heard of, have been thrown away on a man who is positively unable to suffer. Do not mention old John Poindexter to me. And now, if you will be so good, tell the coachman to drive me to my home in Gramercy Park. I have put my finger in the police pie for the last time, Mr. Gryce—positively for the last time." And she sank back on the carriage cushions with an inexorable look, which, nevertheless, did not quite conceal a quiet complacency which argued that she was not altogether dissatisfied with herself or the result of her interference in matters usually considered at variance with a refined woman's natural instincts.

Mr. Gryce, in repressing a smile, bowed lower even than his wont, and, under the shadow of this bow, the carriage drove off. As he walked slowly back, he sighed. Was he wondering if a case of similar interest would ever bring them together again in consultation?

Hand and Ring

Contents

BOOK 1. THE GENTLEMAN FROM TOLEDO

A Startling Coincidence	157
An Appeal to Heaven	166
The Unfinished Letter	174
Imogene	185
Horace Byrd	197
The Skill of an Artist	208
Miss Firman	215
The Thick-Set Man	227
Close Calculations	235
The Final Test	246
Decision	256

BOOK 2. THE WEAVING OF A WEB

The Spider	260
The Fly	265
A Last Attempt	273
The End of a Tortuous Path	279
Storm	283
A Surprise	288
A Brace of Detectives	289
Mr. Ferris	300
A Crisis	307

Heart's Martyrdom   316

Craik Mansell   320

Mr. Orcutt   328

A True Bill   341

Among Telescopes and Charts   345

"He Shall Hear Me!"   350

BOOK 3. THE SCALES OF JUSTICE

The Great Trial   351

The Chief Witness For the Prosecution   355

The Opening of the Defence   372

Byrd Uses His Pencil Again   376

The Chief Witness For the Defence   385

Hickory   394

A Late Discovery   400

What Was Hid Behind Imogene's Veil   413

Pro and Con   428

A Mistake Rectified   445

Under the Great Tree   451

Unexpected Words   467

Mr. Gryce   475

In the Prison   483

A Link Supplied   498

Consultations   506

Mrs. Firman   509

The Widow Clemmens   518

Mr. Gryce Says Goodbye   528

1

A Startling Coincidence

The town clock of Sibley had just struck twelve. Court had adjourned, and Judge Evans, with one or two of the leading lawyers of the county, stood in the doorway of the court-house discussing in a friendly way the eccentricities of criminals as developed in the case then before the court. Mr. Lord had just ventured the assertion that crime as a fine art was happily confined to France; to which district attorney Ferris had replied:

"And why? Because atheism has not yet acquired such a hold upon our upper classes that gentlemen think it possible to meddle with such matters. It is only when a student, a doctor, a lawyer, determines to put aside from his path the secret stumbling-block to his desires or his ambition that the true intellectual crime is developed. That brute whom you see slouching along over the way is the type of the average criminal of the day."

And he indicated with a nod a sturdy, ill-favoured man, who, with pack on his back, was just emerging from a grassy lane that opened out from the street directly opposite the court-house.

"Such men are often seen in the dock," remarked Mr. Orcutt, of more than local reputation as a criminal lawyer. "And often escape the penalty of their crimes," he added, watching, with a curious glance, the lowering brow and furtive look of the man who, upon perceiving the attention he had attracted, increased his pace till he almost broke into a run.

"Looks as if he had been up to mischief," observed Judge Evans.

"Rather as if he had heard the sentence which was passed upon the last tramp who paid his respects to this town," corrected Mr. Lord.

"*Revenons à nos moutons*," resumed the district attorney. "Crime, as an investment, does not pay in this country. The regular burglar leads a

157

dog's life of it; and when you come to the murderer, how few escape suspicion if they do the gallows. I do not know of a case where a murder for money has been really successful in this region."

"Then you must have some pretty cute detective work going on here," remarked a young man who had not before spoken.

"No, no—nothing to brag of. But the brutes are so clumsy—that is the word, clumsy. They don't know how to cover up their tracks."

"The smart ones don't make tracks," interposed a rough voice near them, and a large, red-haired, slightly hump-backed man, who, from the looks of those about, was evidently a stranger in the place, shuffled forward from the pillar against which he had been leaning, and took up the thread of conversation.

"I tell you," he continued, in a gruff tone somewhat out of keeping with the studied abstraction of his keen, gray eye, "that half the criminals are caught because they do make tracks and then resort to such extraordinary means to cover them up. The true secret of success in this line lies in striking your blow with a weapon picked up on the spot, and in choosing for the scene of your tragedy a thoroughfare where, in the natural course of events, other men will come and go and unconsciously tread out your traces, provided you have made any. This dissipates suspicion, or starts it in so many directions that justice is at once confused, if not ultimately baffled. Look at that house yonder," the stranger pursued, pointing to a plain dwelling on the opposite corner. "While we have been standing here, several persons of one kind or another, and among them a pretty rough-looking tramp, have gone into the side gate and so around to the kitchen door and back.

"I don't know who lives there, but say it is a solitary old woman above keeping help, and that an hour from now someone, not finding her in the house, searches through the garden and comes upon her lying dead behind the wood-pile, struck down by her own axe. On whom are you going to lay your hand in suspicion? On the stranger, of course—the rough-looking tramp that everybody thinks is ready for bloodshed at the least provocation. But suspicion is not conviction, and I would dare wager that no court, in face of a persistent denial on his part that he even saw the old woman when he went to her door, would bring in a verdict of murder against him, even though silver from her private drawer were found concealed upon his person. The chance that he spoke the truth, and that she was not in the house when he entered, and that his crime had been merely one of burglary or theft, would be enough to save him from the hangman."

"That is true," assented Mr. Lord, "unless all the other persons who had been seen to go into the yard were not only reputable men, but were willing to testify to having seen the woman alive up to the time he invaded her premises."

But the hump-backed stranger had already lounged away.

"What do you think about this, Mr. Byrd?" inquired the district attorney, turning to the young man before alluded to. "You are an expert in these matters, or ought to be. What would you give for the tramp's chances if the detectives took him in hand?"

"I, sir?" was the response. "I am so comparatively young and inexperienced in such affairs, that I scarcely dare presume to express an opinion. But I have heard it said by Mr. Gryce, who you know stands foremost among the detectives of New York, that the only case of murder in which he utterly failed to get any clue to work upon, was that of a Jew who was knocked down in his own shop in broad daylight. But this will not appear so strange when you learn the full particulars. The store was situated between two alley-ways in Harlem. It had an entrance back and an entrance front. Both were in constant use.

"The man was found behind his counter, having evidently been hit on the head by a slung-shot while reaching for a box of hosiery. But though a succession of people were constantly passing by both doors, there was for that very reason no one to tell which of all the men who were observed to enter the shop, came out again with blood upon his conscience. Nor were the circumstances of the Jew's life such as to assist justice. The most careful investigation failed to disclose the existence of any enemy, nor was he found to possess in this country, at least, any relative who could have hoped to be benefited by the few dollars he had saved from a late bankruptcy. The only conclusion to be drawn is that the man was secretly in the way of someone and was as secretly put out of it, but for what purpose or by whose hand, time has never disclosed."

"There is one, however, who knows both," affirmed Judge Evans, impressively.

"The man himself?"

"God!"

The solemnity with which this was uttered caused a silence, during which Mr. Orcutt looked at his watch.

"I must go to dinner," he announced, withdrawing, with a slight nod, across the street.

159

The rest stood for a few minutes abstractedly contemplating his retreating figure, as with an energetic pace all his own he passed down the little street that opened opposite to where they stood, and entered the unpretending cottage of a widow lady, with whom he was in the habit of taking his mid-day meal whenever he had a case before the court.

A lull was over the whole village, and the few remaining persons on the court-house steps were about to separate, when Mr. Lord uttered an exclamation and pointed to the cottage into which they had just seen Mr. Orcutt disappear. Immediately all eyes looked that way and saw the lawyer standing on the stoop, having evidently issued with the utmost precipitation from the house.

"He is making signs," cried Mr. Lord to Mr. Ferris; and scarcely knowing what they feared, both gentlemen crossed the way and hurried down the street toward their friend, who, with unusual tokens of disturbance in his manner, ran forward to meet them.

"A murder!" he excitedly exclaimed, as soon as he came within speaking distance. "A strange and startling coincidence. Mrs. Clemmens has been struck on the head, and is lying covered with blood at the foot of her dining-room table."

Mr. Lord and the district attorney stared at each other in a maze of surprise and horror easily to be comprehended, and then they rushed forward.

"Wait a moment," the latter suddenly cried, stopping short and looking back. "Where is the fellow who talked so learnedly about murder and the best way of making a success of it. He must be found at once. I don't believe in coincidences." And he beckoned to the person they had called Byrd, who with very pardonable curiosity was hurrying their way. "Go find Hunt, the constable," he cried; "tell him to stop and retain the humpback. A woman here has been found murdered, and that fellow must have known something about it."

The young man stared, flushed with sudden intelligence, and darted off. Mr. Ferris turned, found Mr. Orcutt still at his side, and drew him forward to rejoin Mr. Lord, who by this time was at the door of the cottage.

They all went in together, Mr. Ferris, who was of an adventurous disposition, leading the way. The room into which they first stepped was empty. It was evidently the widow's sitting-room, and was in perfect order, with the exception of Mr. Orcutt's hat, which lay on the centre-table where he had laid it on entering. Neat, without being prim, the entire aspect of the place was one of comfort, ease, and modest luxury. For, though the Widow Clemmens lived alone and without help, she was by no means an indigent person, as a single glance at her house would show. The door leading into the farther room was open, and toward this they hastened, led by the glitter of the fine old china service which loaded the dining-table.

"She is there," said Mr. Orcutt, pointing to the other side of the room.

They immediately passed behind the table, and there, sure enough, lay the prostrate figure of the widow, her head bleeding, her arms extended, one hand grasping her watch, which she had loosened from her belt, the other stretched toward a stick of firewood, that, from the mark of blood upon its side, had evidently been used to fell her to the floor. She was motionless as stone, and was, to all appearance, dead.

"Sickening, sickening!—horrible!" exclaimed Mr. Lord, recoiling upon the district attorney with a gesture, as if he would put the frightful object out of his sight. "What motive could anyone have for killing such an inoffensive woman? The deviltry of man is beyond belief!"

"And after what we have heard, inexplicable," asserted Mr. Ferris. "To be told of a supposable case of murder one minute, and then to see it exemplified in this dreadful way the next, is an experience of no common order. I own I am overcome by it." And he flung open a door that communicated with the lane and let the outside air sweep in.

"That door was unlocked," remarked Mr. Lord, glancing at Mr. Orcutt, who stood with severe, set face, looking down at the outstretched form which, for several years now, had so often sat opposite to him at his noonday meal.

With a start the latter looked up. "What did you say? The door unlocked? There is nothing strange in that. She never locked her doors, though she was so very deaf I often advised her to." And he allowed his eyes to run over the wide stretch of low, uncultivated ground before him, that, in the opinion of many persons, was such a decided blot upon the town. "There is no one in sight," he reluctantly admitted.

"No," responded the other. "The ground is unfavourable for escape. It is marshy and covered with snake grass. A man could make his way, however, between the hillocks into those woods yonder, if he were driven by fear or understood the path well. What is the matter, Orcutt?"

"Nothing," affirmed the latter,—"nothing, I thought I heard a groan."

"You heard me make an exclamation," spoke up Mr. Ferris, who by this time had sufficiently overcome his emotion to lift the head of the prostrate woman and look in her face. "This woman is not dead."

"What!" they both cried, bounding forward.

"See, she breathes," continued the former, pointing to her slowly labouring chest. "The villain, whoever he was, did not do his work well; she may be able to tell us something yet."

"I do not think so," murmured Mr. Orcutt. "Such a blow as that must have destroyed her faculties, if not her life. It was of cruel force."

"However that may be, she ought to be taken care of now," cried Mr. Ferris. "I wish Dr. Tredwell was here."

"I will go for him," signified the other.

But it was not necessary. Scarcely had the lawyer turned to execute this mission, when a sudden murmur was heard at the door, and a dozen or so citizens burst into the house, among them the very person named. Being coroner as well as physician, he at once assumed authority. The widow was carried into her room, which was on the same floor, and a brother practitioner sent for, who took his place at her head and waited for any sign of returning consciousness. The crowd, remanded to the yard, spent their time alternately in furtive questionings of each other's countenances, and in eager look-out for the expected return of the strange young man who had been sent after the incomprehensible humpback of whom all had heard. The coroner, closeted with the district attorney in the dining-room, busied himself in noting certain evident facts.

"I am, perhaps, forestalling my duties in interfering before the woman is dead," intimated the former. "But it is only a matter of a few hours, and any facts we can glean in the interim must be of value to a proper conduct of the inquiry I shall be called upon to hold. I shall therefore make the same note of the position of affairs as I would do if she were dead; and to begin with, I wish you to observe that she was hit while setting the clock." And he pointed to the open door of the huge old-fashioned timepiece which occupied that corner of the room in which she had been found. "She had not even finished her task," he next remarked, "for the clock is still ten minutes slow, while her watch is just right, as you will see by comparing it with your own.

"She was attacked from behind, and to all appearances unexpectedly. Had she turned, her forehead would have been struck, while, as all can see, it is the back of her head that has suffered, and that from a right-hand blow. Her deafness was undoubtedly the cause of her immobility under the approach of such an assailant. She did not hear his step, and, being so busily engaged, saw nothing of the cruel hand uplifted to destroy her. I doubt if she even knew what happened. The mystery is that anyone could have sufficiently desired her death to engage in such a cold-blooded butchery. If plunder were wanted, why was not her watch taken from her? And see, here is a pile of small change lying beside her plate on the table,—a thing a tramp would make for at once."

"It was not a thief that struck her."

"Well, well, we don't know. I have my own theory," admitted the coroner; "but, of course, it will not do for me to mention it here. The stick was taken from that pile laid ready on the hearth," he went on. "Odd, significantly odd, that in all its essential details this affair should tally so completely with the supposable case of crime given a moment before by the deformed wretch you tell me about."

"Not if that man was a madman and the assailant," suggested the district attorney.

"True, but I do not think he was mad—not from what you have told me. But let us see what the commotion is. Someone has evidently arrived."

It was Mr. Byrd, who had entered by the front door, and deaf to the low murmur of the impatient crowd without, stood waiting in silent patience for an opportunity to report to the district attorney the results of his efforts.

Mr. Ferris at once welcomed him.

"What have you done? Did you find the constable or succeed in laying hands on that scamp of a humpback?"

Mr. Byrd, who, to explain at once, was a young and intelligent detective, who had been brought from New York for purposes connected with the case then before the court, glanced carefully in the direction of the coroner and quietly replied:

"The hump-backed scamp, as you call him, has disappeared. Whether he will be found or not I cannot say. Hunt is on his track, and will report to you in an hour. The tramp whom you saw slinking out of this street while we stood on the court-house steps is doubtless the man whom you most want, and him we have captured."

"You have?" repeated Mr. Ferris, eying, with good-natured irony, the young man's gentlemanly but rather indifferent face. "And what makes you think it is the tramp who is the guilty one in this case? Because that ingenious stranger saw fit to make him such a prominent figure in his suppositions?"

"No, sir," replied the detective, flushing with a momentary embarrassment he however speedily overcame; "I do not found my opinions upon any man's remarks. I only——Excuse me," said he, with a quiet air of self-control that was not without its effect upon the sensible man he was addressing. "If you will tell me how, where, and under what circumstances this poor murdered woman was found, perhaps I shall be better able to explain my reasons for believing in the tramp as the guilty party; though the belief, even of a detective, goes for but little in matters of this kind, as you and these other gentlemen very well know."

"Step here, then," signified Mr. Ferris, who, accompanied by the coroner, had already passed around the table. "Do you see that clock? She was winding it when she was struck, and fell almost at its foot. The weapon which did the execution lies over there; it is a stick of firewood, as you see, and was caught up from that pile on the hearth. Now recall what that humpback said about choosing a thoroughfare for a murder (and this house is a thoroughfare), and the peculiar stress which he laid upon the choice of a weapon, and tell me why you think he is innocent of this immediate and most remarkable exemplification of his revolting theory?"

"Let me first ask," ventured the other, with a remaining tinge of embarrassment colouring his cheek, "if you have reason to think this woman had been lying long where she was found, or was she struck soon before the discovery?"

"Soon. The dinner was still smoking in the kitchen, where it had been dished up ready for serving."

"Then," declared the detective with sudden confidence, "a single word will satisfy you that the humpback was not the man who delivered this stroke. To lay that woman low at the foot of this clock would require the presence of the assailant in the room. Now, the humpback was not here this morning, but in the court-room. I know this, for I saw him there."

"You did? You are sure of that?" cried, in a breath, both his hearers, somewhat taken aback by this revelation.

"Yes. He sat down by the door. I noticed him particularly."

"Humph! that is odd," quoth Mr. Ferris, with the testiness of an irritable man who sees himself contradicted in a publicly expressed theory.

"Very odd," repeated the coroner; "so odd, I am inclined to think he did not sit there every moment of the time. It is but a step from the court-house here; he might well have taken the trip and returned while you wiped your eye-glasses or was otherwise engaged."

Mr. Byrd did not see fit to answer this.

"The tramp is an ugly-looking customer," he remarked, in what was almost a careless tone of voice.

Mr. Ferris covered with his hand the pile of loose change that was yet lying on the table, and shortly observed:

"A tramp to commit such a crime must be actuated either by rage or cupidity; that you will acknowledge. Now the fellow who struck this woman could not have been excited by any sudden anger, for the whole position of her body when found proves that she had not even turned to face the intruder, much less engaged in an altercation with him. Yet how could it have been money he was after, when a tempting bit like this remained undisturbed upon the table?"

And Mr. Ferris, with a sudden gesture, disclosed to view the pile of silver coin he had been concealing.

The young detective shook his head but lost none of his seeming indifference. "That is one of the little anomalies of criminal experience that we were talking about this morning," he remarked. "Perhaps the fellow was frightened and lost his head, or perhaps he really heard someone at the door, and was obliged to escape without reaping any of the fruits of his crime."

"Perhaps and perhaps," retorted Mr. Ferris, who was a quick man, and who, once settled in a belief, was not to be easily shaken out of it.

"However that may be," continued Mr. Byrd, without seeming to notice the irritating interruption, "I still think that the tramp, rather than the humpback, will be the man to occupy your future attention."

And with a deprecatory bow to both gentlemen, he drew back and quietly left the room.

Mr. Ferris at once recovered from his momentary loss of temper.

"I suppose the young man is right," he acknowledged; "but, if so, what an encouragement we have received this morning to a belief in clairvoyance." And with less irony and more conviction, he added: "The humpback *must* have known something about the murder."

And the coroner bowed; common-sense undoubtedly agreeing with this assumption.

2

An Appeal to Heaven

It was now half-past one. An hour and a half had elapsed since the widow had been laid upon her bed, and to all appearance no change had taken place in her condition. Within the room where she lay were collected the doctor and one or two neighbours of the female sex, who watched every breath she drew, and stood ready to notice the slightest change in the stony face that, dim with the shadow of death, stared upon them from the unruffled pillows. In the sitting-room Lawyer Orcutt conversed in a subdued voice with Mr. Ferris, in regard to such incidents of the widow's life as had come under his notice in the years of their daily companionship, while the crowd about the gate vented their interest in loud exclamations of wrath against the tramp who had been found, and the unknown humpback who had not. Our story leads us into the crowd in front.

"I don't think she'll ever come to," said one, who from his dusty coat might have been a miller. "Blows like that haven't much let-up about them."

"Doctor says she will die before morning," put in a pert young miss, anxious to have her voice heard.

"Then it will be murder and no mistake, and that brute of a tramp will hang as high as Haman."

"Don't condemn a man before you've had a chance to hear what he has to say for himself," cried another in a strictly judicial tone. "How do you know as he came to this house at all?"

"Miss Perkins says he did, and Mrs. Phillips too; they saw him go into the gate."

"And what else did they see? I warrant he wasn't the only beggar that was roaming round this morning."

"No; there was a tin peddler in the street, for I saw him my own self, and Mrs. Clemmens standing in the door flourishing her broom at him. She was mighty short with such folks. Wouldn't wonder if some of the unholy wretches killed her out of spite. They're a wicked lot, the whole of them."

"Widow Clemmens had a quick temper, but she had a mighty good heart notwithstanding. See how kind she was to them Hubbells."

"And how hard she was to that Pratt girl."

"Well, I know, but———" And so on and so on, in a hum and a buzz about the head of Mr. Byrd, who, engaged in thought seemingly far removed from the subject in hand, stood leaning against the fence, careless and *insouciant*. Suddenly there was a lull, then a short cry, then a woman's voice rose clear, ringing, and commanding, and Mr. Byrd caught the following words:

"What is this I hear? Mrs. Clemmens dead? Struck down by some wandering tramp? Murdered and in her own house?"

In an instant, every eye, including Mr. Byrd's, was fixed upon the speaker. The crowd parted, and the young girl, who had spoken from the street, came into the gate. She was a remarkable-looking person. Tall, large, and majestic in every proportion of an unusually noble figure, she was of a make and possessed a bearing to attract attention had she borne a less striking and beautiful countenance. As it was, the glance lingered but a moment on the grand curves and lithe loveliness of that matchless figure, and passed at once to the face. Once there, it did not soon wander; for though its beauty was incontestable, the something that lay behind that beauty was more incontestable still, and held you, in spite of yourself, long after you had become acquainted with the broad white brow, the clear, deep, changing gray eye, the straight but characteristic nose, and the ruddy, nervous lip. You felt that, young and beautiful as she was, and charming as she might be, she was also one of nature's unsolvable mysteries—a woman whom you might study, obey, adore, but whom you could never hope to understand; a Sphinx without an Œdipus. She was dressed in dark green, and held her gloves in her hand. Her appearance was that of one who had been profoundly startled.

"Why don't someone answer me?" she asked, after an instant's pause, seemingly unconscious that, alike to those who knew her and to those who did not, her air and manner were such as to naturally impose silence. "Must I go into the house in order to find out if this good woman is dead or not?"

167

"Shure she isn't dead yet," spoke up a brawny butcher-boy, bolder than the rest. "But she's sore hurt, miss, and the doctors say as how there is no hope."

A change impossible to understand passed over the girl's face. Had she been less vigorous of body, she would have staggered. As it was, she stood still, rigidly still, and seemed to summon up her faculties, till the very clinch of her fingers spoke of the strong control she was putting upon herself.

"It is dreadful, dreadful!" she murmured, this time in a whisper, and as if to some rising protest in her own soul. "No good can come of it, none." Then, as if awakening to the scene about her, shook her head and cried to those nearest: "It was a tramp who did it, I suppose; at least, I am told so."

"A tramp has been took up, miss, on suspicion, as they call it."

"If a tramp has been taken up on suspicion, then he was the one who assailed her, of course." And pushing on through the crowd that fell back still more awe-struck than before, she went into the house.

The murmur that followed her was subdued but universal. It made no impression on Mr. Byrd. He had leaned forward to watch the girl's retreating form, but, finding his view intercepted by the wrinkled profile of an old crone who had leaned forward too, had drawn impatiently back. Something in that crone's aged face made him address her.

"You know the lady?" he inquired.

"Yes," was the cautious reply, given, however, with a leer he found not altogether pleasant.

"She is a relative of the injured woman, or a friend, perhaps?"

The old woman's face looked frightful.

"No," she muttered grimly; "they are strangers."

At this unexpected response Mr. Byrd made a perceptible start forward. The old woman's hand fell at once on his arm.

"Stay!" she hoarsely whispered. "By strangers I mean they don't visit each other. The town is too small for any of us to be strangers."

Mr. Byrd nodded and escaped her clutch.

"This is worth seeing through," he murmured, with the first gleam of interest he had shown in the affair. And, hurrying forward, he succeeded in following the lady into the house.

The sight he met there did not tend to allay his newborn interest. There she stood in the centre of the sitting-room, tall, resolute, and commanding, her eyes fixed on the door of the room that contained the still breathing sufferer, Mr. Orcutt's eyes fixed upon her. It seemed as if she had asked one question and been answered; there had not been time for more.

"I do not know what to say in apology for my intrusion," she remarked. "But the death, or almost the death, of a person of whom we have all heard, seems to me so terrible that———"

But here Mr. Orcutt interrupted gently, almost tenderly, but with a fatherly authority which Mr. Byrd expected to see her respect.

"Imogene," he observed, "this is no place for you; the horror of the event has made you forget yourself; go home and trust me to tell you on my return all that it is advisable for you to know."

But she did not even meet his glance with her steady eyes. "Thank you," she protested; "but I cannot go till I have seen the place where this woman fell and the weapon with which she was struck. I want to see it all. Mr. Ferris, will you show me?" And without giving any reason for this extraordinary request, she stood waiting with that air of conscious authority which is sometimes given by great beauty when united to a distinguished personal presence.

The district attorney, taken aback, moved toward the dining-room door. "I will consult with the coroner," said he.

But she waited for no man's leave. Following close behind him, she entered upon the scene of the tragedy.

"Where was the poor woman hit?" she inquired.

They told her; they showed her all she desired and asked her no questions. She awed them, all but Mr. Orcutt—him she both astonished and alarmed.

"And a tramp did all this?" she finally exclaimed, in the odd, musing tone she had used once before, while her eye fell thoughtfully to the floor. Suddenly she started, or so Mr. Byrd fondly imagined, and moved a pace, setting her foot carefully down upon a certain spot in the carpet beneath her.

"She has spied something," he thought, and watched to see if she would stoop.

But no, she held herself still more erectly than before, and seemed, by her rather desultory inquiries, to be striving to engage the attention of the others from herself.

"There is someone surely tapping at this door," she intimated, pointing to the one that opened into the lane.

Dr. Tredwell moved to see.

"Is there not?" she repeated, glancing at Mr. Ferris.

He, too, turned to see.

But there was still an eye regarding her from behind the sitting-room door, and, perceiving it, she impatiently ceased her efforts. She was not mistaken about the tapping. A man was at the door whom both gentlemen seemed to know.

"I come from the tavern where they are holding this tramp in custody," announced the newcomer in a voice too low to penetrate into the room. "He is frightened almost out of his wits. Seems to think he was taken up for theft, and makes no bones of saying that he did take a spoon or two from a house where he was let in for a bite. He gave up the spoons and expects to go to jail, but seems to have no idea that any worse suspicion is hanging over him. Those that stand around think he is innocent of the murder."

"Humph! well, we will see," ejaculated Mr. Ferris; and, turning back, he met, with a certain sort of complacence, the eyes of the young lady who had been somewhat impatiently awaiting his reappearance. "It seems there are doubts, after all, about the tramp being the assailant."

The start she gave was sudden and involuntary. She took a step forward and then paused as if hesitating. Instantly, Mr. Byrd, who had not forgotten the small object she had been covering with her foot, sauntered leisurely forward, and, spying a ring on the floor where she had been standing, unconcernedly picked it up.

She did not seem to notice him. Looking at Mr. Ferris with eyes whose startled, if not alarmed, expression she did not succeed in hiding from the detective, she inquired, in a stifled voice:

"What do you mean? What has this man been telling you? You say it was not the tramp. Who, then, was it?"

"That is a question we cannot answer," rejoined Mr. Ferris, astonished at her heat, while Lawyer Orcutt, moving forward, attempted once more to recall her to herself.

"Imogene," he pleaded,—"Imogene, calm yourself. This is not a matter of so much importance to you that you need agitate yourself so violently in regard to it. Come home, I beseech you, and leave the affairs of justice to the attention of those whose duty it is to look after them."

But beyond acknowledging his well-meant interference by a deprecatory glance, she stood immovable, looking from Dr. Tredwell to Mr. Ferris, and back again to Dr. Tredwell, as if she sought in their faces some confirmation of a hideous doubt or fear that had arisen in her own mind. Suddenly she felt a touch on her arm.

"Excuse me, madam, but is this yours?" inquired a smooth and careless voice over her shoulder.

As though awakening from a dream she turned; they all turned. Mr. Byrd was holding out in his open palm a ring blazing with a diamond of no mean lustre or value.

The sight of such a jewel, presented at such a moment, completed the astonishment of her friends. Pressing forward, they stared at the costly ornament and then at her, Mr. Orcutt's face especially assuming a startled expression of mingled surprise and apprehension, that soon attracted the attention of the others, and led to an interchange of looks that denoted a mutual but not unpleasant understanding.

"I found it at your feet," explained the detective, still carelessly, but with just that delicate shade of respect in his voice necessary to express a gentleman's sense of presumption in thus addressing a strange and beautiful young lady.

The tone, if not the explanation, seemed to calm her, as powerful natures are calmed in the stress of a sudden crisis.

"Thank you," she returned, not without signs of great sweetness in her look and manner. "Yes, it is mine," she added slowly, reaching out her hand and taking the ring. "I must have dropped it without knowing it." And meeting the eye of Mr. Orcutt fixed upon her with that startled look of inquiry already alluded to, she flushed, but placed the jewel nonchalantly on her finger.

This cool appropriation of something he had no reason to believe hers, startled the youthful detective immeasurably. He had not expected such a *dénouement* to the little drama he had prepared with such quiet assurance, and, though with the quick self-control that distinguished him he forbore to show his surprise, he none the less felt baffled and ill at ease, all the more that the two gentlemen present, who appeared to be the most disinterested in their regard for this young lady, seemed to accept this act on her part as genuine, and therefore not to be questioned.

"It is a clue that is lost," thought he. "I have made a mess of my first unassisted efforts at real detective work." And, inwardly disgusted with himself, he drew back into the other room and took up his stand at a remote window.

The slight stir he made in crossing the room seemed to break a spell and restore the minds of all present to their proper balance. Mr. Orcutt threw off the shadow that had momentarily disturbed his quiet and assured mien, and advancing once more, held out his arm with even more kindness than before, saying impressively:

"Now you will surely consent to accompany me home. You cannot mean to remain here any longer, can you, Imogene?"

But before she could reply, before her hand could lay itself on his arm, a sudden hush like that of awe passed solemnly through the room, and the physician, who had been set to watch over the dying gasps of the poor sufferer within, appeared on the threshold of the bedroom door, holding up his hand with a look that at once commanded attention and awoke the most painful expectancy in the hearts of all who beheld him:

"She stirs; she moves her lips," he announced, and again paused, listening.

Immediately there was a sound from the dimness behind him, a low sound, inarticulate at first, but presently growing loud enough and plain enough to be heard in the utmost recesses of the furthermost room on that floor.

"Hand! ring!" was the burden of the short ejaculation they heard. "Ring! hand!" till a sudden gasp cut short the fearful iteration, and all was silent again.

"Great heavens!" came in an awe-struck whisper from Mr. Ferris, as he pressed hastily toward the place from which these words had issued.

But the physician at once stopped and silenced him.

"She may speak again," he suggested. "Wait."

But, though they listened breathlessly, and with ever-growing suspense, no further break occurred in the deep silence, and soon the doctor announced:

"She has sunk back into her old state; she may rouse again, and she may not."

As though released from some painful tension, the coroner, the district attorney, and the detective all looked up. They found Miss Dare standing by the open window, with her face turned to the landscape, and Mr. Orcutt gazing at her with an expression of perplexity that had almost the appearance of dismay. This look passed instantly from the lawyer's countenance as he met the eyes of his friends, but Mr. Byrd, who was still smarting under a sense of his late defeat, could not but wonder what that gentleman had seen in Miss Dare, during the period of their late preoccupation, to call up such an expression to his usually keen and composed face.

The clinch of her white hand on the window-sill told nothing; but when in a few moments later she turned toward them again, Mr. Byrd saw, or thought he saw, the last lingering remains of a great horror fading out of her eyes, and was not surprised when she walked up to Mr. Orcutt and said, somewhat hoarsely: "I wish to go home now. This place is a terrible one to be in."

Mr. Orcutt, who was only too glad to comply with her request, again offered her his arm. But anxious as they evidently were to quit the house, they were not allowed to do so without experiencing another shock. Just as they were passing the door of the room where the wounded woman lay, the physician in attendance again appeared before them with that silently uplifted hand.

"Hush!" said he; "she stirs again. I think she is going to speak."

And once more that terrible suspense held each and everyone enthralled: once more that faint, inarticulate murmur eddied through the house, growing gradually into speech that this time took a form that curdled the blood of the listeners, and made Mr. Orcutt and the young woman at his side drop apart from each other as though a dividing sword had passed between them.

"May the vengeance of Heaven light upon the head of him who has brought me to this pass," were the words that now rose ringing and clear from that bed of death. "May the fate that has come upon me be visited upon him, measure for measure, blow for blow, death for death."

Strange and awe-inspiring words, that drew a pall over that house and made the dullest person there gasp for breath. In the silence that followed—a silence that could be felt—the white faces of lawyer and physician, coroner and detective, turned and confronted each other. But the young lady who lingered in their midst looked at no one, turned to no one. Shuddering and white, she stood gazing before her as if she already beheld that retributive hand descending upon the head of the guilty; then, as she awoke to the silence of those around her, gave a quick start and flashed forward to the door and so out into the street before Mr. Orcutt could rouse himself sufficiently from the stupor of the moment to follow her.

3

The Unfinished Letter

"Would there be any indiscretion in my asking who that young lady is?" inquired Mr. Byrd of Mr. Ferris, as, after ascertaining that the stricken sufferer still breathed, they stood together in a distant corner of the dining-room.

"No," returned the other, in a low tone, with a glance in the direction of the lawyer, who was just re-entering the house, after an unsuccessful effort to rejoin the person of whom they were speaking. "She is a Miss Dare, a young lady much admired in this town, and believed by many to be on the verge of matrimony with——" He nodded toward Mr. Orcutt, and discreetly forbore to finish the sentence.

"Ah!" exclaimed the youthful detective, "I understand." And he cast a look of suddenly awakened interest at the man who, up to this time, he had merely regarded as a more than usually acute criminal lawyer.

He saw a small, fair, alert man, of some forty years of age, of a good carriage, easy manner, and refined cast of countenance, overshadowed now by a secret anxiety he vainly tried to conceal. He was not as handsome as Coroner Tredwell, nor as well built as Mr. Ferris, yet he was, without doubt, the most striking-looking man in the room, and, to the masculine eyes of the detective, seemed at first glance to be a person to win the admiration, if not the affection, of women.

"She appears to take a great interest in this affair," he ventured again, looking back at Mr. Ferris.

"Yes, that is woman's way," replied the other, lightly, without any hint of secret feeling or curiosity. "Besides, she is an inscrutable girl, always surprising you by her emotions—or by her lack of them," he added, dismissing the topic with a wave of his hand.

"Which is also woman's way," remarked Mr. Byrd, retiring into his shell, from which he had momentarily thrust his head.

"Does it not strike you that there are rather more persons present than are necessary for the purposes of justice?" asked the lawyer, now coming forward with a look of rather pointed significance at the youthful stranger.

Mr. Ferris at once spoke up. "Mr. Orcutt," said he, "let me introduce to you Mr. Byrd, of New York. He is a member of the police force, and has been rendering me assistance in the case just adjourned."

"A detective!" repeated the other, eying the young man with a critical eye. "It is a pity, sir," he finally observed, "that your present duties will not allow you to render service to justice in this case of mysterious assault." And with a bow of more kindness than Mr. Byrd had reason to look for, he went slowly back to his former place near the door that hid the suffering woman from sight.

However kindly expressed, Mr. Byrd felt that he had received his dismissal, and was about to withdraw, when the coroner, who had been absent from their midst for the last few minutes, approached them from the foot of the stairs, and tapped the detective on the arm.

"I want you," said he.

Mr. Byrd bowed, and with a glance toward the district attorney, who returned him a nod of approval, went quickly out with the coroner.

"I hear you are a detective," observed the latter, taking him up stairs into a room which he carefully locked behind them. "A detective on the spot in a case like this is valuable; are you willing to assume the duties of your profession and act for justice in this matter?"

"Dr. Tredwell," returned the young man, instantly conscious of a vague, inward shrinking from meddling further in the affair, "I am not at present master of my proceedings. To say nothing of the obedience I owe my superiors at home, I am just now engaged in assisting Mr. Ferris in the somewhat pressing matter now before the court, and do not know whether it would meet with his approval to have me mix up matters in this way."

"Mr. Ferris is a reasonable man," said the coroner. "If his consent is all that is necessary——"

"But it is not, sir. I must have orders from New York."

"Oh, as to that, I will telegraph at once."

But still the young man hesitated, lounging in his easy way against the table by which he had taken his stand.

"Dr. Tredwell," he suggested, "you must have men in this town amply able to manage such a matter as this. A woman struck in broad daylight and a man already taken up on suspicion! 'Tis simple, surely; intricate measures are not wanted here."

"So you still think it is the tramp that struck her?" quoth the coroner, a trifle baffled by the other's careless manner.

"I still think it was not the man who sat in court all the morning and held me fascinated by his eye."

"Ah, he held you fascinated, did he?" repeated the other, a trifle suspiciously.

"Well, that is," Mr. Byrd allowed, with the least perceptible loss of his easy bearing, "he made me look at him more than once. A wandering eye always attracts me, and his wandered constantly."

"Humph! and you are sure he was in the court every minute of the morning?"

"There must be other witnesses who can testify to that," answered the detective, with the perceptible irritation of one weary of a subject which he feels he has already amply discussed.

"Well," declared the other, dropping his eyes from the young man's countenance to a sheet of paper he was holding in his hand, "whatever *rôle* this humpback has played in the tragedy now occupying us, whether he be a wizard, a secret accomplice, a fool who cannot keep his own secret, or a traitor who cannot preserve that of his tools, this affair, as you call it, is not likely to prove the simple matter you seem to consider it. The victim, if not her townsfolk, knew she possessed an enemy, and this half-finished letter which I have found on her table, raises the question whether a common tramp, with no motive but that of theft or brutal revenge, was the one to meditate the fatal blow, even if he were the one to deal it."

A perceptible light flickered into the eyes of Mr. Byrd, and he glanced with a new but unmistakable interest at the letter, though he failed to put out his hand for it, even though the coroner held it toward him.

"Thank you," said he; "but if I do not take the case, it would be better for me not to meddle any further with it."

"But you are going to take it," insisted the other, with temper, his anxiety to secure this man's services increasing with the opposition he so unaccountably received. "The officers at the detective bureau in New York are not going to send another man up here when there is already one on the spot. And a man from New York I am determined to have. A crime like this shall not go unpunished in this town, whatever it may do in a great city like yours. We don't have so many murder cases that we need to stint ourselves in the luxury of professional assistance."

"But," protested the young man, still determined to hold back, whatever arguments might be employed or inducements offered him, "how do you know I am the man for your work? We have many sorts and kinds of detectives in our bureau. Some for one kind of business, some for another; the following up of a criminal is not mine."

"What, then, is yours?" asked the coroner, not yielding a jot of his determination.

The detective was silent.

"Read the letter," persisted Dr. Tredwell, shrewdly conscious that if once the young man's professional instinct was aroused, all the puerile objections which influenced him would immediately vanish.

There was no resisting that air of command. Taking the letter in his hand, the young man read:

Dear Emily:—I don't know why I sit down to write to you today. I have plenty to do, and morning is no time for indulging in sentimentalities; but I feel strangely lonely and strangely anxious. Nothing goes just to my mind, and somehow the many causes for secret fear which I have always had, assume an undue prominence in my mind. It is always so when I am not quite well. In vain I reason with myself, saying that respectable people do not lightly enter into crime. But there are so many to whom my death would be more than welcome, that I constantly see myself in the act of being——

"Struck, shot, murdered," suggested Dr. Tredwell, perceiving the young man's eye lingering over the broken sentence.

"The words are not there," remonstrated Mr. Byrd; but the tone of his voice showed that his professional complacency had been disturbed at last.

The other did not answer, but waited with the wisdom of the trapper who sees the quarry nosing round the toils.

"There is evidently some family mystery," the young man continued, glancing again at the letter. "But," he remarked, "Mr. Orcutt is a good friend of hers, and can probably tell us what it all means."

"Very likely," the other admitted, "if we choose to ask him."

Quick as lightning the young man's glance flashed to the coroner's face.

"You would rather not put the question to him?" he inquired.

"No. As he is the lawyer who, in all probability, will be employed by the criminal in this case, I am sure he would rather not be mixed up in any preliminary investigation of the affair."

The young man's eye did not waver. He appeared to take a secret resolve.

"Has it not struck you," he insinuated, "that Mr. Orcutt might have other reasons for not wishing to give any expression of opinion in regard to it?"

The surprise in the coroner's eye was his best answer.

"No," he rejoined.

Mr. Byrd at once resumed all his old nonchalance.

"The young lady who was here appeared to show such agitated interest in this horrible crime, I thought that, in kindness to her, he might wish to keep out of the affair as much as possible."

"Miss Dare? Bless your heart, she would not restrict him in any way. Her interest in the matter is purely one of curiosity. It has been carried, perhaps, to a somewhat unusual length for a woman of her position and breeding. But that is all, I assure you. Miss Dare's eccentricities are well known in this town."

"Then the diamond ring was really hers?" Mr. Byrd was about to inquire, but stopped; something in his memory of this beautiful woman made it impossible for him to disturb the confidence of the coroner in her behalf, at least while his own doubts were so vague and shadowy.

The coroner, however, observed the young detective's hesitation, and smiled.

"Are you thinking of Miss Dare as having anything to do with this shocking affair?" he asked.

Mr. Byrd shook his head, but could not hide the flush that stole up over his forehead.

The coroner actually laughed, a low, soft, decorous laugh, but none the less one of decided amusement. "Your line is not in the direction of spotting criminals, I must allow," said he. "Why, Miss Dare is not only as irreproachable a young lady as we have in this town, but she is a perfect stranger to this woman and all her concerns. I doubt if she even knew her name till today."

A laugh is often more potent than argument. The face of the detective lighted up, and he looked very manly and very handsome as he returned the letter to the coroner, saying, with a sweep of his hand as if he tossed an unworthy doubt away forever:

"Well, I do not wish to appear obstinate. If this woman dies, and the inquest fails to reveal who her assailant is, I will apply to New York for leave to work up the case; that is, if you continue to desire my assistance. Meanwhile——"

"You will keep your eyes open," intimated the coroner, taking back the letter and putting it carefully away in his breast-pocket. "And now, mum!"

Mr. Byrd bowed, and they went together down the stairs.

It was by this time made certain that the dying woman was destined to linger on for some hours. She was completely unconscious, and her breath barely lifted the clothes that lay over the slowly labouring breast; but such vitality as there was held its own with scarcely perceptible change, and the doctor thought it might be midnight before the solemn struggle would end. "In the meantime, expect nothing," he exclaimed; "she has said her last word. What remains will be a mere sinking into the eternal sleep."

This being so, Mr. Orcutt and Mr. Ferris decided to leave. Mr. Byrd saw them safely out, and proceeded to take one or two private observations of his own. They consisted mostly in noting the precise position of the various doors in reference to the hearth where the stick was picked up, and the clock where the victim was attacked. Or, so the coroner gathered from the direction which Mr. Byrd's eye took in its travels over the scene of action, and the diagram which he hastily drew on the back of an envelope. The table was noticed, too, and an inventory of its articles taken, after which he opened the side-door and looked carefully out into the lane.

To observe him now with his quick eye flashing from spot to spot, his head lifted, and a visible air of determination infused through his whole bearing, you would scarcely recognize the easy, gracefully indolent youth who, but a little while before, lounged against the tables and chairs, and met the most penetrating eye with the sleepy gaze of a totally uninterested man. Dr. Tredwell, alert to the change, tapped the letter in his pocket complacently. "I have roused up a weasel," he mentally decided, and congratulated himself accordingly.

It was two o'clock when Mr. Byrd went forth to join Mr. Ferris in the court-room. As he stepped from the door, he encountered, to all appearance, just the same crowd that had encumbered its entrance a half hour before. Even the old crone had not moved from her former position, and seeing him, fairly pounced upon him with question after

179

question, all of which he parried with a nonchalant dexterity that drew shout after shout from those who stood by, and, finally, as he thought, won him the victory, for, with an angry shake of the head, she ceased her importunities, and presently let him pass. He hastened to improve the chance to gain for himself the refuge of the streets; and, having done this, stood for an instant parleying with a trembling young girl, whose real distress and anxiety seemed to merit some attention. Fatal delay. In that instant the old woman had got in front of him, and when he arrived at the head of the street he found her there.

"Now," said she, with full-blown triumph in her venomous eyes, "perhaps you will tell me something! You think I am a mumbling old woman who don't know what she is bothering herself about. But I tell you I've not kept my eyes and ears open for seventy-five years in this wicked world without knowing a bit of the devil's own work when I see it." Here her face grew quite hideous, and her eyes gleamed with an aspect of gloating over the evil she alluded to, that quite sickened the young man, accustomed though he was to the worst phases of moral depravity. Leaning forward, she peered inquiringly in his face. "What has *she* to do with it?" she suddenly asked, emphasizing the pronoun with an expressive leer.

"She?" he repeated, starting back.

"Yes, she; the pretty young lady, the pert and haughty Miss Dare, that had but to speak to make the whole crowd stand back. What had she to do with it, I say? Something, or she wouldn't be here!"

"I don't know what you are talking about," he replied, conscious of a strange and unaccountable dismay at thus hearing his own passing doubt put into words by this vile and repellent being. "Miss Dare is a stranger. She has nothing to do either with this affair or the poor woman who has suffered by it. Her interest is purely one of sympathy."

"Hi! and you call yourself a smart one, I dare say." And the old creature ironically chuckled. "Well, well, well, what fools men are! They see a pretty face, and blind themselves to what is written on it as plain as black writing on a white wall. They call it sympathy, and never stop to ask why she, of all the soft-hearted gals in the town, should be the only one to burst into that house like an avenging spirit! But it's all right," she went on, in a bitterly satirical tone. "A crime like this can't be covered up, however much you may try; and sooner or later we will all know whether this young lady has had anything to do with Mrs. Clemmens' murder or not."

"Stop!" cried Mr. Byrd, struck in spite of himself by the look of meaning with which she said these last words. "Do you know anything against Miss Dare which other folks do not? If you do, speak, and let me hear at once what it is. But——" he felt very angry, though he could not for the moment tell why——"if you are only talking to gratify your spite, and have nothing to tell me except the fact that Miss Dare appeared shocked and anxious when she came from the widow's house just now, look out what use you make of her name, or you will get yourself into trouble. Mr. Orcutt and Mr. Ferris are not men to let you go babbling round town about a young lady of estimable character." And he tightened the grip he had taken upon her arm and looked at her threateningly.

The effect was instantaneous. Slipping from his grasp, she gazed at him with a sinister expression and edged slowly away.

"I know anything?" she repeated. "What should I know? I only say the young lady's face tells a very strange story. If you are too dull or too obstinate to read it, it's nothing to me." And with another leer and a quick look up and down the street, as if she half feared to encounter one or both of the two lawyers whose names he had mentioned, she marched quickly away, wagging her head and looking back as she went, as much as to say: "You have hushed me up for this time, young man, but don't congratulate yourself too much. I have still a tongue in my head, and the day may come when I can use it without any fear of being stopped by you."

Mr. Byrd, who was not very well pleased with himself or the way he had managed this interview, watched her till she was out of sight, and then turned thoughtfully toward the court-house. The fact was, he felt both agitated and confused. In the first place, he was disconcerted at discovering the extent of the impression that had evidently been made upon him by the beauty of Miss Dare, since nothing short of a deep, unconscious admiration for her personal attributes, and a strong and secret dread of having his lately acquired confidence in her again disturbed, could have led him to treat the insinuations of this babbling old wretch in such a cavalier manner.

Any other detective would have seized with avidity upon the opportunity of hearing what she had to say on such a subject, and would not only have cajoled her into confidence, but encouraged her to talk until she had given utterance to all that was on her mind. But in the stress of a feeling to which he was not anxious to give a name, he had forgotten that he was a detective, and remembered only that he was a man; and the consequence was that he had frightened the old creature, and cut short words that it was possibly his business to hear.

In the second place, he felt himself in a quandary as regarded Miss Dare. If, as was more than possible, she was really the innocent woman the coroner considered her, and the insinuations, if not threats, to which he had been listening were simply the result of a wicked old woman's privately nurtured hatred, how could he reconcile it to his duty as a man, or even as a detective, to let the day pass without warning her, or the eminent lawyer who honoured her with his regard, of the danger in which she stood from this creature's venomous tongue.

As he sat in court that afternoon, with his eye upon Mr. Orcutt, beneath whose ordinary aspect of quiet, sarcastic attention he thought he could detect the secret workings of a deep, personal perplexity, if not of actual alarm, he asked himself what he would wish done if he were that man, and a scandal of a debasing character threatened the peace of one allied to him by the most endearing ties. "Would I wish to be informed of it?" he queried. "I most certainly should," was his inward reply.

And so it was that, after the adjournment of court, he approached Mr. Orcutt, and leading him respectfully aside, said, with visible reluctance:

"I beg your pardon, sir, but a fact has come to my knowledge today with which I think you ought to be made acquainted. It is in reference to the young lady who was with us at Mrs. Clemmens' house this morning. Did you know, sir, that she had an enemy in this town?"

Mr. Orcutt, whose thoughts had been very much with that young lady since she left him so unceremoniously a few hours before, started and looked at Mr. Byrd with surprise which was not without its element of distrust.

"An enemy?" he repeated. "An enemy? What do you mean?"

"What I say, Mr. Orcutt. As I came out of Mrs. Clemmens' house this afternoon, an old hag whose name I do not know, but whom you will probably have no difficulty in recognizing, seized me by the arm and made me the recipient of insinuations and threats against Miss Dare, which, however foolish and unfounded, betrayed an animosity and a desire to injure her that is worthy your attention."

"You are very kind," returned Mr. Orcutt, with increased astonishment and a visible constraint, "but I do not understand you. What insinuations or threats could this woman have to make against a young lady of Miss Dare's position and character?"

182

"It is difficult for me to tell you," acknowledged Mr. Byrd; "but the vicious old creature presumed to say that Miss Dare must have had a special and secret interest in this murder, or she would not have gone as she did to that house. Of course," pursued the detective, discreetly dropping his eyes from the lawyer's face, "I did what I could to show her the folly of her suspicions, and tried to make her see the trouble she would bring upon herself if she persisted in expressing them; but I fear I only succeeded in quieting her for the moment, and that she will soon be attacking others with this foolish story."

Mr. Orcutt who, whatever his own doubts or apprehensions, could not fail to be totally unprepared for a communication of this kind, gave utterance to a fierce and bitter exclamation, and fixed upon the detective his keen and piercing eye.

"Tell me just what she said," he demanded.

"I will try to do so," returned Mr. Byrd. And calling to his aid a very excellent memory, he gave a *verbatim* account of the conversation that had passed between him and the old woman. Mr. Orcutt listened, as he always did, without interruption or outward demonstration; but when the recital was over and Mr. Byrd ventured to look at him once more, he noticed that he was very pale and greatly changed in expression. Being himself in a position to understand somewhat of the other's emotion, he regained by an effort the air of polite nonchalance that became him so well, and quickly suggested: "Miss Dare will, of course, be able to explain herself."

The lawyer flashed upon him a quick glance.

"I hope you have no doubts on the subject," he said; then, as the detective's eye fell a trifle before his, paused and looked at him with the self-possession gained in fifteen years of practice in the criminal courts, and said: "I am Miss Dare's best friend. I know her well, and can truly say that not only is her character above reproach, but that I am acquainted with no circumstances that could in any way connect her with this crime. Nevertheless, the incidents of the day have been such as to make it desirable for her to explain herself, and this, as you say, she will probably have no difficulty in doing. If you will, therefore, wait till tomorrow before taking anyone else into your confidence, I promise you to see Miss Dare myself, and, from her own lips, learn the cause of her peculiar interest in this affair. Meanwhile, let me request you to put a curb upon your imagination, and not allow it to soar too high into the regions of idle speculation."

And he held out his hand to the detective with a smile whose vain attempt at unconcern affected Mr. Byrd more than a violent outbreak would have done. It betrayed so unmistakably that his own secret doubts were not without an echo in the breast of this eminent lawyer.

4

Imogene

Mr. Orcutt was a man who for many years had turned a deaf ear and a cold eye to the various attractions and beguilements of woman. Either from natural coldness of disposition, or for some other latent cause, traceable, perhaps, to some fact in his past history, and not to be inquired into by gossiping neighbours and so-called friends, he had resisted, even to the point of disdain, both the blandishments of acknowledged belles, and the more timid but no less pleasing charms of the shy country misses that he met upon his travels.

But one day all this was changed. Imogene Dare entered his home, awakening a light in the dim old place that melted his heart and made a man out of what was usually considered a well-ordered machine.

She had been a foundling. Yes, this beautiful, disdainful, almost commanding woman, had in the beginning been that most unfortunate of beings—a child without a name. But though this fact may have influenced the course of her early days, it gradually disappeared from notice as she grew up and developed, till in Sibley, at least, it became well-nigh a fact forgotten. Her beauty, as well as the imposing traits of her character, was the cause. There are some persons so gifted with natural force that, once brought in contact with them, you forget their antecedents, and, indeed, everything but themselves. Either their beauty overawes you or they, by conversation or bearing, so completely satisfy you of their right to your respect, that indifference takes the place of curiosity, and you yield your regard as if you have already yielded your admiration, without question and without stint.

The early years of her life were passed in the house of a poor widow, to whom the appearance of this child on her door-step one fine day had been nothing more nor less than a veritable godsend. First, because she was herself alone in the world, and needed the mingled companionship and care which a little one invariably gives; and, secondly, because Imogene, from the very first, had been a noticeable child, who early attracted the attention of the neighbours, and led to many a substantial evidence of favour from them, as well as from the strangers who passed their gate or frequented their church. Insensibly to herself, and without help of circumstances or rearing, the girl was a magnet toward which all good things insensibly tended; and the widow saw this, and, while reaping the reward, stinted neither her affection nor her gratitude.

When Imogene was eleven, this protector of her infancy died. But another home instantly offered. A wealthy couple of much kindness, if little culture, adopted her as their child, and gave her every benefit in life save education. This never having possessed themselves, they openly undervalued. But she was not to be kept down by the force of any circumstances, whether favourable or otherwise. All the graces of manner and refinements of thought which properly belong to the station she had now attained, but which, in the long struggle after wealth, had escaped the honest couple that befriended her, became by degrees her own, tempering without destroying her individuality, any more than the new life of restraint that now governed her physical powers, was able to weaken or subdue that rare and splendid physique which had been her fairest birthright.

In the lap of luxury, therefore, and in full possession of means to come and go and conform herself to the genteel world and its fashions, she passed the next four years; but scarcely had she attained the age of fifteen, when bankruptcy, followed by death, again robbed her of her home and set her once more adrift upon the world.

This time she looked to no one for assistance. Refusing all offers, many of them those of honourable marriage, she sought for work, and after a short delay found it in the household of Mr. Orcutt. The aged sister who governed his home and attended to all its domestic details, hired her as a sort of assistant, rightly judging that the able young body and the alert hand would bring into the household economy just that life and interest which her own failing strength had now for some time refused to supply.

That the girl was a beauty and something more, who could not from the nature of things be kept in that subordinate position, she either failed to see, or, seeing, was pleased to disregard. She never sought to impose restraint upon the girl any more than she did upon her brother, when in the course of events she saw that his eye was at last attracted and his imagination fired by the noble specimen of girlhood that made its daily appearance at his own board.

That she had introduced a dangerous element into that quiet home, that ere long would devastate its sacred precincts, and endanger, if not destroy, its safety and honour, she had no reason to suspect. What was there in youth, beauty, and womanly power that one should shrink from their embodiment and tremble as if an evil instead of a good had entered that hitherto undisturbed household? Nothing, if they had been all. But alas for her, and alas for him—they were not all! Mixed with the youth, beauty, and power was a something else not to be so readily understood—a something, too, which, without offering explanation to the fascinated mind that studied her, made the beauty unique, the youth a charm, and the power a controlling force. She was not to be sounded. Going and coming, smiling and frowning, in movement or at rest, she was always a mystery; the depths of her being remaining still in hiding, however calmly she spoke or however graciously she turned upon you the light of her deep gray eyes.

Mr. Orcutt loved her. From the first vision he had of her face and form dominating according to their nature at his board and fireside, he had given up his will into her unconscious keeping. She was so precisely what all other women he had known were not. At first so distant, so self-contained, so unapproachable in her pride; then as her passion grew for books, so teachable, so industrious, so willing to listen to his explanations and arguments; and lastly——

But that did not come at once. A long struggle took place between those hours when he used to encourage her to come into his study and sit at his side, and read from his books, and the more dangerous time still, when he followed her into the drawing-room and sat at her side, and sought to read, not from books, but from her eyes, the story of his own future fate.

For, powerful as was his passion and deeply as his heart had been touched, he did not yield to the thought of marriage which such a passion involves, without a conflict. He would make her his child, the heiress of his wealth, and the support of his old age; this was his first resolve. But it did not last; the first sight he had of her on her return from a visit to Buffalo, which he had insisted upon her making during the time of his greatest mental conflict, had assured him that this could never be; that he must be husband and she wife, or else their relations must entirely cease. Perhaps the look with which she met him had something to do with this. It was such a blushing, humble—yes, for her, really humble and beautiful—look. He could not withstand it. Though no one could have detected it in his manner, he really succumbed in that hour. Doubt and hesitation flew to the winds, and to make her his own became the sole aim and object of his life.

He did not, however, betray his purpose at once. Neighbours and friends might and did suspect the state of his feelings, but to her he was silent. That vague something which marked her off from the rest of her sex, seemed to have deepened in her temporary sojourn from his side, and whatever it meant of good or of ill, it taught him at least to be wary. At last, was it with premeditation or was it in some moment of uncontrollable impulse, he spoke; not with definite pleading, or even with any very clear intimation that he desired some day to make her his wife, but in a way that sufficed to tear the veil from their previous intercourse and let her catch a glimpse, if no more, of his heart, and its devouring passion.

He was absolutely startled at the result. She avowed that she had never thought of his possessing such a regard for her; and for two days shut herself up in her room and refused to see either him or his sister. Then she came down, blooming like a rose, but more distant, more quiet, and more inscrutable than ever. Pride, if pride she felt, was subdued under a general aspect of womanly dignity that for a time held all further avowals in check, and made all intercourse between them at once potent in its attraction and painful in its restraint.

"She is waiting for a distinct offer of marriage," he decided.

And thus matters stood, notwithstanding the general opinion of their friends, when the terrible event recorded in the foregoing chapters of this story brought her in a new light before his eyes, and raised a question, shocking as it was unexpected, as to whether this young girl, immured as he had believed her to be in his own home, had by some unknown and inexplicable means run upon the secret involving, if not explaining, the mystery of this dreadful and daring crime.

Such an idea was certainly a preposterous one to entertain. He neither could nor would believe she knew more of this matter than any other disinterested person in town, and yet there had certainly been something in her bearing upon the scene of tragedy, that suggested a personal interest in the affair; nor could he deny that he himself had been struck by the incongruity of her behaviour long before it attracted the attention of others.

But then he had opportunities for judging of her conduct which others did not have. He not only had every reason to believe that the ring to which she had so publicly laid claim was not her own, but he had observed how, at the moment the dying woman had made that tell-tale exclamation of "*Ring* and *Hand!*" Miss Dare had looked down at the jewel she had thus appropriated, with a quick horror and alarm that seemed to denote she had some knowledge of its owner, or some suspicion, at least, as to whose hand had worn it before she placed it upon her own.

It was not, therefore, a matter of wonder that he was visibly affected at finding her conduct had attracted the attention of others, and one of those a detective, or that the walk home after his interview with Mr. Byrd should have been fraught with a dread to which he scarcely dared to give a name.

The sight of Miss Dare coming down the path as he reached his own gate did not tend to greatly allay his apprehensions, particularly as he observed she was dressed in travelling costume, and carried a small satchel on her arm.

"Imogene," he cried, as she reached him, "what is the meaning of this? Where are you going?"

Her face, which wore a wholly unnatural and strained expression, turned slowly toward his.

"I am going to Buffalo," she said.

"To Buffalo?"

"Yes."

This was alarming, surely. She was going to leave the town—leave it suddenly, without excuse or explanation!

Looking at her with eyes which, for all their intense inquiry, conveyed but little of the serious emotions that were agitating his mind, he asked, hurriedly:

"What takes you to Buffalo—today—so suddenly?"

Her answer was set and mechanical.

"I have had news. One of my—my friends is not well. I must go. Do not detain me."

And she moved quickly toward the gate.

But his tremulous hand was upon it, and he made no offer to open a passage for her.

"Pardon me," said he, "but I cannot let you go till I have had some conversation with you. Come with me to the house, Imogene. I will not detain you long."

But with a sad and abstracted gesture she slowly shook her head.

"It is too late," she murmured. "I shall miss the train if I stop

189

"Taking her hand in his, he looked at her long and
searchingly. 'Imogene,' he exclaimed, 'there is something weighing on your heart.'"

now."

"Then you must miss it," he cried, bitterly, forgetting everything else in the torture of his uncertainty. "What I have to say cannot wait. Come!"

This tone of command from one who had hitherto adapted himself to her every whim, seemed to strike her. Paling quickly, she for the first time looked at him with something like a comprehension of his feelings, and quietly replied:

"Forgive me. I had forgotten for the moment the extent of your claims upon me. I will wait till tomorrow before going." And she led the way back to the house.

When they were alone together in the library, he turned toward her with a look whose severity was the fruit of his condition of mind rather than of any natural harshness or imperiousness.

"Now, Imogene," said he, "tell me why you desire to leave my house."

Her face, which had assumed a mask of cold impassiveness, confronted him like that of a statue, but her voice, when she spoke, was sufficiently gentle.

"Mr. Orcutt," was her answer, "I have told you. I have a call elsewhere which must be attended to. I do not leave your house; I merely go to Buffalo for a few days."

But he could not believe this short statement of her intentions. In the light of these new fears of his, this talk of Buffalo, and a call there, looked to him like the merest subterfuge. Yet her gentle tone was not without its effect, and his voice visibly softened as he said:

"You are intending, then, to return?"

Her reply was prefaced by a glance of amazement.

"Of course," she responded at last. "Is not this my home?"

Something in the way she said this carried a ray of hope to his heart. Taking her hand in his, he looked at her long and searchingly.

"Imogene!" he exclaimed, "there is something serious weighing upon your heart. What is it? Will you not make me the confidant of your troubles? Tell me what has made such a change in you since— since noon, and its dreadful event."

But her expression did not soften, and her manner became even more reserved than before.

"I have not anything to tell," said she.

"Not anything?" he repeated.

"Not anything."

191

Dropping her hand, he communed a moment with himself. That a secret of possible consequence lay between them he could not doubt. That it had reference to and involved the crime of the morning, he was equally sure. But how was he to make her acknowledge it? How was he to reach her mind and determine its secrets without alarming her dignity or wounding her heart?

To press her with questions seemed impossible. Even if he could have found words with which to formulate his fears, her firm, set face, and steady, unrelenting eye, assured him only too plainly that the attempt would be met by failure, if it did not bring upon him her scorn and contempt. No; some other method must be found; some way that would completely and at once ease his mind of a terrible weight, and yet involve no risk to the love that had now become the greatest necessity of his existence. But what way? With all his acumen and knowledge of the world, he could think of but one. He would ask her hand in marriage—aye, at this very moment—and from the tenor of her reply judge of the nature of her thoughts.

For, looking in her face, he felt forced to acknowledge that whatever doubts he had ever cherished in reference to the character of this remarkable girl, upon one point he was perfectly clear, and this was, that she was at basis honourable in her instincts, and would never do herself or another a real injustice. If a distinct wrong or even a secret of an unhappy or debasing nature lay between them, he knew that nothing, not even the bitterest necessity or the most headlong passion, would ever drive her into committing the dishonour of marrying him.

No; if with his declaration in her ears, and with his eyes fixed upon hers, she should give any token of her willingness to accept his addresses, he felt he might know, beyond doubt or cavil, that whatever womanish excitability may have moved her in her demonstrations that day, they certainly arose from no private knowledge or suspicion detrimental to his future peace or to hers.

Bracing himself, therefore, to meet any result that might follow his attempt, he drew her gently toward him and determinedly addressed her.

"Imogene, I told you at the gate that I had something to say to you. So I have; and though it may not be wholly unexpected to you, yet I doubt if it would have left my lips tonight if the events of the day had not urged me to offer you my sympathy and protection."

He paused, almost sickened; at that last phrase she had grown so terribly white and breathless. But something in her manner, notwithstanding, seemed to encourage him to proceed, and smothering his doubts, trampling, as it were, upon his rising apprehensions, he calmed down his tone and went quietly on:

"Imogene, I love you."

She did not shrink.

"Imogene, I want you for my wife. Will you listen to my prayer, and make my home forever happy with your presence?"

Ah, now she showed feeling; now she started and drew back, putting out her hands as if the idea he had advanced was insupportable to her. But it was only for a moment. Before he could say to himself that it was all over, that his worst fears had been true, and that nothing but the sense of some impassable gulf between them could have made her recoil from him like this, she had dropped her hands and turned toward him with a look whose deep inquiry and evident struggle after an understanding of his claims, spoke of a mind clouded by trouble, but not alienated from himself by fear.

She did not speak, however,—not for some few minutes, and when she did, her words came in short and hurried gasps.

"You are kind," was what she said. "To be your—wife"—she had difficulty in uttering the word, but it came at last—"would be an honour and a protection. I appreciate both. But I am in no mood tonight to listen to words of love from any man. Perhaps six months hence——"

But he already had her in his arms. The joy and relief he felt were so great he could not control himself. "Imogene," he murmured, "my Imogene!" And scarcely heeded her when, in a burst of subdued agony, she asked to be released, saying that she was ill and tired, and must be allowed to withdraw to her room.

But a second appeal woke him from his dream. If his worst fears were without foundation; if her mind was pure of aught that unfitted her to be his wife, there was yet much that was mysterious in her conduct, and, consequently, much which he longed to have explained.

"Imogene," he said, "I must ask you to remain a moment longer. Hard as it is for me to distress you, there is a question which I feel it necessary to put to you before you go. It is in reference to the fearful crime which took place today. Why did you take such an interest in it, and why has it had such an effect upon you that you look like a changed woman tonight?"

Disengaging herself from his arms, she looked at him with the set composure of one driven to bay, and asked:

"Is there anything strange in my being interested in a murder perpetrated on a person whose name I have frequently heard mentioned in this house?"

"No," he murmured, "no; but what led you to her home? It was not a spot for a young lady to be in, and any other woman would have shrunk from so immediate a contact with crime."

Imogene's hand was on the door, but she turned back.

"I am not like other women," she declared. "When I hear of anything strange or mysterious, I want to understand it. I did not stop to ask what people would think of my conduct."

"But your grief and terror, Imogene? They are real, and not to be disguised. Look in the glass over there, and you will yourself see what an effect all this has had upon you. If Mrs. Clemmens is a stranger to you; if you know no more of her than you have always led me to suppose, why should you have been so unnaturally impressed by today's tragedy?"

It was a searching question, and her eye fell slightly, but her steady demeanour did not fail her.

"Still," said she, "because I am not like other women. I cannot forget such horrors in a moment." And she advanced again to the door, upon which she laid her hand.

Unconsciously his eye followed the movement, and rested somewhat inquiringly upon that hand. It was gloved, but to all appearance was without the ring which he had seen her put on at the widow's house.

She seemed to comprehend his look. Meeting his eye with unshaken firmness, she resumed, in a low and constrained voice:

"You are wondering about the ring that formed a portion of the scene we are discussing. Mr. Orcutt, I told the gentleman who handed it to me today that it was mine. That should be enough for the man who professes sufficient confidence in me to wish to make me his wife. But since your looks confess a curiosity in regard to this diamond, I will say that I was as much astonished as anybody to see it picked up from the floor at my feet. The last time I had seen it was when I dropped it, somewhat recklessly, into a pocket. How or when it fell out, I cannot say. As for the ring itself," she haughtily added, "young ladies frequently possess articles of whose existence their friends are unconscious."

Here was an attempt at an explanation which, though meagre and

194

far from satisfactory, had at least a basis in possibility. But Mr. Orcutt, as I have before said, was certain that the ring was lying on the floor of the room where it was picked up, before Imogene had made her appearance there, and was therefore struck with dismay at this conclusive evidence of her falsehood.

Yet, as he said to himself, she might have some association with the ring, might even have an owner's claim upon it, incredible as this appeared, without being in the possession of such knowledge as definitely connected it with this crime. And led by this hope he laid his hand on hers as it was softly turning the knob of the door, and said, with emotion:

"Imogene, one moment. This is a subject which I am as anxious to drop as you are. In your condition it is almost cruelty to urge it upon you, but of one thing I must be assured before you leave my presence, and that is, that whatever secrets you may hide in your soul, or whatever motive may have governed your treatment of me and my suit tonight, they do not spring from any real or supposed interest in this crime, which ought from its nature to separate you and me. I ask," he quickly added, as he saw her give a start of injured pride or irrepressible dismay, "not because I have any doubts on the subject myself, but because some of the persons who have unfortunately been witness to your strange and excited conduct today, have presumed to hint that nothing short of a secret knowledge of the crime or criminal could explain your action upon the scene of tragedy."

And with a look which, if she had observed it, might have roused her to a sense of the critical position in which she stood, he paused and held his breath for her reply.

It did not come.

"Imogene?"

"I hear."

Cold and hard the words sounded—his hand went like lightning to his heart.

"Are you going to answer?" he asked, at last.

"Yes."

"What is that answer to be, Yes or No?"

She turned upon him her large gray eyes. There was misery in their depths, but there was a haughtiness, also, which only truth could impart.

"My answer is No!" said she.

And, without another word, she glided from the room.

Next morning, Mr. Byrd found three notes awaiting his perusal. The first was a notification from the coroner to the effect that the Widow Clemmens had quietly breathed her last at midnight. The second, a hurried line from Mr. Ferris, advising him to make use of the day in concluding a certain matter of theirs in the next town; and the third, a letter from Mr. Orcutt, couched in the following terms:

Mr. Byrd: *Dear Sir*—I have seen the person named between us, and I here state, upon my honour, that she is in possession of no facts which it concerns the authorities to know.

Tremont B. Orcutt.

5

Horace Byrd

Horace Byrd was by birth and education a gentleman. He was the son of a man of small means but great expectations, and had been reared to look forward to the day when he should be the possessor of a large income. But his father dying, both means and expectations vanished into thin air, and at the age of twenty, young Horace found himself thrown upon the world without income, without business, and, what was still worse, without those habits of industry that serve a man in such an emergency better than friends and often better than money itself.

He had also an invalid mother to look after, and two young sisters whom he loved with warm and devoted affection; and though by the kindness and forethought of certain relatives he was for a time spared all anxiety on their account, he soon found that some exertion on his part would be necessary to their continued subsistence, and accordingly set about the task of finding suitable employment, with much spirit and no little hope.

But a long series of disappointments taught him that young men cannot leap at a bound into a fine salary or even a promising situation; and baffled in every wish, worn out with continued failures, he sank from one state of hope to another, till he was ready to embrace any prospect that would insure ease and comfort to the helpless beings he so much loved.

It was while he was in this condition that Mr. Gryce—a somewhat famous police detective of New York—came upon him, and observing, as he thought, some signs of natural aptitude for *fine work*, as he called it, in this elegant but decidedly hard-pushed young gentleman, seized upon him with an avidity that can only be explained by this detective's long-cherished desire to ally to himself a man of real refinement and breeding; having, as he privately admitted more than once to certain chosen friends, a strong need of such a person to assist him in certain cases where great houses were to be entered and fine gentlemen if not fair ladies subjected to interviews of a delicate and searching nature.

To join the police force and be a detective was the last contingency that had occurred to Horace Byrd. But men in decidedly straitened circumstances cannot pick and choose too nicely; and after a week of uncertainty and fresh disappointment, he went manfully to his mother and told her of the offer that had been made him. Meeting with less discouragement than he had expected from the broken-down and unhappy woman, he gave himself up to the guiding hand of Mr. Gryce, and before he realized it, was enrolled among the secret members of the New York force.

He was not recognized publicly as a detective. His name was not even known to any but the highest officials. He was employed for special purposes, and it was not considered desirable that he should be seen at police head-quarters. But being a man of much ability and of a solid, reliable nature, he made his way notwithstanding, and by the time he had been in the service a year, was looked upon as a good-fellow and a truly valuable acquisition to the bureau. Indeed, he possessed more than the usual qualifications for his calling, strange as the fact appeared not only to himself but to the few friends acquainted with his secret.

In the first place, he possessed much acuteness without betraying it. Of an easy bearing and a polished address, he was a man to please all and alarm none, yet he always knew what he was about and what you were about, too, unless indeed you possessed a power of dissimulation much beyond ordinary, when the chances were that his gentlemanly instincts would get in his way, making it impossible for him to believe in a guilt that was too hardy to betray itself, and too insensible to shame to blush before the touch of the inquisitor.

In the second place, he liked the business. Yes, notwithstanding the theories of that social code to which he once paid deference, notwithstanding the frankness and candour of his own disposition, he found in this pursuit a nice adjustment of cause to effect and effect to cause that at once pleased and satisfied his naturally mathematical mind.

He did not acknowledge the fact, not even to himself. On the contrary, he was always threatening that in another month he should look up some new means of livelihood, but the coming month would invariably bring a fresh case before his notice, and then it would be: "Well, after this matter is probed to the bottom," or, "When that criminal is made to confess his guilt," till even his little sisters caught the infection, and would whisper over their dolls:

"Brother Horace is going to be a great man when all the bad and naughty people in the world are put in prison."

As a rule, Mr. Byrd was not sent out of town. But, on the occasion of Mr. Ferris desiring a man of singular discretion to assist him in certain inquiries connected with the case then on trial in Sibley, there happened to be a deficiency of capable men in the bureau, and the superintendent was obliged to respond to the call by sending Mr. Byrd. He did not do it, however, without making the proviso that all public recognition of this officer, in his real capacity, was to be avoided. And so far the wishes of his superiors had been respected. No one outside of the few persons mentioned in the first chapter of this story suspected that the easy, affable, and somewhat distinguished-looking young gentleman who honoured the village hotel with his patronage was a secret emissary of the New York police.

Mr. Byrd was, of all men, then, the very one to feel the utmost attraction toward, and at the same time the greatest shrinking from, the pursuit of such investigations as were likely to ensue upon the discovery of the mysterious case of murder which had so unexpectedly been presented to his notice. As a professional, he could not fail to experience that quick start of the blood which always follows the recognition of a "big affair," while as a gentleman, he felt himself recoil from probing into a matter that was blackened by a possibility against which every instinct in his nature rebelled.

It was, therefore, with oddly mingled sensations that he read Mr. Orcutt's letter, and found himself compelled to admit that the coroner had possessed a truer insight than himself into the true cause of Miss Dare's eccentric conduct upon the scene of the tragedy. His main feeling, however, was one of relief. It was such a comfort to think he could proceed in the case without the dread of stumbling upon a clue that, in some secret and unforeseen way, should connect this imposing woman with a revolting crime. Or so he fondly considered.

But he had not spent five minutes at the railroad station, where, in pursuance to the commands of Mr. Ferris, he went to take the train for Monteith, before he saw reason to again change his mind. For, there among the passengers awaiting the New York express, he saw Miss Dare, with a travelling-bag upon her arm and a look on her face that, to say the least, was of most uncommon character in a scene of so much bustle and hurry. She was going away, then—going to leave Sibley and its mystery behind her! He was not pleased with the discovery. This sudden departure looked too much like escape, and gave him, notwithstanding the assurance he had received from Mr. Orcutt, an uneasy sense of having tampered with his duty as an officer of justice, in thus providing this mysterious young woman with a warning that could lead to a result like this.

Yet, as he stood at the depot surveying Miss Dare, in the few minutes they both had to wait, he asked himself over and over again how any thought of her possessing a personal interest in the crime which had just taken place could retain a harbour in his mind. She looked so noble in her quiet aspect of solemn determination, so superior in her young, fresh beauty—a determination that, from the lofty look it imparted, must have its birth in generous emotion, even if her beauty was but the result of a rarely modelled frame and a health of surpassing perfection.

He resolved he would think of her no more in that or any other connection; that he would follow the example of her best friend, and give his doubts to the wind.

And yet such a burr is suspicion, that he no sooner saw a young man approaching her with the evident intention of speaking, than he felt an irresistible desire to hear what she would have to say, and, led by this impulse, allowed himself to saunter nearer and nearer the pair, till he stood almost at their backs.

The first words he heard were:

"How long do you expect to remain in Buffalo, Miss Dare?"

To which she replied:

"I have no idea whether I shall stay a week or a month."

Then the whistle of the advancing train was heard, and the two pressed hurriedly forward.

The business which had taken Mr. Byrd to Monteith kept him in that small town all day. But though he thus missed the opportunity of attending the opening of the inquest at Sibley, he did not experience the vivid disappointment which might have been expected, his interest in that matter having in some unaccountable way subsided from the moment he saw Imogene Dare take the cars for Buffalo.

It was five o'clock when he again returned to Sibley, the hour at which the western train was also due. In fact, it came steaming in while he stood there, and, as was natural, perhaps, he paused a moment to watch the passengers alight. There were not many, and he was about to turn toward home, when he saw a lady step upon the platform whose appearance was so familiar that he stopped, disbelieving the evidence of his own senses. Miss Dare returned? Miss Dare, who but a few hours before had left this very depot for the purpose, as she said, of making a visit of more or less length in the distant city of Buffalo? It could not be. And yet there was no mistaking her, disguised though she was by the heavy veil that covered her features. She had come back, and the interest which Mr. Byrd had lost in Sibley and its possible mystery, revived with a suddenness that called up a self-conscious blush to his hardy cheek.

But why had she so changed her plans? What could have occurred during the few hours that had elapsed since her departure, to turn her about on her path and drive her homeward before her journey was half completed? He could not imagine. True, it was not his present business to do so; and yet, however much he endeavoured to think of other things, he found this question occupying his whole mind long after his return to the village hotel.

She was such a mystery, this woman, it might easily be that she had never intended to go to Buffalo; that she had only spoken of that place as the point of her destination under the stress of her companion's importunities, and that the real place for which she was bound had been some spot very much nearer home.

The fact, that her baggage had consisted only of a small bag that she carried on her arm, would lend probability to this idea, yet, such was the generous character of the young detective, he hesitated to give credit to this suspicion, and indeed took every pains to disabuse himself of it by inquiring of the ticket-agent, whether it was true, as he had heard, that Miss Dare had left town on that day for a visit to her friends in Buffalo.

He received for his reply that she had bought a ticket for that place, though she evidently had not used it, a fact which seemed at least to prove she was honest in the expression of her intentions that morning, whatever alteration may have taken place in her plans during the course of her journey.

Mr. Byrd did not enjoy his supper that night, and was heartily glad when, in a few moments after its completion, Mr. Ferris came in for a chat and a cigar.

They had many things to discuss. First, their own case now drawing to a successful close; next, the murder of the day before; and lastly, the few facts which had been elicited in regard to that murder, in the inquiry which had that day been begun before the coroner.

Of the latter Mr. Ferris spoke with much interest. He had attended the inquest himself, and, though he had not much to communicate— the time having been mainly taken up in selecting and swearing in a jury—a few witnesses had been examined and certain conclusions reached, which certainly added greatly to the impression already made upon the public mind, that an affair of great importance had arisen; an affair, too, promising more in the way of mystery than the simple nature of its earlier manifestations gave them reason to suppose.

In the first place, the widow had evidently been assaulted with a deliberate purpose and a serious intent to slay.

Secondly, no immediate testimony was forthcoming calculated to point with unerring certainty to the guilty party.

To be sure, the tramp and the hunchback still offered possibilities of suspicion; but even they were slight, the former having been seen to leave the widow's house without entering, and the latter having been proved beyond a question to have come into town on the morning train and to have gone at once to court where he remained till the time they all saw him disappear down the street.

That the last-mentioned individual may have had some guilty knowledge of the crime was possible enough. The fact of his having wiped himself out so completely as to elude all search, was suspicious in itself, but if he was connected with the assault it must have been simply as an accomplice employed to distract public attention from the real criminal; and in a case like this, the interest naturally centres with the actual perpetrator; and the question was now and must be: Who was the man who, in broad daylight, dared to enter a house situated like this in a thickly populated street, and kill with a blow an inoffensive woman?

"I cannot imagine," declared Mr. Ferris, as his communication reached this point. "It looks as if she had an enemy, but what enemy could such a person as she possess—a woman who always did her own work, attended to her own affairs, and made it an especial rule of her life never to meddle with those of anybody else?"

"Was she such a woman?" inquired Mr. Byrd, to whom as yet no knowledge had come of the widow's life, habits, or character.

"Yes. In all the years I have been in this town I have never heard of her visiting anyone or encouraging anyone to visit her. Had it not been for Mr. Orcutt, she would have lived the life of a recluse. As it was, she was the most methodical person in her ways that I ever knew. At just such an hour she rose; at just such an hour put on her kettle, cooked her meal, washed her dishes, and sat herself down to her sewing or whatever work it was she had to do. The dinner was the only meal that waited, and that, Mr. Orcutt says, was always ready and done to a turn at whatever moment he chose to present himself."

"Had she no intimates, no relatives?" asked Mr. Byrd, remembering that fragment of a letter he had read—a letter which certainly contradicted this assertion in regard to her even and quiet life.

"None that I am aware of," was the response. "Wait, I believe I have been told she has a nephew somewhere—a sister's son, for whom she had some regard and to whom she intended to leave her money."

"She had money, then?"

"Some five thousand, maybe. Reports differ about such matters."

"And this nephew, where does he live?"

"I cannot tell you. I don't know as anyone can. My remembrances in regard to him are of the vaguest character."

"Five thousand dollars is regarded as no mean sum in a town like this," quoth Mr. Byrd, carelessly.

"I know it. She is called quite rich by many. How she got her money no one knows; for when she first came here she was so poor she had to eat and sleep all in one room. Mr. Orcutt paid her something for his daily dinner, of course, but that could not have enabled her to put ten dollars in the bank as she has done every week for the last ten years. And to all appearances she has done nothing else for her living. You see, we have paid attention to her affairs, if she has paid none to ours."

Mr. Byrd again remembered that scrap of a letter which had been shown him by the coroner, and thought to himself that their knowledge was in all probability less than they supposed.

"Who was that horrid crone I saw shouldering herself through the crowd that collected around the gate yesterday?" was his remark, however. "Do you remember a wizen, toothless old wretch, whose eye has more of the Evil One in it than that of many a young thief you see locked up in the county jails?"

"No; that is, I wonder if you mean Sally Perkins. She is old enough and ugly enough to answer your description; and, now I think of it, she *has* a way of leering at you as you go by that is slightly suggestive of a somewhat bitter knowledge of the world. What makes you ask about her?"

"Because she attracted my attention, I suppose. You must remember that I don't know any of these people, and that an especially vicious-looking person like her would be apt to awaken my curiosity."

"I see, I see; but, in this case, I doubt if it leads to much. Old Sally is a hard one, no doubt. But I don't believe she ever contemplated a murder, much less accomplished it. It would take too much courage, to say nothing of strength. It was a man's hand struck that blow, Mr. Byrd."

"Yes," was the quick reply—a reply given somewhat too quickly, perhaps, for it made Mr. Ferris look up inquiringly at the young man.

"You take considerable interest in the affair," he remarked, shortly. "Well, I do not wonder. Even my old blood has been somewhat fired by its peculiar features. I foresee that your detective instinct will soon lead you to risk a run at the game."

"Ah, then, you see no objection to my trying for the scent, if the coroner persists in demanding it?" inquired Mr. Byrd, as he followed the other to the door.

"On the contrary," was the polite response.

And Mr. Byrd found himself satisfied on that score.

Mr. Ferris had no sooner left the room than the coroner came in.

"Well," cried he, with no unnecessary delay, "I want you."

Mr. Byrd rose.

"Have you telegraphed to New York?" he asked.

"Yes, and expect an answer every minute. There will be no difficulty about that. The superintendent is my friend, and will not be likely to cross me in my expressed wish."

"But——" essayed the detective.

"We have no time for buts," broke in the coroner. "The inquest begins in earnest tomorrow, and the one witness we most want has not yet been found. I mean the man or the woman who can swear to seeing someone approach or enter the murdered woman's house between the time the milkman left it at half-past eleven and the hour she was found by Mr. Orcutt, lying upon the floor of her dining-room in a dying condition. That such a witness exists I have no doubt. A street in which there are six houses, everyone of which has to be passed by the person entering Widow Clemmens' gate, must produce one individual, at least, who can swear to what I want. To be sure, all whom I have questioned so far say that they were either eating dinner at the time or were in the kitchen serving it up; but, for all that, there were plenty who saw the tramp, and two women, at least, who are ready to take their oath that they not only saw him, but watched him long enough to observe him go around to the Widow Clemmens' kitchen door and turn about again and come away as if for some reason he had changed his mind about entering.

"Now, if there were two witnesses to see all that, there must have been one somewhere to notice that other person, known or unknown, who went through the street but a few minutes before the tramp. At all events, I believe such a witness can be found, and I mean to have him if I call up every man, woman, and child who was in the lane at the time. But a little foreknowledge helps a coroner wonderfully, and if you will aid me by making judicious inquiries round about, time will be gained, and, perhaps, a clue obtained that will lead to a direct knowledge of the perpetrator of this crime."

"But," inquired the detective, willing, at least, to discuss the subject with the coroner, "is it absolutely necessary that the murderer should have advanced from the street? Is there no way he could have reached the house from the back, and so have eluded the gaze of the neighbours round about?"

"No; that is, there is no regular path there, only a stretch of swampy ground, anything but pleasant to travel through. Of course a man with a deliberate purpose before him might pursue that route and subject himself to all its inconveniences; but I would scarcely expect it of one who—who chose such an hour for his assault," the coroner explained, with a slight stammer of embarrassment that did not escape the detective's notice. "Nor shall I feel ready to entertain the idea till it has been proved that no person, with the exception of those already named, was seen any time during that fatal half-hour to advance by the usual way to the widow's house."

"Have you questioned the tramp, or in any way received from him an intimation of the reason why he did not go into the house after he came to it?"

"He said he heard voices quarrelling."

"Ah!"

"Of course he was not upon his oath, but as the statement was volunteered, we have some right to credit it, perhaps."

"Did he say"—it was Mr. Byrd now who lost a trifle of his fluen-cy—"what sort of voices he heard?"

"No; he is an ignorant wretch, and is moreover thoroughly fright-ened. I don't believe he would know a cultivated from an uncultivated voice, a gentleman's from a quarryman's. At all events, we cannot trust to his discrimination."

Mr. Byrd started. This was the last construction he had expected to be put upon his question. Flushing a trifle, he looked the coroner earnestly in the face. But that gentleman was too absorbed in the train of thought raised by his own remark to notice the look, and Mr. Byrd, not feeling any too well assured of his own position, forbore to utter the words that hovered on his tongue.

"I have another commission for you," resumed the coroner, after a moment. "Here is a name which I wish you would look at——"

But at this instant a smart tap was heard at the door, and a boy entered with the expected telegram from New York. Dr. Tredwell took it, and, after glancing at its contents with an annoyed look, folded up the paper he was about to hand to Mr. Byrd and put it slowly back into his pocket. He then referred again to the telegram.

"It is not what I expected," he said, shortly, after a moment of perplexed thought. "It seems that the superintendent is not disposed to accommodate me." And he tossed over the telegram.

Mr. Byrd took it and read:

"Expect a suitable man by the midnight express. He will bring a letter."

A flush mounted to the detective's brow.

"You see, sir," he observed, "I was right when I told you I was not the man."

"I don't know," returned the other, rising. "I have not changed my opinion. The man they send may be very keen and very well-up in his business, but I doubt if he will manage this case any better than you would have done," and he moved quietly toward the door.

"Thank you for your too favourable opinion of my skill," said Mr. Byrd, as he bowed the other out. "I am sure the superintendent is right. I am not much accustomed to work for myself, and was none too eager to take the case in the first place, as you will do me the justice to remember. I can but feel relieved at this shifting of the responsibility upon shoulders more fitted to bear it."

Yet, when the coroner was gone, and he sat down alone by himself to review the matter, he found he was in reality more disappointed than he cared to confess. Why, he scarcely knew. There was no lessening of the shrinking he had always felt from the possible developments which an earnest inquiry into the causes of this crime might educe. Yet, to be severed in this way from all professional interest in the pursuit cut him so deeply that, in despite of his usual good-sense and correct judgement, he was never nearer sending in his resignation than he was in that short half-hour which followed the departure of Dr. Tredwell. To distract his thoughts, he at last went down to the bar-room.

6

The Skill of an Artist

He found it occupied by some half-dozen men, one of whom immediately attracted his attention, by his high-bred air and total absorption in the paper he was reading. He was evidently a stranger, and, though not without some faint marks of a tendency to gentlemanly dissipation, was, to say the least, more than ordinarily good-looking, possessing a large, manly figure, and a fair, regular-featured face, above which shone a thick crop of short curly hair of a peculiarly bright blond colour. He was sitting at a small table, drawn somewhat apart from the rest, and was, as I have said, engrossed with a newspaper, to the utter exclusion of any apparent interest in the talk that was going on at the other end of the room.

And yet this talk was of the most animated description, and was seemingly of a nature to attract the attention of the most indifferent. At all events Mr. Byrd considered it so; and, after one comprehensive glance at the elegant stranger, that took in not only the personal characteristics I have noted, but also the frown of deep thought or anxious care that furrowed a naturally smooth forehead, he passed quietly up the room and took his stand among the group of loungers there assembled.

Mr. Byrd was not unknown to the *habitués* of that place, and no cessation took place in the conversation. They were discussing an occurrence slight enough in itself, but made interesting and dramatic by the unconscious enthusiasm of the chief speaker, a young fellow of indifferent personal appearance, but with a fervid flow of words and a knack at presenting a subject that reminded you of the actor's power, and made you as anxious to watch his gesticulations as to hear the words that accompanied them.

"I tell you," he was saying, "that it was just a leaf out of a play. I

208

never saw its equal off the stage. She was so handsome, so impressive in her trouble or anxiety, or whatever it was that agitated her, and he so dark, and so determined in *his* trouble or anxiety, or whatever it was that agitated him. They came in at different doors, she at one side of the depot and he at another, and they met just where I could see them both, directly in the centre of the room. 'You!' was her involuntary cry, and she threw up her hands before her face just as if she had seen a ghost or a demon.

"An equal exclamation burst from him, but he did not cover his eyes, only stood and looked at her as if he were turned to stone. In another moment she dropped her hands. 'Were you coming to see *me?*' came from her lips in a whisper so fraught with secret horror and anguish that it curdled my blood to hear it. 'Were you coming to see *me?*' was his response, uttered in an equally suppressed voice and with an equal intensity of expression. And then, without either giving an answer to the other's question, they both shrank back, and, turning, fled with distracted looks, each by the way they had come, the two doors closing with a simultaneous bang that echoed through that miserable depot like a knell. There were not many folks in the room just at that minute, but I tell you those that were looked at each other as they had not done before and would not be likely to do again. Some unhappy tragedy underlies such a meeting and parting, gentlemen, and I for one would rather not inquire what."

"But the girl—the man—didn't you see them again before you left?" asked an eager voice from the group.

"The young lady," remarked the other, "was on the train that brought me here. The gentleman went the other way."

"Oh!" "Ah!" and "Where did she get off?" rose in a somewhat deafening clamor around him.

"I did not observe. She seemed greatly distressed, if not thoroughly overcome, and observing her pull down her veil, I thought she did not relish my inquiring looks, and as I could not sit within view of her and not watch her, I discreetly betook myself into the smoking-car, where I stayed till we arrived at this place."

"Hum!" "Ha!" "Curious!" rose in chorus once more, and then, the general sympathies of the crowd being exhausted, two or three or more of the group sauntered up to the bar, and the rest sidled restlessly out of the room, leaving the enthusiastic speaker alone with Mr. Byrd.

"A strange scene!" exclaimed the latter, infusing just enough of seeming interest into his usually nonchalant tone to excite the vanity of the person he addressed, and make him more than ever ready to talk. "I wish I had been in your place," continued Mr. Byrd, almost enthusiastically. "I am sure I could have made a picture of that scene that would have been very telling in the gazette I draw for."

"Do you make pictures for papers?" the young fellow inquired, his respect visibly rising.

"Sometimes," the imperturbable detective replied, and in so doing told no more than the truth. He had a rare talent for off-hand sketching, and not infrequently made use of it to increase the funds of the family.

"Well, that is something I would like to do," acknowledged the youth, surveying the other over with curious eyes. "But I haven't a cent's worth of talent for it. I can see a scene in my mind now—this one for instance—just as plain as I can see you; all the details of it, you know, the way they stood, the clothes they wore, the looks on their faces, and all that, but when I try to put it on paper, why, I just can't, that's all."

"Your forte lies another way," remarked Mr. Byrd. "You can present a scene so vividly that a person who had not seen it for himself, might easily put it on paper just from your description. See now!" And he caught up a sheet of paper from the desk and carried it to a side table. "Just tell me what depot this was in."

The young fellow, greatly interested at once, leaned over the detective's shoulder and eagerly replied: "The depot at Syracuse."

Mr. Byrd nodded and made a few strokes with his pencil on the paper before him.

"How was the lady dressed?" he next asked.

"In blue; dark blue cloth, fitting like a glove. Fine figure, you know, very tall and unusually large, but perfect, I assure you, perfect. Yes, that is very like it," he went on watching the quick, assured strokes of the other with growing wonder and an unbounded admiration. "You have caught the exact poise of the head, as I live, and—yes, a large hat with two feathers, sir, two feathers drooping over the side, so; a bag on the arm; two flounces on the skirt; a—oh! the face? Well, handsome, sir, very handsome; straight nose, large eyes, determined mouth, strong, violently agitated expression. Well, I will give up! A photograph couldn't have done her better justice. You are a genius, sir, a genius!"

Mr. Byrd received this tribute to his skill with some confusion and a deep blush, which he vainly sought to hide by bending lower over his work.

"The man, now," he suggested, with the least perceptible change in his voice, that, however, escaped the attention of his companion. "What was he like; young or old?"

"Well, young—about twenty-five I should say; medium height, but very firmly and squarely built, with a strong face, large moustache, brilliant eyes, and a look—I cannot describe it, but you have caught that of the lady so well, you will, doubtless, succeed in getting his also."

But Mr. Byrd's pencil moved with less certainty now, and it was some time before he could catch even the peculiarly sturdy aspect of the figure which made this unknown gentleman, as the young fellow declared, look like a modern Hercules, though he was far from being either large or tall. The face, too, presented difficulties he was far from experiencing in the case of the lady, and the young fellow at his side was obliged to make several suggestions such as:—"A little more hair on the forehead, if you please—there was quite a lock showing beneath his hat;" or, "A trifle less sharpness to the chin,—so;" or, "Stay, you have it too square now; tone it down a hair's breadth, and you will get it," before he received even the somewhat hesitating acknowledgment from the other of: "There, that is something like him!"

But he had not expected to succeed very well in this part of the picture, and was sufficiently pleased to have gained a very correct notion of the style of clothing the gentleman wore, which, it is needless to state, was most faithfully reproduced in the sketch, even if the exact expression of the strong and masculine face was not.

"A really remarkable bit of work," admitted the young fellow when the whole was completed. "And as true to the scene, too, as half the illustrations given in the weekly papers. Would you mind letting me have it as a *souvenir?*" he eagerly inquired. "I would like to show it to a chap who was with me at the time. The likeness to the lady is wonderful."

But Mr. Byrd, with his most careless air, had already thrust the picture into his pocket, from which he refused to withdraw it, saying, with an easy laugh, that it might come in play with him some time, and that he could not afford to part with it. At which remark the young fellow looked disappointed and vaguely rattled some coins he had in his pocket; but, meeting with no encouragement from the other, forbore to press his request, and turned it into an invitation to join him in a social glass at the bar.

To this slight token of appreciation Mr. Byrd did not choose to turn a deaf ear. So the drinks being ordered, he proceeded to clink glasses with the youthful stranger, taking the opportunity, at the same time, of glancing over to the large, well-built man whose quiet absorption in the paper he was reading had so attracted his attention when he first came in.

To his surprise he found that person just as engrossed in the news as ever, not a feature or an eyelash appearing to have moved since the time he looked at him last.

Mr. Byrd was so astonished at this that when he left the room a few minutes later he took occasion in passing the gentleman, to glance at the paper he was studying so industriously, and, to his surprise, found it to be nothing more nor less than the advertising sheet of the New York *Herald*.

"A fellow of my own craft," was his instantaneous conclusion. But a moment's consideration assured him that this could not be, as no detective worthy the name would place so little value upon the understanding of those about him as to sit for a half-hour with his eyes upon a sheet of paper totally devoid of news, no matter what his purpose might be, or how great was his interest in the conversation to which he was secretly listening. No; this gentleman was doubtless what he seemed to be, a mere stranger, with something of a serious and engrossing nature upon his mind, or else he was an amateur, who for some reason was acting the part of a detective without either the skill or experience of one.

Whichever theory might be true, this gentleman was a person who at this time and in this place was well worth watching: that is, if a man had any reason for interesting himself in the pursuit of possible clues to the mystery of Mrs. Clemmens' murder. But Mr. Byrd felt that he no longer possessed a professional right to such interest; so, leaving behind him this fine-looking gentleman, together with all the inevitable conjectures which the latter's peculiar manner had irresistibly awakened, he proceeded to regain his room and enter upon that contemplation of the picture he had just made, which was naturally demanded by his regard for one of the persons there depicted.

It was a vigorous sketch, and the slow blush crept up and dyed Mr. Byrd's forehead as he gazed at it and realized the perfection of the likeness he had drawn of Miss Dare. Yes, that was her form, her face, her expression, her very self. She it was and no other who had been the heroine of the strange scene enacted that day in the Syracuse depot; a scene to which, by means of this impromptu sketch, he had now become as nearly a witness as anyone could hope for who had not been actually upon the spot. Strange! And he had been so anxious to know what had altered the mind of this lady and sent her back to Sibley before her journey was half completed—had pondered so long and vainly upon the whys and wherefores of an action whose motive he had never expected to understand, but which he now saw suggested in a scene that seriously whetted, if it did not thoroughly satisfy, his curiosity.

The moment he had chosen to portray was that in which the eyes of the two met and their first instinctive recoil took place. Turning his attention from the face of the lady and bestowing it upon that of the man, he perceived there the horror and shrinking which he had imprinted so successfully upon hers. That the expression was true, though the countenance was not, he had no doubt. The man, whatever his name, nature, calling, or history, recoiled from a meeting with Imogene Dare as passionately as she did from one with him. Both had started from home with a simultaneous intention of seeking the other, and yet, at the first recognition of this fact, both had started and drawn back as if death rather than life had confronted them in each other's faces. What did it mean?

What secret of a deep and deadly nature could lie between these two, that a scene of such evident import could take place between them? He dared not think; he could do nothing but gaze upon the figure of the man he had portrayed, and wonder if he would be able to identify the original in case he ever met him. The face was more or less a failure, of course, but the form, the cut of the clothes, the manner of carriage, and the general aspect of strong and puissant manhood which distinguished the whole figure, could not be so far from correct but that, with a hint from surrounding circumstances, he would know the man himself when he saw him. At all events, he meant to imprint the possible portrait upon his mind in case——in case what? Pausing he asked himself this question with stern determination, and could find no answer.

"I will burn the sketch at once, and think of it and her no more," he muttered, half-rising.

But he did not do it. Some remembrance crossed his mind of what the young fellow downstairs had said about retaining it as a *souvenir*, and he ended in folding it up and putting it away somewhat carefully in his memorandum-book, with a vow that he would leave Sibley and its troublous mystery at the first moment of release that he could possibly obtain. The pang which this decision cost him convinced him that it was indeed high time he did so.

Miss Firman

Mr. Byrd, upon waking next morning, found himself disturbed by a great perplexity. Were the words then ringing in his ears, real words, which he had overheard spoken outside of his door sometime during the past night, or were they merely the empty utterances of a more than usually vivid dream?

He could not tell. He could remember the very tone of voice in which he fancied them to have been spoken—a tone which he had no difficulty in recognizing as that of the landlord of the hotel; could even recall the faint sounds of bustle which accompanied them, as though the person using them had been showing another person through the hall; but beyond that, all was indistinct and dream-like.

The words were these:

Glad to see you back, sir. This murder following so close upon your visit must have been a great surprise. A sad occurrence, that, sir, and a very mysterious one. Hope you have some information to give.

"If it is a remembrance and such words were uttered outside of my door last night," argued the young detective to himself, "the guest who called them forth can be no other than the tall and florid gentleman whom I encountered in the bar-room. But is it a remembrance, or only a *chimera* of my own overwrought brain struggling with a subject it will not let drop? As Shakespeare says, *That is the question!*"

Fortunately, it was not one which it behoved him to decide. So, for the twentieth time, he put the subject by and resolved to think of it no more.

But perplexities of this kind are not so easily dismissed, and more than once during his hurried and solitary breakfast, did he ask himself whether, in case the words were real, he had not found in the land-lord of this very hotel the one witness for which the coroner was so diligently seeking.

A surprise awaited him after breakfast, in the sudden appearance at his room door of the very gentleman last alluded to.

"Ha, Byrd," said he, with cheerful vivacity: "here is a line from the superintendent which may prove interesting to you."

And with a complacent smile, Dr. Tredwell handed over a letter which had been brought to him by the detective who had that morning arrived from New York.

With a dim sense of foreboding which he would have found difficult to explain, Mr. Byrd opened the note and read the following words:

Dear Sir,—I send with this a man fully competent to conduct a case of any ordinary difficulty. I acknowledge it is for our interest that you employ him to the exclusion of the person mentioned in your letter. But if you or that person think that he can render you any real assistance by his interference, he is at liberty to act in his capacity of detective in as far as he can do so without divulging too widely the secret of his connection with the force. —— ——.

"The superintendent need not be concerned," said Mr. Byrd, returning the note with a constrained bow. "I shall not interfere in this matter."

"You will miss a good thing, then," remarked the coroner, shortly, looking keenly at the young man.

"I cannot help it," observed the other, with a quick sigh of impatience or regret. "I should have to see my duty very clearly and possess the very strongest reasons for interfering before I presumed to offer either advice or assistance after a letter of this kind."

"And who knows but what such reasons may yet present themselves?" ventured the coroner. Then seeing the young man shake his head, made haste to add in the business-like tone of one preparing to take his leave, "At all events the matter stands open for the present; and if during the course of today's inquiry you see fit to change your mind, it will be easy enough for you to notify me." And without waiting for any further remonstrance, he gave a quick nod and passed hastily out.

The state of mind in which he left Mr. Byrd was anything but enviable. Not that the young man's former determination to let this matter alone had been in any wise shaken by the unexpected concession on the part of the superintendent, but that the final hint concerning the inquest had aroused his old interest to quite a formidable degree, and, what was worse, had reawakened certain feelings which since last night it had been his most earnest endeavour to subdue. He felt like a man pursued by an implacable fate, and dimly wondered whether he would be allowed to escape before it was too late to save himself from lasting uneasiness, if not lifelong regret.

A final stroke of business for Mr. Ferris kept him at the courthouse most of the morning; but his duty in that direction being at an end, he no longer found any excuse for neglecting the task imposed upon him by the coroner. He accordingly proceeded to the cottage where the inquest was being held, and finding each and every available room there packed to its uttermost by interested spectators, took up his stand on the outside of a curtained window, where with but a slight craning of his neck he could catch a very satisfactory view of the different witnesses as they appeared before the jury.

The day was warm and he was by no means uncomfortable, though he could have wished that the advantages of his position had occasioned less envy in the breasts of the impatient crowd that was slowly gathering at his back; or, rather, that their sense of these advantages might have been expressed in some more pleasing way than by the various pushes he received from the more or less adventurous spirits who endeavoured to raise themselves over his shoulder or insinuate themselves under his arms.

The room into which he looked was the sitting-room, and it was, so far as he could judge in the first casual glance he threw into it, occupied entirely by strangers. This was a relief. Since it had become his duty to attend this inquiry, he wished to do so with a free mind, unhindered by the watchfulness of those who knew his interest in the affair, or by the presence of persons around whom his own imagination had involuntarily woven a network of suspicion that made his observation of them at once significant and painful.

The proceedings were at a standstill when he first came upon the scene.

A witness had just stepped aside, who, from the impatient shrugs of many persons present, had evidently added little if anything to the testimony already given. Taking advantage of the moment, Mr. Byrd leaned forward and addressed a burly man who sat directly under

217

him.

"What have they been doing all the morning?" he asked. "Anything important?"

"No," was the surly reply. "A score of folks have had their say, but not one of them has told anything worth listening to. Nobody has seen anything, nobody knows anything. The murderer might have risen up through the floor to deal his blow, and having given it, sunk back again with the same supernatural claptrap, for all these stupid people seem to know about him."

The man had a loud voice, and as he made no attempt to modulate it, his words were heard on all sides. Naturally many heads were turned toward him, and more than one person looked at him with an amused smile. Indeed, of all the various individuals in his immediate vicinity, only one forbore to take any notice of his remark. This was a heavy, lymphatic, and somewhat abstracted-looking fellow of nondescript appearance, who stood stiff and straight as an exclamation point against the jamb of the doorway that led into the front hall.

"But have no facts been obtained, no conclusions reached, that would serve to awaken suspicion or put justice on the right track?" pursued Mr. Byrd, lowering his voice in intimation for the other to do the same.

But that other was of an obstinate tendency, and his reply rose full and loud.

"No, unless it can be considered proved that it is only folly to try and find out who commits a crime in these days. Nothing else has come to light, as far as I can see, and that much we all knew before."

A remark of this kind was not calculated to allay the slight inclination to mirth which his former observation had raised; but the coroner rapping with his gavel on the table at this moment, every other consideration was lost in the natural curiosity which everyone felt as to who the next witness would be.

But the coroner had something to say before he called for further testimony.

"Gentlemen," he remarked, in a clear and commanding tone that at once secured attention and awakened interest, "we have spent the morning in examining the persons who live in this street, with a view to ascertaining, if possible, who was in conversation with Mrs. Clemmens at the time the tramp went up to her door."

Was it a coincidence, or was there something in the words themselves that called forth the stir that at this moment took place among the people assembled directly before Mr. Byrd? It was of the slightest character, and was merely momentary in its duration; nevertheless, it attracted his attention, especially as it seemed to have its origin in a portion of the room shut off from his observation by the corner of the wall already alluded to.

The coroner proceeded without pause.

"The result, as you know, has not been satisfactory. No one seems to be able to tell us who it was that visited Mrs. Clemmens on that day. I now propose to open another examination of a totally different character, which I hope may be more conclusive in its results. Miss Firman, are you prepared to give your testimony?"

Immediately a tall, gaunt, but pleasant-faced woman arose from the dim recesses of the parlour. She was dressed with decency, if not taste, and took her stand before the jury with a lady-like yet perfectly assured air that promised well for the correctness and discretion of her answers. The coroner at once addressed her.

"Your full name, madam?"

"Emily Letitia Firman, sir."

"Emily!" ejaculated Mr. Byrd, to himself, with a throb of sudden interest. "That is the name of the murdered woman's correspondent."

"Your birthplace," pursued the coroner, "and the place of your present residence?"

"I was born in Danbury, Connecticut," was the reply, "and I am living in Utica, where I support my aged mother by dress-making."

"How are you related to Mrs. Clemmens, the lady who was found murdered here two days ago?"

"I am her second cousin; her grandmother and my mother were sisters."

"Upon what terms have you always lived, and what can you tell us of her other relatives and connections?"

"We have always been friends, and I can tell you all that is generally known of the two or three remaining persons of her blood and kindred. They are, first, my mother and myself, who, as I have before said, live in Utica, where I am connected with the dress-making establishment of Madame Trebelle; and, secondly, a nephew of hers, the son of a favourite brother, whom she has always supported, and to whom she has frequently avowed her intention of leaving her accumulated savings."

"The name of this gentleman and his place of residence?"

"His name is Mansell—Craik Mansell—and he lives in Buffalo,

where he has a situation of some trust in the large paper manufactory of Harrison, Goodman, & Chamberlin."

Buffalo! Mr. Byrd gave an involuntary start, and became, if possible, doubly attentive.

The coroner's questions went on.

"Do you know this young man?"

"Yes, sir. He has been several times to our house in the course of the last five years."

"What can you tell us of his nature and disposition, as well as of his regard for the woman who proposed to benefit him so materially by her will?"

"Well, sir," returned Miss Firman, "it is hard to read the nature and feelings of any man who has much character, and Craik Mansell has a good deal of character. But I have always thought him a very honest and capable young man, who might do us credit some day, if he were allowed to have his own way and not be interfered with too much. As for his feelings toward his aunt, they were doubtless those of gratitude, though I have never heard him express himself in any very affection-ate terms toward her, owing, no doubt, to a natural reticence of dispo-sition which has been observable in him from childhood."

"You have, however, no reason to believe he cherished any feelings of animosity toward his benefactress?" continued the coroner, some-what carelessly, "or possessed any inordinate desire after the money she was expecting to leave him at her death?"

"No, sir. Both having minds of their own, they frequently disa-greed, especially on business matters; but there was never any bit-terness between them, as far as I know, and I never heard him say anything about his expectations one way or the other. He is a man of much natural force, of strong, if not violent, traits of character; but he has too keen a sense of his own dignity to intimate the existence of desires so discreditable to him."

There was something in this reply and the impartial aspect of the lady delivering it that was worthy of notice, perhaps. And such it would have undoubtedly received from Mr. Byrd, at least, if the words she had used in characterizing this person had not struck him so deeply that he forgot to note anything further.

"A man of great natural force—of strong, if not violent traits of character," he kept repeating to himself. "The description, as I live, of the person whose picture I attempted to draw last night."

And, ignoring everything else, he waited with almost sickening expectation for the question that would link this nephew of Mrs. Clemmens either to the tragedy itself, or to that person still in the background, of whose secret connection with a man of this type, he had obtained so curious and accidental a knowledge.

But it did not come. With a quiet abandonment of the by no means exhausted topic, which convinced Mr. Byrd that the coroner had plans and suspicions to which the foregoing questions had given no clue, Dr. Tredwell leaned slowly forward, and, after surveying the witness with a glance of cautious inquiry, asked in a way to concentrate the attention of all present:

"You say that you knew the Widow Clemmens well; that you have always been on friendly terms with her, and are acquainted with her affairs. Does that mean you have been made a confidante of her troubles, her responsibilities, and her cares?"

"Yes, sir; that is, in as far as she ever made a confidant of anyone. Mrs. Clemmens was not of a complaining disposition, neither was she by nature very communicative. Only at rare times did she make mention of herself or her troubles: but when she did, it was invariably to me, sir—or so she used to say; and she was not a woman to deceive you in such matters."

"Very well, then, you are in a position to tell us something of her history, and why it is she kept herself so close after she came to this town?"

But Miss Firman uttered a vigorous disclaimer to this. "No, sir," said she, "I am not. Mrs. Clemmens' history was simple enough, but her reasons for living as she did have never been explained. She was not naturally a quiet woman, and, when a girl, was remarkable for her spirits and fondness for company."

"Has she had any great sorrow since you knew her—any serious loss or disappointment that may have soured her disposition, and turned her, as it were, against the world?"

"Perhaps; she felt the death of her husband very much—indeed, has never been quite the same since she lost him."

"And when was that, if you please?"

"Full fifteen years ago, sir; just before she came to this town."

"Did you know Mr. Clemmens?"

"No, sir; none of us knew him. They were married in some small village out West, where he died—well, I think she wrote—a month if not less after their marriage. She was inconsolable for a time, and, though she consented to come East, refused to take up her abode with

221

any of her relatives, and so settled in this place, where she has remained ever since."

The manner of the coroner suddenly changed to one of great impressiveness.

"Miss Firman," he now asked, "did it ever strike you that the hermit life she led was due to any fear or apprehension which she may have secretly entertained?"

"Sir?"

The question was peculiar and no one wondered at the start which the good woman gave. But what mainly struck Mr. Byrd, and gave to the moment a seeming importance, was the fact that she was not alone in her surprise or even her expression of it; that the indefinable stir he had before observed had again taken place in the crowd before him, and that this time there was no doubt about its having been occasioned by the movements of a person whose elbow he could just perceive projecting beyond the door-way that led into the hall.

But there was no time for speculation as to whom this person might be. The coroner's questions were every moment growing more rapid, and Miss Firman's answers more interesting.

"I asked," here the coroner was heard to say, "whether, in your intercourse with Mrs. Clemmens, you have ever had reason to suppose she was the victim of any secret or personal apprehension that might have caused her to seclude herself as she did? Or let me put it in another way. Can you tell me whether you know of any other person besides this nephew of hers who is likely to be benefited by Mrs. Clemmens' death?"

"Oh, sir," was the hasty and somewhat excited reply, "you mean young Mr. Hildreth!"

The way in which this was said, together with the slight flush of satisfaction or surprise which rose to the coroner's brow, naturally awoke the slumbering excitement of the crowd and made a small sensation. A low murmur ran through the rooms, amid which Mr. Byrd thought he heard a suppressed but bitter exclamation. He could not be sure of it, however, and had just made up his mind that his ears had deceived him, when his attention was attracted by a shifting in the position of the sturdy, thick-set man who had been leaning against the opposite wall, but who now crossed and took his stand beside the jamb, on the other side of which sat the unknown individual toward whom so many inquiring glances had hitherto been directed.

The quietness with which this change was made, and the slight,

almost imperceptible, alteration in the manner of the person making it, brought a sudden enlightenment to Mr. Byrd, and he at once
made up his mind that this dull, abstracted-looking nonentity leaning
with such apparent unconcern against the wall, was the new detective
who had been sent up that morning from New York. His curiosity
in regard to the identity of the individual round the corner was not
lessened by this.

Meantime the coroner had answered the hasty exclamation of the
witness, by disclaiming the existence of any special meaning of his
own, and had furthermore pressed the question as to who this Mr.
Hildreth was.

She immediately answered: "A gentleman of Toledo, sir; a young
man who could only come into his property by the death of Mrs.
Clemmens."

"How? You have not spoken of any such person as connected with
her."

"No," was her steady response; "nor was he so connected by any
tie of family or friendship. Indeed, I do not know as they were ever
acquainted, or, as for that matter, ever saw each other's faces. The fact
to which I allude was simply the result of a will, sir, made by Mr. Hildreth's grandfather."

"A will? Explain yourself. I do not understand."

"Well, sir, I do not know much about the law, and may make a
dozen mistakes in telling you what you wish to know; but what I
understand about the matter is this: Mr. Hildreth, the grandfather of
the gentleman of whom I have just spoken, having a large property,
which he wanted to leave in bulk to his grandchildren,—their father
being a very dissipated and reckless man,—made his will in such a
way as to prevent its distribution among his heirs till after the death
of two persons whom he mentioned by name. Of these two persons
one was the son of his head clerk, a young boy, who sickened and died
shortly after Mr. Hildreth himself, and the other my cousin, the poor
murdered woman, who was then a little girl visiting the family. I do
not know how she came to be chosen by him for this purpose, unless
it was that she was particularly round and ruddy as a child, and looked
as if she might live for many years."

"And the Hildreths? What of them during these years?"

"Well, I cannot exactly say, as I never had any acquaintance with
them myself. But I know that the father, whose dissipated habits were
the cause of this peculiar will tying up the property, died some little

time ago; also one or two of his children, but beyond that I know little, except that the remaining heirs are a young gentleman and one or two young girls, all of the worldliest and most fashionable description."

The coroner, who had followed all this with the greatest interest, now asked if she knew the first name of the young gentleman.

"Yes," said she, "I do. It is Gouverneur."

The coroner gave a satisfied nod, and remarked casually, "It is not a common name," and then, leaning forward, selected a paper from among several that lay on the table before him. "Miss Firman," he inquired, retaining this paper in his hand, "do you know when it was that Mrs. Clemmens first became acquainted with the fact of her name having been made use of in the elder Mr. Hildreth's will?"

"Oh, years ago; when she first came of age, I believe."

"Was it an occasion of regret to her? Did she ever express herself as sorry for the position in which she stood toward this family?"

"Yes, sir; she did."

The coroner's face assumed a yet greater gravity, and his manner became more and more impressive.

"Can you go a step farther and say that she ever acknowledged herself to have cherished apprehensions of her personal safety, during these years of weary waiting on the part of the naturally impatient heirs?"

A distressed look crossed the amiable spinster's face, and she looked around at the jury with an expression almost deprecatory in its nature.

"I scarcely know what answer to give," she hesitatingly declared. "It is a good deal to say that she was apprehensive; but I cannot help remembering that she once told me her peace of mind had left her since she knew there were persons in the world to whom her death would be a matter of rejoicing. 'It makes me feel as if I were keeping people out of their rights,' she remarked at the same time. 'And, though it is not my fault, I should not be surprised if some day I had to suffer for it.'"

"Was there ever any communication made to Mrs. Clemmens by persons cognizant of the relation in which she stood to these Hildreths?—or any facts or gossip detailed to her concerning them, that would seem to give colour to her fears and supply her with any actual grounds for her apprehensions?"

"No; only such tales as came to her of their expensive ways of living and somewhat headlong rush into all fashionable freaks and follies."

"And Gouverneur Hildreth? Any special gossip in regard to him?"

"No!"

There are some noes that are equivalent to affirmations. This was one of them. Naturally the coroner pressed the question.

"I must request you to think again," he persisted. Then, with a change of voice: "Are you sure you have never heard anything specially derogatory to this young man, or that Mrs. Clemmens had not?"

"I have friends in Toledo who speak of him as the fastest man about town, if that could be called derogatory. As for Mrs. Clemmens, she may have heard as much, and she may have heard more, I cannot say. I know she always frowned when his father's name was mentioned."

"Miss Firman," proceeded the coroner, "in the long years in which you have been more or less separated from Mrs. Clemmens, you have, doubtless, kept up a continued if not frequent correspondence with her?"

"Yes, sir."

"Do you think, from the commencement and general tone of this letter, which I found lying half finished on her desk, that it was written and intended for yourself?"

Taking the letter from his outstretched hand, she fumbled nervously for her glasses, put them on, and then glanced hurriedly at the sheet, saying as she did so:

"There can be no doubt of it. She had no other friend whom she would have been likely to address as 'Dear Emily.'"

"Gentlemen of the Jury, you have a right to hear the words written by the deceased but a few hours, if not a few minutes, previous to the brutal assault that has led to the present inquiry. Miss Firman, as the letter was intended for yourself, will you be kind enough to read it aloud, after which you will hand it over to the jury."

With a gloomy shake of her head, and a certain trembling in her voice, that was due, perhaps, as much to the sadness of her task as to any foreboding of the real nature of the words she had to read, she proceeded to comply:

Dear Emily:—I don't know why I sit down to write to you today. I have plenty to do, and morning is no time for indulging in sentimentalities. But I feel strangely lonely and strangely anxious. Nothing goes just to my mind, and somehow the many causes for secret fear which I have always had, assume an undue prominence in my mind. It is always so when I am not quite well. In vain I reason with myself, saying that respectable people do not lightly enter into crime. But there are so many to whom my death would be more than welcome, that I constantly see myself in the act of being——

"Good heavens!" ejaculated the spinster, dropping the paper from her hand and looking dismally around upon the assembled faces of the now deeply interested spectators.

Seeing her dismay, a man who stood at the right of the coroner, and who seemed to be an officer of the law, quietly advanced, and picking up the paper she had let fall, handed it to the jury. The coroner meanwhile recalled her attention to herself.

"Miss Firman," said he, "allow me to put to you one final question which, though it might not be called a strictly legal one, is surely justified by the gravity of the situation. If Mrs. Clemmens had finished this letter, and you in due course had received it, what conclusion would you have drawn from the words you have just read?"

"I could have drawn but one, sir. I should have considered that the solitary life led by my cousin was telling upon her mind."

"But these terrors of which she speaks? To what and whom would you have attributed them?"

"I don't like to say it, and I don't know as I am justified in saying it, but it would have been impossible for me, under the circumstances, to have thought of any other source for them than the one we have already mentioned."

"And that is?" inexorably pursued the coroner.

"Mr. Gouverneur Hildreth."

8

The Thick-Set Man

In the pause that followed, Miss Firman stepped aside, and Mr. Byrd, finding his attention released, stole a glance toward the hall-way and its nearly concealed occupant. He found the elbow in agitated movement, and, as he looked at it, saw it disappear and a hand project into view, groping for the handkerchief which was, doubtless, hidden in the hat which he now perceived standing on the floor in the corner of the doorway. He looked at that hand well. It was large, white, and elegantly formed, and wore a seal ring of conspicuous size upon the little finger. He had scarcely noticed this ring, and wondered if others had seen it too, when the hand plunged into the hat, and drawing out the kerchief, vanished with it behind the jamb that had already hidden so much from his view.

"A fine gentleman's hand, and a fine gentleman's ring," was Mr. Byrd's mental comment; and he was about to glance aside, when, to his great astonishment, he saw the hand appear once more with the handkerchief in it, but without the ring which a moment since had made it such a conspicuous mark for his eyes.

"Our fine gentleman is becoming frightened," he thought, watching the hand until it dropped the handkerchief back into the hat. "One does not take off a ring in a company like this without a good reason." And he threw a quick glance at the man he considered his rival in the detective business.

But that worthy was busily engaged in stroking his chin in a feeling way, strongly suggestive of a Fledgerby-like interest in his absent whisker; and well versed as was Mr. Byrd in the ways of his fellow-detectives, he found it impossible to tell whether the significant action he had just remarked had escaped the attention of this man or not. Confused if not confounded, he turned back to the coroner, in a maze of new sensations, among which a growing hope that his own former suspicions had been of a wholly presumptuous character, rose predominant.

He found that functionary preparing to make a remark.

"Gentlemen," said he; "you have listened to the testimony of Mrs. Clemmens' most confidential friend, and heard such explanations as she had to give, of the special fears which Mrs. Clemmens acknowledges herself to have entertained in regard to her personal safety. Now, while duly impressing upon you the necessity of not laying too much stress upon the secret apprehensions of a woman living a life of loneliness and seclusion, I still consider it my duty to lay before you another bit of the widow's writing, in which——"

Here he was interrupted by the appearance at his side of a man with a telegram in his hand. In the pause which followed his reading of the same, Mr. Byrd, with that sudden impulse of interference which comes upon us all at certain junctures, tore out a leaf from his memorandum-book, and wrote upon it some half dozen or so words indicative of the advisability of examining the proprietor of the Eastern Hotel as to the name and quality of the several guests entertained by him on the day of the murder; and having signed this communication with his initial letters H. B., looked about for a messenger to carry it to the coroner. He found one in the person of a small boy, who was pressing with all his might against his back, and having despatched him with the note, regained his old position at the window, and proceeded to watch, with a growing interest in the drama before him, the result of his interference upon the coroner.

He had not long to wait. The boy had no sooner shown himself at the door with the note, than Dr. Tredwell laid down the telegram he was perusing and took this new communication. With a slight smile Mr. Byrd was not slow in attributing to its true source, he read the note through, then turned to the officer at his side and gave him some command that sent him from the room. He then took up the slip he was on the point of presenting to the jury at the time he was first interrupted, and continuing his remarks in reference to it, said quietly:

"Gentlemen, this paper which I here pass over to you, was found by me in the recess of Mrs. Clemmens' desk at the time I examined it for the address of Miss Firman. It was in an envelope that had never been sealed, and was, if I may use the expression, tucked away under a pile of old receipts. The writing is similar to that used in the letter you have just read, and the signature attached to it is 'Mary Ann Clemmens.' Will Mr. Black of the jury read aloud the words he will there find written?"

Mr. Black, in whose hand the paper then rested, looked up with a flush, and slowly, if not painfully, complied:

> I desire—(such was the language of the writing before him)—that in case of any sudden or violent death on my part, the authorities should inquire into the possible culpability of a gentleman living in Toledo, Ohio, known by the name of Gouverneur Hildreth. He is a man of no principle, and my distinct conviction is, that if such a death should occur to me, it will be entirely due to his efforts to gain possession of property which cannot be at his full disposal until my death.
>
> Mary Ann Clemmens, Sibley, N.Y.

"A serious charge!" quoth a juryman, breaking the universal silence occasioned by this communication from the dead.

"I should think so," echoed the burly man in front of Mr. Byrd.

But Mr. Byrd himself and the quiet man who leaned so stiffly and abstractedly against the wall, said nothing. Perhaps they found themselves sufficiently engaged in watching that half-seen elbow, which since the reading of this last slip of paper had ceased all movement and remained as stationary as though it had been paralyzed.

"A charge which, as yet, is nothing but a charge," observed the coroner. "But evidence is not wanting," he went on, "that Mr. Hildreth is not at home at this present time, but is somewhere in this region, as will be seen by the following telegram from the superintendent of the Toledo police." And he held up to view, not the telegram he had just received, but another which he had taken from among the papers on the table before him:

> Party mentioned not in Toledo. Left for the East on midnight train of Wednesday the 27th inst. When last heard from was in Albany. He has been living fast, and is well known to be in pecuniary difficulties, necessitating a large and immediate amount of money. Further particulars by letter.

"That, gentlemen, I received last night. Today," he continued, taking up the telegram that had just come in, "the following arrives:

> Fresh advices. Man you are in search of talked of suicide at his club the other night. Seemed in a desperate way, and said that if something did not soon happen he should be a lost man. Horse-

flesh and unfortunate speculations have ruined him. They say it will take all he will ultimately receive to pay his debts.

"And below":

Suspected that he has been in your town.

A crisis was approaching round the corner. This, to the skilled eyes of Mr. Byrd, was no longer doubtful. Even if he had not observed the wondering glances cast in that direction by persons who could see the owner of that now immovable elbow, he would have been assured that all was not right, by the alert expression which had now taken the place of the stolid and indifferent look which had hitherto character-ized the face of the man he believed to be a detective.

A panther about to spring could not have looked more threatening, and the wonder was, that there were no more to observe this exciting by-play. Yet the panther did not spring, and the inquiry went on.

"The witness I now propose to call," announced the coroner, after a somewhat trying delay, "is the proprietor of the Eastern Hotel. Ah, here he is. Mr. Symonds, have you brought your register for the past week?"

"Yes, sir," answered the newcomer, with a good deal of flurry in his manner and an embarrassed look about him, which convinced Mr. Byrd that the words in regard to whose origin he had been so doubt-ful that morning, had been real words and no dream.

"Very well, then, submit it, if you please, to the jury, and tell us in the meantime whether you have entertained at your house this week any guest who professed to come from Toledo?"

"I don't know. I don't remember any such," began the witness, in a stammering sort of way. "We have always a great many men from the West stopping at our house, but I don't recollect any special one who registered himself as coming from Toledo."

"You, however, always expect your guests to put their names in your book?"

"Yes, sir."

There was something in the troubled look of the man which aroused the suspicion of the coroner, and he was about to address him with another question when one of the jury, who was looking over the register, spoke up and asked:

"Who is this Clement Smith who writes himself down here as coming from Toledo?"

"Smith?—Smith?" repeated Symonds, going up to the juryman

and looking over his shoulder at the book. "Oh, yes, the gentleman who came yesterday. He——"

But at this moment a slight disturbance occurring in the other room, the witness paused and looked about him with that same embarrassed look before noted. "He is at the hotel now," he added, with an attempt at ease, transparent as it was futile.

The disturbance to which I have alluded was of a peculiar kind. It was occasioned by the thick-set man making the spring which, for some minutes, he had evidently been meditating. It was not a tragic leap, however, but a decidedly comic one, and had for its end and aim the recovery of a handkerchief which he had taken from his pocket at the moment when the witness uttered the name of Smith, and, by a useless flourish in opening it, flirted from his hand to the floor. At least, so the amused throng interpreted the sudden dive which he made, and the heedless haste that caused him to trip over the gentleman's hat that stood on the floor, causing it to fall and another handkerchief to tumble out.

But Mr. Byrd, who had a detective's insight into the whole matter, saw something more than appeared in the profuse apologies which the thick-set man made, and the hurried manner in which he gathered up the handkerchiefs and stood looking at them before returning one to his pocket and the other to its place in the gentleman's hat. Nor was Mr. Byrd at all astonished to observe that the stand which his fellow-detective took, upon resettling himself, was much nearer the unseen gentleman than before, or that in replacing the hat, he had taken pains to put it so far to one side that the gentleman would be obliged to rise and come around the corner in order to obtain it. The drift of the questions propounded to the witness at this moment opened his eyes too clearly for him to fail any longer to understand the situation.

"Now at the hotel?" the coroner was repeating. "And came yesterday? Why, then, did you look so embarrassed when I mentioned his name?"

"Oh—well—ah," stammered the man, "because he was there once before, though his name is not registered but once in the book."

"He was? And on what day?"

"On Tuesday," asserted the man, with the sudden decision of one who sees it is useless to attempt to keep silence.

"The day of the murder?"

"Yes, sir."

"And why is his name not on the book at that time if he came to your house and put up?"

"Because he did not put up; he merely called in, as it were, and did not take a meal or hire a room."

"How did you know, then, that he was there? Did you see him or talk to him?"

"Yes, sir."

"And what did you say?"

"He asked me for directions to a certain house, and I gave them."

"Whose house?"

"The Widow Clemmens', sir."

Ah, light at last! The long-sought-for witness had been found! Coroner and jury brightened visibly, while the assembled crowd gave vent to a deep murmur, that must have sounded like a knell of doom—in one pair of ears, at least.

"He asked you for directions to the house of Widow Clemmens. At what time was this?"

"At about half-past eleven in the morning."

The very hour!

"And did he leave then?"

"Yes, sir; after taking a glass of brandy."

"And did you not see him again?"

"Not till yesterday, sir."

"Ah, and at what time did you see him yesterday?"

"At bedtime, sir. He came with other arrivals on the five o'clock train; but I was away all the afternoon and did not see him till I went into the bar-room in the evening."

"Well, and what passed between you then?"

"Not much, sir. I asked if he was going to stay with us, and when he said 'Yes,' I inquired if he had registered his name. He replied 'No.' At which I pointed to the book, and he wrote his name down and then went up-stairs with me to his room."

"And is that all? Did you say nothing beyond what you have mentioned? ask him no questions or make no allusions to the murder?"

"Well, sir, I did make some attempt that way, for I was curious to know what took him to the Widow Clemmens' house, but he snubbed me so quickly, I concluded to hold my tongue and not trouble myself any further about the matter."

"And do you mean to say you haven't told anyone that an unknown man had been at your house on the morning of the murder inquiring after the widow?"

"Yes, sir. I am a poor man, and believe in keeping out of all sort of messes. Policy demands that much of me, gentlemen."

The look he received from the coroner may have convinced him that policy can be carried too far.

"And now," said Dr. Tredwell, "what sort of a man is this Clement Smith?"

"He is a gentleman, sir, and not at all the sort of person with whom you would be likely to connect any unpleasant suspicion."

The coroner surveyed the hotel-keeper somewhat sternly.

"We are not talking about suspicions!" he cried; then, in a different tone, repeated: "This gentleman, you say, is still at your house?"

"Yes, sir, or was at breakfast-time. I have not seen him since."

"We will have to call Mr. Smith as a witness," declared the coroner, turning to the officer at his side. "Go and see if you cannot bring him as soon as you did Mr. Symonds."

But here a voice spoke up full and loud from the other room.

"It is not necessary, sir. A witness you will consider more desirable than he is in the building." And the thick-set man showed himself for an instant to the coroner, then walking back, deliberately laid his hand on the elbow which for so long a time had been the centre of Mr. Byrd's wondering conjectures.

In an instant the fine, gentlemanly figure of the stranger, whom he had seen the night before in the bar-room, appeared with a bound from beyond the jamb, and pausing excitedly before the man, now fully discovered to all around as a detective, asked him, in shaking tones of suppressed terror or rage, what it was he meant.

"I will tell you," was the ready assurance, "if you will step out here in view of the coroner and jury."

With a glance that for some reason disturbed Mr. Byrd in his newly acquired complacency, the gentleman stalked hurriedly forward and took his stand in the door-way leading into the room occupied by the persons mentioned.

"Now," he cried, "what have you to say?"

But the detective, who had advanced behind him, still refrained from replying, though he gave a quick look at the coroner, which led that functionary to glance at the hotel-keeper and instantly ask:

"You know this gentleman?"

"It is Mr. Clement Smith."

A flush so violent and profuse, that even Mr. Byrd could see it from his stand outside the window, inundated for an instant the face and neck of the gentleman, but was followed by no words, though the detective at his side waited for an instant before saying:

"I think you are mistaken; I should call him now Mr. Gouverneur Hildreth!"

With a start and a face grown as suddenly white as it had but an instant before been red, the gentleman turned and surveyed the detective from head to foot, saying, in a tone of mock politeness:

"And why, if you please? I have never been introduced to you that I remember."

"No," rejoined the detective, taking from his pocket the handkerchief which he had previously put there, and presenting it to the other with a bow, "but I have read the monogram upon your handkerchief and it happens to be———"

"Enough!" interrupted the other, in a stern if not disdainful voice. "I see I have been the victim of espionage." And stepping into the other room, he walked haughtily up to the coroner and exclaimed: "I am Gouverneur Hildreth, and I come from Toledo. Now, what is it you have to say to me?"

9

Close Calculations

The excitement induced by the foregoing announcement had, in a degree, subsided. The coroner, who appeared to be as much startled as anyone at the result of the day's proceedings, had manifested his desire of putting certain questions to the young man, and had begun by such inquiries into his antecedents, and his connection with Mrs. Clemmens, as elicited the most complete corroboration of all Miss Firman's statements.

An investigation into his motives for coming East at this time next followed, in the course of which he acknowledged that he undertook the journey solely for the purpose of seeing Mrs. Clemmens. And when asked why he wished to see her at this time, admitted, with some manifestation of shame, that he desired to see for himself whether she was really in as strong and healthy a condition as he had always been told; his pecuniary embarrassments being such that he could not prevent his mind from dwelling upon possibilities which, under any other circumstances, he would have been ashamed to consider.

"And did you see Mrs. Clemmens?" the coroner inquired.

"Yes, sir; I did."

"When?"

"On Tuesday, sir; about noon."

The answer was given almost with bravado, and the silence among the various auditors became intense.

"You admit, then, that you were in the widow's house the morning she was murdered, and that you had an interview with her a few minutes before the fatal blow was struck?"

"I do."

There was doggedness in the tone, and doggedness in the look that accompanied it. The coroner moved a little forward in his chair and uttered his next question with deep gravity.

"Did you approach the widow's house by the road and enter into it by means of the front door overlooking the lane?"

"I did."

"And did you meet no one in the lane, or see no one at the windows of any of the houses as you came by?"

"No, sir."

"How long did you stay in this house, and what was the result of the interview which you had with Mrs. Clemmens?"

"I stayed, perhaps, ten minutes, and I learned nothing from Mrs. Clemmens, save that she was well and hearty, and likely to live out her threescore years and ten for all hint that her conversation or appearance gave me."

He spoke almost with a tone of resentment; his eyes glowed darkly, and a thrill of horror sped through the room as if they felt that the murderer himself stood before them.

"You will tell me what was said in this interview, if you please, and whether the widow knew who you were; and, if so, whether any words of anger passed between you?"

The face of the young man burned, and he looked at the coroner and then at the jurymen, as if he would like to challenge the whole crew, but the colour that showed in his face was the flush of shame, or, so thought Mr. Byrd, and in his reply, when he gave it, there was a bitterness of self-scorn that reminded the detective more of the mortification of a gentleman caught in an act of meanness than the secret alarm of a man who had been beguiled into committing a dastardly crime.

"Mrs. Clemmens was evidently a woman of some spirit," said he, forcing out his words with sullen desperation. "She may have used sharp language; I believe indeed she did; but she did not know who I was, for—for I pretended to be a seller of patent medicine, warranted to cure all ills, and she told me she had no ills, and—and—Do you want a man to disgrace himself in your presence?" he suddenly flashed out, cringing under the gaze of the many curious and unsympathetic eyes fixed upon him.

But the coroner, with a sudden assumption of severity, pardonable, perhaps, in a man with a case of such importance on his hands, recommended the witness to be calm and not to allow any small feelings of personal mortification to interfere with a testimony of so much evident value. And without waiting for the witness to recover himself, asked again:

"What did the widow say, and with what words did you leave?"

"The widow said she abominated drugs, and never took them. I replied that she made a great mistake, if she had any ailments. Upon which she retorted that she had no ailment, and politely showed me the door. I do not remember that anything else passed between us."

His tone, which had been shrill and high, dropped at the final sentence, and by the nervous workings of his lips, Mr. Byrd perceived that he dreaded the next question. The persons grouped around him evidently dreaded it too.

But it was less searching than they expected, and proved that the coroner preferred to approach his point by circuitous rather than direct means.

"In what room was the conversation held, and by what door did you come in and go out?"

"I came in by the front door, and we stood in that room"—pointing to the sitting-room from which he had just issued.

"Stood! Did you not sit down?"

"No."

"Stood all the time, and in that room to which you have just pointed?"

"Yes."

The coroner drew a deep breath, and looked at the witness long and searchingly. Mr. Hildreth's way of uttering this word had been anything but pleasant, and consequently anything but satisfactory. A low murmur began to eddy through the rooms.

"Gentlemen, silence!" commanded the coroner, venting in this injunction some of the uncomfortable emotion with which he was evidently surcharged; for his next words were spoken in a comparatively quiet voice, though the fixed severity of his eye could have given the witness but little encouragement.

"You say," he declared, "that in coming through the lane you encountered no one. Was this equally true of your return?"

"Yes, sir; I believe so. I don't remember. I was not looking up," was the slightly confused reply.

"You passed, however, through the lane, and entered the main street by the usual path?"

"Yes."

"And where did you go then?"

"To the depot."

"Ah!"

"I wished to leave the town. I had done with it."

"And did you do so, Mr. Hildreth?"

"I did."

"Where did you go?"

"To Albany, where I had left my traps."

"You took the noon train, then?"

"Yes, sir."

"Which leaves precisely five minutes after twelve?"

"I suppose so."

"Took it without stopping anywhere on the way?"

"Yes, sir."

"Did you buy a ticket at the office?"

"No, sir."

"Why?"

"I did not have time."

"Ah, the train was at the station, then?"

Mr. Hildreth did not reply; he had evidently been driven almost to the end of his patience, or possibly of his courage, by this quick fire of small questions.

The coroner saw this and pressed his advantage.

"Was the train at the station or not when you arrived there, Mr. Hildreth?"

"I do not see why it can interest you to know," the witness retorted, with a flash of somewhat natural anger; "but since you insist, I will tell you that it was just going out, and that I had to run to reach it, and only got a foothold upon the platform of the rear car at the risk of my life."

He looked as if he wished it had been at the cost of his[134]life, and compressed his lips and moved restlessly from side to side as if the battery of eyes levelled upon his face were so many points of red-hot steel burning into his brain.

But the coroner, intent upon his duty, released not one jot of the steady hold he had taken upon his victim.

"Mr. Hildreth," said he, "your position as the only person who acknowledges himself to have been in this house during the half-hour that preceded the assault, makes everything you can tell us in reference to your visit of the highest importance. Was the widow alone, do you think, or did you see anything —pause now and consider well— *anything* that would lead you to suppose there was anyone beside her and yourself in the house?"

It was the suggestion of a just man, and Mr. Byrd looked to see the witness grasp with all the energy of despair at the prospect of release it held out. But Mr. Hildreth either felt his cause beyond the reach of any such assistance, or his understanding was so dulled by misery he could not see the advantage of acknowledging the presence of a third party in the cottage. Giving a dreary shake of the head, he slowly answered:

"There may have been somebody else in the house, I don't know; but if so, I didn't hear him or see him. I thought we were alone."

The frankness with which he made the admission was in his favour, but the quick and overpowering flush that rose to his face the moment he had given utterance to it, betrayed so unmistakable a consciousness of what the admission implied that the effect was immediately reversed. Seeing that he had lost rather than gained in the opinions of the merciless inquisitors about him, he went back to his old bravado, and haughtily lifted his head.

"One question more," resumed the coroner. "You have said that Mrs. Clemmens was a spirited woman. Now, what made you think so? Any expression of annoyance on her part at the interruption in her work which your errand had caused her, or merely the expression of her face and the general way she had of speaking?"

"The latter, I think, though she did use a harsh word or two when she showed me the door."

"And raised her voice?"

"Yes, yes."

"Mr. Hildreth," intimated the coroner, rising, "will you be kind enough to step with me into the adjoining room?"

With a look of wonder not unmixed with alarm, the young man prepared to comply.

"I should like the attention of the jury," Dr. Tredwell signified as he passed through the door.

There was no need to give them this hint. Not a man of them but was already on his feet in eager curiosity as to what their presiding officer was about to do.

"I wish you to tell me now," the coroner demanded of Mr. Hildreth, as they paused in the centre of the sitting-room, "where it was you stood during your interview with Mrs. Clemmens, and, if possible, take the very position now which you held at that time."

"There are too many persons here," the witness objected, visibly rebelling at a request of which he could not guess the full significance.

"The people present will step back," declared the coroner; "you will have no trouble in taking your stand on the spot you occupied the other day."

"Here, then!" exclaimed the young man, taking a position near the centre of the room.

"And the widow?"

"Stood there."

"Facing you?"

"Yes."

"I see," intimated the coroner, pointing toward the windows. "Her back was to the yard while you stood with your face toward it." Then with a quick motion, summoning the witness back into the other room, asked, amid the breathless attention of the crowd, whom this bit of by-play had wrought up to expectation: "Did you observe anyone go around to the back door while you stood there, and go away again without attempting to knock?"

Mr. Hildreth knitted his brow and seemed to think.

"Answer," persisted the coroner; "it is not a question that requires thought."

"Well, then, I did not," cried the witness, looking the other directly in the eye, with the first gleam of real manly feeling which he had yet displayed.

"You did not see a tramp come into the yard, walk around to the kitchen door, wait a moment as if hesitating whether he would rap, and then turn and come back again without doing so?"

"No, sir."

The coroner drew a piece of paper before him and began figuring on it. Earnestly, almost wildly, the young man watched him, drawing a deep breath and turning quite pale as the other paused and looked up.

"Yet," affirmed the coroner, as if no delay had occurred since he received his last answer, "such a person did approach the house while you were in it, and if you had stood where you say, you must have seen him."

It was a vital thrust, a relentless presentation of fact, and as such shook the witness out of his lately acquired composure. Glancing hastily about, he sought the assistance of someone both capable and willing to advise him in this crisis, but seeing no one, he made a vigorous effort and called together his own faculties.

"Sir," he protested, a tremor of undisguised anxiety finding way into his voice, "I do not see how you make that all out. What proof have you that this tramp of which you speak came to the house while I was in it? Could he not have come before? Or, what was better, could he not have come after?"

The ringing tone with which the last question was put startled everybody. No such sounds had issued from his lips before. Had he caught a glimpse of hope, or was he driven to an extremity in his defence that forced him to assert himself? The eyes of Miss Firman and of a few other women began to soften, and even the face of Mr. Byrd betrayed that a change was on the verge of taking place in his feelings.

But the coroner's look and tone dashed cold water on this young and tender growth of sympathy. Passing over to the witness the paper on which he had been scribbling, he explained with dry significance:

"It is only a matter of subtraction and addition, Mr. Hildreth. You have said that upon quitting this house you went directly to the depot, where you arrived barely in time to jump on the train as it was leaving the station. Now, to walk from this place to the depot at any pace you would be likely to use, would occupy—well, let us say seven minutes. At two minutes before twelve, then, you were still in this house. Well!" he ejaculated, interrupting himself as the other opened his lips, "have you anything to say?"

"No," was the dejected and hesitating reply.

The coroner at once resumed:

"But at five minutes before twelve, Mr. Hildreth, the tramp walked into the widow's yard. Now, allowing only two minutes for your interview with that lady, the conclusion remains that you were in the house when he came up to it. Yet you declare that, although you stood in full view of the yard, you did not see him."

"You figure closer than an astronomer calculating an eclipse," burst from the young man's lips in a flash of that resolution which had for the last few minutes animated him. "How do you know your witnesses have been so exact to a second when they say this and that of the goings and comings you are pleased to put into an arithmetical problem. A minute or two one way or the other would make a sad discrepancy in your calculations, Mr. Coroner."

"I know it," assented Dr. Tredwell, quietly ignoring the other's heat; "but if the jury will remember, there were four witnesses, at least, who testified to the striking of the town clock just as the tramp finally issued from the lane, and one witness, of well-known accuracy in matters of detail, who declared on oath that she had just dropped her eyes from that same clock when she observed the tramp go into the widow's gate, and that it was five minutes to twelve exactly. But, lest I do seem too nice in my calculations," the coroner inexorably pursued, "I will take the trouble of putting it another way. At what time did you leave the hotel, Mr. Hildreth?"

"I don't know," was the testy response.

"Well, I can tell you," the coroner assured him. "It was about twenty minutes to twelve, or possibly earlier, but no later. My reason for saying this," he went on, drawing once more before him the fatal sheet of paper "is that Mrs. Dayton's children next door were out playing in front of this house for some few minutes previous to the time the tramp came into the lane. As you did not see them you must have arrived here before they began their game, and that, at the least calculation, would make the time as early as a quarter to twelve."

"Well," the fierce looks of the other seemed to say, "and what if it was?"

"Mr. Hildreth," continued the coroner, "if you were in this house at a quarter to twelve and did not leave it till two minutes before, and the interview was as you say a mere interchange of a dozen words or so, that could not possibly have occupied more than three minutes; *where were you during all the rest of the time* that must have elapsed after you finished your interview and the moment you left the house?"

It was a knock-down question. This aristocratic-looking young gentleman who had hitherto held himself erect before them, notwithstanding the humiliating nature of the inquiries which had been propounded to him, cringed visibly and bowed his head as if a stroke of vital force had descended upon it. Bringing his fist down on the table near which he stood, he seemed to utter a muttered curse, while the veins swelled on his forehead so powerfully that more than one person present dropped their eyes from a spectacle which bore so distinctly the stamp of guilt.

"You have not answered," intimated the coroner, after a moment of silent waiting.

"No!" was the loud reply, uttered with a force that startled all present, and made the more timid gaze with some apprehension at his suddenly antagonistic attitude. "It is not pleasant for a gentleman"— he emphasized the word bitterly—"for a *gentleman* to acknowledge himself caught at a time like this in a decided equivocation. But you have cornered me fairly and squarely, and I am bound to tell the truth. Gentlemen, I did not leave the widow's house as immediately as I said. I stayed for fully five minutes or so alone in the small hall that leads to the front door. In all probability I was there when the tramp passed by on his way to the kitchen-door, and there when he came back again." And Mr. Hildreth fixed his eyes on the coroner as if he dared him to push him further.

But Dr. Tredwell had been in his present seat before. Merely confronting the other with that cold official gaze which seems to act like a wall of ice between a witness and the coroner, he said the two words: "What doing?"

The effect was satisfactory. Paling suddenly, Mr. Hildreth dropped his eyes and replied humbly, though with equal laconism, "I was thinking." But scarcely had the words left his lips, than a fresh flame of feeling started up within him, and looking from juryman to juryman he passionately exclaimed: "You consider that acknowledgment suspicious. You wonder why a man should give a few minutes to thought after the conclusion of an interview that terminated all hope. I wonder at it now myself. I wonder I did not go straight out of the house and rush headlong into any danger that promised an immediate extinction of my life."

No language could have more forcibly betrayed the real desperation of his mind at the critical moment when the widow's life hung in the balance. He saw this, perhaps, when it was too late, for the sweat started on his brow, and he drew himself up like a man nerving himself to meet a blow he no longer hoped to avert. One further remark, however, left his lips.

"Whatever I did or of whatever I was thinking, one thing I here declare to be true, and that is, that I did not see the widow again after she left my side and went back to her kitchen in the rear of the house. The hand that struck her may have been lifted while I stood in the hall, but if so, I did not know it, nor can I tell you now who it was that killed her."

It was the first attempt at direct disavowal which he had made, and it had its effect. The coroner softened a trifle of his austerity, and the jurymen glanced at each other relieved. But the weight of suspicion against this young man was too heavy, and his manner had been too unfortunate, for this effect to last long. Gladly as many would have been to credit this denial, if only for the name he bore and a certain fine aspect of gentlemanhood that surrounded him in spite of his present humiliation, it was no longer possible to do so without question, and he seemed to feel this and do his best to accept the situation with patience.

An inquiry which was put to him at this time by a juryman showed the existent state of feeling against him.

"May I ask," that individual dryly interrogated, "why you came back to Sibley, after having left it?"

The response came clear and full. Evidently the gravity of his position had at last awakened the latent resources of Mr. Hildreth's mind.

"I heard of the death of this woman, and my surprise caused me to return."

"How did you hear of it?"

"Through the newspapers."

"And you were surprised?"

"I was astounded; I felt as if I had received a blow myself, and could not rest till I had come back where I could learn the full particulars."

"So, then, it was curiosity that brought you to the inquest today?"

"It was."

The juryman looked at him astonished; so did all the rest. His manner was so changed, his answers so prompt and ringing.

"And what was it," broke in the coroner, "that led you to register yourself at the hotel under a false name?"

"I scarcely know," was the answer, given with less fire and some show of embarrassment. "Perhaps I thought that, under the circumstances, it would be better for me not to use my own."

"In other words, you were afraid?" exclaimed the coroner, with the full impressiveness of his somewhat weighty voice and manner.

It was a word to make the weakest of men start. Mr. Hildreth, who was conspicuous in his own neighbourhood for personal if not for moral courage, flushed till it looked as if the veins would burst on his forehead, but he made no other reply than a proud and angry look and a short:

"I was not aware of fear; though, to be sure, I had no premonition of the treatment I should be called upon to suffer here today."

The flash told, the coroner sat as if doubtful, and looked from man to man of the jury as if he would question their feelings on this vital subject. Meantime the full shame of his position settled heavier and heavier upon Mr. Hildreth; his head fell slowly forward, and he seemed to be asking himself how he was to meet the possibly impending ignominy of a direct accusation. Suddenly he drew himself erect, and a gleam shot from his eyes that, for the first time, revealed him as a man of latent pluck and courage.

"Gentlemen," he began, looking first at the coroner and then at the jury, "you have not said you consider me guilty of this crime, but you evidently harbour the suspicion. I do not wonder; my own words have given me away, and any man would find it difficult to believe in my innocence after what has been testified to in this place. Do not hesitate, then. The shock of finding myself suspected of a horrible murder is passed. I am willing to be arrested. Indeed, after what has here taken place, I not only am willing but even anxious. I want to be tried, if only to prove to the world my complete and entire innocence."

The effect of this speech, uttered at a moment so critical, may be easily imagined. All the impressible people present at once signified their belief in his honesty, and gave him looks of sympathy, if not approval; while the cooler and possibly the more judicious of his auditors calmly weighed these assertions against the evidence that had been advanced, and finding the result unsatisfactory, shook their heads as if unconvinced, and awaited further developments.

They did not come. The inquiry had reached its climax, and little, if anything, more was left to be said. Mr. Hildreth was examined more fully, and some few of the witnesses who had been heard in the early part of the day were recalled, but no new facts came to light, and no fresh inquiries were started.

Mr. Byrd, who from the attitude of the coroner could not fail to see Mr. Hildreth was looked upon with a suspicion that would ultimately end in arrest, decided that his interest in the inquest was at an end, and being greatly fatigued, gave up his position at the window and quietly stole away.

10

The Final Test

The fact was, he wanted to think. Detective though he was and accustomed to the bravado with which every sort of criminal will turn to meet their fate when fully driven to bay, there had been something in the final manner of this desperate but evidently cultured gentleman, which had impressed him against his own will, and made him question whether the suspected man was not rather the victim of a series of extraordinary circumstances, than the selfish and brutal criminal which the evidence given seemed to suggest.

Not that Mr. Byrd ever allowed his generous heart to blind him to the plain language of facts. His secret and not to be smothered doubts in another direction were proof enough of this; and had it not been for those very doubts, the probabilities are that he would have agreed with the cooler-headed portion of the crowd, which listened unmoved to that last indignant burst of desperate manhood.

But with those doubts still holding possession of his mind, he could not feel so sure of Mr. Hildreth's guilt; and the struggle that was likely to ensue between his personal feelings on the one side and his sense of duty on the other did not promise to be so light as to make it possible for him to remain within eye and earshot of an unsympathetic crowd.

"If only the superintendent had not left it to my judgement to interfere," thought he, pacing the streets with ever-increasing uneasiness, "the responsibility would have been shifted from my shoulders, and I would have left the young man to his fate in peace. But now I would be criminally at fault if I were to let him drift hopelessly to his doom, when by a lift of my finger I might possibly turn the attention of justice toward the real culprit."

Yet the making up of his mind to interfere was a torture to Horace Byrd. If he was not conscious of any love for Imogene Dare, he was sufficiently under the dominion of her extraordinary fascinations to feel that any movement on his part toward the unravelling of the mystery that enveloped her, would be like subjecting his own self to the rack of public inquiry and suspicion.

Nor, though he walked the streets for hours, each moment growing more and more settled in his conviction of Mr. Hildreth's innocence, could he bring himself to the point of embracing the duty presented to him, till he had subjected Miss Dare to a new test, and won for himself absolute certainty as to the fact of her possessing a clue to the crime, which had not been discovered in the coroner's inquiry.

"The possibility of innocence on her part is even greater than on that of Mr. Hildreth," he considered, "and nothing, not even the peril of those dearest to me, could justify me in shifting the weight of suspicion from a guiltless man to an equally guiltless woman."

It was, therefore, for the purpose of solving this doubt, that he finally sought Mr. Ferris, and after learning that Mr. Hildreth was under surveillance, and would in all probability be subjected to arrest on the morrow, asked for some errand that would take him to Mr. Orcutt's house.

"I have a great admiration for that gentleman and would like to make his acquaintance," he remarked carelessly, hiding his true purpose under his usual nonchalant tones. "But I do not want to seem to be pushing myself forward; so if you could give me some papers to carry to him, or some message requiring an introduction to his presence, I should feel very much obliged."

Mr. Ferris, who had no suspicions of his own to assist him in understanding the motives that led to this request, easily provided the detective with the errand he sought. Mr. Byrd at once started for the lawyer's house.

It was fully two miles away, but once arrived there, he was thankful that the walk had been so long, as the fatigue, following upon the activity of the afternoon, had succeeded in quieting his pulses and calming down the fierce excitement which had held him under its control ever since he had taken the determination to satisfy his doubts by an interview with Miss Dare.

Ringing the bell of the rambling old mansion that spread out its wide extensions through the vines and bushes of an old-fashioned and most luxuriant garden, he waited the issue with beating heart. A respectable-looking negro servant came to the door.

"Is Mr. Orcutt in?" he asked; "or, if not, Miss Dare? I have a message from Mr. Ferris and would be glad to see one of them."

This, in order to ascertain at a word if the lady was at home.

"Miss Dare is not in," was the civil response, "and Mr. Orcutt is very busily engaged; but if you will step into the parlour I will tell him you are here."

"No," returned the disappointed detective, handing her the note he held in his hand. "If your master is busy I will not disturb him." And, turning away, he went slowly down the steps.

"If I only knew where she was gone!" he muttered, bitterly.

But he did not consider himself in a position to ask.

Inwardly chafing over his ill-luck, Mr. Byrd proceeded with reluctant pace to regain the street, when, hearing the gate suddenly click, he looked up, and saw advancing toward him a young gentleman of a peculiarly spruce and elegant appearance.

"Ha! another visitor for Miss Dare," was the detective's natural inference. And with a sudden movement he withdrew from the path, and paused as if to light his cigar in the shadow of the thick bushes that grew against the house.

In an instant the young stranger was on the stoop. Another, and he had rung the bell, which was answered almost as soon as his hand dropped from the knob.

"Is Miss Dare in?" was the inquiry, uttered in loud and cheery tones.

"No, sir. She is spending a few days with Miss Tremaine," was the clear and satisfactory reply. "Shall I tell her you have been here?"

"No. I will call myself at Miss Tremaine's," rejoined the gentleman. And, with a gay swing of his cane and a cheerful look overhead where the stars were already becoming visible, he sauntered easily off, followed by the envious thoughts of Mr. Byrd.

"Miss Tremaine," repeated the latter, musingly. "Who knows Miss Tremaine?"

While he was asking himself this question, the voice of the young man rose melodiously in a scrap of old song, and instantly Mr. Byrd recognized in the seeming stranger the well-known tenor singer of the church he had himself attended the Sunday before—a gentleman, too, to whom he had been introduced by Mr. Ferris, and with whom he had exchanged something more than the passing civilities of the moment.

To increase his pace, overtake the young man, recall himself to his attention, and join him in his quick walk down the street, was the work of a moment. The natural sequence followed. Mr. Byrd made himself so agreeable that by the time they arrived at Miss Tremaine's the other felt loath to part with him, and it resulted in his being urged to join this chance acquaintance in his call.

Nothing could have pleased Mr. Byrd better. So, waiving for once his instinctive objection to any sort of personal intrusion, he signified his acquiescence to the proposal, and at once accompanied his new friend into the house of the unknown Miss Tremaine. He found it lit up as for guests. All the rooms on the ground floor were open, and in one of them he could discern a dashing and coquettish young miss holding court over a cluster of eager swains.

"Ah, I forgot," exclaimed Mr. Byrd's companion, whose name, by-the-way, was Duryea. "It is Miss Tremaine's reception night. She is the daughter of one of the professors of the High School," he went on, whispering his somewhat late explanations into the ear of Mr. Byrd. "Every Thursday evening she throws her house open for callers, and the youth of the academy are only too eager to avail themselves of the opportunity of coming here. Well, it is all the better for us. Miss Dare despises boys, and in all likelihood we shall have her entirely to ourselves."

A quick pang contracted the breast of Mr. Byrd. If this easy, almost rakish, fellow at his side but knew the hideous errand which brought him to this house, what a scene would have ensued!

But he had no time for reflection, or even for that irresistible shrinking from his own designs which he now began to experience. Before he realized that he was fully committed to this venture, he found himself in the parlour bowing before the *naïve* and laughing-eyed Miss Tremaine, who rose to receive him with all the airy graciousness of a finished coquette.

Miss Dare was not visible, and Mr. Byrd was just wondering if he would be called upon to enter into a sustained conversation with his pretty hostess, when a deep, rich voice was heard in the adjoining room, and, looking up, he saw the stately figure he so longed and yet dreaded to encounter, advancing toward them through the open door. She was very pale, and, to Mr. Byrd's eyes, looked thoroughly worn out, if not ill. Yet, she bore herself with a steadiness that was evidently the result of her will; and manifested neither reluctance nor impatience when the eager Mr. Duryea pressed forward with his compliments, though from the fixedness of her gaze and the immobility of her lip, Mr. Byrd too truly discovered that her thoughts were far away from the scene of mirth and pleasure in which she found herself.

"You see I have presumed to follow you, Miss Dare," was the greeting with which Mr. Duryea hailed her approach. And he immediately became so engrossed with his gallantries he forgot to introduce his companion.

Mr. Byrd was rather relieved at this. He was not yet ready to submit her to the test he considered necessary to a proper understanding of the situation; and he had not the heart to approach her with any mere civility on his tongue, while matters of such vital importance to her happiness, if not to her honour, trembled in the balance.

He preferred to talk to Miss Tremaine, and this he continued to do till the young fellows at his side, one by one, edged away, leaving no one in that portion of the room but himself and Miss Tremaine, Mr. Duryea and Miss Dare.

The latter two stood together some few feet behind him, and were discussing in a somewhat languid way, the merits of a *musicale* which they had lately attended. They were approaching, however, and he felt that if he did not speak at once he might not have another opportunity for doing so during the whole evening. Turning, therefore, to Miss Tremaine, with more seriousness than her gay and totally inconsequent conversation had hitherto allowed, he asked, in what he meant to be a simply colloquial and courteous manner, if she had heard the news.

"News," she repeated, "no; is there any news?"

"Yes, I call it news. But, perhaps, you are not interested in the murder that has lately taken place in this town?"

"Oh, yes, I am," she exclaimed, all eagerness at once, while he felt rather than perceived that the couple at his back stood suddenly still, as if his words had worked their spell over one heart there at least. "Papa knew Mrs. Clemmens very well," the little lady proceeded with a bewitchingly earnest look. "Have they found the murderer, do you think? Anything less than that would be no news to me."

"There is every reason to suppose——" he began, and stopped, something in the deadly silence behind him making it impossible for him to proceed. Happily he was not obliged to. An interruption occurred in the shape of a new-comer, and he was left with the fatal word on his lips to await the approach of that severely measured step behind him, which by this time he knew was bringing the inscrutable Miss Dare to his side.

"Miss Dare, allow me to present to you Mr. Byrd. Mr. Byrd, Miss Dare."

The young detective bowed. With rigid attention to the forms of etiquette, he uttered the first few acknowledgments necessary to the occasion, and then glanced up.

She was looking him full in the face.

"We have met before," he was about to observe, but not detecting the least sign of recognition in her gaze, restrained the words and hastily dropped his eyes.

"Mr. Duryea informs me you are a stranger in the town," she remarked, moving slowly to one side in a way to rid herself of that gentleman's too immediate presence. "Have you a liking for the place, or do you meditate any lengthy stay?"

"No. That is," he rejoined, somewhat shaken in his theories by the self-possession of her tone and the ease and quietness with which she evidently prepared to enter into a sustained conversation, "I may go away tomorrow, and I may linger on for an indefinite length of time. It all depends upon certain matters that will be determined for me tonight. Sibley is a very pretty place," he observed, startled at his own temerity in venturing the last remark.

"Yes."

The word came as if forced, and she looked at Mr. Duryea.

"Do you wish anything, Miss Dare?" that gentleman suddenly asked. "You do not look well."

"I am not well," she acknowledged. "No, thank you," she cried, as he pushed a chair toward her. "It is too warm here. If you do not object, we will go into the other room." And with a courteous glance that included both gentlemen in its invitation, she led the way into the adjoining apartment. Could it have been with the purpose of ridding herself of the assiduities of Mr. Duryea? The room contained half a dozen or more musical people, and no sooner did they perceive their favourite tenor approach than they seized upon him and, without listening to his excuses, carried him off to the piano, leaving Miss Dare alone with Mr. Byrd.

She seemed instantly to forget her indisposition. Drawing herself up till every queenly attribute she possessed flashed brilliantly before his eyes, she asked, with sudden determination, if she had been right in understanding him to say that there was news in regard to the murder of Mrs. Clemmens?

Subduing, by a strong inward effort, every token of the emotion

251

which her own introduction of this topic naturally evoked, he replied in his easiest tones:

"Yes; there was an inquest held today, and the authorities evidently think they have discovered the person who killed her." And obliging himself to meet halfway the fate that awaited him, he bestowed upon the lady before him a casual glance that hid beneath its easy politeness the greatest anxiety of his life.

The test worked well. From the pallor of sickness, grief, or apprehension, her complexion whitened to the deadlier hue of mortal terror.

"Impossible!" her lips seemed to breathe; and Mr. Byrd could almost fancy he saw the hair rise on her forehead.

Cursing in his heart the bitter necessity that had forced him into this duty, he was about to address her in a way calculated to break the spell occasioned by his last words, when the rich and tuneful voice of the melodious singer rose suddenly on the air, and they heard the words:

Come rest in this bosom, my own stricken deer,
Though the herd have fled from thee, thy home is still here;
Here still is the smile that no cloud can o'ercast,
And a heart and a hand all thy own to the last.

Instantly Mr. Byrd perceived that he should not be obliged to speak. Though the music, or possibly the words, struck her like a blow, it likewise served to recall her to herself. Dropping her gaze, which had remained fixed upon his own, she turned her face aside, saying with forced composure:

"This near contact with crime is dreadful." Then slowly, and with a quietness that showed how great was her power of self-control when she was not under the influence of surprise, she inquired: "And who do they think this person is? What name do they presume to associate with the murderer of this woman?"

With something of the feeling of a surgeon who nerves himself to bury the steel in his patient's quivering flesh, he gave his response unhesitatingly.

"A gentleman's, I believe. A young man connected with her, in some strange way, by financial interests. A Mr. Hildreth, of Toledo—Gouverneur Hildreth, I think they call him."

It was not the name she expected. He saw this by the relaxation that took place in all her features, by the look of almost painful relief

252

that flashed for a moment into the eyes she turned like lightning upon him.

"Gouverneur Hildreth!" she repeated. And he knew from the tone that it was not only a different name from what she anticipated, but that it was also a strange one to her. "I never heard of such a person," she went on after a minute, during which the relentless mellow voice of the unconscious singer filled the room with the passionate appeal:

> *Oh, what was love made for, if 't is not the same,*
> *Through joy and through sorrow, through glory and shame!*

"That is not strange," explained Mr. Byrd, drawing nearer, as if to escape that pursuing sweetness of incongruous song. "He is not known in this town. He only came here the morning the unfortunate woman was murdered. Whether he really killed her or not," he proceeded, with forced quietness, "no one can tell, of course. But the facts are very much against him, and the poor fellow is under arrest."

"What?"

The word was involuntary. So was the tone of horrified surprise in which it was uttered. But the music, now swelling to a crescendo, drowned both word and tone, or so she seemed to fondly imagine; for, making another effort at self-control, she confined herself to a quiet repetition of his words, "'Under arrest'?" and then waited with only a suitable display of emotion for whatever further enlightenment he chose to give her.

He mercifully spoke to the point.

"Yes, under arrest. You see he was in the house at or near the time the deadly blow was struck. He was in the front hall, he says, and nowhere near the woman or her unknown assailant, but there is no evidence against anyone else, and the facts so far proved, show he had an interest in her death, and so he has to pay the penalty of circumstances. And he may be guilty, who knows," the young detective pursued, seeing she was struck with horror and dismay, "dreadful as it is to imagine that a gentleman of culture and breeding could be brought to commit such a deed."

But she seemed to have ears for but one phrase of all this.

"He was in the front hall," she repeated. "How did he get there? What called him there?"

"He had been visiting the widow, and was on his way out. He paused to collect his thoughts, he said. It seems unaccountable, Miss Dare; but the whole thing is strange and very mysterious."

She was deaf to his explanations.

"Do you suppose he heard the widow scream?" she asked, tremblingly, "or——"

A sinking of the ringing tones whose powerful vibration had made this conversation possible, caused her to pause. When the notes grew loud enough again for her to proceed, she seemed to have forgotten the question she was about to propound, and simply inquired:

"Had he anything to say about what he overheard—or saw?"

"No. If he spoke the truth and stood in the hall as he said, the sounds, if sounds there were, stopped short of the sitting-room door, for he has nothing to say about them."

A change passed over Miss Dare. She dropped her eyes, and an instant's pause followed this last acknowledgment.

"Will you tell me," she inquired, at last, speaking very slowly, in an attempt to infuse into her voice no more than a natural tone of interest, "how it was he came to say he stood in that place during the assault?"

"He did not say he stood in that place during the assault," was again the forced rejoinder of Mr. Byrd. "It was by means of a nice calculation of time and events, that it was found he must have been in the house at or near the fatal moment."

Another pause; another bar of that lovely music.

"And he is a gentleman, you say?" was her hurried remark at last.

"Yes, and a very handsome one."

"And they have put him in prison?"

"Yes, or will on the morrow."

She turned and leaned against a window-frame nearby, looking with eyes that saw nothing into the still vast night.

"I suppose he has friends," she faintly suggested.

"Two sisters, if no one nearer and dearer."

Thou hast called me thy angel in moments of bliss,
And thy angel I'll be, 'mid the horrors of this—
Through the furnace, unshrinking, thy steps to pursue,
And shield thee, and save thee—or perish there too,

rang the mellow song.

"I am not well," she suddenly cried, leaving the window and turning quickly toward Mr. Byrd. "I am much obliged to you," said she, lowering her voice to a whisper, for the last note of the song was dying away in a quivering *pianissimo*. "I have been deeply interested in this tragedy, and am thankful for any information in regard to it. I must now bid you good-evening."

And with a stately bow into which she infused the mingled courtesy and haughtiness of her nature, she walked steadily away through the crowd that vainly sought to stay her, and disappeared, almost without a pause, behind the door that opened into the hall.

Mr. Byrd remained for a full half-hour after that, but he never could tell what he did, or with whom he conversed, or how or when he issued from the house and made his way back to his room in the hotel. He only knew that at midnight he was still walking the floor, and had not yet made up his mind to take the step which his own sense of duty now inexorably demanded.

11

Decision

The next morning Mr. Ferris was startled by the appearance in his office of Mr. Byrd, looking wretchedly anxious and ill.

"I have come," said the detective, "to ask you what you think of Mr. Hildreth's prospects. Have you made up your mind to have him arrested for this crime?"

"Yes," was the reply. "The evidence against him is purely circumstantial, but it is very strong; and if no fresh developments occur, I think there can be no doubt about my duty. Each and every fact that comes to light only strengthens the case against him. When he came to be examined last night, a ring was found on his person, which he acknowledged to having worn on the day of the murder."

"He took it off during the inquest," murmured Mr. Byrd; "I saw him."

"It is said by Hickory—the somewhat questionable *cognomen* of your fellow-detective from New York—that the young man manifested the most intense uneasiness during the whole inquiry. That in fact his attention was first drawn to him by the many tokens which he gave of suppressed agitation and alarm. Indeed, Mr. Hickory at one time thought he should be obliged to speak to this stranger in order to prevent a scene. Once Mr. Hildreth got up as if to go, and, indeed, if he had been less hemmed in by the crowd, there is every reason to believe he would have attempted an escape."

"Is this Hickory a man of good judgement?" inquired Mr. Byrd, anxiously.

"Why, yes, I should say so. He seems to understand his business. The way he procured us the testimony of Mr. Hildreth was certainly satisfactory."

"I wish that, without his knowing it, I could hear him give his opinion of this matter," intimated the other.

"Well, you can," rejoined Mr. Ferris, after a quick and comprehensive survey of Mr. Byrd's countenance. "I am expecting him here any moment, and if you see fit to sit down behind that screen, you can, without the least difficulty to yourself or him, hear all he has to impart."

"I will, then," the detective declared, a gloomy frown suddenly corrugating his brow; and he stepped across to the screen which had been indicated to him, and quietly withdrew from view.

He had scarcely done this, when a short, quick step was heard at the door, and a wide-awake voice called out, cheerily:

"Are you alone, sir?"

"Ah!" ejaculated Mr. Ferris, "come in, come in. I have been awaiting you for some minutes," he declared, ignoring the look which the man threw hastily around the room. "Any news this morning?"

"No," returned the other, in a tone of complete self-satisfaction. "We've caged the bird and mustn't expect much more in the way of news. I'm on my way to Albany now, to pick up such facts about him as may be lying around there loose, and shall be ready to start for Toledo any day next week that you may think proper."

"You are, then, convinced that Mr. Hildreth is undeniably the guilty party in this case?" exclaimed the district attorney, taking a whiff at his cigar.

"Convinced? That is a strong word, sir. A detective is never convinced," protested the man. "He leaves that for the judge and jury. But if you ask me if there is any doubt about the direction in which all the circumstantial evidence in this case points, I must retort by asking you for a clue, or the tag-end of a clue, guiding me elsewhere. I know," he went on, with the volubility of a man whose work is done, and who feels he has the right to a momentary indulgence in conversation, "that it is not an agreeable thing to subject a gentleman like Mr. Hildreth to the shame of a public arrest. But facts are not partial, sir; and the gentleman has no more rights in law than the coarsest fellow that we take up for butchering his mother. But you know all this without my telling you, and I only mention it to excuse any obstinacy I may have manifested on the subject.

"He is mightily cut up about it," he again proceeded, as he found Mr. Ferris forbore to reply. "I am told he didn't sleep a wink all night, but spent his time alternately in pacing the floor like a caged lion, and in a wild sort of stupor that had something of the hint of madness in it. 'If my grandfather had only known!' was the burden of his song; and when anyone approached him he either told them to keep their eyes off him, or else buried his face in his hands with an entreaty for them not to disturb the last hours of a dying man. He evidently has no hope of escaping the indignity of arrest, and as soon as it was light enough for him to see, he asked for paper and pencil. They were brought him, and a man stood over him while he wrote. It proved to be a letter to his sisters enjoining them to believe in his innocence, and wound up with what was very much like an attempt at a will. Altogether, it looks as if he meditated suicide, and we have been careful to take from him every possible means for his effecting his release in this way, as well as set a strict though secret watch upon him."

A slight noise took place behind the screen, which at any other time Mr. Hickory would have been the first to notice and inquire into. As it was, it had only the effect of unconsciously severing his train of thought and starting him alertly to his feet.

"Well," said he, facing the district attorney with cheerful vivacity, "any orders?"

"No," responded Mr. Ferris. "A run down to Albany seems to be the best thing for you at present. On your return we will consult again."

"Very well, sir. I shall not be absent more than two days, and, in the meantime, you will let me know if anything important occurs?" And, handing over his new address, Hickory speedily took his leave.

"Well, Byrd, what do you think of him?"

For reply, Mr. Byrd stepped forth and took his stand before the district attorney.

"Has Coroner Tredwell informed you," said he, "that the super-intendent has left it to my discretion to interfere in this matter if I thought that by so doing I could further the ends of justice?"

"Yes," was the language of the quick, short nod he received.

"Very well," continued the other, "you will pardon me, then, if I ask you to convey to Mr. Hildreth the following message: That if he is guiltless of this crime he need have no fear of the results of the arrest to which he may be subjected; that a man has interested himself in this matter who pledges his word not to rest till he has discovered the guilty party and freed the innocent from suspicion."

"What!" cried Mr. Ferris, astonished at the severe but determined bearing of the young man who, up to this time, he had only seen un-der his lighter and more indifferent aspect. "You don't agree with this

258

fellow, then, in his conclusions regarding Mr. Hildreth?"

"No, sir. Hickory, as I judge, is an egotist. He discovered Mr. Hildreth and brought him to the notice of the jury, therefore Mr. Hildreth is guilty."

"And you?"

"I am open to doubt about it. Not that I would acknowledge it to anyone but you, sir."

"Why?"

"Because if I work in this case at all, or make any efforts to follow up the clue which I believe myself to have received, it must be done secretly, and without raising the suspicion of anyone in this town. I am not in a position, as you know, to work openly, even if it were advisable to do so, which it certainly is not. What I do must be accomplished under cover, and I ask you to help me in my self-imposed and by no means agreeable task, by trusting me to pursue my inquiries alone, until such time as I assure myself beyond a doubt that my own convictions are just, and that the man who murdered Mrs. Clemmens is someone entirely separated from Mr. Hildreth and any interests that he represents."

"You are, then, going to take up this case?"

The answer given was short, but it meant the deliberate shivering of the fairest dream of love that had ever visited Mr. Byrd's imagination.

"I am."

12

The Spider

In the interview which Mr. Byrd had held with Miss Dare he had been conscious of omitting one test which many another man in his place would have made. This was the utterance of the name of him whom he really believed to be the murderer of Mrs. Clemmens. Had he spoken this name, had he allowed himself to breathe the words "Craik Mansell" into the ears of this agitated woman, or even gone so far as to allude in the most careless way to the widow's nephew, he felt sure his daring would have been rewarded by some expression on her part that would have given him a substantial basis for his theories to rest upon.

But he had too much natural chivalry for this. His feelings as a man got in the way of his instinct as a detective. Nevertheless, he felt positive that his suspicions in regard to this nephew of Mrs. Clemmens were correct, and set about the task of fitting facts to his theory, with all that settled and dogged determination which follows the pursuit of a stern duty unwillingly embraced.

Two points required instant settling.

First, the truth or falsehood of his supposition as to the identification of the person confronted by Miss Dare in the Syracuse depot with the young man described by Miss Firman as the nephew of Widow Clemmens.

Secondly, the existence or non-existence of proof going to show the presence of this person at or near the house of Mrs. Clemmens, during the time of the assault.

But before proceeding to satisfy himself in regard to these essentials, he went again to the widow's house and there spent an hour in a careful study of its inner and outer arrangements, with a view to the formation of a complete theory as to the manner and method of the

murder. He found that in default of believing Mr. Hildreth the assailant, one supposition was positively necessary, and this was that the
murderer was in the house when this gentleman came to it. A glance
at the diagram on next page will explain why.

The house, as you will see, has but three entrances: the front door,
at which Mr. Hildreth unconsciously stood guard; the kitchen door,
also unconsciously guarded during the critical moment by the coming and going of the tramp through the yard; and the dining-room
door, which, though to all appearance free from the surveillance of
any eye, was so situated in reference to the clock at which the widow
stood when attacked, that it was manifestly impossible for anyone to
enter it and cross the room to the hearth without attracting the attention of her eye if not of her ear.

To be sure, there was the bare possibility of his having come in by
the kitchen-door, after the departure of the tramp, but such a contingency was scarcely worth considering. The almost certain conclusion
was that he had been in the house for some time, and was either in
the dining-room when Mrs. Clemmens returned to it from her interview with Mr. Hildreth, or else came down to it from the floor above
by means of the staircase that so strangely descended into that very
room.

Another point looked equally clear. The escape of the murderer—
still in default of considering Mr. Hildreth as such—must have been
by means of one of the back doors, and must have been in the direction of the woods. To be sure there was a stretch of uneven and marshy
ground to be travelled over before the shelter of the trees could be
reached; but a person driven by fear could, at a pinch, travel it in five
minutes or less; and a momentary calculation on the part of Mr. Byrd
sufficed to show him that more time than this had elapsed from the
probable instant of assault to the moment when Mr. Ferris opened the
side door and looked out upon the swamp.

The dearth of dwellings on the left-hand side of the street, and,
consequently, the comparative immunity from observation which was
given to that portion of the house which over-looked the swamp,
made him conclude that this outlet from the dining-room had been
the one made use of in the murderer's flight. A glance down the yard
to the broken fence that separated the widow's land from the boggy
fields beyond, only tended to increase the probabilities of this supposition, and, alert to gain for himself that full knowledge of the situation
necessary to a successful conduct of this mysterious affair, he hastily

left the house and started across the swamp, with the idea of penetrating the woods and discovering for himself what opportunity they afforded for concealment or escape.

He had more difficulty in doing this than he expected. The ground about the hillocks was half-sunk in water, and the least slip to one side invariably precipitated him among the brambles that encumbered this spot. Still, he compassed his task in little more than five minutes, arriving at the firm ground, and its sturdy growth of beeches and maples, well covered with mud, but so far thoroughly satisfied with the result of his efforts.

The next thing to be done was to search the woods, not for the purpose of picking up clues—it was too late for that—but to determine what sort of a refuge they afforded, and whether, in the event of a man's desiring to penetrate them quickly, many impediments would arise in the shape of tangled underground or loose-lying stones.

He found them remarkably clear; so much so, indeed, that he travelled for some distance into their midst before he realized that he had passed beyond their borders. More than this, he came ere long upon something like a path, and, following it, emerged into a sort of glade, where, backed up against a high rock, stood a small and seemingly deserted hut. It was the first object he had met with that in any way suggested the possible presence of man, and advancing to it with cautious steps, he looked into its open doorway. Nothing met his eyes but an empty interior, and without pausing to bestow upon the building a further thought, he hurried on through a path he saw opening beyond it, till he came to the end of the wood.

Stepping forth, he paused in astonishment. Instead of having penetrated the woods in a direct line, he found that he had merely described a half circle through them, and now stood on a highway leading directly back into the town.

Likewise, he was in full sight of the terminus of a line of horse-cars that connected this remote region of Sibley with its business portion, and though distant a good mile from the railway depot, was, to all intents and purposes, as near that means of escape as he would have been in the street in front of Widow Clemmens' house.

Full of thoughts and inly wondering over the fatality that had confined the attention of the authorities to the approaches afforded by the lane, to the utter exclusion of this more circuitous, but certainly more elusive, road of escape, he entered upon the highway, and proceeded to gain the horse-car he saw standing at the head of the road, a few rods away. As he did so, he for the first time realized just where he was. The elegant villa of Professor Darling rising before him on the ridge that ran along on the right-hand side of the road, made it at once evident that he was on the borders of that choice and aristocratic quarter known as the West Side. It was a new region to him, and, pausing for a moment, he cast his eyes over the scene which lay stretched out before him. He had frequently heard it said that the view commanded by the houses on the ridge was the finest in the town, and he was not disappointed in it.

As he looked across the verdant basin of marshy ground around which the road curved like a horseshoe, he could see the city spread out like a map before him. So unobstructed, indeed, was the view he had of its various streets and buildings, that he thought he could even detect, amid the taller and more conspicuous dwellings, the humble walls and newly-shingled roof of the widow's cottage.

But he could not be sure of this; his eyesight was anything but trustworthy for long distances, and hurrying forward to the car, he took his seat just as it was about to start.

It carried him straight into town, and came to a standstill not ten feet from the railroad depot. As he left it and betook himself back to his hotel, he gave to his thoughts a distinct though inward expression.

"If," he mused, "my suppositions in regard to this matter are true, and another man than Mr. Hildreth struck the fatal blow, then I have just travelled over the self-same route he took in his flight."

But were his suppositions true? It remained for him to determine.

13

The Fly

The paper mill of Harrison, Goodman & Chamberlain was situated in one of the main thoroughfares of Buffalo. It was a large but otherwise unpretentious building, and gave employment to a vast number of operatives, mostly female.

Some of these latter might have been surprised, and possibly a little fluttered, one evening, at seeing a well-dressed young gentleman standing at the gate as they came forth, gazing with languid interest from one face to another, as if he were on the look-out for someone of their number.

But they would have been yet more astonished could they have seen him still lingering after the last one had passed, watching with unabated patience the opening and shutting of the small side door devoted to the use of the firm, and such *employés* as had seats in the office. It was Mr. Byrd, and his purpose there at this time of day was to see and review the whole rank and file of the young men employed in the place, in the hope of being able to identify the nephew of Mrs. Clemmens by his supposed resemblance to the person whose character of face and form had been so minutely described to him.

For Mr. Byrd was a just man and a thoughtful one, and knowing this identification to be the key-stone of his lately formed theory, desired it to be complete and of no doubtful character. He accordingly held fast to his position, watching and waiting, seemingly in vain, for the dark, powerful face and the sturdily-built frame of the gentleman whose likeness he had attempted to draw in conjunction with that of Miss Dare. But, though he saw many men of all sorts and kinds issue from one door or another of this vast building, not one of them struck him with that sudden and unmistakable sense of familiarity which he had a right to expect, and he was just beginning to doubt if the whole framework of his elaborately-formed theory was not destined to fall into ruins, when the small door, already alluded to, opened once more, and a couple of gentlemen came out.

The appearance of one of them gave Mr. Byrd a start. He was young, powerfully built, wore a large moustache, and had a complexion of unusual swarthiness. There was character, too, in his face, though not so much as Mr. Byrd had expected to see in the nephew of Mrs. Clemmens. Still, people differ about degrees of expression, and to his informant this face might have appeared strong. He was dressed in a business suit, and was without an overcoat—two facts that made it difficult for Mr. Byrd to get any assistance from the cut and colour of his clothes.

But there was enough in the general style and bearing of this person to make Mr. Byrd anxious to know his name. He, therefore, took it upon himself to follow him—a proceeding which brought him to the corner just in time to see the two gentlemen separate, and the especial one in whom he was interested, step into a car.

He succeeded in getting a seat in the same car, and for some blocks had the pleasure of watching the back of the supposed Mansell, as he stood on the front platform with the driver. Then others got in, and the detective's view was obstructed, and presently—he never could tell how it was—he lost track of the person he was shadowing, and when the chance came for another sight of the driver and platform, the young man was gone.

Annoyed beyond expression, Mr. Byrd went to a hotel, and next day sent to the mill and procured the address of Mr. Mansell. Going to the place named, he found it to be a very respectable boarding-house, and, chancing upon a time when more or less of the rooms were empty, succeeded in procuring for himself an apartment there.

So here he was a fixture in the house supposed by him to hold the murderer of Mrs. Clemmens. When the time for dinner came, and with it an opportunity for settling the vexed question of Mr. Mansell's identity not only with the man in the Syracuse depot, but with the person who had eluded his pursuit the day before, something of the excitement of the hunter in view of his game seized upon this hitherto imperturbable detective, and it was with difficulty he could sustain his usual *rôle* of fashionable indifference.

He arrived at the table before any of the other boarders, and presently a goodly array of amiable matrons, old and young gentlemen, and pretty girls came filing into the room, and finally—yes, finally—

the gentleman whom he had followed from the mill the day before, and whom he now had no hesitation in fixing upon as Mr. Mansell.

But the satisfaction occasioned by the settlement of this perplexing question was dampened somewhat by a sudden and uneasy sense of being himself at a disadvantage. Why he should feel thus he did not know. Perhaps the almost imperceptible change which took place in that gentleman's face as their eyes first met, may have caused the unlooked-for sensation; though why Mr. Mansell should change at the sight of one who must have been a perfect stranger to him, was more than Mr. Byrd could understand. It was enough that the latter felt he had made a mistake in not having donned a disguise before entering this house, and that, oppressed by the idea, he withdrew his attention from the man he had come to watch, and fixed it upon more immediate and personal matters.

The meal was half over. Mr. Byrd who, as a stranger of more than ordinary good looks and prepossessing manners, had been placed by the obliging landlady between her own daughter and a lady of doubtful attractions, was endeavouring to improve his advantages and make himself as agreeable as possible to both of his neighbours, when he heard a lady near him say aloud, "You are late, Mr. Mansell," and, looking up in his amazement, saw entering the door—— Well, in the presence of the real owner of this name, he wondered he ever could have fixed upon the other man as the original of the person that had been described to him. The strong face, the sombre expression, the herculean frame, were unique, and in the comparison which they inevitably called forth, made all other men in the room look dwarfed if not actually commonplace.

Greatly surprised at this new turn of affairs, and satisfied that he at last had before him the man who had confronted Miss Dare in the Syracuse depot, he turned his attention back to the ladies. He, however, took care to keep one ear open on the side of the new-comer, in the hope of gleaning from his style and manner of conversation some notion of his disposition and nature.

But Craik Mansell was at no time a talkative man, and at this especial period of his career was less inclined than ever to enter into the trivial debates or good-natured repartee that was the staple of conversation at Mrs. Hart's table.

So Mr. Byrd's wishes in this regard were foiled. He succeeded, however, in assuring himself by a square look, into the other's face, that to whatever temptation this man may have succumbed, or of whatever crime he may have been guilty, he was by nature neither cold, cruel, nor treacherous, and that the deadly blow, if dealt by him, was the offspring of some sudden impulse or violent ebullition of temper, and was being repented of with every breath he drew.

But this discovery, though it modified Mr. Byrd's own sense of personal revolt against the man, could not influence him in the discharge of his duty, which was to save another of less interesting and perhaps less valuable traits of character from the consequences of a crime he had never committed. It was, therefore, no more than just, that, upon withdrawing from the table, he should endeavour to put himself in the way of settling that second question, upon whose answer in the affirmative depended the rightful establishment of his secret suspicions.

That was, whether this young man was at or near the house of his aunt at the time when she was assaulted.

Mrs. Hart's parlours were always thrown open to her boarders in the evening.

There, at any time from seven to ten, you might meet a merry crowd of young people intent upon enjoying themselves, and usually highly successful in their endeavours to do so. Into this throng Mr. Byrd accordingly insinuated himself, and being of the sort to win instant social recognition, soon found he had but to make his choice in order to win for himself that *tête-à-tête* conversation from which he hoped so much. He consequently surveyed the company with a critical eye, and soon made up his mind as to which lady was the most affable in her manners and the least likely to meet his advances with haughty reserve, and having won an introduction to her, sat down at her side with the stern determination of making her talk about Mr. Mansell.

"You have a very charming company here," he remarked; "the house seems to be filled with a most cheerful class of people."

"Yes," was the not-unlooked-for reply. "We are all merry enough if we except Mr. Mansell. But, of course, there is excuse for him. No one expects him to join in our sports."

"Mr. Mansell? the gentleman who came in late to supper?" repeated Mr. Byrd, with no suggestion of the secret satisfaction he felt at the immediate success of his scheme.

"Yes, he is in great trouble, you know; is the nephew of the woman who was killed a few days ago at Sibley, don't you remember? The widow lady who was struck on the head by a man of the name of Hildreth, and who died after uttering something about a ring, supposed by many to be an attempt on her part to describe the murderer?"

"Yes," was the slow, almost languid, response; "and a dreadful thing, too; quite horrifying in its nature. And so this Mr. Mansell is her nephew?" he suggestively repeated. "Odd! I suppose he has told you all about the affair?"

"He? Mercy! I don't suppose you could get him to say anything about it to save your life. He isn't of the talking sort. Besides, I don't believe he knows any more about it than you or I. He hasn't been to Sibley."

"Didn't he go to the funeral?"

"No; he said he was too ill; and indeed he was shut up one whole day with a terrible sore throat. He is the heir, too, of all her savings, they say; but he won't go to Sibley. Some folks think it is queer, but I——"

Here her eyes wandered and her almost serious look vanished in a somewhat *coquettish* smile. Following her gaze with his own, Mr. Byrd perceived a gentleman approaching. It was the one he had first taken for Mr. Mansell.

"Beg pardon," was the somewhat abrupt salutation with which this person advanced. "But they are proposing a game in the next room, and Miss Clayton's assistance is considered absolutely indispensable."

"Mr. Brown, first allow me to make you acquainted with Mr. Byrd," said the light-hearted damsel, with a gracious inclination. "As you are both strangers, it is well for you to know each other, especially as I expect you to join in our games."

"Thank you," protested Mr. Brown, "but I don't play games." Then seeing the deep bow of acquiescence which Mr. Byrd was making, added, with what appeared to be a touch of jealousy, "Except under strong provocation," and holding out his arm, offered to escort the young lady into the next room.

With an apologetic glance at Mr. Byrd, she accepted the attention proffered her, and speedily vanished into the midst of the laughing group that awaited her.

Mr. Byrd found himself alone.

"Check number one," thought he; and he bestowed anything but an amiable benediction upon the man who had interrupted him in the midst of so promising a conversation.

His next move was in the direction of the landlady's daughter, who, being somewhat shy, favoured a retired nook behind the piano. They had been neighbours at table, and he could at once address her with–

out fear of seeming obtrusive.

"I do not see here the dark young gentleman whom you call Mr. Mansell?" he remarked, inquiringly.

"Oh, no; he is in trouble. A near relative of his was murdered in cold blood the other day, and under the most aggravating circumstances. Haven't you heard about it? She was a Mrs. Clemmens, and lived in Sibley. It was in all the papers."

"Ah, yes; I remember about it very well. And so he is her nephew," he went on, recklessly repeating himself in his determination to elicit all he could from these young and thoughtless misses. "A peculiar-looking young man; has the air of thoroughly understanding himself."

"Yes, he is very smart, they say."

"Does he never talk?"

"Oh, yes; that is, he used to; but, since his aunt's death, we don't expect it. He is very much interested in machinery, and has invented something——"

"Oh, Clara, you are not going to sit here," interposed the reproachful voice of a saucy-eyed maiden, who at this moment peeped around the corner of the piano. "We want all the recruits we can get," she cried, with a sudden blush, as she encountered the glance of Mr. Byrd. "Do come, and bring the gentleman too." And she slipped away to join that very Mr. Brown who, by his importunities, had been the occasion of the former interruption from which Mr. Byrd had suffered.

"That man and I will quarrel yet," was the mental exclamation with which the detective rose. "Shall we join your friends?" asked he, assuming an unconcern he was far from feeling.

"Yes, if you please," was the somewhat timid, though evidently pleased, reply.

And Mr. Byrd noted down in his own mind check number two.

The game was a protracted one. Twice did he think to escape from the merry crowd he had entered, and twice did he fail to do so. The indefatigable Brown would not let him slip, and it was only by a positive exertion of his will that he finally succeeded in withdrawing himself.

"I wish to have a word with your mother," he explained, in reply to the look of protest with which Miss Hart honoured his departure. "I hear she retires early; so you will excuse me if I leave somewhat abruptly."

And to Mrs. Hart's apartment he at once proceeded, and, by dint of his easy assurance, soon succeeded in leading her, as he had already done the rest, into a discussion of the one topic for which he had an interest. He had not time, however, to glean much from her, for, just as she was making the admission that Mr. Mansell had not been home at the time of the murder, a knock was heard at the door, and, with an affable bow and a short, quick stare of surprise at Mr. Byrd, the ubiquitous Mr. Brown stepped in and took a seat on the sofa, with every appearance of intending to make a call.

At this third check, Mr. Byrd was more than annoyed. Rising, however, with the most amiable courtesy, he bowed his acknowledgments to the landlady, and, without heeding her pressing invitation to remain and make the acquaintance of Mr. Brown, left the room and betook himself back to the parlours.

He was just one minute too late. The last of the boarders had gone up-stairs, and only an empty room met his eyes.

He at once ascended to his own apartment. It was on the fourth floor. There were many other rooms on this floor, and for a moment he could not remember which was his own door. At last, however, he felt sure it was the third one from the stairs, and, going to it, gave a short knock in case of mistake, and, hearing no reply, opened it and went in.

The first glance assured him that his recollection had played him false, and that he was in the wrong room. The second, that he was in that of Mr. Mansell. The sight of the small model of a delicate and intricate machine that stood in full view on a table before him would have been sufficient assurance of this fact, even if the inventor himself had been absent. But he was there. Seated at a table, with his back to the door, and his head bowed forward on his arms, he presented such a picture of misery or despair, that Mr. Byrd felt his sympathies touched in spite of himself, and hastily stumbling backward, was about to confusedly withdraw, when a doubt struck him as to the condition of the deathly, still, and somewhat pallid figure before him, and, stepping hurriedly forward, he spoke the young man's name, and, failing to elicit a response, laid his hand on his shoulder, with an apology for disturbing him, and an inquiry as to how he felt.

The touch acted where the voice had failed. Leaping from his partly recumbent position, Craik Mansell faced the intruder with indignant inquiry written in every line of his white and determined face.

"To what do I owe this intrusion?" he cried, his nostrils expanding

271

and contracting with an anger that proved the violence of his nature when aroused.

"First, to my carelessness," responded Mr. Byrd; "and, secondly——" But there he paused, for the first time in his life, perhaps, absolutely robbed of speech. His eye had fallen upon a picture that the other held clutched in his vigorous right hand. It was a photograph of Imogene Dare, and it was made conspicuous by two heavy black lines which had been relentlessly drawn across the face in the form of a cross. "Secondly," he went on, after a moment, resolutely tearing his gaze away from this startling and suggestive object, "to my fears. I thought you looked ill, and could not forbear making an effort to reassure myself that all was right."

"Thank you," ejaculated the other, in a heavy weariful tone. "I am perfectly well." And with a short bow he partially turned his back, with a distinct intimation that he desired to be left alone.

Mr. Byrd could not resist this appeal. Glad as he would have been for even a moment's conversation with this man, he was, perhaps unfortunately, too much of a gentleman to press himself forward against the expressed wishes even of a suspected criminal. He accordingly withdrew to the door, and was about to open it and go out, when it was flung violently forward, and the ever-obtrusive Brown stepped in.

This second intrusion was more than unhappy Mr. Mansell could stand. Striding passionately forward, he met the unblushing Brown at full tilt, and angrily pointing to the door, asked if it was not the custom of gentlemen to knock before entering the room of strangers.

"I beg pardon," said the other, backing across the threshold, with a profuse display of confusion. "I had no idea of its being a stranger's room. I thought it was my own. I—I was sure that my door was the third from the stairs. Excuse me, excuse me." And he bustled noisily out.

This precise reproduction of his own train of thought and action confounded Mr. Byrd.

Turning with a deprecatory glance to the perplexed and angry occupant of the room, he said something about not knowing the person who had just left them; and then, conscious that a further contemplation of the stern and suffering countenance before him would unnerve him for the duty he had to perform, hurriedly withdrew.

14

A Last Attempt

The sleep of Horace Byrd that night was anything but refreshing. In the first place, he was troubled about this fellow Brown, whose last impertinence showed he was a man to be watched, and, if possible, understood. Secondly, he was haunted by a vision of the unhappy youth he had just left; seeing, again and again, both in his dreams and in the rush of heated fancies which followed his awaking, that picture of utter despair which the opening of his neighbour's door had revealed. He could not think of that poor mortal as sleeping. Whether it was the result of his own sympathetic admiration for Miss Dare, or of some subtle clairvoyance bestowed upon him by the darkness and stillness of the hour, he felt assured that the quiet watch he had interrupted by his careless importunity, had been again established, and that if he could tear down the partition separating their two rooms, he should see that bowed form and buried face crouched despairingly above the disfigured picture.

The depths of human misery and the maddening passions that underlie all crime had been revealed to him for the first time, perhaps, in all their terrible suggestiveness, and he asked himself over and over as he tossed on his uneasy pillow, if he possessed the needful determination to carry on the scheme he had undertaken, in face of the unreasoning sympathies which the fathomless misery of this young man had aroused. Under the softening influences of the night, he answered, No; but when the sunlight came and the full flush of life with its restless duties and common necessities awoke within him, he decided, Yes.

Mr. Mansell was not at the breakfast-table when Mr. Byrd came down. His duties at the mill were peremptory, and he had already taken his coffee and gone. But Mr. Brown was there, and at sight of him

Mr. Byrd's caution took alarm, and he bestowed upon this intrusive busybody a close and searching scrutiny. It, however, elicited nothing in the way of his own enlightenment beyond the fact that this fellow, total stranger though he seemed, was for some inexplicable reason an enemy to himself or his plans.

Not that Mr. Brown manifested this by any offensive token of dislike or even of mistrust. On the contrary, he was excessively polite, and let slip no opportunity of dragging Mr. Byrd into the conversation. Yet, for all that, a secret influence was already at work against the detective, and he could not attribute it to any other source than the jealous efforts of this man. Miss Hart was actually curt to him, and in the attitude of the various persons about the board he detected a certain reserve which had been entirely absent from their manner the evening before.

But while placing, as he thought, due weight upon this fellow's animosity, he had no idea to what it would lead, till he went up-stairs. Mrs. Hart, who had hitherto treated him with the utmost cordiality, now called him into the parlour, and told him frankly that she would be obliged to him if he would let her have his room. To be sure, she qualified the seeming harshness of her request by an intimation that a permanent occupant had applied for it, and offered to pay his board at the hotel till he could find a room to suit him in another house; but the fact remained that she was really in a flutter to rid herself of him, and no subterfuge could hide it, and Mr. Byrd, to whose plans the full confidence of those around him was essential, found himself obliged to acquiesce in her desires, and announce at once his willingness to depart.

Instantly she was all smiles, and overwhelmed him with overtures of assistance; but he courteously declined her help, and, flying from her apologies with what speed he could, went immediately to his room. Here he sat down to deliberate.

The facts he had gleaned, despite the interference of his unknown enemy, were three:

First, that Craik Mansell had found excuses for not attending the inquest, or even the funeral, of his murdered aunt.

Secondly, that he had a strong passion for invention, and had even now the model of a machine on hand.

And third, that he was not at home, wherever else he may have been, on the morning of the murder in Sibley.

"A poor and meagre collection of insignificant facts," thought

Mr. Byrd. "Too poor and meagre to avail much in stemming the tide threatening to overwhelm Gouverneur Hildreth."

But what opportunity remained for making them weightier? He was turned from the house that held the few persons from whom he could hope to glean more complete and satisfactory information, and he did not know where else to seek it unless he went to the mill. And this was an alternative from which he shrank, as it would, in the first place, necessitate a revelation of his real character; and, secondly, make known the fact that Mr. Mansell was under the surveillance of the police, if not in the actual attitude of a suspected man.

A quick and hearty, "Shure, you are very good, sir!" uttered in the hall without roused him from his meditations and turned his thoughts in a new direction. What if he could learn something from the servants? He had not thought of them. This girl, now, whose work constantly carried her into the various rooms on this floor, would, of course, know whether Mr. Mansell had been away on the day of the murder, even if she could not tell the precise time of his return. At all events, it was worthwhile to test her with a question or two before he left, even if he had to resort to the means of spurring her memory with money. His failure in other directions did not necessitate a failure here.

He accordingly called her in, and showing her a bright silver dollar, asked her if she thought it good enough pay for a short answer to a simple question.

To his great surprise she blushed and drew back, shaking her head and muttering that her mistress didn't like to have the girls talk to the young men about the house, and finally going off with a determined toss of her frowsy head, that struck Mr. Byrd aghast, and made him believe more than ever that his evil star hung in the ascendant, and that the sooner he quit the house the better.

In ten minutes he was in the street.

But one thing now remained for him to do. He must make the acquaintance of one of the mill-owners, or possibly of an overseer or accountant, and from him learn where Mr. Mansell had been at the time of his aunt's murder. To this duty he devoted the day; but here also he was met by unexpected difficulties. Though he took pains to disguise himself before proceeding to the mill, all the endeavours which he made to obtain an interview there with any responsible person were utterly fruitless. Whether his ill-luck at the house had followed him to this place he could not tell, but, for some reason or other, there was not one of the gentlemen for whom he inquired but had some excuse for not seeing him; and, worn out at last with repeated disappointments, if not oppressed by the doubtful looks he received from the various subordinates who carried his messages, he left the building, and proceeded to make use of the only means now left him of compassing his end.

This was to visit Mr. Goodman, the one member of the firm who was not at his post that day, and see if from him he could gather the single fact he was in search of.

"Perhaps the atmosphere of distrust with which I am surrounded in this quarter has not reached this gentleman's house," thought he. And having learned from the directory where that house was, he proceeded immediately to it.

His reception was by no means cordial. Mr. Goodman had been ill the night before, and was in no mood to see strangers.

"Mansell?" he coolly repeated, in acknowledgment of the other's inquiry as to whether he had a person of that name in his employ. "Yes, our book-keeper's name is Mansell. May I ask"—and here Mr. Byrd felt himself subjected to a thorough, if not severe, scrutiny— "why you come to me with inquiries concerning him?"

"Because," the determined detective responded, adopting at once the bold course, "you can put me in possession of a fact which it eminently befits the cause of justice to know. I am an emissary, sir, from the district attorney at Sibley, and the point I want settled is, where Mr. Mansell was on the morning of the twenty-sixth of September?"

This was business, and the look that involuntarily leaped into Mr. Goodman's eye proved that he considered it so. He did not otherwise betray this feeling, however, but turned quite calmly toward a chair, into which he slowly settled himself before replying:

"And why do you not ask the gentleman himself where he was? He probably would be quite ready to tell you."

The inflection he gave to these words warned Mr. Byrd to be careful. The truth was, Mr. Goodman was Mr. Mansell's best friend, and as such had his own reasons for not being especially communicative in his regard, to this stranger. The detective vaguely felt this, and immediately changed his manner.

"I have no doubt of that, sir," he ingenuously answered. "But Mr. Mansell has had so much to distress him lately, that I was desirous of saving him from the unpleasantness which such a question would necessarily cause. It is only a small matter, sir. A person—it is not essential to state whom—has presumed to raise the question among the authorities in Sibley as to whether Mr. Mansell, as heir of poor Mrs. Clemmens' small property, might not have had some hand in her dreadful death. There was no proof to sustain the assumption, and Mr. Mansell was not even known to have been in the town on or after the day of her murder; but justice, having listened to the aspersion, felt bound to satisfy itself of its falsity; and I was sent here to learn where Mr. Mansell was upon that fatal day. I find he was not in Buffalo. But this does not mean he was in Sibley, and I am sure that, if you will, you can supply me with facts that will lead to a complete and satisfactory *alibi* for him."

But the hard caution of the other was not to be moved.

"I am sorry," said he, "but I can give you no information in regard to Mr. Mansell's travels. You will have to ask the gentleman himself."

"You did not send him out on business of your own, then?"

"No."

"But you knew he was going?"

"Yes."

"And can tell when he came back?"

"He was in his place on Wednesday."

The cold, dry nature of these replies convinced Mr. Byrd that something more than the sullen obstinacy of an uncommunicative man lay behind this determined reticence. Looking at Mr. Goodman inquiringly, he calmly remarked:

"You are a friend of Mr. Mansell?"

The answer came quick and coldly:

"He is a constant visitor at my house."

Mr. Byrd made a respectful bow.

"You can, then, have no doubts of his ability to prove an *alibi?*"

"I have no doubts concerning Mr. Mansell," was the stern and uncompromising reply.

Mr. Byrd at once felt he had received his dismissal. But before making up his mind to go, he resolved upon one further effort. Calling to his aid his full power of acting, he slowly shook his head with a thoughtful air, and presently murmured half aloud and half, as it were, to himself:

"I thought, possibly, he might have gone to Washington." Then, with a casual glance at Mr. Goodman, added: "He is an inventor, I believe?"

"Yes," was again the laconic response.

"Has he not a machine at present which he desires to bring to the notice of some capitalist?"

"I believe he has," was the forced and none too amiable answer.

Mr. Byrd at once leaned confidingly forward.

"Don't you think," he asked, "that he may have gone to New York to consult with someone about this pet hobby of his? It would certainly be a natural thing for him to do, and if I only knew it was so, I could go back to Sibley with an easy conscience."

His disinterested air, and the tone of kindly concern which he had adopted, seemed at last to produce its effect on his companion. Relaxing a trifle of his austerity, Mr. Goodman went so far as to admit that Mr. Mansell had told him that business connected with his patent had called him out of town; but beyond this he would allow nothing; and Mr. Byrd, baffled in his attempts to elicit from this man any distinct acknowledgment of Mr. Mansell's whereabouts at the critical time of Mrs. Clemmens' death, made a final bow and turned toward the door.

It was only at this moment he discovered that Mr. Goodman and himself had not been alone in the room; that curled up in one of the window-seats was a little girl of some ten or twelve years of age, who at the first tokens of his taking his departure slipped shyly down to the floor and ran before him out into the hall. He found her by the front door when he arrived there. She was standing with her hand on the knob, and presented such a picture of childish eagerness, tempered by childish timidity, that he involuntarily paused before her with a smile. She needed no further encouragement.

"Oh, sir, I know about Mr. Mansell!" she cried. "He wasn't in that place you talk about, for he wrote a letter to papa just the day before he came back, and the postmark on the envelope was Monteith. I remember, because it was the name of the man who made our big map." And, looking up with that eager zeal which marks the liking of very little folks for someone favourite person among their grown acquaintances, she added, earnestly: "I do hope you won't let them say anything bad about Mr. Mansell, he is so good."

And without waiting for a reply, she ran off, her curls dancing, her eyes sparkling, all her little innocent form alive with the joy of having done a kindness, as she thought, for her favourite, Mr. Mansell.

Mr. Byrd, on the contrary, felt a strange pang that the information he had sought for so long and vainly should come at last from the lips of an innocent child.

Monteith, as you remember, was the next station to Sibley.

15

The End of a Tortuous Path

The arrest of Mr. Hildreth had naturally quieted public suspicion by fixing attention upon a definite point, so that when Mr. Byrd returned to Sibley he found that he could pursue whatever inquiries he chose without awakening the least mistrust that he was on the lookout for the murderer of Mrs. Clemmens.

The first use he made of his time was to find out if Mr. Mansell, or any man answering to his description, had been seen to take the train from the Sibley station on the afternoon or evening of the fatal Tuesday. The result was unequivocal. No such person had been seen there, and no such person was believed to have been at the station at any time during that day. This was his first disappointment.

He next made the acquaintance of the conductors on that line of street-cars by means of which he believed Mr. Mansell to have made his escape. But with no better result. Not one of them remembered having taken up, of late, any passenger from the terminus, of the appearance described by Mr. Byrd.

And this was his second disappointment.

His next duty was obviously to change his plan of action and make the town of Monteith the centre of his inquiries. But he hesitated to do this till he had made one other visit to the woods in whose recesses he still believed the murderer to have plunged immediately upon dealing the fatal blow.

He went by the way of the street railroad, not wishing to be again seen crossing the bog, and arrived at the hut in the centre of the glade without meeting anyone or experiencing the least adventure.

This time he went in, but nothing was to be seen save bare logs, a rough hearth where a fire had once been built, and the rudest sort of bench and table; and hurrying forth again, he looked doubtfully up and down the glade in pursuit of some hint to guide him in his future researches.

Suddenly he received one. The thick wall of foliage which at first glance revealed but the two outlets already traversed by him, showed upon close inspection a third path, opening well behind the hut, and leading, as he soon discovered, in an entirely opposite direction from that which had taken him to West Side. Merely stopping to cast one glance at the sun, which was still well overhead, he set out on this new path. It was longer and much more intricate than the other. It led through hollows and up steeps, and finally out into an open blackberry patch, where it seemed to terminate. But a close study of the surrounding bushes, soon disclosed signs of a narrow and thread-like passage curving about a rocky steep.

Entering this he presently found himself drawn again into the woods, which he continued to traverse till he came to a road cut through the heart of the forest, for the use of the lumbermen. Here he paused. Should he turn to the right or left? He decided to turn to the right. Keeping in the road, which was rough with stones where it was not marked with the hoofs of both horses and cattle, he walked for some distance. Then he emerged into open space again, and discovered that he was on the hillside overlooking Monteith, and that by a mile or two's further walk over the highway that was dimly to be descried at the foot of the hill, he would reach the small station devoted to the uses of the quarrymen that worked in this place.

There was no longer any further doubt that this route, and not the other, had been the one taken by Mr. Mansell on that fatal afternoon. But he was determined not to trust any further to mere surmises; so hastening down the hill, he made his way in the direction of the highway, meaning to take the walk alluded to, and learn for himself what passengers had taken the train at this point on the Tuesday afternoon so often mentioned.

But a barrier rose in his way. A stream which he had barely noticed in the quick glance he threw over the landscape from the brow of the hill, separated with quite a formidable width of water the hillside from the road, and it was not till he wandered back for some distance along its banks, that he found a bridge. The time thus lost was considerable, but he did not think of it; and when, after a long and weary tramp, he stepped upon the platform of the small station, he was so eager to learn if he had correctly followed the scent, that he forgot to remark that the road he had taken was anything but an easy or feasible one for a hasty escape.

The accommodation-trains, which alone stop at this point, had both passed, and he found the station-master at leisure. A single glance into his honest and intelligent face convinced the detective that he had a reliable man to deal with. He at once commenced his questions.

"Do many persons besides the quarrymen take the train at this place?" asked he.

"Not many," was the short but sufficiently good-natured rejoinder. "I guess I could easily count them on the fingers of one hand," he laughed.

"You would be apt to notice, then, if a strange gentleman got on board here at any time, would you not?"

"Guess so; not often troubled that way, but sometimes—sometimes."

"Can you tell me whether a young man of very dark complexion, heavy moustache, and a determined, if not excited, expression, took the cars here for Monteith, say, any day last week?"

"I don't know," mused the man. "Dark complexion, you say, large moustache; let me see."

"No dandy," Mr. Byrd carefully explained, "but a strong man, who believes in work. He was possibly in a state of somewhat nervous hurry," he went on, suggestively, "and if he wore an overcoat at all, it was a gray one."

The face of the man lighted up.

"I seem to remember," said he. "Did he have a very bright blue eye and a high colour?"

Mr. Byrd nodded.

"And did he carry a peculiarly shaped bag, of which he was very careful?"

"I don't know," said Mr. Byrd, but remembering the model, added with quick assurance, "I have no doubt he did"; which seemed to satisfy the other, for he at once cried:

"I recollect such a person very well. I noticed him before he got to the station; as soon in fact as he came in sight. He was walking down the highway, and seemed to be thinking about something. He's of the kind to attract attention. What about him, sir?"

"Nothing. He was in trouble of some kind, and he went from home without saying where he was going; and his friends are anxious about him, that is all. Do you think you could swear to his face if you saw it?"

"I think I could. He was the only stranger that got on to the cars that afternoon."

"Do you remember, then, the day?"

"Well, no, now, I don't."

"But can't you, if you try? Wasn't there something done by you that day which will assist your memory?"

Again that slow "Let me see" showed that the man was pondering. Suddenly he slapped his thigh and exclaimed:

"You might be a lawyer's clerk now, mightn't you; or, perhaps, a lawyer himself? I do remember that a large load of stone was sent off that day, and a minute's look at my book—— It was Tuesday," he presently affirmed.

Mr. Byrd drew a deep breath. There is sadness mixed with the satisfaction of such a triumph.

"I am much obliged to you," he said, in acknowledgment of the other's trouble. "The friends of this gentleman will now have little difficulty in tracing him. There is but one thing further I should like to make sure of."

And taking from his memorandum-book the picture he kept concealed there, he showed him the face of Mr. Mansell, now altered to a perfect likeness, and asked him if he recognized it.

The decided Yes which he received made further questions unnecessary.

16

Storm

A day had passed. Mr. Byrd, who no longer had any reason to doubt that he was upon the trail of the real assailant of the Widow Clemmens, had resolved upon a third visit to the woods, this time with the definite object of picking up any clew, however trifling, in support of the fact that Craik Mansell had passed through the glade behind his aunt's house.

The sky, when he left the hotel, was one vast field of blue; but by the time he reached the terminus of the car-route, and stepped out upon the road leading to the woods, dark clouds had overcast the sun, and a cool wind replaced the quiet zephyrs which had all day fanned the brilliant autumn foliage.

He did not realize the condition of the atmosphere, however, and proceeded on his way, thinking more of the person he had just perceived issuing from the door-way of Professor Darling's lofty mansion, than of the low mutterings of distant thunder that now and then disturbed the silence of the woods, or of the ominous, brazen tint which was slowly settling over the huge bank of cloud that filled the northern sky. For that person was Miss Dare, and her presence here, or anywhere near him, at this time, must of necessity, awaken a most painful train of thought.

But, though unmindful of the storm, he was dimly conscious of the darkness that was settling about him. Quicker and quicker grew his pace, and at last he almost broke into a run as the heavy pall of a large black cloud swept up over the zenith, and wiped from the heavens the last remnant of blue sky. One drop fell, then another, then a slow, heavy patter, that bent double the leaves they fell upon, as if a shower of lead had descended upon the heavily writhing forest. The wind had risen, too, and the vast aisles of that clear and beautiful wood thundered with the swaying of boughs, and the crash here and there of an old and falling limb. But the lightning delayed.

The blindest or most abstracted man could be ignorant no longer of what all this turmoil meant. Stopping in the path along which he had been speeding, Mr. Byrd glanced before him and behind, in a momentary calculation of distances, and deciding he could not regain the terminus before the storm burst, pushed on toward the hut.

He reached it just as the first flash of lightning darted down through the heavy darkness, and was about to fling himself against the door, when something—was it the touch of an invisible hand, or the crash of awful thunder which at this instant ploughed up the silence of the forest and woke a pandemonium of echoes about his head?—stopped him.

He never knew. He only realized that he shuddered and drew back, with a feeling of great disinclination to enter the low building before him, alone; and that presently taking advantage of another loud crash of falling boughs, he crept around the corner of the hut, and satisfied his doubts by looking into the small, square window opening to the west.

He found there was ample reason for all the hesitation he had felt. A man was sitting there, who, at the first glimpse, appeared to him to be none other than Craik Mansell. But reason soon assured him this could not be, though the shape, the attitude—that old attitude of despair which he remembered so well—was so startlingly like that of the man whose name was uppermost in his thoughts, that he recoiled in spite of himself.

A second flash swept blinding through the wood. Mr. Byrd advanced his head and took another glance at the stranger. It *was* Mr. Mansell. No other man would sit so quiet and unmoved during the rush and clatter of a terrible storm.

Look! not a hair of his head has stirred, not a movement has taken place in the hands clasped so convulsively beneath his brow. He is an image, a stone, and would not hear though the roof fell in.

Mr. Byrd himself forgot the storm, and only queried what his duty was in this strange and surprising emergency.

But before he could come to any definite conclusion, he was subjected to a new sensation. A stir that was not the result of the wind or the rain had taken place in the forest before him. A something—he could not tell what—was advancing upon him from the path he had himself travelled so short a time before, and its step, if step it were, shook him with a vague apprehension that made him dread to lift his eyes. But he conquered the unmanly instinct, and merely taking the precaution to step somewhat further back from view, looked in the direction of his fears, and saw a tall, firmly-built woman, whose grandly poised head, held high, in defiance of the gale, the lightning, and the rain, proclaimed her to be none other than Imogene Dare.

It was a juxtaposition of mental, moral, and physical forces that almost took Mr. Byrd's breath away. He had no doubt whom she had come to see, or to what sort of a tryst he was about to be made an unwilling witness. But he could not have moved if the blast then surging through the trees had uprooted the huge pine behind which he had involuntarily drawn at the first impression he had received of her approach. He must watch that white face of hers slowly evolve itself from the surrounding darkness, and he must be present when the dreadful bolt swept down from heaven, if only to see her eyes in the flare of its ghostly flame.

It came while she was crossing the glade. Fierce, blinding, more vivid and searching than at any time before, it flashed down through the cringing boughs, and, like a mantle of fire, enveloped her form, throwing out its every outline, and making of the strong and beautiful face an electric vision which Mr. Byrd was never able to forget.

A sudden swoop of wind followed, flinging her almost to the ground, but Mr. Byrd knew from that moment that neither wind nor lightning, not even the fear of death, would stop this woman if once she was determined upon any course.

Dreading the next few moments inexpressibly, yet forcing himself, as a detective, to remain at his post, though every instinct of his nature rebelled, Mr. Byrd drew himself up against the side of the low hut and listened. Her voice, rising between the mutterings of thunder and the roar of the ceaseless gale, was plainly to be heard.

"Craik Mansell," said she, in a strained tone, that was not without its severity, "you sent for me, and I am here."

Ah, this was her mode of greeting, was it? Mr. Byrd felt his breath come easier, and listened for the reply with intensest interest.

But it did not come. The low rumbling of the thunder went on, and the wind howled through the gruesome forest, but the man she had addressed did not speak.

"Craik!" Her voice still came from the door-way, where she had seemingly taken her stand. "Do you not hear me?"

A stifled groan was the sole reply.

She appeared to take one step forward, but no more.

"I can understand," said she, and Mr. Byrd had no difficulty in hearing her words, though the turmoil overhead was almost deafening, "why the restlessness of despair should drive you into seeking this interview. I have longed to see you too, if only to tell you that I wish heaven's thunderbolts had fallen upon us both on that day when we sat and talked of our future prospects and——"

A lurid flash cut short her words. Strange and awesome sounds awoke in the air above, and the next moment a great branch fell crashing down upon the roof of the hut, beating in one corner, and sliding thence heavily to the ground, where it lay with all its quivering leaves uppermost, not two feet from the door-way where this woman stood.

A shriek like that of a lost spirit went up from her lips.

"I thought the vengeance of heaven had fallen!" she gasped. And for a moment not a sound was heard within or without the hut, save that low flutter of the disturbed leaves. "It is not to be," she then whispered, with a return of her old calmness, that was worse than any shriek. "Murder is not to be avenged thus." Then, shortly: "A dark and hideous line of blood is drawn between you and me, Craik Mansell. I cannot pass it, and you must not, forever and forever and forever. But that does not hinder me from wishing to help you, and so I ask, in all sincerity, What is it you want me to do for you today?"

A response came this time.

"Show me how to escape the consequences of my act," were his words, uttered in a low and muffled voice.

She did not answer at once.

"Are you threatened?" she inquired at last, in a tone that proved she had drawn one step nearer to the bowed form and hidden face of the person she addressed.

"My conscience threatens me," was the almost stifled reply.

Again that heavy silence, all the more impressive that the moments before had been so prolific of heaven's most terrible noises.

"You suffer because another man is forced to endure suspicion for a crime he never committed," she whisperingly exclaimed.

Only a groan answered her; and the moments grew heavier and heavier, more and more oppressive, though the hitherto accompanying outcries of the forest had ceased, and a faint lightening of the heavy darkness was taking place overhead. Mr. Byrd felt the pressure of the situation so powerfully, he drew near to the window he had hitherto avoided, and looked in. She was standing a foot behind the crouched figure of the man, between whom and herself she had avowed a line of blood to be drawn. As he looked she spoke.

"Craik," said she, and the deathless yearning of love spoke in her voice at last, "there is but one thing to do. Expiate your guilt by acknowledging it. Save the innocent from unmerited suspicion, and trust to the mercy of God. It is the only advice I can give you. I know no other road to peace. If I did——" She stopped, choked by the terror of her own thoughts. "Craik," she murmured, at last, "on the day I hear of your having made this confession, I vow to take an oath of celibacy for life. It is the only recompense I can offer for the misery and sin into which our mutual mad ambitions have plunged you."

And subduing with a look of inexpressible anguish an evident longing to lay her hand in final caress upon that bended head, she gave him one parting look, and then, with a quick shudder, hurried away, and buried herself amid the darkness of the wet and shivering woods.

17

A Surprise

When all was still again, Mr. Byrd advanced from his place of concealment, and softly entered the hut. Its solitary occupant sat as before, with his head bent down upon his clasped hands. But at the first sound of Mr. Byrd's approach he rose and turned. The shock of the discovery which followed sent the detective reeling back against the door. The person who faced him with such quiet assurance was *not* Craik Mansell.

18

A Brace of Detectives

"So there are two of us! I thought as much when I first set eyes upon your face in Buffalo!"

This exclamation, uttered in a dry and musing tone, woke Mr. Byrd from the stupor into which this astonishing discovery had thrown him. Advancing upon the stranger, who in size, shape, and colouring was almost the *facsimile* of the person he had so successfully represented, Mr. Byrd looked him scrutinizingly over.

The man bore the ordeal with equanimity; he even smiled.

"You don't recognize me, I see."

Mr. Byrd at once recoiled.

"Ah!" cried he, "you are that Jack-in-the-box, Brown!"

"*Alias* Frank Hickory, at your service."

This name, so unexpected, called up a flush of mingled surprise and indignation to Mr. Byrd's cheek.

"I thought——" he began.

"Don't think," interrupted the other, who, when excited, affected laconicism, "know." Then, with affability, proceeded, "You are the gentleman——" he paid that much deference to Mr. Byrd's air and manner, "who I was told might lend me a helping hand in this Clemmens affair. I didn't recognize you before, sir. Wouldn't have stood in your way if I had. Though, to be sure, I did want to see this matter through myself. I thought I had the right. And I've done it, too, as you must acknowledge, if you have been present in this terrible place very long."

This self-satisfied, if not boastful, allusion to a scene in which this strange being had played so unworthy, if not unjustifiable, a part, sent a thrill of revulsion through Mr. Byrd. Drawing hastily back with an instinct of dislike he could not conceal, he cast a glance through the thicket of trees that spread beyond the open door, and pointedly asked:

"Was there no way of satisfying yourself of the guilt of Craik Mansell, except by enacting a farce that may lead to the life-long remorse of the woman out of whose love you have made a trap?"

A slow flush, the first, possibly, that had visited the hardy cheek of this thick-skinned detective for years, crept over the face of Frank Hickory.

"I don't mean she shall ever know," he sullenly protested, kicking at the block upon which he had been sitting. "But it *was* a mean trick," he frankly enough admitted the next moment. "If I hadn't been the tough old hickory knot that I am, I couldn't have done it, I suppose. The storm, too, made it seem a bit trifling. But—— Well, well!" he suddenly interjected, in a more cheerful tone, "'tis too late now for tears and repentance. The thing is done, and can't be undone. And, at all events, I reckon we are both satisfied *now* as to who killed Widow Clemmens!"

Mr. Byrd could not resist a slight sarcasm. "I thought you were satisfied in that regard before?" said he. "At least, I understood that at a certain time you were very positive it was Mr. Hildreth."

"So I was," the fellow good-naturedly allowed; "so I was. The by-ways of a crime like this are dreadful dark and uncertain. It isn't strange that a fellow gets lost sometimes. But I got a jog on my elbow that sent me into the right path," said he, "as, perhaps, you did too, sir, eh?"

Not replying to this latter insinuation, Mr. Byrd quietly repeated:

"You got a jog on your elbow? When, may I ask?"

"Three days ago, *just!*" was the emphatic reply.

"And from whom?"

Instead of replying, the man leaned back against the wall of the hut and looked at his interlocutor in silence.

"Are we going to join hands over this business?" he cried, at last, "or are you thinking of pushing your way on alone after you have got from me all that I know?"

The question took Mr. Byrd by surprise.

He had not thought of the future. He was as yet too much disturbed by his memories of the past. To hide his discomfiture, he began to pace the floor, an operation which his thoroughly wet condition certainly made advisable.

"I have no wish to rob you of any glory you may hope to reap from the success of the plot you have carried on here today," he presently declared, with some bitterness; "but if this Craik Mansell *is* guilty, I suppose it is my duty to help you in the collection of all suitable and proper evidence against him."

"Then," said the other, who had been watching him with rather an anxious eye, "let us to work." And, sitting down on the table, he motioned to Mr. Byrd to take a seat upon the block at his side.

But the latter kept up his walk.

Hickory surveyed him for a moment in silence, then he said:

"You must have something against this young man, or you wouldn't be here. What is it? What first set you thinking about Craik Mansell?"

Now, this was a question Mr. Byrd could not and would not answer. After what had just passed in the hut, he felt it impossible to mention to this man the name of Imogene Dare in connection with that of the nephew of Mrs. Clemmens. He therefore waived the other's interrogation and remarked:

"My knowledge was rather the fruit of surmise than fact. I did not believe in the guilt of Gouverneur Hildreth, and so was forced to look about me for someone whom I could conscientiously suspect. I fixed upon this unhappy man in Buffalo; how truly, your own suspicions, unfortunately, reveal."

"And I had to have my wits started by a horrid old woman," murmured the evidently abashed Hickory.

"Horrid old woman!" repeated Mr. Byrd. "Not Sally Perkins?"

"Yes. A sweet one, isn't she?"

Mr. Byrd shuddered.

"Tell me about it," said he, coming and sitting down in the seat the other had previously indicated to him.

"I will, sir; I will: but first let's look at the weather. Some folks would think it just as well for you to change that toggery of yours. What do you say to going home first, and talking afterward?"

"I suppose it would be wise," admitted Mr. Byrd, looking down at his garments, whose decidedly damp condition he had scarcely noticed in his excitement. "And yet I hate to leave this spot till I learn how you came to choose it as the scene of the tragi-comedy you have enacted here today, and what position it is likely to occupy in the testimony which you have collected against this young man."

"Wait, then," said the bustling fellow, "till I build you the least bit of a fire to warm you. It won't take but a minute," he averred, piling together some old sticks that cumbered the hearth, and straightway setting a match to them. "See! isn't that pleasant? And now, just cast your eye at this!" he continued, drawing a comfortable-looking flask out of his pocket and handing it over to the other with a dry laugh. "Isn't *this* pleasant?" And he threw himself down on the floor and stretched out his hands to the blaze, with a gusto which the dreary hour he had undoubtedly passed made perfectly natural, if not excusable.

"I thank you," said Mr. Byrd; "I didn't know I was so chilled," and he, too, enjoyed the warmth. "And, now," he pursued, after a moment, "go on; let us have the thing out at once."

But the other was in no hurry. "Very good, sir," he cried; "but, first, if you don't mind, suppose you tell me what brought *you* to this hut today?"

"I was on the lookout for clues. In my study of the situation, I decided that the murderer of Mrs. Clemmens escaped, not from the front, but from the back, of the house. Taking the path I imagined him to have trod, I came upon this hut. It naturally attracted my attention, and today I came back to examine it more closely in the hope of picking up some signs of his having been here, or at least of having passed through the glade on his way to the deeper woods."

"And what, if you had succeeded in this, sir? What, if some token of his presence had rewarded your search?"

"I should have completed a chain of proof of which only this one link is lacking. I could have shown how Craik Mansell fled from this place on last Tuesday afternoon, making his way through the woods to the highway, and thence to the Quarry Station at Monteith, where he took the train which carried him back to Buffalo."

"You could!—show me how?"

Mr. Byrd explained himself more definitely.

Hickory at once rose.

"I guess we can give you the link," he dryly remarked. "At all events, suppose you just step here and tell me what conclusion you draw from the appearance of this pile of brush."

Mr. Byrd advanced and looked at a small heap of hemlock that lay in a compact mass in one corner.

"I have not disturbed it," pursued the other. "It is just as it was when I found it."

"Looks like a pillow," declared Mr. Byrd. "Has been used for such, I am sure; for see, the dust in this portion of the floor lies lighter than elsewhere. You can almost detect the outline of a man's recumbent form," he went on, slowly, leaning down to examine the floor more closely. "As for the boughs, they have been cut from the tree with a knife, and——" Lifting up a sprig, he looked at it, then passed it over to Hickory, with a meaning glance that directed attention to one or two short hairs of a dark brown colour, that were caught in the rough bark. "He did not even throw his pocket-handkerchief over the heap before lying down," he observed.

Mr. Hickory smiled. "You're up in your business, I see." And drawing his new colleague to the table, he asked him what he saw there.

At first sight Mr. Byrd exclaimed: "Nothing," but in another moment he picked up an infinitesimal chip from between the rough logs that formed the top of this somewhat rustic piece of furniture, and turning it over in his hand, pronounced it to be a piece of wood from a lead-pencil.

"Here are several of them," remarked Mr. Hickory, "and what is more, it is easy to tell just the colour of the pencil from which they were cut. It was blue."

"That is so," assented Mr. Byrd.

"Quarrymen, charcoal-burners, and the like are not much in the habit of sharpening pencils," suggested Hickory.

"Is the pencil now to be found in the pocket of Mr. Mansell a blue one?"

"It is."

"Have you anything more to show me?" asked Mr. Byrd.

"Only this," responded the other, taking out of his pocket the torn-off corner of a newspaper. "I found this blowing about under the bushes out there," said he. "Look at it and tell me from what paper it was torn."

"I don't know," said Mr. Byrd; "none that I am acquainted with."

"You don't read the Buffalo *Courier?*"

"Oh, is this——"

"A corner from the Buffalo *Courier?* I don't know, but I mean to find out. If it is, and the date proves to be correct, we won't have much trouble about the little link, will we?"

Mr. Byrd shook his head and they again crouched down over the fire.

"And, now, what did you learn in Buffalo?" inquired the persistent Hickory.

"Not much," acknowledged Mr. Byrd. "The man Brown was entirely too ubiquitous to give me my full chance. Neither at the house nor at the mill was I able to glean anything beyond an admission from the landlady that Mr. Mansell was not at home at the time of his aunt's murder. I couldn't even learn where he was on that day, or where he had ostensibly gone? If it had not been for the little girl of Mr. Goodman——"

"Ah, I had not time to go to that house," interjected the other, suggestively.

"I should have come home as wise as I went," continued Mr. Byrd. "She told me that on the day before Mr. Mansell returned, he wrote to her father from Monteith, and *that* settled my mind in regard to him. It was pure luck, however."

The other laughed long and loud.

"I didn't know I did it up so well," he cried. "I told the landlady you were a detective, or acted like one, and she was very ready to take the alarm, having, as I judge, a motherly liking for her young boarder. Then I took Messrs. Chamberlin and Harrison into my confidence, and having got from them all the information they could give me, told them there was evidently another man on the track of this Mansell, and warned them to keep silence till they heard from the prosecuting attorney in Sibley. But I didn't know who you were, or, at least, I wasn't sure; or, as I said before, I shouldn't have presumed."

The short, dry laugh with which he ended this explanation had not ceased, when Mr. Byrd observed:

"You have not told me what *you* gathered in Buffalo."

"Much," quoth Hickory, reverting to his favourite laconic mode of speech. "First, that Mansell went from home on Monday, the day before the murder, for the purpose, as he said, of seeing a man in New York about his wonderful invention. Secondly, that he never went to New York, but came back the next evening, bringing his model with him, and looking terribly used up and worried. Thirdly, that to get this invention before the public had been his pet aim and effort for a whole year. That he believed in it as you do in your Bible, and would have given his heart's blood, if it would have done any good, to start the thing, and prove himself right in his estimate of its value. That the money to do this was all that was lacking, no one believing in him sufficiently to advance him the five thousand dollars considered necessary to build the machine and get it in working order. That, in short, he was a fanatic on the subject, and often said he would be willing to die within the year if he could first prove to the unbelieving capitalists whom he had vainly importuned for assistance, the worth of the discovery he believed himself to have made. Fourthly—but what is it you wish to say, sir?"

"Five thousand dollars is just the amount Widow Clemmens is supposed to leave him," remarked Mr. Byrd.

"Precisely," was the short reply.

"And fourthly?" suggested the former.

"Fourthly, he was in the mill on Wednesday morning, where he went about his work as usual, until someone who knew his relation to Mrs. Clemmens looked up from the paper he was reading, and, in pure thoughtlessness, cried, 'So they have killed your aunt for you, have they?' A barbarous jest, that caused everybody near him to start in indignation, but which made him recoil as if one of these thunderbolts we have been listening to this afternoon had fallen at his feet. And he didn't get over it," Hickory went on. "He had to beg permission to go home. He said the terrible news had made him ill, and indeed he looked sick enough, and continued to look sick enough for days. He had letters from Sibley, and an invitation to attend the inquest and be present at the funeral services, but he refused to go. He was threatened with diphtheria, he declared, and remained away from the mill until the day before yesterday. Someone, I don't remember who, says he went out of town the very Wednesday he first heard the news; but if so, he could not have been gone long, for he was at home Wednesday night, sick in bed, and threatened, as I have said, with the diphtheria. Fifthly——"

"Well, fifthly?"

"I am afraid of your criticisms," laughed the rough detective. "Fifthly is the result of my poking about among Mr. Mansell's traps."

"Ah!" frowned the other, with a vivid remembrance of that picture of Miss Dare, with its beauty blotted out by the ominous black lines.

"You are too squeamish for a detective," the other declared. "Guess you're kept for the fancy business, eh?"

The look Mr. Byrd gave him was eloquent. "Go on," said he; "let us hear what lies behind your fifthly."

"Love," returned the man. "Locked in the drawer of this young gentleman's table, I found some half-dozen letters tied with a black ribbon. I knew they were written by a lady, but squeamishness is not a fault of mine, and so I just allowed myself to glance over them. They were from Miss Dare, of course, and they revealed the fact that love, as well as ambition, had been a motive power in determining this Mansell to make a success out of his invention."

Leaning back, the now self-satisfied detective looked at Mr. Byrd.

"The name of Miss Dare," he went on, "brings me to the point from which we started. I haven't yet told you what old Sally Perkins had to say to me."

"No," rejoined Mr. Byrd.

"Well," continued the other, poking with his foot the dying embers of the fire, till it started up into a fresh blaze, "the case against this young fellow wouldn't be worth very much without that old crone's testimony, I reckon; but with it I guess we can get along."

"Let us hear," said Mr. Byrd.

"The old woman is a wretch," Hickory suddenly broke out. "She seems to gloat over the fact that a young and beautiful woman is in trouble. She actually trembled with eagerness as she told her story. If I hadn't been rather anxious myself to hear what she had to say, I could have thrown her out of the window. As it was, I let her go on; duty before pleasure, you see—duty before pleasure."

"But her story," persisted Mr. Byrd, letting some of his secret irritation betray itself.

"Well, her story was this: Monday afternoon, the day before the murder, you know, she was up in these very woods hunting for witch-hazel. She had got her arms full and was going home across the bog when she suddenly heard voices. Being of a curious disposition, like myself, I suppose, she stopped, and seeing just before her a young gentleman and lady sitting on an old stump, crouched down in the shadow of a tree, with the harmless intent, no doubt, of amusing herself with their conversation. It was more interesting than she expected, and she really became quite tragic as she related her story to me. I cannot do justice to it myself, and I shan't try. It is enough that the man whom she did not know, and the woman whom she immediately recognized as Miss Dare, were both in a state of great indignation.

"That he spoke of selfishness and obstinacy on the part of his aunt, and that she, in the place of rebuking him, replied in a way to increase his bitterness, and lead him finally to exclaim: 'I cannot bear it! To think that with just the advance of the very sum she proposes to give me some day, I could make her fortune and my own, and win *you* all in one breath! It is enough to drive a man mad to see all that he craves in this world so near his grasp, and yet have nothing, not even hope, to comfort him.' And at that, it seems, they both rose, and she, who had not answered anything to this, struck the tree before which they stood, with her bare fist, and murmured a word or so which the old woman couldn't catch, but which was evidently something to the effect that she wished she knew Mrs. Clemmens; for Mansell—

296

of course it was he—said, in almost the same breath, 'And if you did know her, what then?'

"A question which elicited no reply at first, but which finally led her to say: 'Oh! I think that, possibly, I might be able to persuade her.' All this," the detective went on, "old Sally related with the greatest force; but in regard to what followed, she was not so clear. Probably they interrupted their conversation with some lovers' by-play, for they stood very near together, and he seemed to be earnestly pleading with her. 'Do take it,' old Sally heard him say. 'I shall feel as if life held some outlook for me, if you only will gratify me in this respect.' But she answered: 'No; it is of no use. I am as ambitious as you are, and fate is evidently against us,' and put his hand back when he endeavoured to take hers, but finally yielded so far as to give it to him for a moment, though she immediately snatched it away again, crying: 'I cannot; you must wait till tomorrow.'

"And when he asked: 'Why tomorrow?' she answered: 'A night has been known to change the whole current of a person's affairs.' To which he replied: 'True,' and looked thoughtful, very thoughtful, as he met her eyes and saw her raise that white hand of hers and strike the tree again with a passionate force that made her fingers bleed. And she was right," concluded the speaker. "The night, or if not the night, the next twenty-four hours, *did* make a change, as even old Sally Perkins observed. Widow Clemmens was struck down and Craik Mansell became the possessor of the five thousand dollars he so much wanted in order to win for himself a fortune and a bride."

Mr. Byrd, who had been sitting with his face turned aside during this long recital, slowly rose to his feet. "Hickory," said he, and his tone had an edge of suppressed feeling in it that made the other start, "don't let me ever hear you say, in my presence, that you think this young and beautiful woman was the one to suggest murder to this man, for I won't hear it. And now," he continued, more calmly, "tell me why this babbling old wretch did not enliven the inquest with her wonderful tale. It would have been a fine offset to the testimony of Miss Firman."

"She said she wasn't fond of coroners and had no wish to draw the attention of twelve of her own townsfolk upon herself. She didn't mean to commit herself with me," pursued Hickory, rising also. "She was going to give me a hint of the real state of affairs; or, rather, set me working in the right direction, as this little note which she tucked under the door of my room at the hotel will show. But I was too quick for her, and had her by the arm before she could shuffle down the stairs. It was partly to prove her story was true and not a romance made up for the occasion, that I lured this woman here this afternoon."

"You are not as bad a fellow as I thought," Mr. Byrd admitted, after a momentary contemplation of the other's face. "If I might only know how you managed to effect this interview."

"Nothing easier. I found in looking over the scraps of paper which Mansell had thrown into the waste-paper basket in Buffalo, the draft of a note which he had written to Miss Dare, under an impulse which he afterward probably regretted. It was a summons to their usual place of tryst at or near this hut, and though unsigned, was of a character, as I thought, to effect its purpose. I just sent it to her, that's all."

The nonchalance with which this was said completed Mr. Byrd's astonishment.

"You are a worthy disciple of Gryce," he asserted, leading the way to the door.

"Think so?" exclaimed the man, evidently flattered at what he considered a great compliment. "Then shake hands," he cried, with a frank appeal Mr. Byrd found it hard to resist. "Ah, you don't want to," he somewhat ruefully declared. "Will it change your feelings any if I promise to ignore what happened here today—my trick with Miss Dare and what she revealed and all that? If it will, I swear I won't even think of it any more if I can help it. At all events, I won't tattle about it even to the superintendent. It shall be a secret between you and me, and she won't know but what it was her lover she talked to, after all."

"You are willing to do all this?" inquired Mr. Byrd.

"Willing and ready," cried the man. "I believe in duty to one's superiors, but duty doesn't always demand of one to tell everything he knows. Besides, it won't be necessary, I imagine. There is enough against this poor fellow without that."

"I fear so," ejaculated Mr. Byrd.

"Then it is a bargain?" said Hickory.

"Yes."

And Mr. Byrd held out his hand.

The rain had now ceased and they prepared to return home. Before leaving the glade, however, Mr. Byrd ran his eye over the other's person and apparel, and in some wonder inquired:

"How do you fellows ever manage to get up such complete disguises? I declare you look enough like Mr. Mansell in the back to make me doubt even now who I am talking to."

"Oh," laughed the other, "it is easy enough. It's my specialty, you see, and one in which I *am* thought to excel. But, to tell the truth, I hadn't much to contend with in this case. In build I am famously like this man, as you must have noticed when you saw us together in Buffalo. Indeed, it was our similarity in this respect that first put the idea of personifying him into my head. My complexion had been darkened already, and, as for such accessories as hair, voice, manner, dress, etc., a five-minutes' study of my model was sufficient to prime me up in all that—enough, at least, to satisfy the conditions of an interview which did not require me to show my face."

"But you did not know when you came here that you would not have to show your face," persisted Mr. Byrd, anxious to understand how this man dared risk his reputation on an undertaking of this kind.

"No, and I did not know that the biggest thunderstorm of the season was going to spring up and lend me its darkness to complete the illusion I had attempted. I only trusted my good fortune—and my wits," he added, with a droll demureness. "Both had served me before, and both were likely to serve me again. And, say she had detected me in my little game, what then? Women like her don't babble."

There was no reply to make to this, and Mr. Byrd's thoughts being thus carried back to Imogene Dare and the unhappy revelations she had been led to make, he walked on in a dreary silence his companion had sufficient discretion not to break.

19

Mr. Ferris

Mr. Ferris sat in his office in a somewhat gloomy frame of mind. There had been bad news from the jail that morning. Mr. Hildreth had attempted suicide the night before, and was now lying in a critical condition at the hospital.

Mr. Ferris himself had never doubted this man's guilt. From Hildreth's first appearance at the inquest, the district attorney had fixed upon him as the murderer of Mrs. Clemmens, and up to this time he had seen no good and substantial reason for altering his opinion.

Even the doubts expressed by Mr. Byrd had moved him but little. Mr. Byrd was an enthusiast, and, naturally enough, shrank from believing a gentleman capable of such a crime. But the other detective's judgement was unswayed, and he considered Hildreth guilty. It was not astonishing, then, that the opinion of Mr. Ferris should coincide with that of the older and more experienced man.

But the depth of despair or remorse which had led Mr. Hildreth to this desperate attempt upon his own life had struck the district attorney with dismay. Though not over-sensitive by nature, he could not help feeling sympathy for the misery that had prompted such a deed, and while secretly regarding this unsuccessful attempt at suicide as an additional proof of guilt, he could not forbear satisfying himself by a review of the evidence elicited at the inquest, that the action of the authorities in arresting this man had been both warrantable and necessary.

The result was satisfactory in all but one point. When he came to the widow's written accusation against one by the name of Gouverneur Hildreth, he was impressed by a fact that had hitherto escaped his notice. This was the yellowness of the paper upon which the words were written. If they had been transcribed a dozen years before, they would not have looked older, nor would the ink have presented a more faded appearance. Now, as the suspected man was under twenty-five years of age, and must, therefore, have been a mere child when the paper was drawn up, the probability was that the Gouverneur intended was the prisoner's father, their names being identical.

But this discovery, while it robbed the affair of its most dramatic feature, could not affect in any serious way the extreme significance of the remaining real and compromising facts which told so heavily against this unfortunate man. Indeed, the well-known baseness of the father made it easier to distrust the son, and Mr. Ferris had just come to the conclusion that his duty compelled him to draw up an indictment of the would-be suicide, when the door opened, and Mr. Byrd and Mr. Hickory came in.

To see these two men in conjunction was a surprise to the district attorney. He, however, had no time to express himself on the subject, for Mr. Byrd, stepping forward, immediately remarked:

"Mr. Hickory and I have been in consultation, sir; and we have a few facts to give you that we think will alter your opinion as to the person who murdered Mrs. Clemmens."

"Is this so?" cried Mr. Ferris, looking at Hickory with a glance indicative of doubt.

"Yes, *sir*," exclaimed that not easily abashed individual, with an emphasis decided enough to show the state of his feelings on the subject. "After I last saw you a woman came in my way and put into my hands so fresh and promising a clue, that I dropped the old scent at once and made instanter for the new game. But I soon found I was not the only sportsman on this trail. Before I had taken a dozen steps I ran upon this gentleman, and, finding him true grit, struck up a partnership with him that has led to our bringing down the quarry together."

"Humph!" quoth the district attorney. "Some very remarkable discoveries must have come to light to influence the judgement of two such men as yourselves."

"You are right," rejoined Mr. Byrd. "In fact, I should not be surprised if this case proved to be one of the most remarkable on record. It is not often that equally convincing evidence of guilt is found against two men having no apparent connection."

"And have you collected such evidence?"

"We have."

"And who is the person you consider equally open to suspicion with Mr. Hildreth?"

"Craik Mansell, Mrs. Clemmens' nephew."

The surprise of the district-attorney was, as Mr. Hickory in later days remarked, nuts to him. The solemn nature of the business he was engaged upon never disturbed this hardy detective's sense of the ludicrous, and he indulged in one of his deepest chuckles as he met the eye of Mr. Ferris.

"One never knows what they are going to run upon in a chase of this kind, do they, sir?" he remarked, with the greatest cheerfulness. "Mr. Mansell is no more of a gentleman than Mr. Hildreth; yet, because he is the second one of his caste who has attracted our attention, you are naturally very much surprised. But wait till you hear what we have to tell you. I am confident you will be satisfied with our reasons for suspecting this new party." And he glanced at Mr. Byrd, who, seeing no cause for delay, proceeded to unfold before the district attorney the evidence they had collected against Mr. Mansell.

It was strong, telling, and seemingly conclusive, as we already know; and awoke in the mind of Mr. Ferris the greatest perplexity of his life. It was not simply that the facts urged against Mr. Mansell were of the same circumstantial character and of almost the same significance as those already urged against Mr. Hildreth, but that the association of Miss Dare's name with this new theory of suspicion presented difficulties, if it did not involve consequences, calculated to make any friend of Mr. Orcutt quail. And Mr. Ferris was such a friend, and knew very well the violent nature of the shock which this eminent lawyer would experience at discovering the relations held by this trusted woman toward a man suspected of crime.

Then Miss Dare herself! Was this beautiful and cherished woman, hitherto believed by all who knew her to be set high above the reach of reproach, to be dragged down from her pedestal and submitted to the curiosity of the rabble, if not to its insinuations and reproach? It seemed hard; even to this stern, dry searcher among dead men's bones, it seemed both hard and bitter. And yet, because he was an honest man, he had no thought of paltering with his duty. He could only take time to make sure what that duty was. He accordingly refrained from expressing any opinion in regard to Mr. Mansell's culpability to the two detectives, and finally dismissed them without any special orders.

But a day or two after this he sent for them again, and said:

"Since I have seen you I have considered, with due carefulness, the various facts presented me in support of your belief that Craik Mansell is the man who assailed the Widow Clemmens, and have weighed them against the equally significant facts pointing toward Mr. Hildreth as the guilty party, and find but one link lacking in the former chain of evidence which is not lacking in the latter; and that is this: Mrs. Clemmens, in the one or two lucid moments which returned to her after the assault, gave utterance to an exclamation which many think was meant to serve as a guide in determining the person of her murderer. She said, 'Ring,' as Mr. Byrd here will doubtless remember, and then 'Hand,' as if she wished to fix upon the minds of those about her that the hand uplifted against her wore a ring.

"At all events, such a conclusion is plausible enough, and led to my making an experiment yesterday, which has, for ever, set the matter at rest in my own mind. I took my stand at the huge clock in her house, just in the attitude she was supposed to occupy when struck, and, while in this position, ordered my clerk to advance upon me from behind with his hands clasped about a stick of wood, which he was to bring down within an inch of my head. This was done, and while his arm was in the act of descending, I looked to see if by a quick glance from the corner of my eye I could detect the broad seal ring I had previously pushed upon his little finger. I discovered that I could; that indeed it was all of the man which I could distinctly see without turning my head completely around.

"The ring, then, is an important feature in this case, a link without which any chain of evidence forged for the express purpose of connecting a man with this murder must necessarily remain incomplete and consequently useless. But amongst the suspicious circumstances brought to bear against Mr. Mansell, I discern no token of a connection between him and any such article, while we all know that Mr. Hildreth not only wore a ring on the day of the murder, but considered the circumstance so much in his own disfavour, that he slipped it off his finger when he began to see the shadow of suspicion falling upon him."

"You have, then, forgotten the diamond I picked up from the floor of Mrs. Clemmens' dining-room on the morning of the murder?" suggested Mr. Byrd with great reluctance.

"No," answered the district attorney, shortly. "But Miss Dare distinctly avowed that ring to be hers, and you have brought me no evidence as yet to prove her statement false. If you can supply such proof, or if you can show that Mr. Mansell had that ring on his hand when he entered Mrs. Clemmens' house on the fatal morning—another fact, which, by-the-way, rests as yet upon inference only—I shall consider the case against him as strong as that against Mr. Hildreth;

otherwise, not."

Mr. Byrd, with the vivid remembrance before him of Miss Dare's looks and actions in the scene he had witnessed between her and the supposed Mansell in the hut, smiled with secret bitterness over this attempt of the district attorney to shut his eyes to the evident guiltiness of this man.

Mr. Ferris saw this smile and instantly became irritated.

"I do not doubt any more than yourself," he resumed, in a changed voice, "that this young man allowed his mind to dwell upon the possible advantages which might accrue to himself if his aunt should die. He may even have gone so far as to meditate the commission of a crime to insure these advantages. But whether the crime which did indeed take place the next day in his aunt's house was the result of his meditations, or whether he found his own purpose forestalled by an attack made by another person possessing no less interest than himself in seeing this woman dead, is not determined by the evidence you bring."

"Then you do not favour his arrest?" inquired Mr. Byrd.

"No. The vigorous measures which were taken in Mr. Hildreth's case, and the unfortunate event to which they have led, are terrible enough to satisfy the public craving after excitement for a week at least. I am not fond of driving men to madness myself, and unless I can be made to see that my duty demands a complete transferral of my suspicions from Hildreth to Mansell, I can advise nothing more than a close but secret surveillance of the latter's movements until the action of the grand jury determines whether the evidence against Mr. Hildreth is sufficient to hold him for trial."

Mr. Byrd, who had such solid, if private and uncommunicable, reasons for believing in the guilt of Craik Mansell, was somewhat taken aback at this unlooked-for decision of Mr. Ferris, and, remembering the temptation which a man like Hickory must feel to make his cause good at all hazards, cast a sharp look toward that blunt-spoken detective, in some doubt as to whether he could be relied upon to keep his promise in the face of this manifest disappointment.

But Hickory had given his word, and Hickory remained firm; and Mr. Byrd, somewhat relieved in his own mind, was about to utter his acquiescence in the district attorney's views, when a momentary interruption occurred, which gave him an opportunity to exchange a few words aside with his colleague.

"Hickory," he whispered, "what do you think of this objection which Mr. Ferris makes?"

"I?" was the hurried reply. "Oh, I think there is something in it."

"Something in it?"

"Yes. Mr. Mansell is the last man to wear a ring, I must acknowledge. Indeed, I took some pains while in Buffalo to find out if he ever indulged in any such vanity, and was told decidedly No. As to the diamond you mentioned, that is certainly entirely too rich a jewel for a man like him to possess. I—I am a afraid the absence of this link in our chain of evidence is fatal. I shouldn't wonder if the old scent was the best, after all."

"But Miss Dare—her feelings and her convictions, as manifested by the words she made use of in the hut?" objected Mr. Byrd.

"Oh! *she* thinks he is guilty, of course!"

She thinks! Mr. Byrd stared at his companion for a minute in silence. *She* thinks! Then there was a possibility, it seems, that it was only her thought, and that Mr. Mansell was not really the culpable man he had been brought to consider him.

But here an exclamation, uttered by Mr. Ferris, called their attention back to that gentleman. He was reading a letter which had evidently been just brought in, and his expression was one of amazement, mixed with doubt. As they looked toward him they met his eye, that had a troubled and somewhat abashed expression, which convinced them that the communication he held in his hand was in some way connected with the matter under consideration.

Surprised themselves, they unconsciously started forward, when, in a dry and not altogether pleased tone, the district attorney observed:

"This affair seems to be full of coincidences. You talk of a missing link, and it is immediately thrust under your nose. Read that!"

And he pushed toward them the following epistle, roughly scrawled on a sheet of common writing-paper:

If Mr. Ferris is anxious for justice, and can believe that suspicion does not always attach itself to the guilty, let him, or someone whose business it is, inquire of Miss Imogene Dare, of this town, how she came to claim as her own the ring that was picked up on the floor of Mrs. Clemmens' house.

"Well!" cried Mr. Byrd, glancing at Hickory, "what are we to think of this?"

"Looks like the work of old Sally Perkins," observed the other, pointing out the lack of date and signature.

"So it does," acquiesced Mr. Byrd, in a relieved tone. "The miserable old wretch is growing impatient."

But Mr. Ferris, with a gloomy frown, shortly said:

"The language is not that of an ignorant old creature like Sally Perkins, whatever the writing may be. Besides, how could she have known about the ring? The persons who were present at the time it was picked up are not of the gossiping order."

"Who, then, do you think wrote this?" inquired Mr. Byrd.

"That is what I wish you to find out," declared the district attorney.

Mr. Hickory at once took it in his hand.

"Wait," said he, "I have an idea." And he carried the letter to one side, where he stood examining it for several minutes. When he came back he looked tolerably excited and somewhat pleased. "I believe I can tell you who wrote it," said he.

"Who?" inquired the district attorney.

For reply the detective placed his finger upon a name that was written in the letter.

"Imogene Dare?" exclaimed Mr. Ferris, astonished.

"She herself," proclaimed the self-satisfied detective.

"What makes you think that?" the district attorney slowly asked.

"Because I have seen her writing, and studied her signature, and, ably as she has disguised her hand in the rest of the letter, it betrays itself in her name. See here." And Hickory took from his pocket-book a small slip of paper containing her autograph, and submitted it to the test of comparison.

The similarity between the two signatures was evident, and both Mr. Byrd and Mr. Ferris were obliged to allow the detective might be right, though the admission opened up suggestions of the most formidable character.

"It is a turn for which I am not prepared," declared the district attorney.

"It is a turn for which *we* are not prepared," repeated Mr. Byrd, with a controlling look at Hickory.

"Let us, then, defer further consideration of the matter till I have had an opportunity to see Miss Dare," suggested Mr. Ferris.

And the two detectives were very glad to acquiesce in this, for they were as much astonished as he at this action of Miss Dare, though, with their better knowledge of her feelings, they found it comparatively easy to understand how her remorse and the great anxiety she doubtless felt for Mr. Hildreth had sufficed to drive her to such an extreme and desperate measure.

20

A Crisis

That my readers may understand even better than Byrd and Hickory how it was that Imogene came to write this letter, I must ask them to consider certain incidents that had occurred in a quarter far removed from the eye of the detectives.

Mr. Orcutt's mind had never been at rest concerning the peculiar attitude assumed by Imogene Dare at the time of Mrs. Clemmens' murder. Time and thought had not made it any more possible for him to believe now than then that she knew anything of the matter beyond what appeared to the general eye: but he could not forget the ring. It haunted him. Fifty times a day he asked himself what she had meant by claiming as her own a jewel which had been picked up from the floor of a strange house at a time so dreadful, and which, in despite of her explanations to him, he found it impossible to believe was hers or ever could have been hers? He was even tempted to ask her; but he never did.

The words would not come. Though they faltered again and again upon his lips, he could not give utterance to them; no, though with every passing day he felt that the bond uniting her to him was growing weaker and weaker, and that if something did not soon intervene to establish confidence between them, he would presently lose all hope of the treasure for the possession of which he was now ready to barter away half the remaining years of his life.

Her increasing reticence, and the almost stony look of misery that now confronted him without let or hindrance from her wide gray eyes, were not calculated to reassure him or make his future prospects look any brighter. Her pain, if pain it were, or remorse, if remorse it could be, was not of a kind to feel the influence of time; and, struck with dismay, alarmed in spite of himself, if not for her reason at least for his own, he watched her from day to day, feeling that now he would give his life not merely to possess her, but to understand her and the secret that was gnawing at her heart.

At last there came a day when he could no longer restrain himself. She had been seated in his presence, and had been handed a letter which for the moment seemed to thoroughly overwhelm her. We know what that letter was. It was the note which had been sent as a decoy by the detective Hickory, but which she had no reason to doubt was a real communication from Craik Mansell, despite the strange handwriting on the envelope. It prayed her for an interview. It set the time and mentioned the place of meeting, and created for the instant such a turmoil in her usually steady brain that she could not hide it from the searching eyes that watched her.

"What is it, Imogene?" inquired Mr. Orcutt, drawing near her with a gesture of such uncontrollable anxiety, it looked as if he were about to snatch the letter from her hand.

For reply she rose, walked to the grate, in which a low wood fire was burning, and plunged the paper in among the coals. When it was all consumed she turned and faced Mr. Orcutt.

"You must excuse me," she murmured; "but the letter was one which I absolutely desired no one to see."

But he did not seem to hear her apology. He stood with his gaze fixed on the fire, and his hand clenched against his heart, as if something in the fate of that wretched sheet of paper reminded him of the love and hope that were shrivelling up before his eyes.

She saw his look and drooped her head with a sudden low moan of mingled shame and suffering.

"Am I killing *you?*" she faintly cried. "Are my strange, wild ways driving *you* to despair? I had not thought of that. I am so selfish, I had not thought of that!"

This evidence of feeling, the first she had ever shown him, moved Mr. Orcutt deeply. Advancing toward her, with sudden passion, he took her by the hand.

"Killing me?" he repeated. "Yes, you are killing me. Don't you see how fast I am growing old? Don't you see how the dust lies thick upon the books that used to be my solace and delight? I do not understand you, Imogene. I love you and I do not understand your grief, or what it is that is affecting you in this terrible way. Tell me. Let me know the nature of the forces with which I have to contend, and I can bear all the rest."

This appeal, forced as it was from lips unused to prayer, seemed to strike her, absorbed though she was in her own suffering. Looking at him with real concern, she tried to speak, but the words faltered on her tongue. They came at last, however, and he heard her say:

"I wish I could weep, if only to show you I am not utterly devoid of womanly sympathy for an anguish I cannot cure. But the fountain of my tears is dried at its source. I do not think I can ever weep again. I am condemned to tread a path of misery and despair, and must traverse it to the end without weakness and without help. Do not ask me why, for I can never tell you. And do not detain me now, or try to make me talk, for I must go where I can be alone and silent."

She was slipping away, but he caught her by the wrist and drew her back. His pain and perplexity had reached their climax.

"You must speak," he cried. "I have paltered long enough with this matter. You must tell me what it is that is destroying your happiness and mine."

But her eyes, turning toward him, seemed to echo that *must* in a look of disdain eloquent enough to scorn all help from words, and in the indomitable determination of her whole aspect he saw that he might slay her, but that he could never make her speak.

Loosing her with a gesture of despair, he turned away. When he glanced back again she was gone.

The result of this interview was naturally an increased doubt and anxiety on his part. He could not attend to his duties with any degree of precision, he was so haunted by uneasy surmises as to what might have been the contents of the letter which he had thus seen her destroy before his eyes. As for her words, they were like her conduct, an insolvable mystery, for which he had no key.

His failure to find her at home when he returned that night added to his alarm, especially as he remembered the vivid thunderstorm that had deluged the town in the afternoon. Nor, though she came in very soon and offered both excuses and explanations for her absence, did he experience any appreciable relief, or feel at all satisfied that he was not threatened with some secret and terrible catastrophe. Indeed, the air of vivid and feverish excitement which pervaded every look of hers from this time, making each morning and evening distinctive in his memory as a season of fresh fear and renewed suspense, was enough of itself to arouse this sense of an unknown, but surely approaching, danger.

He saw she was on the lookout for some event, he knew not what, and studied the papers as sedulously as she, in the hope of coming upon some revelation that should lay bare the secret of this new condition of hers. At last he thought he had found it. Coming home one day from the court, he called her into his presence, and, without pause or preamble, exclaimed, with almost cruel abruptness:

"An event of possible interest to you has just taken place. The murderer of Mrs. Clemmens has just cut his throat."

He saw before he had finished the first clause that he had struck at the very citadel of her terrors and her woe. At the end of the second sentence he knew, beyond all doubt now, what it was she had been fearing, if not expecting. Yet she said not a word, and by no movement betrayed that the steel had gone through and through her heart.

A demon—the maddening demon of jealousy—gripped him for the first time with relentless force.

"Ah, you have been looking for it?" he cried in a choked voice. "You know this man, then—knew him, perhaps, before the murder of Mrs. Clemmens; knew him, and—and, perhaps, loved him?"

She did not reply.

He struck his forehead with his hand, as if the moment was perfectly intolerable to him.

"Answer," he cried. "Did you know Gouverneur Hildreth or not?"

"*Gouverneur Hildreth?*" Oh, the sharp surprise, the wailing anguish of her tone! Mr. Orcutt stood amazed. "It is not he who has made this attempt upon his life!—not he!" she shrieked like one appalled.

Perhaps because all other expression or emotion failed him, Mr. Orcutt broke forth into a loud and harrowing laugh. "And who else should it be?" he cried. "What other man stands accused of having murdered Widow Clemmens? You are mad, Imogene; you don't know what you say or what you do."

"Yes, I am mad," she repeated—"mad!" and leaned her forehead forward on the back of a high chair beside which she had been standing, and hid her face and struggled with herself for a moment, while the clock went on ticking, and the wretched surveyor of her sorrow stood looking at her bended head like a man who does not know whether it is he or she who is in the most danger of losing his reason.

At last a word struggled forth from between her clasped hands.

"When did it happen?" she gasped, without lifting her head. "Tell me all about it. I think I can understand."

The noted lawyer smiled a bitter smile, and spoke for the first time, without pity and without mercy.

"He has been trying for some days to effect his death. His arrest and the little prospect there is of his escaping trial seem to have maddened his gentlemanly brain. Firearms were not procurable, neither was poison nor a rope, but a pewter plate is enough in the hands of a desperate man. He broke one in two last night, and——"

He paused, sick and horror-stricken. Her face had risen upon him from the back of the chair, and was staring upon him like that of a Medusa. Before that gaze the flesh crept on his bones and the breath of life refused to pass his lips. Gazing at her with rising horror, he saw her stony lips slowly part.

"Don't go on," she whispered. "I can see it all without the help of words." Then, in a tone that seemed to come from some far-off world of nightmare, she painfully gasped, "Is he dead?"

Mr. Orcutt was a man who, up to the last year, had never known what it was to experience a real and controlling emotion. Life with him had meant success in public affairs, and a certain social pre-eminence that made his presence in any place the signal of admiring looks and respectful attentions. But let no man think that, because his doom delays, it will never come. Passions such as he had deprecated in others, and desires such as he had believed impossible to himself, had seized upon him with ungovernable power, and in this moment especially he felt himself yielding to their sway with no more power of resistance than a puppet experiences in the grasp of a whirlwind. Meeting that terrible eye of hers, burning with an anxiety for a man he despised, and hearing that agonized question from lips whose touch he had never known, he experienced a sudden wild and almost demoniac temptation to hurl back the implacable "Yes" that he felt certain would strike her like a dead woman to the ground. But the horrid impulse passed, and, with a quick remembrance of the claims of honour upon one bearing his name and owning his history, he controlled himself with a giant resolution, and merely dropping his eyes from an anguish he dared no longer confront, answered, quietly:

"No; he has hurt himself severely and has disfigured his good looks for life, but he will not die; or so the physicians think."

A long, deep, shuddering sigh swept through the room.

"Thank God!" came from her lips, and then all was quiet again.

He looked up in haste; he could not bear the silence.

"Imogene——" he began, but instantly paused in surprise at the

"HE PAUSED, SICK AND HORROR-STRICKEN. HER
FACE HAD RISEN UPON HIM FROM THE BACK OF THE
CHAIR, AND WAS STARING AT HIM LIKE THAT OF A
MEDUSA."

change which had taken place in her expression. "What do you intend to do?" was his quick demand. "You look as I have never seen you look before."

"Do not ask me!" she returned. "I have no words for what I am going to do. What *you* must do is to see that Gouverneur Hildreth is released from prison. He is not guilty, mind you; he never committed this crime of which he is suspected, and in the shame of which suspicion he has this day attempted his life. If he is kept in the restraint which is so humiliating to him, and if he dies there, it will be murder—do you hear? murder! And he *will* die there if he is not released; I know his feelings only too well."

"But, Imogene——"

"Hush! don't argue. 'Tis a matter of life and death, I tell you. He must be released! I know," she went on, hurriedly, "what it is you want to say. You think you cannot do this; that the evidence is all against him; that he went to prison of his own free will and cannot hope for release till his guilt or innocence has been properly inquired into. But I know you can effect his enlargement if you will. You are a lawyer, and understand all the crooks and turns by which a man can sometimes be made to evade the grasp of justice. Use your knowledge. Avail yourself of your influence with the authorities, and I——" she paused and gave him a long, long look.

He was at her side in an instant.

"You would—what?" he cried, taking her hand in his and pressing it impulsively.

"I would grant you whatever you ask," she murmured, in a weariful tone.

"Would you be my wife?" he passionately inquired.

"Yes," was the choked reply; "if I did not die first."

He caught her to his breast in rapture. He knelt at her side and threw his arms about her waist.

"You shall not die," he cried. "You shall live and be happy. Only marry me today."

"Not till Gouverneur Hildreth be released," she interposed, gently.

He started as if touched by a galvanic battery, and slowly rose up and coldly looked at her.

"Do you love him so madly you would sell yourself for his sake?" he sternly demanded.

With a quick gesture she threw back her head as though the indignant "No" that sprang to her lips would flash out whether she would or not. But she restrained herself in time.

"I cannot answer," she returned.

But he was master now—master of this dominating spirit that had held him in check for so long a time, and he was not to be put off.

"You must answer," he sternly commanded. "I have the right to know the extent of your feeling for this man, and I will. Do you *love* him, Imogene Dare? Tell me, or I here swear that I will do nothing for him, either now or at a time when he may need my assistance more than you know."

This threat, uttered as he uttered it, could have but one effect. Turning aside, so that he should not see the shuddering revolt in her eyes, she mechanically whispered:

"And what if I did? Would it be so very strange? Youth admires youth, Mr. Orcutt, and Mr. Hildreth is very handsome and very unfortunate. Do not oblige me to say more."

Mr. Orcutt, across whose face a dozen different emotions had flitted during the utterance of these few words, drew back till half the distance of the room lay between them.

"Nor do I wish to hear any more," he rejoined, slowly. "You have said enough, quite enough. I understand now all the past—all your terrors and all your secret doubts and unaccountable behaviour. The man you loved was in danger, and you did not know how to manage his release. Well, well, I am sorry for you, Imogene. I wish I could help you. I love you passionately, and would make you my wife in face of your affection for this man if I could do for you what you request. But it is impossible. Never during the whole course of my career has a blot rested upon my integrity as a lawyer. I am known as an honest man, and honest will I remain known to the last. Besides, I could do nothing to effect his enlargement if I tried. Nothing but the plainest proof that he is innocent, or that another man is guilty, would avail now to release him from the suspicion which his own admissions have aroused."

"Then there is no hope?" was her slow and despairing reply.

"None at present, Imogene," was his stern, almost as despairing, answer.

As Mr. Orcutt sat over his lonely hearth that evening, a servant brought to him the following letter:

Dear Friend,—It is not fit that I should remain any longer under your roof. I have a duty before me which separates me forever from the friendship and protection of honourable men and women. No home but such as I can provide for myself by the work of my own hands shall henceforth shelter the disgraced head of Imogene Dare. Her fate, whatever it may prove to be, she bears alone, and you, who have been so kind, shall never suffer from any association with one whose name must henceforth become the sport of the crowd, if not the execration of the virtuous. If your generous heart rebels at this, choke it relentlessly down. I shall be already gone when you read these lines, and nothing you could do or say would make me come back. Goodbye, and may Heaven grant you forgetfulness of one whose only return to your benefactions has been to make you suffer almost as much as she suffers herself.

As Mr. Orcutt read these last lines, District Attorney Ferris was unsealing the anonymous missive which has already been laid before my readers.

21

Heart's Martyrdom

Mr. Ferris' first impulse upon dismissing the detectives had been to carry the note he had received to Mr. Orcutt. But a night's careful consideration of the subject convinced him that the wisest course would be to follow the suggestions conveyed in the letter, and seek a direct interview with Imogene Dare.

It was not an agreeable task for him to undertake. Miss Dare was a young lady whom he had always held in the highest esteem. He had hoped to see her the wife of his friend, and would have given much from his own private stock of hope and happiness to have kept her name free from the contumely which any association with this dreadful crime must necessarily bring upon it. But his position as prosecuting attorney of the county would not allow him to consult his feelings any further in a case of such serious import. The condition of Mr. Hildreth was, to say the least, such as demanded the most impartial action on the part of the public officials, and if through any explanation of Miss Dare the one missing link in the chain of evidence against another could be supplied, it was certainly his duty to do all he could to insure it.

Accordingly at a favourable hour the next day, he made his appearance at Mr. Orcutt's house, and learning that Miss Dare had gone to Professor Darling's house for a few days, followed her to her new home and requested an interview.

She at once responded to his call. Little did he think as she came into the parlour where he sat, and with even more than her usual calm self-possession glided down the length of that elegant apartment to his side, that she had just come from a small room on the top floor, where, in the position of a hired seamstress, she had been engaged in cutting out the wedding garments of one of the daughters of the house.

Her greeting was that of a person attempting to feign a surprise she did not feel.

"Ah," said she, "Mr. Ferris! This is an unexpected pleasure."

But Mr. Ferris had no heart for courtesies.

"Miss Dare," he began, without any of the preliminaries which might be expected of him, "I have come upon a disagreeable errand. I have a favour to ask. You are in the possession of a piece of information which it is highly necessary for me to share."

"I?"

The surprise betrayed in this single word was no more than was to be expected from a lady thus addressed, neither did the face she turned so steadily toward him alter under his searching gaze.

"If I can tell you anything that you wish to know," she quietly declared, "I am certainly ready to do so, sir."

Deceived by the steadiness of her tone and the straightforward look of her eyes, he proceeded, with a sudden releasement from his embarrassment, to say:

"I shall have to recall to your mind a most painful incident. You remember, on the morning when we met at Mrs. Clemmens' house, claiming as your own a diamond ring which was picked up from the floor at your feet?"

"I do."

"Miss Dare, was this ring really yours, or were you misled by its appearance into merely thinking it your property? My excuse for asking this is that the ring, if not yours, is likely to become an important factor in the case to which the murder of this unfortunate woman has led."

"Sir——" The pause which followed the utterance of this one word was but momentary, but in it what faint and final hope may have gone down into the depths of everlasting darkness God only knows. "Sir, since you ask me the question, I will say that in one sense of the term it was mine, and in another it was not. The ring was mine, because it had been offered to me as a gift the day before. The ring was not mine, because I had refused to take it when it was offered."

At these words, spoken with such quietness they seemed like the mechanical utterances of a woman in a trance, Mr. Ferris started to his feet. He could no longer doubt that evidence of an important nature lay before him.

"And may I ask," he inquired, without any idea of the martyrdom he caused, "what was the name of the person who offered you this ring, and from whom you refused to take it?"

"The name?" She quavered for a moment, and her eyes flashed up toward heaven with a look of wild appeal, as if the requirement of this moment was more than even she had strength to meet. Then a certain terrible calm settled upon her, blotting the last hint of feeling from her face, and, rising up in her turn, she met Mr. Ferris' inquiring eye, and slowly and distinctly replied:

"It was Craik Mansell, sir. He is a nephew of Mrs. Clemmens."

It was the name Mr. Ferris had come there to hear, yet it gave him a slight shock when it fell from her lips—perhaps because his mind was still running upon her supposed relations with Mr. Orcutt. But he did not show his feelings, however, and calmly asked:

"And was Mr. Mansell in this town the day before the assault upon his aunt?"

"He was."

"And you had a conversation with him?"

"I had."

"May I ask where?"

For the first time she flushed; womanly shame had not yet vanished entirely from her stricken breast; but she responded as steadily as before:

"In the woods, sir, back of Mrs. Clemmens' house. There were reasons"—she paused—"there were good reasons, which I do not feel obliged to state, why a meeting in such a place was not discreditable to us."

Mr. Ferris, who had received from other sources a full version of the interview to which she thus alluded, experienced a sudden revulsion of feeling against one he could not but consider as a detected coquette; and, drawing quickly back, made a gesture such as was not often witnessed in those elegant apartments.

"You mean," said he, with a sharp edge to his tone that passed over her dreary soul unheeded, "that you were lovers?"

"I mean," said she, like the automaton she surely was at that moment, "that he had paid me honourable addresses, and that I had no reason to doubt his motives or my own in seeking such a meeting."

"Miss Dare,"—all the district attorney spoke in the manner of Mr. Ferris now,—"if you refused Mr. Mansell his ring, you must have returned it to him?"

She looked at him with an anguish that bespoke her full appreciation of all this question implied, but unequivocally bowed her head.

"It was in his possession, then," he continued, "when you left him on that day and returned to your home?"

"Yes," her lips seemed to say, though no distinct utterance came from them.

"And you did not see it again till you found it on the floor of Mrs. Clemmens' dining-room the morning of the murder?"

"No."

"Miss Dare," said he, with greater mildness, after a short pause, "you have answered my somewhat painful inquiries with a straight-forwardness I cannot sufficiently commend. If you will now add to my gratitude by telling me whether you have informed anyone else of the important facts you have just given me, I will distress you by no further questions."

"Sir," said she, and her attitude showed that she could endure but little more, "I have taken no one else into my confidence. Such knowledge as I had to impart was not matter for idle gossip."

And Mr. Ferris, being thus assured that his own surmises and that of Hickory were correct, bowed with the respect her pale face and rigid attitude seemed to demand, and considerately left the house.

22

Craik Mansell

"He is here."

Mr. Ferris threw aside his cigar, and looked up at Mr. Byrd, who was standing before him.

"You had no difficulty, then?"

"No, sir. He acted like a man in hourly expectation of some such summons. At the very first intimation of your desire to see him in Sibley, he rose from his desk, with what I thought was a meaning look at Mr. Goodman, and after a few preparations for departure, signified he was ready to take the next train."

"And did he ask no questions?"

"Only one. He wished to know if I were a detective. And when I responded 'Yes,' observed with an inquiring look: 'I am wanted as a witness, I suppose.' A suggestion to which I was careful to make no reply."

Mr. Ferris pushed aside his writing and glanced toward the door. "Show him in, Mr. Byrd," said he.

A moment after Mr. Mansell entered the room.

The district attorney had never seen this man, and was struck at once by the force and manliness of his appearance. Half-rising from his seat to greet the visitor, he said:

"I have to beg your pardon, Mr. Mansell. Feeling it quite necessary to see you, I took the liberty of requesting you to take this journey, my own time being fully occupied at present."

Mr. Mansell bowed—a slow, self-possessed bow,—and advancing to the table before which the district attorney sat, laid his hand firmly upon it and said:

"No apologies are needed." Then shortly, "What is it you want of me?"

The words were almost the same as those which had been used by Mr. Hildreth under similar circumstances, but how different was their effect! The one was the utterance of a weak man driven to bay, the other of a strong one. Mr. Ferris, who was by no means of an impressible organization, flashed a look of somewhat uneasy doubt at Mr. Byrd, and hesitated slightly before proceeding.

"We have sent for you in this friendly way," he remarked, at last, "in order to give you that opportunity for explaining certain matters connected with your aunt's sudden death which your well-known character and good position seem to warrant. We think you can do this. At all events I have accorded myself the privilege of so supposing; and any words you may have to say will meet with all due consideration. As Mrs. Clemmens' nephew, you, of course, desire to see her murderer brought to justice."

The slightly rising inflection given to the last few words made them to all intents and purposes a question, and Mr. Byrd, who stood nearby, waited anxiously for the decided Yes which seemed the only possible reply under the circumstances, but it did not come.

Surprised, and possibly anxious, the district attorney repeated himself.

"As her nephew," said he, "and the inheritor of the few savings she has left behind her, you can have but one wish on this subject, Mr. Mansell?"

But this attempt succeeded no better than the first. Beyond a slight compression of the lips, Mr. Mansell gave no manifestation of having heard this remark, and both Mr. Ferris and the detective found themselves forced to wonder at the rigid honesty of a man who, whatever death-giving blow he may have dealt, would not allow himself to escape the prejudice of his accusers by assenting to a supposition he and they knew to be false.

Mr. Ferris did not press the question.

"Mr. Mansell," he remarked instead, "a person by the name of Gouverneur Hildreth is, as you must know, under arrest at this time, charged with the crime of having given the blow that led to your aunt's death. The evidence against him is strong, and the public generally have no doubt that his arrest will lead to trial, if not to conviction. But, unfortunately for us, however fortunately for him, another person has lately been found, against whom an equal show of evidence can be raised, and it is for the purpose of satisfying ourselves that it is but a show, we have requested your presence here today."

A spasm, vivid as it was instantaneous, distorted for a moment the powerful features of Craik Mansell at the words, "another person," but it was gone before the sentence was completed; and when Mr. Ferris ceased, he looked up with the steady calmness which made his bearing so remarkable.

"I am waiting to hear the name of this freshly suspected person," he observed.

"Cannot you imagine?" asked the district attorney, coldly, secretly disconcerted under a gaze that held his own with such steady persistence.

The eyeballs of the other flashed like coals of fire.

"I think it is my right to hear it spoken," he returned.

This display of feeling restored Mr. Ferris to himself.

"In a moment, sir," said he. "Meanwhile, have you any objections to answering a few questions I would like to put to you?"

"I will hear them," was the steady reply.

"You know," said the district attorney, "you are at perfect liberty to answer or not, as you see fit. I have no desire to entrap you into any acknowledgments you may hereafter regret."

"Speak," was the sole response he received.

"Well, sir," said Mr. Ferris, "are you willing to tell me where you were when you first heard of the assault which had been made upon your aunt?"

"I was in my place at the mill."

"And—pardon me if I go too far—were you also there the morning she was murdered?"

"No, sir."

"Mr. Mansell, if you could tell us where you were at that time, it would be of great benefit to us, and possibly to yourself."

"To myself?"

Having shown his surprise, or, possibly, his alarm, by the repetition of the other's words, Craik Mansell paused and looked slowly around the room until he encountered Mr. Byrd's eye. There was a steady compassion in the look he met there that seemed to strike him with great force, for he at once replied that he was away from home, and stopped—his glance still fixed upon Mr. Byrd, as if, by the very power of his gaze, he would force the secrets of that detective's soul to the surface.

"Mr. Mansell," pursued the district attorney, "a distinct avowal on your part of the place where you were at that time, would be best for us both, I am sure."

"Do you not already know?" inquired the other, his eye still upon Horace Byrd.

"We have reason to think you were in this town," averred Mr. Ferris, with an emphasis calculated to recall the attention of his visitor to himself.

"And may I ask," Craik Mansell quietly said, "what reason you can have for such a supposition? No one could have seen me here, for, till today I have not entered the streets of this place since my visit to my aunt three months ago."

"It was not necessary to enter the streets of this town to effect a visit to Mrs. Clemmens' house, Mr. Mansell."

"No?"

There was the faintest hint of emotion in the intonation he gave to that one word, but it vanished before he spoke his next sentence.

"And how," asked he, "can a person pass from Sibley Station to the door of my aunt's house without going through the streets?"

Instead of replying, Mr. Ferris inquired:

"Did you get out at Sibley Station, Mr. Mansell?"

But the other, with unmoved self-possession, returned:

"I have not said so."

"Mr. Mansell," the district attorney now observed, "we have no motive in deceiving or even in misleading you. You were in this town on the morning of your aunt's murder, and you were even in her house. Evidence which you cannot dispute proves this, and the question that now arises, and of whose importance we leave you to judge, is whether you were there prior to the visit of Mr. Hildreth, or after. Any proof you may have to show that it was before will receive its due consideration."

A change, decided as it was involuntary, took place in the hitherto undisturbed countenance of Craik Mansell. Leaning forward, he surveyed Mr. Ferris with great earnestness.

"I asked that man," said he, pointing with a steady forefinger at the somewhat abashed detective, "if I were not wanted here simply as a witness, and he did not say No. Now, sir," he continued, turning back with a slight gesture of disdain to the district attorney, "was the man right in allowing me to believe such a fact, or was he not? I would like an answer to my question before I proceed further, if you please."

"You shall have it, Mr. Mansell. If this man did not answer you, it was probably because he did not feel justified in so doing. He knew I had summoned you here in the hope of receiving such explanations of your late conduct as should satisfy me you had nothing to do with your aunt's murder. The claims upon my consideration, which are held by certain persons allied to you in this matter"—Mr. Ferris' look was eloquent of his real meaning here—"are my sole justification for this somewhat unusual method of dealing with a suspected man."

A smile, bitter, oh, how bitter in its irony! traversed the firm-set lips of Craik Mansell for a moment, then he bowed with a show of deference to the district attorney, and settling into the attitude of a man willing to plead his own cause, responded:

"It would be more just, perhaps, if I first heard the reasons you have for suspecting me, before I attempt to advance arguments to prove the injustice of your suspicions."

"Well," said Mr. Ferris, "you shall have them. If frankness on my part can do aught to avert the terrible scandal which your arrest and its consequent developments would cause, I am willing to sacrifice thus much to my friendship for Mr. Orcutt. But if I do this, I shall expect an equal frankness in return. The matter is too serious for subterfuge."

The other merely waved his hand.

"The reasons," proceeded Mr. Ferris, "for considering you a party as much open to suspicion as Mr. Hildreth, are several. First, we have evidence to prove your great desire for a sum of money equal to your aunt's savings, in order to introduce an invention which you have just patented.

"Secondly, we can show that you left your home in Buffalo the day before the assault, came to Monteith, the next town to this, alighted at the remote station assigned to the use of the quarrymen, crossed the hills and threaded the woods till you came to a small hut back of your aunt's house, where you put up for the night.

"Thirdly, evidence is not lacking to prove that while there you visited your aunt's once, if not twice; the last time on the very morning she was killed, entering the house in a surreptitious way by the back door, and leaving it in the same suspicious manner.

"And fourthly, we can prove that you escaped from this place as you had come, secretly, and through a difficult and roundabout path over the hills.

"Mr. Mansell, these facts, taken with your reticence concerning a visit so manifestly of importance to the authorities to know, must strike even you as offering grounds for a suspicion as grave as that attaching to Mr. Hildreth."

With a restraint marked as it was impressive, Mr. Mansell looked at the district attorney for a moment, and then said:

"You speak of proof. Now, what proof have you to give that I put up, as you call it, for a night, or even for an hour, in the hut which stands in the woods back of my aunt's house?"

"This," was Mr. Ferris' reply. "It is known you were in the woods the afternoon previous to the assault upon your aunt, because you were seen there in company with a young lady with whom you were holding a tryst. Did you speak, sir?"

"No!" was the violent, almost disdainful, rejoinder.

"You did not sleep at your aunt's, for her rooms contained not an evidence of having been opened for a guest, while the hut revealed more than one trace of having been used as a dormitory. I could even tell you where you cut the twigs of hemlock that served you for a pillow, and point to the place where you sat when you scribbled over the margin of the Buffalo *Courier* with a blue pencil, such as that I now see projecting from your vest pocket."

"It is not necessary," replied the young man, heavily frowning. Then with another short glance at Mr. Ferris, he again demanded:

"What is your reason for stating I visited my aunt's house on the morning she was murdered? Did anyone see me do it? or does the house, like the hut, exhibit traces of my presence there at that particular time?"

There was irony in his tone, and a disdain almost amounting to scorn in his wide-flashing blue eyes; but Mr. Ferris, glancing at the hand clutched about the railing of the desk, remarked quietly:

"You do not wear the diamond ring you carried away with you from the tryst I mentioned? Can it be that the one which was picked up after the assault, on the floor of Mrs. Clemmens' dining-room, could have fallen from your finger, Mr. Mansell?"

A start, the first this powerfully repressed man had given, showed that his armour of resistance had been pierced at last.

"How do you know," he quickly asked, "that I carried away a diamond ring from the tryst you speak of?"

"Circumstances," returned the district attorney, "prove it beyond a doubt. Miss Dare——"

"Miss Dare!"

Oh, the indescribable tone of this exclamation! Mr. Byrd shuddered as he heard it, and looked at Mr. Mansell with a new feeling, for which he had no name.

"Miss Dare," repeated the district attorney, without, apparently, regarding the interruption, "acknowledges she returned you the ring which you endeavoured at that interview to bestow upon her."

"Ah!" The word came after a moment's pause. "I see the case has been well worked up, and it only remains for me to give you such explanations as I choose to make. Sir," declared he, stepping forward, and bringing his clenched hand down upon the desk at which Mr. Ferris was sitting, "I did not kill my aunt. I admit that I paid her a visit. I admit that I stayed in the woods back of her house, and even slept in the hut, as you have said; but that was on the day previous to her murder, and not after it. I went to see her for the purpose of again urging the claims of my invention upon her. I went secretly, and by the roundabout way you describe, because I had another purpose in visiting Sibley, which made it expedient for me to conceal my presence in the town.

"I failed in my efforts to enlist the sympathies of my aunt in regard to my plans, and I failed also in compassing that other desire of my heart of which the ring you mention was a token. Both failures unnerved me, and I lay in that hut all night. I even lay there most of the next morning; but I did not see my aunt again, and I did not lift my hand against her life."

There was indescribable quiet in the tone, but there was indescribable power also, and the look he levelled upon the district attorney was unwaveringly solemn and hard.

"You deny, then, that you entered the widow's house on the morning of the murder?"

"I do."

"It is, then, a question of veracity between you and Miss Dare?"

Silence.

"She asserts she gave you back the ring you offered her. If this is so, and that ring was in your possession after you left her on Monday evening, how came it to be in the widow's dining-room the next morning, if you did not carry it there?"

"I can only repeat my words," rejoined Mr. Mansell.

The district attorney replied impatiently. For various reasons he did not wish to believe this man guilty.

"You do not seem very anxious to assist me in my endeavours to reach the truth," he observed. "Cannot you tell me what you did with the ring after you left Miss Dare? Whether you put it on your finger, or thrust it into your pocket, or tossed it into the marsh? If you did not carry it to the house, someone else must have done so, and you ought to be able to help us in determining who."

But Mr. Mansell shortly responded:

"I have nothing to say about the ring. From the moment Miss Dare returned it to me, as you say, it was, so far as I am concerned, a thing forgotten. I do not know as I should ever have thought of it again, if you had not mentioned it to me today. How it vanished from my possession only to reappear upon the scene of murder, some more clever conjurer than myself must explain."

"And this is all you have to say, Mr. Mansell?"

"This is all I have to say."

"Byrd," suggested the district attorney, after a long pause, during which the subject of his suspicions had stood before him as rigid and inscrutable as a statue in bronze, "Mr. Mansell would probably like to go to the hotel, unless, indeed, he desires to return immediately to Buffalo."

Craik Mansell at once started forward.

"Do you intend to allow me to return to Buffalo?" he asked.

"Yes," was the district attorney's reply.

"You are a good man," broke involuntarily from the other's lips, and he impulsively reached out his hand, but as quickly drew it back with a flush of pride that greatly became him.

"I do not say," quoth Mr. Ferris, "that I exempt you from surveillance. As prosecuting attorney of this district, my duty is to seek out and discover the man who murdered Mrs. Clemmens, and your explanations have not been as full or as satisfactory as I could wish."

"Your men will always find me at my desk in the mill," said Mr. Mansell, coldly. And, with another short bow, he left the attorney's side and went quickly out.

"That man is innocent," declared Mr. Ferris, as Horace Byrd leaned above him in expectation of instructions to keep watch over the departing visitor.

"The way in which he held out his hand to me spoke volumes."

The detective cast a sad glance at Craik Mansell's retreating figure.

"You could not convince Hickory of that fact," said he.

23

Mr. Orcutt

These words rang in the ears of Mr. Ferris. For he felt himself disturbed by them. Hickory did not believe Mr. Mansell innocent.

At last he sent for that detective.

"Hickory," he asked, "why do you think Mansell, rather than Hildreth, committed this crime?"

Now this query, on the part of the district attorney, put Hickory into a quandary. He wished to keep his promise to Horace Byrd, and yet he greatly desired to answer his employer's question truthfully. Without any special sympathies of his own, he yet had an undeniable leaning toward justice, and justice certainly demanded the indictment of Mansell. He ended by compromising matters.

"Mr. Ferris," said he, "when you went to see Miss Dare the other day, what did you think of her state of mind?"

"That it was a very unhappy one."

"Didn't you think more than that, sir? Didn't you think she believed Mr. Mansell guilty of this crime?"

"Yes," admitted the other, with reluctance.

"If Miss Dare is attached to Mr. Mansell, she must feel certain of his guilt to *offer* testimony against him. Her belief should go for something, sir; for much, it strikes me, when you consider what a woman she is."

This conversation increased Mr. Ferris' uneasiness. Much as he wished to spare the feelings of Miss Dare, and, through her, those of his friend, Mr. Orcutt, the conviction of Mansell's criminality was slowly gaining ground in his mind. He remembered the peculiar manner of the latter during the interview they had held together; his quiet acceptance of the position of a suspected man, and his marked reticence in regard to the ring. Though the delicate nature of the interests involved might be sufficient to explain his behaviour in the latter regard, his whole conduct could not be said to be that of a disinterested man, even if it were not necessarily that of a guilty one. In whatever way Mr. Ferris looked at it, he could come to but one conclusion, and that was, that justice to Hildreth called for such official attention to the evidence which had been collected against Mansell as should secure the indictment of that man against whom could be brought the more convincing proof of guilt.

Not that Mr. Ferris meant, or in anywise considered it good policy, to have Mansell arrested at this time. As the friend of Mr. Orcutt, it was manifestly advisable for him to present whatever evidence he possessed against Mansell directly to the grand jury. For in this way he would not only save the lawyer from the pain and humiliation of seeing the woman he so much loved called up as a witness against the man who had successfully rivalled him in her affections, but would run the chance, at least, of eventually preserving from open knowledge, the various details, if not the actual facts, which had led to this person being suspected of crime.

For the grand jury is a body whose business it is to make secret inquisition into criminal offences. Its members are bound by oath to the privacy of their deliberations. If, therefore, they should find the proofs presented to them by the district attorney insufficient to authorize an indictment against Mansell, nothing of their proceedings would transpire. While, on the contrary, if they decided that the evidence was such as to oblige them to indict Mansell instead of Hildreth, neither Mr. Orcutt nor Miss Dare could hold the district attorney accountable for the exposures that must follow.

The course, therefore, of Mr. Ferris was determined upon. All the evidence in his possession against both parties, together with the verdict of the coroner's jury, should go at once before the grand jury; Mansell, in the meantime, being so watched that a bench-warrant issuing upon the indictment would have him safely in custody at any moment.

But this plan for saving Mr. Orcutt's feelings did not succeed as fully as Mr. Ferris hoped. By some means or other the rumour got abroad that another man than Hildreth had fallen under the suspicion of the authorities, and one day Mr. Ferris found himself stopped on the street by the very person he had for a week been endeavouring to avoid.

"Mr. Orcutt!" he cried, "how do you do? I did not recognize you at first."

"No?" was the sharp rejoinder. "I'm not myself nowadays. I have a bad cold." With which impatient explanation he seized Mr. Ferris by the arm and said: "But what is this I hear? You have your eye on another party suspected of being Mrs. Clemmens' murderer?"

The district attorney bowed uneasily. He had hoped to escape the discussion of this subject with Mr. Orcutt.

The lawyer observed the embarrassment his question had caused, and instantly turned pale, notwithstanding the hardihood which a long career at the bar had given him.

"Ferris," he pursued, in a voice he strove hard to keep steady, "we have always been good friends, in spite of the many tilts we have had together before the court. Will you be kind enough to inform me if your suspicions are founded upon evidence collected by yourself, or at the instigation of parties professing to know more about this murder than they have hitherto revealed?"

Mr. Ferris could not fail to understand the true nature of this question, and out of pure friendship answered quietly:

"I have allowed myself to look with suspicion upon this Mansell— for it is Mrs. Clemmens' nephew who is at present occupying our attention,—because the facts which have come to light in his regard are as criminating in their nature as those which have transpired in reference to Mr. Hildreth. The examination into this matter, which my duty requires, has been anything but pleasant to me, Mr. Orcutt. The evidence of such witnesses as will have to be summoned before the Grand Jury, is of a character to bring open humiliation, if not secret grief, upon persons for whom I entertain the highest esteem."

The pointed way in which this was said convinced Mr. Orcutt that his worst fears had been realized. Turning partly away, but not losing his hold upon the other's arm, he observed with what quietness he could:

"You say that so strangely, I feel forced to put another question to you. If what I have to ask strikes you with any surprise, remember that my own astonishment and perplexity at being constrained to interrogate you in this way, are greater than any sensation you can yourself experience. What I desire to know is this. Among the witnesses you have collected against this last suspected party, there are some women, are there not?"

The district attorney gravely bowed.

"Ferris, is Miss Dare amongst them?"

"Orcutt, she is."

With a look that expressed his secret mistrust the lawyer gave way to a sudden burst of feeling.

"Ferris," he wrathfully acknowledged, "I may be a fool, but I don't see what she can have to say on this subject. It is impossible she should know anything about the murder; and, as for this Mansell——" He made a violent gesture with his hand, as if the very idea of her having any acquaintance with the nephew of Mrs. Clemmens were simply preposterous.

The district attorney, who saw from this how utterly ignorant the other was concerning Miss Dare's relations to the person named, felt his embarrassment increase.

"Mr. Orcutt," he replied, "strange as it may appear to you, Miss Dare *has* testimony to give of value to the prosecution, or she would not be reckoned among its witnesses. What that testimony is, I must leave to her discretion to make known to you, as she doubtless will, if you question her with sufficient consideration. I never forestall matters myself, nor would you wish me to tell you what would more becomingly come from her own lips. But, Mr. Orcutt, this I can say: that if it had been given me to choose between the two alternatives of resigning my office and of pursuing an inquiry which obliges me to submit to the unpleasantness of a judicial investigation a person held in so much regard by yourself, I would have given up my office with pleasure, so keenly do I feel the embarrassment of my position and the unhappiness of yours. But any mere resignation on my part would have availed nothing to save Miss Dare from appearing before the Grand Jury. The evidence she has to give in this matter makes the case against Mansell as strong as that against Hildreth, and it would be the duty of any public prosecutor to recognize the fact and act accordingly."

Mr. Orcutt, who had by the greatest effort succeeded in calming himself through this harangue, flashed sarcastically at this last remark, and surveyed Mr. Ferris with a peculiar look.

"Are you sure," he inquired in a slow, ironical tone, "that she has not succeeded in making it stronger?"

The look, the tone, were unexpected, and greatly startled Mr. Ferris. Drawing nearer to his friend, he returned his gaze with marked earnestness.

"What do you mean?" he asked, with secret anxiety.

But the wary lawyer had already repented this unwise betrayal of his own doubts. Meeting his companion's eye with a calmness that amazed himself, he remarked, instead of answering:

"It was through Miss Dare, then, that your attention was first drawn to Mrs. Clemmens' nephew?"

"No," disclaimed Mr. Ferris, hastily. "The detectives already had their eyes upon him. But a hint from her went far toward determining me upon pursuing the matter," he allowed, seeing that his friend was determined upon hearing the truth.

"So then," observed the other, with a stern dryness that recalled his manner at the bar, "she opened a communication with you herself?"

"Yes."

It was enough. Mr. Orcutt dropped the arm of Mr. Ferris, and, with his usual hasty bow, turned shortly away. The revelation which he believed himself to have received in this otherwise far from satisfactory interview, was one that he could not afford to share—that is, not yet; not while any hope remained that circumstances would so arrange themselves as to make it unnecessary for him to do so. If Imogene Dare, out of her insane desire to free Gouverneur Hildreth from the suspicion that oppressed him, had resorted to perjury and invented evidence tending to show the guilt of another party—and remembering her admissions at their last interview and the language she had used in her letter of farewell, no other conclusion offered itself,—what alternative was left him but to wait till he had seen her before he proceeded to an interference that would separate her from himself by a gulf still greater than that which already existed between them?

To be sure, the jealousy which consumed him, the passionate rage that seized his whole being when he thought of all she dared do for the man she loved, or that he thought she loved, counselled him to nip this attempt of hers in the bud, and by means of a word to Mr. Ferris throw such a doubt upon her veracity as a witness against this new party as should greatly influence the action of the former in the critical business he had in hand. But Mr. Orcutt, while a prey to unwonted passions, had not yet lost control of his reason, and reason told him that impulse was an unsafe guide for him to follow at this time.

Thought alone—deep and concentrated thought—would help him out of this crisis with honour and safety. But thought would not come at call. In all his quick walk home but one mad sentence formulated itself in his brain, and that was: "She loves him so, she is willing to perjure herself for his sake!" Nor, though he entered his door with his usual bustling air and went through all the customary observances of the hour with an appearance of no greater abstraction and gloom than had characterized him ever since the departure of Miss Dare, no other idea obtruded itself upon his mind than this: "She loves him so, she is willing to perjure herself for his sake!"

Even the sight of his books, his papers, and all that various paraphernalia of work and study which gives character to a lawyer's library, was insufficient to restore his mind to its usual condition of calm thought and accurate judgement. Not till the clock struck eight and he found himself almost without his own volition at Professor Darling's house, did he realize all the difficulties of his position and the almost intolerable nature of the undertaking which had been forced upon him by the exigencies of the situation.

Miss Dare, who had refused to see him at first, came into his presence with an expression that showed him with what reluctance she had finally responded to his peremptory message. But in the few heavy moments he had been obliged to wait, he had schooled himself to expect coldness if not absolute rebuff. He therefore took no heed of the haughty air of inquiry which she turned upon him, but came at once to the point, saying almost before she had closed the door:

"What is this you have been doing, Imogene?"

A flush, such as glints across the face of a marble statue, visited for a moment the still whiteness of her set features, then she replied:

"Mr. Orcutt, when I left your house I told you I had a wretched and unhappy duty to perform, that, when once accomplished, would separate us forever. I have done it, and the separation has come; why attempt to bridge it?"

There was a sad weariness in her tone, a sad weariness in her face, but he seemed to recognize neither. The demon jealousy—that hindrance to all unselfish feeling—had gripped him again, and the words that came to his lips were at once bitter and masterful.

"Imogene," he cried, with as much wrath in his tone as he had ever betrayed in her presence, "you do not answer my question. I ask you what you have been doing, and you reply, your duty. Now, what do you mean by duty? Tell me at once and distinctly, for I will no longer be put off by any roundabout phrases concerning a matter of such vital importance."

"Tell you?" This repetition of his words had a world of secret anguish in it which he could not help but notice. She did not succumb to it, however, but continued in another moment: "You said to me, in the last conversation we held together, that Gouverneur Hildreth could not be released from his terrible position without a distinct proof of innocence or the advancement of such evidence against another as should turn suspicion aside from him into a new and more justifiable quarter. I could not, any more than he, give a distinct proof of his innocence; but I could furnish the authorities with testimony calculated to arouse suspicion in a fresh direction, and I did it. For Gouverneur Hildreth had to be saved at any price—*at any price.*"

The despairing emphasis she laid upon the last phrase went like hot steel to Mr. Orcutt's heart, and made his eyes blaze with almost uncontrollable passion.

"*Je ne vois pas la necessité,*" said he, in that low, restrained tone of bitter sarcasm which made his invective so dreaded by opposing counsel. "If Gouverneur Hildreth finds himself in an unfortunate position, he has only his own follies and inordinate desire for this woman's death to thank for it. Because you love him and compassionate him beyond all measure, that is no reason why you should perjure yourself, and throw the burden of his shame upon a man as innocent as Mr. Mansell."

But this tone, though it had made many a witness quail before it, neither awed nor intimidated her.

"You—you do not understand," came from her white lips. "It is Mr. Hildreth who is perfectly innocent, and not——" But here she paused. "You will excuse me from saying more," she said. "You, as a lawyer, ought to know that I should not be compelled to speak on a subject like this except under oath."

"Imogene!" A change had passed over Mr. Orcutt. "Imogene, do you mean to affirm that you really have charges to make against Craik Mansell; that this evidence you propose to give is real, and not manufactured for the purpose of leading suspicion aside from Hildreth?"

It was an insinuation against her veracity he never could have made, or she have listened to, a few weeks before; but the shield of her pride was broken between them, and neither he nor she seemed to give any thought to the reproach conveyed in these words.

"What I have to say is the truth," she murmured. "I have not manufactured anything ."

With an astonishment he took no pains to conceal, Mr. Orcutt anxiously surveyed her. He could not believe this was so, yet how could he convict her of falsehood in face of that suffering expression of resolve which she wore. His methods as a lawyer came to his relief.

"Imogene," he slowly responded, "if, as you say, you are in possession of positive evidence against this Mansell, how comes it that you jeopardized the interests of the man you loved by so long withholding your testimony?"

But instead of the flush of confusion which he expected, she flashed upon him with a sudden revelation of feeling that made him involuntarily start.

"Shall I tell you?" she replied. "You will have to know some time, and why not now? I kept back the truth," she replied, advancing a step, but without raising her eyes to his, "because it is not the aspersed Hildreth that I love, but——"

Why did she pause? What was it she found so hard to speak? Mr. Orcutt's expression became terrible.

"But the other," she murmured at last.

"The other!"

It was now her turn to start and look at him in surprise, if not in some fear.

"What other?" he cried, seizing her by the hand. "Name him. I will have no further misunderstanding between us."

"Is it necessary?" she asked, with bitterness. "Will Heaven spare me nothing?" Then, as she saw no relenting in the fixed gaze that held her own, whispered, in a hollow tone: "You have just spoken the name yourself—Craik Mansell."

"Ah!"

Incredulity, anger, perplexity, all the emotions that were seething in this man's troubled soul, spoke in that simple exclamation. Then silence settled upon the room, during which she gained control over herself, and he the semblance of it if no more. She was the first to speak.

"I know," said she, "that this avowal on my part seems almost incredible to you; but it is no more so than that which you so readily received from me the other day in reference to Gouverneur Hildreth. A woman who spends a month away from home makes acquaintances which she does not always mention when she comes back. I saw Mr. Mansell in Buffalo, and——" turning, she confronted the lawyer with her large gray eyes, in which a fire burned such as he had never seen there before—"and grew to esteem him," she went on. "For the first time in my life I found myself in the presence of a man whose nature commanded mine.

"His ambition, his determination, his unconventional and forcible character woke aspirations within me such as I had never known my-

335

self capable of before. Life, which had stretched out before me with a somewhat monotonous outlook, changed to a panorama of varied and wonderful experiences, as I listened to his voice and met the glance of his eye; and soon, before he knew it, and certainly before I realized it, words of love passed between us, and the agony of that struggle began which has ended—— Ah, let me not think how, or I shall go mad!"

Mr. Orcutt, who had watched her with a lover's fascination during all this attempted explanation, shivered for a moment at this last bitter cry of love and despair, but spoke up when he did speak, with a coldness that verged on severity.

"So you loved another man when you came back to my home and listened to the words of passion which came from *my* lips, and the hopes of future bliss and happiness that welled up from *my* heart?"

"Yes," she whispered, "and, as you will remember, I tried to suppress those hopes and turn a deaf ear to those words, though I had but little prospect of marrying a man whose fortunes depended upon the success of an invention he could persuade no one to believe in."

"Yet you brought yourself to listen to those hopes on the afternoon of the murder," he suggested, ironically.

"Can you blame me for that?" she cried, "remembering how you pleaded, and what a revulsion of feeling I was labouring under?"

A smile bitter as the fate which loomed before him, and scornful as the feelings that secretly agitated his breast, parted Mr. Orcutt's pale lips for an instant, and he seemed about to give utterance to some passionate rejoinder, but he subdued himself with a determined effort, and quietly waiting till his voice was under full control, remarked with lawyer-like brevity at last:

"You have not told me what evidence you have to give against young Mansell?"

Her answer came with equal brevity if not equal quietness.

"No; I have told Mr. Ferris; is not that enough?"

But he did not consider it so. "Ferris is a district attorney," said he, "and has demanded your confidence for the purposes of justice, while I am your friend. The action you have taken is peculiar, and you may need advice. But how can I give it or how can you receive it unless there is a complete understanding between us?"

Struck in spite of herself, moved perhaps by a hope she had not allowed herself to contemplate before, she looked at him long and earnestly.

"And do you really wish to help me?" she inquired. "Are you so generous as to forgive the pain, and possibly the humiliation, I have inflicted upon you, and lend me your assistance in case my testimony works its due effect, and he be brought to trial instead of Mr. Hildreth?"

It was a searching and a pregnant question, for which Mr. Orcutt was possibly not fully prepared, but his newly gained control did not give way.

"I must insist upon hearing the facts before I say anything of my intentions," he averred. "Whatever they may be, they cannot be more startling in their character than those which have been urged against Hildreth."

"But they are," she whispered. Then with a quick look around her, she put her mouth close to Mr. Orcutt's ear and breathed:

"Mr. Hildreth is not the only man who, unseen by the neighbours, visited Mrs. Clemmens' house on the morning of the murder. Craik Mansell was there also."

"Craik Mansell! How do you know that? Ah," he pursued, with the scornful intonation of a jealous man, "I forgot that you are lovers."

The sneer, natural as it was, perhaps, seemed to go to her heart and wake its fiercest indignation.

"Hush," cried she, towering upon him with an ominous flash of her proud eye. "Do not turn the knife in *that* wound or you will seal my lips forever." And she moved hastily away from his side. But in another instant she determinedly returned, saying: "This is no time for indulging in one's sensibilities. I affirm that Craik Mansell visited his aunt on that day, because the ring which was picked up on the floor of her dining-room—you remember the ring, Mr. Orcutt?"

Remember it! Did he not? All his many perplexities in its regard crowded upon him as he made a hurried bow of acquiescence.

"It belonged to him," she continued. "He had bought it for me, or, rather, had had the diamond reset for me—it had been his mother's. Only the day before, he had tried to put it on my finger in a meeting we had in the woods back of his aunt's house. But I refused to allow him. The prospect ahead was too dismal and unrelenting for us to betroth ourselves, whatever our hopes or wishes might be."

"You—you had a meeting with this man in the woods the day before his aunt was assaulted," echoed Mr. Orcutt, turning upon her with an amazement that swallowed up his wrath.

337

"Yes."

"And he afterward visited her house?"

"Yes."

"And dropped that ring there?"

"Yes."

Starting slowly, as if the thoughts roused by this short statement of facts were such as demanded instant consideration, Mr. Orcutt walked to the other side of the room, where he paced up and down in silence for some minutes. When he returned it was the lawyer instead of the lover who stood before her.

"Then, it was the simple fact of finding this gentleman's ring on the floor of Mrs. Clemmens' dining-room that makes you consider him the murderer of his aunt?" he asked, with a tinge of something like irony in his tone.

"No," she breathed rather than answered. "That was a proof, of course, that he had been there, but I should never have thought of it as an evidence of guilt if the woman herself had not uttered, in our hearing that tell-tale exclamation of 'Ring and Hand,' and if, in the talk I held with Mr. Mansell the day before, he had not betrayed—— Why do you stop me?" she whispered.

"I did not stop you," he hastily assured her. "I am too anxious to hear what you have to say. Go on, Imogene. What did this Mansell betray? I—I ask as a father might," he added, with some dignity and no little effort.

But her fears had taken alarm, or her caution been aroused, and she merely said:

"The five thousand dollars which his aunt leaves him is just the amount he desired to start him in life."

"Did he wish such an amount?" Mr. Orcutt asked.

"Very much."

"And acknowledged it in the conversation he had with you?"

"Yes."

"Imogene," declared the lawyer, "if you do not want to insure Mr. Mansell's indictment, I would suggest to you not to lay too great stress upon any *talk* you may have held with him."

But she cried with unmoved sternness, and a relentless crushing down of all emotion that was at once amazing and painful to see:

"The innocent is to be saved from the gallows, no matter what the fate of the guilty may be."

And a short but agitated silence followed which Mr. Orcutt broke at last by saying:

"Are these all the facts you have to give me?"

She started, cast him a quick look, bowed her head, and replied: "Yes."

There was something in the tone of this assertion that made him repeat his question.

"Are these *all* the facts you have to give me?"

Her answer came ringing and emphatic now.

"Yes," she avowed—"all."

With a look of relief, slowly smoothing out the deep furrows of his brow, Mr. Orcutt, for the second time, walked thoughtfully away in evident consultation with his own thoughts. This time he was gone so long, the suspense became almost intolerable to Imogene. Feeling that she could endure it no longer, she followed him at last, and laid her hand upon his arm.

"Speak," she impetuously cried. "Tell me what you think; what I have to expect."

But he shook his head.

"Wait," he returned; "wait till the grand jury has brought in a bill of indictment. It will, doubtless, be against one of these two men; but I must know which, before I can say or do anything ."

"And do you think there can be any doubt about which of these two it will be?" she inquired, with sudden emotion.

"There is always doubt," he rejoined, "about anything or everything a body of men may do. This is a very remarkable case, Imogene," he resumed, with increased sombreness; "the most remarkable one, perhaps, that has ever come under my observation. What the grand jury will think of it; upon which party, Mansell or Hildreth, the weight of their suspicion will fall, neither I nor Ferris, nor any other man, can prophesy with any assurance. The evidence against both is, in so far as we know, entirely circumstantial. That you believe Mr. Mansell to be the guilty party——"

"Believe!" she murmured; "I know it."

"That you *believe* him to be the guilty party," the wary lawyer pursued, as if he had not heard her "does not imply that they will believe it too. Hildreth comes of a bad stock, and his late attempt at suicide tells wonderfully against him; yet, the facts you have to give in Mansell's disfavour are strong also, and Heaven only knows what the upshot will be. However, a few weeks will determine all that, and then——" Pausing, he looked at her, and, as he did so, the austerity and self-command of the lawyer vanished out of sight, and the passionate gleam of a fierce and overmastering love shone again in his eyes. "And then," he cried, "then we will see what Tremont Orcutt can do to bring order out of this chaos."

There was so much resolve in his look, such a hint of promise in his tone, that she flushed with something almost akin to hope.

"Oh, generous——" she began.

But he stopped her before she could say more.

"Wait," he repeated; "wait till we see what action will be taken by the grand jury." And taking her hand, he looked earnestly, if not passionately, in her face. "Imogene," he commenced, "if I should succeed——"But there he himself stopped short with a quick recalling of his own words, perhaps. "No," he cried, "I will say no more till we see which of these two men is to be brought to trial." And, pressing her hand to his lips, he gave her one last look in which was concentrated all the secret passions which had been called forth by this hour, and hastily left the room.

24

A True Bill

The town of Sibley was in a state of excitement. About the court-house especially the crowd was great and the interest manifested intense. The grand jury was in session, and the case of the Widow Clemmens was before it.

As all the proceedings of this body are private, the suspense of those interested in the issue was naturally very great. The name of the man lastly suspected of the crime had transpired, and both Hildreth and Mansell had their partisans, though the mystery surrounding the latter made his friends less forward in asserting his innocence than those of the more thoroughly understood Hildreth. Indeed, the ignorance felt on all sides as to the express reasons for associating the name of Mrs. Clemmens' nephew with his aunt's murder added much to the significance of the hour. Conjectures were plenty and the wonder great, but the causes why this man, or any other, should lie under a suspicion equal to that raised against Hildreth at the inquest was a mystery that none could solve.

But what is the curiosity of the rabble to us? Our interest is in a little room far removed from this scene of excitement, where the young daughter of Professor Darling kneels by the side of Imogene Dare, striving by caress and entreaty to win a word from her lips or a glance from her heavy eyes.

"Imogene," she pleaded,—"Imogene, what is this terrible grief? Why did you have to go to the court-house this morning with papa, and why have you been almost dead with terror and misery ever since you got back? Tell me, or I shall perish of mere fright. For weeks now, ever since you were so good as to help me with my wedding-clothes, I have seen that something dreadful was weighing upon your mind, but this which you are suffering now is awful; this I cannot bear. Cannot you speak dear? Words will do you good."

"Words!"

Oh, the despair, the bitterness of that single exclamation! Miss Darling drew back in dismay. As if released, Imogene rose to her feet and surveyed the sweet and ingenuous countenance uplifted to her own, with a look of faint recognition of the womanly sympathy it conveyed.

"Helen," she resumed, "you are happy. Don't stay here with me, but go where there are cheerfulness and hope."

"But I cannot while you suffer so. I love you, Imogene. Would you drive me away from your side when you are so unhappy? You don't care for me as I do for you or you could not do it."

"Helen!" The deep tone made the sympathetic little bride-elect quiver. "Helen, some griefs are best borne alone. Only a few hours now and I shall know the worst. Leave me."

But the gentle little creature was not to be driven away. She only clung the closer and pleaded the more earnestly:

"Tell me, tell me!"

The reiteration of this request was too much for the pallid woman before her. Laying her two hands on the shoulders of this child, she drew back and looked her earnestly in the face.

"Helen," she cried, "what do you know of earthly anguish? A pet-ted child, the favourite of happy fortune, you have been kept from evil as from a blight. None of the annoyances of life have been allowed to enter your path, much less its griefs and sins. Terror with you is but a name, remorse an unknown sensation. Even your love has no depths in it such as suffering gives. Yet, since you do love, and love well, per-haps you can understand something of what a human soul can endure who sees its only hope and only love tottering above a gulf too hor-rible for words to describe—a gulf, too, which her own hand—— But no, I cannot tell you. I overrated my strength. I——"

She sank back, but the next moment started again to her feet: a servant had opened the door.

"What is it!" she exclaimed; "speak, tell me."

"Only a gentleman to see you, miss."

"Only a——" But she stopped in that vain repetition of the girl's simple words, and looked at her as if she would force from her lips the name she had not the courage to demand; but, failing to obtain it, turned away to the glass, where she quietly smoothed her hair and adjusted the lace at her throat, and then catching sight of the tear-stained face of Helen, stooped and gave her a kiss, after which she moved mechanically to the door and went down those broad flights, one after one, till she came to the parlour, when she went in and encountered—Mr. Orcutt.

A glance at his face told her all she wanted to know.

"Ah!" she gasped, "it is then——"

"Mansell!"

It was five minutes later. Imogene leaned against the window where she had withdrawn herself at the utterance of that one word. Mr. Orcutt stood a couple of paces behind her.

"Imogene," said he, "there is a question I would like to have you answer."

The feverish agitation expressed in his tone made her look around.

"Put it," she mechanically replied.

But he did not find it easy to do this, while her eyes rested upon him in such despair. He felt, however, that the doubt in his mind must be satisfied at all hazards; so choking down an emotion that was almost as boundless as her own, he ventured to ask:

"Is it among the possibilities that you could ever again contemplate giving yourself in marriage to Craik Mansell, no matter what the issue of the coming trial may be?"

A shudder quick and powerful as that which follows the withdrawal of a dart from an agonizing wound shook her whole frame for a moment, but she answered, steadily:

"No; how can you ask, Mr. Orcutt?"

A gleam of relief shot across his somewhat haggard features.

"Then," said he, "it will be no treason in me to assure you that never has my love been greater for you than today. That to save you from the pain which you are suffering, I would sacrifice everything, even my pride. If, therefore, there is any kindness I can show you, any deed I can perform for your sake, I am ready to attempt it, Imogene.

"Would you—" she hesitated, but gathered courage as she met his eye—"would you be willing to go to him with a message from me?"

His glance fell and his lips took a line that startled Imogene, but his answer, though given with bitterness was encouraging.

"Yes," he returned; "even that."

"Then," she cried, "tell him that to save the innocent, I had to betray the guilty, but in doing this I did not spare myself; that whatever his doom may be, I shall share it, even though it be that of death."

"Imogene!"

"Will you tell him?" she asked.

But he would not have been a man, much less a lover, if he could answer that question now. Seizing her by the arm, he looked her wildly in the face.

"Do you mean to kill yourself?" he demanded.

"I feel I shall not live," she gasped, while her hand went involuntarily to her heart.

He gazed at her in horror.

"And if he is cleared?" he hoarsely ejaculated.

"I—I shall try to endure my fate."

He gave her another long, long look.

"So this is the alternative you give me?" he bitterly exclaimed. "I must either save this man or see you perish. Well," he declared, after a few minutes' further contemplation of her face, "I will save this man— that is, if he will allow me to do so."

A flash of joy such as he had not perceived on her countenance for weeks transformed its marble-like severity into something of its pristine beauty.

"And you will take him my message also?" she cried.

But to this he shook his head.

"If I am to approach him as a lawyer willing to undertake his cause, don't you see I can give him no such message as that?"

"Ah, yes, yes. But you can tell him Imogene Dare has risked her own life and happiness to save the innocent."

"I will tell him whatever I can to show your pity and your misery."

And she had to content herself with this. In the light of the new hope that was thus unexpectedly held out to her, it did not seem so difficult. Giving Mr. Orcutt her hand, she endeavoured to thank him, but the reaction from her long suspense was too much, and, for the first time in her brave young life, Imogene lost consciousness and fainted quite away.

25

Among Telescopes and Charts

Gouverneur Hildreth was discharged and Craik Mansell committed to prison to await his trial.

Horace Byrd, who no longer had any motive for remaining in Sibley, had completed all his preparations to return to New York. His valise was packed, his *adieus* made, and nothing was left for him to do but to step around to the station, when he bethought him of a certain question he had not put to Hickory.

Seeking him out, he propounded it.

"Hickory," said he, "have you ever discovered in the course of your inquiries where Miss Dare was on the morning of the murder?"

The stalwart detective, who was in a very contented frame of mind, answered up with great cheeriness:

"Haven't I, though! It was one of the very first things I made sure of. She was at Professor Darling's house on Summer Avenue."

"At Professor Darling's house?" Mr. Byrd felt a sensation of dismay. Professor Darling's house was, as you remember, in almost direct communication with Mrs. Clemmens' cottage by means of a path through the woods. As Mr. Byrd recalled his first experience in threading those woods, and remembered with what suddenness he had emerged from them only to find himself in full view of the West Side and Professor Darling's spacious villa, he stared uneasily at his colleague and said:

"It is train time, Hickory, but I cannot help that. Before I leave this town I must know just what she was doing on that morning, and whom she was with. Can you find out?"

"*Can I find out?*"

The hardy detective was out of the door before the last word of this scornful repetition had left his lips.

He was gone an hour. When he returned he looked very much

excited.

"Well!" he ejaculated, breathlessly, "I have had an experience."

Mr. Byrd gave him a look, saw something he did not like in his face, and moved uneasily in his chair.

"You have?" he retorted. "What is it? Speak."

"Do you know," the other resumed, "that the hardest thing I ever had to do was to keep my head down in the hut the other day, and deny myself a look at the woman who could bear herself so bravely in the midst of a scene so terrible. Well," he went on, "I have today been rewarded for my self-control. I have seen Miss Dare."

Horace Byrd could scarcely restrain his impatience.

"Where?" he demanded. "How? Tell a fellow, can't you?"

"I am going to," protested Hickory. "Cannot you wait a minute? *I* had to wait forty. Well," he continued more pleasantly as he saw the other frown, "I went to Professor Darling's. There is a girl there I have talked to before, and I had no difficulty in seeing her or getting a five minutes' chat with her at the back-gate. Odd how such girls will talk! She told me in three minutes all I wanted to know. Not that it was so much, only——"

"Do get on," interrupted Mr. Byrd. "When did Miss Dare come to the house on the morning Mrs. Clemmens was murdered, and what did she do while there?"

"She came early; by ten o'clock or so, I believe, and she sat, if she did sit, in an observatory they have at the top of the house: a place where she often used to go, I am told, to study astronomy with Professor Darling's oldest daughter."

"And was Miss Darling with her that morning? Did they study together all the time she was in the house?"

"No; that is, the girl said no one went up to the observatory with Miss Dare; that Miss Darling did not happen to be at home that day, and Miss Dare had to study alone. Hearing this," pursued Hickory, answering the look of impatience in the other's face, "I had a curiosity to interview the observatory, and being—well, not a clumsy fellow at soft-soaping a girl—I at last succeeded in prevailing upon her to take me up. Byrd, will you believe me when I tell you that we did it without going into the house?"

"What?"

"I mean," corrected the other, "without entering the main part of the building. The professor's house has a tower, you know, at the upper angle toward the woods, and it is in the top of that tower he keeps his telescopes and all that kind of thing. The tower has a special staircase of its own. It is a spiral one, and opens on a door below that connects directly with the garden. We went up these stairs."

"You dared to?"

"Yes; the girl assured me everyone was out of the house but the servants, and I believed her. We went up the stairs, entered the observatory——"

"It is not kept locked, then?"

"It was not locked today—saw the room, which is a curious one—glanced out over the view, which is well worth seeing, and then——"

"Well, what?"

"I believe I stood still and asked the girl a question or two more. I inquired," he went on, deprecating the other's impatience by a wave of his nervous hand, "when Miss Dare came down from this place on the morning you remember. She answered that she couldn't quite tell; that she wouldn't have remembered anything about it at all, only that Miss Tremaine came to the house that morning, and wanting to see Miss Dare, ordered her to go up to the observatory and tell that lady to come down, and that she went, but to her surprise did not find Miss Dare there, though she was sure she had not gone home, or, at least, hadn't taken any of the cars that start from the front of the house, for she had looked at them everyone as they went by the basement window where she was at work."

"The girl said this?"

"Yes, standing in the door of this small room, and looking me straight in the eye."

"And did you ask her nothing more? Say nothing about the time, Hickory, or—or inquire where she supposed Miss Dare to have gone?"

"Yes, I asked her all this. I am not without curiosity any more than you are, Mr. Byrd."

"And she replied?"

"Oh, as to the time, that it was somewhere before noon. Her reason for being sure of this was that Miss Tremaine declined to wait till another effort had been made to find Miss Dare, saying she had an engagement at twelve which she did not wish to break."

"And the girl's notions about where Miss Dare had gone?"

"Such as you expect, Byrd. She said she did not know anything about it, but that Miss Dare often went strolling in the garden, or even in the woods when she came to Professor Darling's house, and that she supposed she had gone off on some such walk at this time, for, at one o'clock or thereabouts, she saw her pass in the horse-car on her way back to the town."

"Hickory, I wish you had not told me this just as I am going back to the city."

"Wish I had not told it, or wish I had not gone to Professor Darling's house as you requested?"

"Wish you had not told it. I dare not wish the other. But you spoke of seeing Miss Dare; how was that? Where did you run across her?"

"Do you want to hear?"

"Of course, of course."

"But I thought——"

"Oh, never mind, old boy; tell me the whole now, as long as you have told me any. Was she in the house?"

"I will tell you. I had asked the girl all these questions, as I have said, and was about to leave the observatory and go below when I thought I would cast another glance around the curious old place, and in doing so caught a glimpse of a huge portfolio of charts, as I supposed, standing upright in a rack that stretched across the further portion of the room. Somehow my heart misgave me when I saw this rack, and, scarcely conscious what it was I feared, I crossed the floor and looked behind the portfolio. Byrd, there was a woman crouched there—a woman whose pallid cheeks and burning eyes lifted to meet my own, told me only too plainly that it was Miss Dare. I have had many experiences," Hickory allowed, after a moment, "and some of them anything but pleasant to myself, but I don't think I ever felt just as I did at that instant.

"I believe I attempted a bow—I don't remember; or, at least, tried to murmur some excuse, but the look that came into her face paralyzed me, and I stopped before I had gotten very far, and waited to hear what she would say. But she did not say much; she merely rose, and, turning toward me, exclaimed: 'No apologies; you are a detective, I suppose?' And when I nodded, or made some other token that she had guessed correctly, she merely remarked, flashing upon me, however, in a way I do not yet understand: 'Well, you have got what you desired, and now can go.' And I went, Byrd, went; and I felt puzzled, I don't know why, and a little bit sore about the heart, too, as if—— Well, I can't even tell what I mean by that *if*. The only thing I am sure of is, that Mansell's cause hasn't been helped by this day's job, and that if this lady is asked on the witness stand where she was during the hour everyone believed her to be safely shut up with the telescopes and charts, we shall hear——"

"What?"

"Well, that she *was* shut up with them, most likely. Women like her are not to be easily disconcerted even on the witness stand."

26

"He Shall Hear Me!"

The time is midnight, the day the same as that which saw this ir-
ruption of Hickory into Professor Darling's observatory; the scene
that of Miss Dare's own room in the northeast tower. She is standing
before a table with a letter in her hand and a look upon her face that,
if seen, would have added much to the puzzlement of the detectives.

The letter was from Mr. Orcutt and ran thus:

> I have seen Mr. Mansell, and have engaged myself to undertake
> his defence. When I tell you that out of the hundreds of cases I
> have tried in my still short life, I have lost but a small percent-
> age, you will understand what this means.
> In pursuance to your wishes, I mentioned your name to the
> prisoner with an intimation that I had a message from you
> to deliver. But he stopped me before I could utter a word. "I
> receive no communication from Miss Dare!" he declared, and,
> anxious as I really was to do your bidding, I was compelled to
> refrain; for his tone was one of hatred and his look that of inef-
> fable scorn.

This was all, but it was enough. Imogene had read these words over
three times, and now was ready to plunge the letter into the flame of
a candle to destroy it. As it burned, her grief and indignation took
words:

"He is alienated, completely alienated," she gasped; "and I do not
wonder. But," and here the full majesty of her nature broke forth in
one grand gesture, "he shall hear me yet! As there is a God above, he
shall hear me yet, even if it has to be in the open court and in the
presence of judge and jury!"

27

The Great Trial

Sibley was in a stir. Sibley was the central point of interest for the whole country. The great trial was in progress and the curiosity of the populace knew no bounds.

In a room of the hotel sat our two detectives. They had just come from the court-house. Both seemed inclined to talk, though both showed an indisposition to open the conversation. A hesitation lay between them; a certain thin veil of embarrassment that either one would have found it hard to explain, and yet which sufficed to make their intercourse a trifle uncertain in its character, though Hickory's look had lost none of its rude good-humour, and Byrd's manner was the same mixture of easy nonchalance and quiet self-possession it had always been.

It was Hickory who spoke at last.

"Well, Byrd?" was his suggestive exclamation.

"Well, Hickory?" was the quiet reply.

"What do you think of the case so far?"

"I think"—the words came somewhat slowly—"I think that it looks bad. Bad for the prisoner, I mean," he explained the next moment with a quick flush.

"Your sympathies are evidently with Mansell," Hickory quietly remarked.

"Yes," was the slow reply. "Not that I think him innocent, or would turn a hair's breadth from the truth to serve him."

"He *is* a manly fellow," Hickory bluntly admitted, after a moment's puff at the pipe he was smoking. "Do you remember the peculiar straightforwardness of his look when he uttered his plea of 'Not guilty,' and the tone he used too, so quiet, yet so emphatic? You could have heard a pin drop."

"Yes," returned Mr. Byrd, with a quick contraction of his usually smooth brow.

"Have you noticed," the other broke forth, after another puff, "a certain curious air of disdain that he wears?"

"Yes," was again the short reply.

"I wonder what it means?" queried Hickory carelessly, knocking the ashes out of his pipe.

Mr. Byrd flashed a quick askance look at his colleague from under his half-fallen lids, but made no answer.

"It is not pride alone," resumed the rough-and-ready detective, half-musingly; "though he's as proud as the best of 'em. Neither is it any sort of make-believe, or *I* wouldn't be caught by it. 'Tis—'tis—what?" And Hickory rubbed his nose with his thoughtful forefinger, and looked inquiringly at Mr. Byrd.

"How should I know?" remarked the other, tossing his stump of a cigar into the fire. "Mr. Mansell is too deep a problem for me."

"And Miss Dare too?"

"*And* Miss Dare."

Silence followed this admission, which Hickory broke at last by observing:

"The day that sees *her* on the witness stand will be interesting, eh?"

"It is not far off," declared Mr. Byrd.

"No?"

"I think she will be called as a witness tomorrow."

"Have you noticed," began Hickory again, after another short interval of quiet contemplation, "that it is only when Miss Dare is present that Mansell wears the look of scorn I have just mentioned."

"Hickory," said Mr. Byrd, wheeling directly about in his chair and for the first time surveying his colleague squarely, "I have noticed *this*. That ever since the day she made her first appearance in the court-room, she has sat with her eyes fixed earnestly upon the prisoner, and that he has never answered her look by so much as a glance in her direction. This has but one explanation as I take it. He never forgets that it is through her he has been brought to trial for his life."

Mr. Byrd uttered this very distinctly, and with a decided emphasis. But the impervious Hickory only settled himself farther back in his chair, and stretching his feet out toward the fire, remarked dryly:

"Perhaps I am not much of a judge of human nature, but I should have said now that this Mansell was not a man to treat her contemptuously for that. Rage he might show or hatred, but this quiet ignoring of her presence seems a little too dignified for a criminal facing a person he has every reason to believe is convinced of his guilt."

"Ordinary rules don't apply to this man. Neither you nor I can sound his nature. If he displays contempt, it is because he is of the sort to feel it for the woman who has betrayed him."

"You make him out mean-spirited, then, as well as wicked?"

"I make him out human. More than that," Mr. Byrd resumed, after a moment's thought, "I make him out consistent. A man who lets his passions sway him to the extent of committing a murder for the purpose of satisfying his love or his ambition, is not of the unselfish cast that would appreciate such a sacrifice as Miss Dare has made. This under the supposition that our reasons for believing him guilty are well founded. If our suppositions are false, and the crime was not committed by him, his contempt needs no explanation."

"Just so!"

The peculiar tone in which this was uttered caused Mr. Byrd to flash another quick look at his colleague. Hickory did not seem to observe it.

"What makes you think Miss Dare will be called to the witness stand tomorrow?" he asked.

"Well I will tell you," returned Byrd, with the sudden vivacity of one glad to turn the current of conversation into a fresh channel. "If you have followed the method of the prosecution as I have done, you will have noticed that it has advanced to its point by definite stages. First, witnesses were produced to prove the existence of motive on the part of the accused. Mr. Goodman was called to the witness stand, and, after him, other business men of Buffalo, all of whom united in unqualified assertions of the prisoner's frequently-expressed desire for a sum of money sufficient to put his invention into practical use. Next, the amount considered necessary for this purpose was ascertained and found to be just covered by the legacy bequeathed him by his aunt; after which, ample evidence was produced to show that he knew the extent of her small fortune, and the fact that she had by her will made him her heir.

"Motive for the crime being thus established, they now proceeded to prove that he was not without actual opportunity for perpetrating it. He was shown to have been in Sibley at the time of the murder. The station-master at Monteith was confronted with the prisoner, also old Sally Perkins. Then you and I came before the court with

353

our testimony, and whatever doubt may have remained as to his having been in a position to effect his aunt's death, and afterward escape unnoticed by means of the path leading over the hills to Monteith Quarry station, was swept away. What remains? To connect him with the murder itself, by some, strong link of circumstantial evidence, such as the ring provides. And who is it that can give testimony regarding the ring?—Miss Dare."

"Hem! Well, she will do it," was the dry remark of Hickory.

"She will be obliged to do it," was the emphatic response of Byrd.

And again their glances crossed in a furtive way both seemed ready to ignore.

"What do you think of Orcutt?" Hickory next inquired.

"He is very quiet."

"Too quiet, eh?"

"Perhaps. Folks that know him well declare they never before saw him conduct a case in so temperate a manner. He has scarcely made an effort at cross-examination, and, in fact, has thus far won nothing for the defence except that astonishing tribute to the prisoner's character given by Mr. Goodman."

"Mr. Goodman is Mansell's friend."

"I know it; but his short, decisive statements told upon the jury. Such a man as he made Mansell out to be is just the sort to create an impression on a body of men like them."

"Orcutt understands a jury."

"Orcutt understands his case. He knows he can make nothing by attempting to shake the evidence which has been presented by the prosecution; the facts are too clear, and the witnesses which have been called to testify are of too reliable a character. Whatever defence he contemplates, it will not rest upon a denial of any of the facts brought to light through our efforts, or the evidence of such persons as Messrs. Goodman and Harrison."

"No."

"The question is, then, in what will it lie? Some strong point, I warrant you, or he would not hold himself and his plans so completely in reserve. But what strong point? I acknowledge the uncertainty troubles me."

"I don't wonder," rejoined Hickory. "So it does me."

And a constraint again fell between them that lasted till Hickory put his pipe in his pocket and signified his intention of returning to his own apartments.

28

The Chief Witness For
the Prosecution

Mr. Byrd's countenance after the departure of his companion was anything but cheerful. The fact is, he was secretly uneasy. He dreaded the morrow. He dreaded the testimony of Miss Dare. He had not yet escaped so fully from under the dominion of her fascinations as to regard with equanimity this unhappy woman forcing herself to give testimony compromising to the man she loved.

Yet when the morrow came he was among the first to secure a seat in the court-room. Though the scene was likely to be harrowing to his feelings, he had no wish to lose it, and, indeed, chose such a position as would give him the best opportunity for observing the prisoner and surveying the witnesses.

He was not the only one on the lookout for the testimony of Miss Dare. The increased number of the spectators and the general air of expectation visible in more than one of the chief actors in this terrible drama gave suspicious proof of the fact; even if the deadly pallor of the lady herself had not revealed her own feelings in regard to the subject.

The entrance of the prisoner was more marked, too, than usual. His air and manner were emphasized, so to speak, and his face, when he turned it toward the jury, wore an iron look of resolution that would have made him conspicuous had he occupied a less prominent position than that of the dock.

Miss Dare, who had flashed her eyes toward him at the moment of his first appearance, dropped them again, contrary to her usual custom. Was it because she knew the moment was at hand when their glances would be obliged to meet?

Mr. Orcutt, whom no movement on the part of Miss Dare ever escaped, leaned over and spoke to the prisoner.

"Mr. Mansell," said he, "are you prepared to submit with composure to the ordeal of confronting Miss Dare?"

"Yes," was the stern reply.

"I would then advise you to look at her now," proceeded his counsel. "She is not turned this way, and you can observe her without encountering her glance. A quick look at this moment may save you from betraying any undue emotion when you see her upon the stand."

The accused smiled with a bitterness Mr. Orcutt thought perfectly natural, and slowly prepared to obey. As he raised his eyes and allowed them to traverse the room until they settled upon the countenance of the woman he loved, this other man who, out of a still more absorbing passion for Imogene, was at that very moment doing all that lay in his power for the saving of this his openly acknowledged rival, watched him with the closest and most breathless attention. It was another instance of that peculiar fascination which a successful rival has for an unsuccessful one. It was as if this great lawyer's thoughts reverted to his love, and he asked himself: "What is there in this Mansell that she should prefer him to me?"

And Orcutt himself, though happily unaware of the fact, was at that same instant under a scrutiny as narrow as that he bestowed upon his client. Mr. Ferris, who knew his secret, felt a keen interest in watching how he would conduct himself at this juncture. Not an expression of the lawyer's keen and puzzling eye but was seen by the district attorney and noted, even if it was not understood.

Of the three, Mr. Ferris was the first to turn away, and his thoughts if they could have been put into words might have run something like this: "That man"—meaning Orcutt—"is doing the noblest work one human being can perform for another, and yet there is something in his face I do not comprehend. Can it be he hopes to win Miss Dare by his effort to save his rival?"

As for the thoughts of the person thus unconsciously subjected to the criticism of his dearest friend, let our knowledge of the springs that govern his action serve to interpret both the depth and bitterness of his curiosity; while the sentiments of Mansell—— But who can read what lurks behind the iron of that sternly composed countenance? Not Imogene, not Orcutt, not Ferris. His secret, if he owns one, he keeps well, and his lids scarcely quiver as he drops them over the eyes that but a moment before reflected the grand beauty of the unfortunate woman for whom he so lately protested the most fervent love.

The next moment the court was opened and Miss Dare's name was called by the district attorney.

With a last look at the unresponsive prisoner, Imogene rose, took her place on the witness stand and faced the jury.

It was a memorable moment. If the curious and impressible crowd of spectators about her had been ignorant of her true relations to the accused, the deadly stillness and immobility of her bearing would have convinced them that emotion of the deepest nature lay behind the still, white mask she had thought fit to assume. That she was beautiful and confronted them from that common stand as from a throne, did not serve to lessen the impression she made.

The officer held the Bible toward her. With a look that Mr. Byrd was fain to consider one of natural shrinking only, she laid her white hand upon it; but at the intimation from the officer, "The right hand, if you please, miss," she started and made the exchange he suggested, while at the same moment there rang upon her ear the voice of the clerk as he administered the awful adjuration that she should, as she believed and hoped in Eternal mercy, tell the truth as between this man and the law and keep not one tittle back. The book was then lifted to her lips by the officer, and withdrawn.

"Take your seat, Miss Dare," said the district attorney. And the examination began.

"Your name, if you please?"

"Imogene Dare."

"Are you married or single?"

"I am single."

"Where were you born?"

Now this was a painful question to one of her history. Indeed, she showed it to be so by the flush which rose to her cheek and by the decided trembling of her proud lip. But she did not seek to evade it.

"Sir," she said, "I cannot answer you. I never heard any of the particulars of my birth. I was a foundling."

The mingled gentleness and dignity with which she made this acknowledgment won for her the instantaneous sympathy of all present. Mr. Orcutt saw this, and the flash of indignation that had involuntarily passed between him and the prisoner subsided as quickly as it arose.

Mr. Ferris went on.

"Where do you live?"

"In this town?"

"With whom do you live?"

"I am boarding at present with a woman of the name of Kennedy. I support myself by my needle," she hurriedly added, as though anxious to forestall his next question.

Seeing the prisoner start at this, Imogene lifted her head still higher. Evidently this former lover of hers knew little of her movements since they parted so many weeks ago.

"And how long is it since you supported yourself in this way?" asked the district attorney.

"For a few weeks only. Formerly," she said, making a slight inclination in the direction of the prisoner's counsel, "I lived in the household of Mr. Orcutt, where I occupied the position of assistant to the lady who looks after his domestic affairs." And her eye met the lawyer's with a look of pride that made him inwardly cringe, though not even the jealous glance of the prisoner could detect that an eyelash quivered or a flicker disturbed the studied serenity of his gaze.

The district attorney opened his lips as if to pursue this topic, but, meeting his opponent's eye, concluded to waive further preliminaries and proceed at once to the more serious part of the examination.

"Miss Dare," said he, "will you look at the prisoner and tell us if you have any acquaintance with him?"

Slowly she prepared to reply; slowly she turned her head and let her glance traverse that vast crowd till it settled upon her former lover. The look which passed like lightning across her face as she encountered his gaze fixed for the first time steadily upon her own, no one in that assemblage ever forgot.

"Yes," she returned, quietly, but in a tone that made Mansell quiver and look away, despite his iron self-command; "I know him."

"Will you be kind enough to say how long you have known him and where it was you first made his acquaintance?"

"I met him first in Buffalo some four months since," was the steady reply. "He was calling at a friend's house where I was staying."

"Did you at that time know of his relation to your townswoman, Mrs. Clemmens?"

"No, sir. It was not till I had seen him several times that I learned he had any connections in Sibley."

"Miss Dare, you will excuse me, but it is highly desirable for the court to know if the prisoner ever paid his addresses to you?"

The deep, almost agonizing blush that coloured her white cheek answered as truly as the slow "Yes," that struggled painfully to her lips.

"And—excuse me again, Miss Dare—did he propose marriage to you?"

"He did."

"Did you accept him?"

"I did not."

"Did you refuse him?"

"I refused to engage myself to him."

"Miss Dare, will you tell us when you left Buffalo?"

"On the nineteenth day of August last."

"Did the prisoner accompany you?"

"He did not."

"Upon what sort of terms did you part?"

"Good terms, sir."

"Do you mean friendly terms, or such as are held by a man and a woman between whom an attachment exists which, under favourable circumstances, may culminate in marriage?"

"The latter, sir, I think."

"Did you receive any letters from the prisoner after your return to Sibley?"

"Yes, sir."

"And did you answer them?"

"I did."

"Miss Dare, may I now ask what reasons you gave the prisoner for declining his offer—that is, if my friend does not object to the question?" added the district attorney, turning with courtesy toward Mr. Orcutt.

The latter, who had started to his feet, bowed composedly and prepared to resume his seat.

"I desire to put nothing in the way of your eliciting the whole truth concerning this matter," was his quiet, if somewhat constrained, response.

Mr. Ferris at once turned back to Miss Dare.

"You will, then, answer," he said.

Imogene lifted her head and complied.

"I told him," she declared, with thrilling distinctness, "that he was in no condition to marry. I am by nature an ambitious woman, and, not having suffered at that time, thought more of my position before the world than of what constitutes the worth and dignity of a man."

No one who heard these words could doubt they were addressed to the prisoner. Haughtily as she held herself, there was a deprecatory humility in her tone that neither judge nor jury could have elicited from her. Naturally many eyes turned in the direction of the prisoner. They saw two white faces before them, that of the accused and that of his counsel, who sat near him. But the pallor of the one was of scorn, and that of the other—— Well, no one who knew the relations of Mr. Orcutt to the witness could wonder that the renowned lawyer shrank from hearing the woman he loved confess her partiality for another man.

Mr. Ferris, who understood the situation as well as anyone, but who had passed the point where sympathy could interfere with his action, showed a disposition to press his advantage.

"Miss Dare," he inquired, "in declining the proposals of the prisoner, did you state to him in so many words these objections you have here mentioned?"

"I did."

"And what answer did he give you?"

"He replied that he was also ambitious, and hoped and intended to make a success in life."

"And did he tell you how he hoped and intended to make a success?"

"He did."

"Miss Dare, were these letters written by you?"

She looked at the packet he held toward her, started as she saw the broad black ribbon that encircled it, and bowed her head.

"I have no doubt these are my letters," she rejoined, a little tremulously for her. And unbinding the packet, she examined its contents. "Yes," she answered, "they are. These letters were all written by me."

And she handed them back with such haste that the ribbon which bound them remained in her fingers, where consciously or unconsciously she held it clutched all through the remaining time of her examination.

"Now," said the district attorney, "I propose to read two of these letters. Does my friend wish to look at them before I offer them in evidence?" holding them out to Mr. Orcutt.

Every eye in the court-room was fixed upon the latter's face, as the letters addressed to his rival by the woman he wished to make his wife, were tendered in this public manner to his inspection. Even the iron face of Mansell relaxed into an expression of commiseration as he turned and surveyed the man who, in despite of the anomalous position they held toward each other, was thus engaged in battling for his life before the eyes of the whole world. At that instant there was not a spectator who did not feel that Tremont Orcutt was the hero of the moment.

He slowly turned to the prisoner:

"Have you any objection to these letters being read?"

"No," returned the other, in a low tone.

Mr. Orcutt turned firmly to the district attorney:

"You may read them if you think proper," said he.

Mr. Ferris bowed; the letters were marked as exhibits by the stenographic reporter who was taking the minutes of testimony, and handed back to Ferris, who proceeded to read the following in a clear voice to the jury:

Sibley, N.Y., September 7, 1882.

Dear Friend,—You show signs of impatience, and ask for a word to help you through this period of uncertainty and unrest. What can I say more than I have said? That I believe in you and in your invention, and proudly wait for the hour when you will come to claim me with the fruit of your labours in your hand. I am impatient myself, but I have more trust than you. Someone will see the value of your work before long, or else your aunt will interest herself in your success, and lend you that practical assistance which you need to start you in the way of fortune and fame. I cannot think you are going to fail. I will not allow myself to look forward to anything less than success for you and happiness for myself. For the one involves the other, as you must know by this time, or else believe me to be the most heartless of *coquettes*.

Wishing to see you, but of the opinion that further meetings between us would be unwise till our future looks more settled, I remain, hopefully yours,

Imogene Dare.

"The other letter I propose to read," continued Mr. Ferris, "is dated September 23rd, three days before the widow's death.

Dear Craik,—Since you insist upon seeing me, and say that you have reasons of your own for not visiting me openly, I will consent to meet you at the trysting spot you mention, though all such underhand dealings are as foreign to my nature as I believe them to be to yours.

Trusting that fortune will so favour us as to make it unnecessary for us to meet in this way more than once, I wait in anxiety for your coming.

Imogene Dare.

These letters, unfolding relations that, up to this time, had been barely surmised by the persons congregated before her, created a great impression. To those especially who knew her and believed her to be engaged to Mr. Orcutt the surprise was well-nigh thrilling. The witness seemed to feel this, and bestowed a short, quick glance upon the lawyer, that may have partially recompensed him for the unpleasantness of the general curiosity.

The prosecuting attorney went on without pause:

"Miss Dare," said he, "did you meet the prisoner as you promised?"

"I did."

"Will you tell me when and where?"

"On the afternoon of Monday, September 27th, in the glade back of Mrs. Clemmens' house."

"Miss Dare, we fully realize the pain it must cost you to refer to these matters, but I must request you to tell us what passed between you at this interview?"

"If you will ask me questions, sir, I will answer them with the truth the subject demands."

The sorrowful dignity with which this was said, called forth a bow from the prosecuting attorney.

"Very well," he rejoined, "did the prisoner have anything to say about his prospects?"

"He did."

"How did he speak of them?"

"Despondingly."

"And what reason did he give for this?"

"He said he had failed to interest any capitalist in his invention."

"Any other reason?"

"Yes."

"What was that?"

"That he had just come from his aunt whom he had tried to persuade to advance him a sum of money to carry out his wishes, but that she had refused."

"He told you that?"

"Yes, sir."

"Did he also tell you what path he had taken to his aunt's house?"

"No, sir."

"Was there anything said by him to show he did not take the secret path through the woods and across the bog to her back door?"

"No, sir."

"Or that he did not return in the same way?"

"No, sir."

"Miss Dare, did the prisoner express to you at this time irritation as well as regret at the result of his efforts to elicit money from his aunt?"

"Yes," was the evidently forced reply.

"Can you remember any words that he used which would tend to show the condition of his mind?"

"I have no memory for words," she began, but flushed as she met the eye of the Judge, and perhaps remembered her oath. "I do recollect, however, one expression he used. He said: 'My life is worth nothing to me without success. If only to win you, I must put this matter through; and I will do it yet.'"

She repeated this quietly, giving it no emphasis and scarcely any inflection, as if she hoped by her mechanical way of uttering it to rob it of any special meaning. But she did not succeed, as was shown by the compassionate tone in which Mr. Ferris next addressed her.

"Miss Dare, did you express any anger yourself at the refusal of Mrs. Clemmens to assist the prisoner by lending him such moneys as he required?"

"Yes, sir; I fear I did. It seemed unreasonable to me then, and I was very anxious he should have that opportunity to make fame and fortune which I thought his genius merited."

"Miss Dare," inquired the district attorney, calling to his aid such words as he had heard from old Sally in reference to this interview, "did you make use of any such expression as this: 'I wish I knew Mrs. Clemmens'?"

"I believe I did."

"And did this mean you had no acquaintance with the murdered woman at that time?" pursued Mr. Ferris, half-turning to the prisoner's counsel, as if he anticipated the objection which that gentleman might very properly make to a question concerning the intention of a witness.

And Mr. Orcutt, yielding to professional instinct, did indeed make a slight movement as if to rise, but became instantly motionless. Nothing could be more painful to him than to wrangle before the crowded court-room over these dealings between the woman he loved and the man he was now defending.

Mr. Ferris turned back to the witness and awaited her answer. It came without hesitation.

"It meant that, sir."

"And what did the prisoner say when you gave utterance to this wish?"

"He asked me why I desired to know her."

"And what did you reply?"

"That if I knew her I might be able to persuade her to listen to his request."

"And what answer had he for this?"

"None but a quick shake of his head."

"Miss Dare; up to the time of this interview had you ever received any gift from the prisoner—jewelry, for instance—say, a ring!"

"No, sir."

"Did he offer you such a gift then?"

"He did."

"What was it?"

"A gold ring set with a diamond."

"Did you receive it?"

"No, sir. I felt that in taking a ring from him I would be giving an irrevocable promise, and I was not ready to do that."

"Did you allow him to put it on your finger?"

"I did."

"And it remained there?" suggested Mr. Ferris, with a smile.

"A minute, may be."

"Which of you, then, took it off?"

"I did."

"And what did you say when you took it off?"

"I do not remember my words."

Again recalling old Sally's account of this interview, Mr. Ferris asked:

"Were they these: 'I cannot. Wait till tomorrow'?"

"Yes, I believe they were."

"And when he inquired: 'Why tomorrow?' did you reply: 'A night has been known to change the whole current of one's affairs'?"

"I did."

"Miss Dare, what did you mean by those words?"

"I object!" cried Mr. Orcutt, rising. Unseen by any save himself, the prisoner had made him an eloquent gesture, slight, but peremptory.

"I think it is one I have a right to ask," urged the district attorney.

But Mr. Orcutt, who manifestly had the best of the argument, maintained his objection, and the court instantly ruled in his favour.

Mr. Ferris prepared to modify his question. But before he could speak the voice of Miss Dare was heard.

"Gentlemen," said she, "there was no need of all this talk. I intended to seek an interview with Mrs. Clemmens and try what the effect would be of confiding to her my interest in her nephew."

The dignified simplicity with which she spoke, and the air of quiet candour that for that one moment surrounded her, gave to this voluntary explanation an unexpected force that carried it quite home to the hearts of the jury. Even Mr. Orcutt could not preserve the frown with which he had confronted her at the first movement of her lips, but turned toward the prisoner with a look almost congratulatory in its character. But Mr. Byrd, who for reasons of his own kept his eyes upon that prisoner, observed that it met with no other return than that shadow of a bitter smile which now and then visited his otherwise unmoved countenance.

Mr. Ferris, who, in his friendship for the witness, was secretly rejoiced in an explanation which separated her from the crime of her lover, bowed in acknowledgment of the answer she had been pleased to give him in face of the ruling of the court, and calmly proceeded:

"And what reply did the prisoner make you when you uttered this remark in reference to the change that a single day sometimes makes in one's affairs?"

"Something in the way of assent."

"Cannot you give us his words?"

"No, sir."

"Well, then, can you tell us whether or not he looked thoughtful when you said this?"

"He may have done so, sir."

"Did it strike you at the time that he reflected on what you said?"

"I cannot say how it struck me at the time."

"Did he look at you a few minutes before speaking, or in any way conduct himself as if he had been set thinking?"

"He did not speak for a few minutes."

"And looked at you?"

"Yes, sir."

The district attorney paused a moment as if to let the results of his examination sink into the minds of the jury; then he went on:

"Miss Dare, you say you returned the ring to the prisoner?"

"Yes, sir."

"You say positively the ring passed from you to him; that you saw it in his hand after it had left yours?"

"No, sir. The ring passed from me to him, but I did not see it in his hand, because I did not return it to him that way. I dropped it into his pocket."

At this acknowledgment, which made both the prisoner and his counsel look up, Mr. Byrd felt himself nudged by Hickory.

"Did you hear that?" he whispered.

"Yes," returned the other.

"And do you believe it?"

"Miss Dare is on oath," was the reply.

"Pooh!" was Hickory's whispered exclamation.

The district attorney alone showed no surprise.

"You dropped it into his pocket?" he resumed. "How came you to do that?"

"I was weary of the strife which had followed my refusal to accept this token. He would not take it from me himself, so I restored it to him in the way I have said."

"Miss Dare, will you tell us what pocket this was?"

"The outside pocket on the left side of his coat," she returned, with a cold and careful exactness that caused the prisoner to drop his eyes from her face, with that faint but scornful twitch of the muscles about his mouth, which gave to his countenance now and then the proud look of disdain which both the detectives had noted.

"Miss Dare," continued the prosecuting attorney, "did you see this ring again during the interview?"

"No, sir."

"Did you detect the prisoner making any move to take it out of his pocket, or have you any reason to believe that it was taken out of the pocket on the left-hand side of his coat while you were with him?"

"No, sir."

"So that, as far as you know, it was still in his pocket when you parted?"

"Yes, sir."

"Miss Dare, have you ever seen that ring since?"

"I have."

"When and where?"

"I saw it on the morning of the murder. It was lying on the floor of Mrs. Clemmens' dining-room. I had gone to the house, in my surprise at hearing of the murderous assault which had been made upon her, and, while surveying the spot where she was struck, perceived this ring lying on the floor before me."

"What made you think it was this ring which you had returned to the prisoner the day before?"

"Because of its setting, and the character of the gem, I suppose."

"Could you see all this where it was lying on the floor?"

"It was brought nearer to my eyes, sir. A gentleman who was standing near, picked it up and offered it to me, supposing it was mine. As he held it out in his open palm I saw it plainly."

"Miss Dare, will you tell us what you did when you first saw this ring lying on the floor?"

"I covered it with my foot."

"Was that before you recognized it?"

"I cannot say. I placed my foot upon it instinctively."

"How long did you keep it there?"

"Some few minutes."

"What caused you to move at last?"

"I was surprised."

"What surprised you?"

"A man came to the door."

"What man."

"I don't know. A stranger to me. Someone who had been sent on an errand connected with this affair."

"What did he say or do to surprise you?"

"Nothing. It was what you said yourself after the man had gone."

"And what did I say, Miss Dare?"

She cast him a look of the faintest appeal, but answered quietly:

"Something about its not being the tramp who had committed this crime."

"That surprised you?"

"That made me start."

"Miss Dare, were you present in the house when the dying woman spoke the one or two exclamations which have been testified to in

367

this trial?"

"Yes, sir."

"What was the burden of the first speech you heard?"

"The words *Hand*, sir, and *Ring*. She repeated the two half a dozen times."

"Miss Dare, what did you say to the gentleman who showed you the ring and asked if it were yours?"

"I told him it was mine, and took it and placed it on my finger."

"But the ring was not yours?"

"My acceptance of it made it mine. In all but that regard it had been mine ever since Mr. Mansell offered it to me the day before."

Mr. Ferris surveyed the witness for a moment before saying:

"Then you considered it damaging to your lover to have this ring found in that apartment?"

Mr. Orcutt instantly rose to object.

"I won't press the question," said the district attorney, with a wave of his hand and a slight look at the jury.

"You ought never to have asked it?" exclaimed Mr. Orcutt, with the first appearance of heat he had shown.

"You are right," Mr. Ferris coolly responded. "The jury could see the point without any assistance from you or me."

"And the jury," returned Mr. Orcutt, with equal coolness, "is scarcely obliged to you for the suggestion."

"Well, we won't quarrel about it," declared Mr. Ferris.

"We won't quarrel about anything ," retorted Mr. Orcutt. "We will try the case in a legal manner."

"Have you got through?" inquired Mr. Ferris, nettled.

Mr. Orcutt took his seat with the simple reply:

"Go on with the case."

The district attorney, after a momentary pause to regain the thread of his examination and recover his equanimity, turned to the witness.

"Miss Dare," he asked, "how long did you keep that ring on your finger after you left the house?"

"A little while—five or ten minutes, perhaps."

"Where were you when you took it off?"

Her voice sank just a trifle:

"On the bridge at Warren Street."

"What did you do with it then?"

Her eyes which had been upon the attorney's face, fell slowly.

"I dropped it into the water," she said.

And the character of her thoughts and suspicions at that time stood revealed.

The prosecuting attorney allowed himself a few more questions.

"When you parted with the prisoner in the woods, was it with any arrangement for meeting again before he returned to Buffalo?"

"No, sir."

"Give us the final words of your conversation, if you please."

"We were just parting, and I had turned to go, when he said: 'Is it goodbye, then, Imogene?' and I answered, 'That tomorrow must decide.' 'Shall I stay, then?' he inquired; to which I replied, 'Yes.'"

'Twas a short, seemingly literal, repetition of possibly innocent words, but the whisper into which her voice sank at the final "Yes" endowed it with a thrilling effect for which even she was not prepared. For she shuddered as she realized the deathly quiet that followed its utterance, and cast a quick look at Mr. Orcutt that was full of question, if not doubt.

"I was calculating upon the interview I intended to have with Mrs. Clemmens," she explained, turning toward the judge with indescribable dignity.

"We understand that," remarked the prosecuting attorney, kindly, and then inquired:

"Was this the last you saw of the prisoner until today?"

"No, sir."

"When did you see him again?"

"On the following Wednesday."

"Where?"

"In the *depôt* at Syracuse."

"How came you to be in Syracuse the day after the murder?"

"I had started to go to Buffalo."

"What purpose had you in going to Buffalo?"

"I wished to see Mr. Mansell."

"Did he know you were coming?"

"No, sir."

"Had no communication passed between you from the time you parted in the woods till you came upon each other in the *depôt* you have just mentioned?"

"No, sir."

"Had he no reason to expect to meet you there?"

"No, sir."

"With what words did you accost each other?"

"I don't know. I have no remembrance of saying anything . I was utterly dumbfounded at seeing him in this place, and cannot say into what exclamation I may have been betrayed."

"And he? Don't you remember what he said?"

"No, sir. I only know he started back with a look of great surprise. Afterward he asked if I were on my way to see him."

"And what did you answer?"

"I don't think I made any answer. I was wondering if he was on his way to see me."

"Did you put the question to him?"

"Perhaps. I cannot tell. It is all like a dream to me."

If she had said horrible dream, everyone there would have believed her.

"You can tell us, however, if you held any conversation?"

"We did not."

"And you can tell us how the interview terminated?"

"Yes, sir. I turned away and took the train back home, which I saw standing on the track without."

"And he?"

"Turned away also. Where he went I cannot say."

"Miss Dare"—the district attorney's voice was very earnest—"can you tell us which of you made the first movement to go?"

"What does he mean by that?" whispered Hickory to Byrd.

"I think——" she commenced and paused. Her eyes in wandering over the throng of spectators before her, had settled on these two detectives, and noting the breathless way in which they looked at her, she seemed to realize that more might lie in this question than at first appeared.

"I do not know," she answered at last. "It was a simultaneous movement, I think."

"Are you sure?" persisted Mr. Ferris. "You are on oath, Miss Dare? Is there no way in which you can make certain whether he or you took the initiatory step in this sudden parting after an event that so materially changed your mutual prospects?"

"No, sir. I can only say that in recalling the sensations of that hour, I am certain my own movement was not the result of any I saw him take. The instinct to leave the place had its birth in my own breast."

"I told you so," commented Hickory, in the ear of Byrd. "She is not going to give herself away, whatever happens."

"But can you positively say he did not make the first motion to leave?"

"No, sir."

Mr. Ferris bowed, turned toward the opposing counsel and said:
"The witness is yours."

Mr. Ferris sat down perfectly satisfied. He had dexterously brought
out Imogene's suspicions of the prisoner's guilt, and knew that the
jury must be influenced in their convictions by those of the woman
who, of all the world, ought to have believed, if she could, in the innocence of her lover. He did not even fear the cross-examination which
he expected to follow. No amount of skill on the part of Orcutt could
extract other than the truth, and the truth was that Imogene believed
the prisoner to be the murderer of his aunt. He, therefore, surveyed
the court-room with a smile, and awaited the somewhat slow proceedings of his opponent with equanimity.

But, to the surprise of everyone, Mr. Orcutt, after a short consultation with the prisoner, rose and said he had no questions to put to
the witness.

And Miss Dare was allowed to withdraw from the stand, to the
great satisfaction of Mr. Ferris, who found himself by this move in a
still better position than he had anticipated.

"Byrd," whispered Hickory, as Miss Dare returned somewhat tremulously to her former seat among the witnesses—"Byrd, you could
knock me over with a feather. I thought the defence would have no
difficulty in riddling this woman's testimony, and they have not even
made the effort. Can it be that Orcutt has such an attachment for her
that he is going to let his rival hang?"

"No. Orcutt isn't the man to deliberately lose a case for any woman. He looks at Miss Dare's testimony from a different standpoint than
you do. He believes what she says to be true, and you do not."

"Then, all I've got to say, 'So much the worse for Mansell!'" was
the whispered response. "He was a fool to trust his case to that man."

The judge, the jury, and all the bystanders in court, it must be confessed, shared the opinion of Hickory—Mr. Orcutt was standing on
slippery ground.

29

The Opening of the Defence

Late that afternoon the prosecution rested. It had made out a case of great strength and seeming impregnability. Favourably as everyone was disposed to regard the prisoner, the evidence against him was such that, to quote a man who was pretty free with his opinions in the lobby of the court-room: "Orcutt will have to wake up if he is going to clear his man in face of facts like these."

The moment, therefore, when this famous lawyer and distinguished advocate rose to open the defence, was one of great interest to more than the immediate actors in the scene. It was felt that hitherto he had rather idled with his case, and curiosity was awake to his future course. Indeed, in the minds of many the counsel for the prisoner was on trial as well as his client.

He rose with more of self-possession, quiet and reserved strength, than could be hoped for, and his look toward the court and then to the jury tended to gain for him the confidence which up to this moment he seemed to be losing. Never a handsome man or even an imposing one, he had the advantage of always rising to the occasion, and whether pleading with a jury or arguing with opposing counsel, flashed with that unmistakable glitter of keen and ready intellect which, once observed in a man, marks him off from his less gifted fellows and makes him the cynosure of all eyes, however insignificant his height, features, or ordinary expression.

Today he was even cooler, more brilliant, and more confident in his bearing than usual. Feelings, if feelings he possessed—and we who have seen him at his hearth can have no doubt on this subject,—had been set aside when he rose to his feet and turned his face upon the expectant crowd before him. To save his client seemed the one predominating impulse of his soul, and, as he drew himself up to speak,

Mr. Byrd, who was watching him with the utmost eagerness and anticipation, felt that, despite appearances, despite evidence, despite probability itself, this man was going to win his case.

"May it please your Honour and Gentlemen of the Jury," he began, and those who looked at him could not but notice how the prisoner at his side lifted his head at this address, till it seemed as if the words issued from his lips instead of from those of his counsel, "I stand before you today not to argue with my learned opponent in reference to the evidence which he has brought out with so much ingenuity. I have a simpler duty than that to perform. I have to show you how, in spite of this evidence, in face of all this accumulated testimony showing the prisoner to have been in possession of both motive and opportunities for committing this crime, he is guiltless of it; that a physical impossibility stands in the way of his being the assailant of the Widow Clemmens, and that to whomever or whatsoever her death may be due, it neither was nor could have been the result of any blow struck by the prisoner's hand.

"In other words, we dispute, not the facts which have led the prosecuting attorney of this district, and perhaps others also, to infer guilt on the part of the prisoner,"—here Mr. Orcutt cast a significant glance at the bench where the witnesses sat,—"but the inference itself. Something besides proof of motive and opportunity must be urged against *this* man in order to convict him of guilt. Nor is it sufficient to show he was on the scene of murder some time during the fatal morning when Mrs. Clemmens was attacked; you must prove he was there at the time the deadly blow was struck; for it is not with him as with so many against whom circumstantial evidence of guilt is brought. *This* man, gentlemen, has an answer for those who accuse him of crime— an answer, too, before which all the circumstantial evidence in the world cannot stand. Do you want to know what it is? Give me but a moment's attention and you shall hear."

Expectation, which had been rising through this exordium, now stood at fever-point. Byrd and Hickory held their breaths, and even Miss Dare showed feeling through the icy restraint which had hitherto governed her secret anguish and suspense. Mr. Orcutt went on:

"First, however, as I have already said, the prisoner desires it to be understood that he has no intention of disputing the various facts which have been presented before you at this trial. He does not deny that he was in great need of money at the time of his aunt's death; that he came to Sibley to entreat her to advance to him certain sums he deemed necessary to the furtherance of his plans; that he came secretly and in the roundabout way you describe. Neither does he refuse to allow that his errand was also one of love, that he sought and obtained a private interview with the woman he wished to make his wife, in the place and at the time testified to; that the scraps of conversation which have been sworn to as having passed between them at this interview are true in as far as they go, and that he did place upon the finger of Miss Dare a diamond ring.

"Also, he admits that she took this ring off immediately upon receiving it, saying she could not accept it, at least not then, and that she entreated him to take it back, which he declined to do, though he cannot say she did not restore it in the manner she declares, for he remembers nothing of the ring after the moment he put her hand aside as she was offering it back to him. The prisoner also allows that he slept in the hut and remained in that especial region of the woods until near noon the next day; but, your Honour and Gentlemen of the Jury, what the prisoner does not allow and will not admit is that he struck the blow which eventually robbed Mrs. Clemmens of her life, and the proof which I propose to bring forward in support of this assertion is this:

"Mrs. Clemmens received the blow which led to her death at some time previously to three minutes past twelve o'clock on Tuesday, September 26th. This the prosecution has already proved. Now, what I propose to show is, that Mrs. Clemmens, however or whenever assailed, was still living and unhurt up to ten minutes before twelve on that same day. A witness, whom you must believe, saw her at that time and conversed with her, proving that the blow by which she came to her death must have occurred after that hour, that is, after ten minutes before noon. But, your Honour and Gentlemen of the Jury, the prosecution has already shown that the prisoner stepped on to the train at Monteith Quarry Station at twenty minutes past one of that same day, and has produced witnesses whose testimony positively proves that the road he took there from Mrs. Clemmens' house was the same he had traversed in his secret approach to it the day before—viz., the path through the woods; the only path, I may here state, that connects those two points with anything like directness.

"But, Sirs, what the prosecution has not shown you, and what it now devolves upon me to show, is that this path which the prisoner is allowed to have taken is one which no man could traverse without encountering great difficulties and many hindrances to speed. It is

374

not only a narrow path filled with various encumbrances in the way of brambles and rolling stones, but it is so flanked by an impenetrable undergrowth in some places, and by low, swampy ground in others, that no deviation from its course is possible, while to keep within it and follow its many turns and windings till it finally emerges upon the highway that leads to the Quarry Station would require many more minutes than those which elapsed between the time of the murder and the hour the prisoner made his appearance at the Quarry Station.

"In other words, I propose to introduce before you as witnesses two gentlemen from New York, both of whom are experts in all feats of pedestrianism, and who, having been over the road themselves, are in position to testify that the time necessary for a man to pass by means of this path from Mrs. Clemmens' house to the Quarry Station is, by a definite number of minutes, greater than that allowed to the prisoner by the evidence laid before you. If, therefore, you accept the testimony of the prosecution as true, and believe that the prisoner took the train for Buffalo, which he has been said to do, it follows, as a physical impossibility, for him to have been at Mrs. Clemmens' cottage, or anywhere else except on the road to the station, at the moment when the fatal blow was dealt.

"Your Honour, this is our answer to the terrible charge which has been made against the prisoner; it is simple, but it is effective, and upon it, as upon a rock, we found our defence."

And with a bow, Mr. Orcutt sat down, and, it being late in the day, the court adjourned.

30

Byrd Uses His Pencil Again

"Byrd, you look dazed."

"I am."

Hickory paused till they were well clear of the crowd that was pouring from the court-room; then he said:

"Well, what do you think of this as a defence?"

"I am beginning to think it is good," was the slow, almost hesitating, reply.

"Beginning to think?"

"Yes. At first it seemed puerile. I had such a steadfast belief in Mansell's guilt, I could not give much credit to any argument tending to shake me loose from my convictions. But the longer I think of it the more vividly I remember the difficulties of the road he had to take in his flight. I have travelled it myself, you remember, and I don't see how he could have got over the ground in ninety minutes."

Hickory's face assumed a somewhat quizzical expression.

"Byrd," said he, "whom were you looking at during the time Mr. Orcutt was making his speech?"

"At the speaker, of course."

"Bah!"

"Whom were *you* looking at?"

"At the person who would be likely to give me some return for my pains."

"The prisoner?"

"No."

"Whom, then?"

"Miss Dare."

Byrd shifted uneasily to the other side of his companion.

"And what did you discover from her, Hickory?" he asked.

"Two things. First, that she knew no more than the rest of us what the defence was going to be. Secondly, that she regarded it as a piece of great cleverness on the part of Orcutt, but that she didn't believe in it anymore—well, any more than I do."

"Hickory!"

"Yes, *sir!* Miss Dare is a smart woman, and a resolute one, and could have baffled the penetration of all concerned if she had only remembered to try. But she forgot that others might be more interested in making out what was going on in her mind at this critical moment than in watching the speaker or noting the effect of his words upon the court. In fact, she was too eager herself to hear what he had to say to remember her *rôle*, I fancy."

"But, I don't see——" began Byrd.

"Wait," interrupted the other. "You believe Miss Dare loves Craik Mansell?"

"Most certainly," was the gloomy response.

"Very well, then. If she had known what the defence was going to be she would have been acutely alive to the effect it was going to have upon the jury. That would have been her first thought and her only thought all the time Mr. Orcutt was speaking, and she would have sat with her eyes fixed upon the men upon whose acceptance or non-acceptance of the truth of this argument her lover's life ultimately depended. But no; her gaze, like yours, remained fixed upon Mr. Orcutt, and she scarcely breathed or stirred till he had fully revealed what his argument was going to be. Then——"

"Well, then?"

"Instead of flashing with the joy of relief which any devoted woman would experience who sees in this argument a proof of her lover's innocence, she merely dropped her eyes and resumed her old mask of impassiveness."

"From all of which you gather——"

"That her feelings were not those of relief, but doubt. In other words, that the knowledge she possesses is of a character which laughs to scorn any such subterfuge of defence as Orcutt advances."

"Hickory," ventured Byrd, after a long silence, "it is time we understood each other. What is your secret thought in relation to Miss Dare?"

"My secret thought? Well," drawled the other, looking away, "I think she knows more about this crime than she has yet chosen to reveal."

"More than she evinced today in her testimony?"

"Yes."

"I should like to know why you think so. What special reasons have you for drawing any such conclusions?"

"Well, one reason is, that she was no more shaken by the plausible argument advanced by Mr. Orcutt. If her knowledge of the crime was limited to what she acknowledged in her testimony, and her conclusions as to Mansell's guilt were really founded upon such facts as she gave us in court today, why didn't she grasp at the possibility of her lover's innocence which was held out to her by his counsel? No facts that she had testified to, not even the fact of his ring having been found on the scene of murder, could stand before the proof that he left the region of Mrs. Clemmens' house before the moment of assault; yet, while evincing interest in the argument, and some confidence in it, too, as one that would be likely to satisfy the jury, she gave no tokens of being surprised by it into a reconsideration of her own conclusions, as must have happened if she told the truth, the whole truth, and nothing but the truth, when she was on the stand today."

"I see," remarked Byrd, "that you are presuming to understand Miss Dare after all."

Hickory smiled.

"You call this woman a mystery," proceeded Byrd; "hint at great possibilities of acting on her part, and yet in a moment, as it were, profess yourself the reader of her inmost thoughts, and the interpreter of looks and expressions she has manifestly assumed to hide those thoughts."

Hickory's smile broadened into a laugh.

"Just so," he cried. "One's imbecility has to stop somewhere." Then, as he saw Byrd look grave, added: "I haven't a single fact at my command that isn't shared by you. My conclusions are different, that is all."

Horace Byrd did not answer. Perhaps if Hickory could have sounded his thoughts he would have discovered that their conclusions were not so far apart as he imagined.

"Hickory," Byrd at last demanded, "what do you propose to do with your conclusions?"

"I propose to wait and see if Mr. Orcutt proves his case. If he don't, I have nothing more to say; but if he does, I think I shall call the attention of Mr. Ferris to one question he has omitted to ask Miss Dare."

"And what is that?"

"Where she was on the morning of Mrs. Clemmens' murder. You remember you took some interest in that question yourself a while ago."

"But——"

"Not that I think anything will come of it, only my conscience will be set at rest."

"Hickory,"—Byrd's face had quite altered now—"where do you think Miss Dare was at that time?"

"Where do I think she was?" repeated Hickory.

"Well, I will tell you. I think she was *not* in Professor Darling's observatory."

"Do you think she was in the glade back of Widow Clemmens' house?"

"Now you ask me conundrums."

"Hickory!" Byrd spoke almost violently, "Mr. Orcutt shall not prove his case."

"No?"

"I will make the run over the ground supposed to have been taken by Mansell in his flight, and show in my own proper person that it can be done in the time specified."

Hickory's eye, which had taken a rapid survey of his companion's form during the utterance of the above, darkened, then he slowly shook his head.

"You couldn't," he rejoined laconically. "Too little staying power; you'd give out before you got clear of the woods. Better delegate the job to me."

"To you?"

"Yes. I'm of the make to stand long runs; besides I am no novice at athletic sports of any kind. More than one race has owed its interest to the efforts of your humble servant. 'Tis my pet amusement, you see, as off-hand drawing is yours, and is likely to be of as much use to me, eh?"

"Hickory, you are chaffing me."

"Think so? Do you see that five-barred gate over there? Well, now keep your eye on the top rail and see if I clear it without a graze or not."

"Stop!" exclaimed Mr. Byrd, "don't make a fool of yourself in the public street. I'll believe you if you say you understand such things."

"Well, I do, and what is more, I'm an adept at them. If I can't make that run in the time requisite to show that Mansell could have committed the murder, and yet arrive at the station the moment he did, I don't know of a chap who can."

"Hickory, do you mean to say you *will* make this run?"

"Yes."

"With a conscientious effort to prove that Orcutt's scheme of defence is false?"

"Yes."

"When?"

"Tomorrow."

"While we are in court?"

"Yes."

Byrd turned square around, gave Hickory a look and offered his hand.

"You are a good fellow," he declared, "May luck go with you."

Hickory suddenly became unusually thoughtful.

"A little while ago," he reflected, "this fellow's sympathies were all with Mansell; now he would risk my limbs and neck to have the man proved guilty. He does not wish Miss Dare to be questioned again, I see."

"Hickory," resumed Byrd, a few minutes later, "Orcutt has not rested the defence upon this one point without being very sure of its being unassailable."

"I know that."

"He has had more than one expert make that run during the weeks that have elapsed since the murder. It has been tested to the uttermost."

"I know *that.*"

"If you succeed then in doing what none of these others have, it must be by dint of a better understanding of the route you have to take and the difficulties you will have to overcome. Now, do you understand the route?"

"I think so."

"You will have to start from the widow's door, you know?"

"Certain."

"Cross the bog, enter the woods, skirt the hut—but I won't go into details. The best way to prove you know exactly what you have to do is to see if you can describe the route yourself. Come into my room, old fellow, and let us see if you can give me a sufficiently exact account of the ground you will have to pass over, for me to draw up a chart by it. An hour spent with paper and pencil tonight may save you from an

uncertainty tomorrow that would lose you a good ten minutes."

"Good! that's an idea; let's try it," rejoined Hickory.

And being by this time at the hotel, they went in. In another moment they were shut up in Mr. Byrd's room, with a large sheet of foolscap before them.

"Now," cried Horace, taking up a pencil, "begin with your description, and I will follow with my drawing."

"Very well," replied Hickory, setting himself forward in a way to watch his colleague's pencil. "I leave the widow's house by the dining-room door—a square for the house, Byrd, well down in the left-hand corner of the paper, and a dotted line for the path I take,—run down the yard to the fence, leap it, cross the bog, and make straight for the woods."

"Very good," commented Byrd, sketching rapidly as the other spoke.

"Having taken care to enter where the trees are thinnest, I find a path along which I rush in a bee-line till I come to the glade—an ellipse for the glade, Byrd, with a dot in it for the hut. Merely stopping to dash into the hut and out again——"

"Wait!" put in Byrd, pausing with his pencil in mid-air; "what did you want to go into the hut for?"

"To get the bag which I propose to leave there tonight."

"Bag?"

"Yes; Mansell carried a bag, didn't he? Don't you remember what the station-master said about the curious portmanteau the fellow had in his hand when he came to the station?"

"Yes, but——"

"Byrd, if I run that fellow to his death it must be fairly. A man with an awkward bag in his hand cannot run like a man without one. So I handicap myself in the same way he did, do you see?"

"Yes."

"Very well, then; I rush into the hut, pick up the bag, carry it out, and dash immediately into the woods at the opening behind the hut.—What are you doing?"

"Just putting in a few landmarks," explained Byrd, who had run his pencil off in an opposite direction. "See, that is the path to West Side which I followed in my first expedition through the woods—the path, too, which Miss Dare took when she came to the hut at the time of the fearful thunderstorm. And wait, let me put in Professor Darling's house, too, and the ridge from which you can see Mrs. Clemmens' cottage. It will help us to understand——"

"What?" cried Hickory, with quick suspiciousness, as the other paused.

But Byrd, impatiently shaking his head, answered:

"The whole situation, of course."Then, pointing hastily back to the hut, exclaimed: "So you have entered the woods again at this place? Very well; what then?"

"Well, then," resumed Hickory, "I make my way along the path I find there—run it at right angles to the one leading up to the glade—till I come to a stony ledge covered with blackberry bushes. (A very cleverly drawn blackberry patch that, Byrd.) Here I fear I shall have to pause."

"Why?"

"Because, deuce take me if I can remember where the path runs after that."

"But I can. A big hemlock-tree stands just at the point where the woods open again. Make for that and you will be all right."

"Good enough; but it's mighty rough travelling over that ledge, and I shall have to go at a foot's pace. The stones are slippery as glass, and a fall would scarcely be conducive to the final success of my scheme."

"I will make the path serpentine."

"That will be highly expressive."

"And now, what next?"

"The Foresters' Road, Byrd, upon which I ought to come about this time. Run it due east and west—not that I have surveyed the ground, but it looks more natural so—and let the dotted line traverse it toward the right, for that is the direction in which I shall go."

"It's done," said Byrd.

"Well, description fails me now. All I know is, I come out on a hillside running straight down to the river-bank and that the highway is visible beyond, leading directly to the station; but the way to get to it——"

"I will show you," interposed Byrd, mapping out the station and the intervening river with a few quick strokes of his dexterous pencil. "You see this point where you issue from the woods? Very good; it is, as you say, on a hillside overlooking the river. Well, it seems unfortunate, but there is no way of crossing that river at this point. The falls above and below make it no place for boats, and you will have to go back along its banks for some little distance before you come to a bridge. But there is no use in hesitating or looking about for a shorter path. The woods just here are encumbered with a mass of tangled undergrowth which make them simply impassable except as you keep in the road, while the river curves so frequently and with so much abruptness—see, I will endeavour to give you some notion of it here—that you would only waste time in attempting to make any short cuts. But, once over the bridge——"

"I have only to foot it," burst in Hickory, taking up the sketch which the other had now completed, and glancing at it with a dubious eye. "Do you know, Byrd," he remarked in another moment, "that it strikes me Mansell did not take this roundabout road to the station?"

"Why?"

"Because it *is* so roundabout, and he is such a clearheaded fellow. Couldn't he have got there by some shorter cut?"

"No. Don't you remember how Orcutt cross-examined the station-master about the appearance which Mansell presented when he came upon the platform, and how that person was forced to acknowledge that, although the prisoner looked heated and exhausted, his clothes were neither muddied nor torn? Now, I did not think of it at the time, but this was done by Orcutt to prove that Mansell did take the road I have jotted down here, since any other would have carried him through swamps knee-deep with mud, or amongst stones and briers which would have put him in a state of disorder totally unfitting him for travel."

"That is so," acquiesced Hickory, after a moment's thought. "Mansell must be kept in the path. Well, well, we will see tomorrow if wit and a swift foot can make anything out of this problem."

"Wit? Hickory, it *will* be wit and not a swift foot. Or luck, maybe I should call it, or rather providence. If a wagon should be going along the highway, now——"

"Let me alone for availing myself of it," laughed Hickory. "Wagon! I would jump on the back of a mule sooner than lose the chance of gaining a minute on these experts whose testimony we are to hear tomorrow. Don't lose confidence in old Hickory yet. He's the boy for this job if he isn't for any other."

And so the matter was settled.

31

The Chief Witness For the Defence

The crowd that congregated at the court-house the next morning was even greater than at any previous time. The opening speech of Mr. Orcutt had been telegraphed all over the country, and many who had not been specially interested in the case before felt an anxiety to hear how he would substantiate the defence he had so boldly and confidently put forth.

To the general eye, however, the appearance of the court-room was much the same as on the previous day. Only to the close observer was it evident that the countenances of the several actors in this exciting drama wore a different expression. Mr. Byrd, who by dint of the most energetic effort had succeeded in procuring his old seat, was one of these, and as he noted the significant change, wished that Hickory had been at his side to note it with him.

The first person he observed was, naturally, the Judge.

Judge Evans, who has been but barely introduced to the reader, was a man of great moral force and discretion. He had occupied his present position for many years, and possessed not only the confidence but the affections of those who came within the sphere of his jurisdiction. The reason for this undoubtedly lay in his sympathetic nature. While never accused of weakness, he so unmistakably retained the feeling heart under the official ermine that it was by no means an uncommon thing for him to show more emotion in uttering a sentence than the man he condemned did in listening to it.

His expression, then, upon this momentous morning was of great significance to Mr. Byrd. In its hopefulness and cheer was written the extent of the effect made upon the unprejudiced mind by the promised defence.

As for Mr. Orcutt himself, no advocate could display a more confident air or prepare to introduce his witnesses with more dignity or quiet assurance. His self-possession was so marked, indeed, that Mr. Byrd, who felt a sympathetic interest in what he knew to be seething in this man's breast, was greatly surprised, and surveyed, with a feeling almost akin to awe, the lawyer who could so sink all personal considerations in the cause he was trying.

Miss Dare, on the contrary, was in a state of nervous agitation. Though no movement betrayed this, the very force of the restraint she put upon herself showed the extent of her inner excitement.

The prisoner alone remained unchanged. Nothing could shake his steady soul from its composure, not the possibility of death or the prospect of release. He was absolutely imposing in his quiet presence, and Mr. Byrd could not but admire the power of the man even while recoiling from his supposed guilt.

The opening of the defence carried the minds of many back to the inquest. The nice question of time was gone into, and the moment when Mrs. Clemmens was found lying bleeding and insensible at the foot of her dining-room clock, fixed at three or four minutes past noon. The next point to be ascertained was when she received the deadly blow.

And here the great surprise of the defence occurred. Mr. Orcutt rose, and in clear, firm tones said:

"Gouverneur Hildreth, take the stand."

Instantly, and before the witness could comply, Mr. Ferris was on his feet.

"Who? what?" he cried.

"Gouverneur Hildreth," repeated Mr. Orcutt.

"Did you know this gentleman has already been in custody upon suspicion of having committed the crime for which the prisoner is now being tried?"

"I do," returned Mr. Orcutt, with imperturbable *sang froid*.

"And is it your intention to save your client from the gallows by putting the halter around the neck of the man you now propose to call as a witness?"

"No," retorted Mr. Orcutt; "*I* do not propose to put the halter about any man's neck. That is the proud privilege of my learned and respected opponent."

With an impatient frown Mr. Ferris sat down, while Mr. Hildreth, who had taken advantage of this short passage of arms between the lawyers to retain his place in the remote corner where he was more or less shielded from the curiosity of the crowd, rose, and, with a slow and painful movement that at once attracted attention to his carefully bandaged throat and the general air of debility which surrounded him, came hesitatingly forward and took his stand in face of the judge and jury.

Necessarily a low murmur greeted him from the throng of interested spectators who saw in this appearance before them of the man who, by no more than a hair's-breadth, had escaped occupying the position of the prisoner, another of those dramatic incidents with which this trial seemed fairly to bristle.

It was hushed by one look from the judge, but not before it had awakened in Mr. Hildreth's weak and sensitive nature those old emotions of shame and rage whose token was a flush so deep and profuse it unconsciously repelled the gaze of all who beheld it. Immediately Mr. Byrd, who sat with bated breath, as it were, so intense was his excitement over the unexpected turn of affairs, recognized the full meaning of the situation, and awarded to Mr. Orcutt all the admiration which his skill in bringing it about undoubtedly deserved. Indeed, as the detective's quick glance flashed first at the witness, cringing in his old unfortunate way before the gaze of the crowd, and then at the prisoner sitting unmoved and quietly disdainful in his dignity and pride, he felt that, whether Mr. Orcutt succeeded in getting all he wished from his witness, the mere conjunction of these two men before the jury, with the opportunity for comparison between them which it inevitably offered, was the master-stroke of this eminent lawyer's legal career.

Mr. Ferris seemed to feel the significance of the moment also, for his eyes fell and his brow contracted with a sudden doubt that convinced Mr. Byrd that, mentally, he was on the point of giving up his case.

The witness was at once sworn.

"Orcutt believes Hildreth to be the murderer, or, at least, is willing that others should be impressed with this belief," was the comment of Byrd to himself at this juncture.

He had surprised a look which had passed between the lawyer and Miss Dare—a look of such piercing sarcasm and scornful inquiry that it might well arrest the detective's attention and lead him to question the intentions of the man who could allow such an expression of his feelings to escape him.

But whether the detective was correct in his inferences, or whether Mr. Orcutt's glance at Imogene meant no more than the natural emotion of a man who suddenly sees revealed to the woman he loves the face of him for whose welfare she has expressed the greatest concern and for whose sake, while unknown, she has consented to make the heaviest of sacrifices, the wary lawyer was careful to show neither scorn nor prejudice when he turned toward the witness and began his interrogations.

On the contrary, his manner was highly respectful, if not considerate, and his questions while put with such art as to keep the jury constantly alert to the anomalous position which the witness undoubtedly held, were of a nature mainly to call forth the one fact for which his testimony was presumably desired. This was, his presence in the widow's house on the morning of the murder, and the fact that he saw her and conversed with her and could swear to her being alive and unhurt up to a few minutes before noon. To be sure, the precise minute of his leaving her in this condition Mr. Orcutt failed to gather from the witness, but, like the coroner at the inquest, he succeeded in eliciting enough to show that the visit had been completed prior to the appearance of the tramp at the widow's kitchen-door, as it had been begun after the disappearance of the Danton children from the front of the widow's house.

This fact being established and impressed upon the jury, Mr. Orcutt with admirable judgement cut short his own examination of the witness, and passed him over to the district attorney, with a grim smile, suggestive of his late taunt, that to this gentleman belonged the special privilege of weaving halters for the necks of unhappy criminals.

Mr. Ferris who understood his adversary's tactics only too well, but who in his anxiety for the truth could not afford to let such an opportunity for reaching it slip by, opened his cross-examination with great vigour.

The result could not but be favourable to the defence and damaging to the prosecution. The position which Mr. Hildreth must occupy if the prisoner was acquitted, was patent to all understandings, making each and every admission on his part tending to exculpate the latter, of a manifest force and significance.

Mr. Ferris, however, was careful not to exceed his duty or press his inquiries beyond due bounds. The man they were trying was not Gouverneur Hildreth but Craik Mansell, and to press the witness too close, was to urge him into admissions seemingly so damaging to himself as, in the present state of affairs, to incur the risk of distracting attention entirely from the prisoner.

Mr. Hildreth's examination being at an end, Mr. Orcutt proceeded with his case, by furnishing proof calculated to fix the moment at which Mr. Hildreth had made his call. This was done in much the same way as it was at the inquest. Mrs. Clemmens' next-door neighbour, Mrs. Danton, was summoned to the stand, and after her her two children, the testimony of the three, taken with Mr. Hildreth's own acknowledgments, making it very evident to all who listened that he could not have gone into Mrs. Clemmens' house before a quarter to twelve.

The natural inference followed. Allowing the least possible time for his interview with Mrs. Clemmens, the moment at which the witness swore to having seen her alive and unhurt must have been as late as ten minutes before noon.

Taking pains to impress this time upon the jury, Mr. Orcutt next proceeded to fix the moment at which the prisoner arrived at Monteith Quarry Station. As the fact of his having arrived in time to take the afternoon train to Buffalo had been already proved by the prosecution, it was manifestly necessary only to determine at what hour the train was due, and whether it had come in on time.

The hour was ascertained, by direct consultation with the road's time-table, to be just twenty minutes past one, and the station-master having been called to the stand, gave it as his best knowledge and belief that the train had been on time.

This, however, not being deemed explicit enough for the purposes of the defence, there was submitted to the jury a telegram bearing the date of that same day, and distinctly stating that the train was on time. This was testified to by the conductor of the train as having been sent by him to the superintendent of the road who was awaiting the cars at Monteith; and was received as evidence and considered as conclusively fixing the hour at which the prisoner arrived at the Quarry Station as twenty minutes past one.

This settled, witnesses were called to testify as to the nature of the path by which he must have travelled from the widow's house to the station. A chart similar to that Mr. Byrd had drawn, but more explicit and nice in its details, was submitted to the jury by an actual surveyor of the ground; after which, and the establishment of other minor details not necessary to enumerate here, a man of well-known proficiency in running and other athletic sports, was summoned to the stand.

Mr. Byrd, who up to this moment had shared in the interest everywhere displayed in the defence, now felt his attention wandering. The fact is, he had heard the whistle of the train on which Hickory had promised to return to Sibley, and interesting as was the testimony given by the witness, he could not prevent his eyes from continually turning toward the door by which he expected Hickory to enter.

Strange to say, Mr. Orcutt seemed to take a like interest in that same door, and was more than once detected by Byrd flashing a hurried glance in its direction, as if he, too, were on the look-out for someone.

Meantime the expert in running was saying:

"It took me one hundred and twenty minutes to go over the ground the first time, and one hundred and fifteen minutes the next. I gained five minutes the second time, you see," he explained, "by knowing my ground better and by saving my strength where it was of no avail to attempt great speed. The last time I made the effort, however, I lost three minutes on my former time. The wood road which I had to take for some distance was with mud, and my feet sank with every step. The shortest time, then, which I was able to make in three attempts, was one hundred and fifteen minutes."

Now, as the time between the striking of the fatal blow and the hour at which the prisoner arrived at the Quarry Station was only ninety minutes, a general murmur of satisfaction followed this announcement. It was only momentary, however, for Mr. Ferris, rising to cross-examine the witness, curiosity prevailed over all lesser emotions, and an immediate silence followed without the intervention of the Court.

"Did you make these three runs from Mrs. Clemmens' house to Monteith Quarry Station entirely on foot?"

"I did, sir."

"Was that necessary?"

"Yes, sir; as far as the highway, at least. The path through the woods is not wide enough for a horse, unless it be for that short distance where the Foresters' Road intervenes."

"And you ran there?"

"Yes, sir, twice at full speed; the third time I had the experience I have told you of."

"And how long do you think it took you to go over that especial portion of ground?"

"Five minutes, maybe."

"And, supposing you had had a horse?"

"Well, sir, *if* I had had a horse, and *if* he had been waiting there, all ready for me to jump on his back, and *if* he had been a good runner and used to the road, I think I could have gone over it in two minutes, if I had not first broken my neck on some of the jagged stones that roughen the road."

"In other words, you could have saved three minutes if you had been furnished with a horse at that particular spot?"

"Yes, *if*."

Mr. Orcutt, whose eye had been fixed upon the door at this particular juncture, now looked back at the witness and hurriedly rose to his feet.

"Has my esteemed friend any testimony on hand to prove that the prisoner had a horse at this place? if he has not, I object to these questions."

"What testimony I have to produce will come in at its proper time," retorted Mr. Ferris. "Meanwhile, I think I have a right to put this or any other kind of similar question to the witness."

The judge acquiescing with a nod, Mr. Orcutt sat down.

Mr. Ferris went on.

"Did you meet anyone on the road during any of these three runs which you made?"

"No, sir. That is, I met no one in the woods. There were one or two persons on the highway the last time I ran over it."

"Were they riding or walking?"

"Walking."

Here Mr. Orcutt interposed.

"Did you say that in passing over the highway you ran?"

"Yes, sir."

"Why did you do this? Had you not been told that the prisoner was seen to be walking when he came down the road to the station?"

"Yes, sir. But I was in for time, you see."

"And you did not make it even with that advantage?"

"No, sir."

The second expert had the same story to tell, with a few variations. He had made one of his runs in five minutes less than the other had done, but it was by a great exertion that left him completely exhausted when he arrived at the station. It was during his cross-examination that Hickory at last came in.

Horace Byrd, who had been growing very impatient during the last few minutes, happened to be looking at the door when it opened to admit this late comer.

So was Mr. Orcutt. But Byrd did not notice this, or Hickory either. If they had, perhaps Hickory would have been more careful to hide his feelings. As it was, he no sooner met his colleague's eye than he gave a quick, despondent shake of the head in intimation that he had *failed*.

Mr. Byrd, who had anticipated a different result, was greatly disappointed. His countenance fell and he cast a glance of compassion at Miss Dare, now flushing with a secret but slowly growing hope. The defence, then, was good, and she ran the risk of being interrogated again. It was a prospect from which Mr. Byrd recoiled.

As soon as Hickory got the chance, he made his way to the side of Byrd.

"No go," was his low but expressive salutation. "One hundred and five minutes is the shortest time in which I can get over the ground, and that by a deuced hard scramble of it too."

"But that's five minutes' gain on the experts," Byrd whispered.

"Is it? Hope I could gain something on them, but what's five minutes' gain in an affair like this? Fifteen is what's wanted."

"I know it."

"And fifteen I cannot make, nor ten either, unless a pair of wings should be given me to carry me over the river."

"Sure?"

"Sure!"

Here there was some commotion in their vicinity, owing to the withdrawal of the last witness from the stand. Hickory took advantage of the bustle to lean over and whisper in Byrd's ear:

"Do you know I think I have been watched today. There was a fellow concealed in Mrs. Clemmens' house, who saw me leave it, and who, I have no doubt, took express note of the time I started. And there was another chap hanging round the station at the quarries, whom I am almost sure had no business there unless it was to see at what moment I arrived. He came back to Sibley when I did, but he telegraphed first, and it is my opinion that Orcutt——"

Here he was greatly startled by hearing his name spoken in a loud and commanding tone of voice. Stopping short, he glanced up, encountered the eye of Mr. Orcutt fixed upon him from the other side of the court-room, and realized he was being summoned to the witness stand.

"The deuce!" he murmured, with a look at Byrd to which none but an artist could do justice.

32

Hickory

Hickory's face was no new one to the court. He had occupied a considerable portion of one day in giving testimony for the prosecution, and his rough manner and hardy face, twinkling, however, at times with an irrepressible humour that redeemed it and him from all charge of ugliness, were well known not only to the jury but to all the *habitués* of the trial. Yet, when he stepped upon the stand at the summons of Mr. Orcutt, every eye turned toward him with curiosity, so great was the surprise with which his name had been hailed, and so vivid the interest aroused in what a detective devoted to the cause of the prosecution might have to say in the way of supporting the defence.

The first question uttered by Mr. Orcutt served to put them upon the right track.

"Will you tell the court where you have been today, Mr. Hickory?"

"Well," replied the witness in a slow and ruminating tone of voice, as he cast a look at Mr. Ferris, half apologetic and half reassuring, "I have been in a good many places——"

"You know what I mean," interrupted Mr. Orcutt. "Tell the court where you were between the hours of eleven and a quarter to one," he added, with a quick glance at the paper he held in his hand.

"Oh, *then*," cried Hickory, suddenly relaxing into his drollest self. "Well, *then*, I was all along the route from Sibley to Monteith Quarry Station. I don't think I was stationary at anyone minute of the time, sir."

"In other words——" suggested Mr. Orcutt, severely.

"I was trying to show myself smarter than my betters;" bowing with a great show of respect to the two experts who sat near. "*Or,* in other words still, I was trying to make the distance between Mrs. Clemmens' house and the station I have mentioned, in time sufficient to upset the defence, sir."

And the look he cast at Mr. Ferris was wholly apologetic now.

"Ah, I understand, and at whose suggestion did you undertake to do this, Mr. Hickory?"

"At the suggestion of a friend of mine, who is also somewhat of a detective."

"And when was this suggestion given?"

"After your speech, sir, yesterday afternoon."

"And where?"

"At the hotel, sir, where I and my friend put up."

"Did not the counsel for the prosecution order you to make this attempt?"

"No, sir."

"Did he not know you were going to make it?"

"No, sir."

"Who did know it?"

"My friend."

"No one else?"

"Well, sir, judging from my present position, I should say there seems to have been someone else," the witness slyly retorted.

The calmness with which Mr. Orcutt carried on this examination suffered a momentary disturbance.

"You know what I mean," he returned. "Did you tell anyone but your friend that you were going to undertake this run?"

"No, sir."

"Mr. Hickory," the lawyer now pursued, "will you tell us why you considered yourself qualified to succeed in an attempt where you had already been told regular experts had failed?"

"Well, sir, I don't know unless you find the solution in the slightly presumptive character of my disposition."

"Had you ever run before or engaged in athletic sports of any kind?"

"Oh, yes, I have run before."

"And engaged in athletic sports?"

"Yes, sir."

"Mr. Hickory, have you ever run in a race with men of well-known reputation for speed?"

"Well, yes, I have."

"Did you ever win in running such a race?"

"Once."

"No more?"

"Well, then, twice."

The dejection with which this last assent came forth roused the mirth of some light-hearted, feather-headed people, but the officers of the court soon put a stop to that.

"Mr. Hickory, will you tell us whether on account of having twice beaten in a race requiring the qualifications of a professional runner, you considered yourself qualified to judge of the feasibility of any other man's making the distance from Mrs. Clemmens' house to Monteith Quarry Station in ninety minutes by your own ability or non-ability to do so?"

"Yes, sir, I did; but a man's judgement of his own qualifications don't go very far, I've been told."

"I did not ask you for any remarks, Mr. Hickory. This is a serious matter and demands serious treatment. I asked if in undertaking to make this run in ninety minutes you did not presume to judge of the feasibility of the prisoner having made it in that time, and you answered, 'Yes.' It was enough."

The witness bowed with an air of great innocence.

"Now," resumed the lawyer, "you say you made a run from Mrs. Clemmens' house to Monteith Quarry Station today. Before telling us in what time you did it, will you be kind enough to say what route you took?"

"The one, sir, which has been pointed out by the prosecution as that which the prisoner undoubtedly took—the path through the woods and over the bridge to the highway. I knew no other."

"Did you know *this?*"

"Yes, sir."

"How came you to know it?"

"I had been over it before."

"The whole distance?"

"Yes, sir."

"Mr. Hickory, were you well enough acquainted with the route not to be obliged to stop at any point during your journey to see if you were in the right path or taking the most direct road to your destination?"

"Yes, sir."

"And when you got to the river?"

"I turned straight to the right and made for the bridge."

"Did you not pause long enough to see if you could not cross the stream in some way?"

"No, sir. I don't know how to swim in my clothes and keep them dry, and as for my wings, I had unfortunately left them at home."

Mr. Orcutt frowned.

"These attempts at humour," said he, "are very *mal à propos*, Mr. Hickory." Then, with a return to his usual tone: "Did you cross the bridge at a run?"

"Yes, sir."

"And did you keep up your pace when you got to the highroad?"

"No, I did not."

"You did not?"

"No, sir."

"And why, may I ask?"

"I was tired."

"Tired?"

"Yes, sir."

There was a droll demureness in the way Hickory said this which made Mr. Orcutt pause. But in another minute he went on.

"And what pace do you take when you are tired?"

"A horse's pace when I can get it," was the laughing reply. "A team was going by, sir, and I just jumped up with the driver."

"Ah, you rode, then, part of the way? Was it a fast team, Mr. Hickory?"

"Well, it wasn't one of Bonner's."

"Did they go faster than a man could run?"

"Yes, sir, I am obliged to say they did."

"And how long did you ride behind them?"

"Till I got in sight of the station."

"Why did you not go farther?"

"Because I had been told the prisoner was seen to walk up to the station, and I meant to be fair to him when I knew how."

"Oh, you did; and do you think it was fair to him to steal a ride on the highway?"

"Yes, sir."

"And why?"

"Because no one has ever told me he didn't ride down the highway, at least till he came within sight of the station."

"Mr. Hickory," inquired the lawyer, severely, "are you in possession of any knowledge proving that he did?"

"No, sir."

Mr. Byrd, who had been watching the prisoner breathlessly through all this, saw or thought he saw the faintest shadow of an odd, disdainful smile cross his sternly composed features at this moment. But he could not be sure. There was enough in the possibility, however, to make the detective thoughtful; but Mr. Orcutt proceeding rapidly with his examination, left him no time to formulate his sensations into words.

"So that by taking this wagon you are certain you lost no time?"

"Yes, sir."

"Rather gained some?"

"Yes, sir."

"Mr. Hickory, will you now state whether you put forth your full speed today in going from Mrs. Clemmens' house to the Quarry Station?"

"I did not."

"What?"

"I did not put forth anything like my full speed, sir," the witness repeated, with a twinkle in the direction of Byrd that fell just short of being a decided wink.

"And why, may I ask? What restrained you from running as fast as you could? Sympathy for the defence?"

The ironical suggestion conveyed in this last question gave Hickory an excuse for indulging in his peculiar humour.

"No, sir; sympathy for the prosecution. I feared the loss of one of its most humble but valuable assistants. In other words, I was afraid I should break my neck."

"And why should you have any special fears of breaking your neck?"

"The path is so uneven, sir. No man could run for much of the way without endangering his life or at least his limbs."

"Did you run when you could?"

"Yes, sir."

"And in those places where you could not run, did you proceed as fast as you knew how?"

"Yes, sir."

"Very well; now I think it is time you told the jury just how many minutes it took you to go from Mrs. Clemmens' door to the Monteith Quarry Station."

"Well, sir, according to *my* watch, it took one hundred and five minutes."

Mr. Orcutt glanced impressively at the jury.

"One hundred and five minutes," he repeated. He then turned to the witness with his concluding questions.

"Mr. Hickory, were you present in the court-room just now when the two experts whom I have employed to make the run gave their testimony?"

"No, sir."

"Do you know in what time they made it?"

"I believe I do. I was told by the person whom I informed of my failure that I had gained five minutes upon them."

"And what did you reply?"

"That I hoped I could make something on *them;* but that five minutes wasn't much when a clean fifteen was wanted," returned Hickory, with another droll look at the experts and an askance appeal at Byrd, which being translated might read:"How in the deuce could this man have known what I was whispering to you on the other side of the court-room? Is he a wizard, this Orcutt?"

He forgot that a successful lawyer is always more or less of a wizard.

33

A Late Discovery

With the cross-examination of Hickory, the defence rested, and the day being far advanced, the court adjourned.

During the bustle occasioned by the departure of the prisoner, Mr. Byrd took occasion to glance at the faces of those most immediately concerned in the trial.

His first look naturally fell upon Mr. Orcutt. Ah! all was going well with the great lawyer. Hope, if not triumph, beamed in his eye and breathed in every movement of his alert and nervous form. He was looking across the court-room at Imogene Dare, and his features wore a faint smile that indelibly impressed itself upon Mr. Byrd's memory. Perhaps because there was something really peculiar and remarkable in its expression, and perhaps because of the contrast it offered to his own feelings of secret doubt and dread.

His next look naturally followed that of Mr. Orcutt and rested upon Imogene Dare. Ah! she was under the spell of awakening hope also. It was visible in her lightened brow, her calmer and less studied aspect, her eager and eloquently speaking gaze yet lingering on the door through which the prisoner had departed. As Mr. Byrd marked this look of hers and noted all it revealed, he felt his emotions rise till they almost confounded him. But strong as they were, they deepened still further when, in another moment, he beheld her suddenly drop her eyes from the door and turn them slowly, reluctantly but gratefully, upon Mr. Orcutt. All the story of her life was in that change of look; all the story of her future, too, perhaps, if—— Mr. Byrd dared not trust himself to follow the contingency that lurked behind that *if*, and, to divert his mind, turned his attention to Mr. Ferris.

But he found small comfort there. For the district attorney was not alone. Hickory stood at his side, and Hickory was whispering in his ear, and Mr. Byrd, who knew what was weighing on his colleague's mind, found no difficulty in interpreting the mingled expression of perplexity and surprise that crossed the dark, aquiline features of the district attorney as he listened with slightly bended head to what the detective had to say. That look and the deep, anxious frown which crossed his brow as he glanced up and encountered Imogene's eye, remained in Mr. Byrd's mind long after the court-room was empty and he had returned to his hotel. It mingled with the smile of strange satisfaction which he had detected on Mr. Orcutt's face, and awakened such a turmoil of contradictory images in his mind that he was glad when Hickory at last came in to break the spell.

Their meeting was singular, and revealed, as by a flash, the difference between the two men. Byrd contented himself with giving Hickory a look and saying nothing, while Hickory bestowed upon Byrd a hearty "Well, old fellow!" and broke out into a loud and by no means unenjoyable laugh.

"You didn't expect to see me mounting the rostrum in favour of the defence, did you?" he asked, after he had indulged himself as long as he saw fit in the display of this somewhat unseasonable mirth. "Well, it was a surprise. But I've done it for Orcutt now!"

"You have?"

"Yes, I have."

"But the prosecution has closed its case?"

"Bah! what of that?" was the careless reply. "The district attorney can get it reopened. No court would refuse that."

Horace surveyed his colleague for a moment in silence.

"So Mr. Ferris was struck with the point you gave him?" he ventured, at last.

"Well, sufficiently so to be uneasy," was Hickory's somewhat dry response.

The look with which Byrd answered him was eloquent. "And that makes you cheerful?" he inquired, with ill-concealed sarcasm.

"Well, it has a slight tendency that way," drawled the other, seemingly careless of the other's expression, if, indeed, he had noted it. "You see," he went on, with a meaning wink and a smile of utter unconcern, "all my energies just now are concentrated on getting myself even with that somewhat too wide-awake lawyer." And his smile broadened till it merged into a laugh that was rasping enough to Byrd's more delicate and generous sensibilities.

"Sufficiently so to be uneasy!" Yes, that was it. From the minute

Mr. Ferris listened to the suggestion that Miss Dare had not told all she knew about the murder, and that a question relative to where she had been at the time it was perpetrated would, in all probability, bring strange revelations to light, he had been awakened to a most uncomfortable sense of his position and the duty that was possibly required of him. To be sure, the time for presenting testimony to the court was passed, unless it was in the way of rebuttal; but how did he know but what Miss Dare had a fact at her command which would help the prosecution in overturning the strange, unexpected, yet simple theory of the defence?

At all events, he felt he ought to know whether, in giving her testimony she had exhausted her knowledge on this subject, or whether, in her sympathy for the accused, she had kept back certain evidence which if presented might bring the crime more directly home to the prisoner. Accordingly, somewhere toward eight o'clock in the evening, he sought her out with the bold resolution of forcing her to satisfy him on this point.

He did not find his task so easy, however, when he came into direct contact with her stately and far from encouraging presence, and met the look of surprise not unmixed with alarm with which she greeted him. She looked very weary, too, and yet unnaturally excited, as if she had not slept for many nights, if indeed she had rested at all since the trial began. It struck him as cruel to further disturb this woman, and yet the longer he surveyed her, the more he studied her pale, haughty, inscrutable face, he became the more assured that he would never feel satisfied with himself if he did not give her an immediate opportunity to disperse at once and forever these freshly awakened doubts.

His attitude or possibly his expression must have betrayed something of his anxiety if not of his resolve, for her countenance fell as she watched him, and her voice sounded quite unnatural as she strove to ask to what she was indebted for this unexpected visit.

He did not keep her in suspense.

"Miss Dare," said he, not without kindness, for he was very sorry for this woman, despite the inevitable prejudice which her relations to the accused had awakened, "I would have given much not to have been obliged to disturb you tonight, but my duty would not allow it. There is a question which I have hitherto omitted to ask——"

He paused, shocked; she was swaying from side to side before his eyes, and seemed indeed about to fall. But at the outreaching of his hand she recovered herself and stood erect, the noblest spectacle of a woman triumphing over the weakness of her body by the mere force of her indomitable will, that he had ever beheld.

"Sit down," he gently urged, pushing toward her a chair. "You have had a hard and dreary week of it; you are in need of rest."

She did not refuse to avail herself of the chair, though, as he could not help but notice, she did not thereby relax one *iota* of the restraint she put upon herself.

"I do not understand," she murmured; "what question?"

"Miss Dare, in all you have told the court, in all that you have told me, about this fatal and unhappy affair, you have never informed us how it was you first came to hear of it. You were———"

"I heard it on the street corner," she interrupted, with what seemed to him an almost feverish haste.

"First?"

"Yes, first."

"Miss Dare, had you been in the street long? Were you in it at the time the murder happened, do you think?"

"I in the street?"

"Yes," he repeated, conscious from the sudden strange alteration in her look that he had touched upon a point which, to her, was vital with some undefined interest, possibly that to which the surmises of Hickory had supplied a clue. "Were you in the street, or anywhere out-of-doors at the time the murder occurred? It strikes me that it would be well for me to know."

"Sir," she cried, rising in her sudden indignation, "I thought the time for questions had passed. What means this sudden inquiry into a matter we have all considered exhausted, certainly as far as I am concerned."

"Shall I show you?" he cried, taking her by the hand and leading her toward the mirror nearby, under one of those impulses which sometimes effect so much. "Look in there at your own face and you will see why I press this question upon you."

Astonished, if not awed, she followed with her eyes the direction of his pointing finger, and anxiously surveyed her own image in the glass. Then, with a quick movement, her hands went up before her face—which till that moment had kept its counsel so well—and, tottering back against a table, she stood for a moment communing with herself, and possibly summoning up her courage for the conflict she evidently saw before her.

"What is it you wish to know?" she faintly inquired, after a long period of suspense and doubt.

"Where were you when the clock struck twelve on the day Mrs. Clemmens was murdered?"

Instantly dropping her hands, she turned toward him with a sudden lift of her majestic figure that was as imposing as it was unexpected.

"I was at Professor Darling's house," she declared, with great steadiness.

Mr. Ferris had not expected this reply, and looked at her for an instant almost as if he felt inclined to repeat his inquiry.

"Do you doubt my word?" she queried. "Is it possible you question my truth at a time like this?"

"No, Miss Dare," he gravely assured her. "After the great sacrifice you have publicly made in the interests of justice, it would be worse than presumptuous in me to doubt your sincerity now."

She drew a deep breath, and straightened herself still more proudly.

"Then am I to understand you are satisfied with the answer you have received?"

"Yes, if you will also add that you were in the observatory at Professor Darling's house," he responded quickly, convinced there was some mystery here, and seeing but one way to reach it.

"Very well, then, I was," she averred, without hesitation.

"You were!" he echoed, advancing upon her with a slight flush on his middle-aged cheek, that evinced how difficult it was for him to pursue this conversation in face of the haughty and repellant bearing she had assumed. "You will, perhaps, tell me, then, why you did not see and respond to the girl who came into that room at this very time, with a message from a lady who waited below to see you?"

"Ah!" she cried, succumbing with a suppressed moan to the inexorable destiny that pursued her in this man, "you have woven a net for me!"

And she sank again into a chair, where she sat like one stunned, looking at him with a hollow gaze which filled his heart with compassion, but which had no power to shake his purpose as a district attorney.

"Yes," he acknowledged, after a moment, "I have woven a net for you, but only because I am anxious for the truth, and desirous of furthering the ends of justice. I am confident you know more about this crime than you have ever revealed, Miss Dare; that you are acquainted with some fact that makes you certain Mr. Mansell committed this murder, notwithstanding the defence advanced in his favour. What is this fact? It is my office to inquire. True," he admitted, seeing her draw back with denial written on every line of her white face, "you have a right to refuse to answer me here, but you will have no right to refuse to answer me tomorrow when I put the same question to you in the presence of judge and jury."

"And"—her voice was so husky he could but with difficulty distinguish her words—"do you intend to recall me to the stand tomorrow?"

"I am obliged to, Miss Dare."

"But I thought the time for examination was over; that the witnesses had all testified, and that nothing remained now but for the lawyers to sum up."

"When in a case like this the prisoner offers a defence not anticipated by the prosecution, the latter, of course, has the right to meet such defence with proof in rebuttal."

"Proof in rebuttal? What is that?"

"Evidence to rebut or prove false the matters advanced in support of the defence."

"Ah!"

"I must do it in this case—if I can, of course."

She did not reply.

"And even if the testimony I desire to put in is not rebuttal in its character, no unbiased judge would deny to counsel the privilege of reopening his case when any new or important fact has come to light."

As if overwhelmed by a prospect she had not anticipated, she hurriedly arose and pointed down the room to a curtained recess.

"Give me five minutes," she cried; "five minutes by myself where no one can look at me, and where I can think undisturbed upon what I had better do."

"Very well," he acquiesced; "you shall have them."

She at once crossed to the small retreat.

"Five minutes," she reiterated huskily, as she lifted the curtains aside; "when the clock strikes nine I will come out."

"You will?" he repeated, doubtfully.

"I will."

The curtains fell behind her, and for five long minutes Mr. Ferris paced the room alone. He was far from easy. All was so quiet behind that curtain,—so preternaturally quiet. But he would not disturb her;

no, he had promised, and she should be left to fight her battle alone. When nine o'clock struck, however, he started, and owned to himself some secret dread. Would she come forth or would he have to seek her in her place of seclusion? It seemed he would have to seek her, for the curtains did not stir, and by no sound from within was any token given that she had heard the summons. Yet he hesitated, and as he did so, a thought struck him. Could it be there was any outlet from the refuge she had sought? Had she taken advantage of his consideration to escape him? Moved by the fear, he hastily crossed the room. But before he could lay his hand upon the curtains, they parted, and disclosed the form of Imogene.

"I am coming," she murmured, and stepped forth more like a faintly-breathing image than a living woman.

His first glance at her face convinced him she had taken her resolution. His second, that in taking it she had drifted into a state of feeling different from any he had observed in her before, and of a sort that to him was wholly inexplicable. Her words when she spoke only deepened this impression.

"Mr. Ferris," said she, coming very near to him in evident dread of being overheard, "I have decided to tell you all. I hoped never to be obliged to do this. I thought enough had been revealed to answer your purpose. I—I believed Heaven would spare me this last trial, let me keep this last secret. It was of so strange a nature, so totally out of the reach of any man's surmise. But the finger of God is on me. It has followed this crime from the beginning, and there is no escape. By some strange means, some instinct of penetration, perhaps, you have discovered that I know something concerning this murder of which I have never told you, and that the hour I spent at Professor Darling's is accountable for this knowledge. Sir, I cannot struggle with Providence. I will tell you all I have hitherto hidden from the world if you will promise to let me know if my words will prove fatal, and if he— he who is on trial for his life—will be lost if I give to the court my last evidence against him?"

"But, Miss Dare," remonstrated the district attorney, "no man can tell——" He did not finish his sentence. Something in the feverish gaze she fixed upon him stopped him. He felt that he could not palter with a woman in the grasp of an agony like this. So, starting again, he observed: "Let me hear what you have to say, and afterward we will consider what the effect of it may be; though a question of expediency should not come into your consideration, Miss Dare, in telling

"The curtains parted and disclosed the form of Imogene. 'I am coming,' she murmured, and stepped forth."

such truths as the law demands."

"No?" she broke out, giving way for one instant to a low and terrible laugh which curdled Mr. Ferris' blood and made him wish his duty had led him into the midst of any other scene than this.

But before he could remonstrate with her, this harrowing expression of misery had ceased, and she was saying in quiet and suppressed tones:

"The reason I did not see and respond to the girl who came into the observatory on the morning of Mrs. Clemmens' murder is, that I was so absorbed in the discoveries I was making behind the high rack which shuts off one end of the room, that any appeal to me at that time must have passed unnoticed. I had come to Professor Darling's house, according to my usual custom on Tuesday mornings, to study astronomy with his daughter Helen. I had come reluctantly, for my mind was full of the secret intention I had formed of visiting Mrs. Clemmens in the afternoon, and I had no heart for study. But finding Miss Darling out, I felt a drawing toward the seclusion I knew I should find in the observatory, and mounting to it, I sat down by myself to think.

"The rest and quiet of the place were soothing to me, and I sat still a long time, but suddenly becoming impressed with the idea that it was growing late, I went to the window to consult the town-clock. But though its face could be plainly seen from the observatory, its hands could not, and I was about to withdraw from the window when I remembered the telescope, which Miss Darling and I had, in a moment of caprice a few days before, so arranged as to command a view of the town. Going to it, I peered through it at the clock." Stopping, she surveyed the district attorney with breathless suspense. "It was just five minutes to twelve," she impressively whispered.

Mr. Ferris felt a shock.

"A critical moment!" he exclaimed. Then, with a certain intuition of what she was going to say next, inquired: "And what then, Miss Dare?"

"I was struck by a desire to see if I could detect Mrs. Clemmens' house from where I was, and shifting the telescope slightly, I looked through it again, and——"

"What did you see, Miss Dare?"

"I saw her dining-room door standing ajar and a man leaping headlong over the fence toward the bog."

The district attorney started, looked at her with growing interest, and inquired:

"Did you recognize this man, Miss Dare?"

She nodded in great agitation.

"Who was he?"

"Craik Mansell."

"Miss Dare," ventured Mr. Ferris, after a moment, "you say this was five minutes to twelve?"

"Yes, sir," was the faint reply.

"Five minutes later than the time designated by the defence as a period manifestly too late for the prisoner to have left Mrs. Clemmens' house and arrived at the Quarry Station at twenty minutes past one?"

"Yes," she repeated, below her breath.

The district attorney surveyed her earnestly, perceiving she had not only spoken the truth, but realized all which that truth implied, and drew back a few steps muttering ironically to himself:

"Ah, Orcutt! Orcutt!"

Breathlessly she watched him, breathlessly she followed him step by step like some white and haunting spirit.

"You believe, then, this fact will cost him his life?" came from her lips at last.

"Don't ask me that, Miss Dare. You and I have no concern with the consequences of this evidence."

"No concern?" she repeated, wildly. "You and I no concern? Ah!" she went on, with heart-piercing sarcasm, "I forgot that the sentiments of the heart have no place in judicial investigation. A criminal is but lawful prey, and it is every good citizen's duty to push him to his doom. No matter if one is bound to that criminal by the dearest ties which can unite two hearts; no matter if the trust he has bestowed upon you has been absolute and unquestioning, the law does not busy itself with that. The law says if you have a word at your command which can destroy this man, give utterance to it; and the law must be obeyed."

"But, Miss Dare——" the district attorney hastily intervened, startled by the feverish gleam of her hitherto calm eye.

But she was not to be stopped, now that her misery had at last found words.

"You do not understand my position, perhaps," she continued. "You do not see that it has been my hand, and mine only, which, from the first, has slowly, remorselessly pushed this man back from the point of safety, till now, now, I am called upon to drag from his hand the one poor bending twig to which he clings, and upon which he relies to support him above the terrible gulf that yawns at his feet. You do not see——"

"Pardon me," interposed Mr. Ferris again, anxious, if possible, to restore her to herself. "I see enough to pity you profoundly. But you must allow me to remark that your hand is not the only one which has been instrumental in hurrying this young man to his doom. The detectives——"

"Sir," she interrupted in her turn, "can you, dare you say, that without my testimony he would have stood at any time in a really critical position?—or that he would stand in jeopardy of his life even now, if it were not for this fact I have to tell?"

Mr. Ferris was silent.

"Oh, I knew it, I knew it!" she cried. "There will be no doubt concerning whose testimony it was that convicted him, if he is sentenced by the court for this crime. Ah, ah, what an enviable position is mine! What an honourable deed I am called upon to perform! To tell the truth at the expense of the life most dear to you. It is a Roman virtue! I shall be held up as a model to my sex. All the world must shower plaudits upon the woman who, sooner than rob justice of its due, delivered her own lover over to the hangman."

Pausing in her passionate burst, she turned her hot, dry eyes in a sort of desperation upon his face.

"Do you know," she gurgled in his ear, "some women would kill themselves before they would do this deed."

Struck to his heart in spite of himself, Mr. Ferris looked at her in alarm—saw her standing there with her arms hanging down at her sides, but with her two hands clinched till they looked as if carved from marble—and drew near to her with the simple hurried question of:

"But you?"

"I?" she laughed again—a low, gurgling laugh, that yet had a tone in it that went to the other's heart and awoke strange sensations there. "Oh, I shall live to respond to your questions. Do not fear that I shall not be in the court-room tomorrow."

There was something in her look and manner that was new. It awed him, while it woke all his latent concern.

"Miss Dare," he began, "you can believe how painful all this has been to me, and how I would have spared you this misery if I could.

But the responsibilities resting upon me are such——"

He did not go on; why should he? She was not listening. To be sure, she stood before him, seemingly attentive, but the eyes with which she met his were fixed upon other objects than any which could have been apparent to her in his face; and her form, which she had hitherto held upright, was shaking with long, uncontrollable shudders, which, to his excited imagination, threatened to lay her at his feet.

He at once started toward the door for help. But she was alive to his movements if not to his words. Stopping him with a gesture, she cried:

"No—no! do not call for anyone; I wish to be alone; I have *my* duty to face, you know; my testimony to prepare." And rousing herself she cast a peculiar look about the room, like one suddenly introduced into a strange place, and then moving slowly toward the window, threw back the curtain and gazed without. "Night!" she murmured, "night!" and after a moment added, in a deep, unearthly voice that thrilled irresistibly upon Mr. Ferris' ear: "And a heaven full of stars!"

Her face, as she turned it upward, wore so strange a look, Mr. Ferris involuntarily left his position and crossed to her side. She was still murmuring to herself in seeming unconsciousness of his presence. "Stars!" she was repeating; "and above them God!" And the long shudders shook her frame again, and she dropped her head and seemed about to fall into her old abstraction when her eye encountered that of the district attorney, and she hurriedly aroused herself.

"Pardon me," she exclaimed, with an ill-concealed irony, particularly impressive after her tone of the moment before, "have you anything further to exact of me?"

"No," he made haste to reply; "only before I go I would entreat you to be calm——"

"And say the word I have to say tomorrow without a balk and without an unnecessary display of feeling," she coldly interpolated. "Thanks, Mr. Ferris, I understand you. But you need fear nothing from me. There will be no scene—at least on my part—when I rise before the court to give my testimony tomorrow. Since my hand must strike the fatal blow, it shall strike—firmly!" and her clenched fist fell heavily on her own breast, as if the blow she meditated must first strike there.

The district attorney, more moved than he had deemed it possible for him to be, made her a low bow and withdrew slowly to the door.

"I leave you, then, till tomorrow," he said.

411

"Till tomorrow."

Long after he had passed out, the deep meaning which informed those two words haunted his memory and disturbed his heart. Till tomorrow! Alas, poor girl! and after tomorrow, what then?

34

What Was Hid Behind Imogene's Veil

The few minutes that elapsed before the formal opening of court the next morning were marked by great cheerfulness. The crisp frosty air had put everybody in a good-humour. Even the prisoner looked less sombre than before, and for the first time since the beginning of his trial, deigned to turn his eyes toward the bench where Imogene sat, with a look that, while it was not exactly kind, had certainly less disdain in it than before he saw his way to a possible acquittal on the theory advanced by his counsel.

But this look, though his first, did not prove to be his last. Something in the attitude of the woman he gazed at—or was it the mystery of the heavy black veil that enveloped her features?—woke a strange doubt in his mind. Beckoning to Mr. Orcutt, he communicated with him in a low tone.

"Can it be possible," asked he, "that anything new could have transpired since last night to give encouragement to the prosecution?"

The lawyer, startled, glanced hastily about him and shook his head.

"No," he cried; "impossible! What could have transpired?"

"Look at Mr. Ferris," whispered the prisoner, "and then at the witness who wears a veil."

With an unaccountable feeling of reluctance, Mr. Orcutt hastily complied. His first glance at the district attorney made him thoughtful. He recognized the look which his opponent wore; he had seen it many a time before this, and knew what it indicated. As for Imogene, who could tell what went on in that determined breast? The close black veil revealed nothing. Mr. Orcutt impatiently turned back to his client.

"I think you alarm yourself unnecessarily," he whispered. "Ferris

413

means to fight, but what of that? He wouldn't be fit for his position if he didn't struggle to the last gasp even for a failing cause."

Yet in saying this his lip took its sternest line, and from the glitter of his eye and the close contraction of his brow it looked as if he were polishing his own weapons for the conflict he thus unexpectedly saw before him.

Meantime, across the court-room, another whispered conference was going on.

"Hickory, where have you been ever since last night? I have not been able to find you anywhere."

"I was on duty; I had a bird to look after."

"A bird?"

"Yes, a wild bird; one who is none too fond of its cage; a desperate one who might find means to force aside its bars and fly away."

"What do you mean, Hickory? What nonsense is this?"

"Look at Miss Dare and perhaps you will understand."

"Miss Dare?"

"Yes."

Horace's eyes opened in secret alarm.

"Do you mean——"

"I mean that I spent the whole night in tramping up and down in front of her window. And a dismal task it was too. Her lamp burned till daylight."

Here the court was called to order and Byrd had only opportunity to ask:

"Why does she wear a veil?"

To which the other whisperingly retorted:

"Why did she spend the whole night in packing up her worldly goods and writing a letter to the Congregational minister to be sent after the adjournment of court today?"

"Did she do that?"

"She did."

"Hickory, don't *you* know—haven't you been told what she is expected to say or do here today?"

"No."

"You only guess?"

"No, I don't guess."

"You fear, then?"

"Fear! Well, that's a big word to a fellow like me. I don't know as I fear anything ; I'm curious, that is all."

Mr. Byrd drew back, looked over at Imogene, and involuntarily shook his head. What was in the mind of this mysterious woman? What direful purpose or shadow of doom lay behind the veil that separated her from the curiosity and perhaps the sympathy of the surrounding crowd? It was in vain to question; he could only wait in secret anxiety for the revelations which the next few minutes might bring.

The defence having rested the night before, the first action of the judge on the opening of the court was to demand whether the prosecution had any rebuttal testimony to offer.

Mr. Ferris instantly rose.

"Miss Dare, will you retake the stand," said he.

Immediately Mr. Orcutt, who up to the last moment had felt his case as secure as if it had indeed been founded on a rock, bounded to his feet, white as the witness herself.

"I object!" he cried. "The witness thus recalled by the counsel of the prosecution has had ample opportunity to lay before the court all the evidence in her possession. I submit it to the court whether my learned opponent should not have exhausted his witness before he rested his case."

"Mr. Ferris," asked the judge, turning to the district attorney, "do you recall this witness for the purpose of introducing fresh testimony in support of your case or merely to disprove the defence?"

"Your honour," was the district attorney's reply, "I ought to say in fairness to my adversary and to the court, that since the case was closed a fact has come to my knowledge of so startling and conclusive a nature that I feel bound to lay it before the jury. From this witness alone can we hope to glean this fact; and as I had no information on which to base a question concerning it in her former examination, I beg the privilege of reopening my case to that extent."

"Then the evidence you desire to submit is not in rebuttal?" queried the Judge.

"I do not like to say that," rejoined the district attorney, adroitly. "I think it may bear directly upon the question whether the prisoner could catch the train at Monteith Quarry if he left the widow's house after the murder. If the evidence I am about to offer be true, he certainly could."

Thoroughly alarmed now and filled with the dismay which a mysterious threat is always calculated to produce, Mr. Orcutt darted a wild look of inquiry at Imogene, and finding her immovable behind her thick veil, turned about and confronted the district attorney with a most sarcastic smile upon his blanched and trembling lips.

"Does my learned friend suppose the court will receive any such ambiguous explanation as this? If the testimony sought from this witness is by way of rebuttal, let him say so; but if it is not, let him be frank enough to admit it, that I may in turn present my objections to the introduction of any irrelevant evidence at this time."

"The testimony I propose to present through this witness *is* in the way of rebuttal," returned Mr Ferris, severely. "The argument advanced by the defence, that the prisoner could not have left Mrs. Clemmens' house at ten minutes before twelve and arrived at Monteith Quarry Station at twenty minutes past one, is not a tenable one, and I purpose to prove it by this witness."

Mr. Orcutt's look of anxiety changed to one of mingled amazement and incredulity.

"By *this* witness! You have chosen a peculiar one for the purpose," he ironically exclaimed, more and more shaken from his self-possession by the quiet bearing of his opponent, and the silent air of waiting which marked the stately figure of her whom, as he had hitherto believed, he thoroughly comprehended. "Your Honour," he continued, "I withdraw my objections; I should really like to hear how Miss Dare or any lady can give evidence on this point."

And he sank back into his seat with a look at his client in which professional bravado strangely struggled with something even deeper than alarm.

"This must be an exciting moment to the prisoner," whispered Hickory to Byrd.

"So, so. But mark his control, will you? He is less cut up than Orcutt."

"Look at his eyes, though. If anything could pierce that veil of hers, you would think such a glance might."

"Ah, he is trying his influence over her at last."

"But it is too late."

Meantime the district attorney had signified again to Miss Dare his desire that she should take the stand. Slowly, and like a person in a dream, she arose, unloosed her veil, dragged it from before her set features, and stepped mechanically forward to the place assigned her. What was there in the face thus revealed that called down an instantaneous silence upon the court, and made the momentary pause that ensued memorable in the minds of all present? It was not that she was so pale, though her close-fitting black dress, totally unrelieved by any suspicion of white, was of a kind to bring out any startling change in her complexion; nor was there visible in her bearing any trace of the feverish excitement which had characterized it the evening before; yet of all the eyes that were fixed upon her—and there were many in that crowd whose only look a moment before had been one of heartless curiosity—there were none which were not filled with compassion and more or less dread.

Meanwhile, she remained like a statue on the spot where she had taken her stand, and her eyes, which in her former examination had met the court with the unflinching gaze of an automaton, were lowered till the lashes swept her cheek.

"Miss Dare," asked the district attorney, as soon as he could recover from his own secret emotions of pity and regret, "will you tell us where you were at the hour of noon on the morning Mrs. Clemmens was murdered?"

Before she could answer, before in fact her stiff and icy lips could part, Mr. Orcutt had risen impetuously to his feet, like a man bound to contend every step of the way with the unknown danger that menaced him.

"I object!" he cried, in the changed voice of a deeply disturbed man, while those who had an interest in the prisoner at this juncture, could not but notice that he, too, showed signs of suppressed feeling, and for the first time since the beginning of the trial, absolutely found his self-command insufficient to keep down the rush of colour that swept up to his swarthy cheek.

"The question," continued Mr. Orcutt, "is not to elicit testimony in rebuttal."

"Will my learned friend allow the witness to give her answer, instead of assuming what it is to be?"

"I will not," retorted his adversary. "A child could see that such a question is not admissible at this stage of the case."

"I am sure my learned friend would not wish me to associate *him* with any such type of inexperience?" suggested Mr. Ferris, grimly.

But the sarcasm, which at one time would have called forth a stinging retort from Mr. Orcutt, passed unheeded. The great lawyer was fighting for his life, for his heart's life, for the love and hand of Imogene—a recompense which at this moment her own unconsidered action, or the constraining power of a conscience of whose might he had already received such heart-rending manifestation, seemed about to snatch from his grasp forever. Turning to the judge, he said:

"I will not delay the case by bandying words with my esteemed friend, but appeal at once to the court as to whether the whereabouts of Miss Dare on that fatal morning can have anything to do with the defence we have proved."

"Your Honour," commenced the district attorney, calmly following the lead of his adversary, "I am ready to stake my reputation on the declaration that this witness is in possession of a fact that overturns the whole fabric of the defence. If the particular question I have made use of, in my endeavour to elicit this fact, is displeasing to my friend, I will venture upon another less ambiguous, if more direct and perhaps leading." And turning again to the witness, Mr. Ferris calmly inquired:

"Did you or did you not see the prisoner on the morning of the assault, at a time distinctly known by you to be after ten minutes to twelve?"

It was out. The line of attack meditated by Mr. Ferris was patent to everybody. A murmur of surprise and interest swept through the court-room, while Mr. Orcutt, who in spite of his vague fears was anything but prepared for a thrust of this vital nature, started and cast short demanding looks from Imogene to Mansell, as if he would ask them what fact this was which through ignorance or presumption they had conspired to keep from him. The startled look which he surprised on the stern face of the prisoner, showed him there was everything to fear in her reply, and bounding again to his feet, he was about to make some further attempt to stave off the impending calamity, when the rich voice of Imogene was heard saying:

"Gentlemen, if you will allow me to tell my story unhindered, I think I shall soonest satisfy both the district attorney and the counsel for the prisoner."

And raising her eyes with a slow and heavy movement from the floor, she fixed them in a meaning way upon the latter.

At once convinced that he had been unnecessarily alarmed, Mr. Orcutt sank back into his seat, and Imogene slowly proceeded.

She commenced in a forced tone and with a sudden quick shudder that made her words come hesitatingly and with strange breaks: "I have been asked—two questions by Mr. Ferris—I prefer—to answer the first. He asked me—where I was at the hour Mrs. Clemmens was murdered."

She paused so long one had time to count her breaths as they came in gasps to her white lips.

"I have no further desire to hide from you the truth. I was with Mrs. Clemmens in her own house."

At this acknowledgment so astonishing, and besides so totally different from the one he had been led to expect, Mr. Ferris started as if a thunder-bolt had fallen at his feet.

"In Mrs. Clemmens' house!" he repeated, amid the excited hum of a hundred murmuring voices. "Did you say, in Mrs. Clemmens' house?"

"Yes," she returned, with a wild, ironical smile that at once assured Mr. Ferris of his helplessness. "I am on oath *now*, and I assert that on the day and at the hour Mrs. Clemmens was murdered, I was in her house and in her dining-room. I had come there secretly," she proceeded, with a sudden feverish fluency that robbed Mr. Ferris of speech, and in fact held all her auditors spell-bound. "I had been spending an hour or so at Professor Darling's, whose house in West Side is, as many here know, at the very end of Summer Avenue, and close to the woods that run along back of Mrs. Clemmens' cottage. I had been sitting alone in the observatory, which is at the top of one of the towers, but being suddenly seized with a desire to see the widow and make that promised attempt at persuading her to reconsider her decision in regard to the money her—her—the prisoner wanted, I came down, and unknown to anyone in the house, stole away to the woods and so to the widow's cottage. It was noon when I got there, or very near it, for her company, if she had had any, was gone, and she was engaged in setting the clock where——"

Why did she pause? The district attorney, utterly stupefied by his surprise, had made no sign; neither had Mr. Orcutt. Indeed, it looked as if the latter could not have moved, much less spoken, even if he had desired it. Thought, feeling, life itself, seemed to be at a standstill within him as he sat with a face like clay, waiting for words whose import he perhaps saw foreshadowed in her wild and terrible mien. But though his aspect was enough to stop her, it was not upon him she was gazing when the words tripped on her lips. It was upon the prisoner, on the man who up to this time had borne himself with such iron-like composure and reserve, but who now, with every sign of feeling and alarm, had started forward and stood surveying her, with his hand uplifted in the authoritative manner of a master.

The next instant he sank back, feeling the eye of the judge upon him; but the signal had been made, and many in that court-room looked to see Imogene falter or break down. But she, although fascinated, perhaps moved, by this hint of feeling from one who had hitherto met all the exigencies of the hour with a steady and firm composure, did not continue silent at his bidding. On the contrary, her purpose, whatever it was, seemed to acquire new force, for turning from him with a strange, unearthly glare on her face, she fixed her glances on the jury and went steadily on.

"I have said," she began, "that Mrs. Clemmens was winding her clock. When I came in she stepped down, and a short and angry colloquy commenced between us. She did not like my coming there. She did not appreciate my interest in her nephew. She made me furious, frenzied, mad. I—I turned away—then I came back. She was standing with her face lifted toward her clock, as though she no longer heeded or remembered my presence. I—I don't know what came to me; whether it was hatred or love that maddened my brain—but——"

She did not finish; she did not need to. The look she gave, the attitude she took, the appalling gesture which she made, supplied the place of language. In an instant Mr. Ferris, Mr. Orcutt, all the many and confused spectators who hung upon her words as if spell-bound, realized that instead of giving evidence inculpating the prisoner, she was giving evidence *accusing* herself; that, in other words, Imogene Dare, goaded to madness by the fearful alternative of either destroying her lover or sacrificing herself, had yielded to the claims of her love or her conscience, and in hearing of judge and jury, proclaimed herself to be the murderess of Mrs. Clemmens.

The moment that followed was frightful. The prisoner, who was probably the only man present who foresaw her intention when she began to speak, had sunk back into his seat and covered his face with his hands long before she reached the fatal declaration. But the spectacle presented by Mr. Orcutt was enough, as with eyes dilated and lips half parted in consternation, he stood before them a victim of overwhelming emotion; so overcome, indeed, as scarcely to be able to give vent to the one low and memorable cry that involuntarily left his lips as the full realization of what she had done smote home to his stricken breast.

As for Mr. Ferris, he stood dumb, absolutely robbed of speech by this ghastly confession he had unwillingly called from his witness' lips; while slowly from end to end of that court-room the wave of horror spread, till Imogene, her cause, and that of the wretched prisoner himself, seemed swallowed up in one fearful tide of unreality and nightmare.

420

The first gleam of relief came from the judge.

"Miss Dare," said he, in his slow, kindly way that nothing could impair, "do you realize the nature of the evidence you have given to the court?"

Her slowly falling head and white face, from which all the fearful excitement was slowly ebbing in a dead despair, gave answer for her.

"I fear that you are not in a condition to realize the effect of your words," the judge went on. "Sympathy for the prisoner or the excitement of being recalled to the stand has unnerved or confused you. Take time, Miss Dare, the court will wait; reconsider your words, and then tell us the truth about this matter."

But Imogene, with white lips and drooped head, answered hurriedly:

"I have nothing to consider. I have told, or attempted to tell, how Mrs. Clemmens came to her death. She was struck down by me; Craik Mansell there is innocent."

At this repetition in words of what she had before merely intimated by a gesture, the judge ceased his questions, and the horror of the multitude found vent in one long, low, but irrepressible murmur. Taking advantage of the momentary disturbance, Byrd turned to his colleague with the agitated inquiry:

"Hickory, is *this* what you have had in your mind for the last few days?"

"This," repeated the other, with an air of careful consideration, assumed, as Byrd thought, to conceal any emotion which he might have felt; "no, no, not really. I—I don't know what I thought. Not this though." And he fixed his eyes upon Imogene's fallen countenance, with an expression of mingled doubt and wonder, as baffling in its nature as the tone of voice he had used.

"But," stammered Byrd, with an earnestness that almost partook of the nature of pleading, "she is not speaking the truth, of course. What we heard her say in the hut——"

"Hush!" interposed the other, with a significant gesture and a sudden glance toward the prisoner and his counsel; "watching is better than talking just now. Besides, Orcutt is going to speak."

It was so. After a short and violent conflict with the almost overwhelming emotions that had crushed upon him with the words and actions of Imogene, the great lawyer had summoned up sufficient control over himself to reassume the duties of his position and face once more the expectant crowd, and the startled, if not thoroughly benumbed, jury.

His first words had the well-known ring, and, like a puff of cool air through a heated atmosphere, at once restored the court-room to its usual condition of formality and restraint.

"This is not evidence, but the raving of frenzy," he said, in impassioned tones. "The witness has been tortured by the demands of the prosecution, till she is no longer responsible for her words." And turning toward the district attorney, who, at the first sound of his adversary's voice, had roused himself from the stupor into which he had been thrown by the fearful and unexpected turn which Imogene's confession had taken, he continued: "If my learned friend is not lost to all feelings of humanity, he will withdraw from the stand a witness labouring under a mental aberration of so serious a nature."

Mr. Ferris was an irritable man, but he was touched with sympathy for his friend, reeling under so heavy a blow. He therefore forbore to notice this taunt save by a low bow, but turned at once to the judge.

"Your Honour," said he, "I desire to be understood by the court, that the statement which has just been made in your hearing by this witness, is as much of a surprise to me as to anyone in this courtroom. The fact which I proposed to elicit from her testimony was of an entirely different nature. In the conversation which we held last night——"

But Mr. Orcutt, vacillating between his powerful concern for Imogene, and his duty to his client, would not allow the other to proceed.

"I object," said he, "to any attempt at influencing the jury by the statement of any conversation which may have passed between the district attorney and the witness. From its effects we may judge something of its nature, but with its details we have nothing to do."

And raising his voice till it filled the room like a clarion, Mr. Orcutt said:

"The moment is too serious for wrangling. A spectacle, the most terrible that can be presented to the eyes of man, is before you. A young, beautiful, and hitherto honoured woman, caught in the jaws of a cruel fate and urged on by the emotions of her sex, which turn ever toward self-sacrifice, has, in a moment of mistaken zeal or frantic terror, allowed herself to utter words which sound like a criminal confession. May it please your Honour and Gentlemen of the Jury, this is an act to awaken compassion in the breast of every true man. Neither my client nor myself can regard it in any other light. Though his case were ten times more critical than it is, and condemnation awaited him at your hands instead of a triumphant acquittal, he is not the man I believe him, if he would consent to accept a deliverance founded upon utterances so manifestly frenzied and devoid of truth. I therefore repeat the objection I have before urged. I ask your Honour now to strike out all this testimony as irrelevant in rebuttal, and I beg our learned friend to close an examination as unprofitable to his own cause as to mine."

"I agree with my friend," returned Mr. Ferris, "that the moment is one unfit for controversy. If it please the court, therefore, I will withdraw the witness, though by so doing I am forced to yield all hope of eliciting the important fact I had relied upon to rebut the defence."

And obedient to the bow of acquiescence he received from the judge, the district attorney turned to Miss Dare and considerately requested her to leave the stand.

But she, roused by the sound of her name perhaps, looked up, and meeting the eye of the judge, said:

"Pardon me, your Honour, but I do not desire to leave the stand till I have made clear to all who hear me that it is I, not the prisoner, who am responsible for Mrs. Clemmens' death. The agony which I have been forced to undergo in giving testimony against him, has earned me the right to say the words that prove his innocence and my own guilt."

"But," said the Judge, "we do not consider you in any condition to give testimony in court today, even against yourself. If what you say is true, you shall have ample opportunities hereafter to confirm and establish your statements, for you must know, Miss Dare, that no confession of this nature will be considered sufficient without testimony corroborative of its truth."

"But, your Honour," she returned, with a dreadful calmness, "I have corroborative testimony." And amid the startled looks of all present, she raised her hand and pointed with steady forefinger at the astounded and by-no-means gratified Hickory. "Let that man be recalled," she cried, "and asked to repeat the conversation he had with a young servant-girl called Roxana, in Professor Darling's observatory some ten weeks ago."

The suddenness of her action, the calm assurance with which it was made, together with the intention it evinced of summoning actual evidence to substantiate her confession, almost took away the breath of the assembled multitude. Even Mr. Orcutt seemed shaken by it, and stood looking from the outstretched hand of this woman he so adored, to the abashed countenance of the rough detective, with a wonder that for the first time betrayed the presence of alarm. Indeed, to him as to others, the moment was fuller of horror than when she made her first self-accusation, for what at that time partook of the vagueness of a dream, seemed to be acquiring the substance of an awful reality.

Imogene alone remained unmoved. Still with her eyes fixed on Hickory, she continued:

"He has not told you all he knows about this matter, any more than I. If my word needs corroboration, look to him."

And taking advantage of the sensation which this last appeal occasioned, she waited where she was for the judge to speak, with all the calmness of one who has nothing more to fear or hope for in this world.

But the judge sat aghast at this spectacle of youth and beauty insisting upon its own guilt, and neither Mr. Ferris nor Mr. Orcutt having words for this emergency, a silence, deep as the feeling which had been aroused, gradually settled over the whole court. It was fast becoming oppressive, when suddenly a voice, low but firm, and endowed with a strange power to awake and hold the attention, was heard speaking in that quarter of the room whence Mr. Orcutt's commanding tones had so often issued. It was an unknown voice, and for a minute a doubt seemed to rest upon the assembled crowd as to whom it belonged.

But the change that had come into Imogene's face, as well as the character of the words that were uttered, soon convinced them it was the prisoner himself. With a start, everyone turned in the direction of the dock. The sight that met their eyes seemed a fit culmination of the scene through which they had just passed. Erect, noble, as commanding in appearance and address as the woman who still held her place on the witness stand, Craik Mansell faced the judge and jury with a quiet, resolute, but courteous assurance, that seemed at once to rob him of the character of a criminal, and set him on a par with the able and honourable men by whom he was surrounded. Yet his words were not those of a belied man, nor was his plea one of innocence.

"I ask pardon," he was saying, "for addressing the court directly; first of all, the pardon of my counsel, whose ability has never been so conspicuous as in this case, and whose just resentment, if he were less magnanimous and noble, I feel I am now about to incur."

Mr. Orcutt turned to him a look of surprise and severity, but the prisoner saw nothing but the face of the judge, and continued:

"I would have remained silent if the disposition which your Honour and the district attorney proposed to make of this last testimony were not in danger of reconsideration from the appeal which the witness has just made. I believe, with you, that her testimony should be disregarded. I intend, if I have the power, that it shall be disregarded."

The judge held up his hand, as if to warn the prisoner and was about to speak.

"I entreat that I may be heard," said Mansell, with the utmost calmness. "I beg the court not to imagine that I am about to imitate the witness in any sudden or ill-considered attempt at a confession. All I intend is that her self-accusation shall not derive strength or importance from any doubts of my guilt which may spring from the defence which has been interposed in my behalf."

Mr. Orcutt, who, from the moment the prisoner began to speak, had given evidences of a great indecision as to whether he should allow his client to continue or not, started at these words, so unmistakably pointing toward a demolishment of his whole case, and hurriedly rose. But a glance at Imogene seemed to awaken a new train of thought, and he as hurriedly reseated himself.

The prisoner, seeing he had nothing to fear from his counsel's interference, and meeting with no rebuke from the judge, went calmly on:

"Yesterday I felt differently in regard to this matter. If I could be saved from my fate by a defence seemingly so impregnable, I was willing to be so saved, but today I would be a coward and a disgrace to my sex if, in face of the generous action of this woman, I allowed a falsehood of whatever description to place her in peril, or to stand between me and the doom that probably awaits me. Sir," he continued, turning for the first time to Mr. Orcutt, with a gesture of profound respect, "you had been told that the path from Mrs. Clemmens' house to the bridge, and so on to Monteith Quarry Station, could not be traversed in ninety minutes, and you believed it. You were not wrong. It cannot be gone over in that time.

"But I now say to your Honour and to the jury, that the distance from my aunt's house to the Quarry Station can be made in that number of minutes if a way can be found to cross the river without going around by the bridge. I know," he proceeded, as a torrent of muttered exclamations rose on his ear, foremost among which was that of the much-discomfited Hickory, "that to many of you, to all of you, perhaps, all means for doing this seem to be lacking to the chance wayfarer, but if there were a lumberman here, he would tell you that the logs which are frequently floated down this stream to the station afford an easy means of passage to one accustomed to ride them, as I have been when a lad, during the year I spent in the Maine woods.

"At all events, it was upon a log that happened to be lodged against the banks, and which I pushed out into the stream by means of the 'pivy' or long spiked pole which I found lying in the grass at its side, that I crossed the river on that fatal day; and if the detective, who has already made such an effort to controvert the defence, will risk an attempt at this expedient for cutting short his route, I have no doubt he will be able to show you that a man can pass from Mrs. Clemmens' house to the station at Monteith Quarry, not only in ninety minutes, but in less, if the exigencies of the case seem to demand it. I did it."

And without a glance at Imogene, but with an air almost lofty in its pride and manly assertion, the prisoner sank back into his seat, and resumed once more his quiet and unshaken demeanour.

This last change in the kaleidoscope of events, that had been shifting before their eyes for the last half hour, was too much for the continued equanimity of a crowd already worked up into a state of feverish excitement. It had become apparent that by stripping away his defence, Mansell left himself naked to the law. In this excitement of the jury, consequent upon the self-accusation of Imogene, the prisoner's admission might prove directly fatal to him. He was on trial for this crime; public justice demanded blood for blood, and public excitement clamoured for a victim. It was dangerous to toy with a feeling but one degree removed from the sentiment of a mob. The jury might not stop to sympathize with the self-abnegation of these two persons willing to die for each other. They might say: "The way is clear as to the prisoner at least; he has confessed his defence is false; the guilty interpose false defences; we are acquit before God and men if we convict him out of his own mouth."

The crowd in the court-room was saying all this and more, each man to his neighbour. A clamour of voices next to impossible to suppress rose over the whole room, and not even the efforts of the officers of the court, exerted to their full power in the maintenance of order, could have hushed the storm, had not the spectators become mute with expectation at seeing Mr. Ferris and Mr. Orcutt, summoned by a sign from the judge, advance to the front of the bench and engage in an earnest conference with the court. A few minutes afterward the judge turned to the jury and announced that the disclosures of the morning demanded a careful consideration by the prosecution, that an adjournment was undoubtedly indispensable, and that the jury should refrain from any discussion of the case, even among themselves, until it was finally given them under the charge of the court. The jury expressed their concurrence by an almost unanimous gesture of assent, and the crier proclaimed an adjournment until the next day at ten o'clock.

Imogene, still sitting in the witness chair, saw the prisoner led forth by the jailer without being able to gather, in the whirl of the moment, any indication that her dreadful sacrifice—for she had made wreck of her life in the eyes of the world whether her confession were true or false—had accomplished anything save to drive the man she loved to the verge of that doom from which she had sought to deliver him.

35

Pro and Con

Shortly after the adjournment of court, Mr. Ferris summoned the two detectives to his office.

"We have a serious question before us to decide," said he. "Are we to go on with the prosecution or are we to stop? I should like to hear your views on the subject."

Hickory was, as usual, the first to speak.

"I should say, stop," he cried. "This fresh applicant for the honour of having slain the Widow Clemmens deserves a hearing at least."

"But," hurriedly interposed Byrd, "you don't give any credit to her story now, even if you did before the prisoner spoke? You know she did not commit the crime herself, whatever she may choose to declare in her anxiety to shield the prisoner. I hope, sir," he proceeded, glancing at the district attorney, "that *you* have no doubts as to Miss Dare's innocence?"

But Mr. Ferris, instead of answering, turned to Hickory and said:

"Miss Dare, in summoning you to confirm her statement, relied, I suppose, upon the fact of your having been told by Professor Darling's servant-maid that she—that is, Miss Dare—was gone from the observatory when the girl came for her on the morning of the murder?"

"Yes, sir."

"A strong corroborative fact, if true?"

"Yes, sir."

"But is it true? In the explanation which Miss Dare gave me last night of this affair, she uttered statements essentially different from those she made in court today. She then told me she *was* in the observatory when the girl came for her; that she was looking through a telescope which was behind a high rack filled with charts; and that——
Why do you start?"

"I didn't start," protested Hickory.

"I beg your pardon," returned Mr. Ferris.

"Well, then, if I did make such a fool of myself, it was because so far her story is plausible enough. She was in that very position when *I* visited the observatory, you remember, and she was so effectually concealed I didn't see her or know she was there, till I looked behind the rack."

"Very good!" interjected Mr. Ferris. "And that," he resumed, "she did not answer the girl or make known her presence, because at the moment the girl came in she was deeply interested in watching something that was going on in the town."

"In the town!" repeated Byrd.

"Yes; the telescope was lowered so as to command a view of the town, and she had taken advantage of its position (as she assured me last night) to consult the church clock."

"The church clock!" echoed Byrd once more. "And what time did she say it was?" breathlessly cried both detectives.

"Five minutes to twelve."

"A critical moment," ejaculated Byrd. "And what was it she saw going on in the town at that especial time?"

"I will tell you," returned the district attorney, impressively. "She said—and I believed her last night and so recalled her to the stand this morning—that she saw Craik Mansell fleeing toward the swamp from Mrs. Clemmens' dining-room door."

Both men looked up astonished.

"That was what she told me last night. Today she comes into court with this contradictory story of herself being the assailant and sole cause of Mrs. Clemmens' death."

"But all that is frenzy," protested Byrd. "She probably saw from your manner that the prisoner was lost if she gave this fact to the court, and her mind became disordered. She evidently loves this Mansell, and as for me, I pity her."

"So do I," assented the district attorney; "still——"

"Is it possible," Byrd interrupted, with feeling, as Mr. Ferris hesitated, "that you do doubt her innocence? After the acknowledgments made by the prisoner too?"

Rising from his seat, Mr. Ferris began slowly to pace the floor.

"I should like each of you," said he, without answering the appeal of Byrd, "to tell me why I should credit what she told me in conversation last night rather than what she uttered upon oath in the court-room today?"

"Let me speak first," rejoined Byrd, glancing at Hickory. And, rising also, he took his stand against the mantel-shelf where he could partially hide his face from those he addressed. "Sir," he proceeded, after a moment, "both Hickory and myself know Miss Dare to be innocent of this murder. A circumstance which we have hitherto kept secret, but which in justice to Miss Dare I think we are now bound to make known, has revealed to us the true criminal. Hickory, tell Mr. Ferris of the deception you practised upon Miss Dare in the hut."

The surprised, but secretly gratified, detective at once complied. *He* saw no reason for keeping quiet about that day's work. He told how, by means of a letter purporting to come from Mansell, he had decoyed Imogene to an interview in the hut, where, under the supposition she was addressing her lover, she had betrayed her conviction of his guilt, and advised him to confess it.

Mr. Ferris listened with surprise and great interest.

"That seems to settle the question," he said.

But it was now Hickory's turn to shake his head.

"I don't know," he remonstrated. "I have sometimes thought she saw through the trick and turned it to her own advantage."

"How to her own advantage?"

"To talk in such a way as to make us think Mansell was guilty."

"Stuff!" said Byrd; "that woman?"

"More unaccountable things have happened," was the weak reply of Hickory, his habitual state of suspicion leading him more than once into similar freaks of folly.

"Sir," said Mr. Byrd, confidingly, to the district attorney, "let us run over this matter from the beginning. Starting with the supposition that the explanation she gave you last night was the true one, let us see if the whole affair does not hang together in a way to satisfy us all as to where the real guilt lies. To begin, then, with the meeting in the woods——"

"Wait," interrupted Hickory; "there is going to be an argument here; so suppose you give your summary of events from the lady's standpoint, as that seems to be the one which interests you most."

"I was about to do so," Horace assured him, heedless of the rough fellow's good-natured taunt. "To make my point, it is absolutely necessary for us to transfer ourselves into her position and view matters as they gradually unfolded themselves before her eyes. First, then, as I have before suggested, let us consider the interview held by this man and woman in the woods. Miss Dare, as we must remember, was not engaged to Mr. Mansell; she only loved him. Their engagement, to say nothing of their marriage, depended upon his success in life—a success which to them seemed to hang solely upon the decision of Mrs. Clemmens concerning the small capital he desired her to advance him. But in the interview which Mansell had held with his aunt previous to the meeting between the lovers, Mrs. Clemmens had refused to loan him this money, and Miss Dare, whose feelings we are endeavouring to follow, found herself beset by the entreaties of a man who, having failed in his plans for future fortune, feared the loss of her love as well. What was the natural consequence? Rebellion against the widow's decision, of course,—a rebellion which she showed by the violent gesture which she made;—and then a determination to struggle for her happiness, as she evinced when, with most unhappy ambiguity of expression, she begged him to wait till the next day before pressing his ring upon her acceptance, because, as she said:

"'A night has been known to change the whole current of a person's affairs.'

"To her, engrossed with the one idea of making a personal effort to alter Mrs. Clemmens' mind on the money question, these words seemed innocent enough. But the look with which he received them, and the pause that followed, undoubtedly impressed her, and prepared the way for the interest she manifested when, upon looking through the telescope the next day, she saw him flying in that extraordinary way from his aunt's cottage toward the woods. Not that she then thought of his having committed a crime. As I trace her mental experience, she did not come to that conclusion till it was forced upon her. I do not know, and so cannot say, how she first heard of the murder——"

"She was told of it on the street-corner," interpolated Mr. Ferris.

"Ah, well, then, fresh from this vision of her lover hasting from his aunt's door to hide himself in the woods beyond, she came into town and was greeted by the announcement that Mrs. Clemmens had just been assaulted by a tramp in her own house. I know this was the way in which the news was told her, from the expression of her face as she entered the house. I was standing at the gate, you remember, when she came up, and her look had in it determination and horror, but no special fear. In fact, the words she dropped show the character of her thoughts at that time. She distinctly murmured in my hearing: 'No good can come of it, none.'

"As if her mind were dwelling upon the advantages which might

431

accrue to her lover from his aunt's death, and weighing them against the foul means by which that person's end had been hastened. Yet I will not say but she may have been influenced in the course which she took by some doubt or apprehension of her own. The fact that she came to the house at all, and, having come, insisted upon knowing all the details of the assault, seem to prove she was not without a desire to satisfy herself that suspicion rightfully attached itself to the tramp.

"But not until she saw her lover's ring on the floor (the ring which she had with her own hand dropped into the pocket of his coat the day before) and heard that the tramp had justified himself and was no longer considered the assailant, did her true fear and horror come. Then, indeed, all the past rose up before her, and, believing her lover guilty of this crime, she laid claim to the jewel as the first and only alternative that offered by which she might stand between him and the consequences of his guilt. Her subsequent agitation when the dying woman made use of the exclamation that indissolubly connected the crime with a ring, speaks for itself.

"Nor was her departure from the house any too hurried or involuntary, when you consider that the vengeance invoked by the widow, was, in Miss Dare's opinion, called down upon one to whom she had nearly plighted her troth. What is the next act in the drama? The scene in the Syracuse depot. Let me see if I cannot explain it. A woman who has once allowed herself to suspect the man she loves of a murderous deed, cannot rest till she has either convinced herself that her suspicions are false, or until she has gained such knowledge of the truth as makes her feel justified in her seeming treason. A woman of Miss Dare's generous nature especially. What does she do, then? With the courage that characterizes all her movements, she determines upon seeing him, and from his own lips, perhaps, win a confession of guilt or innocence. Conceiving that his flight was directed toward the Quarry Station, and thence to Buffalo, she embraced the first opportunity to follow him to the latter place.

"As I have told you, her ticket was bought for Buffalo, and to Buffalo she evidently intended going. But chancing to leave the cars at Syracuse, she was startled by encountering in the depot the very man with whom she had been associating thoughts of guilt. Shocked and thrown off her guard by the unexpectedness of the occurrence, she betrays her shrinking and her horror. 'Were you coming to see me?' she asks, and recoils, while he, conscious at the first glimpse of her face that his guilt has cost him her love, starts back also, uttering, in his shame and despair, words that were similar to hers, 'Were you coming to see me?'"

"Convinced without further speech, that her worst fears had foundation in fact, she turns back toward her home. The man she loved had committed a crime. That it was partly for her sake only increased her horror sevenfold. She felt as if she were guilty also, and, with sudden remorse, remembered how, instead of curbing his wrath the day before she had inflamed it by her words, if not given direction to it by her violent gestures. That fact, and the self-blame it produced, probably is the cause why her love did not vanish with her hopes. Though he was stained by guilt, she felt that it was the guilt of a strong nature driven from its bearings by the conjunction of two violent passions,— ambition and love; and she being passionate and ambitious herself, remained attached to the man while she recoiled from his crime.

"This being so, she could not, as a woman, wish him to suffer the penalty of his wickedness. Though lost to her, he must not be lost to the world. So, with the heroism natural to such a nature, she shut the secret up in her own breast, and faced her friends with courage, wishing, if not hoping, that the matter would remain the mystery it promised to be when she stood with us in the presence of the dying woman.

"But this was not to be, for suddenly, in the midst of her complacency, fell the startling announcement that another man—an innocent man—one, too, of her lover's own standing, if not hopes, had by a curious conjunction of events so laid himself open to the suspicion of the authorities as to be actually under arrest for this crime. 'Twas a danger she had not foreseen, a result for which she was not prepared.

"Startled and confounded she let a few days go by in struggle and indecision, possibly hoping, with the blind trust of her sex, that Mr. Hildreth would be released without her interference. But Mr. Hildreth was not released, and her anxiety was fast becoming unendurable, when that decoy letter sent by Hickory reached her, awakening in her breast for the first time, perhaps, the hope that Mansell would show himself to be a true man in this extremity, and by a public confession of guilt release her from the task of herself supplying the information which would lead to his commitment.

"And, perhaps, if it had really fallen to the lot of Mansell to confront her in the hut and listen to her words of adjuration and appeal, he might have been induced to consent to her wishes. But a detective sat there instead of her lover, and the poor woman lived to see the days go by without any movement being made to save Mr. Hildreth. At last—was it the result of the attempt made by this man upon his life?—she put an end to the struggle by acting for herself. Moved by a sense of duty, despite her love, she sent the letter which drew attention to her lover, and paved the way for that trial which has occupied our attention for so many days.

"But—mark this, for I think it is the only explanation of her whole conduct—the sense of justice that upheld her in this duty was mingled with the hope that her lover would escape conviction if he did not trial. The one fact which told the most against him—I allude to his flight from his aunt's door on the morning of the murder, as observed by her through the telescope—was as yet a secret in her own breast, and there she meant it to remain unless it was drawn forth by actual question. But it was not a fact likely to be made the subject of question, and drawing hope from that consideration, she prepared herself for the ordeal before her, determined, as I actually believe, to answer with truth all the inquiries that were put to her.

"But in an unexpected hour she learned that the detectives were anxious to know where she was during the time of the murder. She heard Hickory question Professor Darling's servant-girl, as to whether she was still in the observatory, and at once feared that her secret was discovered. Feared, I say—I conjecture this,—but what I do not conjecture is that with the fear, or doubt, or whatever emotion it was she cherished, a revelation came of the story she might tell if worst came to worst, and she found herself forced to declare what she saw when the clock stood at five minutes to twelve on that fatal day. Think of your conversation with the girl Roxana," he went on to Hickory, "and then think of that woman crouching behind the rack, listening to your words, and see if you can draw any other conclusion from the expression of her face than that of triumph at seeing a way to deliver her lover at the sacrifice of herself."

As Byrd waited for a reply, Hickory reluctantly acknowledged:

"Her look was a puzzler, that I will allow. She seemed glad——"

"There," cried Byrd, "you say she seemed glad; that is enough. Had she had the weight of this crime upon her conscience, she would have betrayed a different emotion from that. I pray you to consider the situation," he proceeded, turning to the district attorney, "for on it hangs your conviction of her innocence. First, imagine her guilty. What would her feelings be, as, hiding unseen in that secret corner, she hears a detective's voice inquiring where she was when the fatal blow was struck, and hears the answer given that she was not where she was supposed to be, but in the woods—the woods which she and everyone know lead so directly to Mrs. Clemmens' house, she could without the least difficulty hasten there and back in the hour she was observed to be missing? Would she show gladness or triumph even of a wild or delirious order?

"No, even Hickory cannot say she would. Now, on the contrary, see her as I do, crouched there in the very place before the telescope which she occupied when the girl came to the observatory before, but unseen now as she was unseen then, and watch the change that takes place in her countenance as she hears question and answer and realizes what confirmation she would receive from this girl if she ever thought fit to declare that she was not in the observatory when the girl sought her there on the day of the murder. That by this act she would bring execration if not death upon herself, she does not stop to consider. Her mind is full of what she can do for her lover, and she does not think of herself.

"But an enthusiasm like this is too frenzied to last. As time passes by and Craik Mansell is brought to trial, she begins to hope she may be spared this sacrifice. She therefore responds with perfect truth when summoned to the stand to give evidence, and does not waver, though question after question is asked her, whose answers cannot fail to show the state of her mind in regard to the prisoner's guilt. Life and honour are sweet even to one in her condition; and if her lover could be saved without falsehood it was her natural instinct to avoid it.

"And it looked as if he would be saved. A defence both skilful and ingenious had been advanced for him by his counsel—a defence which only the one fact so securely locked in her bosom could controvert. You can imagine, then, the horror and alarm which must have seized her when, in the very hour of hope, you approached her with the demand which proved that her confidence in her power to keep silence had been premature, and that the alternative was yet to be submitted to her of destroying her lover or sacrificing herself. Yet, because a great nature does not succumb without a struggle, she tried even now the effect of the truth upon you, and told you the one fact she considered so detrimental to the safety of her lover.

"The result was fatal. Though I cannot presume to say what passed between you, I can imagine how the change in your countenance warned her of the doom she would bring upon Mansell if she went into court with the same story she told you. Nor do I find it difficult to imagine how, in one of her history and temperament, a night of continuous brooding over this one topic should have culminated in the act which startled us so profoundly in the court-room this morning. Love, misery, devotion are not mere names to her, and the greatness which sustained her through the ordeal of denouncing her lover in order that an innocent man might be relieved from suspicion, was the same that made it possible for her to denounce herself that she might redeem the life she had thus deliberately jeopardized.

"That she did this with a certain calmness and dignity proves it to have been the result of design. A murderess forced by conscience into confession would not have gone into the details of her crime, but blurted out her guilt, and left the details to be drawn from her by question. Only the woman anxious to tell her story with the plausibility necessary to insure its belief would have planned and carried on her confession as she did.

"The action of the prisoner, in face of this proof of devotion, though it might have been foreseen by a man, was evidently not foreseen by her. To me, who watched her closely at the time, her face wore a strange look of mingled satisfaction and despair,—satisfaction in having awakened his manhood, despair at having failed in saving him. But it is not necessary for me to dilate on this point. If I have been successful in presenting before you the true condition of her mind during this struggle, you will see for yourself what her feelings must be now that her lover has himself confessed to a fact, to hide which she made the greatest sacrifice of which mortal is capable."

Mr. Ferris, who, during this lengthy and exhaustive harangue, had sat with brooding countenance and an anxious mien, roused himself as the other ceased, and glanced with a smile at Hickory.

"Well," said he, "that's good reasoning; now let us hear how you will go to work to demolish it."

The cleared brow, the playful tone of the district attorney showed the relieved state of his mind. Byrd's arguments had evidently convinced him of the innocence of Imogene Dare.

Hickory, seeing it, shook his head with a gloomy air.

"Sir," said he, "I can't demolish it. If I could tell why Mansell fled from Widow Clemmens' house at five minutes to twelve I might be able to do so, but that fact stumps me. It is an act consistent with guilt. It may be consistent with innocence, but, as we don't know all the facts, we can't say so. But this I do know, that my convictions with regard to that man have undergone a change. I now as firmly believe in his innocence as I once did in his guilt."

"What has produced the change?" asked Mr. Ferris.

"Well," said Hickory, "it all lies in this. From the day I heard Miss Dare accuse him so confidently in the hut, I believed him guilty; from the moment he withdrew his defence, I believed him innocent."

Mr. Ferris and Mr. Byrd looked at him astonished. He at once brought down his fist in vigorous assertion on the table.

"I tell you," said he, "that Craik Mansell is innocent. The truth is, he believes Miss Dare guilty, and so stands his trial, hoping to save her."

"And be hung for her crime?" asked Mr. Ferris.

"No; he thinks his innocence will save him, in spite of the evidence on which we got him indicted."

But the district attorney protested at this.

"That can't be," said he; "Mansell has withdrawn the only defence he had."

"On the contrary," asserted Hickory, "that very thing only proves my theory true. He is still determined to save Miss Dare by everything short of a confession of his own guilt. He won't lie. That man is innocent."

"And Miss Dare is guilty?" said Byrd.

"Shall I make it clear to you in the way it has become clear to Mr. Mansell?"

As Byrd only answered by a toss of his head, Hickory put his elbows on the table, and checking off every sentence with the forefinger of his right hand, which he pointed at Mr. Ferris' shirt-stud, as if to instil from its point conviction into that gentleman's bosom, he proceeded with the utmost composure as follows:

"To commence, then, with the scene in the woods. He meets her. She is as angry at his aunt as he is. What does she do? She strikes the tree with her hand, and tells him to wait till tomorrow, since a night has been known to change the whole current of a person's affairs. Now tell me what does that mean? Murder? If so, she was the one to originate it. He can't forget that. It has stamped itself upon Mansell's memory, and when, after the assassination of Mrs. Clemmens, he recalls those words, he is convinced that she has slain Mrs. Clemmens to help him."

"But, Mr. Hickory," objected Mr. Ferris, "this assumes that Mr. Mansell is innocent, whereas we have exceedingly cogent proof that he is the guilty party. There is the circumstance of his leaving Widow

Clemmens' house at five minutes to twelve."

To which Hickory, with a twinkle in his eye, replied:

"I won't discuss that; it hasn't been proved, you know. Miss Dare told you she saw him do this, but she wouldn't swear to it. Nothing is to be taken for granted against my man."

"Then you think Miss Dare spoke falsely?"

"I don't say that. I believe that whatever he did could be explained if we knew as much about it as he does. But I'm not called upon to explain anything which has not appeared in the evidence against him."

"Well, then, we'll take the evidence. There is his ring, found on the scene of murder."

"Exactly," rejoined Hickory. "Dropped there, as he must suppose, by Miss Dare, because he didn't know she had secretly restored it to his pocket."

Mr. Ferris smiled.

"You don't see the force of the evidence," said he. "As she *had* restored it to his pocket, he must have been the one to drop it there."

"I am willing to admit he dropped it there, not that he killed Mrs. Clemmens. I am now speaking of his suspicions as to the assassin. When the betrothal ring was found there, he suspects Miss Dare of the crime, and nothing has occurred to change his suspicions."

"But," said the district attorney, "how does your client, Mr. Mansell, get over this difficulty; that Miss Dare, who has committed a murder to put five thousand dollars into his pocket, immediately afterward turns round and accuses him of the crime—nay more, furnishes evidence against him!"

"You can't expect the same consistency from a woman as from a man. They can nerve themselves up one moment to any deed of desperation, and take every pains the next to conceal it by a lie."

"Men will do the same; then why not Mansell?"

"I am showing you why I know that Mansell believes Miss Dare guilty of a murder. To continue, then. What does he do when he hears that his aunt has been murdered? He scratches out the face of Miss Dare in a photograph; he ties up her letters with a black ribbon as if she were dead and gone to him. Then the scene in the Syracuse depot! The rule of three works both ways, Mr. Byrd, and if she left her home to solve *her* doubts, what shall be said of him? The recoil, too—was it less on his part than hers? And, if she had cause to gather guilt from his manner, had he not as much cause to gather it from hers? If his mind was full of suspicion when he met her, it became conviction before he left; and, bearing that fact in your mind, watch how he henceforth conducted himself. He does not come to Sibley; the woman he fears to encounter is there.

"He hears of Mr. Hildreth's arrest, reads of the discoveries which led to it, and keeps silent. So would any other man have done in his place, at least till he saw whether this arrest was likely to end in trial. But he cannot forget he had been in Sibley on the fatal day, or that there may be someone who saw his interview with Miss Dare. When Byrd comes to him, therefore, and tells him he is wanted in Sibley, his first question is, 'Am I wanted as a witness?' and, even you have acknowledged, Mr. Ferris, that he seemed surprised to find himself accused of the crime. But, accused, he takes his course and keeps to it. Brought to trial, he remembers the curious way in which he crossed the river, and thus cut short the road to the station; and, seeing in it great opportunities for a successful defence, chooses Mr. Orcutt for his counsel, and trusts the secret to him.

"The trial goes on; acquittal seems certain, when suddenly she is recalled to the stand, and he hears words which make him think she is going to betray him by some falsehood, when, instead of following the lead of the prosecution, she launches into a personal confession. What does he do? Why, rise and hold up his hand in a command for her to stop. But she does not heed, and the rest follows as a matter of course. The life she throws away he will not accept. He is innocent, but his defence is false! He says so, and leaves the jury to decide on the verdict. There can be no doubt," Hickory finally concluded, "that some of these circumstances are consistent only with his belief that Miss Dare is a murderess: such, for instance, as his scratching out her face in the picture.

"Others favour the theory in a less degree, but this is what I want to impress upon both your minds," he declared, turning first to Mr. Ferris and then to Mr. Byrd: "*If any fact, no matter how slight, leads us to the conviction that Craik Mansell, at any time after the murder, entertained the belief that Miss Dare committed it, his innocence follows as a matter of course. For the guilty could never entertain a belief in the guilt of any other person.*"

"Yes," said Mr. Ferris, "I admit that, but we have got to see into Mr. Mansell's mind before we can tell what his belief really was."

"No," was Hickory's reply; "let us look at his actions. I say that that defaced picture is conclusive. One day he loves that woman and wants her to marry him; the next, he defaces her picture. Why? She had not offended him. Not a word, not a line, passes between them to cause him to commit this act. But he does hear of his aunt's murder, and he does recall her sinister promise: 'Wait; there is no telling what a day will bring forth.' I say that no other cause for his act is shown except his conviction that she is a murderess."

"But," persisted Mr. Ferris, "his leaving the house, as he acknowledges he did, by this unfrequented and circuitous road?"

"I have said before that I cannot explain his presence there, or his flight. All I am now called upon to show is, some fact inconsistent with anything except a belief in this young woman's guilt. I claim I have shown it, and, as you admit, Mr. Ferris, if I show *that*, he is innocent."

"Yes," said Byrd, speaking for the first time; "but we have heard of people manufacturing evidence in their own behalf."

"Come, Byrd," replied Hickory, "you don't seriously mean to attack my position with that suggestion. How could a man dream of manufacturing evidence of such a character? A murderer manufactures evidence to throw suspicion on other people. No fool could suppose that scratching out the face of a girl in a photograph and locking it up in his own desk, would tend to bring her to the scaffold, or save him from it."

"And, yet," rejoined Byrd, "that very act acquits him in your eyes. All that is necessary is to give him credit for being smart enough to foresee that it would have such a tendency in the eyes of any person who discovered the picture."

"Then," said Hickory, "he would also have to foresee that she would accuse herself of murder when he was on trial for it, and that he would thereupon withdraw his defence. Byrd, you are foreseeing too much. My friend Mansell possesses no such power of looking into the future as that."

"Your friend Mansell!" repeated Mr. Ferris, with a smile. "If you were on his jury, I suppose your bias in his favour would lead you to acquit him of this crime?"

"I should declare him 'Not guilty,' and stick to it, if I had to be locked up for a year."

Mr. Ferris sank into an attitude of profound thought. Horace Byrd, impressed by this, looked at him anxiously.

"Have your convictions been shaken by Hickory's ingenious theory?" he ventured to inquire at last.

Mr. Ferris abstractedly replied:

"This is no time for me to state my convictions. It is enough that you comprehend my perplexity." And, relapsing into his former condition, he remained for a moment wrapped in silence, then he said: "Byrd, how comes it that the humpback who excited so much attention on the day of the murder was never found?"

Byrd, astonished, surveyed the district attorney with a doubtful look that gradually changed into one of quiet satisfaction as he realized the significance of this recurrence to old theories and suspicions. His answer, however, was slightly embarrassed in tone, though frank enough to remind one of Hickory's blunt-spoken admissions.

"Well," said he, "I suppose the main reason is that I made no attempt to find him."

"Do you think that you were wise in that, Mr. Byrd?" inquired Mr. Ferris, with some severity.

Horace laughed.

"I can find him for you today, if you want him," he declared.

"You can? You know him, then?"

"Very well. Mr. Ferris," he courteously remarked, "I perhaps should have explained to you at the time, that I recognized this person and knew him to be an honest man; but the habits of secrecy in our profession are so fostered by the lives we lead, that we sometimes hold our tongue when it would be better for us to speak. The humpback who talked with us on the court-house steps the morning Mrs. Clemmens was murdered, was not what he seemed, sir. He was a detective; a detective in disguise; a man with whom I never presume to meddle—in other words, our famous Mr. Gryce."

"Gryce!—that man!" exclaimed Mr. Ferris, astounded.

"Yes, sir. He was in disguise, probably for some purpose of his own, but I knew his eye. Gryce's eye isn't to be mistaken by anyone who has much to do with him."

"And that famous detective was actually on the spot at the time this murder was discovered, and you let him go without warning me of his presence?"

"Sir," returned Mr. Byrd, "neither you nor I nor anyone at that time could foresee what a serious and complicated case this was going to be. Besides, he did not linger in this vicinity, but took the cars only a few minutes after he parted from us. I did not think he wanted to be dragged into this affair unless it was necessary. He had important matters of his own to look after. However, if suspicion had continued to follow him, I should have notified him of the fact, and let him speak

441

for himself. But it vanished so quickly in the light of other developments, I just let the matter drop."

The impatient frown with which Mr. Ferris received this acknowledgment showed he was not pleased.

"I think you made a mistake," said he. Then, after a minute's
thought, added: "You have seen Gryce since?"

"Yes, sir; several times."

"And he acknowledged himself to have been the humpback?"

"Yes, sir."

"You must have had some conversation with him, then, about this
murder? He was too nearly concerned in it not to take some interest
in the affair?"

"Yes, sir; Gryce takes an interest in all murder cases."

"Well, then, what did he have to say about this one? He gave an
opinion, I suppose?"

"No, sir. Gryce never gives an opinion without study, and we detectives have no time to study up an affair not our own. If you want
to know what Gryce thinks about a crime, you have got to put the
case into his hands."

Mr. Ferris paused and seemed to ruminate. Seeing this, Mr. Byrd
flushed and cast a side glance at Hickory, who returned him an expressive shrug.

"Mr. Ferris," ventured the former, "if you wish to consult with Mr.
Gryce on this matter, do not hesitate because of us. Both Hickory
and myself acknowledge we are more or less baffled by this case, and
Gryce's judgement is a good thing to have in a perplexity."

"You think so?" queried the district attorney.

"I do," said Byrd.

Mr. Ferris glanced at Hickory.

"Oh, have the old man here if you want him," was that detective's
blunt reply. "I have nothing to say against your getting all the light you
can on this affair."

"Very good," returned Mr. Ferris. "You may give me his address
before you go."

"His address for tonight is Utica," observed Byrd. "He could be
here before morning, if you wanted him."

"I am in no such hurry as that," returned Mr. Ferris, and he sank
again into thought.

The detectives took advantage of his abstraction to utter a few
private condolences in each other's ears.

"So it seems we are to be laid on the shelf," whispered Hickory.

"Yes, for which let us be thankful," answered Byrd.

"Why? Are you getting tired of the affair?"

"Yes."

A humorous twinkle shone for a minute in Hickory's eye.

"Pooh!" said he, "it's just getting interesting."

"Opinions differ," quoth Byrd.

"Not much," retorted Hickory.

Something in the way he said this made Byrd look at him more intently. He instantly changed his tone.

"Old fellow," said he, "you don't believe Miss Dare committed this crime any more than I do."

A sly twinkle answered him from the detective's half-shut eye.

"All that talk of having seen through your disguise in the hut is just nonsense on your part to cover up your real notion about it. What is that notion, Hickory? Come, out with it; let us understand each other thoroughly at last."

"Do I understand you?"

"You shall, when you tell me just what your convictions are in this matter."

"Well, then," replied Hickory, with a short glance at Mr. Ferris, "I believe (it's hard as pulling teeth to own it) that neither of them did it: that she thought him guilty and he thought her so, but that in reality the crime lies at the door of some third party totally disconnected with either of them."

"Such as Gouverneur Hildreth?" whispered Byrd.

"Such—as—Gouverneur Hildreth," drawled Hickory.

The two detectives eyed each other, smiled, and turned with relieved countenances toward the district attorney. He was looking at them with great earnestness.

"That is your joint opinion?" he remarked.

"It is mine," cried Hickory, bringing his fist down on the table with a vim that made every individual article on it jump.

"It is and it is not mine," acquiesced Byrd, as the eye of Mr. Ferris turned in his direction. "Mr. Mansell may be innocent—indeed, after hearing Hickory's explanation of his conduct, I am ready to believe he is—but to say that Gouverneur Hildreth is guilty comes hard to me after the long struggle I have maintained in favour of his innocence. Yet, what other conclusion remains after an impartial view of the subject? None. Then why should I shrink from acknowledging I was at fault, or hesitate to admit a defeat where so many causes combined to mislead me?"

"Which means you agree with Hickory?" ventured the district attorney.

Mr. Byrd slowly bowed.

Mr. Ferris continued for a moment looking alternately from one to the other; then he observed:

"When two such men unite in an opinion, it is at least worthy of consideration." And, rising, he took on an aspect of sudden determination. "Whatever may be the truth in regard to this matter," said he, "one duty is clear. Miss Dare, as you inform me, has been—with but little idea of the consequences, I am sure—allowed to remain under the impression that the interview which she held in the hut was with her lover. As her belief in the prisoner's guilt doubtless rests upon the admissions which were at that time made in her hearing, it is palpable that a grave injustice has been done both to her and to him by leaving this mistake of hers uncorrected. I therefore consider it due to Miss Dare, as well as to the prisoner, to undeceive her on this score before another hour has passed over our heads. I must therefore request you, Mr. Byrd, to bring the lady here. You will find her still in the court-house, I think, as she requested leave to remain in the room below till the crowd had left the streets."

Mr. Byrd, who, in the new light which had been thrown on the affair by his own and Hickory's suppositions, could not but see the justice of this, rose with alacrity to obey.

"I will bring her if she is in the building," he declared, hurriedly leaving the room.

"And if she is not," Mr. Ferris remarked, with a glance at the consciously rebuked Hickory, "we shall have to follow her to her home, that is all. I am determined to see this woman's mind cleared of all misapprehensions before I take another step in the way of my duty.

36

A Mistake Rectified

If Mr. Ferris, in seeking this interview with Miss Dare, had been influenced by any hope of finding her in an unsettled and hesitating state of mind, he was effectually undeceived, when, after a few minutes' absence, Mr. Byrd returned with her to his presence. Though her physical strength was nearly exhausted, and she looked quite pale and worn, there was a steady gleam in her eye, which spoke of an unshaken purpose.

Seeing it, and noting the forced humility with which she awaited his bidding at the threshold, the district attorney, for the first time perhaps, realized the power of this great, if perverted, nature, and advancing with real kindness to the door, he greeted her with as much deference as he ever showed to ladies, and gravely pushed toward her a chair.

She did not take it. On the contrary, she drew back a step, and looked at him in some doubt, but a sudden glimpse of Hickory's sturdy figure in the corner seemed to reassure her, and merely stopping to acknowledge Mr. Ferris' courtesy by a bow, she glided forward and took her stand by the chair he had provided.

A short and, on his part, somewhat embarrassing pause followed. It was broken by her.

"You sent for me," she suggested. "You perhaps want some explanation of my conduct, or some assurance that the confession I made before the court today was true?"

If Mr. Ferris had needed any further proof than he had already received that Imogene Dare, in presenting herself before the world as a criminal, had been actuated by a spirit of devotion to the prisoner, he would have found it in the fervour and unconscious dignity with which she uttered these few words. But he needed no such proof.

445

Giving her, therefore, a look full of grave significance, he replied:

"No, Miss Dare. After my experience of the ease with which you can contradict yourself in matters of the most serious import, you will pardon me if I say that the truth or falsehood of your words must be arrived at by some other means than any you yourself can offer. My business with you at this time is of an entirely different nature. Instead of listening to further confessions from you, it has become my duty to offer one myself. Not on my own behalf," he made haste to explain, as she looked up, startled, "but on account of these men, who, in their anxiety to find out who murdered Mrs. Clemmens, made use of means and resorted to deceptions which, if their superiors had been consulted, would not have been countenanced for a moment."

"I do not understand," she murmured, looking at the two detectives with a wonder that suddenly merged into alarm as she noticed the embarrassment of the one and the decided discomfiture of the other.

Mr. Ferris at once resumed:

"In the weeks that have elapsed since the commission of this crime, it has been my lot to subject you to much mental misery, Miss Dare. Provided by yourself with a possible clue to the murder, I have probed the matter with an unsparing hand. Heedless of the pain I was inflicting, or the desperation to which I was driving you, I asked you questions and pressed you for facts as long as there seemed questions to ask or facts to be gained. My duty and the claims of my position demanded this, and for it I can make no excuse, notwithstanding the unhappy results that have ensued. But, Miss Dare, whatever anxiety I may have shown in procuring the conviction of a man I believed to be a criminal, I have never wished to win my case at the expense of justice and right; and had I been told before you came to the stand that you had been made the victim of a deception calculated to influence your judgement, I should have hastened to set you right with the same anxiety as I do now."

"Sir—sir——" she began.

But Mr. Ferris would not listen.

"Miss Dare," he proceeded with all the gravity of conviction, "you have uttered a deliberate perjury in the court-room today. You said that you alone were responsible for the murder of Mrs. Clemmens, whereas you not only did not commit the crime yourself but were not even an accessory to it. Wait!" he commanded, as she flashed upon him a look full of denial, "I would rather you did not speak. The motive for this calumny you uttered upon yourself lies in a fact which may be modified by what I have to reveal. Hear me, then, before you stain yourself still further by a falsehood you will not only be unable to maintain, but which you may no longer see reason for insisting upon. Hickory, turn around so Miss Dare can see your face.

"Miss Dare, when you saw fit to call upon this man to upbear you in the extraordinary statements you made today, did you realize that in doing this you appealed to the one person best qualified to prove the falsehood of what you had said? I see you did not; yet it is so. He if no other can testify that a few weeks ago, no idea of taking this crime upon your own shoulders had ever crossed your mind; that, on the contrary, your whole heart was filled with sorrow for the supposed guilt of another, and plans for inducing that other to make a confession of his guilt before the world."

"This man!" was her startled exclamation. "It is not possible; I do not know him; he does not know me. I never talked with him but once in my life, and that was to say words I am not only willing but anxious for him to repeat."

"Miss Dare," the district attorney pursued, "when you say this you show how completely you have been deceived. The conversation to which you allude is not the only one which has passed between you two. Though you did not know it, you held a talk with this man at a time in which you so completely discovered the secrets of your heart, you can never hope to deceive us or the world by any story of personal guilt which you may see fit to manufacture."

"I reveal my heart to this man!" she repeated, in a maze of doubt and terror that left her almost unable to stand. "You are playing with my misery, Mr. Ferris."

The district attorney took a different tone.

"Miss Dare," he asked, "do you remember a certain interview you held with a gentleman in the hut back of Mrs. Clemmens' house, a short time after the murder?"

"Did this man overhear my words that day?" she murmured, reaching out her hand to steady herself by the back of the chair near which she was standing.

"Your words that day were addressed to this man."

"To him!" she repeated, staggering back.

"Yes, to him, disguised as Craik Mansell. With an unjustifiable zeal to know the truth, he had taken this plan for surprising your secret thoughts, and he succeeded, Miss Dare, remember that, even if he did you and your lover the cruel wrong of leaving you undisturbed in the impression that Mr. Mansell had admitted his guilt in your presence."

But Imogene, throwing out her hands, cried impetuously:

"It is not so; you are mocking me. This man never could deceive me like that!"

But even as she spoke she recoiled, for Hickory, with ready art, had thrown his arms and head forward on the table before which he sat, in the attitude and with much the same appearance he had preserved on the day she had come upon him in the hut. Though he had no assistance from disguise and all the accessories were lacking which had helped forward the illusion on the former occasion, there was still a sufficient resemblance between this bowed figure and the one that had so impressed itself upon her memory as that of her wretched and remorseful lover, that she stood rooted to the ground in her surprise and dismay.

"You see how it was done, do you not?" inquired Mr. Ferris. Then, as he saw she did not heed, added: "I hope you remember what passed between you two on that day?"

As if struck by a thought which altered the whole atmosphere of her hopes and feelings, she took a step forward with a power and vigour that recalled to mind the Imogene of old.

"Sir," she exclaimed, "let that man turn around and face me!"

Hickory at once rose.

"Tell me," she demanded, surveying him with a look it took all his well-known hardihood to sustain unmoved, "was it all false—all a trick from the beginning to the end? I received a letter—was that written by your hand too? Are you capable of forgery as well as of other deceptions?"

The detective, who knew no other way to escape from his embarrassment, uttered a short laugh. But finding a reply was expected of him, answered with well-simulated indifference:

"No, only the address on the envelope was mine; the letter was one which Mr. Mansell had written but never sent. I found it in his wastepaper basket in Buffalo."

"Ah! and you could make use of that?"

"I know it was a mean trick," he acknowledged, dropping his eyes from her face. "But things do look different when you are in the thick of 'em than when you take a stand and observe them from the outside. I—I was ashamed of it long ago, Miss Dare"—this was a lie; Hickory never was really ashamed of it—"and would have told you about it, but I thought 'mum' was the word after a scene like that."

She did not seem to hear him.

"Then Mr. Mansell did not send me the letter inviting me to meet him in the hut on a certain day, some few weeks after Mrs. Clemmens was murdered?"

"No."

"Nor know that such a letter had been sent?"

"No."

"Nor come, as I supposed he did, to Sibley? nor admit what I supposed he admitted in my hearing? nor listen, as I supposed he did, to the insinuations I made use of in the hut?"

"No."

Imbued with sudden purpose and energy, she turned upon the district attorney.

"Oh, what a revelation to come to me now!" she murmured.

Mr. Ferris bowed.

"You are right," he assented; "it should have come to you before. But I can only repeat what I have previously said, that if I had known of this deception myself, you would have been notified of it previous to going upon the stand. For your belief in the prisoner's guilt has necessarily had its effect upon the jury, and I cannot but see how much that belief must have been strengthened, if it was not actually induced, by the interview which we have just been considering."

Her eyes took on fresh light; she looked at Mr. Ferris as if she would read his soul.

"Can it be possible——" she breathed, but stopped as suddenly as she began. The district attorney was not the man from whom she could hope to obtain any opinion in reference to the prisoner's innocence.

Mr. Ferris, noting her hesitation and understanding it too, perhaps, moved toward her with a certain kindly dignity, saying:

"I should be glad to utter words that would give you some comfort, Miss Dare, but in the present state of affairs I do not feel as if I could go farther than bid you trust in the justice and wisdom of those who have this matter in charge. As for your own wretched and uncalled-for action in court today, it was a madness which I hope will be speedily forgotten, or, if not forgotten, laid to a despair almost too heavy for mortal strength to endure."

"Thank you," she murmured; but her look, the poise of her head, the colour that quivered through the pallor of her cheek, showed she was not thinking of herself. Doubt, the first which had visited her since she became convinced that Craik Mansell was the destroyer of his aunt's life, had cast a momentary gleam over her thoughts, and she was conscious of but one wish, and that was to understand the feelings of the men before her.

But she soon saw the hopelessness of this, and, sinking back again into her old distress as she realized how much reason she still had for believing Craik Mansell guilty, she threw a hurried look toward the door as if anxious to escape from the eyes and ears of men interested, as she knew, in gleaning her every thought and sounding her every impulse.

Mr. Ferris at once comprehended her intention, and courteously advanced.

"Do you wish to return home?" he asked.

"If a carriage can be obtained."

"There can be no difficulty about that," he answered; and he gave Hickory a look, and whispered a word to Mr. Byrd, that sent them both speedily from the room.

When he was left alone with her, he said:

"Before you leave my presence, Miss Dare, I wish to urge upon you the necessity of patience. Any sudden or violent act on your part now would result in no good, and lead to much evil. Let me, then, pray you to remain quiet in your home, confident that Mr. Orcutt and myself will do all in our power to insure justice and make the truth evident."

She bowed, but did not speak; while her impatient eye, resting feverishly on the door, told of her anxiety to depart.

"She will need watching," commented Mr. Ferris to himself, and he, too, waited impatiently for the detectives' return. When they came in he gave Imogene to their charge, but the look he cast Byrd contained a hint which led that gentleman to take his hat when he went below to put Miss Dare into her carriage.

37

Under the Great Tree

Imogene went to her home. Confused, disordered, the prey of a thousand hopes and a thousand fears, she sought for solitude and found it within the four walls of the small room which was now her only refuge.

The two detectives who had followed her to the house—the one in the carriage, the other on foot—met, as the street-door closed upon her retreating form, and consulted together as to their future course.

"Mr. Ferris thinks we ought to keep watch over the house, to make sure she does not leave it again," announced Mr. Byrd.

"Does he? Well, then, I am the man for that job," quoth Hickory. "I was on this very same beat last night."

"Good reason why you should rest and give me a turn at the business," declared the other.

"Do you want it?"

"I am willing to take it," said Byrd.

"Well, then, after nine o'clock you shall."

"Why after nine?"

"Because if she's bent on skylarking, she'll leave the house before then," laughed the other.

"And you want to be here if she goes out?"

"Well, yes, *rather!*"

They compromised matters by both remaining, Byrd within view of the house and Hickory on a corner within hail. Neither expected much from this effort at surveillance, there seeming to be no good reason why she should venture forth into the streets again that night. But the watchfulness of the true detective mind is unceasing.

Several hours passed. The peace of evening had come at last to the troubled town. In the streets, especially, its gentle influence was felt,

451

and regions which had seethed all day with a restless and impatient throng were fast settling into their usual quiet and solitary condition. A new moon hung in the west, and to Mr. Byrd, pacing the walk in front of Imogene's door, it seemed as if he had never seen the town look more lovely or less like the abode of violence and crime. All was so quiet, especially in the house opposite him, he was fast becoming convinced that further precautions were needless, and that Imogene had no intention of stirring abroad again, when the window where her light burned suddenly became dark, and he perceived the street door cautiously open, and her tall, veiled figure emerge and pass rapidly up the street. Merely stopping to give the signal to Hickory, he hastened after her with rapid but cautious steps.

She went like one bound on no uncertain errand. Though many of the walks were heavily shaded, and the light of the lamps was not brilliant, she speeded on from corner to corner, threading the business streets with rapidity, and emerging upon the large and handsome avenue that led up toward the eastern district of the town before Hickory could overtake Byrd, and find sufficient breath to ask:

"Where is she bound for? Who lives up this way?"

"I don't know," answered Byrd, lowering his voice in the fear of startling her into a knowledge of their presence. "It may be she is going to Miss Tremaine's; the High School is somewhere in this direction."

But even as they spoke, the gliding figure before them turned into another street, and before they knew it, they were on the car-track leading out to Somerset Park.

"Ha! I know now," whispered Hickory. "It is Orcutt she is after." And pressing the arm of Byrd in his enthusiasm, he speeded after her with renewed zeal.

Byrd, seeing no reason to dispute a fact that was every moment becoming more evident, hurried forward also, and after a long and breathless walk—for she seemed to be urged onward by flying feet— they found themselves within sight of the grand old trees that guarded the entrance to the lawyer's somewhat spacious grounds.

"What are we going to do now?" asked Byrd, stopping, as they heard the gate click behind her.

"Wait and watch," said Hickory. "She has not led us this wild-goose chase for nothing." And leaping the hedge, he began creeping up toward the house, leaving his companion to follow or not, as he saw fit.

Meantime Imogene had passed up the walk and paused before the front door. But a single look at it seemed to satisfy her, for, moving hurriedly away, she flitted around the corner of the house and stopped just before the long windows whose brightly illumined sashes proclaimed that the master of the house was still in his library.

She seemed to feel relieved at this sight. Pausing, she leaned against the frame of a trellis-work nearby to gather up her courage or regain her breath before proceeding to make her presence known to the lawyer. As she thus leaned, the peal of the church clock was heard, striking the hour of nine. She started, possibly at finding it so late, and bending forward, looked at the windows before her with an anxious eye that soon caught sight of a small opening left by the curtains having been drawn together by a too hasty or a too careless hand, and recognizing the opportunity it afforded for a glimpse into the room before her, stepped with a light tread upon the *piazza* and quietly peered within.

The sight she saw never left her memory.

Seated before a deadened fire, she beheld Mr. Orcutt. He was neither writing nor reading, nor, in the true sense of the word, thinking. The papers he had evidently taken from his desk, lay at his side undisturbed, and from one end of the room to the other, solitude, suffering, and despair seemed to fill the atmosphere and weigh upon its dreary occupant, till the single lamp which shone beside him burned dimmer and dimmer, like a life going out or a purpose vanishing in the gloom of a stealthily approaching destiny.

Imogene, who had come to this place thus secretly and at this late hour of the day with the sole intent of procuring the advice of this man concerning the deception which had been practised upon her before the trial, felt her heart die within her as she surveyed this rigid figure and realized all it implied. Though his position was such she could not see his face, there was that in his attitude which bespoke hopelessness and an utter weariness of life, and as ash after ash fell from the grate, she imagined how the gloom deepened on the brow which till this hour had confronted the world with such undeviating courage and confidence.

It was therefore a powerful shock to her when, in another moment, he looked up, and, without moving his body, turned his head slowly around in such a way as to afford her a glimpse of his face. For, in all her memory of it—and she had seen it distorted by many and various emotions during the last few weeks—she had never beheld it wear such a look as now. It gave her a new idea of the man; it filled her with dismay, and sent the life-blood from her cheeks. It fascinated her, as the glimpse of any evil thing fascinates, and held her spell-bound long after he had turned back again to his silent contemplation of the fire and its ever-drifting ashes. It was as if a veil had been rent before her eyes, disclosing to her a living soul writhing in secret struggle with its own worst passions; and horrified at the revelation, more than horrified at the remembrance that it was her own action of the morning which had occasioned this change in one she had long reverenced, if not loved, she sank helplessly upon her knees and pressed her face to the window in a prayer for courage to sustain this new woe and latest, if not heaviest, disappointment.

It came while she was kneeling—came in the breath of the cold night wind, perhaps; for, rising up, she turned her forehead gratefully to the breeze, and drew in long draughts of it before she lifted her hand and knocked upon the window.

The sharp, shrill sound made by her fingers on the pane reassured her as much as it startled him. Gathering up her long cloak, which had fallen apart in her last hurried movement, she waited with growing self-possession for his appearance at the window.

He came almost immediately—came with his usual hasty step and with much of his usual expression on his well-disciplined features. Flinging aside the curtains, he cried impatiently: "Who is there?" But at sight of the tall figure of Imogene standing upright and firm on the *piazza* without, he drew back with a gesture of dismay, which was almost forbidding in its character.

She saw it, but did not pause. Pushing up the window, she stepped into the room; then, as he did not offer to help her, turned and shut the window behind her and carefully arranged the curtains. He meantime stood watching her with eyes in whose fierce light burned equal love and equal anger.

When all was completed, she faced him. Instantly a cry broke from his lips:

"You here!" he exclaimed, as if her presence were more than he could meet or stand. But in another moment the forlornness of her position seemed to strike him, and he advanced toward her, saying in a voice husky with passion: "Wretched woman, what have you done? Was it not enough that for weeks, months now, you have played with my love and misery as with toys, that you should rise up at the last minute and crush me before the whole world with a story, mad as it is false, of yourself being a criminal and the destroyer of the woman for whose death your miserable lover is being tried? Had you no consideration, no pity, if not for yourself, ruined by this day's work, for me, who have sacrificed everything, done everything the most devoted man or lawyer could do to save this fellow and win you for my wife?"

"Sir," said she, meeting the burning anger of his look with the coldness of a set despair, as if in the doubt awakened by his changed demeanour she sought to probe his mind for its hidden secret, "I did what any other woman would have done in my place. When we are pushed to the wall we tell the truth."

"The truth!" Was that his laugh that rang startlingly through the room? "The truth! You told the truth! Imogene, Imogene, is any such farce necessary with me?"

Her lips, which had opened, closed again, and she did not answer for a moment; then she asked:

"How do you know that what I said was not the truth?"

"How do I know?" He paused as if to get his breath. "How do I know?" he repeated, calling up all his self-control to sustain her gaze unmoved. "Do you think I have lost my reason, Imogene, that you put me such a question as that? How do I know you are innocent? Recall your own words and acts since the day we met at Mrs. Clemmens' house, and tell me how it would be possible for me to think anything else of you?"

But her purpose did not relax, neither did she falter as she returned:

"Mr. Orcutt, will you tell me what has ever been said by me or what you have ever known me to do that would make it certain I did not commit this crime myself?"

His indignation was too much for his courtesy.

"Imogene," he commanded, "be silent! I will not listen to any further arguments of this sort. Isn't it enough that you have destroyed my happiness, that you should seek to sport with my good-sense? I say you are innocent as a babe unborn, not only of the crime itself but of any complicity in it. Every word you have spoken, every action you have taken, since the day of Mrs. Clemmens' death, proves you to be the victim of a fixed conviction totally at war with the statement you were pleased to make today. Only your belief in the guilt of another and your—your——"

He stopped, choked. The thought of his rival maddened him.

She immediately seized the opportunity to say:

"Mr. Orcutt, I cannot argue about what I have done. It is over and cannot be remedied. It is true I have destroyed myself, but this is no time to think of that. All I can think of or mourn over now is that, by destroying myself, I have not succeeded in saving Craik Mansell."

If her purpose was to probe the lawyer's soul for the deadly wound that had turned all his sympaties to gall, she was successful at last. Turning upon her with a look in which despair and anger were strangely mingled, he cried:

"And me, Imogene—have you no thought for me?"

"Sir," said she, "any thought from one disgraced as I am now, would be an insult to one of your character and position."

It was true. In the eyes of the world Tremont Orcutt and Imogene Dare henceforth stood as far apart as the poles. Realizing it only too well, he uttered a half-inarticulate exclamation, and trod restlessly to the other end of the room. When he came back, it was with more of the lawyer's aspect and less of the baffled lover's.

"Imogene," he said, "what could have induced you to resort to an expedient so dreadful? Had you lost confidence in me? Had I not told you I would save this man from his threatened fate?"

"You cannot do everything," she replied. "There are limits even to a power like yours. I knew that Craik was lost if I gave to the court the testimony which Mr. Ferris expected from me."

"Ah, then," he cried, seizing with his usual quickness at the admission which had thus unconsciously, perhaps, slipped from her, "you acknowledge you uttered a perjury to save yourself from making declarations you believed to be hurtful to the prisoner?"

A faint smile crossed her lips, and her whole aspect suddenly changed.

"Yes," she said; "I have no motive for hiding it from you now. I perjured myself to escape destroying Craik Mansell. I was scarcely the mistress of my own actions. I had suffered so much I was ready to do anything to save the man I had so relentlessly pushed to his doom. I forgot that God does not prosper a lie."

The jealous gleam which answered her from the lawyer's eyes was a revelation.

"You regret, then," he said, "that you tossed my happiness away with a breath of your perjured lips?"

"I regret I did not tell the truth and trust God."

At this answer, uttered with the simplicity of a penitent spirit, Mr.

Orcutt unconsciously drew back.

"And, may I ask, what has caused this sudden regret?" he inquired, in a tone not far removed from mockery; "the generous action of the prisoner in relieving you from your self-imposed burden of guilt by an acknowledgment that struck at the foundation of the defence I had so carefully prepared?"

"No," was her short reply; "that could but afford me joy. Of whatever sin he may be guilty, he is at least free from the reproach of accepting deliverance at the expense of a woman. I am sorry I said what I did today, because a revelation has since been made to me, which proves I could never have sustained myself in the position I took, and that it was mere suicidal folly in me to attempt to save Craik Mansell by such means."

"A revelation?"

"Yes." And, forgetting all else in the purpose which had actuated her in seeking this interview, Imogene drew nearer to the lawyer and earnestly said: "There have been some persons—I have perceived it—who have wondered at my deep conviction of Craik Mansell's guilt. But the reasons I had justified it. They were great, greater than anyone knew, greater even than *you* knew. His mother—were she living—must have thought as I did, had she been placed beside me and seen what I have seen, and heard what I have heard from the time of Mrs. Clemmens' death. Not only were all the facts brought against him in the trial known to me, but I saw him—saw him with my own eyes, running from Mrs. Clemmens' dining-room door at the very time we suppose the murder to have been committed; that is, at five minutes before noon on the fatal day."

"Impossible!" exclaimed Mr. Orcutt, in his astonishment. "You are playing with my credulity, Imogene."

But she went on, letting her voice fall in awe of the lawyer's startled look.

"No," she persisted; "I was in Professor Darling's observatory. I was looking through a telescope, which had been pointed toward the town. Mrs. Clemmens was much in my mind at the time, and I took the notion to glance at her house, when I saw what I have described to you. I could not help remembering the time," she added, "for I had looked at the clock but a moment before."

"And it was five minutes before noon?" broke again from the lawyer's lips, in what was almost an awe-struck tone.

Troubled at an astonishment which seemed to partake of the na-

457

ture of alarm, she silently bowed her head.

"And you were looking at him—actually looking at him—that very moment through a telescope perched a mile or so away?"

"Yes," she bowed again.

Turning his face aside, Mr. Orcutt walked to the hearth and began kicking the burnt-out logs with his restless foot. As he did so, Imogene heard him mutter between his set teeth:

"It is almost enough to make one believe in a God!"

Struck, horrified, she glided anxiously to his side.

"Do not you believe in a God?" she asked.

He was silent.

Amazed, almost frightened, for she had never heard him breathe a word of scepticism before,—though, to be sure, he had never mentioned the name of the Deity in her presence,—she stood looking at him like one who had received a blow; then she said:

"I believe in God. It is my punishment that I do. It is He who wills blood for blood; who dooms the guilty to a merited death. Oh, if He only would accept the sacrifice I so willingly offer!—take the life I so little value, and give me in return——"

"Mansell's?" completed the lawyer, turning upon her in a burst of fury he no longer had power to suppress. "Is that your cry—always and forever your cry? You drive me too far, Imogene. This mad and senseless passion for a man who no longer loves you——"

"Spare me!" rose from her trembling lips. "Let me forget that."

But the great lawyer only laughed.

"You make it worth my while to save you the bitterness of such a remembrance," he cried. Then, as she remained silent, he changed his tone to one of careless inquiry, and asked:

"Was it to tell this story of the prisoner having fled from his aunt's house that you came here tonight?"

Recalled to the purpose of the hour, she answered, hurriedly:

"Not entirely; that story was what Mr. Ferris expected me to testify to in court this morning. You see for yourself in what a position it would have put the prisoner."

"And the revelation you have received?" the lawyer coldly urged.

"Was of a deception that has been practised upon me—a base deception by which I was led to think long ago that Craik Mansell had admitted his guilt and only trusted to the excellence of his defence to escape punishment."

"I do not understand," said Mr. Orcutt. "Who could have practised such deception upon you?"

"The detectives," she murmured; "that rough, heartless fellow they call Hickory." And, in a burst of indignation, she told how she had been practised upon, and what the results had been upon her belief, if not upon the testimony which grew out of that belief.

The lawyer listened with a strange apathy. What would once have aroused his fiercest indignation and fired him to an exertion of his keenest powers, fell on him now like the tedious repetition of an old and worn-out tale. He scarcely looked up when she was done; and despair—the first, perhaps, she had ever really felt—began to close in around her as she saw how deep a gulf she had dug between this man and herself by the inconsiderate act which had robbed him of all hope of ever making her his wife. Moved by this feeling, she suddenly asked:

"Have you lost all interest in your client, Mr. Orcutt? Have you no wish or hope remaining of seeing him acquitted of this crime?"

"My client," responded the lawyer, with bitter emphasis, "has taken his case into his own hands. It would be presumptuous in me to attempt anything further in his favour."

"Mr. Orcutt!"

"Ah!" he scornfully laughed, with a quick yielding to his passion as startling as it was unexpected, "you thought you could play with me as you would; use my skill and ignore the love that prompted it. You are a clever woman, Imogene, but you went too far when you considered my forbearance unlimited."

"And you forsake Craik Mansell, in the hour of his extremity?"

"Craik Mansell has forsaken me."

This was true; for her sake her lover had thrown his defence to the winds and rendered the assistance of his counsel unavailable. Seeing her droop her head abashed, Mr. Orcutt dryly proceeded.

"I do not know what may take place in court tomorrow," said he. "It is difficult to determine what will be the outcome of so complicated a case. The district attorney, in consideration of the deception which has been practised upon you, may refuse to prosecute any further; or, if the case goes on and the jury is called upon for a verdict, they may or may not be moved by its peculiar aspects to acquit a man of such generous dispositions. If they are, I shall do nothing to hinder an acquittal; but ask for no more active measures on my part. I cannot plead for the lover of the woman who has disgraced me."

This decision, from one she had trusted so implicitly, seemed to crush her.

"Ah," she murmured, "if you did not believe him guilty you would not leave him thus to his fate."

He gave her a short, side-long glance, half-mocking, half-pitiful.

"If," she pursued, "you had felt even a passing gleam of doubt, such as came to me when I discovered that he had never really admitted his guilt, you would let no mere mistake on the part of a woman turn you from your duty as counsellor for a man on trial for his life."

His glance lost its pity and became wholly mocking.

"And do *you* cherish but passing gleams?" he sarcastically asked.

She started back.

"I laugh at the inconsistency of women," he cried. "You have sacrificed everything, even risked your life for a man you really believe guilty of crime; yet if another man similarly stained asked you for your compassion only, you would fly from him as from a pestilence."

But no words he could utter of this sort were able to raise any emotion in her now.

"Mr. Orcutt," she demanded, "do *you* believe Craik Mansell innocent?"

His old mocking smile came back.

"Have I conducted his case as if I believed him guilty?" he asked.

"No, no; but you are his lawyer; you are bound not to let your real thoughts appear. But in your secret heart you did not, could not, believe he was free from a crime to which he is linked by so many criminating circumstances?"

But his strange smile remaining unchanged, she seemed to waken to a sudden doubt, and leaping impetuously to his side, laid her hand on his arm and exclaimed:

"Oh, sir, if you have ever cherished one hope of his innocence, no matter how faint or small, tell me of it, even if this last disclosure has convinced you of its folly!"

Giving her an icy look, he drew his arm slowly from her grasp and replied:

"Mr. Mansell has never been considered guilty by me."

"Never?"

"Never."

"Not even now?"

"Not even now."

It seemed as if she could not believe his words.

"And yet you know all there is against him; all that I do now!"

"I know he visited his aunt's house at or after the time she was murdered, but that is no proof he killed her, Miss Dare."

"No," she admitted with slow conviction, "no. But why did he fly in that wild way when he left it? Why did he go straight to Buffalo and not wait to give me the interview he promised?"

"Shall I tell you?" Mr. Orcutt inquired, with a dangerous sneer on his lips. "Do you wish to know why this man—the man you have so loved—the man for whom you would die this moment, has conducted himself with such marked discretion?"

"Yes," came like a breath from between Imogene's parted lips.

"Well," said the lawyer, dropping his words with cruel clearness, "Mr. Mansell has a great faith in women. He has such faith in you, Imogene Dare, he thinks you are all you declare yourself to be; that in the hour you stood up before the court and called yourself a murderer, you spoke but the truth; that——" He stopped; even his scornful *aplomb* would not allow him to go on in the face of the look she wore.

"Say—say those words again!" she gasped. "Let me hear them once more. He thinks what?"

"That you are what you proclaimed yourself to be this day, the actual assailant and murderer of Mrs. Clemmens. He has thought so all along, Miss Dare, why, I do not know. Whether he saw anything or heard anything in that house from which you saw him fly so abruptly, or whether he relied solely upon the testimony of the ring, which you must remember he never acknowledged having received back from you, I only know that from the minute he heard of his aunt's death, his suspicions flew to you, and that, in despite of such suggestions as I felt it judicious to make, they have never suffered shock or been turned from their course from that day to this. *Such* honour," concluded Mr. Orcutt, with dry sarcasm, "does the man you love show to the woman who has sacrificed for his sake all that the world holds dear."

"I—I cannot believe it. You are mocking me," came inarticulately from her lips, while she drew back, step by step, till half the room lay between them.

"Mocking you? Miss Dare, he has shown his feelings so palpably, I have often trembled lest the whole court should see and understand them."

"You have trembled"—she could scarcely speak, the rush of her emotion was so great—"*you* have trembled lest the whole court should see he suspected me of this crime?"

"Yes."

"Then," she cried, "you must have been convinced,—Ah!" she hurriedly interposed, with a sudden look of distrust, "you are not amusing yourself with me, are you, Mr. Orcutt? So many traps have been laid for me from time to time, I dare not trust the truth of my best friend. Swear you believe Craik Mansell to have thought this of me! Swear you have seen this dark thing lying in his soul, or I——"

"What?"

"Will confront him myself with the question, if I have to tear down the walls of the prison to reach him. His mind I must and will know."

"Very well, then, you do. I have told you," declared Mr. Orcutt. "Swearing would not make it any more true."

Lifting her face to heaven, she suddenly fell on her knees.

"O God!" she murmured, "help me to bear this great joy!"

"*Joy!*"

The icy tone, the fierce surprise it expressed, started her at once to her feet.

"Yes," she murmured, "joy! Don't you see that if he thinks me guilty, he *must* be innocent? I am willing to perish and fall from the ranks of good men and honourable women to be sure of a fact like this!"

"Imogene, Imogene, would you drive me mad?"

She did not seem to hear.

"Craik, are you guiltless, then?" she was saying. "Is the past all a dream! Are we two nothing but victims of dread and awful circumstances? Oh, we will see; life is not ended yet!" And with a burst of hope that seemed to transfigure her into another woman, she turned toward the lawyer with the cry: "If he is innocent, he can be saved. Nothing that has been done by him or me can hurt him if this be so. God who watches over this crime has His eye on the guilty one. Though his sin be hidden under a mountain of deceit, it will yet come forth. Guilt like his cannot remain hidden."

"You did not think this when you faced the court this morning with perjury on your lips," came in slow, ironical tones from her companion.

"Heaven sometimes accepts a sacrifice," she returned. "But who will sacrifice himself for a man who could let the trial of one he knew to be innocent go on unhindered?"

"Who, indeed!" came in almost stifled tones from the lawyer's lips.

"If a stranger and not Craik Mansell slew Mrs. Clemmens," she went on, "and nothing but an incomprehensible train of coincidences unites him and me to this act of violence, then may God remember the words of the widow, and in His almighty power call down such a doom——"

She ended with a gasp. Mr. Orcutt, with a sudden movement, had laid his hand upon her lips.

"Hush!" he said, "let no curses issue from *your* mouth. The guilty can perish without that."

Releasing herself from him in alarm, she drew back, her eyes slowly dilating as she noted the dead whiteness that had settled over his face, and taken even the hue of life from his nervously trembling lip.

"Mr. Orcutt," she whispered, with a solemnity which made them heedless that the lamp which had been burning lower and lower in its socket was giving out its last fitful rays, "if Craik Mansell did not kill the Widow Clemmens who then did?"

Her question—or was it her look and tone?—seemed to transfix Mr. Orcutt. But it was only for a moment. Turning with a slight gesture to the table at his side, he fumbled with his papers, still oblivious of the flaring lamp, saying slowly:

"I have always supposed Gouverneur Hildreth to be the true author of this crime."

"Gouverneur Hildreth?"

Mr. Orcutt bowed.

"I do not agree with you," she returned, moving slowly toward the window. "I am no reader of human hearts, as all my past history shows, but something—is it the voice of God in my breast?—tells me that Gouverneur Hildreth is as innocent as Craik Mansell, and that the true murderer of Mrs. Clemmens——" Her words ended in a shriek. The light, which for so long a time had been flickering to its end, had given one startling flare in which the face of the man before her had flashed on her view in a ghastly flame that seemed to separate it from all surrounding objects, then as suddenly gone out, leaving the room in total darkness.

In the silence that followed, a quick sound as of rushing feet was heard, then the window was pushed up and the night air came moaning in. Imogene had fled.

★★★★★★

Horace Byrd had not followed Hickory in his rush toward the

463

house. He had preferred to await results under the great tree which, standing just inside the gate, cast its mysterious and far-reaching shadow widely over the wintry lawn. He was, therefore, alone during most of the interview which Miss Dare held with Mr. Orcutt in the library, and, being alone, felt himself a prey to his sensations and the weirdness of the situation in which he found himself.

Though no longer a victim to the passion with which Miss Dare had at first inspired him, he was by no means without feeling for this grand if somewhat misguided woman, and his emotions, as he stood there awaiting the issue of her last desperate attempt to aid the prisoner, were strong enough to make any solitude welcome, though this solitude for some reason held an influence which was anything but enlivening, if it was not actually depressing, to one of his ready sensibilities.

The tree under which he had taken his stand was, as I have intimated, an old one. It had stood there from time immemorial, and was, as I have heard it since said, at once the pride of Mr. Orcutt's heart and the chief ornament of his grounds. Though devoid of foliage at the time, its vast and symmetrical canopy of interlacing branches had caught Mr. Byrd's attention from the first moment of his entrance beneath it, and, preoccupied as he was, he could not prevent his thoughts from reverting now and then with a curious sensation of awe to the immensity of those great limbs which branched above him. His imagination was so powerfully affected at last, he had a notion of leaving the spot and seeking a nearer lookout in the belt of evergreens that hid the crouching form of Hickory; but a spell seemed to emanate from the huge trunk against which he leaned that restrained him when he sought to go, and noticing almost at the same moment that the path which Miss Dare would have to take in her departure ran directly under this tree, he yielded to the apathy of the moment and remained where he was.

Soon after he was visited by Hickory.

"I can see nothing and hear nothing," was that individual's hurried salutation. "She and Mr. Orcutt are evidently still in the library, but I cannot get a clue to what is going on. I shall keep up my watch, however, for I want to catch a glimpse of her face as she steps from the window." And he was off again before Byrd could reply.

But the next instant he was back, panting and breathless.

"The light is out in the library," he cried; "we shall see her no more tonight."

But scarcely had the words left his lips when a faint sound was heard from the region of the *piazza*, and looking eagerly up the path, they saw the form of Miss Dare coming hurriedly toward them.

To slip around into the deepest shadow cast by the tree was but the work of a moment. Meantime, the moon shone brightly on the walk down which she was speeding, and as, in the agitation of her departure, she had forgotten to draw down her veil, they succeeded in obtaining a view of her face. It was pale, and wore an expression of fear, while her feet hasted as though she were only filled with thoughts of escape.

Seeing this, the two detectives held their breaths, preparing to follow her as soon as she had passed the tree. But she did not pass the tree. Just as she got within reach of its shadow, a commanding voice was heard calling upon her to stop, and Mr. Orcutt came hurrying, in his turn, down the path.

"I cannot let you go thus," he cried, pausing beside her on the walk directly under the tree. "If you command me to save Craik Mansell I must do it. What you wish must be done, Imogene."

"My wishes should not be needed to lead you to do your duty by the man you believe to be innocent of the charge for which he is being tried," was her earnest and strangely cold reply.

"Perhaps not," he muttered, bitterly; "but—ah, Imogene," he suddenly broke forth, in a way to startle these two detectives, who, however suspicious they had been of his passion, had never before had the opportunity of seeing him under its control, "what have you made of me with your bewildering graces and indomitable soul? Before I knew you, life was a round of honourable duties and serene pleasures. I lived in my profession, and found my greatest delight in its exercise. But now——"

"What now?" she asked.

"I seem"—he said, and the hard, cold selfishness that underlay all his actions, however generous they may have been in appearance, was apparent in his words and tones,—"I seem to forget everything, even my standing and fame as a lawyer, in the one fear that, although lost to me, you will yet live to give yourself to another."

"If you fear that I shall ever be so weak as to give myself to Craik Mansell," was her steady reply, "you have only to recall the promise I made you when you undertook his case."

"Yes," said he, "but that was when you yourself believed him guilty."

"I know," she returned; "but if he were not good enough for me then, I am not good enough for him now. Do you forget that I am blotted with a stain that can never be effaced? When I stood up in court today and denounced myself as guilty of crime, I signed away all my chances of future happiness."

There was a pause; Mr. Orcutt seemed to be thinking. From the position occupied by the two detectives his shadow could be seen oscillating to and fro on the lawn, then, amid the hush of night—a deathly hush—undisturbed, as Mr. Byrd afterward remarked, by so much as the cracking of a twig, his voice rose quiet, yet vaguely sinister, in the words:

"You have conquered. If any man suffers for this crime it shall not be Craik Mansell, but——"

The sentence was never finished. Before the words could leave his mouth a sudden strange and splitting sound was heard above their heads, then a terrifying rush took place, and a great limb lay upon the walk where but a moment before the beautiful form of Imogene Dare lifted itself by the side of the eminent lawyer.

When a full sense of the terrible nature of the calamity which had just occurred swept across the minds of the benumbed detectives, Mr. Byrd, recalling the words and attitude of Imogene in face of a similar, if less fatal, catastrophe at the hut, exclaimed under his breath:

"It is the vengeance of Heaven! Imogene Dare must have been more guilty than we believed."

But when, after a superhuman exertion of strength, and the assistance of many hands, the limb was at length raised, it was found that, although both had been prostrated by its weight, only one remained stretched and senseless upon the ground, and that was not Imogene Dare, but the great lawyer, Mr. Orcutt.

38

Unexpected Words

"Mr. Orcutt dead?"

"Dying, sir."

"How, when, where?"

"In his own house, sir. He has been struck down by a falling limb."

The district attorney, who had been roused from his bed to hear these evil tidings, looked at the perturbed face of the messenger before him—who was none other than Mr. Byrd—and with difficulty restrained his emotion.

"I sympathize with your horror and surprise," exclaimed the detective, respectfully. Then, with a strange mixture of embarrassment and agitation, added: "It is considered absolutely necessary that you come to the house. He may yet speak—and—and—you will find Miss Dare there," he concluded, with a peculiarly hesitating glance and a rapid movement toward the door.

Mr. Ferris, who, as we know, cherished a strong feeling of friendship for Mr. Orcutt, stared uneasily at the departing form of the detective.

"What do you say?" he repeated. "Miss Dare there, in Mr. Orcutt's house?"

The short "Yes," and the celerity with which Mr. Byrd vanished, gave him the appearance of one anxious to escape further inquiries.

Astonished, as well as greatly distressed, the district attorney made speedy preparations for following him, and soon was in the street. He found it all alive with eager citizens, who, notwithstanding the lateness of the hour, were rushing hither and thither in search of particulars concerning this sudden calamity; and upon reaching the house itself, found it well-nigh surrounded by an agitated throng of neighbours and friends.

Simply pausing at the gate to cast one glance at the tree and its fallen limb, he made his way to the front door. It was immediately opened. Dr. Tredwell, whose face it was a shock to encounter in this place, stood before him, and farther back a group of such favoured friends as had been allowed to enter the house. Something in the look of the coroner, as he silently reached forth his hand in salutation, added to the mysterious impression which had been made upon Mr. Ferris by the manner, if not words, of Mr. Byrd. Feeling that he was losing his self-command, the district attorney grasped the hand that was held out to him, and huskily inquired if Mr. Orcutt was still alive.

The coroner, who had been standing before him with a troubled brow and lowered eyes, gravely bowed, and quietly leading the way, ushered him forward to Mr. Orcutt's bedroom door. There he paused and looked as if he would like to speak, but hastily changing his mind, opened the door and motioned the district attorney in. As he did so, he cast a meaning and solemn look toward the bed, then drew back, watching with evident anxiety what the effect of the scene before him would have upon this new witness.

A stupefying one it seemed, for Mr. Ferris, pausing in his approach, looked at the cluster of persons about the bed, and then drew his hand across his eyes like a man in a maze. Suddenly he turned upon Dr. Tredwell with the same strange look he had himself seen in the eyes of Byrd, and said, almost as if the words were forced from his lips:

"This is no new sight to us, doctor; we have been spectators of a scene like this before."

That was it. As nearly as the alteration in circumstances and surroundings would allow, the spectacle before him was the same as that which he had encountered months before in a small cottage at the other end of the town. On the bed a pallid, senseless, but slowly breathing form, whose features, stamped with the approach of death, stared at them with marble-like rigidity from beneath the heavy bandages which proclaimed the injury to be one to the head. At his side the doctor—the same one who had been called in to attend Mrs. Clemmens—wearing, as he did then, a look of sombre anticipation which Mr. Ferris expected every instant to see culminate in the solemn gesture which he had used at the widow's bedside before she spoke.

Even the group of women who clustered about the foot of the couch wore much the same expression as those who waited for movement on the part of Mrs. Clemmens; and had it not been for the sight of Imogene Dare sitting immovable and watchful on the farther side of the bed, he might almost have imagined he was transported back to the old scene, and that all this new horror under which he was labouring was a dream from which he would speedily be awakened.

But Imogene's face, her look, her air of patient waiting, were not to be mistaken. Attention once really attracted to her, it was not possible for it to wander elsewhere. Even the face of the dying man and the countenance of the watchful physician paled in interest before that fixed look which, never wavering, never altering, studied the marble visage before her, for the first faint signs of reawakening consciousness. Even his sister, who, if weak of mind, was most certainly of a loving disposition, seemed to feel the force of the tie that bound Imogene to that pillow; and, though she hovered nearer and nearer the beloved form as the weariful moments sped by, did not presume to interpose her grief or her assistance between the burning eye of Imogene and the immovable form of her stricken brother.

The hush that lay upon the room was unbroken save by the agitated breaths of all present.

"Is there no hope?" whispered Mr. Ferris to Dr. Tredwell, as, seeing no immediate prospect of change, they sought for seats at the other side of the room.

"No; the wound is strangely like that which Mrs. Clemmens received. He will rouse, probably, but he will not live. Our only comfort is that in this case it is not a murder."

The district attorney made a gesture in the direction of Imogene.

"How came she to be here?" he asked.

Dr. Tredwell rose and drew him from the room.

"It needs some explanation," he said; and began to relate to him how Mr. Orcutt was escorting Miss Dare to the gate when the bough fell which seemed likely to rob him of his life.

Mr. Ferris, through whose mind those old words of the widow were running in a way that could only be accounted for by the memories which the scene within had awakened—"May the vengeance of Heaven light upon the head of him who has brought me to this pass! May the fate that has come upon me be visited upon him, measure for measure, blow for blow, death for death!"—turned with impressive gravity and asked if Miss Dare had not been hurt.

But Dr. Tredwell shook his head.

"She is not even bruised," said he.

"And yet was on his arm?"

"Possibly, though I very much doubt it."

"She was standing at his side," uttered the quiet voice of Mr. Byrd in their ear; "and disappeared when he did, under the falling branch. She must have been bruised, though she says not. I do not think she is in a condition to feel her injuries."

"You were present, then," observed Mr. Ferris, with a meaning glance at the detective.

"I was present," he returned, with a look the district attorney did not find it difficult to understand.

"Is there anything you ought to tell me?" Mr. Ferris inquired, when a moment or so later the coroner had been drawn away by a friend.

"I do not know," said Byrd. "Of the conversation that passed between Miss Dare and Mr. Orcutt, but a short portion came to our ears. It is her manner, her actions, that have astonished us, and made us anxious to have you upon the spot." And he told with what an expression of fear she had fled from her interview with Mr. Orcutt in the library, and then gave, as nearly as he could, an account of what had passed between them before the falling of the fatal limb. Finally he said: "Hickory and I expected to find her lying crushed and bleeding beneath, but instead of that, no sooner was the bough lifted than she sprang to her knees, and seeing Mr. Orcutt lying before her insensible, bent over him with that same expression of breathless awe and expectation which you see in her now. It looks as if she were waiting for him to rouse and finish the sentence that was cut short by this catastrophe."

"And what was that sentence?"

"As near as I can recollect, it was this: 'If any man suffers for this crime it shall not be Craik Mansell, but——'He did not have time to say whom."

"My poor friend!" ejaculated Mr. Ferris, "cut down in the exercise of his duties! It is a mysterious providence—a very mysterious providence!" And crossing again to the sick-room, he went sadly in.

He found the aspect unchanged. On the pillow the same white, immovable face; at the bedside the same constant and expectant watchers. Imogene especially seemed scarcely to have made a move in all the time of his absence. Like a marble image watching over a form of clay she sat silent, breathless, intent—a sight to draw all eyes and satisfy none; for her look was not one of grief, nor of awe, nor of hope, yet it had that within it which made her presence there seem a matter of right even to those who did not know the exact character of the bond which united her to the unhappy sufferer.

Mr. Ferris, who had been only too ready to accept Mr. Byrd's explanation of her conduct, allowed himself to gaze at her unhindered.

Overwhelmed, as he was, by the calamity which promised to rob the bar of one of its most distinguished advocates, and himself of a long-tried friend, he could not but feel the throb of those deep interests which, in the estimation of this woman at least, hung upon a word which those dying lips might utter. And swayed by this feeling, he unconsciously became a third watcher, though for what, and in hope of what, he could scarcely have told, so much was he benumbed by the suddenness of this great catastrophe, and the extraordinary circumstances by which it was surrounded.

And so one o'clock came and passed.

It was not the last time the clock struck before a change came. The hour of two went by, then that of three, and still, to the casual eye, all remained the same. But ere the stroke of four was heard, Mr. Ferris, who had relaxed his survey of Imogene to bestow a fuller attention upon his friend, felt an indefinable sensation of dismay assail him, and rising to his feet, drew a step or so nearer the bed, and looked at its silent occupant with the air of a man who would fain shut his eyes to the meaning of what he sees before him. At the same moment Mr. Byrd, who had just come in, found himself attracted by the subtle difference he observed in the expression of Miss Dare.

The expectancy in her look was gone, and its entire expression was that of awe. Advancing to the side of Mr. Ferris, he glanced down at the dying lawyer. He at once saw what it was that had so attracted and moved the district attorney. A change had come over Mr. Orcutt's face. Though rigid still, and unrelieved by any signs of returning conscious ness, it was no longer that of the man they knew, but a strange face, owning the same features, but distinguished now by a look sinister as it was unaccustomed, filling the breasts of those who saw it with dismay, and making any contemplation of his countenance more than painful to those who loved him.

Nor did it decrease as they watched him. Like that charmed writing which appears on a blank paper when it is subjected to the heat, the subtle, unmistakable lines came out, moment by moment, on the mask of his unconscious face, till even Imogene trembled, and turned an appealing glance upon Mr. Ferris, as if to bid him note this involuntary evidence of nature against the purity and good intentions of

471

the man who had always stood so high in the world's regard. Then, satisfied, perhaps, with the expression she encountered on the face of the district attorney, she looked back; and the heavy minutes went on, only more drearily, and perhaps more fearfully, than before.

Suddenly—was it at a gesture of the physician, or a look from Imogene?—a thrill of expectation passed through the room, and Dr. Tredwell, Mr. Ferris, and a certain other gentleman who had but just entered at a remote corner of the apartment, came hurriedly forward and stood at the foot of the bed. At the same instant Imogene rose, and motioning them a trifle aside, with an air of mingled entreaty and command, bent slowly down toward the injured man. A look of recognition answered her from the face upon the pillow, but she did not wait to meet it, nor pause for the word that evidently trembled on his momentarily conscious lip.

Shutting out with her form the group of anxious watchers behind her, she threw all her soul into the regard with which she held him enchained; then slowly, solemnly, but with unyielding determination, uttered these words, which no one there could know were but a repetition of a question made a few eventful hours ago: "If Craik Mansell is not the man who killed Mrs. Clemmens, do you, Mr. Orcutt, tell us who is!" and, pausing, remained with her gaze fixed demandingly on that of the lawyer, undeterred by the smothered exclamations of those who witnessed this scene and missed its clue or found it only in the supposition that this last great shock had unsettled her mind.

The panting sufferer just trembling on the verge of life thrilled all down his once alert and nervous frame, then searching her face for one sign of relenting, unclosed his rigid lips and said, with emphasis:

"Has not Fate spoken?"

Instantly Imogene sprang erect, and, amid the stifled shrieks of the women and the muttered exclamations of the men, pointed at the recumbent figure before them, saying:

"You hear! Tremont Orcutt declares upon his death-bed that it is the voice of Heaven which has spoken in this dreadful calamity. You who were present when Mrs. Clemmens breathed her imprecations on the head of her murderer, must know what that means."

Mr. Ferris, who of all present, perhaps, possessed the greatest regard for the lawyer, gave an ejaculation of dismay at this, and bounding forward, lifted her away from the bedside he believed her to have basely desecrated.

"Madwoman," he cried, "where will your ravings end? He will tell no such tale to me."

But when he bent above the lawyer with the question forced from him by Miss Dare's words, he found him already lapsed into that strange insensibility which was every moment showing itself more and more to be the precursor of death.

The sight seemed to rob Mr. Ferris of his last grain of self-command. Rising, he confronted the dazed faces of those about him with a severe look.

"This charge," said he, "is akin to that which Miss Dare made against herself in the court yesterday morning. When a woman has become crazed she no longer knows what she says."

But Imogene, strong in the belief that the hand of Heaven had pointed out the culprit for whom they had so long been searching, shook her head in quiet denial, and simply saying, "None of you know this man as I do," moved quietly aside to a dim corner, where she sat down in calm expectation of another awakening on the part of the dying lawyer.

It came soon—came before Mr. Ferris had recovered himself, or Dr. Tredwell had had a chance to give any utterance to the emotions which this scene was calculated to awaken.

Rousing as the widow had done, but seeming to see no one, not even the physician who bent close at his side, Mr. Orcutt lifted his voice again, this time in the old stentorian tones which he used in court, and clearly, firmly exclaimed:

"Blood will have blood!" Then in lower and more familiar accents, cried: "Ah, Imogene, Imogene, it was all for you!" And with her name on his lips, the great lawyer closed his eyes again, and sank for the last time into a state of insensibility.

Imogene at once rose.

"I must go," she murmured; "my duty in this place is done." And she attempted to cross the floor.

But the purpose which had sustained her being at an end, she felt the full weight of her misery, and looking in the faces about her, and seeing nothing there but reprobation, she tottered and would have fallen had not a certain portly gentleman who stood nearby put forth his arm to sustain her. Accepting the support with gratitude, but scarcely pausing to note from what source it came, she turned for an instant to Mr. Ferris.

"I realize," said she, "with what surprise you must have heard the revelation which has just come from Mr. Orcutt's lips. So unexpected is it that you cannot yet believe it, but the time will come when, of all the words I have spoken, these alone will be found worthy your full credit: that not Craik Mansell, not Gouverneur Hildreth, not even unhappy Imogene Dare herself, could tell you so much of the real cause and manner of Mrs. Clemmens' death as this man who lies stricken here a victim of Divine justice."

And merely stopping to cast one final look in the direction of the bed, she stumbled from the room. A few minutes later and she reached the front door; but only to fall against the lintel with the moan:

"My words are true, but who will ever believe them?"

"Pardon me," exclaimed a bland and fatherly voice over her shoulder, "I am a man who can believe in anything . Put your confidence in me, Miss Dare, and we will see—we will see."

Startled by her surprise into new life, she gave one glance at the gentleman who had followed her to the door. It was the same who had offered her his arm, and whom she supposed to have remained behind her in Mr. Orcutt's room. She saw before her a large comfortable-looking personage of middle age, of no great pretensions to elegance or culture, but bearing that within his face which oddly enough baffled her understanding while it encouraged her trust. This was the more peculiar in that he was not looking at her, but stood with his eyes fixed on the fading light of the hall-lamp, which he surveyed with an expression of concern that almost amounted to pity.

"Sir, who are you?" she tremblingly asked.

Dropping his eyes from the lamp, he riveted them upon the veil she held tightly clasped in her right hand.

"If you will allow me the liberty of whispering in your ear, I will soon tell you," said he.

She bent her weary head downward; he at once leaned toward her and murmured a half-dozen words that made her instantly start erect with new light in her eyes.

"And you will help me?" she cried.

"What else am I here for?" he answered.

And turning toward a quiet figure which she now saw for the first time standing on the threshold of a small room nearby, he said with the calmness of a master:

"Hickory, see that no one enters or leaves the sick-room till I return." And offering Imogene his arm, he conducted her into the library, the door of which he shut to behind them.

Chapter 39

Mr. Gryce

An hour later, as Mr. Ferris was leaving the house in company with Dr. Tredwell, he felt himself stopped by a slight touch on his arm. Turning about he saw Hickory.

"Beg pardon, sirs," said the detective, with a short bow, "but there's a gentleman, in the library who would like to see you before you go."

They at once turned to the room indicated. But at sight of its well-known features—its huge cases of books, its large centre-table profusely littered with papers, the burnt-out grate, the empty arm-chair—they paused, and it was with difficulty they could recover themselves sufficiently to enter. When they did, their first glance was toward the gentleman they saw standing in a distant window, apparently perusing a book.

"Who is it?" inquired Mr. Ferris of his companion.

"I cannot imagine," returned the other.

Hearing voices, the gentleman advanced.

"Ah," said he, "allow me to introduce myself. I am Mr. Gryce, of the New York Detective Service."

"Mr. Gryce!" repeated the district attorney, in astonishment.

The famous detective bowed. "I have come," said he, "upon a summons received by me in Utica not six hours ago. It was sent by a subordinate of mine interested in the trial now going on before the court. Horace Byrd is his name. I hope he is well liked here and has your confidence."

"Mr. Byrd is well enough liked," rejoined Mr. Ferris, "but I gave him no orders to send for you. At what hour was the telegram dated?"

"At half-past eleven; immediately after the accident to Mr. Orcutt."

"I see."

"He probably felt himself inadequate to meet this new emergency. He is a young man, and the affair is certainly a complicated one."

The district attorney, who had been studying the countenance of the able detective before him, bowed courteously.

"I am not displeased to see you," said he. "If you have been in the room above——"

The other gravely bowed.

"You know probably of the outrageous accusation which has just been made against our best lawyer and most-esteemed citizen. It is but one of many which this same woman has made; and while it is to be regarded as the ravings of lunacy, still your character and ability may weigh much in lifting the opprobrium which any such accusation, however unfounded, is calculated to throw around the memory of my dying friend."

"Sir," returned Mr. Gryce, shifting his gaze uneasily from one small object to another in that dismal room, till all and every article it contained seemed to partake of his mysterious confidence, "this is a world of disappointment and deceit. Intellects we admired, hearts in which we trusted, turn out frequently to be the abodes of falsehood and violence. It is dreadful, but it is true."

Mr. Ferris, struck aghast, looked at the detective with severe disapprobation.

"Is it possible," he asked, "that you have allowed yourself to give any credence to the delirious utterances of a man suffering from a wound on the head, or to the frantic words of a woman who has already abused the ears of the court by a deliberate perjury?" While Dr. Tredwell, equally indignant and even more impatient, rapped with his knuckles on the table by which he stood, and cried:

"Pooh, pooh, the man cannot be such a fool!"

A solemn smile crossed the features of the detective.

"Many persons have listened to the aspersion you denounce. Active measures will be needed to prevent its going farther."

"I have commanded silence," said Dr. Tredwell. "Respect for Mr. Orcutt will cause my wishes to be obeyed."

"Does Mr. Orcutt enjoy the universal respect of the town?"

"He does," was the stern reply.

"It behoves us, then," said Mr. Gryce, "to clear his memory from every doubt by a strict inquiry into his relations with the murdered woman."

"They are known," returned Mr. Ferris, with grim reserve. "They were such as any man might hold with the woman at whose house he finds it convenient to take his daily dinner. She was to him the provider of a good meal."

Mr. Gryce's eye travelled slowly toward Mr. Ferris' shirt stud.

"Gentlemen," said he, "do you forget that Mr. Orcutt was on the scene of murder some minutes before the rest of you arrived? Let the attention of people once be directed toward him as a suspicious party, and they will be likely to remember this fact."

Astounded, both men drew back.

"What do you mean by that remark?" they asked.

"I mean," said Mr. Gryce, "that Mr. Orcutt's visit to Mrs. Clemmens' house on the morning of the murder will be apt to be recalled by persons of a suspicious tendency as having given him an opportunity to commit the crime."

"People are not such fools," cried Dr. Tredwell; while Mr. Ferris, in a tone of mingled incredulity and anger, exclaimed:

"And do you, a reputable detective, and, as I have been told, a man of excellent judgement, presume to say that there could be found anyone in this town, or even in this country, who could let his suspicions carry him so far as to hint that Mr. Orcutt struck this woman with his own hand in the minute or two that elapsed between his going into her house and his coming out again with tidings of her death?"

"Those who remember that he had been a participator in the lengthy discussion which had just taken place on the court-house steps as to how a man might commit a crime without laying himself open to the risk of detection, might—yes, sir."

Mr. Ferris and the coroner, who, whatever their doubts or fears, had never for an instant seriously believed the dying words of Mr. Orcutt to be those of confession, gazed in consternation at the detective, and finally inquired:

"Do you realize what you are saying?"

Mr. Gryce drew a deep breath, and shifted his gaze to the next stud in Mr. Ferris' shirt-front.

"I have never been accused of speaking lightly," he remarked. Then, with quiet insistence, asked: "Where was Mrs. Clemmens believed to get the money she lived on?"

"It is not known," rejoined the district attorney.

"Yet she left a nice little sum behind her?"

"Five thousand dollars," declared the coroner.

"Strange that, in a town like this, no one should know where it came from?" suggested the detective.

The two gentlemen were silent.

"It was a good deal to come from Mr. Orcutt in payment of a single meal a day!" continued Mr. Gryce.

"No one has ever supposed it did come from Mr. Orcutt," remarked Mr. Ferris, with some severity.

"But does anyone know it did not?" ventured the detective.

Dr. Tredwell and the district attorney looked at each other, but did not reply.

"Gentlemen," pursued Mr. Gryce, after a moment of quiet waiting, "this is without exception the most serious moment of my life. Never in the course of my experience—and that includes much—have I been placed in a more trying position than now. To allow one's self to doubt, much less to question, the integrity of so eminent a man, seems to me only less dreadful than it does to you; yet, for all that, were I his friend, as I certainly am his admirer, I would say: 'Sift this matter to the bottom; let us know if this great lawyer has any more in favour of his innocence than the other gentlemen who have been publicly accused of this crime.'"

"But," protested Dr. Tredwell, seeing that the district attorney was too much moved to speak, "you forget the evidences which underlay the accusation of these *other* gentlemen; also that of all the persons who, from the day the widow was struck till now, have been in any way associated with suspicion, Mr. Orcutt is the only one who could have had no earthly motive for injuring this humble woman, even if he were all he would have to be to first perform such a brutal deed and then carry out his hypocrisy to the point of using his skill as a criminal lawyer to defend another man falsely accused of the crime."

"I beg your pardon, sir," said the detective, "but I forget nothing. I only bring to the consideration of this subject a totally unprejudiced mind and an experience which has taught me never to omit testing the truth of a charge because it seems at first blush false, preposterous, and without visible foundation. If you will recall the conversation to which I have just alluded as having been held on the court-house steps on the morning Mrs. Clemmens was murdered, you will remember that it was the intellectual crime that was discussed—the crime of an intelligent man, safe in the knowledge that his motive for doing such a deed was a secret to the world."

"My God!" exclaimed Mr. Ferris, under his breath, "the man seems to be in earnest!"

"Gentlemen," pursued Mr. Gryce, with more dignity than he had hitherto seen fit to assume, "it is not my usual practice to express myself as openly as I have done here today. In all ordinary cases I consider it expedient to reserve intact my suspicions and my doubts till I have completed my discoveries and arranged my arguments so as to bear out with some show of reason whatever statement I may feel obliged to make. But the extraordinary features of this affair, and the fact that so many were present at the scene we have just left, have caused me to change my usual tactics. Though far from ready to say that Mr. Orcutt's words were those of confession, I still see much reason to doubt his innocence, and, feeling thus, am quite willing you should know it in time to prepare for the worst."

"Then you propose making what has occurred here public?" asked Mr. Ferris, with emotion.

"Not so," was the detective's ready reply. "On the contrary, I was about to suggest that you did something more than lay a command of silence upon those who were present."

The district attorney, who, as he afterward said, felt as if he were labouring under some oppressive nightmare, turned to the coroner and said:

"Dr. Tredwell, what do you advise me to do? Terrible as this shock has been, and serious as is the duty it possibly involves, I have never allowed myself to shrink from doing what was right simply because it afforded suffering to myself or indignity to my friends. Do you think I am called upon to pursue this matter?"

The coroner, troubled, anxious, and nearly as much overwhelmed as the district attorney, did not immediately reply. Indeed, the situation was one to upset any man of whatever calibre. Finally he turned to Mr. Gryce.

"Mr. Gryce," said he, "we are, as you have observed, friends of the dying man, and, being so, may miss our duty in our sympathy. What do you think ought to be done, in justice to him, the prisoner, and the positions which we both occupy?"

"Well, sirs," rejoined Mr. Gryce, "it is not usual, perhaps, for a man in my position to offer actual advice to gentlemen in yours; but if you wish to know what course I should pursue if I were in your places, I should say: First, require the witnesses still lingering around the dying man to promise that they will not divulge what was there said till a week has fully elapsed; next, adjourn the case now before the court for the same decent length of time; and, lastly, trust me and the two men you have hitherto employed, to find out if there is anything in Mr. Orcutt's past history of a nature to make you tremble if the world hears of the words which escaped him on his death-bed. We shall probably need but a week."

"And Miss Dare?"

"Has already promised secrecy."

There was nothing in all this to alarm their fears; everything, on the contrary, to allay them.

The coroner gave a nod of approval to Mr. Ferris, and both signified their acquiescence in the measures proposed.

Mr. Gryce at once assumed his usual genial air.

"You may trust me," said he, "to exercise all the discretion you would yourselves show under the circumstances. I have no wish to see the name of such a man blasted by an ineffaceable stain." And he bowed as if about to leave the room.

But Mr. Ferris, who had observed this movement with an air of some uneasiness, suddenly stepped forward and stopped him.

"I wish to ask," said he, "whether superstition has had anything to do with this readiness on your part to impute the worst meaning to the chance phrases which have fallen from the lips of our severely injured friend. Because his end seems in some regards to mirror that of the widow, have you allowed a remembrance of the words she made use of in the face of death to influence your good judgement as to the identity of Mr. Orcutt with her assassin?"

The face of Mr. Gryce assumed its grimmest aspect.

"Do you think this catastrophe was necessary to draw my attention to Mr. Orcutt? To a man acquainted with the extraordinary coincidence that marked the discovery of Mrs. Clemmens' murder, the mystery must be that Mr. Orcutt has gone unsuspected for so long." And assuming an argumentative air, he asked:

"Were either of you two gentlemen present at the conversation I have mentioned as taking place on the court-house steps the morning Mrs. Clemmens was murdered?"

"I was," said the district attorney.

"You remember, then, the hunchback who was so free with his views?"

"Most certainly."

"And know, perhaps, who that hunchback was?"

"Yes."

"You will not be surprised, then, if I recall to you the special incidents of that hour. A group of lawyers, among them Mr. Orcutt, are amusing themselves with an off-hand chat concerning criminals and the clumsy way in which, as a rule, they plan and execute their crimes. All seem to agree that a murder is usually followed by detection, when suddenly a stranger speaks and tells them that the true way to make a success of the crime is to choose a thoroughfare for the scene of tragedy, and employ a weapon that has been picked up on the spot. What happens? Within five minutes after this piece of gratuitous information, or as soon as Mr. Orcutt can cross the street, Mrs. Clemmens is found lying in her blood, struck down by a stick of wood picked up from her own hearth-stone. Is this chance? If so, 'tis a very curious one."

"I don't deny it," said Doctor Tredwell.

"I believe you never did deny it," quickly retorted the detective. "Am I not right in saying that it struck you so forcibly at the time as to lead you into supposing some collusion between the hunchback and the murderer?"

"It certainly did," admitted the coroner.

"Very well," proceeded Mr. Gryce. "Now as there could have been no collusion between these parties, the hunchback being no other person than myself, what are we to think of this murder? That it was a coincidence, or an actual result of the hunchback's words?"

Dr. Tredwell and Mr. Ferris were both silent.

"Sirs," continued Mr. Gryce, feeling, perhaps, that perfect openness was necessary in order to win entire confidence, "I am not given to boasting or to a too-free expression of my opinion, but if I had been ignorant of this affair, and one of my men had come to me and said: 'A mysterious murder has just taken place, marked by this extraordinary feature, that it is a precise reproduction of a supposable case of crime which has just been discussed by a group of indifferent persons in the public street,' and then had asked me where to look for the assassin, I should have said: 'Search for that man who heard the discussion through, was among the first to leave the group, and was the first to show himself upon the scene of murder.' To be sure, when Byrd did come to me with this story, I was silent, for the man who fulfilled these conditions was Mr. Orcutt."

"Then," said Mr. Ferris, "you mean to say that you would have suspected Mr. Orcutt of this crime long ago if he had not been a man of such position and eminence?"

"Undoubtedly," was Mr. Gryce's reply.

If the expression was unequivocal, his air was still more so. Shocked and disturbed, both gentlemen fell back. The detective at once advanced and opened the door.

It was time. Mr. Byrd had been tapping upon it for some minutes, and now hastily came in. His face told the nature of his errand before he spoke.

"I am sorry to be obliged to inform you——" he began.

"Mr. Orcutt is dead?" quickly interposed Mr. Ferris.

The young detective solemnly bowed.

CHAPTER 40

In the Prison

Mr. Mansell sat in his cell, the prey of gloomy and perturbed thought. He knew Mr. Orcutt was dead; he had been told of it early in the morning by his jailer, but of the circumstances which attended that death he knew nothing, save that the lawyer had been struck by a limb falling from a tree in his own garden.

The few moments during which the court had met for the purpose of re-adjournment had added but little to his enlightenment. A marked reserve had characterized the whole proceedings; and though an indefinable instinct had told him that in some mysterious way his cause had been helped rather than injured by this calamity to his counsel, he found no one ready to volunteer those explanations which his great interest in the matter certainly demanded. The hour, therefore, which he spent in solitude upon his return to prison was one of great anxiety, and it was quite a welcome relief when the cell door opened and the keeper ushered in a strange gentleman. Supposing it to be the new counsel he had chosen at haphazard from a list of names that had been offered him, Mr. Mansell rose. But a second glance assured him he had made a mistake in supposing this person to be a lawyer, and stepping back he awaited his approach with mingled curiosity and reserve.

The stranger, who seemed to be perfectly at home in the narrow quarters in which he found himself, advanced with a frank air.

"My name is Gryce," said he, "and I am a detective. The district attorney, who, as you know, has been placed in a very embarrassing situation by the events of the last two days, has accepted my services in connection with those of the two men already employed by him, in the hope that my greater experience may assist him in determining which, of all the persons who have been accused, or who have accused themselves, of murdering Mrs. Clemmens, is the actual perpetrator of that deed. Do you require any further assurance of my being in the confidence of Mr. Ferris than the fact that I am here, and in full liberty to talk with you?"

"No," returned the other, after a short but close study of his visitor.

"Very well, then," continued the detective, with a comfortable air of ease, "I will speak to the point; and the first thing I will say is, that upon looking at the evidence against you, and hearing what I have heard from various sources since I came to town, I know you are not the man who killed Mrs. Clemmens. To be sure, you have declined to explain certain points, but I think you can explain them, and if you will only inform me——"

"Pardon me," interrupted Mr. Mansell, gravely; "but you say you are a detective. Now, I have no information to give a detective."

"Are you sure?" was the imperturbable query.

"Quite," was the quick reply.

"You are then determined upon going to the scaffold, whether or no?" remarked Mr. Gryce, somewhat grimly.

"Yes, if to escape it I must confide in a detective."

"Then you do wrong," declared the other; "as I will immediately proceed to show you. Mr. Mansell, you are, of course, aware of the manner of Mr. Orcutt's death?"

"I know he was struck by a falling limb."

"Do you know what he was doing when this occurred?"

"No."

"He was escorting Miss Dare down to the gate."

The prisoner, whose countenance had brightened at the mention of his lawyer, turned a deadly white at this.

"And—and was Miss Dare hurt?" he asked.

The detective shook his head.

"Then why do you tell me this?"

"Because it has much to do with the occasion of my coming here, Mr. Mansell," proceeded Mr. Gryce, in that tone of completely understanding himself which he knew so well how to assume with men of the prisoner's stamp. "I am going to speak to you without circumlocution or disguise. I am going to put your position before you just as it is. You are on trial for a murder of which not only yourself, but another man, was suspected. Why are you on trial instead of him? Because you were reticent in regard to certain matters which common-sense would say you ought to be able to explain. Why were you reticent? There can be but one answer. Because you feared to implicate another person, for whose happiness and honour you had more regard than for your own. Who was that other person? The woman who stood up in court yesterday and declared she had herself committed this crime. What is the conclusion? You believe, and have always believed, Miss Dare to be the assassin of Mrs. Clemmens."

The prisoner, whose pallor had increased with every word the detective uttered, leaped to his feet at this last sentence.

"You have no right to say that!" he vehemently asseverated. "What do you know of my thoughts or my beliefs? Do I carry my convictions on my sleeve? I am not the man to betray my ideas or feelings to the world."

Mr. Gryce smiled. To be sure, this expression of silent complacency was directed to the grating of the window overhead, but it was none the less effectual on that account. Mr. Mansell, despite his self-command, began to look uneasy.

"Prove your words!" he cried. "Show that these have been my convictions!"

"Very well," returned Mr. Gryce. "Why were you so long silent about the ring? Because you did not wish to compromise Miss Dare by declaring she did not return it to you, as she had said. Why did you try to stop her in the midst of her testimony yesterday? Because you saw it was going to end in confession. Finally, why did you throw aside your defence, and instead of proclaiming yourself guilty, simply tell how you were able to reach Monteith Quarry Station in ninety minutes? Because you feared her guilt would be confirmed if her statements were investigated, and were willing to sacrifice everything but the truth in order to save her."

"You give me credit for a great deal of generosity," coldly replied the prisoner. "After the evidence brought against me by the prosecution, I should think my guilt would be accepted as proved the moment I showed that I had not left Mrs. Clemmens' house at the time she was believed to be murdered."

"And so it would," responded Mr. Gryce, "if the prosecution had not seen reason to believe that the moment of Mrs. Clemmens' death has been put too early. We now think she was not struck till some time after twelve, instead of five minutes before."

"Indeed?" said Mr. Mansell, with stern self-control.

Mr. Gryce, whose carelessly roving eye told little of the close study with which he was honouring the man before him, nodded with grave decision.

"You could add very much to our convictions on this point," he observed, "by telling what it was you saw or heard in Mrs. Clemmens' house at the moment you fled from it so abruptly."

"How do you know I fled from it abruptly?"

"You were seen. The fact has not appeared in court, but a witness we might name perceived you flying from your aunt's door to the swamp as if your life depended upon the speed you made."

"And with that fact added to all the rest you have against me, you say you believe me innocent?" exclaimed Mr. Mansell.

"Yes; for I have also said I believe Mrs. Clemmens not to have been assaulted till after the hour of noon. You fled from the door at precisely five minutes before it."

The uneasiness of Mr. Mansell's face increased, till it amounted to agitation.

"And may I ask," said he, "what has happened to make you believe she was not struck at the moment hitherto supposed?"

"Ah, now," replied the detective, "we come down to facts." And leaning with a confidential air toward the prisoner, he quietly said: "Your counsel has died, for one thing."

Astonished as much by the tone as the tenor of these words, Mr. Mansell drew back from his visitor in some distrust. Seeing it, Mr. Gryce edged still farther forward, and calmly continued:

"If no one has told you the particulars of Mr. Orcutt's death, you probably do not know why Miss Dare was at his house last evening?"

The look of the prisoner was sufficient reply.

"She went there," resumed Mr. Gryce, with composure, "to tell him that her whole evidence against you had been given under the belief that you were guilty of the crime with which you had been charged; that by a trick of my fellow-detectives, Hickory and Byrd, she had been deceived into thinking you had actually admitted your guilt to her; and that she had only been undeceived after she had uttered the perjury with which she sought to save you yesterday morning."

"Perjury?" escaped involuntarily from Craik Mansell's lips.

"Yes," repeated the detective, "perjury. Miss Dare lied when she said she had been to Mrs. Clemmens' cottage on the morning of the murder. She was not there, nor did she lift her hand against the widow's life. That tale she told to escape telling another which she thought would insure your doom."

"You have been talking to Miss Dare?" suggested the prisoner, with subdued sarcasm.

"I have been talking to my two men," was the unmoved retort, "to Hickory and to Byrd, and they not only confirm this statement of hers in regard to the deception they played upon her, but say enough to show she could not have been guilty of the crime, because at that time she honestly believed you to be so."

"I do not understand you," cried the prisoner, in a voice that, despite his marked self-control, showed the presence of genuine emotion.

Mr. Gryce at once went into particulars. He was anxious to have Craik Mansell's mind disabused of the notion that Imogene had committed this crime, since upon that notion he believed his unfortunate reticence to rest. He therefore gave him a full relation of the scene in the hut, together with all its consequences.

Mr. Mansell listened like a man in a dream. Some fact in the past evidently made this story incredible to him.

Seeing it, Mr. Gryce did not wait to hear his comments, but upon finishing his account, exclaimed, with a confident air:

"Such testimony is conclusive. It is impossible to consider Miss Dare guilty, after an insight of this kind into the real state of her mind. Even she has seen the uselessness of persisting in her self-accusation, and, as I have already told you, went to Mr. Orcutt's house in order to explain to him her past conduct, and ask his advice for the future. She learned something else before her interview with Mr. Orcutt ended," continued the detective, impressively. "She learned that she had not only been mistaken in supposing you had admitted your guilt, but that you could not have been guilty, because you had always believed her to be so. It has been a mutual case of suspicion, you see, and argues innocence on the part of you both. Or so it seems to the prosecution. How does it seem to you?"

"Would it help my cause to say?"

"It would help your cause to tell what sent you so abruptly from Mrs. Clemmens' house the morning she was murdered."

"I do not see how," returned the prisoner.

The glance of Mr. Gryce settled confidentially on his right hand where it lay outspread upon his ample knee.

"Mr. Mansell," he inquired, "have you no curiosity to know any details of the accident by which you have unexpectedly been deprived of a counsel?"

487

Evidently surprised at this sudden change of subject, Craik replied:

"If I had not hoped you would understand my anxiety and presently relieve it, I could not have shown you as much patience as I have."

"Very well," rejoined Mr. Gryce, altering his manner with a suddenness that evidently alarmed his listener. "Mr. Orcutt did not die immediately after he was struck down. He lived some hours; lived to say some words that have materially changed the suspicions of persons interested in the case he was defending."

"Mr. Orcutt?"

The tone was one of surprise. Mr. Gryce's little finger seemed to take note of it, for it tapped the leg beneath it in quite an emphatic manner as he continued: "It was in answer to a question put to him by Miss Dare. To the surprise of everyone, she had not left him from the moment they were mutually relieved from the weight of the fallen limb, but had stood over him for hours, watching for him to rouse from his insensibility. When he did, she appealed to him in a way that showed she expected a reply, to tell her who it was that killed the Widow Clemmens."

"And did Mr. Orcutt know?" was Mansell's half-agitated, half-incredulous query.

"His answer seemed to show that he did. Mr. Mansell, have you ever had any doubts of Mr. Orcutt?"

"Doubts?"

"Doubts as to his integrity, good-heartedness, or desire to serve you?"

"No."

"You will, then, be greatly surprised," Mr. Gryce went on, with increased gravity, "when I tell you that Mr. Orcutt's reply to Miss Dare's question was such as to draw attention to himself as the assassin of Widow Clemmens, and that his words and the circumstances under which they were uttered have so impressed Mr. Ferris, that the question now agitating his mind is not, 'Is Craik Mansell innocent, but was his counsel, Tremont Orcutt, guilty?'"

The excited look which had appeared on the face of Mansell at the beginning of this speech, changed to one of strong disgust.

"This is too much!" he cried. "I am not a fool to be caught by any such make-believe as this! Mr. Orcutt thought to be an assassin? You might as well say that people accuse Judge Evans of killing the Widow

Clemmens."

Mr. Gryce, who had perhaps stretched a point when he so un-equivocally declared his complete confidence in the innocence of the man before him, tapped his leg quite affectionately at this burst of natural indignation, and counted off another point in favour of the prisoner. His words, however, were dry as sarcasm could make them.

"No," said he, "for people know that Judge Evans was without the opportunity for committing this murder, while everyone remembers how Mr. Orcutt went to the widow's house and came out again with tidings of her death."

The prisoner's lip curled disdainfully.

"And do you expect me to believe you regard this as a ground-work for suspicion? I should have given you credit for more penetra-tion, sir."

"Then you do not think Mr. Orcutt knew what he was saying when, in answer to Miss Dare's appeal for him to tell who the mur-derer was, he answered: 'Blood will have blood!' and drew attention to his own violent end?"

"Did Mr. Orcutt say that?"

"He did."

"Very well, a man whose whole mind has for some time been engrossed with defending another man accused of murder, might say anything while in a state of delirium."

Mr. Gryce uttered his favourite "Humph!" and gave his leg an-other pat, but added, gravely enough: "Miss Dare believes his words to be those of confession."

"You say Miss Dare once believed me to have confessed."

"But," persisted the detective, "Miss Dare is not alone in her opin-ion. Men in whose judgement you must rely, find it difficult to explain the words of Mr. Orcutt by means of any other theory than that he is himself the perpetrator of that crime for which you are yourself being tried."

"I find it difficult to believe that possible," quietly returned the prisoner. "What!" he suddenly exclaimed; "suspect a man of Mr. Or-cutt's abilities and standing of a hideous crime—the very crime, too, with which his client is charged, and in defence of whom he has brought all his skill to bear! The idea is preposterous, unheard of!"

"I acknowledge that," dryly assented Mr. Gryce; "but it has been my experience to find that it is the preposterous things which hap-pen."

For a minute the prisoner stared at the speaker incredulously; then he cried:

"You really appear to be in earnest."

"I was never more so in my life," was Mr. Gryce's rejoinder.

Drawing back, Craik Mansell looked at the detective with an emotion that had almost the character of hope. Presently he said:

"If you do distrust Mr. Orcutt, you must have weightier reasons for it than any you have given me. What are they? You must be willing I should know, or you would not have gone as far with me as you have."

"You are right," Gryce assured him. "A case so complicated as this calls for unusual measures. Mr. Ferris, feeling the gravity of his position, allows me to take you into our confidence, in the hope that you will be able to help us out of our difficulty."

"I help you! You'd better release me first."

"That will come in time."

"*If* I help you?"

"Whether you help or not, if we can satisfy ourselves and the world that Mr. Orcutt's words were a confession. You may hasten that conviction."

"How?"

"By clearing up the mystery of your flight from Mrs. Clemmens' house."

The keen eyes of the prisoner fell; all his old distrust seemed on the point of returning.

"That would not help you at all," said he.

"*I* should like to be the judge," said Mr. Gryce.

The prisoner shook his head.

"My word must go for it," said he.

The detective had been the hero of too many such scenes to be easily discouraged. Bowing as if accepting this conclusion from the prisoner, he quietly proceeded with the recital he had planned. With a frankness certainly unusual to him, he gave the prisoner a full account of Mr. Orcutt's last hours, and the interview which had followed between himself and Miss Dare. To this he added his own reasons for doubting the lawyer, and, while admitting he saw no motive for the deed, gave it as his serious opinion, that the motive would be found if once he could get at the secret of Mr. Orcutt's real connection with the deceased. He was so eloquent, and so manifestly in earnest, Mr. Mansell's eye brightened in spite of himself, and when the detective

490

ceased he looked up with an expression which convinced Mr. Gryce that half the battle was won. He accordingly said, in a tone of great confidence:

"A knowledge of what went on in Mrs. Clemmens' house before he went to it would be of great help to us. With that for a start, all may be learned. I therefore put it to you for the last time whether it would not be best for you to explain yourself on this point. I am sure you will not regret it."

"Sir," said Mansell, with undisturbed composure, "if your purpose is to fix this crime on Mr. Orcutt, I must insist upon your taking my word that I have no information to give you that can in any way affect him."

"You could give us information, then, that would affect Miss Dare?" was the quick retort. "Now, I say," the astute detective declared, as the prisoner gave an almost imperceptible start, "that whatever your information is, Miss Dare is not guilty."

"You say it!" exclaimed the prisoner. "What does your opinion amount to if you haven't heard the evidence against her?"

"There is no evidence against her but what is purely circumstantial."

"How do you know that?"

"Because she is innocent. Circumstantial evidence may exist alike against the innocent and the guilty; real evidence only against the guilty. I mean to say that as I am firmly convinced Miss Dare once regarded you as guilty of this crime, I must be equally convinced she didn't commit it herself. This is unanswerable."

"You have stated that before."

"I know it; but I want you to see the force of it; because, once convinced with me that Miss Dare is innocent, you will be willing to tell all you know, even what apparently implicates her."

Silence answered this remark.

"You didn't *see* her strike the blow?"

Mansell roused indignantly.

"No, of course not!" he cried.

"You did not see her with your aunt that moment you fled from the house immediately before the murder!"

"I didn't *see* her."

That emphasis, unconscious, perhaps, was fatal. Gryce, who never lost anything, darted on this small gleam of advantage as a hungry pike darts upon an innocent minnow.

"But you thought you heard her," he cried; "her voice, or her laugh, or perhaps merely the rustle of her dress in another room?"

"No," said Mansell, "I didn't *hear* her."

"Of course not," was the instantaneous reply. "But something said or done by somebody—a something which amounts to nothing as evidence—gives you to understand she was there, and so you hold your tongue for fear of compromising her."

"Amounts to nothing as evidence?" echoed Mansell. "How do you know that?"

"Because Miss Dare was not in the house with your aunt at that time. Miss Dare was in Professor Darling's observatory, a mile or so away."

"Does she say that?"

"We will *prove* that."

Aroused, excited, the prisoner turned his flashing blue eyes on the detective.

"I should be glad to have you," he said.

"But you must first tell me in what room you were when you received this intimation of Miss Dare's presence?"

"I was in no room; I was on the stone step outside of the dining-room door. I did not go into the house at all that morning, as I believe I have already told Mr. Ferris."

"*Very* good! It will all be simpler than I thought. You came up to the house and went away again without coming in; ran away, I may say, taking the direction of the swamp."

The prisoner did not deny it.

"You remember all the incidents of that short flight?"

The prisoner's lip curled.

"Remember leaping the fence and stumbling a trifle when you came down?"

"Yes."

"Very well; now tell me how could Miss Dare see you do that from Mrs. Clemmens' house?"

"Did Miss Dare tell you she saw me trip after I jumped the fence?"

"She did."

"And yet was in Professor Darling's observatory, a mile or so away?"

"Yes."

A satirical laugh broke from the prisoner.

"I think," said he, "that instead of my telling you how she could have seen this from Mrs. Clemmens' house, you should tell me how she could have seen it from Professor Darling's observatory."

"That is easy enough. She was looking through a telescope."

"What?"

"At the moment you were turning from Mrs. Clemmens' door, Miss Dare, perched in the top of Professor Darling's house, was looking in that very direction through a telescope."

"I—I would like to believe that story," said the prisoner, with suppressed emotion. "It would——"

"What?" urged the detective, calmly.

"Make a new man of me," finished Mansell, with a momentary burst of feeling.

"Well, then, call up your memories of the way your aunt's house is situated. Recall the hour, and acknowledge that, if Miss Dare was with her, she must have been in the dining-room."

"There is no doubt about that."

"Now, how many windows has the dining-room?"

"One."

"How situated?"

"It is on the same side as the door."

"There is none, then, which looks down to that place where you leaped the fence?"

"No."

"How account for her seeing that little incident, then, of your stumbling?"

"She might have come to the door, stepped out, and so seen me."

"Humph! I see you have an answer for everything."

Craik Mansell was silent.

A look of admiration slowly spread itself over the detective's face.

"We must probe the matter a little deeper," said he. "I see I have a hard head to deal with." And, bringing his glance a little nearer to the prisoner, he remarked:

"If she had been standing there you could not have turned round without seeing her?"

"No."

"Now, did you see her standing there?"

"No."

"Yet you turned round?"

"I did?"

"Miss Dare says so."

The prisoner struck his forehead with his hand.

"And it *is* so," he cried. "I remember now that some vague desire to know the time made me turn to look at the church clock. Go on. Tell me more that Miss Dare saw."

His manner was so changed—his eye burned so brightly—the detective gave himself a tap of decided self-gratulation.

"She saw you hurry over the bog, stop at the entrance of the wood, take a look at your watch, and plunge with renewed speed into the forest."

"It is so. It is so. And, to have seen that, she must have had the aid of a telescope."

"Then she describes your appearance. She says you had your pants turned up at the ankles, and carried your coat on your left arm."

"*Left* arm?"

"Yes."

"I think I had it on my right."

"It was on the arm toward her, she declares. If she was in the observatory, it was your left side that she saw."

"Yes, yes; but the coat was over the other arm. I remember using my left hand in vaulting over the fence when I came up to the house."

"It is a vital point," said Mr. Gryce, with a quietness that concealed his real anxiety and chagrin. "If the coat was on the arm *toward* her, the fact of its being on the right———"

"Wait!" exclaimed Mr. Mansell, with an air of sudden relief. "I recollect now that I changed it from one arm to the other after I vaulted the fence. It was just at the moment I turned to come back to the side door, and, as she does not pretend to have seen me till after I left the door, of course the coat was, as she says, on my left arm."

"I thought you could explain it," returned Mr. Gryce, with an air of easy confidence. "But what do you mean when you say that you changed it at the moment you turned to come back to the side door? Didn't you go at once to the dining-room door from the swamp?"

"No. I had gone to the front door on my former visit, and was going to it this time; but when I got to the corner of the house I saw the tramp coming into the gate, and not wishing to encounter anyone, turned round and came back to the dining-room door."

"I see. And it was then you heard———"

"What I heard," completed the prisoner, grimly.

494

"Mr. Mansell," said the other, "are you not sufficiently convinced by this time that Miss Dare was not with Mrs. Clemmens, but in the observatory of Professor Darling's house, to tell me what that was?"

"Answer me a question and I will reply. Can the entrance of the woods be seen from the position which she declares herself to have occupied?"

"It can. Not two hours ago I tried the experiment myself, using the same telescope and kneeling in the same place where she did. I found I could not only trace the spot where you paused, but could detect quite readily every movement of my man Hickory, whom I had previously placed there to go through the motions. I should not have come here if I had not made myself certain on that point."

Yet the prisoner hesitated.

"I not only made myself sure of that," resumed Mr. Gryce, "but I also tried if I could see as much with my naked eye from Mrs. Clemmens' side door. I found I could not, and my sight is very good."

"Enough," said Mansell; "hard as it is to explain, I must believe Miss Dare was not where I thought her."

"Then you will tell me what you heard?"

"Yes; for in it may lie the key to this mystery, though how, I cannot see, and doubt if you can. I am all the more ready to do it," he pursued, "because I can now understand how she came to think me guilty, and, thinking so, conducted herself as she has done from the beginning of my trial. All but the fact of her denouncing herself yesterday; that I cannot comprehend."

"A woman in love can do anything ," quoth Mr. Gryce. Then admonished by the flush of the prisoner's cheek that he was treading on dangerous ground, he quickly added: "But she will explain all that herself some day. Let us hear what you have to tell me."

Craik Mansell drooped his head and his brow became gloomy.

"Sir," said he, "it is unnecessary for me to state that your surmise in regard to my past convictions is true. If Miss Dare was not with my aunt just before the murder, I certainly had reasons for thinking she was. To be sure, I did not see her or hear her voice, but I heard my aunt address her distinctly and by name."

"You did?" Mr. Gryce's interest in the tattoo he was playing on his knee became intense.

"Yes. It was just as I pushed the door ajar. The words were these: 'You think you are going to marry him, Imogene Dare; but I tell you you *never shall*, not while *I* live.'"

"Humph!" broke involuntarily from the detective's lips, and, though his face betrayed nothing of the shock this communication occasioned him, his fingers stopped an instant in their restless play.

Mr. Mansell saw it and cast him an anxious look. The detective instantly smiled with great unconcern. "Go on," said he, "what else did you hear?"

"Nothing else. In the mood in which I was this very plain intimation that Miss Dare had sought my aunt, had pleaded with her for me and failed, struck me as sufficient. I did not wait to hear more, but hurried away in a state of passion that was little short of frenzy. To leave the place and return to my work was now my one wish. When I found, then, that by running I might catch the train at Monteith, I ran, and so unconsciously laid myself open to suspicion."

"I see," murmured the detective; "I see."

"Not that I suspected any evil then," pursued Mr. Mansell, earnestly. "I was only conscious of disappointment and a desire to escape from my own thoughts. It was not till next day——"

"Yes—yes," interrupted Mr. Gryce, abstractedly, "but your aunt's words! She said: 'You think you are going to marry him, Imogene Dare; but you never shall, not while I live.' Yet Imogene Dare was not there. Let us solve that problem."

"You think you can?"

"I think I must."

"How? how?"

The detective did not answer. He was buried in profound thought. Suddenly he exclaimed:

"It is, as you say, the key-note to the tragedy. It must be solved." But the glance he dived deep into space seemed to echo that "How? how?" of the prisoner, with a gloomy persistence that promised little for an immediate answer to the enigma before them. It occurred to Mansell to offer a suggestion.

"There is but one way *I* can explain it," said he. "My aunt was speaking to herself. She was deaf and lived alone. Such people often indulge in soliloquizing."

The slap which Mr. Gryce gave his thigh must have made it tingle for a good half-hour.

"There," he cried, "who says extraordinary measures are not useful at times? You've hit the very explanation. Of course she was speaking to herself. She was just the woman to do it. Imogene Dare was in her thoughts, so she addressed Imogene Dare. If you had opened the door

496

you would have seen her standing there alone, venting her thoughts into empty space."

"I wish I had," said the prisoner.

Mr. Gryce became exceedingly animated. "Well, that's settled," said he. "Imogene Dare was not there, save in Mrs. Clemmens' imagination. And now for the conclusion. She said: 'You think you are going to marry him, Imogene Dare; but you never shall, not while I live.' That shows her mind was running on you."

"It shows more than that. It shows that, if Miss Dare was not with her then, she must have been there earlier in the day. For, when I left my aunt the day before, she was in entire ignorance of my attachment to Miss Dare, and the hopes it had led to."

"Say that again," cried Gryce.

Mr. Mansell repeated himself, adding: "That would account for the ring being found on my aunt's dining-room floor———"

But Mr. Gryce waved that question aside.

"What I want to make sure of is that your aunt had not been informed of your wishes as concerned Miss Dare."

"Unless Miss Dare was there in the early morning and told her herself."

"There were no neighbours to betray you?"

"There wasn't a neighbour who knew anything about the matter."

The detective's eye brightened till it vied in brilliancy with the stray gleam of sunshine which had found its way to the cell through the narrow grating over their heads.

"A clue!" he murmured; "I have received a clue," and rose as if to leave.

The prisoner, startled, rose also.

"A clue to what?" he cried.

But Mr. Gryce was not the man to answer such a question.

"You shall hear soon. Enough that you have given me an idea that may eventually lead to the clearing up of this mystery, if not to your own acquittal from a false charge of murder."

"And Miss Dare?"

"Is under no charge, and never will be."

"And Mr. Orcutt?"

"Wait," said Mr. Gryce—"wait."

41

A Link Supplied

Mr. Gryce did not believe that Imogene Dare had visited Mrs. Clemmens before the assault, or, indeed, had held any communication with her. Therefore, when Mansell declared that he had never told his aunt of the attachment between himself and this young lady, the astute detective at once drew the conclusion that the widow had never known of that attachment, and consequently that the words which the prisoner had overheard must have referred, not to himself, as he supposed, but to some other man, and, if to some other man—why to the only one with whom Miss Dare's name was at that time associated; in other words, to Mr. Orcutt!

Now it was not easy to measure the importance of a conclusion like this. For whilst there would have been nothing peculiar in this solitary woman, with the few thousands in the bank, boasting of her power to separate her nephew from the lady of his choice, there was everything that was significant in her using the same language in regard to Miss Dare and Mr. Orcutt. Nothing but the existence of some unsuspected bond between herself and the great lawyer could have accounted, first, for her feeling on the subject of his marriage; and, secondly, for the threat of interference contained in her very emphatic words,—a bond which, while evidently not that of love, was still of a nature to give her control over his destiny, and make her, in spite of her lonely condition, the selfish and determined arbitrator of his fate.

What was that bond? A secret shared between them? The knowledge on her part of some fact in Mr. Orcutt's past life, which, if revealed, might serve as an impediment to his marriage? In consideration that the great mystery to be solved was what motive Mr. Orcutt could have had for killing this woman, an answer to this question was manifestly of the first importance.

But before proceeding to take any measures to insure one, Mr. Gryce sat down and seriously asked himself whether there was any known fact, circumstantial or otherwise, which refused to fit into the theory that Mr. Orcutt actually committed this crime with his own hand, and at the time he was seen to cross the street and enter Mrs. Clemmens' house. For, whereas the most complete chain of circumstantial evidence does not necessarily prove the suspected party to be guilty of a crime, the least break in it is fatal to his conviction. And Mr. Gryce wished to be as fair to the memory of Mr. Orcutt as he would have been to the living man.

Beginning, therefore, with the earliest incidents of the fatal day, he called up, first, the letter which the widow had commenced but never lived to finish. It was a suggestive epistle. It was addressed to her most intimate friend, and showed in the few lines written a certain foreboding or apprehension of death remarkable under the circumstances. Mr. Gryce recalled one of its expressions. "There are so many," wrote she, "to whom my death would be more than welcome." So many! Many is a strong word; many means more than one, more than two; many means *three* at least.

Now where were the three? Hildreth, of course, was one, Mansell might very properly be another, but who was the third? To Mr. Gryce, but one name suggested itself in reply. So far, then, his theory stood firm. Now what was the next fact known? The milkman stopped with his milk; that was at half-past eleven. He had to wait a few minutes, from which it was concluded she was upstairs when he rapped. Was it at this time she was interrupted in her letter-writing? If so, she probably did not go back to it, for when Mr. Hildreth called, some fifteen minutes later, she was on the spot to open the door. Their interview was short; it was also stormy. Medicine was the last thing she stood in need of; besides, her mind was evidently preoccupied. Showing him the door, she goes back to her work, and, being deaf, does not notice that he does not leave the house as she expected. Consequently her thoughts go on unhindered, and, her condition being one of anger, she mutters aloud and bitterly to herself as she flits from dining-room to kitchen in her labour of serving up her dinner.

The words she made use of have been overheard, and here another point appears. For, whereas her temper must have been disturbed by the demand which had been made upon her the day before by her favourite relative and heir, her expressions of wrath at this moment were not levelled against him, but against a young lady who is said to have been a stranger to her, her language being: "You think you are going to marry him, Imogene Dare; but I tell you you never shall, not while I live." Her chief grievance, then, and the one thing uppermost in her thoughts, even at a time when she felt that there were many who desired her death, lay in this fact that a young and beautiful woman had manifested, as she supposed, a wish to marry Mr. Orcutt, the word *him* which she had used, necessarily referring to the lawyer, as she knew nothing of Imogene's passion for her nephew.

But this is not the only point into which it is necessary to inquire. For to believe Mr. Orcutt guilty of this crime one must also believe that all the other persons who had been accused of it were truthful in the explanations which they gave of the events which had seemingly connected them with it. Now, were they? Take the occurrences of that critical moment when the clock stood at five minutes to twelve. If Mr. Hildreth is to be believed, he was at that instant in the widow's front hall musing on his disappointment and arranging his plans for the future; the tramp, if those who profess to have watched him are to be believed, was on the kitchen portico; Craik Mansell on the dining-room door-step; Imogene Dare before her telescope in Professor Darling's observatory.

Mr. Hildreth, with two doors closed between him and the back of the house, knew nothing of what was said or done there, but the tramp heard loud talking, and Craik Mansell the actual voice of the widow raised in words which were calculated to mislead him into thinking she was engaged in angry altercation with the woman he loved. What do all three do, then? Mr. Hildreth remains where he is; the tramp skulks away through the front gate; Craik Mansell rushes back to the woods. And Imogene Dare? She has turned her telescope toward Mrs. Clemmens' cottage, and, being on the side of the dining-room door, sees the flying form of Craik Mansell, and marks it till it disappears from her sight. Is there anything contradictory in these various statements? No. Everything, on the contrary, that is reconcilable.

Let us proceed then. What happens a few minutes later? Mr. Hildreth, tired of seclusion and anxious to catch the train, opens the front door and steps out. The tramp, skulking round some other back door, does not see him; Imogene, with her eye on Craik Mansell, now vanishing into the woods, does not see him; nobody sees him. He goes, and the widow for a short interval is as much alone as she believed herself to be a minute or two before when three men stood, unseen by each other, at each of the three doors of her house. What does she do now?

Why, she finishes preparing her dinner, and then, observing that the clock is slow, proceeds to set it right. Fatal task! Before she has had an opportunity to finish it, the front door has opened again, Mr. Orcutt has come in, and, tempted perhaps by her defenceless position, catches up a stick of wood from the fireplace and, with one blow, strikes her down at his feet, and rushes forth again with tidings of her death.

Now, is there anything in all *this* that is contradictory? No; there is only something left out. In the whole of this description of what went on in the widow's house, there has been no mention made of the ring—the ring which it is conceded was either in Craik Mansell's or Imogene Dare's possession the evening before the murder, and which was found on the dining-room floor within ten minutes after the assault took place. If Mrs. Clemmens' exclamations are to be taken as an attempt to describe her murderer, then this ring must have been on the hand which was raised against her, and how could that have been if the hand was that of Mr. Orcutt?

Unimportant as it seemed, the discovery of this ring on the floor, taken with the exclamations of the widow, make a break in the chain that is fatal to Mr. Gryce's theory. Yet does it? The consternation displayed by Mr. Orcutt when Imogene claimed the ring and put it on her finger may have had a deeper significance than was thought at the time. Was there any way in which he could have come into possession of it before she did? and could it have been that he had had it on his hand when he struck the blow? Mr. Gryce bent all his energies to inquire.

First, where was the ring when the lovers parted in the wood the day before the murder? Evidently in Mr. Mansell's coat-pocket. Imogene had put it there, and Imogene had left it there. But Mansell did not know it was there, so took no pains to look after its safety. It accordingly slipped out; but when? Not while he slept, or it would have been found in the hut. Not while he took the path to his aunt's house, or it would have been found in the lane, or, at best, on the dining-room door-step. When, then? Mr. Gryce could think of but one instant, and that was when the young man threw his coat from one arm to the other at the corner of the house toward the street.

If it rolled out then it would have been under an impetus, and, as the coat was flung from the right arm to the left, the ring would have flown in the direction of the gate and fallen, perhaps, directly on the walk in front of the house. If it had, its presence in the dining-room seemed to show it had been carried there by Mr. Orcutt, since he was the next person who went into the house.

But did it fall there? Mr. Gryce took the only available means to find out.

Sending for Horace Byrd, he said to him:

"You were on the court-house steps when Mr. Orcutt left and crossed over to the widow's house?"

"Yes, sir."

"Were you watching him? Could you describe his manner as he entered the house; how he opened the gate; or whether he stopped to look about him before going in?"

"No, sir," returned Byrd; "my eyes may have been on him, but I don't remember anything especial that he did."

Somewhat disappointed, Mr. Gryce went to the district attorney and put to him the same question. The answer he received from him was different. With a gloomy contraction of his brow, Mr. Ferris said:

"Yes, I remember his look and appearance very well. He stepped briskly, as he always did, and carried his head—— Wait!" he suddenly exclaimed, giving the detective a look in which excitement and decision were strangely blended. "You think Mr. Orcutt committed this crime; that he left us standing on the court-house steps and crossed the street to Mrs. Clemmens' house with the deliberate intention of killing her, and leaving the burden of his guilt to be shouldered by the tramp. Now, you have called up a memory to me that convinces me this could not have been. Had he had any such infernal design in his breast he would not have been likely to have stopped as he did to pick up something which he saw lying on the walk in front of Mrs. Clemmens' house."

"And did Mr. Orcutt do that?" inquired Mr. Gryce, with admirable self-control.

"Yes, I remember it now distinctly. It was just as he entered the gate. A man meditating a murder of this sort would not be likely to notice a pin lying in his path, much less pause to pick it up."

"How if it were a diamond ring?"

"A diamond ring?"

"Mr. Ferris," said the detective, gravely, "you have just supplied a very important link in the chain of evidence against Mr. Orcutt. The question is, how could the diamond ring which Miss Dare is believed to have dropped into Mr. Mansell's coat-pocket have been carried into Mrs. Clemmens' house without the agency of either herself or

Mr. Mansell? I think you have just shown." And the able detective, in a few brief sentences, explained the situation to Mr. Ferris, together with the circumstances of Mansell's flight, as gleaned by him in his conversation with the prisoner.

The district attorney was sincerely dismayed. The guilt of the renowned lawyer was certainly assuming positive proportions. Yet, true to his friendship for Mr. Orcutt, he made one final effort to controvert the arguments of the detective, and quietly said:

"You profess to explain how the ring might have been carried into Mrs. Clemmens' house, but how do you account for the widow having used an exclamation which seems to signify it was *on* the hand which she saw lifted against her life?"

"By the fact that it was on that hand."

"Do you think that probable if the hand was Mr. Orcutt's?"

"Perfectly so. Where else would he be likely to put it in the preoccupied state of mind in which he was? In his pocket? The tramp might have done that, but not the gentleman."

Mr. Ferris looked at the detective with almost an expression of fear.

"And how came it to be on the floor if Mr. Orcutt put it on his finger?"

"By the most natural process in the world. The ring made for Miss Dare's third finger was too large for Mr. Orcutt's little finger, and so slipped off when he dropped the stick of wood from his hand."

"And he left it lying where it fell?"

"He probably did not notice its loss. If, as I suppose, he had picked it up and placed it on his finger, mechanically, its absence at such a moment would not be observed. Besides, what clue could he suppose a diamond ring he had never seen before, and which he had had on his finger but an instant, would offer in a case like this?"

"You reason close," said the district attorney; "too close," he added, as he recalled, with painful distinctness, the look and attitude of Mr. Orcutt at the time this ring was first brought into public notice, and realized that so might a man comport himself who, conscious of this ring's association with the crime he had just secretly perpetrated, sees it claimed and put on the finger of the woman he loves.

Mr. Gryce, with his usual intuition, seemed to follow the thoughts of the district attorney.

"If our surmises are correct," he remarked, "it was a grim moment for the lawyer when, secure in his immunity from suspicion, he saw

Miss Dare come upon the scene with eager inquiries concerning this murder. To you, who had not the clue, it looked as if he feared she was not as innocent as she should be; but, if you will recall the situation now, I think you will see that his agitation can only be explained by his apprehension of her intuitions and an alarm lest her interest sprang from some mysterious doubt of himself."

Mr. Ferris shook his head with a gloomy air, but did not respond.

"Miss Dare tells me," the detective resumed, "that his first act upon their meeting again at his house was to offer himself to her in marriage. Now you, or anyone else, would say this was to show he did not mistrust her, but I say it was to find out if she mistrusted him."

Still Mr. Ferris remained silent.

"The same reasoning will apply to what followed," continued Mr. Gryce. "You cannot reconcile the thought of his guilt with his taking the case of Mansell and doing all he could to secure his acquittal. But you will find it easier to do so when I tell you that, without taking into consideration any spark of sympathy which he might feel for the man falsely accused of his crime, he knew from Imogene's lips that she would not survive the condemnation of her lover, and that, besides this, his only hope of winning her for his wife lay in the gratitude he might awaken in her if he succeeded in saving his rival."

"You are making him out a great villain," murmured Mr. Ferris, bitterly.

"And was not that the language of his own countenance as he lay dying?" inquired the detective.

Mr. Ferris could not say No. He had himself been too deeply impressed by the sinister look he had observed on the face of his dying friend. He therefore confined himself to remarking, not without sarcasm:

"And now for the motive of this hideous crime—for I suppose your ingenuity has discovered one before this."

"It will be found in his love for Miss Dare," returned the detective; "but just how I am not prepared today to say."

"His love for Miss Dare? What had this plain and homespun Mrs. Clemmens to do with his love for Miss Dare?"

"She was an interference."

"How?"

"Ah, that, sir, is the question."

"So then you do not know?"

Mr. Gryce was obliged to shake his head.

The district attorney drew himself up. "Mr. Gryce," said he, "the charge which has been made against this eminent man demands the very strongest proof in order to substantiate it. The motive, especially, must be shown to have been such as to offer a complete excuse for suspecting him. No trivial or imaginary reason for his wishing this woman out of the world will answer in his case. You must prove that her death was absolutely necessary to the success of his dearest hopes, or your reasoning will only awaken distrust in the minds of all who hear it. The fame of a man like Mr. Orcutt is not to be destroyed by a passing word of delirium, or a specious display of circumstantial evidence such as you evolve from the presence of the ring on the scene of murder."

"I know it," allowed Mr. Gryce, "and that is why I have asked for a week."

"Then you still believe you can find such a motive?"

The smile which Mr. Gryce bestowed upon the favoured object then honoured by his gaze haunted the district attorney for the rest of the week.

42

Consultations

Mr. Gryce was perfectly aware that the task before him was a difficult one. To be himself convinced that Mr. Orcutt had been in possession of a motive sufficient to account for, if not excuse, this horrible crime was one thing; to find out that motive and make it apparent to the world was another. But he was not discouraged. Summoning his two subordinates, he laid the matter before them.

"I am convinced," said he, "that Mrs. Clemmens was a more important person to Mr. Orcutt than her plain appearance and humble manner of life would suggest. Do either of you know whether Mr. Orcutt's name has ever been associated with any private scandal, the knowledge of which might have given her power over him?"

"I do not think he was that kind of a man," said Byrd. "Since morning I have put myself in the way of such persons as I saw disposed to converse about him, and though I have been astonished to find how many there are who say they never quite liked or altogether trusted this famous lawyer, I have heard nothing said in any way derogatory to his private character. Indeed, I believe, as far as the ladies were concerned, he was particularly reserved. Though a bachelor, he showed no disposition to marry, and until Miss Dare appeared on the scene was not known to be even attentive to one of her sex."

"Someone, however, I forget who, told me that for a short time he was sweet on a certain Miss Pratt," remarked Hickory.

"Pratt? Where have I heard that name?" murmured Byrd to himself.

"But nothing came of it," Hickory continued. "She was not over and above smart they say, and though pretty enough, did not hold his fancy. Some folks declare she was so disappointed she left town."

"Pratt, Pratt!" repeated Byrd to himself. "Ah! I know now," he suddenly exclaimed. "While I stood around amongst the crowd, the morning Mrs. Clemmens was murdered, I remember overhearing someone say how hard she was on the Pratt girl."

"Humph!" ejaculated Mr. Gryce. "The widow was hard on anyone Mr. Orcutt chose to admire."

"I don't understand it," said Byrd.

"Nor I," rejoined Mr. Gryce; "but I intend to before the week is out." Then abruptly: "When did Mrs. Clemmens come to this town?"

"Fifteen years ago," replied Byrd.

"And Orcutt—when did he first put in an appearance here?"

"At very much the same time, I believe."

"Humph! And did they seem to be friends at that time?"

"Some say Yes, some say No."

"Where did he come from—have you learned?"

"From some place in Nebraska, I believe."

"And she?"

"Why, she came from some place in Nebraska too!"

"The *same* place?"

"That we must find out."

Mr. Gryce mused for a minute; then he observed:

"Mr. Orcutt was renowned in his profession. Do you know anything about his career—whether he brought a reputation for ability with him, or whether his fame was entirely made in this place?"

"I think it was made here. Indeed, I have heard that it was in this court he pleaded his first case. Don't you know more about it, Hickory?"

"Yes; Mr. Ferris told me this morning that Orcutt had not opened a law-book when he came to this town. That he was a country schoolmaster in some uncivilized district out West, and would never have been anything more, perhaps, if the son of old Stephen Orcutt had not died, and thus made a vacancy in the law-office here which he was immediately sent for to fill."

"Stephen Orcutt? He was the uncle of this man, wasn't he?"

"Yes."

"And quite a lawyer too?"

"Yes, but nothing like Tremont B. *He* was successful from the start. Had a natural aptitude, I suppose—must have had, to pick up the profession in the way he did."

"Boys," cried Mr. Gryce, after another short ruminative pause, "the secret we want to know is of long standing; indeed, I should not be surprised if it were connected with his life out West. I will tell you why I think so. For ten years Mrs. Clemmens has been known to put money in the bank regularly every week. Now, where did she get that money? From Mr. Orcutt, of course. What for? In payment for the dinner he usually took with her? No, in payment of her silence concerning a past he desired kept secret."

"But they have been here fifteen years and she has only received money for ten."

"She has only put money in the bank for ten; she may have been paid before that and may not. I do not suppose he was in a condition to be very lavish at the outset of his career."

"You advise us, then, to see what we can make out of his early life out West?"

"Yes; and I will see what I can make out of hers. The link which connects the two will be found. Mr. Orcutt did not say: 'It was all for you, Imogene,' for nothing."

And, dismissing the two young men, Mr. Gryce proceeded to the house of Mr. Orcutt, where he entered upon an examination of such papers and documents as were open to his inspection, in the hope of discovering some allusion to the deceased lawyer's early history. But he was not successful. Neither did a like inspection of the widow's letters bring any new facts to light. The only result which seemed to follow these efforts was an increased certainty on his part that some dangerous secret lurked in a past that was so determinedly hidden from the world, and resorting to the only expedient now left to him, he resolved to consult Miss Firman, as being the only person who professed to have had any acquaintance with Mrs. Clemmens before she came to Sibley. To be sure, she had already been questioned by the coroner, but Mr. Gryce was a man who had always found that the dryest well could be made to yield a drop or two more of water if the bucket was dropped by a dexterous hand. He accordingly prepared himself for a trip to Utica.

43

Mrs. Firman

"Miss Firman, I believe?" The staid, pleasant-faced lady whom we know, but who is looking older and considerably more careworn than when we saw her at the coroner's inquest, rose from her chair in her own cosy sitting-room, and surveyed her visitor curiously. "I am Mr. Gryce," the genial voice went on. "Perhaps the name is not familiar?"

"I never heard it before," was the short but not ungracious reply.

"Well, then, let me explain," said he. "You are a relative of the Mrs. Clemmens who was so foully murdered in Sibley, are you not? Pardon me, but I see you are; your expression speaks for itself." How he could have seen her expression was a mystery to Miss Firman, for his eyes, if not attention, were seemingly fixed upon some object in quite a different portion of the room. "You must, therefore," he pursued, "be in a state of great anxiety to know who her murderer was. Now, I am in that same state, madam; we are, therefore, in sympathy, you see."

The respectful smile and peculiar intonation with which these last words were uttered, robbed them of their familiarity and allowed Miss Firman to perceive his true character.

"You are a detective," said she, and as he did not deny it, she went on: "You say I must be anxious to know who my cousin's murderer was. Has Craik Mansell, then, been acquitted?"

"A verdict has not been given," said the other. "His trial has been adjourned in order to give him an opportunity to choose a new counsel."

Miss Firman motioned her visitor to be seated, and at once took a chair herself.

"What do you want with me?" she asked, with characteristic bluntness.

The detective was silent. It was but for a moment, but in that moment he seemed to read to the bottom of this woman's mind.

"Well," said he, "I will tell you. You believe Craik Mansell to be innocent?"

"I do," she returned.

"Very well; so do I."

"Let me shake hands with you," was her abrupt remark. And without a smile she reached forth her hand, which he took with equal gravity.

This ceremony over, he remarked, with a cheerful mien:

"We are fortunately not in a court of law, and so can talk freely together. Why do you think Mansell innocent? I am sure the evidence has not been much in his favour."

"Why do *you* think him innocent?" was the brisk retort.

"I have talked with him."

"Ah!"

"I have talked with Miss Dare."

A different "Ah!" this time.

"And I was present when Mr. Orcutt breathed his last."

The look she gave was like cold water on Mr. Gryce's secretly growing hopes.

"What has that to do with it?" she wonderingly exclaimed.

The detective took another tone.

"You did not know Mr. Orcutt then?" he inquired.

"I had not that honour," was the formal reply.

"You have never, then, visited your cousin in Sibley?"

"Yes, I was there once; but that did not give me an acquaintance with Mr. Orcutt."

"Yet he went almost every day to her house."

"And he came while I was there, but *that* did not give me an acquaintance with him."

"He was reserved, then, in his manners, uncommunicative, possibly morose?"

"He was just what I would expect such a gentleman to be at the table with women like my cousin and myself."

"Not morose, then; only reserved."

"Exactly," the short, quick bow of the amiable spinster seemed to assert.

Mr. Gryce drew a deep breath. This well seemed to be destitute of even a drop of moisture.

"Why do you ask me about Mr. Orcutt? Has his death in any way affected young Mansell's prospects?"

"That is what I want to find out," declared Mr. Gryce. Then, without giving her time for another question, said: "Where did Mrs. Clemmens first make the acquaintance of Mr. Orcutt? Wasn't it in some town out West?"

"Out West? Not to my knowledge, sir. I always supposed she saw him first in Sibley."

This well was certainly very dry.

"Yet you are not positive that this is so, are you?" pursued the patient detective. "She came from Nebraska, and so did he; now, why may they not have known each other there?"

"I did not know that he came from Nebraska."

"She has never talked about him then?"

"Never."

Mr. Gryce drew another deep breath and let down his bucket again.

"I thought your cousin spent her childhood in Toledo?"

"She did, sir."

"How came she to go to Nebraska then?"

"Well, she was left an orphan and had to look out for herself. A situation in some way opened to her in Nebraska, and she went there to take it."

"A situation at what?"

"As waitress in some hotel."

"Humph! And was she still a waitress when she married?"

"Yes, I think so, but I am not sure about it or anything else in connection with her at that time. The subject was so painful we never discussed it."

"Why painful?"

"She lost her husband so soon."

"But you can tell me the name of the town in which this hotel was, can you not?"

"It was called Swanson then, but that was fifteen years ago. Its name may have been changed since."

Swanson! This was something to learn, but not much. Mr. Gryce returned to his first question. "You have not told me," said he, "why *you* believe Craik Mansell to be innocent?"

"Well," replied she, "*I* believe Craik Mansell to be innocent because he is the son of his mother. I think I know *him* pretty well, but I am certain I knew *her*. She was a woman who would go through fire and water to attain a purpose she thought right, but who would stop in the midst of any project the moment she felt the least doubt of its being just or wise. Craik has his mother's forehead and eyes, and no one will ever make me believe he has not her principles also."

"I coincide with you, madam," remarked the attentive detective.

"I hope the jury will," was her energetic response.

He bowed and was about to attempt another question, when an interruption occurred. Miss Firman was called from the room, and Mr. Gryce found himself left for a few moments alone. His thoughts, as he awaited her return, were far from cheerful, for he saw a long and tedious line of inquiry opening before him in the West, which, if it did not end in failure, promised to exhaust not only a week, but possibly many months, before certainty of any kind could be obtained. With Miss Dare on the verge of a fever, and Mansell in a position calling for the utmost nerve and self-control, this prospect looked anything but attractive to the benevolent detective; and, carried away by his impatience, he was about to give utterance to an angry ejaculation against the man he believed to be the author of all this mischief, when he suddenly heard a voice raised from some unknown quarter nearby, saying in strange tones he was positive did not proceed from Miss Firman:

"Was it Clemmens or was it Orcutt? Clemmens or Orcutt? I cannot remember."

Naturally excited and aroused, Mr. Gryce rose and looked about him. A door stood ajar at his back. Hastening toward it, he was about to lay his hand on the knob when Miss Firman returned.

"Oh, I beg you," she entreated. "That is my mother's room, and she is not at all well."

"I was going to her assistance," asserted the detective, with grave composure. "She has just uttered a cry."

"Oh, you don't say so!" exclaimed the unsuspicious spinster, and hurrying forward, she threw open the door herself. Mr. Gryce benevolently followed. "Why, she is asleep," protested Miss Firman, turning on the detective with a suspicious look.

Mr. Gryce, with a glance toward the bed he saw before him, bowed with seeming perplexity.

"She certainly appears to be," said he, "and yet I am positive she spoke but an instant ago; I can even tell you the words she used."

"What were they?" asked the spinster, with something like a look of concern.

"She said: 'Was it Clemmens or was it Orcutt? Clemmens or Or-cutt? I cannot remember.'"

"You don't say so! Poor ma! She was dreaming. Come into the other room and I will explain."

And leading the way back to the apartment they had left, she motioned him again toward a chair, and then said:

"Ma has always been a very hale and active woman for her years; but this murder seems to have shaken her. To speak the truth, sir, she has not been quite right in her mind since the day I told her of it; and I often detect her murmuring words similar to those you have just heard."

"Humph! And does she often use his name?"

"Whose name?"

"Mr. Orcutt's."

"Why, yes; but not with any understanding of whom she is speaking."

"Are you *sure?*" inquired Mr. Gryce, with that peculiar impressiveness he used on great occasions.

"What do you mean?"

"I mean," returned the detective, dryly, "that I believe your mother does know what she is talking about when she links the name of Mr. Orcutt with that of your cousin who was murdered. They belong together; Mr. Orcutt was her murderer."

"*Mr. Orcutt?*"

"Hush!" cried Mr. Gryce, "you will wake up your mother."

And, adapting himself to this emergency as to all others, he talked with the astounded and incredulous woman before him till she was in a condition not only to listen to his explanations, but to discuss the problem of a crime so seemingly without motive. He then said, with easy assurance:

"Your mother does not know that Mr. Orcutt is dead?"

"No, sir."

"She does not even know he was counsel for Craik Mansell in the trial now going on."

"How do you know that?" inquired Miss Firman, grimly.

"Because I do not believe you have even told her that Craik Mansell was on trial."

"Sir, you are a magician."

"Have you, madam?"

"No, sir, I have not."

513

"Very good; what *does* she know about Mr. Orcutt, then; and why should she connect his name with Mrs. Clemmens?"

"She knows he was her boarder, and that he was the first one to discover she had been murdered."

"That is not enough to account for her frequent repetition of his name."

"You think not?"

"I am sure not. Cannot your mother have some memories connected with his name of which you are ignorant?"

"No, sir; we have lived together in this house for twenty-five years, and have never had a thought we have not shared together. Ma could not have known anything about him or Mary Ann which I did not. The words she has just spoken sprang from mental confusion. She is almost like a child sometimes."

Mr. Gryce smiled. If the cream-jug he happened to be gazing at on a tray nearby had been full of cream, I am far from certain it would not have turned sour on the spot.

"I grant the mental confusion," said he; "but why should she confuse those two names in preference to all others?" And, with quiet persistence, he remarked again: "She may be recalling some old fact of years ago. Was there never a time, even while you lived here together, when she could have received some confidence from Mrs. Clemmens——"

"Mary Ann, Mary Ann!" came in querulous accents from the other room, "I wish you had not told me; Emily would be a better one to know your secret."

It was a startling interruption to come just at that moment The two surprised listeners glanced toward each other, and Miss Firman coloured.

"That sounds as if your surmise was true," she dryly observed.

"Let us make an experiment," said he, and motioned her to re-enter her mother's room, which she did with a precipitation that showed her composure had been sorely shaken by these unexpected occurrences.

He followed her without ceremony.

The old lady lay as before in a condition between sleeping and waking, and did not move as they came in. Mr. Gryce at once withdrew out of sight, and, with finger on his lip, put himself in the attitude of waiting. Miss Firman, surprised, and possibly curious, took her stand at the foot of the bed.

A few minutes passed thus, during which a strange dreariness seemed to settle upon the room; then the old lady spoke again, this time repeating the words he had first heard, but in a tone which betrayed an increased perplexity.

"*Was* it Clemmens or *was* it Orcutt? I wish somebody would tell me."

Instantly Mr. Gryce, with his soft tread, drew near to the old lady's side, and, leaning over her, murmured gently:

"I think it was Orcutt."

Instantly the old lady breathed a deep sigh and moved.

"Then her name was Mrs. Orcutt," said she, "and I thought you always called her Clemmens."

Miss Firman, recoiling, stared at Mr. Gryce, on whose cheek a faint spot of red had appeared—a most unusual token of emotion with him.

"Did she say it was Mrs. Orcutt," he pursued, in the even tones he had before used.

"She said——" But here the old lady opened her eyes, and, seeing her daughter standing at the foot of her bed, turned away with a peevish air, and restlessly pushed her hand under the pillow.

Mr. Gryce at once bent nearer.

"She said——" he suggested, with careful gentleness.

But the old lady made no answer. Her hand seemed to have touched some object for which she was seeking, and she was evidently oblivious to all else. Miss Firman came around and touched Mr. Gryce on the shoulder.

"It is useless," said she; "she is awake now, and you won't hear anything more; come!"

And she drew the reluctant detective back again into the other room.

"What does it all mean?" she asked, sinking into a chair.

Mr. Gryce did not answer. He had a question of his own to put.

"Why did your mother put her hand under her pillow?" he asked.

"I don't know, unless it was to see if her big envelope was there."

"Her big envelope?"

"Yes; for weeks now, ever since she took to her bed, she has kept a paper in a big envelope under her pillow. What is in it I don't know, for she never seems to hear me when I inquire."

"And have you no curiosity to find out?"

515

"No, sir. Why should I? It might easily be my father's old letters sealed up, or, for that matter, be nothing more than a piece of blank paper. My mother is not herself, as I have said before."

"I should like a peep at the contents of that envelope," he declared.

"You?"

"Is there any name written on the outside?"

"No."

"It would not be violating anyone's rights, then, if you opened it."

"Only my mother's, sir."

"You say she is not in her right mind?"

"All the more reason why I should respect her whims and caprices."

"Wouldn't you open it if she were dead?"

"Yes."

"Will it be very different then from what it is now? A father's letters! a blank piece of paper! What harm would there be in looking at them?"

"My mother would know it if I took them away. It might excite and injure her."

"Put another envelope in the place of this one, with a piece of paper folded up in it."

"It would be a trick."

"I know it; but if Craik Mansell can be saved even by a trick, I should think you would be willing to venture on one."

"Craik Mansell? What has he got to do with the papers under my mother's pillow?"

"I cannot say that he has anything to do with them; but if he has—if, for instance, that envelope should contain, not a piece of blank paper, or even the letters of your father, but such a document, say, as a certificate of marriage——"

"A certificate of marriage?"

"Yes, between Mrs. Clemmens and Mr. Orcutt, it would not take much perspicacity to prophesy an acquittal for Craik Mansell."

"Mary Ann the wife of Mr. Orcutt! Oh, that is impossible!" exclaimed the agitated spinster. But even while making this determined statement, she turned a look full of curiosity and excitement toward the door which separated them from her mother's apartment.

Mr. Gryce smiled in his wise way.

"Less improbable things than that have been found to be true in this topsy-turvy world," said he. "Mrs. Clemmens might very well have been Mrs. Orcutt."

"Do you really think so?" she asked; and yielding with sudden impetuosity to the curiosity of the moment, she at once dashed from his side and disappeared in her mother's room. Mr. Gryce's smile took on an aspect of triumph.

It was some few moments before she returned, but when she did, her countenance was flushed with emotion.

"I have it," she murmured, taking out a packet from under her apron and tearing it open with trembling fingers.

A number of closely written sheets fell out.

44

The Widow Clemmens

"Well, and what have you to say?" It was Mr. Ferris who spoke. The week which Mr. Gryce had demanded for his inquiries had fully elapsed, and the three detectives stood before him ready with their report.

It was Mr. Gryce who replied.

"Sir," said he, "our opinions have not been changed by the discoveries which we have made. It was Mr. Orcutt who killed Mrs. Clemmens, and for the reason already stated that she stood in the way of his marrying Miss Dare. Mrs. Clemmens was his wife."

"His *wife?*"

"Yes, sir; and, what is more, she has been so for years; before either of them came to Sibley, in fact."

The district attorney looked stunned.

"It was while they lived West," said Byrd. "He was a poor schoolmaster, and she a waitress in some hotel. She was pretty then, and he thought he loved her. At all events, he induced her to marry him, and then kept it secret because he was afraid she would lose her place at the hotel, where she was getting very good wages. You see, he had the makings in him of a villain even then."

"And was it a real marriage?"

"There is a record of it," said Hickory.

"And did he never acknowledge it?"

"Not openly," answered Byrd. "The commonness of the woman seemed to revolt him after he was married to her, and when in a month or so he received the summons East, which opened up before him the career of a lawyer, he determined to drop her and start afresh. He accordingly left town without notifying her, and actually succeeded in reaching the railway depot twenty miles away before he was stopped. But here, a delay occurring in the departure of the train, she was enabled to overtake him, and a stormy scene ensued. What its exact nature was, we, of course, cannot say, but from the results it is evident that he told her his prospects had changed, and with them his tastes and requirements; that she was not the woman he thought her, and that he could not and would not take her East with him as his wife: while she, on her side, displayed full as much spirit as he, and replied that if he could desert her like this he wasn't the kind of a man she could live with, and that he could go if he wished; only that he must acknowledge her claims upon him by giving her a yearly stipend, according to his income and success.

"At all events, some such compromise was effected, for he came East and she went back to Swanson. She did not stay there long, however; for the next we know she was in Sibley, where she set up her own little house-keeping arrangements under his very eye. More than that, she prevailed upon him to visit her daily, and even to take a meal at her house, her sense of justice seeming to be satisfied if he showed her this little attention and gave to no other woman the place he denied her. It was the weakness shown in this last requirement that doubtless led to her death. She would stand anything but a rival. He knew this, and preferred crime to the loss of the woman he loved."

"You speak very knowingly," said Mr. Ferris. "May I ask where you received your information?"

It was Mr. Gryce who answered.

"From letters. Mrs. Clemmens was one of those women who delight in putting their feelings on paper. Fortunately for us, such women are not rare. See here!" And he pulled out before the district attorney a pile of old letters in the widow's well-known handwriting.

"Where did you find these?" asked Mr. Ferris.

"Well," said Mr. Gryce, "I found them in rather a curious place. They were in the keeping of old Mrs. Firman, Miss Firman's mother. Mrs. Clemmens, or, rather, Mrs. Orcutt, got frightened some two years ago at the disappearance of her marriage certificate from the place where she had always kept it hidden, and, thinking that Mr. Orcutt was planning to throw her off, she resolved to provide herself with a confidante capable of standing by her in case she wished to assert her rights. She chose old Mrs. Firman. Why, when her daughter would have been so much more suitable for the purpose, it is hard to tell; possibly the widow's pride revolted from telling a woman of her own years the indignities she had suffered. However that may be, it was to

519

the old lady she told her story and gave these letters—letters which, as you will see, are not written to any special person, but are rather the separate leaves of a journal which she kept to show the state of her feelings from time to time."

"And this?" inquired Mr. Ferris, taking up a sheet of paper written in a different handwriting from the rest.

"This is an attempt on the part of the old lady to put on paper the story which had been told her. She evidently thought herself too old to be entrusted with a secret so important, and, fearing loss of memory, or perhaps sudden death, took this means of explaining how she came into possession of her cousin's letters. 'T was a wise precaution. Without it we would have missed the clue to the widow's journal. For the old lady's brain gave way when she heard of the widow's death, and had it not been for a special stroke of good-luck on my part, we might have remained some time longer in ignorance of what very valuable papers she secretly held in her possession."

"I will read the letters," said Mr. Ferris.

Seeing from his look that he only waited their departure to do so, Mr. Gryce and his subordinates arose.

"I think you will find them satisfactory," drawled Hickory.

"If you do not," said Mr. Gryce, "then give a look at this telegram. It is from Swanson, and notifies us that a record of a marriage between Benjamin Orcutt—Mr. Orcutt's middle name was Benjamin—and Mary Mansell can be found in the old town books."

Mr. Ferris took the telegram, the shade of sorrow settling heavier and heavier on his brow.

"I see," said he, "I have got to accept your conclusions. Well, there are those among the living who will be greatly relieved by these discoveries. I will try and think of that."

Yet, after the detectives were gone, and he sat down in solitude before these evidences of his friend's perfidy, it was many long and dreary moments before he could summon up courage to peruse them. But when he did, he found in them all that Mr. Gryce had promised. As my readers may feel some interest to know how the seeming widow bore the daily trial of her life, I will give a few extracts from these letters. The first bears date of fourteen years back, and was written after she came to Sibley:

November 8, 1867.—In the same town! Within a stone's throw of the court-house, where, they tell me, his business will soon take him almost every day! Isn't it a triumph? and am I not to be congratulated upon my bravery in coming here? He hasn't seen me yet, but I have seen *him*. I crept out of the house at nightfall on purpose. He was sauntering down the street and he looked—it makes my blood boil to think of it—he looked *happy*.

November 10, 1867.—Clemmens, Clemmens—that is my name, and I have taken the title of widow. What a fate for a woman with a husband in the next street! He saw *me* today. I met him in the open square, and I looked him right in the face. How he did quail! It just does me good to think of it! Perk and haughty as he is, he grew as white as a sheet when he saw me, and though he tried to put on airs and carry it off with a high hand, he failed, just as I knew he would when he came to meet me on even ground. Oh, I'll have my way now, and if I choose to stay in this place where I can keep my eye on him, he won't dare to say No. The only thing I fear is that he will do me a secret mischief some day. His look was just murderous when he left me.

February 24, 1868.—Can I stand it? I ask myself that question every morning when I get up. Can I stand it? To sit all alone in my little narrow room and know that he is going about as gay as you please with people who wouldn't look at me twice. It's awful hard; but it would be worse still to be where I couldn't see what he was up to. Then I should imagine all sorts of things. No, I will just grit my teeth and bear it. I'll get used to it after a while.

October 7, 1868.—If he says he never loved me he lies. He did, or why did he marry me? I never asked him to. He teased me into it, saying my saucy ways had bewitched him. A month after, it was common ways, rude ways, such ways as he wouldn't have in a wife. That's the kind of man he is.

May 11, 1869.—One thing I will say of him. He don't pay no heed to women. He's too busy, I guess. He don't seem to think of anything but to get along, and he does get along remarkable. I'm awful proud of him. He's taken to defending criminals lately. They almost all get off.

October 5, 1870.—He pays me but a pittance. How can I look like anything , or hold my head up with the ladies here if I cannot get enough together to buy me a new fall hat. I *will* not go to church looking like a farmer's wife, if I haven't any education or any manners. I'm as good as anybody here if they but knew it, and deserve to dress as well. He *must* give me more money.

November 2, 1870.—No, he shan't give me a cent more. If I can't go to church I will stay at home. He shan't say I stood in his way of becoming a great man. He *is* too good for me. I saw it today when he got up in the court to speak. I was there with a thick veil over my face, for I was determined to know whether he was as smart as folks say or not. And he just is! Oh, how beautiful he did look, and how everybody held their breaths while he was speaking! I felt like jumping up and saying:'This is my husband; we were married three years ago.' Wouldn't I have raised a rumpus if I had! I guess the poor man he was pleading for would not have been remembered very long after that. My husband! the thought makes me laugh. No other woman can call him that, anyhow. He is mine, *mine, mine,* and I mean he shall stay so.

January 9, 1871.—I feel awful blue tonight. I have been thinking about those Hildreths. How they would like to have me dead! And so would Tremont, though he don't say nothing. I like to call him Tremont; it makes me feel as if he belonged to me. What if that wicked Gouverneur Hildreth should know I lived so much alone? I don't believe he would stop at killing me! And my husband! He is equal to telling him I have no protector. Oh, what a dreadful wickedness it is in me to put that down on paper! It isn't so—it isn't so; my husband wouldn't do me any harm if he could. If ever I'm found dead in my bed, it will be the work of that Toledo man and of nobody else.

March 2, 1872.—I hope I am going to have some comfort now. Tremont has begun to pay me more money. He *had* to. He isn't a poor man any more, and when he moves into his big house, I am going to move into a certain little cottage I have found, just around the corner. If I can't have no other pleasures, I will at least have a kitchen I can call my own, and a parlour too. What if there don't no company come to it; they would if they *knew.* I've just heard from Adelaide; she says Craik is getting to be a big boy, and is so smart.

June 10, 1872.—What's the use of having a home? I declare I feel just like breaking down and crying. I don't want company: if women folks, they're always talking about their husbands and children; and if men, they're always saying: 'My wife's this, and my wife's that.' But I do want *him.* It's my right; what if I couldn't say three words to him that was agreeable, I could look at him and think: 'This splendid gentleman is my husband, I ain't so much alone in the world as folks think.' I'll put on my bonnet and run down the street. Perhaps I'll see him sitting in the club-house window!

Evening.—I hate him. He has a hard, cruel, wicked heart. When I got to the club-house window he was sitting there, so I just went walking by, and he saw me and came out and hustled me away with terrible words, saying he wouldn't have me hanging round where he was; that I had promised not to bother him, and that I must keep my word, or he would see me—he didn't say where, but it's easy enough to guess. So—so! he thinks he'll put an end to my coming to see him, does he? Well, perhaps he can; but if he does, he shall pay for it by coming to see me. I'll not sit day in and day out alone without the glimpse of a face I love, not while I have a husband in the same town with me. He shall come, if it is only for a moment each day, or I'll dare everything and tell the world I am his wife."

June 16, 1872.—He had to consent! Meek as I have been, he knows it won't do to rouse me too much. So today he came in to dinner, and he had to acknowledge it was a good one. Oh, how I did feel when I saw his face on the other side of the table! I didn't know whether I hated him or loved him. But I am sure now I hated him, for he scarcely spoke to me all the time he was eating, and when he was through, he went away just as a stranger would have done. He means to act like a boarder, and, goodness me, he's welcome to if he isn't going to act like a husband! The hard, selfish—— Oh, oh, I love him!

August 5, 1872.—It is no use; I'll never be a happy woman. Tremont has been in so regularly to dinner lately, and shown me such a kind face, I thought I would venture upon a little familiarity. It was only to lay my hand upon his arm, but it made him very angry, and I thought he would strike me. Am I then actually hateful to him? or is he so proud he cannot bear the thought of my having the right to touch him? I looked in the glass when he went out. I *am* plain and homespun, that's a fact. Even my red cheeks are gone, and the dimples which once took his fancy. I shall never lay the tip of a finger on him again.

February 13, 1873.—What shall I cook for him today? Something that he likes. It is my only pleasure, to see how he does enjoy my meals. I should think they would choke him; they do me sometimes. But men are made of iron—ambitious men, anyhow. Little they care what suffering they cause, so long as they have a good time and get all the praises they want. *He* gets them more and more every day. He will soon be as far above me as if I had married the president himself. Oh, sometimes when I think of it and remember he is my own husband, I just feel as if some awful fate was preparing for him or me!

June 7, 1873.—Would he send for me if he was dying? No. He hates me; he hates me.

September 8, 1874.—Craik was here today; he is just going North to earn a few dollars in the logging business. What a keen eye he has for a boy of his years! I shouldn't wonder if he made a powerful smart man some day. If he's only good, too, and kind to his women-folks, I sh'n't mind. But a smart man who is all for himself is an awful trial to those who love him. Don't I know? Haven't I suffered? Craik must never be like him.

December 21, 1875.—One thousand dollars. That's a nice little sum to have put away in the bank. So much I get out of my husband's fame, anyhow. I think I will make my will, for I want Craik to have what I leave. He's a fine lad.

February 19, 1876.—I was thinking the other day, suppose I did die suddenly. It would be dreadful to have the name of Clemmens put on my tombstone! But it would be. Tremont would never let the truth be known, if he had to rifle my dead body for my marriage certificate. What shall I do, then? Tell anybody who I am? It seems just as if I couldn't. Either the whole world must know it, or just himself and me alone. Oh, I wish I had never been born!

June 17, 1876.—Why wasn't I made handsome and fine and nice? Think where I would be if I was! I'd be in that big house

524

of his, curtseying to all the grand folks as go there. I went to see it last night. It was dark as pitch in the streets, and I went into the gate and all around the house. I walked upon the *piazza* too, and rubbed my hand along the window-ledges and up and down the doors. It's mighty nice, all of it, and there shan't lie a square inch on that whole ground that my foot shan't go over. I wish I could get inside the house once.

July 1, 1876.—I have done it. I went to see Mr. Orcutt's sister. I had a right. Isn't he away, and isn't he my boarder, and didn't I want to know when he was coming home? She's a soft, good-natured piece, and let me peek into the library without saying a word. What a room it is! I just felt like I'd been struck when I saw it and spied his chair setting there and all those books heaped around and the fine things on the mantel-shelf and the pictures on the walls. What would I do in such a place as that? I could keep it clean, but so could any gal he might hire. Oh, me! Oh, me! I wish he'd given me a chance. Perhaps if he had loved me I might have learned to be quiet and nice like that silly sister of his.

January 12, 1877.—Some women would take a heap of delight in having folks know they were the wife of a great man, but I find lots of pleasure in being so without folks knowing it. If I lived in his big house and was called Mrs. Orcutt, why, he would have nothing to be afraid of and might do as he pleased; but now he has to do what *I* please. Sometimes, when I sit down of an evening in my little sitting-room to sew, I think how this famous man whom everybody is afraid of has to come and go just as humble me wants him to; and it makes me hug myself with pride. It's as if I had a string tied round his little finger, which I can pull now and then. I don't pull it much; but I do sometimes."

March 30, 1877.—Gouverneur Hildreth is dead. I shall never be his victim, at any rate. Shall I ever be the victim of anybody? I don't feel as if I cared now. For one kiss I would sell my life and die happy.
There is a young Gouverneur, but it will be years before he will be old enough to make me afraid of him.

November 16, 1878.—I should think that Tremont would be

lonely in that big house of his. If he had a heart he would. They say he reads all the time. How can folks pore so over books? I can't. I'd rather sit in my chair and think. What story in all the books is equal to mine?

April 23, 1879.—I am growing very settled in my ways. Now that Tremont comes in almost every day, I'm satisfied not to see any other company. My house affairs keep me busy too. I like to have it all nice for him. I believe I could almost be happy if he'd only smile once in a while when he meets my eye. But he never does. Oh, well, we all have our crosses, and he's a very great man."

January 18, 1880.—He went to a ball last night. What does it mean? He never seemed to care for things like that. Is there any girl he is after?

February 6, 1880.—Oh, he has been riding with a lady, has he? It was in the next town, and he thought I wouldn't hear. But there's little he does that I don't know about; let him make himself sure of that. I even know her name; it is Selina Pratt. If he goes with her again, look out for a disturbance. I'll not stand his making love to another woman."

"*May 26,* 1880.—My marriage certificate is missing. Can it be that Tremont has taken it? I have looked all through the desk where I have kept it for so many years, but I cannot find it. He was left alone in the house a few minutes the other day. Could he have taken the chance to rob me of the only proof I have that we are man and wife? If he has he is a villain at heart, and is capable of doing anything, even of marrying this Pratt girl who he *has* taken riding again. The worst is that I dare not accuse him of having my certificate; for if he didn't take it and should find out it is gone, he'd throw me off just as quick as if he had. What shall I do then? Something. He shall *never* marry another woman while I live.

May 30, 1880.—The Pratt girl is gone. If he cared for her it was only for a week, like an old love I could mention. I think I feel safe again, only I am convinced someone ought to know my secret besides myself. Shall it be Emily? No. I'd rather tell her mother.

June 9th, 1880.—I am going to Utica. I shall take these letters with me. Perhaps I shall leave them. For the last time, then, let me say 'I am the lawful wife of Tremont Benjamin Orcutt, the lawyer, who lives in Sibley, New York.' We were married in Swanson, Nevada, on the 3rd of July, 1867, by a travelling minister, named George Sinclair.

Mary Ann Orcutt, Sibley, N.Y.

45

Mr. Gryce Says Goodbye

"Helen?"

"Yes, Imogene."

"What noise is that? The people seem to be shouting down the street. What does it mean?"

Helen Richmond—whom we better know as Helen Darling—looked at the worn, fever-flushed countenance of her friend, and for a moment was silent; then she whispered:

"I have not dared to tell you before, you seemed so ill; but I can tell you now, because joyful news never hurts. The people shout because the long and tedious trial of an innocent man has come to an end. Craik Mansell was acquitted from the charge of murder this morning."

"Acquitted! O Helen!"

"Yes, dear. Since you have been ill, very strange and solemn revelations have come to light. Mr. Orcutt——"

"Ah!" cried Imogene, rising up in the great armchair in which she was half-sitting and half-reclining "I know what you are going to say. I was with Mr. Orcutt when he died. I heard him myself declare that fate had spoken in his death. I believe Mr. Orcutt to have been the murderer of Mrs. Clemmens, Helen."

"Yes, there can be no doubt about that," was the reply.

"It has been proved then?"

"Yes."

Moved to the depths of her being, Imogene covered her face with her hands. Presently she murmured:

"I do not understand it. Why should such a great man as he have desired the death of a woman like her? He said it was all for my sake. What did he mean, Helen?"

"Don't you know?" questioned the other, anxiously.

"How should I? It is the mystery of mysteries to me."

"Ah, then you did not suspect that she was his wife?"

"His wife!" Imogene rose in horror.

"Yes," repeated the little bride with decision. "She was his lawfully wedded wife. They were married as long ago as when we were little children."

"Married! And he dared to approach me with words of love! Dared to offer himself to me as a husband while his hands were still wet with the life-blood of his wife! O the horror of it! The amazing wickedness and presumption of it!"

"He is dead," whispered the gentle little lady at her side.

With a sigh of suppressed feeling, Imogene sank back.

"I must not think of him," she cried. "I am not strong enough. I must think only of Craik. He has been acquitted, you say—acquitted."

"Yes, and the whole town is rejoicing."

A smile, exquisite as it was rare, swept like a sunbeam over Imogene's lips.

"And I rejoice with the rest," she cried. Then, as if she felt all speech to be a mockery, she remained for a long time silent, gazing with ever-deepening expression into the space before her, till Helen did not know whether the awe she felt creeping over her sprang from admiration of her companion's suddenly awakened beauty or from a recognition of the depths of that companion's emotions. At last Imogene spoke:

"How came Mr. Mansell to be *acquitted?* Mr. Gryce did not tell me to look for any such reinstatement as that. The most he bade me expect was that Mr. Ferris would decline to prosecute Mr. Mansell any further, in which event he would be discharged."

"I know," said Helen, "but Mr. Mansell was not satisfied with that. He demanded a verdict from the jury. So Mr. Ferris, with great generosity, asked the judge to recommend the jury to bring in a verdict of acquittal, and when the judge hesitated to do this, the foreman of the jury himself rose, and intimated that he thought the jury were ready with their verdict. The judge took advantage of this, and the result was a triumphant acquittal."

"O Helen, Helen!"

"That was just an hour ago," cried the little lady, brightly, "but the people are not through shouting yet. There has been a great excitement in town these last few days."

"And I knew nothing of it!" exclaimed Imogene. Suddenly she looked at Helen. "How did you hear about what took place in the court-room today?" she asked.

"Mr. Byrd told me."

"Ah, Mr. Byrd?"

"He came to leave a goodbye for you. He goes home this afternoon."

"I should like to have seen Mr. Byrd," said Imogene.

"Would you?" queried the little lady, quietly shaking her head. "I don't know; I think it is just as well you did not see him," said she.

But she made no such demur when a little while later Mr. Gryce was announced. The fatherly old gentleman had evidently been in that house before, and Mrs. Richmond was not the woman to withstand a man like him.

He came immediately into the room where Imogene was sitting. Evidently he thought as Helen did, that good news never hurts.

"Well!" he cried, taking her trembling hand in his, with his most expressive smile. "What did I tell you? Didn't I say that if you would only trust me all would come right? And it has, don't you see? Right as a trivet."

"Yes," she returned; "and I never can find words with which to express my gratitude. You have saved two lives, Mr. Gryce: his—and mine."

"Pooh! pooh!" cried the detective, good-humouredly. "You mustn't think too much of anything I have done. It was the falling limb that did the business. If Mr. Orcutt's conscience had not been awakened by the stroke of death, I don't know where we should have been today. Affairs were beginning to look pretty dark for Mansell."

Imogene shuddered.

"But I haven't come here to call up unpleasant memories," he continued. "I have come to wish you joy and a happy convalescence." And leaning toward her, he said, with a complete change of voice: "You know, I suppose, why Mr. Mansell presumed to think *you* guilty of this crime?"

"No," she murmured, wearily; "unless it was because the ring he believed me to have retained was found on the scene of murder."

"Bah!" cried Mr. Gryce, "he had a much better reason than that."

And with the air of one who wishes to clear up all misunderstandings, he told her the words which her lover had overheard Mrs. Clemmens say when he came up to her dining-room door.

The effect on Imogene was very great. Hoping to hide it, she turned away her face, showing in this struggle with herself something of the strength of her old days. Mr. Gryce watched her with interest.

"It is very strange," was her first remark. "I had such reasons for thinking him guilty; he such good cause for thinking me so. What wonder we doubted each other. And yet I can never forgive myself for doubting him; I can sooner forgive him for doubting me. If you see him——"

"If *I* see him?" interrupted the detective, with a smile.

"Yes," said she. "If you see him tell him that Imogene Dare thanks him for his noble conduct toward one he believed to be stained by so despicable a crime, and assure him that I think he was much more justified in his suspicions than I was in mine, for there were weaknesses in my character which he had ample opportunities for observing, while all that I knew of him was to his credit."

"Miss Dare," suggested the detective, "couldn't you tell him this much better yourself?"

"I shall not have the opportunity," she said.

"And why?" he inquired.

"Mr. Mansell and I have met for the last time. A woman who has stained herself by such declarations as I made use of in court the last time I was called to the stand has created a barrier between herself and all earthly friendship. Even he for whom I perjured myself so basely cannot overleap the gulf I dug between us two that day."

"But that is hard," said Mr. Gryce.

"My life *is* hard," she answered.

The wise old man, who had seen so much of life and who knew the human heart so well, smiled, but did not reply. He turned instead to another subject.

"Well," he declared, "the great case is over! Sibley, satisfied with having made its mark in the world, will now rest in peace. I quit the place with some reluctance myself. 'Tis a mighty pretty spot to do business in."

"You are going?" she asked.

"Immediately," was the reply. "We detectives don't have much time to rest." Then, as he saw how deep a shadow lay upon her brow, added, confidentially: "Miss Dare, we all have occasions for great regret. Look at me now. Honest as I hold myself to be, I cannot blind myself to the fact that I am the possible instigator of this crime. If I had not shown

Mr. Orcutt how a man like himself might perpetrate a murder without rousing suspicion, he might never have summoned up courage to attempt it. For a detective with a conscience, that is a hard thought to bear."

"But you were ignorant of what you were doing," she protested. "You had no idea there was anyone present who was meditating crime."

"True; but a detective shouldn't be ignorant. He ought to know men; he has opportunity enough to learn them. But I won't be caught again. Never in any company, not if it is composed of the highest dignitaries in the land, will I ever tell again how a crime of any kind can be perpetrated without risk. One always runs the chance of encountering an Orcutt."

Imogene turned pale. "Do not speak of him," she cried. "I want to forget that such a man ever lived."

Mr. Gryce smiled again.

"It is the best thing you can do," said he. "Begin a new life, my child; begin a new life."

And with this fatherly advice, he said goodbye, and she saw his wise, kind face no more.

The hour that followed was a dreary one for Imogene. Her joy at knowing Craik Mansell was released could not blind her to the realization of her own ruined life. Indeed she seemed to feel it now as never before; and as the slow minutes passed, and she saw in fancy the strong figure of Mansell surrounded by congratulating admirers and friends, the full loneliness of her position swept over her, and she knew not whether to be thankful or not to the fever for having spared her blighted and dishonoured life.

Mrs. Richmond, seeing her so absorbed, made no attempt at consolation. She only listened, and when a step was heard, arose and went out, leaving the door open behind her.

And Imogene mused on, sinking deeper and deeper into melancholy, till the tears, which for so long a time had been dried at their source, welled up to her eyes and fell slowly down her cheeks. Their touch seemed to rouse her. Starting erect, she looked quickly around as if to see if anybody was observing her. But the room seems quite empty, and she is about to sink back again with a sigh when her eyes fall on the door-way and she becomes transfixed. A sturdy form is standing there! A manly, eager form in whose beaming eyes and tender smile shine a love and a purpose which open out before her quite a different future from that which her fancy had been so ruthlessly picturing.

The Doctor, his Wife, and the Clock

Contents

Chapter 1   539

Chapter 2   554

Chapter 3   569

Chapter 1

On the 17th of July, 1851, a tragedy of no little interest occurred in one of the residences of the Colonnade in Lafayette Place.

Mr. Hasbrouck, a well-known and highly respected citizen, was attacked in his room by an unknown assailant, and shot dead before assistance could reach him. His murderer escaped, and the problem offered to the police was, how to identify this person who, by some happy chance or by the exercise of the most remarkable forethought, had left no traces behind him, or any clue by which he could be followed.

The affair was given to a young man, named Ebenezer Gryce, to investigate, and the story, as he tells it, is this:

When, sometime after midnight, I reached Lafayette Place, I found the block lighted from end to end. Groups of excited men and women peered from the open doorways, and mingled their shadows with those of the huge pillars which adorn the front of this picturesque block of dwellings.

The house in which the crime had been committed was near the centre of the row, and, long before I reached it, I had learned from more than one source that the alarm was first given to the street by a woman's shriek, and secondly by the shouts of an old man-servant who had appeared, in a half-dressed condition, at the window of Mr. Hasbrouck's room, crying "Murder! murder!"

But when I had crossed the threshold, I was astonished at the paucity of the facts to be gleaned from the inmates themselves. The old servitor, who was the first to talk, had only this account of the crime to give.

The family, which consisted of Mr. Hasbrouck, his wife, and three servants, had retired for the night at the usual hour and under the usual auspices. At eleven o'clock the lights were all extinguished, and the whole household asleep, with the possible exception of Mr. Hasbrouck himself, who, being a man of large business responsibilities, was frequently troubled with insomnia.

Suddenly Mrs. Hasbrouck woke with a start. Had she dreamed the words that were ringing in her ears, or had they been actually uttered in her hearing? They were short, sharp words, full of terror and menace, and she had nearly satisfied herself that she had imagined them, when there came, from somewhere near the door, a sound she neither understood nor could interpret, but which filled her with inexplicable terror, and made her afraid to breathe, or even to stretch forth her hand towards her husband, whom she supposed to be sleeping at her side. At length another strange sound, which she was sure was not due to her imagination, drove her to make an attempt to rouse him, when she was horrified to find that she was alone in the bed, and her husband nowhere within reach.

Filled now with something more than nervous apprehension, she flung herself to the floor, and tried to penetrate, with frenzied glances, the surrounding darkness. But the blinds and shutters both having been carefully closed by Mr. Hasbrouck before retiring, she found this impossible, and she was about to sink in terror to the floor, when she heard a low gasp on the other side of the room, followed by the suppressed cry:

"God! what have I done!"

The voice was a strange one, but before the fear aroused by this fact could culminate in a shriek of dismay, she caught the sound of retreating footsteps, and, eagerly listening, she heard them descend the stairs and depart by the front door.

Had she known what had occurred—had there been no doubt in her mind as to what lay in the darkness on the other side of the room—it is likely that, at the noise caused by the closing front door, she would have made at once for the balcony that opened out from the window before which she was standing, and taken one look at the flying figure below. But her uncertainty as to what lay hidden from her by the darkness chained her feet to the floor, and there is no knowing when she would have moved, if a carriage had not at that moment passed down Astor Place, bringing with it a sense of companionship which broke the spell that held her, and gave her strength to light the gas, which was in ready reach of her hand.

As the sudden blaze illuminated the room, revealing in a burst the old familiar walls and well-known pieces of furniture, she felt for a moment as if released from some heavy nightmare and restored to the common experiences of life. But in another instant her former dread returned, and she found herself quaking at the prospect of passing around the foot of the bed into that part of the room which was as yet hidden from her eyes.

But the desperation which comes with great crises finally drove her from her retreat; and, creeping slowly forward, she cast one glance at the floor before her, when she found her worst fears realized by the sight of the dead body of her husband lying prone before the open doorway, with a bullet-hole in his forehead.

Her first impulse was to shriek, but, by a powerful exercise of will, she checked herself, and, ringing frantically for the servants who slept on the top-floor of the house, flew to the nearest window and endeavoured to open it. But the shutters had been bolted so securely by Mr. Hasbrouck, in his endeavour to shut out light and sound, that by the time she had succeeded in unfastening them, all trace of the flying murderer had vanished from the street.

Sick with grief and terror, she stepped back into the room just as the three frightened servants descended the stairs. As they appeared in the open doorway, she pointed at her husband's inanimate form, and then, as if suddenly realizing in its full force the calamity which had befallen her, she threw up her arms, and sank forward to the floor in a dead faint.

The two women rushed to her assistance, but the old butler, bounding over the bed, sprang to the window, and shrieked his alarm to the street.

In the interim that followed, Mrs. Hasbrouck was revived, and the master's body laid decently on the bed; but no pursuit was made, nor any inquiries started likely to assist me in establishing the identity of the assailant.

Indeed, every one, both in the house and out, seemed dazed by the unexpected catastrophe, and as no one had any suspicions to offer as to the probable murderer, I had a difficult task before me.

I began, in the usual way, by inspecting the scene of the murder. I found nothing in the room, or in the condition of the body itself, which added an iota to the knowledge already obtained. That Mr. Hasbrouck had been in bed; that he had risen upon hearing a noise; and that he had been shot before reaching the door, were self-evident facts. But there was nothing to guide me further. The very simplicity of the circumstances caused a dearth of clues, which made the difficulty of procedure as great as any I ever encountered.

My search through the hall and down the stairs elicited nothing; and an investigation of the bolts and bars by which the house was secured, assured me that the assassin had either entered by the front door, or had already been secreted in the house when it was locked up for the night.

"I shall have to trouble Mrs. Hasbrouck for a short interview," I hereupon announced to the trembling old servitor, who had followed me like a dog about the house.

He made no demur, and in a few minutes I was ushered into the presence of the newly made widow, who sat quite alone, in a large chamber in the rear. As I crossed the threshold she looked up, and I encountered a good plain face, or without the shadow of guile in it.

"Madam," said I, "I have not come to disturb you. I will ask two or three questions only, and then leave you to your grief. I am told that some words came from the assassin before he delivered his fatal shot. Did you hear these distinctly enough to tell me what they were?"

"I was sound asleep," said she," and dreamt, as I thought, that a fierce, strange voice cried somewhere to some one: 'Ah! you did not expect *me*!' But I dare not say that these words were really uttered to my husband, for he was not the man to call forth hate, and only a man in the extremity of passion could address such an exclamation in such a tone as rings in my memory in connection with the fatal shot which woke me."

"But that shot was not the work of a friend," I argued. "If, as these words seem to prove, the assassin had some other motive than gain in his assault, then your husband had an enemy, though you never suspected it."

"Impossible!" was her steady reply, uttered in the most convincing tone. "The man who shot him was a common burglar, and, frightened at having been betrayed into murder, fled without looking for booty. I am sure I heard him cry out in terror and remorse: 'God! what have I done!'"

"Was that before you left the side of the bed?"

"Yes; I did not move from my place till I heard the front door close. I was paralyzed by my fear and dread."

"Are you in the habit of trusting to the security of a latch-lock only in the fastening of your front door at night? I am told that the big key was not in the lock, and that the bolt at the bottom of the door was not drawn."

"The bolt at the bottom of the door is never drawn. Mr. Hasbrouck was so good a man he never mistrusted anyone. That is why the big lock was not fastened. The key, not working well, he took it some days ago to the locksmith, and when the latter failed to return it, he laughed, and said he thought no one would ever think of meddling with his front door."

"Is there more than one night-key to your house?" I now asked.

She shook her head.

"And when did Mr. Hasbrouck last use his?"

"Tonight, when he came home from prayer-meeting," she answered, and burst into tears.

Her grief was so real and her loss so recent that I hesitated to afflict her by further questions. So returning to the scene of the tragedy, I stepped out upon the balcony which ran in front. Soft voices instantly struck my ears. The neighbours on either side were grouped in front of their own windows, and were exchanging the remarks natural under the circumstances. I paused, as in duty bound, and listened. But I heard nothing worth recording, and would have instantly re-entered the house, if I had not been impressed by the appearance of a very graceful woman who stood at my right. She was clinging to her husband, who was gazing at one of the pillars before him in a strange, fixed way which astonished me till he attempted to move, and then I saw that he was blind. Instantly I remembered that there lived in this row a blind doctor, equally celebrated for his skill and for his uncommon personal attractions, and, greatly interested not only in his affliction, but in the sympathy evinced for him by his young and affectionate wife, I stood still till I heard her say in the soft and appealing tones of love:

"Come in, Constant; you have heavy duties for tomorrow, and you should get a few hours' rest, if possible."

He came from the shadow of the pillar, and for one minute I saw his face with the lamplight shining full upon it. It was as regular of feature as a sculptured Adonis, and it was as white.

"Sleep!" he repeated, in the measured tones of deep but suppressed feeling. "Sleep! with murder on the other side of the wall!" And he stretched out his arms in a dazed way that insensibly accentuated the horror I myself felt of the crime which had so lately taken place in the room behind me.

She, noting the movement, took one of the groping hands in her own and drew him gently towards her.

"This way," she urged; and, guiding him into the house, she closed the window and drew down the shades, making the street seem darker by the loss of her exquisite presence.

This may seem a digression, but I was at the time a young man of thirty, and much under the dominion of woman's beauty. I was therefore slow in leaving the balcony, and persistent in my wish to learn something of this remarkable couple before leaving Mr. Hasbrouck's house.

The story told me was very simple. Dr. Zabriskie had not been born blind, but had become so after a grievous illness which had stricken him down soon after he received his diploma. Instead of succumbing to an affliction which would have daunted most men, he expressed his intention of practicing his profession, and soon became so successful in it that he found no difficulty in establishing himself in one of the best-paying quarters of the city. Indeed, his intuition seemed to have developed in a remarkable degree after his loss of sight, and he seldom, if ever, made a mistake in diagnosis. Considering this fact, and the personal attractions which gave him distinction, it was no wonder that he soon became a popular physician whose presence was a benefaction and whose word a law.

He had been engaged to be married at the time of his illness, and, when he learned what was likely to be its results, had offered to release the young lady from all obligation to him. But she would not be released, and they were married. This had taken place some five years previous to Mr. Hasbrouck's death, three of which had been spent by them in Lafayette Place.

So much for the beautiful woman next door.

There being absolutely no clue to the assailant of Mr. Hasbrouck, I naturally looked forward to the inquest for some evidence upon which to work. But there seemed to be no underlying facts to this tragedy. The most careful study into the habits and conduct of the deceased brought nothing to light save his general beneficence and rectitude, nor was there in his history or in that of his wife any secret or hidden obligation calculated to provoke any such act of revenge as murder. Mrs. Hasbrouck's surmise that the intruder was simply a burglar, and that she had rather imagined than heard the words that pointed to the shooting as a deed of vengeance, soon gained general credence. But, though the police worked long and arduously in this new direction, their efforts were without fruit, and the case bade fair to remain an unsolvable mystery.

But the deeper the mystery the more persistently does my mind cling to it, and some five months after the matter had been delegated to oblivion, I found myself starting suddenly from sleep, with these words ringing in my ears:

"*Who uttered the scream that gave the first alarm of Mr. Hasbrouck's violent death?*"

I was in such a state of excitement that the perspiration stood out on my forehead. Mrs. Hasbrouck's story of the occurrence returned to me, and I remembered as distinctly as if she were then speaking, that she had expressly stated that she did not scream when confronted by the sight of her husband's dead body. But someone had screamed, and that very loudly. Who was it, then? One of the maids, startled by the sudden summons from below, or someone else—some involuntary witness of the crime, whose testimony had been suppressed at the inquest, by fear or influence?

The possibility of having come upon a clue even at this late day, so fired my ambition, that I took the first opportunity of revisiting Lafayette Place. Choosing such persons as I thought most open to my questions, I learned that there were many who could testify to having heard a woman's shrill scream on that memorable night just prior to the alarm given by old Cyrus, but no one who could tell from whose lips it had come. One fact, however, was immediately settled. It had not been the result of the servant-women's fears. Both of the girls were positive that they had uttered no sound, nor had they themselves heard any, till Cyrus rushed to the window with his wild cries. As the scream, by whomever given, was uttered before they descended the stairs, I was convinced by these assurances that it had issued from one of the front windows, and not from the rear of the house, where their own rooms lay. Could it be that it had sprung from the adjoining dwelling, and that—— My thoughts went no further, but I made up my mind to visit the doctor's house at once.

It took some courage to do this, for the doctor's wife had attended the inquest, and her beauty, seen in broad daylight, had worn such an aspect of mingled sweetness and dignity, that I hesitated to encounter it under any circumstances likely to disturb its pure serenity. But a clue, once grasped, cannot be lightly set aside by a true detective, and it would have taken more than a woman's frown to stop me at this point. So I rang Dr. Zabriskie's bell.

I am seventy years old now and am no longer daunted by the charms of a beautiful woman, but I confess that when I found myself in the fine reception parlor on the first-floor, I experienced no little trepidation at the prospect of the interview which awaited me.

But as soon as the fine commanding form of the doctor's wife crossed the threshold, I recovered my senses and surveyed her with as direct a gaze as my position allowed. For her aspect bespoke a degree of emotion that astonished me; and even before I spoke I perceived her to be trembling, though she was a woman of no little natural dignity and self-possession.

"I seem to know your face," she said, advancing courteously towards me, "but your name"—and here she glanced at the card she held in her hand—"is totally unfamiliar to me."

"I think you saw me some eighteen months ago," said I. "I am the detective who gave testimony at the inquest which was held over the remains of Mr. Hasbrouck."

I had not meant to startle her, but at this introduction of myself I saw her naturally pale cheek turn paler, and her fine eyes, which had been fixed curiously upon me, gradually sink to the floor.

"Great heaven!" thought I, "what is this I have stumbled upon!"

"I do not understand what business you can have with me," she presently remarked, with a show of gentle indifference that did not in the least deceive me.

"I do not wonder," I rejoined. "The crime which took place next door is almost forgotten by the community, and even if it were not, I am sure you would find it difficult to conjecture the nature of the question I have to put to you."

"I am surprised," she began, rising in her involuntary emotion and thereby compelling me to rise also. "How can you have any question to ask me on this subject? Yet if you have," she continued, with a rapid change of manner that touched my heart in spite of myself, "I shall, of course, do my best to answer you."

There are women whose sweetest tones and most charming smiles only serve to awaken distrust in men of my calling; but Mrs. Zabriskie was not of this number. Her face was beautiful, but it was also candid in its expression, and beneath the agitation which palpably disturbed her, I was sure there lurked nothing either wicked or false. Yet I held fast by the clue which I had grasped, as it were, in the dark, and without knowing whither I was tending, much less whither I was leading her, I proceeded to say:

"The question which I presume to put to you as the next-door neighbour of Mr. Hasbrouck, is this: Who was the woman who screamed out so loudly that the whole neighbourhood heard her on the night of that gentleman's assassination?"

The gasp she gave answered my question in a way she little realized, and, struck as I was by the impalpable links that had led me to the threshold of this hitherto unsolvable mystery, I was about to press my advantage and ask another question, when she quickly started forward and laid her hand on my lips.

Astonished, I looked at her inquiringly, but her head was turned aside, and her eyes, fixed upon the door, showed the greatest anxiety. Instantly I realized what she feared. Her husband was entering the house, and she dreaded lest his ears should catch a word of our conversation.

Not knowing what was in her mind, and unable to realize the importance of the moment to her, I yet listened to the advance of her blind husband with an almost painful interest. Would he enter the room where we were, or would he pass immediately to his office in the rear? She seemed to wonder too, and almost held her breath as he neared the door, paused, and stood in the open doorway, with his ear turned towards us.

As for myself, I remained perfectly still, gazing at his face in mingled surprise and apprehension. For besides its beauty, which was of a marked order, as I have already observed, it had a touching expression which irresistibly aroused both pity and interest in the spectator. This may have been the result of his affliction, or it may have sprung from some deeper cause; but, whatever its source, this look in his face produced a strong impression upon me and interested me at once in his personality. Would he enter? Or would he pass on? Her look of silent appeal showed me in which direction her wishes lay, but while I answered her glance by complete silence, I was conscious in some indistinct way that the business I had undertaken would be better furthered by his entrance.

The blind have been often said to possess a sixth sense in place of the one they have lost. Though I am sure we made no noise, I soon perceived that he was aware of our presence. Stepping hastily forward he said, in the high and vibrating tone of restrained passion:

"Helen, are you here?"

For a moment I thought she did not mean to answer, but knowing doubtless from experience the impossibility of deceiving him, she answered with a cheerful assent, dropping her hand as she did so from before my lips.

He heard the slight rustle which accompanied the movement, and

547

a look I found it hard to comprehend flashed over his features, altering his expression so completely that he seemed another man.

"You have someone with you," he declared, advancing another step but with none of the uncertainty which usually accompanies the movements of the blind. "Some dear friend," he went on, with an almost sarcastic emphasis and a forced smile that had little of gaiety in it.

The agitated and distressed blush which answered him could have but one interpretation. He suspected that her hand had been clasped in mine, and she perceived his thought and knew that I perceived it also.

Drawing herself up, she moved towards him, saying in a sweet womanly tone that to me spoke volumes:

"It is no friend, Constant, not even an acquaintance. The person whom I now present to you is an agent from the police. He is here upon a trivial errand which will be soon finished, when I will join you in your office."

I knew she was but taking a choice between two evils. That she would have saved her husband the knowledge of a detective's presence in the house, if her self-respect would have allowed it, but neither she nor I anticipated the effect which this presentation produced upon him.

"A police officer," he repeated, staring with his sightless eyes, as if, in his eagerness to see, he half hoped his lost sense would return. "He can have no trivial errand here; he has been sent by God Himself to——"

"Let me speak for you," hastily interposed his wife, springing to his side and clasping his arm with a fervour that was equally expressive of appeal and command. Then turning to me, she explained: "Since Mr. Hasbrouck's unaccountable death, my husband has been labouring under an hallucination which I have only to mention for you to recognize its perfect absurdity. He thinks—oh! do not look like that, Constant; you know it is an hallucination which must vanish the moment we drag it into broad daylight—that he—*he*, the best man in all the world, was himself the assailant of Mr. Hasbrouck."

Good God!

"I say nothing of the impossibility of this being so," she went on in a fever of expostulation. "He is blind, and could not have delivered such a shot even if he had desired to; besides, he had no weapon. But the inconsistency of the thing speaks for itself, and should assure him that his mind is unbalanced and that he is merely suffering from a shock that was greater than we realized. He is a physician and has had many such instances in his own practice. Why, he was very much attached to Mr. Hasbrouck! They were the best of friends, and though he insists that he killed him, he cannot give any reason for the deed."

At these words the doctor's face grew stern, and he spoke like an automaton repeating some fearful lesson.

"I killed him. I went to his room and deliberately shot him. I had nothing against him, and my remorse is extreme. Arrest me, and let me pay the penalty of my crime. It is the only way in which I can obtain peace."

Shocked beyond all power of self-control by this repetition of what she evidently considered the unhappy ravings of a madman, she let go his arm and turned upon me in frenzy.

"Convince him!" she cried. "Convince him by your questions that he never could have done this fearful thing."

I was labouring under great excitement myself, for I felt my youth against me in a matter of such tragic consequence. Besides, I agreed with her that he was in a distempered state of mind, and I hardly knew how to deal with one so fixed in his hallucination and with so much intelligence to support it. But the emergency was great, for he was holding out his wrists in the evident expectation of my taking him into instant custody; and the sight was killing his wife, who had sunk on the floor between us, in terror and anguish.

"You say you killed Mr. Hasbrouck," I began. "Where did you get your pistol, and what did you do with it after you left his house?"

"My husband had no pistol; never had any pistol," put in Mrs. Zabriskie, with vehement assertion. "If I had seen him with such a weapon——"

"I threw it away. When I left the house, I cast it as far from me as possible, for I was frightened at what I had done, horribly frightened."

"No pistol was ever found," I answered, with a smile, forgetting for the moment that he could not see. "If such an instrument had been found in the street after a murder of such consequence it certainly would have been brought to the police."

"You forget that a good pistol is valuable property," he went on stolidly. "Someone came along before the general alarm was given; and seeing such a treasure lying on the sidewalk, picked it up and carried it off. Not being an honest man, he preferred to keep it to drawing the attention of the police upon himself."

"Hum, perhaps," said I; "but where did *you* get it. Surely you can tell where you procured such a weapon, if, as your wife intimates, you did not own one."

"I bought it that self-same night of a friend; a friend whom I will not name, since he resides no longer in this country. I———" He paused; intense passion was in his face; he turned towards his wife, and a low cry escaped him, which made her look up in fear.

"I do not wish to go into any particulars," said he. "God forsook me and I committed a horrible crime. When I am punished, perhaps peace will return to me and happiness to her. I would not wish her to suffer too long or too bitterly for my sin."

"Constant!" What love was in the cry! and what despair! It seemed to move him and turn his thoughts for a moment into a different channel.

"Poor child!" he murmured, stretching out his hands by an irresistible impulse towards her. But the change was but momentary, and he was soon again the stern and determined self-accuser. "Are you going to take me before a magistrate?" he asked. "If so, I have a few duties to perform which you are welcome to witness."

"I have no warrant," I said; "besides, I am scarcely the one to take such a responsibility upon myself. If, however, you persist in your declaration, I will communicate with my superiors, who will take such action as they think best."

"That will be still more satisfactory to me," said he; "for though I have many times contemplated giving myself up to the authorities, I have still much to do before I can leave my home and practice without injury to others. Good-day; when you want me, you will find me here."

He was gone, and the poor young wife was left crouching on the floor alone. Pitying her shame and terror, I ventured to remark that it was not an uncommon thing for a man to confess to a crime he had never committed, and assured her that the matter would be inquired into very carefully before any attempt was made upon his liberty.

She thanked me, and, slowly rising, tried to regain her equanimity; but the manner as well as the matter of her husband's self-condemnation was too overwhelming in its nature for her to recover readily from her emotions.

"I have long dreaded this," she acknowledged. "For months I have foreseen that he would make some rash communication or insane avowal. If I had dared, I would have consulted some physician about this hallucination of his; but he was so sane on other points that I hesitated to give my dreadful secret to the world. I kept hoping that time and his daily pursuits would have their effect and restore him to himself. But his illusion grows, and now I fear that nothing will ever convince him that he did not commit the deed of which he accuses himself. If he were not blind I would have more hope, but the blind have so much time for brooding."

"I think he had better be indulged in his fancies for the present," I ventured. "If he is labouring under an illusion it might be dangerous to cross him."

"*If?*" she echoed in an indescribable tone of amazement and dread. "Can you for a moment harbour the idea that he has spoken the truth?"

"Madam," I returned, with something of the cynicism of my later years, "what caused you to give such an unearthly scream just before this murder was made known to the neighbourhood?"

She stared, paled, and finally began to tremble, not, as I now believe, at the insinuation latent in my words, but at the doubts which my question aroused in her own breast.

"Did I?" she asked; then with a great burst of candour, which seemed inseparable from her nature, she continued: "Why do I try to mislead you or deceive myself? I did give a shriek just before the alarm was raised next door; but it was not from any knowledge I had of a crime having been committed, but because I unexpectedly saw before me my husband whom I supposed to be on his way to Poughkeepsie. He was looking very pale and strange, and for a moment I thought I was beholding his ghost. But he soon explained his appearance by saying that he had fallen from the train and had been only saved by a miracle from being dismembered; and I was just bemoaning his mishap and trying to calm him and myself, when that terrible shout was heard next door of 'Murder! murder!'

"Coming so soon after the shock he had himself experienced, it quite unnerved him, and I think we can date his mental disturbance from that moment. For he began almost immediately to take a morbid interest in the affair next door, though it was weeks, if not months, before he let a word fall of the nature of those you have just heard. Indeed it was not till I repeated to him some of the expressions he was continually letting fall in his sleep, that he commenced to accuse himself of crime and talk of retribution."

"You say that your husband frightened you on that night by appearing suddenly at the door when you thought him on his way to
Poughkeepsie. Is Dr. Zabriskie in the habit of thus going and coming
alone at an hour so late as this must have been?"

"You forget that to the blind, night is less full of perils than the day.
Often and often has my husband found his way to his patients' houses
alone after midnight; but on this especial evening he had Harry with
him. Harry was his driver, and always accompanied him when he
went any distance."

"Well, then," said I, "all we have to do is to summon Harry and
hear what he has to say concerning this affair. He surely will know
whether or not his master went into the house next door."

"Harry has left us," she said. "Dr. Zabriskie has another driver
now. Besides—(I have nothing to conceal from you)—Harry was not
with him when he returned to the house that evening, or the doctor
would not have been without his portmanteau till the next day. Something—I have never known what—caused them to separate, and that
is why I have no answer to give the doctor when he accuses himself
of committing a deed on that night which is wholly out of keeping
with every other act of his life."

"And have you never questioned Harry why they separated and
why he allowed his master to come home alone after the shock he had
received at the station?"

"I did not know there was any reason for doing so till long after
he left us."

"And when did he leave?"

"That I do not remember. A few weeks or possibly a few days after
that dreadful night."

"And where is he now?"

"Ah, that I have not the least means of knowing. But," she suddenly cried, "what do you want of Harry? If he did not follow Dr.
Zabriskie to his own door, he could tell us nothing that would convince my husband that he is labouring under an illusion."

"But he might tell us something which would convince us that Dr.
Zabriskie was not himself after the accident, that he———"

"Hush!" came from her lips in imperious tones. "I will not believe
that he shot Mr. Hasbrouck even if you prove him to have been insane
at the time. How could he? My husband is blind. It would take a man
of very keen sight to force himself into a house that was closed for the
night, and kill a man in the dark at one shot."

"Rather," cried a voice from the doorway, "it is only a blind man who could do this. Those who trust to eyesight must be able to catch some glimpse of the mark they aim at, and this room, as I have been told, was without a glimmer of light. But the blind trust to sound, and as Mr. Hasbrouck spoke——"

"Oh!" burst from the horrified wife, "is there no one to stop him when he speaks like that?"

Chapter 2

When I related to my superiors the details of the foregoing interview, two of them coincided with the wife in thinking that Dr. Zabriskie was in an irresponsible condition of mind which made any statement of his questionable. But the third seemed disposed to argue the matter, and, casting me an inquiring look, seemed to ask what my opinion was on the subject. Answering him as if he had spoken, I gave my conclusion as follows: That whether insane or not, Dr. Zabriskie had fired the shot which terminated Mr. Hasbrouck's life.

It was the inspector's own idea, but it was not shared in by the others, one of whom had known the doctor for years. Accordingly they compromised by postponing all opinion till they had themselves interrogated the doctor, and I was detailed to bring him before them the next afternoon.

He came without reluctance, his wife accompanying him. In the short time which elapsed between their leaving Lafayette Place and entering Headquarters, I embraced the opportunity of observing them, and I found the study equally exciting and interesting. His face was calm but hopeless, and his eye, which should have shown a wild glimmer if there was truth in his wife's hypothesis, was dark and unfathomable, but neither frenzied nor uncertain. He spake but once and listened to nothing, though now and then his wife moved as if to attract his attention, and once even stole her hand toward his, in the tender hope that he would feel its approach and accept her sympathy. But he was deaf as well as blind; and sat wrapped up in thoughts which she, I know, would have given worlds to penetrate.

Her countenance was not without its mystery also. She showed in every lineament passionate concern and misery, and a deep tenderness from which the element of fear was not absent. But she, as well as he, betrayed that some misunderstanding, deeper than any I had previously suspected, drew its intangible veil between them and made the near proximity in which they sat, at once a heart-piercing delight and an unspeakable pain. What was this misunderstanding? and what was the character of the fear that modified her every look of love in his direction? Her perfect indifference to my presence proved that it was not connected with the position in which he had put himself towards the police by his voluntary confession of crime, nor could I thus interpret the expression of frantic question which now and then contracted her features, as she raised her eyes towards his sightless orbs, and strove to read, in his firm-set lips, the meaning of those assertions she could only ascribe to a loss of reason.

The stopping of the carriage seemed to awaken both from thoughts that separated rather than united them. He turned his in her direction, and she, stretching forth her hand, prepared to lead him from the carriage, without any of that display of timidity which had been previously evident in her manner.

As his guide she seemed to fear nothing; as his lover, everything.

"There is another and a deeper tragedy underlying the outward and obvious one," was my inward conclusion, as I followed them into the presence of the gentlemen awaiting them.

Dr. Zabriskie's appearance was a shock to those who knew him; so was his manner, which was calm, straightforward, and quietly determined.

"I shot Mr. Hasbrouck," was his steady affirmation, given without any show of frenzy or desperation "If you ask me why I did it, I cannot answer; if you ask me how, I am ready to state all that I know concerning the matter."

"But, Dr. Zabriskie," interposed his friend, "the why is the most important thing for us to consider just now. If you really desire to convince us that you committed the dreadful crime of killing a totally inoffensive man, you should give us some reason for an act so opposed to all your instincts and general conduct."

But the doctor continued unmoved:

"I had no reason for murdering Mr. Hasbrouck. A hundred questions can elicit no other reply; you had better keep to the how."

A deep-drawn breath from the wife answered the looks of the three gentlemen to whom this suggestion was offered. "You see," that breath seemed to protest, "that he is not in his right mind."

I began to waver in my own opinion, and yet the intuition which has served me in cases as seemingly impenetrable as this, bade me beware of following the general judgement.

"Ask him to inform you how he got into the house," I whispered to Inspector D——, who sat nearest me.

Immediately the inspector put the question I had suggested:

"By what means did you enter Mr. Hasbrouck's house at so late an hour as this murder occurred?"

The blind doctor's head fell forward on his breast, and he hesitated for the first and only time.

"You will not believe me," said he; "but the door was ajar when I came to it. Such things make crime easy; it is the only excuse I have to offer for this dreadful deed."

The front door of a respectable citizen's house ajar at half-past eleven at night. It was a statement that fixed in all minds the conviction of the speaker's irresponsibility. Mrs. Zabriskie's brow cleared, and her beauty became for a moment dazzling as she held out her hands in irrepressible relief towards those who were interrogating her husband. I alone kept my impassibility. A possible explanation of this crime had flashed like lightning across my mind; an explanation from which I inwardly recoiled, even while I was forced to consider it.

"Dr. Zabriskie," remarked the inspector who was most friendly to him, "such old servants as those kept by Mr. Hasbrouck do not leave the front door ajar at twelve o'clock at night."

"Yet ajar it was," repeated the blind doctor, with quiet emphasis; "and finding it so, I went in. When I came out again, I closed it. Do you wish me to swear to what I say? If so, I am ready."

What could we reply? To see this splendid-looking man, hallowed by an affliction so great that in itself it called forth the compassion of the most indifferent, accusing himself of a cold-blooded crime, in tones that sounded dispassionate because of the will that forced their utterance, was too painful in itself for us to indulge in any unnecessary words. Compassion took the place of curiosity, and each and all of us turned involuntary looks of pity upon the young wife pressing so eagerly to his side.

"For a blind man," ventured one, "the assault was both deft and certain. Are you accustomed to Mr. Hasbrouck's house, that you found your way with so little difficulty to his bedroom?"

"I am accustomed——" he began.

But here his wife broke in with irrepressible passion:

"He is not accustomed to that house. He has never been beyond the first-floor. Why, why do you question him? Do you not see——"

His hand was on her lips.

"Hush!" he commanded. "You know my skill in moving about a house; how I sometimes deceive those who do not know me into believing that I can see, by the readiness with which I avoid obstacles and find my way even in strange and untried scenes. Do not try to make them think I am not in my right mind, or you will drive me into the very condition you deprecate."

His face, rigid, cold, and set, looked like that of a mask. Hers, drawn with horror and filled with question that was fast taking the form of doubt, bespoke an awful tragedy from which more than one of us recoiled.

"Can you shoot a man dead without seeing him?" asked the Superintendent, with painful effort.

"Give me a pistol and I will show you," was the quick reply.

A low cry came from the wife. In a drawer near to every one of us there lay a pistol, but no one moved to take it out. There was a look in the Doctor's eye which made us fear to trust him with a pistol just then.

"We will accept your assurance that you possess a skill beyond that of most men," returned the superintendent. And beckoning me forward, he whispered: "This is a case for the doctors and not for the police. Remove him quietly, and notify Dr. Southyard of what I say."

But Dr. Zabriskie, who seemed to have an almost supernatural acuteness of hearing, gave a violent start at this and spoke up for the first time with real passion in his voice:

"No, no, I pray you. I can bear anything but that. Remember, gentlemen, that I am blind; that I cannot see who is about me; that my life would be a torture if I felt myself surrounded by spies watching to catch some evidence of madness in me. Rather conviction at once, death, dishonour, and obloquy. These I have incurred. These I have brought upon myself by crime, but not this worse fate—oh! not this worse fate."

His passion was so intense and yet so confined within the bounds of decorum, that we felt strangely impressed by it. Only the wife stood transfixed, with the dread growing in her heart, till her white, waxen visage seemed even more terrible to contemplate than his passion-distorted one.

"It is not strange that my wife thinks me demented," the doctor continued, as if afraid of the silence that answered him. "But it is your business to discriminate, and you should know a sane man when you see him."

Inspector D—— no longer hesitated.

"Very well," said he, "give us the least proof that your assertions are true, and we will lay your case before the prosecuting attorney."

"Proof? Is not a man's word——"

"No man's confession is worth much without some evidence to support it. In your case there is none. You cannot even produce the pistol with which you assert yourself to have committed the deed."

"True, true. I was frightened by what I had done, and the instinct of self-preservation led me to rid myself of the weapon in any way I could. But someone found this pistol; someone picked it up from the sidewalk of Lafayette Place on that fatal night. Advertise for it. Offer a reward. I will give you the money." Suddenly he appeared to realize how all this sounded. "Alas!" cried he, "I know the story seems improbable; all I say seems improbable; but it is not the probable things that happen in this life, but the improbable, as you should know, who every day dig deep into the heart of human affairs."

Were these the ravings of insanity? I began to understand the wife's terror.

"I bought the pistol," he went on, "of—alas! I cannot tell you his name. Everything is against me. I cannot adduce one proof; yet she, even she, is beginning to fear that my story is true. I know it by her silence, a silence that yawns between us like a deep and unfathomable gulf."

But at these words her voice rang out with passionate vehemence.

"No, no, it is false! I will never believe that your hands have been plunged in blood. You are my own pure-hearted Constant, cold, perhaps, and stern, but with no guilt upon your conscience, save in your own wild imagination."

"Helen, you are no friend to me," he declared, pushing her gently aside. "Believe me innocent, but say nothing to lead these others to doubt my word."

And she said no more, but her looks spoke volumes.

The result was that he was not detained, though he prayed for instant commitment. He seemed to dread his own home, and the surveillance to which he instinctively knew he would henceforth be subjected. To see him shrink from his wife's hand as she strove to lead him from the room was sufficiently painful; but the feeling thus aroused was nothing to that with which we observed the keen and agonized expectancy of his look as he turned and listened for the steps of the officer who followed him.

"I shall never again know whether or not I am alone," was his final observation as he left our presence.

I said nothing to my superiors of the thoughts I had had while listening to the above interrogatories. A theory had presented itself to my mind which explained in some measure the mysteries of the doctor's conduct, but I wished for time and opportunity to test its reasonableness before submitting it to their higher judgment. And these seemed likely to be given me, for the inspectors continued divided in their opinion of the blind physician's guilt, and the district-attorney, when told of the affair, pooh-poohed it without mercy, and declined to stir in the matter unless some tangible evidence were forthcoming to substantiate the poor doctor's self-accusations.

"If guilty, why does he shrink from giving his motives," said he, "and if so anxious to go to the gallows, why does he suppress the very facts calculated to send him there? He is as mad as a March hare, and it is to an asylum he should go and not to a jail."

In this conclusion I failed to agree with him, and as time wore on my suspicions took shape and finally ended in a fixed conviction. Dr. Zabriskie had committed the crime he avowed, but—let me proceed a little further with my story before I reveal what lies beyond that "but."

Notwithstanding Dr. Zabriskie's almost frenzied appeal for solitude, a man had been placed in surveillance over him in the shape of a young doctor skilled in diseases of the brain. This man communicated more or less with the police, and one morning I received from him the following extracts from the diary he had been ordered to keep.

"The doctor is settling into a deep melancholy from which he tries to rise at times, but with only indifferent success. Yesterday he rode around to all his patients for the purpose of withdrawing his services on the plea of illness. But he still keeps his office open, and today I had the opportunity of witnessing his reception and treatment of the many sufferers who came to him for aid. I think he was conscious of my presence, though an attempt had been made to conceal it. For the listening look never left his face from the moment he entered the room, and once he rose and passed quickly from wall to wall, groping with outstretched hands into every nook and corner, and barely escaping contact with the curtain behind which I was hidden. But if he suspected my presence, he showed no displeasure at it, wishing perhaps for a witness to his skill in the treatment of disease.

"And truly I never beheld a finer manifestation of practical insight in cases of a more or less baffling nature than I beheld in him today. He is certainly a most wonderful physician, and I feel bound to record that his mind is as clear for business as if no shadow had fallen upon it.

"Dr. Zabriskie loves his wife, but in a way that tortures both himself and her. If she is gone from the house he is wretched, and yet when she returns he often forbears to speak to her, or if he does speak, it is with a constraint that hurts her more than his silence. I was present when she came in today. Her step, which had been eager on the stairway, flagged as she approached the room, and he naturally noted the change and gave his own interpretation to it. His face, which had been very pale, flushed suddenly, and a nervous trembling seized him which he sought in vain to hide. But by the time her tall and beautiful figure stood in the doorway he was his usual self again in all but the expression of his eyes, which stared straight before him in an agony of longing only to be observed in those who have once seen.

"'Where have you been, Helen?' he asked, as, contrary to his wont, he moved to meet her.

"'To my mother's, to Arnold & Constable's, and to the hospital, as you requested,' was her quick answer, made without faltering or embarrassment.

"He stepped still nearer and took her hand, and as he did so my physician's eye noted how his finger lay over her pulse in seeming unconsciousness.

"'Nowhere else?' he queried.

"She smiled the saddest kind of smile and shook her head; then, remembering that he could not see this movement, she cried in a wistful tone:

"'Nowhere else, Constant; I was too anxious to get back.'

"I expected him to drop her hand at this, but he did not; and his finger still rested on her pulse.

"'And whom did you see while you were gone?' he continued.

"She told him, naming over several names.

"'You must have enjoyed yourself,' was his cold comment, as he let go her hand and turned away. But his manner showed relief, and I could not but sympathize with the pitiable situation of a man who found himself forced to means like these for probing the heart of his young wife.

"Yet when I turned towards her I realized that her position was but little happier than his. Tears are no strangers to her eyes, but those that welled up at this moment seemed to possess a bitterness that promised but little peace for her future. Yet she quickly dried them and busied herself with ministrations for his comfort.

"If I am any judge of woman, Helen Zabriskie is superior to most of her sex. That her husband mistrusts her is evident, but whether this is the result of the stand she has taken in his regard, or only a manifestation of dementia, I have as yet been unable to determine. I dread to leave them alone together, and yet when I presume to suggest that she should be on her guard in her interviews with him, she smiles very placidly and tells me that nothing would give her greater joy than to see him lift his hand against her, for that would argue that he is not accountable for his deeds or for his assertions.

"Yet it would be a grief to see her injured by this passionate and unhappy man.

"You have said that you wanted all details I could give; so I feel bound to say, that Dr. Zabriskie tries to be considerate of his wife, though he often fails in the attempt. When she offers herself as his guide, or assists him with his mail, or performs any of the many acts of kindness by which she continually manifests her sense of his affliction, he thanks her with courtesy and often with kindness, yet I know she would willingly exchange all his set phrases for one fond embrace or impulsive smile of affection. That he is not in the full possession of his faculties would be too much to say, and yet upon what other hypothesis can we account for the inconsistencies of his conduct.

"I have before me two visions of mental suffering. At noon I passed the office door, and looking within, saw the figure of Dr. Zabriskie seated in his great chair, lost in thought or deep in those memories which make an abyss in one's consciousness. His hands, which were clenched, rested upon the arms of his chair, and in one of them I detected a woman's glove, which I had no difficulty in recognizing as one of the pair worn by his wife this morning. He held it as a tiger might hold his prey or a miser his gold, but his set features and sightless eyes betrayed that a conflict of emotions was waging within him, among which tenderness had but little share.

"Though alive, as he usually is, to every sound, he was too absorbed at this moment to notice my presence though I had taken no pains to approach quietly. I therefore stood for a full minute watching him, till an irresistible sense of the shame of thus spying upon a blind man in his moments of secret anguish seized upon me and I turned away. But not before I saw his features relax in a storm of passionate feeling, as he rained kisses after kisses on the senseless kid he had so long held in his motionless grasp. Yet when an hour later he entered the dining-room on his wife's arm, there was nothing in his manner to show that he had in any way changed in his attitude towards her.

"The other picture was more tragic still. I have no business with Mrs. Zabriskie's affairs; but as I passed upstairs to my room an hour ago, I caught a fleeting vision of her tall form, with the arms thrown up over her head in a paroxysm of feeling which made her as oblivious to my presence as her husband had been several hours before. Were the words that escaped her lips 'Thank God we have no children!' or was this exclamation suggested to me by the passion and unrestrained impulse of her action?"

Side by side with these lines, I, Ebenezer Gryce, placed the following extracts from my own diary:

"Watched the Zabriskie mansion for five hours this morning, from the second story window of an adjoining hotel. Saw the Doctor when he drove away on his round of visits, and saw him when he returned. A coloured man accompanied him.

"Today I followed Mrs. Zabriskie. I had a motive for this, the nature of which I think it wisest not to divulge. She went first to a house in Washington Place where I am told her mother lives. Here she stayed some time, after which she drove down to Canal Street, where she did some shopping, and later stopped at the hospital, into which I took the liberty of following her. She seemed to know many there, and passed from cot to cot with a smile in which I alone discerned the sadness of a broken heart. When she left, I left also, without having learned anything beyond the fact that Mrs. Zabriskie is one who does her duty in sorrow as in happiness. A rare and trustworthy woman I should say, and yet her husband does not trust her. Why?

"I have spent this day in accumulating details in regard to Dr. and Mrs. Zabriskie's life previous to the death of Mr. Hasbrouck. I learned from sources it would be unwise to quote just here, that Mrs. Zabriskie had not lacked enemies ready to charge her with coquetry; that while she had never sacrificed her dignity in public, more than one person had been heard to declare, that Dr. Zabriskie was fortunate in being blind, since the sight of his wife's beauty would have but poorly compensated him for the pain he would have suffered in seeing how that beauty was admired.

"That all gossip is more or less tinged with exaggeration I have no

562

doubt, yet when a name is mentioned in connection with such stories, there is usually some truth at the bottom of them. And a name is mentioned in this case, though I do not think it worth my while to repeat it here; and loath as I am to recognize the fact, it is a name that carries with it doubts that might easily account for the husband's jealousy. True, I have found no one who dares to hint that she still continues to attract attention or to bestow smiles in any direction save where they legally belong. For since a certain memorable night which we all know, neither Dr. Zabriskie nor his wife have been seen save in their own domestic circle, and it is not into such scenes that this serpent, of which I have spoken, ever intrudes, nor is it in places of sorrow or suffering that his smile shines, or his fascinations flourish.

"And so one portion of my theory is proved to be sound. Dr. Zabriskie is jealous of his wife: whether with good cause or bad I am not prepared to decide; for her present attitude, clouded as it is by the tragedy in which she and her husband are both involved, must differ very much from that which she held when her life was unshadowed by doubt, and her admirers could be counted by the score.

"I have just found out where Harry is. As he is in service some miles up the river, I shall have to be absent from my post for several hours, but I consider the game well worth the candle.

"Light at last. I have seen Harry, and, by means known only to the police, have succeeded in making him talk. His story is substantially this: That on the night so often mentioned, he packed his master's portmanteau at eight o'clock and at ten called a carriage and rode with the doctor to the Twenty-ninth Street station. He was told to buy tickets for Poughkeepsie where his master had been called in consultation, and having done this, hurried back to join his master on the platform. They had walked together as far as the cars, and Dr. Zabriskie was just stepping on to the train when a man pushed himself hurriedly between them and whispered something into his master's ear, which caused him to fall back and lose his footing. Dr. Zabriskie's body slid half under the car, but he was withdrawn before any harm was done, though the cars gave a lurch at that moment which must have frightened him exceedingly, for his face was white when he rose to his feet, and when Harry offered to assist him again on to the train, he refused to go and said he would return home and not attempt to ride to Poughkeepsie that night.

"The gentleman, whom Harry now saw to be Mr. Stanton, an intimate friend of Dr. Zabriskie, smiled very queerly at this, and taking the doctor's arm led him away to a carriage. Harry naturally followed them, but the doctor, hearing his steps, turned and bade him, in a very peremptory tone, to take the omnibus home, and then, as if on second thought, told him to go to Poughkeepsie in his stead and explain to the people there that he was too shaken up by his mis-step to do his duty, and that he would be with them next morning. This seemed strange to Harry, but he had no reasons for disobeying his master's orders, and so rode to Poughkeepsie. But the doctor did not follow him the next day; on the contrary he telegraphed for him to return, and when he got back dismissed him with a month's wages. This ended Harry's connection with the Zabriskie family.

"A simple story bearing out what the wife has already told us; but it furnishes a link which may prove invaluable. Mr. Stanton, whose first name is Theodore, knows the real reason why Dr. Zabriskie returned home on the night of the seventeenth of July, 1851. Mr. Stanton, consequently, I must see, and this shall be my business tomorrow.

"Checkmate! Theodore Stanton is not in this country. Though this points him out as the man from whom Dr. Zabriskie bought the pistol, it does not facilitate my work, which is becoming more and more difficult.

"Mr. Stanton's whereabouts are not even known to his most intimate friends. He sailed from this country most unexpectedly on the eighteenth of July a year ago, which was *the day after the murder of Mr. Hasbrouck*. It looks like a flight, especially as he has failed to maintain open communication even with his relatives. Was he the man who shot Mr. Hasbrouck? No; but he was the man who put the pistol in Dr. Zabriskie's hand that night, and, whether he did this with purpose or not, was evidently so alarmed at the catastrophe which followed that he took the first outgoing steamer to Europe. So far, all is clear, but there are mysteries yet to be solved, which will require my utmost tact. What if I should seek out the gentleman with whose name that of Mrs. Zabriskie has been linked, and see if I can in any way connect him with Mr. Stanton or the events of that night?

"Eureka! I have discovered that Mr. Stanton cherished a mortal hatred for the gentleman above mentioned. It was a covert feeling, but no less deadly on that account; and while it never led him into any extravagances, it was of force sufficient to account for many a secret misfortune which happened to that gentleman. Now, if I can prove he was the Mephistopheles who whispered insinuations into the ear of our blind Faust, I may strike a fact that will lead me out of this maze.

"But how can I approach secrets so delicate without compromising the woman I feel bound to respect, if only for the devoted love she manifests for her unhappy husband!

"I shall have to appeal to Joe Smithers. This is something which I always hate to do, but as long as he will take money, and as long as he is fertile in resources for obtaining the truth from people I am myself unable to reach, so long must I make use of his cupidity and his genius. He is an honourable fellow in one way, and never retails as gossip what he acquires for our use. How will he proceed in this case, and by what tactics will he gain the very delicate information which we need? I own that I am curious to see.

"I shall really have to put down at length the incidents of this night. I always knew that Joe Smithers was invaluable to the police, but I really did not know he possessed talents of so high an order. He wrote me this morning that he had succeeded in getting Mr. T——'s promise to spend the evening with him, and advised me that if I desired to be present also, his own servant would not be at home, and that an opener of bottles would be required.

"As I was very anxious to see Mr. T—— with my own eyes, I accepted the invitation to play the spy upon a spy, and went at the proper hour to Mr. Smithers's rooms, which are in the University Building. I found them picturesque in the extreme. Piles of books stacked here and there to the ceiling made nooks and corners which could be quite shut off by a couple of old pictures that were set into movable frames that swung out or in at the whim or convenience of the owner.

"As I liked the dark shadows cast by these pictures, I pulled them both out, and made such other arrangements as appeared likely to facilitate the purpose I had in view, then I sat down and waited for the two gentlemen who were expected to come in together.

"They arrived almost immediately, whereupon I rose and played my part with all necessary discretion. While ridding Mr. T——of his overcoat, I stole a look at his face. It is not a handsome one, but it boasts of a gay, devil-may-care expression which doubtless makes it dangerous to many women, while his manners are especially attractive, and his voice the richest and most persuasive that I ever heard. I contrasted him, almost against my will, with Dr. Zabriskie, and decided that with most women the former's undoubted fascinations of speech and bearing would outweigh the latter's great beauty and mental endowments; but I doubted if they would with her.

"The conversation which immediately began was brilliant but desultory, for Mr. Smithers, with an airy lightness for which he is remarkable, introduced topic after topic, perhaps for the purpose of showing off Mr. T——'s versatility, and perhaps for the deeper and more sinister purpose of shaking the kaleidoscope of talk so thoroughly, that the real topic which we were met to discuss should not make an undue impression on the mind of his guest.

"Meanwhile one, two, three bottles passed, and I saw Joe Smithers's eye grow calmer and that of Mr. T—— more brilliant and more uncertain. As the last bottle showed signs of failing, Joe cast me a meaning glance, and the real business of the evening began.

"I shall not attempt to relate the half-dozen failures which Joe made in endeavouring to elicit the facts we were in search of, without arousing the suspicion of his visitor. I am only going to relate the successful attempt. They had been talking now for some hours, and I, who had long before been waved from their immediate presence, was hiding my curiosity and growing excitement behind one of the pictures, when suddenly I heard Joe say:

"'He has the most remarkable memory I ever met. He can tell to a day when any notable event occurred.'

"'Pshaw!' answered his companion, who, by the by, was known to pride himself upon his own memory for dates, 'I can state where I went and what I did on every day in the year. That may not embrace what you call 'notable events,' but the memory required is all the more remarkable, is it not?'

"'Pooh!' was his friend's provoking reply, 'you are bluffing, Ben; I will never believe that.'

"Mr. T——, who had passed by this time into that state of intoxication which makes persistence in an assertion a duty as well as a pleasure, threw back his head, and as the wreaths of smoke rose in airy spirals from his lips, reiterated his statement, and offered to submit to any test of his vaunted powers which the other might dictate.

"'You have a diary——' began Joe.

"'Which is at home,' completed the other.

"'Will you allow me to refer to it tomorrow, if I am suspicious of the accuracy of your recollections?'

"'Undoubtedly,' returned the other.

"'Very well, then, I will wager you a cool fifty, that you cannot tell where you were between the hours of ten and eleven on a certain night which I will name.'

"'Done!' cried the other, bringing out his pocket-book and laying it on the table before him.

"Joe followed his example and then summoned me.

"'Write a date down here,' he commanded, pushing a piece of paper towards me, with a look keen as the flash of a blade. 'Any date, man,' he added, as I appeared to hesitate in the embarrassment I thought natural under the circumstances. 'Put down day, month, and year, only don't go too far back; not farther than two years.'

"Smiling with the air of a flunkey admitted to the sports of his superiors, I wrote a line and laid it before Mr. Smithers, who at once pushed it with a careless gesture towards his companion. You can of course guess the date I made use of: July 17, 1851. Mr. T——, who had evidently looked upon this matter as mere play, flushed scarlet as he read these words, and for one instant looked as if he had rather flee our presence than answer Joe Smithers's nonchalant glance of inquiry.

"'I have given my word and will keep it,' he said at last, but with a look in my direction that sent me reluctantly back to my retreat. 'I don't suppose you want names,' he went on, 'that is, if anything I have to tell is of a delicate nature?'

"'O no,' answered the other, 'only facts and places.'

"'I don't think places are necessary either,' he returned. 'I will tell you what I did and that must serve you. I did not promise to give number and street.'

"'Well, well,' Joe exclaimed; 'earn your fifty, that is all. Show that you remember where you were on the night of'—and with an admirable show of indifference he pretended to consult the paper between them—'the seventeenth of July, 1851, and I shall be satisfied.'

"'I was at the club for one thing,' said Mr. T——; 'then I went to see a lady friend, where I stayed till eleven. She wore a blue muslin—— What is that?'

"I had betrayed myself by a quick movement which sent a glass tumbler crashing to the floor. Helen Zabriskie had worn a blue muslin on that same night. I had noted it when I stood on the balcony watching her and her husband.

"'That noise?' It was Joe who was speaking. 'You don't know Reuben as well as I do or you wouldn't ask. It is his practice, I am sorry to say, to accentuate his pleasure in draining my bottles, by dropping a glass at every third one.'

"Mr. T—— went on.

"'She was a married woman and I thought she loved me; but—and this is the greatest proof I can offer you that I am giving you a true account of that night—she had not had the slightest idea of the extent of my passion, and only consented to see me at all because she thought, poor thing, that a word from her would set me straight, and rid her of attentions that were fast becoming obnoxious. A sorry figure for a fellow to cut who has not been without his triumphs; but you caught me on the most detestable date in my calendar, and——'

"There is where he stopped being interesting, so I will not waste time by quoting further. And now what reply shall I make when Joe Smithers asks me double his usual price, as he will be sure to do, next time? Has he not earned an advance? I really think so.

"I have spent the whole day in weaving together the facts I have gleaned, and the suspicions I have formed, into a consecutive whole likely to present my theory in a favourable light to my superiors. But just as I thought myself in shape to meet their inquiries, I received an immediate summons into their presence, where I was given a duty to perform of so extraordinary and unexpected a nature, that it effectually drove from my mind all my own plans for the elucidation of the Zabriskie mystery.

"This was nothing more nor less than to take charge of a party of people who were going to the Jersey heights for the purpose of testing Dr. Zabriskie's skill with a pistol."

Chapter 3

The cause of this sudden move was soon explained to me. Mrs. Zabriskie, anxious to have an end put to the present condition of affairs, had begged for a more rigid examination into her husband's state. This being accorded, a strict and impartial inquiry had taken place, with a result not unlike that which followed the first one. Three out of his four interrogators judged him insane, and could not be moved from their opinion though opposed by the verdict of the young expert who had been living in the house with him. Dr. Zabriskie seemed to read their thoughts, and, showing extreme agitation, begged as before for an opportunity to prove his sanity by showing his skill in shooting. This time a disposition was evinced to grant his request, which Mrs. Zabriskie no sooner perceived, than she added her supplications to his that the question might be thus settled.

A pistol was accordingly brought; but at sight of it her courage failed, and she changed her prayer to an entreaty that the experiment should be postponed till the next day, and should then take place in the woods away from the sight and hearing of needless spectators.

Though it would have been much wiser to have ended the matter there and then, the Superintendent was prevailed upon to listen to her entreaties, and thus t was that I came to be a spectator, if not a participator, in the final scene of this most sombre drama.

There are some events which impress the human mind so deeply that their memory mingles with all after-experiences. Though I have made it a rule to forget as soon as possible the tragic episodes into which I am constantly plunged, there is one scene in my life which will not depart at my will; and that is the sight which met my eyes from the bow of the small boat in which Dr. Zabriskie and his wife were rowed over to Jersey on that memorable afternoon.

Though it was by no means late in the day, the sun was already sinking, and the bright red glare which filled the heavens and shone full upon the faces of the half-dozen persons before me added much to the tragic nature of the scene, though we were far from comprehending its full significance.

The doctor sat with his wife in the stern, and it was upon their faces my glance was fixed. The glare shone luridly on his sightless eyeballs, and as I noticed his unwinking lids I realized as never before what it was to be blind in the midst of sunshine. Her eyes, on the contrary, were lowered, but there was a look of hopeless misery in her colourless face which made her appearance infinitely pathetic, and I felt confident that if he could only have seen her, he would not have maintained the cold and unresponsive manner which chilled the words on her lips and made all advance on her part impossible.

On the seat in front of them sat the inspector and a doctor, and from some quarter, possibly from under the inspector's coat, there came the monotonous ticking of a small clock, which, I had been told, was to serve as a target for the blind man's aim.

This ticking was all I heard, though the noise and bustle of a great traffic was pressing upon us on every side. And I am sure it was all that she heard, as, with hand pressed to her heart and eyes fixed on the opposite shore, she waited for the event which was to determine whether the man she loved was a criminal or only a being afflicted of God, and worthy of her unceasing care and devotion.

As the sun cast its last scarlet gleam over the water, the boat grounded, and it fell to my lot to assist Mrs. Zabriskie up the bank. As I did so, I allowed myself to say: "I am your friend, Mrs. Zabriskie," and was astonished to see her tremble, and turn toward me with a look like that of a frightened child.

But there was always this characteristic blending in her countenance of the childlike and the severe, such as may so often be seen in the faces of nuns, and beyond an added pang of pity for this beautiful but afflicted woman, I let the moment pass without giving it the weight it perhaps demanded.

"The doctor and his wife had a long talk last night," was whispered in my ear as we wound our way along into the woods. I turned and perceived at my side the expert physician, portions of whose diary I have already quoted. He had come by another boat.

"But it did not seem to heal whatever breach lies between them," he proceeded. Then in a quick, curious tone, he asked: "Do you believe this attempt on his part is likely to prove anything but a farce?"

"I believe he will shatter the clock to pieces with his first shot," I answered, and could say no more, for we had already reached the ground which had been selected for this trial at arms, and the various members of the party were being placed in their several positions.

The doctor, to whom light and darkness were alike, stood with his face towards the western glow, and at his side were grouped the Inspector and the two physicians. On the arm of one of the latter hung Dr. Zabriskie's overcoat, which he had taken off as soon as he reached the field.

Mrs. Zabriskie stood at the other end of the opening, near a tall stump, upon which it had been decided that the clock should be placed when the moment came for the doctor to show his skill. She had been accorded the privilege of setting the clock on this stump, and I saw it shining in her hand as she paused for a moment to glance back at the circle of gentlemen who were awaiting her movements. The hands of the clock stood at five minutes to five, though I scarcely noted the fact at the time, for her eyes were on mine, and as she passed me she spoke:

"If he is not himself, he cannot be trusted. Watch him carefully, and see that he does no mischief to himself or others. Be at his right hand, and stop him if he does not handle his pistol properly."

I promised, and she passed on, setting the clock upon the stump and immediately drawing back to a suitable distance at the right, where she stood, wrapped in her long dark cloak, quite alone. Her face shone ghastly white, even in its environment of snow-covered boughs which surrounded her, and, noting this, I wished the minutes fewer between the present moment and the hour of five, at which he was to draw the trigger.

"Dr. Zabriskie," quoth the inspector, "we have endeavoured to make this trial a perfectly fair one. You are to have one shot at a small clock which has been placed within a suitable distance, and which you are expected to hit, guided only by the sound which it will make in striking the hour of five. Are you satisfied with the arrangement?"

"Perfectly. Where is my wife?"

"On the other side of the field, some ten paces from the stump upon which the clock is fixed."

He bowed, and his face showed satisfaction.

"May I expect the clock to strike soon?"

"In less than five minutes," was the answer.

"Then let me have the pistol; I wish to become acquainted with its size and weight."

We glanced at each other, then across at her.

She made a gesture; it was one of acquiescence.

Immediately the inspector placed the weapon in the blind man's hand. It was at once apparent that the doctor understood the instrument, and my last doubt vanished as to the truth of all he had told us.

"Thank God I am blind this hour and cannot see *her*," fell unconsciously from his lips; then, before the echo of these words had left my ears, he raised his voice and observed calmly enough, considering that he was about to prove himself a criminal in order to save himself from being thought a madman.

"Let no one move. I must have my ears free for catching the first stroke of the clock." And he raised the pistol before him.

There was a moment of torturing suspense and deep, unbroken silence. My eyes were on him, and so I did not watch the clock, but suddenly I was moved by some irresistible impulse to note how Mrs. Zabriskie was bearing herself at this critical moment, and, casting a hurried glance in her direction, I perceived her tall figure swaying from side to side, as if under an intolerable strain of feeling. Her eyes were on the clock, the hands of which seemed to creep with snail-like pace along the dial, when unexpectedly, and a full minute before the minute hand had reached the stroke of five, I caught a movement on her part, saw the flash of something round and white show for an instant against the darkness of her cloak, and was about to shriek warning to the doctor, when the shrill, quick stroke of a clock rung out on the frosty air, followed by the ping and flash of a pistol.

A sound of shattered glass, followed by a suppressed cry, told us that the bullet had struck the mark, but before we could move, or rid our eyes of the smoke which the wind had blown into our faces, there came another sound which made our hair stand on end and sent the blood back in terror to our hearts. Another clock was striking, the clock which we now perceived was still standing upright on the stump where Mrs. Zabriskie had placed it.

Whence came the clock, then, which had struck before the time and been shattered for its pains? One quick look told us. On the ground, ten paces at the right, lay Helen Zabriskie, a broken clock at her side, and in her breast a bullet which was fast sapping the life from her sweet eyes.

We had to tell him, there was such pleading in her looks; and never shall I forget the scream that rang from his lips as he realized the truth. Breaking from our midst, he rushed forward, and fell at her feet as if guided by some supernatural instinct.

"Helen," he shrieked, "what is this? Were not my hands dyed deep enough in blood that you should make me answerable for your life also?"

Her eyes were closed, but she opened them. Looking long and steadily at his agonized face, she faltered forth:

"It is not you who have killed me; it is your crime. Had you been innocent of Mr. Hasbrouck's death, your bullet would never have found my heart. Did you think I could survive the proof that you had killed that good man?"

"I—I did it unwittingly. I——"

"Hush!" she commanded, with an awful look, which, happily, he could not see. "I had another motive. I wished to prove to you, even at the cost of my life, that I loved you, had always loved you, and not——"

It was now his turn to silence her. His hand crept over her lips, and his despairing face turned itself blindly towards us.

"Go," he cried; "leave us! Let me take a last farewell of my dying wife, without listeners or spectators."

Consulting the eye of the physician who stood beside me, and seeing no hope in it, I fell slowly back. The others followed, and the Doctor was left alone with his wife. From the distant position we took, we saw her arms creep round his neck, saw her head fall confidingly on his breast, then silence settled upon them and upon all nature, the gathering twilight deepening, till the last glow disappeared from the heavens above and from the circle of leafless trees which enclosed this tragedy from the outside world.

But at last there came a stir, and Dr. Zabriskie, rising up before us, with the dead body of his wife held closely to his breast, confronted us with a countenance so rapturous that he looked like a man transfigured.

"I will carry her to the boat" said he. "Not another hand shall touch her. She was my true wife, my true wife!" And he towered into an attitude of such dignity and passion, that for a moment he took on heroic proportions and we forgot that he had just proved himself to have committed a cold-blooded and ghastly crime.

The stars were shining when we again took our seats in the boat; and if the scene of our crossing to Jersey was impressive, what shall be said of that of our return.

The doctor, as before, sat in the stern, an awesome figure, upon which the moon shone with a white radiance that seemed to lift his face out of the surrounding darkness and set it, like an image of frozen horror, before our eyes. Against his breast he held the form of his dead wife, and now and then I saw him stoop as if he were listening for some tokens of life at her set lips. Then he would lift himself again, with hopelessness stamped upon his features, only to lean forward in renewed hope that was again destined to disappointment.

The Inspector and the accompanying physician had taken seats in the bow, and unto me had been assigned the special duty of watching over the doctor. This I did from a low seat in front of him. I was therefore so close that I heard his labouring breath, and though my heart was full of awe and compassion, I could not prevent myself from bending towards him and saying these words:

"Dr. Zabriskie, the mystery of your crime is no longer a mystery to me. Listen and see if I do not understand your temptation, and how you, a conscientious and God-fearing man, came to slay your innocent neighbour.

"A friend of yours, or so he called himself, had for a long time filled your ears with tales tending to make you suspicious of your wife and jealous of a certain man whom I will not name. You knew that your friend had a grudge against this man, and so for many months turned a deaf ear to his insinuations. But finally some change which you detected in your wife's bearing or conversation roused your own suspicions, and you began to doubt if all was false that came to your ears, and to curse your blindness, which in a measure rendered you helpless. The jealous fever grew and had risen to a high point, when one night—a memorable night—this friend met you just as you were leaving town, and with cruel craft whispered in your ear that the man you hated was even then with your wife, and that if you would return at once to your home you would find him in her company.

"The demon that lurks at the heart of all men, good or bad, thereupon took complete possession of you, and you answered this false friend by saying that you would not return without a pistol. Whereupon he offered to take you to his house and give you his. You consented, and getting rid of your servant by sending him to Poughkeepsie with your excuses, you entered a coach with your friend.

"You say you bought the pistol, and perhaps you did, but, however that may be, you left his house with it in your pocket and, declining

574

companionship, walked home, arriving at the Colonnade a little before midnight.

"Ordinarily you have no difficulty in recognizing your own doorstep. But, being in a heated frame of mind, you walked faster than usual and so passed your own house and stopped at that of Mr. Hasbrouck's, one door beyond. As the entrances of these houses are all alike, there was but one way by which you could have made yourself sure that you had reached your own dwelling, and that was by feeling for the doctor's sign at the side of the door. But you never thought of that. Absorbed in dreams of vengeance, your sole impulse was to enter by the quickest means possible.

"Taking out your night-key, you thrust it into the lock. It fitted, but it took strength to turn it, so much strength that the key was twisted and bent by the effort. But this incident, which would have attracted your attention at another time, was lost upon you at this moment. An entrance had been effected, and you were in too excited a frame of mind to notice at what cost, or to detect the small differences apparent in the atmosphere and furnishings of the two houses—trifles which would have arrested your attention under other circumstances, and made you pause before the upper floor had been reached.

"It was while going up the stairs that you took out your pistol, so that by the time you arrived at the front-room door you held it ready cocked and drawn in your hand. For, being blind, you feared escape on the part of your victim, and so waited for nothing but the sound of a man's voice before firing. When, therefore, the unfortunate Mr. Hasbrouck, roused by this sudden intrusion, advanced with an exclamation of astonishment, you pulled the trigger, killing him on the spot. It must have been immediately upon his fall that you recognized from some word he uttered, or from some contact you may have had with your surroundings, that you were in the wrong house and had killed the wrong man; for you cried out, in evident remorse, 'God! what have I done!' and fled without approaching your victim.

"Descending the stairs, you rushed from the house, closing the front door behind you and regaining your own without being seen. But here you found yourself baffled in your attempted escape, by two things. First, by the pistol you still held in your hand, and secondly, by the fact that the key upon which you depended for entering your own door was so twisted out of shape that you knew it would be useless for you to attempt to use it. What did you do in this emergency? You have already told us, though the story seemed so improbable at the time, you found nobody to believe it but myself.

"The pistol you flung far away from you down the pavement, from which, by one of those rare chances which sometimes happen in this world, it was presently picked up by some late passer-by of more or less doubtful character. The door offered less of an obstacle than you anticipated; for when you turned to it again you found it, if I am not greatly mistaken, ajar, left so, as we have reason to believe, by one who had gone out of it but a few minutes before in a state which left him but little master of his actions. It was this fact which provided you with an answer when you were asked how you succeeded in getting into Mr. Hasbrouck's house after the family had retired for the night.

"Astonished at the coincidence, but hailing with gladness the deliverance which it offered, you went in and ascended at once into your wife's presence; and it was from her lips, and not from those of Mrs. Hasbrouck, that the cry arose which startled the neighbourhood and prepared men's minds for the tragic words which were shouted a moment later from the next house.

"But she who uttered the scream knew of no tragedy save that which was taking place in her own breast. She had just repulsed a dastardly suitor, and, seeing you enter so unexpectedly in a state of unaccountable horror and agitation, was naturally stricken with dismay, and thought she saw your ghost, or, what was worse, a possible avenger; while you, having failed to kill the man you sought, and having killed a man you esteemed, let no surprise on her part lure you into any dangerous self-betrayal. You strove instead to soothe her, and even attempted to explain the excitement under which you laboured, by an account of your narrow escape at the station, till the sudden alarm from next door distracted her attention, and sent both your thoughts and hers in a different direction. Not till conscience had fully awakened and the horror of your act had had time to tell upon your sensitive nature, did you breathe forth those vague confessions, which, not being supported by the only explanations which would have made them credible, led her, as well as the police, to consider you affected in your mind. Your pride as a man, and your consideration for her as a woman, kept you silent, but did not keep the worm from preying upon your heart.

"Am I not correct in my surmises, Dr. Zabriskie, and is not this the true explanation of your crime?"

With a strange look, he lifted up his face.

"Hush!" said he; "you will awaken her. See how peacefully she sleeps! I should not like to have her awakened now, she is so tired, and I—I have not watched over her as I should."

Appalled at his gesture, his look, his tone, I drew back, and for a few minutes no sound was to be heard but the steady dip-dip of the oars and the lap-lap of the waters against the boat. Then there came a quick uprising, the swaying before me of something dark and tall and threatening, and before I could speak or move, or even stretch forth my hands to stay him, the seat before me was empty and darkness had filled the place where but an instant previous he had sat, a fearsome figure, erect and rigid as a sphinx.

What little moonlight there was only served to show us a few rising bubbles, marking the spot where the unfortunate man had sunk with his much-loved burden. We could not save him. As the widening circles fled farther and farther out, the tide drifted us away, and we lost the spot which had seen the termination of one of earth's saddest tragedies.

The bodies were never recovered. The police reserved to themselves the right of withholding from the public the real facts which made this catastrophe an awful remembrance to those who witnessed it. A verdict of accidental death by drowning answered all purposes, and saved the memory of the unfortunate pair from such calumny as might have otherwise assailed it. It was the least we could do for two beings whom circumstances had so greatly afflicted.

LEONAUR

ALSO FROM LEONAUR
AVAILABLE IN SOFTCOVER OR HARDCOVER WITH DUST JACKET

THE LONG PATROL *by George Berrie*—A Novel of Light Horsemen from Gallipoli to the Palestine campaign of the First World War.

NAPOLEONIC WAR STORIES *by Arthur Quiller-Couch*—Tales of soldiers, spies, battles & sieges from the Peninsular & Waterloo campaingns.

THE FIRST DETECTIVE *by Edgar Allan Poe*—The Complete Auguste Dupin Stories—The Murders in the Rue Morgue, The Mystery of Marie Rogêt & The Purloined Letter.

THE COMPLETE DR NIKOLA—MAN OF MYSTERY: 1 *by Guy Boothby*—*A Bid for Fortune & Dr Nikola Returns*—Guy Boothby's Dr.Nikola adventures continue to fascinate readers and enthusiasts of crime and mystery fiction because—in the manner of Raffles, the gentleman cracksman—here is character far removed from the uncompromising goodness of Holmes and Watson or the uncompromising evil of Professor Moriarty.

THE COMPLETE DR NIKOLA—MAN OF MYSTERY: 2 *by Guy Boothby*—*The Lust of Hate, Dr Nikola's Experiment & Farewell, Nikola*—Guy Boothby's Dr.Nikola adventures continue to fascinate readers and enthusiasts of crime and mystery fiction because—in the manner of Raffles, the gentleman cracksman—here is character far removed from the uncompromising goodness of Holmes and Watson or the uncompromising evil of Professor Moriarty.

THE CASEBOOKS OF MR J. G. REEDER: BOOK 1 *by Edgar Wallace*—*Room 13, The Mind of Mr J. G. Reeder* and *Terror Keep*—Edgar Wallace's sleuth—whose territory is the London of the 1920s—is an unlikely figure, more bank clerk than detective in appearance, ever wearing his square topped bowler, frock coat, cravat and muffler, Mr Reeder is usually inseparable from his umbrella.

THE CASEBOOKS OF MR J. G. REEDER: BOOK 2 *by Edgar Wallace*—*Red Aces, Mr J. G. Reeder Returns, The Guv'nor* and *The Man Who Passed*—Edgar Wallace's sleuth—whose territory is the London of the 1920s—is an unlikely figure, more bank clerk than detective in appearance, ever wearing his square topped bowler, frock coat, cravat and muffler, Mr Reeder is usually inseparable from his umbrella.

THE COMPLETE FOUR JUST MEN: VOLUME 1 *by Edgar Wallace*—*The Four Just Men, The Council of Justice & The Just Men of Cordova*—disillusioned with a world where the wicked and the abusers of power perpetually go unpunished, the Just Men set about to rectify matters according to their own standards, and retribution is dispensed on swift and deadly wings.